CREDITS

Lead Designers: Dan Dillon, Chris Harris, and Jeff Lee

Designers: Wolfgang Baur, Scott Carter, Matthew Corley, Jesse Jordan, Phillip Larwood, Chris Lockey, Greg Marks, Shawn Merwin, Michael Ohl, Carlos Ovalle, Mike Welham, and Steve Winter

Additional Designers: Dan Abrahmsen, John-Michael Albrecht, Steven Andrews, Anonymous (2), Brice Barnett, Mary Beaton, Tor Bittmann, John H. Bookwalter Jr., Carl Brost, Joshua K. Brown, Nick Brown, Peter Bruhn, Steve Collin, Trevor Lee Cooper, Andrew Croft, Kameron Crump, Wally D., Jordan Day, Stephen Diamond, Scott Dornian, Melissa Doucette, Brandon Elms, William Fischer, Alex Fosth, Casey Geyer, Seth Grimes, Kim Hanley, Chris D. Hansen, Randall Hartman, Claire Hogan, Matthew House, Kristopher R. Hunter, Jacob Johnson, John Landis, Frank Licato, Michael Liebhart, James McManus, Andre Montague, Fabrizio Nava, Patrick Martin Frosz Nielsen, Xavier Noé, Brian Oppermann, Conlan Parkman, Kelly Pawlik, Tim Prior, Craig C. Robertson, Abbey Ross, George Sager, Ricardo L. Santiago, Francisco Santos, John Seidler, Skagasaurus, Kenneth Smith, Brian Suskind, Dennis Sustare, Michael Swords, David Truman, Cody Tunison, Nsima Uwah, Andrew Vince, Adam Weiler, Joseph Williams, and John Windsor

Developer: Steve Winter

Editor: Kim Mohan

Additional Editors: Meagan Maricle, Steve Winter, Marcie Wood

Playtest Coordinator: Ben McFarland

Cover Art: Marcel Mercado

Interior Artists: Emile Denis, Rita Fei, Marcel Mercado, Julia Metzger, David Auden Nash, William O'Brien, Corwin Paradinha, Addison Rankin, Florian Stitz, Bryan Syme, Egil Thompson, Mateusz Wilma

2023 EDITION

Lead Designer: Celeste Conowitch

Designers: Wolfgang Baur, Ben McFarland, Marc Radle, Mike Welham

Developers: Celeste Conowitch, Scott Gable

Editor: Scott Gable, Meagan Maricle

Cover Artist: Marcel Mercado

Interior Artists: Brom, Emile Denis, Marcel Mercado, Julia Metzger, David Auden Nash, William O'Brien, Corwin Paradinha, Addison Rankin, Florian Stitz, Bryan Syme, Egil Thompson, Mateusz Wilma

Graphic Designers: Marc Radle, Amber Seger

KOBOLD WARRENS

Publisher: Wolfgang Baur

Chief Operations Officer: T. Alexander Stangroom

Director Of Digital Growth: Blaine McNutt

Art Director: Marc Radle

Art Department: Marc Radle, Amber Seger

Editorial Director: Thomas M. Reid

Editorial Department: Scott Gable, Meagan Maricle, Jeff Quick, Thomas M. Reid

Senior Game Designer: Celeste Conowitch

Marketing Director: Chelsea "Dot" Steverson

Project Manager: Amber Seger

Community Manager: Zachery Newbill

Sales Manager: Kym Weiler

SPECIAL THANKS

A special thanks to the 4,456 backers who made this volume possible! Thanks also to the playtesters who kept us sharp, the fans who wrote in with questions for clarification, and the designers of some of these spells in prior editions of the game going back to the dawn of Zobeck and the ticking pendulum.

On the Cover

A confident spellcaster quickly creates an icy shield to protect her from the oncoming flames in this illustration by Marcel Mercado.

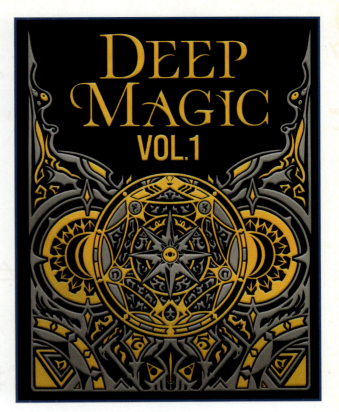

On the Limited Edition Cover

Sigils of arcana are engraved upon the cover, presaging its contents, in this illustration by Addison Rankin.

Product Identity: The following items are hereby identified as Product Identity, as defined in the Open Game License version 1.0a, Section 1(e), and are not Open Content: All trademarks, registered trademarks, proper names (characters, place names, new deities, etc.), dialogue, plots, story elements, locations, characters, artwork, sidebars, and trade dress. (Elements that have previously been designated as Open Game Content are not included in this declaration.)

Kobold Press, Midgard, and Tales of the Valiant are trademarks of Open Design LLC. All rights reserved.

Open Game Content: The Open Content includes the spells previously published and the backer spells. All other material is Product Identity, especially place names, character names, locations, story elements, background, sidebars, and fiction.

No other portion of this work may be reproduced in any form without permission.

©2023 Open Design LLC. All rights reserved.
www.koboldpress.com
PO Box 2811 | Kirkland, WA 98083

Printed in China / FSC Paper

ISBN: 978-1-950789-54-2
Limited Edition ISBN: 978-1-950789-65-8

2 4 6 8 10 9 7 5 3 1

TABLE OF

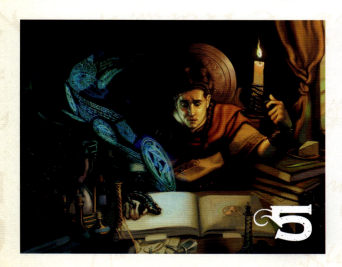

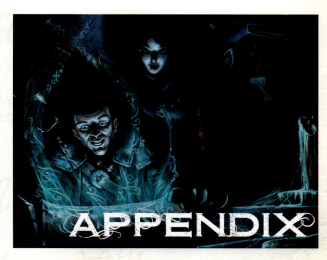

CONTENTS

1 Character Options	**7**
Theurge	7
Dweomercrafter	12
Mystic	13
Spell Siphon	14
Subclasses	15
Arcane Traditions	15
Alkemancer	15
Blood Mage	18
Dragon Mage	18
Elementalist	21
Entropist	23
Illuminator	24
Master of Fiends	25
Necrophage	27
Ring Warden	28
Timekeeper	29
White Necromancer	30
Bard Colleges	31
College of Wyrdsingers	31
Greenleaf College	32
Divine Domains	32
Angelic Scribe	32
Beer Domain	34
Cat Domain	35
Dragon Domain	36
Frost Domain	36
Hunger Domain	38
Hunting Domain	38
Justice Domain	39
Lust Domain	40
Moon Domain	40
Mountain Domain	41
Ocean Domain	42
Prophecy Domain	43
Speed Domain	43
Time Domain	44
Travel Domain	44
Druid Circles	45
Circle of Oaks	45
Circle of Owls	46
Circle of Roses	46
Martial Archetypes	48
Prescient Knight	48
Otherworldly Patrons	49
Frozen One	49
Genie Lord	50
Sibyl	52
Ranger Archetypes	53
Griffon Scout	53
Vampire Slayer	54
Sacred Oaths	54
Oath of Radiance	54
Oath of Thunder	56
Sorcerous Origins	57
Boreal	57
Elemental Essence	58
Farseer	60
Serophage	60
Backgrounds	61
Archivist	61
Fey Hostage	63
Soul Channeler	64
Transformed Familiar	66
2 Styles of Magic	**68**
What Are Magic Styles?	68
How to Use This Section	68
Style Descriptions	69
Alkemancy Magic	69
Recommended Spell List	71
Alkemancy Magic Items	71
Mundane Alkemical Items	73
Angelic Magic	74
Angelic Spells	74
Recommended Spell List	74
Blood Magic	75
Recommended Spell List	75

DEEP MAGIC VOLUME 1

Chaos Magic	76
Chaos Magic Surges	76
Recommended Spell List	80
Dragon Magic	80
Recommended Spell List	80
Fiendish Magic	81
Recommended Spell List	81
Frost Magic	82
Recommended Spell List	82
Hieroglyph Magic	82
Script Carver	82
Script Sage	83
Invoking Hieroglyph Powers	83
Hieroglyph Descriptions	84
Illumination Magic	89
Recommended Spell List	89
Mythos Magic	90
Essence of the Void	90
Recommended Spell List	90
Grimoires of the Cthulhu Mythos	90
Ring Magic	92
Ring Magic Feats	93
Circle Spellcaster	93
Ring-Bound	93
Recommended Spell List	94
Sorcerer Ring Spells	94
Warlock Ring Spells	94
Wizard Ring Spells	94
Rune Magic	95
Rune Powers	95
Rune Knowledge	95
Rune Mastery	96
Invoking Rune Powers	96
Rune Descriptions	96
Temporal Magic	102
Variant: Clockwork Magic	102
Recommended Spell List	103
3 Spellcasting Allies	**104**
Apprentices	104
Arn of Rowan	105
Erolimar	105
Lereilel Cloudwood	106
Terindor Grayveil	107
Xelasora	107
Magic Constructs	108
Bzeldruin's Hundred	108
Leothar's Bust	109
Nisruel's Coachfly	110
Sivvar's Writing Desk	111
Familiar Territory	112
Standard Familiars	113
4 Spell Lists	**125**
5 Spell Descriptions	**141**
6 Appendix: Tales of the Valiant Spell Conversion	**281**
Spell Conversion	281
Circles of Magic	281
Arcane Circle	281
Divine Circle	281
Primordial Circle	282
Wyrd Circle	282
Multi-Circle Spells	282

CHARACTER OPTIONS

This chapter includes an array of new spellcasting-focused character options compatible with any setting. Here are the options featured:

- *Theurge.* Details a new base class.
- *Subclasses.* Presents a variety of subclasses for characters with spellcasting base classes.
- *Backgrounds.* Expands the options for arcane characters with new backgrounds.

THEURGE

The half-elf's eyes glitter as ice shards from the enemy's spell pelt her and her companions. But as her fists clench and eyes flash, the spell harmlessly fizzles in the very air above them.

The tiny gnome thoughtfully strokes his long beard as he contemplates the vile creature slowly moving toward him, its jagged sword flashing in the torchlight. He sneers as the strange, eye-shaped tattoo on his forehead opens to fire a beam of powerful energy at the creature, rendering it momentarily stunned, and quickly follows it up with a barrage of spells from each hand.

Twirling his hands in intricate circles, the human furiously shapes and manipulates his spells in the very act of casting them. A fiery ball made of solid ice erupts from his hand, exploding among friend and foe alike, though only affecting his enemies while leaving his companions unharmed.

Some spend their lives poring over ancient tomes and texts. Others devote themselves to the gods, acting as emissaries of the divine. The theurge seeks to achieve a perfect balance between the arcane and the divine, blending both kinds of magic into a powerful and cohesive whole.

CHAPTER 1 CHARACTER OPTIONS | 7

BLENDING THE ARCANE AND THE DIVINE

Theurges revel in the unbridled wonders of magic, regardless of its source. They strive to refine their magical abilities, driven by their quest to accomplish ever greater feats of spellcasting. Many consider the theurge to be the epitome of what it means to be a spellcaster.

THE DIVINITY OF MAGIC

Although many theurges worship a specific deity, often one devoted to magic, others choose to venerate personifications of magical forces or perhaps even magic itself. Theurges typically possess an unquenchable and obsessive thirst to further their understanding and mastery of spellcasting and magic. Their might lies in their ability to draw upon, combine, and manipulate multiple forms of magical power to overcome any obstacle.

THE THEURGE

Level	Proficiency Bonus	Features	Cantrips Known	1st	2nd	3rd	4th	5th	6th	7th	8th	9th
1st	+2	Spell Nexus, Spellcasting	3	2	—	—	—	—	—	—	—	—
2nd	+2	Summon Libram	3	3	—	—	—	—	—	—	—	—
3rd	+2	Theurgic Devotion	3	4	2	—	—	—	—	—	—	—
4th	+2	Ability Score Improvement	4	4	3	—	—	—	—	—	—	—
5th	+3	Theurgic Insight (d6)	4	4	3	2	—	—	—	—	—	—
6th	+3	Theurgic Devotion Feature	4	4	3	3	—	—	—	—	—	—
7th	+3	Superior Focus	4	4	3	3	1	—	—	—	—	—
8th	+3	Ability Score Improvement	4	4	3	3	2	—	—	—	—	—
9th	+4	Spell Synthesis (3rd Level)	4	4	3	3	3	1	—	—	—	—
10th	+4	Theurgic Devotion Feature	5	4	3	3	3	2	—	—	—	—
11th	+4	Theurgic Insight (d8)	5	4	3	3	3	2	1	—	—	—
12th	+4	Ability Score Improvement	5	4	3	3	3	2	1	—	—	—
13th	+5	Spell Synthesis (4th Level)	5	4	3	3	3	2	1	1	—	—
14th	+5	Theurgic Devotion Feature	5	4	3	3	3	2	1	1	—	—
15th	+5	Innate Spells	5	4	3	3	3	2	1	1	1	—
16th	+5	Ability Score Improvement	5	4	3	3	3	2	1	1	1	—
17th	+6	Innate Spells Improvement, Theurgic Insight (d10)	5	4	3	3	3	2	1	1	1	1
18th	+6	Spell Synthesis (5th Level)	5	4	3	3	3	3	1	1	1	1
19th	+6	Ability Score Improvement	5	4	3	3	3	3	2	1	1	1
20th	+6	Theurge Supreme	5	4	3	3	3	3	2	2	1	1

DEEP MAGIC VOLUME 1

CREATING A THEURGE

When creating a theurge, it is important to decide how and why you can blend such disparate forms of magic. Were you born with this ability? Were your powers a gift from a deity? Did you learn your craft through countless hours of solitary study?

You should also decide if you are a religious individual, actively working to promote the will of one or more particular deities. Alternatively, do you believe magic itself is worthy of divine reverence without the need for gods? Or perhaps you are an academic person, one who treats the acquisition of spells and magical power as a purely intellectual endeavor separate from the acknowledgement of such divinity.

QUICK BUILD

You can make a theurge quickly by following these suggestions. First, Intelligence should be your highest ability score, followed by Wisdom. Second, choose the occultist (see *Tome of Heroes*) background or the acolyte from the core game.

CLASS FEATURES

As a theurge, you gain the following class features.

HIT POINTS

Hit Dice: 1d6 per theurge level
Hit Points at 1st Level: 6 + your Constitution modifier
Hit Points at Higher Levels: 1d6 (or 4) + your Constitution modifier per theurge level after 1st

PROFICIENCIES

Armor: None
Weapons: Daggers, darts, slings, quarterstaffs
Tools: None
Saving Throws: Intelligence, Wisdom
Skills: Choose two from Arcana, History, Insight, Investigation, Medicine, and Religion

EQUIPMENT

You start with the following equipment, in addition to the equipment granted by your background:

- (a) a quarterstaff or (b) a dagger
- (a) a component pouch or (b) an arcane focus or holy symbol
- (a) a scholar's pack or (b) an explorer's pack
- A theurgic libram

SPELLCASTING

As a student of magic, you can cast cleric and wizard spells.

Cantrips

At 1st level, you know one cantrip of your choice from the cleric spell list, one cantrip of your choice from the wizard spell list, and a third cantrip from either the cleric or wizard spell list (your choice). You learn additional cleric or wizard cantrips of your choice at higher levels, as shown in the Cantrips Known column of the Theurge table.

Theurgic Libram

At 1st level, you learn the ritual to create a theurgic libram. This ritual takes 1 hour, during which time you construct your libram and then magically bond with it.

Your theurgic libram contains six 1st-level spells of your choice. You can choose these spells from the cleric or wizard spell lists, but at least two of these spells must be from the cleric spell list and at least two must be from the wizard spell list.

The spells that you add to your theurgic libram as you gain levels reflect the magical and esoteric research you conduct on your own, as well as intellectual breakthroughs you have made about the nature of magic.

Replacing the Libram. If your theurgic libram is lost or destroyed, you can create a new one by performing the same ritual, which requires a number of hours equal to the highest spell level contained in your libram (so if the libram contained 1st-level spells only, the ritual to replace it takes 1 hour, but if the libram contained 1st, 2nd, and 3rd-level spells, the ritual takes 3 hours). The contents of your new libram are identical to the contents of your previous libram.

You can't have more than one theurgic libram at a time. If it still exists, your previous libram vanishes the moment you complete the ritual to create a replacement libram.

Libram's Appearance. Your theurgic libram is a unique compilation of spells with its own decorative flourishes and margin notes. It might appear plain and functional, resembling a gift you once received from your master, or be a finely bound, gilt-edged prayer tome worthy of an ancient temple or even be a simple, dog-eared journal you crafted yourself.

Preparing and Casting Spells

The Theurge table shows how many spell slots you have to cast your cleric or wizard spells of 1st level and higher. To cast one of these spells, you must expend a slot of the spell's level or higher. You regain all expended spell slots when you finish a long rest. For example, if you know the 1st-level spell cure wounds and have a 1st-level and a 2nd-level spell slot available, you can cast cure wounds using either slot.

You prepare the list of cleric and wizard spells that are available for you to cast. To do so, choose a number of cleric or wizard spells from your theurgic libram equal to your Intelligence modifier + your theurge level (minimum of one spell). The spells must be of a level for which you have spell slots.

For example, if you're a 3rd-level theurge, you have four 1st-level and two 2nd-level spell slots. With an Intelligence of 16, your list of prepared spells can include six spells of 1st or 2nd level, in any combination, chosen from your theurgic libram. If you prepare the 1st-level spell *cure wounds* or *magic missile*, you can cast it using a 1st-level or a 2nd-level slot. Casting the spell doesn't remove it from your list of prepared spells.

You can change your list of prepared spells when you finish a long rest. Preparing a new list of spells requires time spent studying your theurgic libram and memorizing the incantations and gestures you must make to cast the spell: at least 1 minute per spell level for each spell on your prepared spell list.

Spellcasting Ability

Intelligence is your spellcasting ability for both your cleric and wizard spells since you learn your spells through dedicated study and mental discipline. You use your Intelligence whenever a spell refers to your spellcasting ability. In addition, you use your Intelligence modifier when setting the saving throw DC for a cleric or wizard spell that you cast and when making an attack roll with one.

Spell save DC = 8 + your proficiency bonus + your Intelligence modifier

Spell attack modifier = your proficiency bonus + your Intelligence modifier

Ritual Casting

You can cast a cleric or wizard spell as a ritual if that spell has the ritual tag and you have the spell in your theurgic libram. You don't need to have the spell prepared to cast it as a ritual.

Spellcasting Focus

You can use either an arcane focus or holy symbol as a spellcasting focus for both your cleric and wizard spells.

Learning Spells of 1st Level and Higher

Each time you gain a theurge level, you can add three spells of your choice from the cleric or wizard spell lists to your libram. At least one of these spells must be from the cleric spell list, and at least one must be from the wizard spell list. Each of these spells must be of a level for which you have spell slots, as shown in the Theurge table.

SPELL NEXUS

While your theurgic libram is on your person, you can use a bonus action to open a magical conduit between you and it, allowing you to instantly replace one spell you currently have prepared with another spell of the same level transcribed within the libram. For example, if you're a 3rd-level theurge, you could instantly replace one 1st-level spell you currently have prepared with another 1st-level spell transcribed in your libram.

You can't use this feature again until you finish a long rest.

SUMMON LIBRAM

At 2nd level, you are able to sense the location of your theurgic libram, as long as it is within 100 feet of you. If your libram is within this range, you can use a bonus action to cause it to instantly teleport to your hand.

Beginning at 9th level, you can sense the location of your theurgic libram and summon it to you as long as it is on the same plane of existence as you. If the libram is not on the same plane of existence, you learn which plane it is on but not the exact location within the plane.

THEURGIC DEVOTION

When you reach 3rd level, you choose a theurgic devotion which shapes your practice of magic. Choose one of the devotions detailed later in this section: the Dweomercrafter, Mystic, or Spell Siphon devotion. Your choice grants you features at 3rd level and again at 6th, 10th, and 14th level.

ABILITY SCORE IMPROVEMENT

When you reach 4th level, and again at 8th, 12th, 16th, and 19th level, you can increase one ability score of your choice by 2, or you can increase two ability scores of your choice by 1. As normal, you can't increase an ability score above 20 using this feature.

THEURGIC INSIGHT

Starting at 5th level, you gain a pool of Theurgic Insight dice. Your Theurgic Insight dice start off as d6, and they become d8 at 11th level and d10 at 17th level. The number of Theurgic Insight dice in this pool is equal to your proficiency bonus.

When you make an ability check that uses either the Arcana or Religion proficiencies, you can expend one Theurgic Insight die and add the number rolled to your ability check. You can choose to do so after you roll the die for the ability check but must do so before the GM tells you whether you succeed or fail.

You regain any expended Theurgic Insight dice when you finish a long rest.

SUPERIOR FOCUS

At 7th level, you can simultaneously maintain two spells that require concentration. One spell must be from the wizard spell list, and the other must be from the cleric spell list.

You must make a Constitution saving throw (DC equals 10 + the highest-level spell cast) at the beginning of each round in which you are attempting to maintain concentration on two spells. If you fail this save, you immediately lose both spells.

Additionally, while concentrating on two spells, you roll with disadvantage on Constitution saving throws to maintain concentration whenever you take damage. Anything that causes you to lose concentration, including being incapacitated or killed, causes you to lose both spells.

SPELL SYNTHESIS

Beginning at 9th level, you can cast one wizard spell and one cleric spell that you have prepared on your turn. Both spells must be of 3rd level or lower, and each must have a casting time of 1 action or a bonus action. You expend spell slots for each spell as normal. Due to the intense effort this requires, you can't take a reaction on the same round you use Spell Synthesis.

You must finish a long rest before you can use Spell Synthesis again.

Beginning at 13th level, you can use Spell Synthesis twice between rests, and the maximum level of the spells you can cast increases to 4th level. At 18th level, you can use Spell Synthesis three times between rests, and the maximum level of the spells you can cast increases to 5th level. When you finish a long rest, you regain any expended uses of Spell Synthesis.

INNATE SPELLS

At 15th level, your mastery over spells allows you to cast a small number of them at will. You can choose a 1st-level cleric spell and a 1st-level wizard in your theurgic libram. These spells may not be from the evocation school of magic. You can cast these spells at their lowest level without expending a spell slot when you have them prepared. If you want to cast either of these spells at a higher level, you must expend a spell slot as normal.

When you reach 17th level, you can add one additional cleric or wizard spell from your theurgic libram to your list of innate spells. This spell can be of either 1st level or 2nd level. In addition, you can now cast your innate spells without needing to prepare them.

As part of a long rest, you can exchange any of your innate spells for different spells in your theurgic libram of the same levels.

THEURGE SUPREME

At 20th level, you can use Spell Nexus a number of times per day equal to your proficiency bonus.

Additionally, when you take damage, you no longer make your Constitution saving throws with disadvantage when using Superior Focus to maintain concentration on two spells.

CHAPTER 1 CHARACTER OPTIONS

THEURGIC DEVOTIONS

The theurge's never-ending quest to unlock the secrets of spellcasting leads to extremely focused areas of magical devotion.

DWEOMERCRAFTER

Due to your extensive research into magic, you have discovered dweomercraft—esoteric methods that allow you to shape, sculpt, and otherwise modify your spells.

Dweomercraft Initiate

Starting at 3rd level, you learn your first two dweomercraft discoveries. Your dweomercraft options are detailed below. You learn an additional such discovery at 6th, 10th, and 14th level.

You can use only one dweomercraft discovery on a spell when you cast it, unless otherwise noted. Spells modified by dweomercraft cannot also be modified by Metamagic:

- *Accurate Spell.* When you cast a spell that requires an attack roll, you have advantage on that roll. If the spell requires multiple attack rolls, you have advantage on only one (your choice).
- *Branding Spell.* When you hit a single creature with a spell that deals acid, cold, fire, force, lightning, necrotic, radiant, or thunder damage, the creature is marked by an invisible rune. Until the end of your next turn, any spell attack rolls against the same target have advantage if they are from spells that deal damage of the same type as the triggering spell.
- *Disarming Spell.* When you hit a single creature with a spell that deals force damage, you can attempt to disarm it. The creature must succeed on a Strength saving throw or drop one object of your choice that it is currently holding. The dropped object lands in the target's space.
- *Forceful Spell.* When you hit a single creature that is Large or smaller with a spell that deals force damage, the creature must succeed on a Strength saving throw or be pushed up to 15 feet away from you.
- *Penetrating Spell.* You increase the spell save DC of the spell by an amount equal to half your Wisdom modifier.
- *Piercing Spell.* When you hit a single creature with a spell that deals damage, the spell ignores the creature's resistance to a single damage type of your choice. Creatures that are normally immune to your chosen damage type take half damage instead of no damage.
- *Redirect Spell.* When you cast a spell that targets a single creature but that has no effect on the target (such as due to a successful saving throw or a missed attack roll), you can redirect the spell to another eligible target within 15 feet of the initial target. If the spell requires any attack rolls, you must roll new ones

against the new target. If the spell has no effect on the new target, the spell is lost.
- *Sculpt Spell.* When you cast a spell that deals acid, cold, fire, force, lightning, necrotic, radiant, or thunder damage, you can change that damage type to another type from that list.
- *Selective Spell.* When you cast a spell that forces targeted creatures to make a saving throw, you can protect some of those targets from the spell's full force. Choose a number of targets up to your Intelligence modifier (minimum of one). A chosen target automatically succeeds on its saving throw against the spell.
- *Upcast Spell.* You cast a spell that is treated as if it were cast using a spell slot of one level higher. This spell does not actually use a higher-level slot though.

You can use any combination of the dweomercraft discoveries you know a total number of times equal to your Intelligence modifier (minimum of one). You cannot use more until you finish a long rest.

Saving Throws. If a dweomercraft discovery requires your target to make a saving throw, it is against your theurge spell save DC.

Spellweaver

Beginning at 6th level, when you cast a spell that affects an area, you can increase or decrease its area of effect. You can do this a number of times equal to your proficiency bonus. You regain any expended uses of this feature upon completing a long rest.

When you reach 11th level, you regain expended uses of Spellweaver when you finish a short or long rest.

Area of Effect	Modification
Cone	Increase or decrease the cone's size by up to 10 feet
Cube	Increase or decrease the cube's sides by up to 10 feet each
Cylinder	Increase or decrease the cylinder's height or diameter by up to 10 feet
Line	Increase or decrease the line's length by up to 10 feet
Sphere	Increase or decrease the sphere's radius by up to 10 feet

Dweomercraft Adept

Beginning at 10th level, you can use the dweomercraft discoveries you know a total number of times equal to your Intelligence modifier + your Wisdom modifier.

In addition, you can use two dweomercraft discoveries you know on a single spell you cast. Alternatively, you can use a dweomercraft discovery on each spell you cast using the Spell Synthesis feature.

Dweomercraft Master

At 14th level, you recover all expended uses of your dweomercraft discoveries when you finish a short or long rest.

MYSTIC

You have learned how to unlock and harness the mystical potential of the mind. This mystical power manifests as a third eye, through which you can unleash psionic abilities.

Third Eye

At 3rd level, a mystical eye appears on your forehead. This eye can take the form of a stylized tattoo, an eye-shaped scar, or it could be an actual eye. The eye opens whenever you use one of your mystic powers. Otherwise, it remains closed.

Your third eye unlocks psionic energy from deep within, represented by a pool of psionic points. The number of psionic points you have is equal to your theurge level + your proficiency bonus.

You regain all spent psionic points when you finish a long rest. When you reach 9th level, you regain all spent psionic points when you finish a short or long rest.

As an action, you can expend one or more psionic points to fuel the mystical powers of your third eye (see below). Each power has a duration of 1 hour. You can only have one such power active at a time:

- You can detect the presence of secret or concealed doors or compartments within 30 feet of you.
  Cost: 1 psionic point
- You can see invisible creatures and objects within 30 feet of you as if they were visible.
  Cost: 2 psionic points
- You can see normally in darkness, both magical and nonmagical, to a distance of 60 feet.
  Cost: 3 psionic points
- You can detect visual illusions within 30 feet of you, and you automatically succeed on saving throws against them. You can also perceive the original form of a shapechanger or a creature transformed by magic.
  Cost: 4 psionic points

Psychic Blast

Starting at 6th level, you can fire a blast of psychic energy from your third eye by expending one or more psionic

points. As a bonus action, make a ranged spell attack against one creature you can see within 60 feet of you. On a hit, the target takes 1d8 psychic damage per psionic point spent, up to a maximum number of points equal to your proficiency bonus.

Psychic blasts are sometimes difficult to control and have the potential to deal significant psychic damage. If you roll an 8 on an individual damage die when you deal damage with your psychic blast, you can roll another d8 and add the result to the total. For example, if you roll 2d8 and the roll resulted in a 3 and an 8, you can roll one additional die (because you rolled one 8) and add the result to the current total of 11. When a damage die results in an 8, it is called a psionic surge.

If you roll an 8 again, you can roll the damage die again and add the result to the total, further increasing the psychic blast damage. Any of the damage dice for a psychic blast, including extra dice from a critical hit, can have a psionic surge and result in a reroll. For each psychic blast attack you make, the maximum number of psionic surge dice you can reroll is equal to your proficiency bonus, regardless of how many damage dice result in an 8. The additional damage dice rolled due to psionic surges do not cost additional psionic points.

For example, a 6th-level theurge mystic unleashes a psychic blast and scores a critical hit. The character spends 3 psionic points and rolls 6d8 damage dice (3d8 for the 3 psionic points spent plus 3d8 for the critical hit damage) which results in a 1, 3, 5, 8, 8 and another 8. The character then rerolls each 8, resulting in a 1, 3, and an 8. The character adds those results to the current damage total for a final damage total of 45. Since the character's proficiency bonus is +3, the character can't reroll the new 8, ending the psionic surge for that psychic blast attack. When that character makes another attack with psychic blast, this process begins anew.

Beginning at 11th level, a target hit by your psychic blast must also succeed on an Intelligence saving throw against your spell save DC or be stunned until the start of your next turn.

Psychic Shield

At 10th level, you gain resistance to psychic damage.

As a bonus action, you can temporarily gain resistance to additional damage types by spending 1 psionic point per additional resistance. You can select resistance to damage types from the following list: acid, cold, fire, force, lightning, necrotic, radiant, or thunder. These additional resistances remain until the start of your next turn. You can keep, add, or remove these temporary resistances each new round by expending the appropriate number of additional psionic points. For example, as a bonus action, you could add resistance to force, radiant, and thunder damage by expending 3 psionic points. At the start of your next turn, you could use a new bonus action to keep resistance to force, radiant, and thunder damage, as well as add resistance to slashing damage, by expending 4 additional psionic points.

You can choose to extend your resistance to psychic damage, plus any additional temporary resistances, to friendly creatures within 10 feet of you. At 14th level, the range of your Psychic Shield increases to 15 feet, and at 18th level, it increases to 20 feet.

Psychic Storm

At 14th level, as an action, you can spend 5 psionic points to release a storm of psychic energy. Each creature within a 30-foot radius of you must make an Intelligence saving throw against your spell save DC. Creatures that fail the save take 5d8 psychic damage and have disadvantage on attacks until the beginning of your next turn. Creatures that succeed on the save take half as much damage and do not have disadvantage on their attacks.

You can increase the damage by 1d8 per each additional psionic point spent beyond the initial 5 points.

Beginning at 18th level, you can use Psychic Storm as a bonus action.

SPELL SIPHON

Your insatiable thirst for new and expanded spell options has led you to discover how to siphon spell energy and knowledge directly from other spellcasters.

Spell Siphon

At 3rd level, you gain the ability to magically siphon the knowledge of how to cast a spell from another spellcaster in the very act of casting the spell. This can potentially allow you to learn a spell from a spell list other than that of the cleric or wizard.

If a creature that you can see within 30 feet of you casts a spell, you can use your reaction to attempt to learn the spell for yourself. To do so, you make an Intelligence check with a DC equal to 12 + the spell's level.

If you succeed, you siphon the knowledge of the spell if it is at least 1st level and of a level you can cast. You can then immediately add this spell to your theurgic libram. You must replace a spell currently in your theurgic libram of the same level as the siphoned spell with the new spell. If you choose not to transfer the spell into your libram, the spell energy immediately fades from your mind with no effect.

Spell Channel

Starting at 6th level, you can immediately use the stored spell energy that you absorbed when using Spell Siphon to cast the siphoned spell, as if you are casting it yourself. Doing so does not expend one of your spell slots or require any material components. Once you cast a spell in this way, the spell energy immediately vanishes from your mind and cannot be transferred into your theurgic libram.

You can use this feature once per short or long rest.

Spell Fizzle

Beginning at 10th level, if a creature casts a spell that targets you or includes you in its area of effect, you can use your reaction to force the creature to make a saving throw against your spell save DC. (The creature uses its spellcasting ability for the save.) If the creature fails the save, you negate the spell's effect against you. If the spell includes other creatures in its area of effect, and the saving throw fails by 5 or more, you can choose to negate the spell's effect on them as well.

You can use Spell Fizzle up to a number of times equal to half your proficiency bonus (rounded down). You regain any expended uses once you finish a long rest.

Spell Cache

Beginning at 14th level, a successful use of Spell Siphon allows you to replace a spell currently in your theurgic libram with the newly siphoned spell as normal. However, the spell knowledge does not immediately vanish. Instead, you can store the spell within you for a number of rounds equal to your proficiency bonus.

As an action, you can release this spell energy on your turn to cast the spell, as if you are casting it yourself. Doing so does not expend one of your spell slots nor require any material components. Once you release the spell energy to cast the spell, the energy vanishes from your mind. If you do not cast the spell within the allotted number of rounds, the spell energy fades from your mind with no effect.

You can do this a number of times equal to half your proficiency bonus (rounded down). You can't do so again until you finish a long rest.

SUBCLASSES

This section includes various subclass options for spellcasting characters.

ARCANE TRADITIONS

At 2nd level, a wizard gains the Arcane Tradition feature, and the following new options become available.

ALKEMANCER

Wizards who combine traditional spellcasting with advanced alchemical practices and concoctions are called alkemancers. They are a mysterious breed sometimes confused with transmuters, with whom they share a complicated rivalry.

Wizard Specialty

Unlike many transmuters, who focus on the physical transformation of objects and creatures, alkemancers are concerned with the search for human perfection and

immortality, and they use alchemy as a means in this pursuit. Still, there is much crossover between the two specialties. Alkemancers and transmuters can be found working toward the same goals, as both allies and rivals.

Alkemancy spells typically blend conjuration, necromancy, and transmutation effects. Few alkemancy spells belong to the schools of evocation or illusion, since spells of these schools summon energy out of nothingness or create things that are not real; both concepts are at odds with the precepts of alkemancy, which seeks to reduce energy and matter to its constituent parts and refine them to a more purified (or useful) state of existence.

Except as noted below, alkemancers function as wizards and use the wizard spell list.

Alchemical Savant

Beginning when you select this specialty at 2nd level, the gold and time you must spend to copy an alkemancy spell into your spellbook are halved.

When you gain a level, one of the two spells you learn for gaining a level can be an alkemancy spell even if you've never encountered the spell before. Similarly, when you learn a new cantrip, it can be an alkemancy cantrip even if you've never previously encountered it.

CHAPTER 1 CHARACTER OPTIONS | 15

Skilled Alchemist

Beginning at 2nd level, you gain proficiency with alchemical supplies if you did not already have it and your proficiency bonus with alchemical supplies is doubled. You also halve the cost of alchemical items you create, enabling you to fashion most basic items in a single day. Finally, you gain proficiency with alchemical weapons, and you add your proficiency bonus to their damage rolls when you use them as weapons.

Essence Mastery

Beginning at 6th level, you can add one of the six fundamental essences to your spells as an additional material component at the cost of 1 gp per spell level. This addition doesn't increase the casting time of the spell or any of its other effects, except as follows:

- Adding brimstone to a spell that deals fire damage gives the flames a bluish hue and releases irritating vapors. A creature damaged by the spell must make a successful Constitution saving throw or become poisoned for a number of rounds equal to your Intelligence modifier (minimum of 1).
- Adding lead to a spell that improves your Armor Class, such as *mage armor* or *shield*, increases the spell's AC bonus by 2. If the spell has a duration longer than 1 round, the duration increases by a number of rounds equal to your Intelligence modifier (minimum of 1). Any visible spell effect modified with the addition of lead takes on a dull gray sheen.
- Adding quicksilver to a spell that changes the form of a creature or an object, such as *alter self* or *polymorph*, increases the spell's duration by a number of minutes equal to your Intelligence modifier (minimum of 1 minute). For any such spell that has a duration of less than 10 minutes, such as *alchemical form*, the increase is measured in rounds instead of minutes. Any change in form modified with quicksilver is accompanied by lustrous wisps or motes of silvery energy.
- Adding quintessence to a necromancy spell that grants temporary hit points, such as *false life* or *life hack*, increases the temporary hit points gained by a number equal to twice your Intelligence modifier (minimum of 2). Adding quintessence to a spell doesn't change the spell's visible aspects.
- Adding salt to a spell that deals acid damage gives the acid a pale, crystalline hue and causes it to become extremely painful. Any creature damaged by the spell must also make a successful Constitution saving throw or lose 1d4 points from its Strength and Dexterity

scores (rolled separately). These lost ability score points return automatically after a number of rounds equal to your Intelligence modifier (minimum of 1).
- Adding void salt to a spell that deals necrotic damage causes the spell to shed palpable strands of darkness. Any creature damaged by the spell is also surrounded by a veil of cloying shadows and must make a successful Constitution saving throw or be restrained for a number of rounds equal to your Intelligence modifier (minimum of 1).

Craft Minor Elixir

Beginning at 10th level, you automatically learn the formulas for a number of elixirs, oils, philters, or potions of your choice equal to 1 + your Intelligence modifier (minimum of one). You do not need to spend time or gold researching these formulas.

When you brew an elixir, oil, philter, or potion based on one of the formulas you obtained, you can add exotic alchemical reagents to the mixture at the cost of additional gold equal to half the potion's standard cost. If you do so, the resulting mixture is more powerful than normal: if the potion's effect is instantaneous (such as a *potion of healing*), it automatically has its maximum effect; if the potion has a duration (such as a *potion of giant strength*), it lasts for twice its normal duration.

Path of the Golden Glower

Beginning at 14th level, you learn the secret formulas for brewing the fabled *Six Elixirs*, magical draughts of incredible potency and rarity. Each elixir takes a full year or more to create from exceedingly rare ingredients, but once finished and consumed or otherwise applied, it grants its user a permanent bonus of some sort. The six elixirs are described below.

Additionally, once you reach 14th level, you become so adept at working with dangerous chemicals and reagents that you gain resistance to acid damage and poison damage and immunity to the poisoned condition.

The Six Elixirs

Alkemancers are responsible for the creation of many astonishing alchemical items, but the pinnacle of their craftsmanship is known collectively as the *Six Elixirs*, magical liquids of such incredible power and rarity that they feature in many tales and legends. Vast resources and even many lives have been expended in the pursuit of these fabled elixirs. A single elixir could be the focus of an entire campaign arc for an alkemancer character or group of adventurers.

Brewing any one of the *Six Elixirs* takes one year of work with rare, mysterious, and sometimes dangerous ingredients. The ingredients needed to create each elixir are given in its description. The GM can modify ingredients to meet the needs of the campaign.

BLACK ELIXIR

Potion, Legendary

This greasy black liquid acts as a poison when drunk or rubbed on flesh. Its unfortunate or foolish user takes 12d6 poison damage, or half as much damage with a successful DC 20 Constitution saving throw.

Its true power is revealed, however, when *black elixir* is smeared on a doorway or other portal; the magical oil acts as a *forbiddance* spell with a duration of one year. Unlike the spell, *black elixir* doesn't incorporate a password and only affects celestials and fiends. Typically, the creator of the elixir determines when the elixir is created whether the *forbiddance* effect deals radiant or necrotic damage.

Ingredients. The heart of a marut, the powdered horn of a ki-rin, and a vial of black mud taken from the bottom of a lake that at least one celestial or fiend has bathed in.

GOLDEN ELIXIR

Potion, Legendary

The most famous of the six elixirs is this thick, golden, syrupy liquid that grants its imbiber eternal life. The potion completely stops the aging process and renders the imbiber immune to all natural and magical diseases and poisons. The drinker can still be harmed or killed through other methods such as violence, but the march of time no longer holds any threat over him or her.

Ingredients. A thimble of distilled sunlight, the breath of a solar, and the hair of a venerable sage who is at least 100 years old.

IRON ELIXIR

Potion, Legendary

This dark, grainy liquid tastes positively awful. Anyone imbibing the elixir gains permanent resistance to bludgeoning, piercing, and slashing damage and gains a damage threshold of 5, but their speed is reduced by 10 feet, and they always make Dexterity saving throws and Dexterity ability checks with disadvantage that can't be overcome or canceled out by any means.

Ingredients. The core of an iron golem, a shard of purest adamantine, and the powdered teeth of a mountain giant.

JADE ELIXIR

Potion, Legendary

This bright green elixir grants its consumer incredible Charisma when dealing with celestials, elementals, fey, and fiends. The drinker always has advantage on Charisma checks when dealing with extraplanar creatures, and when one of the selected creatures is called or conjured, it arrives with maximum hit points.

Ingredients. The tears of an invisible stalker, the claw of a pit fiend, and the tongue of a bard of at least 10th level.

PEARL ELIXIR

Potion, Legendary

This silvery-white elixir has a variety of effects depending on whether it is drunk, rubbed on a creature's feet, or smeared on the hull of a boat. If drunk, the elixir confers the ability to breathe both air and water with equal ease. If rubbed on the feet, the elixir provides a creature with the ability to walk on water as if wearing a *ring of water walking*. If placed on the hull of a boat or similar vessel, the vessel gains a damage threshold of 20 against all environmental effects, and anyone piloting the vessel has advantage on ability checks associated with it. All of these effects are permanent.

Ingredients. The scale of a merfolk princess, a vial of pure elemental water, and the eye of a kraken.

RUBY ELIXIR

Potion, Legendary

This vermilion-hued elixir neutralizes all magical and nonmagical diseases and poisons, all curses of 8th level or lower, and all exhaustion effects, as well as restoring hit points as a *superior healing potion*. If this elixir is poured over a corpse that has been dead for no more than a year, it restores the creature to life (as the *resurrection* spell) even if the corpse could normally not be resurrected.

Ingredients. A mixture of purest cinnabar, the blood of a slain dragon of at least adult age, and the hearts of six celestial tigers willingly donated to the Alkemancer.

BLOOD MAGE

Blood can be a source of magical energy for those willing to make the necessary sacrifices, whether those be personal or dark and forbidden.

Wizard Specialty

A blood mage powers their magic with the secrets they learn from their own blood. Eventually, they learn to manipulate the blood of others as well.

Blood Savant

Beginning when you select this specialty at 2nd level, the gold and time you must spend to copy a blood magic spell into your spellbook is halved.

Bonus Proficiency

At 2nd level, you gain proficiency in Medicine.

Internal Fortitude

At 2nd level, you also gain a greater awareness of the blood flowing through your veins and of the heart that pumps it—and some measure of control over both. When you are subjected to a disease or poison effect that allows a Constitution saving throw to take only half damage, you instead take no damage on a successful save and only half damage on a failed one.

Blood Vision

Beginning at 6th level, you can see a moment of the past through the eyes of a creature by consuming its blood. Upon ingesting a small amount of the blood of another creature, you become stunned. While stunned, you experience one of the creature's memories through its own eyes. (The memory may or may not be about the incident that caused it to bleed.)

Once you have consumed a creature's blood for this purpose, the creature is immune to further uses of this ability.

Absorb Toxins

Beginning at 10th level, you can absorb a poison or a disease from another creature, living or dead, and turn it to your use. By exposing a fresh wound to a source of disease or poison, you can safely absorb it and store it, dormant, in your bloodstream. You can then inflict the disease or poison on another creature by spitting a stream of blood at it. As an action, you make a ranged spell attack. On a hit, the target is exposed to the disease or poison and must proceed with any saving throws required.

If you do not pass the disease or poison along to another living creature within three days, it becomes active in the body, and you must make the first two saving throws required by the disease or poison with disadvantage.

Thicken or Quicken Blood

Beginning at 14th level, you can turn another creature's blood into sludge, hampering the creature, or you can thin it out, giving the creature extra mobility. As an action, you can cause a touched creature that fails a Constitution saving throw to become affected as if by a *slow* spell—or alternatively, to gain the effect of a *haste* spell. The duration of either effect is a number of rounds equal to your Intelligence modifier. The target of the *haste* effect can intentionally fail the saving throw.

You can use this ability once, regaining the use of it upon finishing a long rest.

DRAGON MAGE

Wizards practice the subtle magic of pulling power from thin air and shaping it to fit their needs. Sorcerers tame the chaotic power within themselves, releasing it in barely controlled gouts of magical eruptions. Wizards who walk the path between these two diverse means of using magic are called dragon mages, and they meld the order of wizardry with the chaos of elemental mastery to grant themselves special powers.

Wizard Specialty

Dragon mages manifest their magic in a variety of styles, as diverse as the kinds of dragons and the types of magic that populate the worlds. Kobolds serving as councilors to great wyrms are taught by their masters to harness their innate draconic nature through the use of more traditional spells. A wild-eyed human, oozing sorcerous magic thanks to an ancient draconic ancestor, might find a kindly wizard to help her focus her power. Special legions of dragonborn troops train with a master dragon mage, learning to better defend their homeland from invaders.

How to Start. If you're a wizard who wants to become a dragon mage, you make that decision upon reaching 2nd level, when you are also entitled to choose an arcane tradition. If you decide to follow the path of the dragon mage exclusively, you can forego the selection of an arcane tradition and gain the features of the dragon mage specialty instead.

You can also pursue the dragon mage specialty in conjunction with one of the standard arcane traditions. If you choose to do this, you gain the Savant feature of your chosen school in addition to Dragon Magic Savant (described below). Also at 2nd level, you choose whether to gain Invoke Dragon Mask (see below) or the 2nd-level feature of your chosen school. Thereafter, at 6th, 10th, and 14th level, you choose between the lowest-level features still available. For instance, an enchanter might select Hypnotic Gaze at 2nd level and Invoke Dragon Mask at 6th level, followed by either Instinctive Charm or Invoke Dragon Heart at 10th level.

Dragon Magic Savant
Beginning when you take up this specialty at 2nd level, the gold and time you must spend to copy a dragon magic spell into your spellbook is halved.

Invoke Dragon Mask
Starting at 2nd level, you can invoke a magic dragon mask. You use a bonus action and expend a spell slot to invoke the mask, which lasts for 3 rounds for each level of the expended spell slot. The dragon mask remains as long as you are not incapacitated, until you use a bonus action to dismiss or replace it, or until the duration expires. The mask is a translucent magical force, in the form of a dragon's head, which covers your face. Your face is still visible through the mask, and the mask does not hinder vision.

While you wear your dragon mask, you receive the following benefits and drawbacks:

- You have a bonus to your AC equal to your Intelligence modifier (minimum of –1).
- You gain a bite attack. As an action, make a melee spell attack against one adjacent target. On a hit, the target takes piercing damage equal to 1d8 + your Intelligence modifier. This attack counts as magical for the purpose of overcoming a target's immunity or resistance to piecing damage.

- You have advantage on Wisdom (Perception) checks and Charisma (Intimidation) checks.
- Attack rolls for any ranged or melee attack spells you cast while wearing the mask are made with disadvantage, and saving throws against spells you cast while wearing the mask are made with advantage.
- As a bonus action, you can expend an additional spell slot to augment the damage of your next dragon mask bite attack. The damage increases by 1d8 for each level of the expended spell slot, and you have advantage on the attack roll.

Invoke Dragon Heart

Starting at 6th level, you can invoke a magic dragon heart. You use a bonus action and expend a spell slot to invoke the heart, which lasts for 3 rounds for each level of the expended spell slot. The dragon heart remains as long as you are not incapacitated, until you use a bonus action to dismiss or replace it, or until the duration expires. The heart is a translucent magical force, in the form of a beating heart, which covers your chest. Your body is still visible through the heart.

While you wear your dragon heart, you receive the following benefits:

- You have a bonus to Wisdom and Charisma saving throws equal to your Intelligence modifier (minimum of +1).
- You gain temporary hit points equal to twice your wizard level. These temporary hit points are lost when your heart is no longer active.
- You gain a breath weapon attack. You can use an action to shoot a 30-foot-long, 5-foot-wide line of energy (dealing your choice of acid, cold, fire, or lightning damage) from your dragon heart in a direction you choose. Each creature in the line must make a successful Dexterity saving throw or take 4d6 damage of the chosen type. The damage type cannot be changed while your current dragon heart is active.
- As a bonus action, you can expend an additional spell slot to augment the damage of your next dragon heart breath weapon attack. The damage increases by 2d6 for each level of the expended spell slot, and you can add 10 feet of length to the line for each level of the expended spell slot.

Invoke Dragon Wings

Starting at 10th level, you can invoke a set of magical dragon wings. You use a bonus action and spend a spell slot to invoke the dragon wings, which last for 2 rounds per level of the spent spell slot. The dragon wings remain as long as you are not incapacitated, until the duration ends, or until they are dismissed or replaced by using a bonus action.

While you wear your dragon wings, you receive the following benefits:

- Your speed increases by 10 feet, and you gain a flying speed equal to your walking speed.
- You have resistance to bludgeoning, piercing, and slashing damage from nonmagical attacks.
- You have advantage on any melee or ranged spell attack rolls.
- As a bonus action, you can spend an additional spell slot to augment your wings. Until the start of your next turn, you can add 5 feet of additional speed for each level of the expended spell slot spent. Additionally, you can choose one creature within 10 feet of you for each level of the expended spell slot, and ranged attacks against those creatures are made with disadvantage.

Invoke Dragon Tail

Starting at 14th level, you can invoke a magic dragon tail. You use a bonus action and expend a spell slot to invoke the tail, which lasts for 1 round per level of the spent spell slot. The dragon tail remains as long as you are not incapacitated, until you use a bonus action to dismiss or replace it, or until the duration expires. The dragon tail is a translucent magical force, in the form of a 15-foot-long appendage capable of striking with great impact.

While you wear your dragon tail, you receive the following benefits:

- You are immune to the grappled condition.
- You have proficiency with Strength and Dexterity saving throws and any ability checks using Strength. In addition, you can use your Intelligence modifier instead of the normal modifier for those saving throws and checks.
- You gain a tail slam attack. As an action, you make a separate melee spell attack against each target within 15 feet of you. On a hit, the target takes bludgeoning damage equal to 3d10 + your Intelligence modifier. A creature hit by this attack is pushed up to 10 feet away from you and knocked prone unless it succeeds on a Strength saving throw against your spell save DC. This attack counts as magical for the purpose of overcoming a target's immunity or resistance to bludgeoning damage.
- As a reaction, you can make a tail slam attack against a creature that moves to within 15 feet of your tail.
- As a bonus action, you can spend an additional spell slot to augment your dragon tail. Until the start of your next turn, your dragon tail's slam attack damage increases by 1d10 per level of the spell slot spent. In addition, you heal yourself for 3 hit points per level of the spell slot spent.

ELEMENTALIST

You concentrate your arcane studies on the power inherent to one of the Elemental Planes.

Wizard Specialty

Elementalists believe in the superiority of their chosen element above all others, and they aren't shy about making that fact known. Elementalists are sometimes secluded researchers, but more often they're adventurous types who sign on with groups that can appreciate their singular talents.

Elemental Savant

Beginning when you select this specialty at 2nd level, choose one element from the Elemental Focus table. That element becomes the focus of your study. You can speak, read, and write the language associated with your focus element, and the associated damage type is used by other features as noted.

ELEMENTAL FOCUS

Element	Language	Damage Type
Air	Auran	Lightning or thunder (choose one)
Earth	Terran	Bludgeoning
Fire	Ignan	Fire
Water	Aquan	Cold

The Focus Element spell lists bring together some of the spells associated with your chosen element. The gold and time you must spend to copy a spell associated with your chosen element into your spellbook is halved. Spells marked with an asterisk (*) appear in **Chapter 5**.

FOCUS ELEMENT: AIR

Cantrips—*shocking grasp, wind lash**
1st level—*fog cloud, thunderwave, wind tunnel**
2nd level—*gust of wind, rolling thunder**
3rd level—*call lightning, lightning bolt, wind wall*
4th level—*conjure minor elementals*
5th level—*conjure elemental*
6th level—*chain lightning*
9th level—*storm of vengeance*

FOCUS ELEMENT: EARTH

Cantrips—*acid splash, pummelstone**
2nd level—*acid arrow*
3rd level—*jeweled fissure**
4th level—*conjure minor elementals, earthskimmer*, stone shape*
5th level—*conjure elemental, wall of stone*
6th level—*entomb*, move earth*
8th level—*caustic torrent*, earthquake*

FOCUS ELEMENT: FIRE

Cantrips—*fire bolt, produce flame*
2nd level—*fire darts*, flaming sphere, heat metal, scorching ray*
3rd level—*fireball*
4th level—*conjure minor elementals, fire shield, flame wave*, wall of fire*
5th level—*conjure elemental*
7th level—*delayed blast fireball*
8th level—*incendiary cloud*
9th level—*meteor swarm, pyroclasm**

FOCUS ELEMENT: WATER

Cantrips—*ray of frost*
1st level—*create or destroy water, tidal barrier**
3rd level—*frozen razors*, riptide*, sleet storm*
4th level—*conjure minor elementals, control water*
5th level—*cone of cold, conjure elemental, frostbite**
6th level—*drown*, freezing sphere, wall of ice*

Elemental Mastery

Starting at 2nd level, you learn techniques called masteries to channel elemental magic into your being and your spells.

Masteries. You learn two masteries of your choice, which are detailed below. You learn one additional mastery of your choice at 6th, 10th, and 14th levels. Each time you learn a new mastery, you can also replace one mastery you know with a different one.

Substitute Elements

Beginning at 6th level, you can funnel elemental essence through your damage-dealing spells. When you cast a spell that deals damage, you can change the damage to the type associated with your focus element.

Absorb Elements

Starting at 10th level, when you would take damage of the type associated with your focus element, you can use a reaction to take no damage and regain a number of hit points equal to half the damage you would have taken. You can use this feature even if you have resistance or immunity to that damage type from another source. You can use this feature a number of times equal to your Intelligence modifier (minimum of once). You regain all expended uses when you finish a long rest.

Irresistible Strike

At 14th level, your elemental damage spells are unstoppable. Your spells that deal damage of the type associated with your focus element ignore immunity to that damage type. You can use this feature a number of times equal to your Intelligence modifier (minimum of once). You regain all expended uses when you finish a long rest.

Masteries

Masteries are specialized techniques you can use to augment your spellcasting. Unless noted otherwise, you can use only one mastery on a given spell. The masteries are presented in alphabetical order.

ELEMENTAL ADAPTATION

Prerequisite: 14th level

You add *plane shift* to your spellbook if you don't already have it, and you can cast it once with this mastery without expending a spell slot. You can travel only to the elemental plane associated with your focus element, or to the Material Plane. While you are on the elemental plane, you aren't harmed by the normal conditions of the plane, you can breathe normally, and you can use your speed to move in a manner appropriate to the plane (flying for air, burrowing for earth, and swimming for water). You regain the ability to cast *plane shift* with this mastery when you finish a long rest.

ELEMENTAL BINDING

Prerequisite: 10th level

You add *planar binding* to your spellbook if you don't already have it, and you can cast it once with this mastery without expending a spell slot. When you cast the spell in this way, you must target an elemental creature associated with your focus element. If the elemental fails its saving throw, it gains temporary hit points equal to your wizard level. You regain the ability to cast *planar binding* with this mastery when you finish a long rest.

ELEMENTAL BULWARK

Prerequisite: 6th level

You gain resistance to the damage type associated with your focus element, and you have advantage on Constitution saving throws made to maintain concentration on spells that involve your focus element.

ELEMENTAL COMMAND

As an action, you can charm an elemental creature for as long as you maintain concentration as if concentrating on a spell, for up to 1 hour. If you or your companions damage the charmed elemental or take any harmful action against it, the charmed condition ends immediately. When this condition ends for a given elemental, it is immune to being charmed by you for 24 hours.

ELEMENTAL EROSION

Prerequisite: 10th level

After you damage a target with a spell that deals the damage type associated with your focus element, the target gains vulnerability to that damage type until the end of your next turn. You can use this feature twice. You regain all expended uses when you finish a short or long rest.

IGNITE

Prerequisite: Elemental focus (fire)

When you deal fire damage to a target with a spell of 1st level or higher, you can use a bonus action to cause the target to catch fire. At the start of its next turn, the creature takes half as much fire damage as it originally took from the spell, and the flames go out. This damage can be prevented if an ally within 5 feet uses an action to put out the flames. If you damage more than one target with the spell, choose just one to catch fire.

OVERWHELMING ONSLAUGHT

Prerequisite: 14th level

When you damage a creature with a spell of 1st level or higher that deals the damage type associated with your focus element, you can weave a lingering aura of elemental energy around the target. At the start of its turn, the creature must make a Constitution saving throw. On a failed save, it takes 4d6 damage of the type dealt by the spell and is stunned until the start of its next turn. On a successful save, it takes half the damage and the effect ends.

You can use this feature twice. You regain all expended uses when you finish a short or long rest.

STONY REFUGE

Prerequisite: Elemental focus (earth)

When you cast a spell of 1st level or higher, you can use a bonus action to create a hovering slab of stone that interposes itself between you and one creature of your choice within 60 feet. Until the end of your next turn, the slab provides half cover to you against attacks from the chosen creature.

SWEEPING SWELL

Prerequisite: Elemental focus (water)

When you cast a spell of 1st level or higher, you can use a bonus action to create a sweeping wave of water that drenches a target you can see within 20 feet. The creature must succeed on a Strength saving throw or be pushed 5 feet in the direction of your choice.

WIND BLAST

Prerequisite: Elemental focus (air)

When you cast a spell of 1st level or higher, you can use a bonus action to create a line of wind 20 feet long and 5 feet wide. Each creature in the line must make a successful Strength saving throw or take 1d6 slashing damage and be pushed 10 feet away from you in the direction of the line.

ENTROPIST

Wizards who specialize in chaos magic crave an understanding of probability and life's unpredictable outcomes to the point of obsession.

Wizard Specialty

What starts as an attempt to analyze the patterns of chaos quickly becomes a trip down the rabbit hole to madness.

How to Start. If you're a wizard who wants to become an entropist, you make that decision upon reaching 2nd level, when you are also entitled to choose an arcane tradition. If you decide to follow the path of the entropist exclusively, you can forego the selection of an arcane tradition and gain the features of the entropist specialty instead.

You can also pursue the entropist specialty in conjunction with one of the standard arcane traditions. If you choose to do this, you gain the Savant feature of your chosen school in addition to Chaos Magic Savant (described below). Also at 2nd level, you choose whether to gain Long Odds (see below) or the 2nd-level feature of your chosen school. Thereafter, at 6th, 10th, and 14th level, you choose between the lowest-level features still available. For

instance, a transmuter might select Minor Alchemy at 2nd level and Long Odds at 6th level, followed by either Transmuter's Stone or Twisted Arcana at 10th level.

Chaos Magic Savant

Beginning when you take up this specialty at 2nd level, the gold and time you must spend to copy a chaos spell into your spellbook is halved.

Long Odds

Also starting at 2nd level, you can manipulate the reality-changing forces of chaos to alter the odds in a situation. You can use a bonus action to give yourself, or a reaction to give a creature you can see, advantage on one attack roll, saving throw, or ability check made during this turn. Using this feature causes a chaos magic surge. You must finish a long rest before you can use this feature again.

Twisted Arcana

Starting at 6th level, when you cast a spell that deals damage, you can infuse the effect with greater power by channeling chaos through yourself. You make this choice after determining that the spell has been successfully cast (by making a spell attack roll) but before rolling damage. If you decide to use this feature, roll a d6 + 1; this is the maximum number of your spell's damage dice you can reroll. You can reroll any number of damage dice up to that maximum, and you must use the rerolled results.

In addition, the type of damage your spell deals is replaced randomly. Use the Random Damage Type table to determine the spell's new damage type.

RANDOM DAMAGE TYPE

d10	Damage Type
1	Acid
2	Cold
3	Fire
4	Force
5	Lightning
6	Necrotic
7	Poison
8	Psychic
9	Radiant
10	Thunder

Using this feature has a chance of causing a chaos magic surge. You must finish a long rest before you can use this feature again.

Shifting Resistance

Beginning at 10th level, when you cast a chaos spell, you gain resistance to a random damage type for a number of rounds equal to 1 + your Intelligence modifier (minimum of 1). You can try to narrow the spell's focus to a damage type you prefer, but doing so has an element of risk; you can roll twice on the Random Damage Type table and choose the result you prefer, but you must also roll to see if a chaos magic surge occurs. You must finish a long rest before you can use this feature again.

Master of Chaos

Starting at 14th level, anytime you cause a chaos magic surge, you regain one use of Long Odds, Twisted Arcana, or Shifting Resistance without needing to finish a long rest. In addition, every time you cast a chaos spell, you gain temporary hit points equal to your Intelligence modifier + the spell's level.

ILLUMINATOR

Wizards who pursue illumination magic, called illuminators, use the stars to predict when danger is near, and they draw on the power of light to attack their foes.

Wizard Specialty

This branch of magic is popular with those who delve underground because its spells work best where light is dim or absent.

How to Start. If you're a wizard who wants to become an illuminator, you make that decision upon reaching 2nd level, when you are also entitled to choose an arcane tradition. If you decide to follow the path of the illuminator exclusively, you can forego the selection of an arcane tradition and gain the features of the illuminator specialty instead.

You can also pursue the illuminator specialty in conjunction with one of the standard arcane traditions. If you choose to do this, you gain the Savant feature of your chosen school in addition to Illumination Magic Savant (described below). Also at 2nd level, you choose whether to gain Omen of Warning (see below) or the 2nd-level feature of your chosen school. Thereafter, at 6th, 10th, and 14th level, you choose between the lowest-level features still available. For instance, a diviner might select Portent at 2nd level and Omen of Warning at 6th level, followed by either Expert Divination or Master of the Radiant Heavens at 10th level.

Illumination Magic Savant

Beginning when you select this school at 2nd level, the gold and time needed to copy illumination spells into your spellbook is halved.

Omen of Warning

Starting at 2nd level, you can forecast danger for the next 24 hours by studying the stars for 1 hour. The stars must be visible to you for you to use this feature. Studying the stars in this way gives you advantage on up to two initiative rolls. The bonus remains for 24 hours or until the end of your next long rest.

ability. The insight you gather is stored as a small reserve of magic inside an item that has meaning to you; a star chart or an astrolabe is commonly used, but any item that can be held in your hand will suffice. When the item is in your hand, you can consume that stored magic as a bonus action to produce one of the effects described below. The insight is expended in one use, and it is lost if it hasn't been used within 24 hours or by the time you start your next long rest:

- *Comet.* Comets are the harbingers of change and instability. You can change your appearance as if you had cast an *alter self* spell, but the effect doesn't require concentration and lasts until you finish a long rest.
- *Conjunction.* Planetary conjunctions destabilize minds and emotions. You can give one creature you can see disadvantage on a saving throw against one enchantment or illusion spell you cast.
- *Eclipse.* Eclipses plunge the world into darkness and strengthen connections to the shadow plane. When you cast a spell of 5th level or lower that deals necrotic damage, you can reroll a number of damage dice equal to your Intelligence modifier (minimum of one die). You must use the new rolls.

MASTER OF FIENDS

Some individuals are willing to do anything in exchange for power. They delve into forbidden knowledge to expand their command of magic—trafficking with fiends and endangering their immortal soul in exchange for arcane might.

Wizard Specialty

Beings of the Lower Planes dangle promises of power as bait, hoping to lure careless folk into their clutches. Some of those who take the bait have a keen intellect, enabling them to use careful planning that circumvents this damnation—or at least delays it. In this way, power-hungry mages strike bargains and increase their magical might with the knowledge the fiends offer. A master of fiends, as these individuals are called, is either a diabolist (one who deals with devils) or a demonologist (one who traffics with demons). Most common folk care little about the distinction, seeing both simply as servants of evil, but the differences between the two are significant.

Diabolists are masters of language and context, knowing that the contracts proffered by devils are complex and meant to mislead, and must be read carefully and fully understood so as to avoid any trickery. Demons have little use for subtlety; they understand and respect only one thing—power. A demonologist must have the magical power to compel such fiends to do their bidding, or they will surely be rent asunder and have their soul carried screaming back to the Abyss by the demon. Either path takes a person willing to risk their immortal soul in the pursuit of power, and few dare to do so.

Instead of using this feature on yourself, you can grant advantage on an initiative roll to one other creature you can see when initiative rolls are made, but doing this prevents you from using the benefit on yourself in that combat. You can choose whether to use this feature at the moment initiative is rolled, but you must make the decision before rolling the die.

Master of the Radiant Heavens

Starting when you reach 6th level, the spell attack modifier and spell save DC for any cantrips you cast in dim light or darkness increases by 1.

Illusions of Permanence

Beginning at 10th level, illusion spells you cast that require concentration last for 1 round after you stop concentrating, as long as the spell hasn't exceeded its duration.

Comprehension of the Starry Sky

Starting at 14th level, during a long rest you can consult the stars and comprehend some meaning in a cosmic event. The stars must be visible to you for you to use this

Dark Arts

Beginning at 2nd level, you gain a bonus spell you can copy to your spellbook at half the cost. You gain a new spell at each level indicated on the following list if you have not already learned the spell. You acquire knowledge of these spells through your trafficking with fiends.

When you attain the appropriate wizard level, add the indicated spell to your spellbook: 2nd level, *hellish rebuke*; 4th level, *enthrall*; 6th level, *nest of infernal vipers*; 8th level, *conjure fiends*; 10th level, *channel fiendish power*; 12th level, *aura of wrath*; 14th level, *plane shift*; 16th level, *dominate monster*; and 18th level, *imprisonment*.

Fiendish Presence

At 2nd level, you develop a dark aura of either allure or menace. You gain proficiency in Deception, Intimidation, or Persuasion. You can bring this talent to the fore to gain advantage on a single check using the chosen skill. Once you use this feature, you can't use it again until you finish a short or long rest.

Hellbound

Due to your dealings with fiends, your soul is damned, and after your death it is collected by the fiends with whom you bargained. Such creatures do not give up their prizes willingly. Starting when you reach 2nd level, a caster using a spell to return you to life must make a DC 12 Wisdom saving throw. The DC of this save increases by 1 for every five levels you gain hereafter, to a maximum of DC 15 at 17th level. On a successful save, your soul is retrieved, and the spell works normally. On a failed save, the spell ends, and you remain dead. (The GM can opt to allow either you or the caster trying to revive you to strike a bargain that allows you to be raised. The details of this deal are left up to the GM, but typically such bargaining involves extremely valuable items, magic, and—especially—souls.)

Communion at the Crossroads

Tradition states that the devil awaits at the crossroads, looking to bargain with those who seek to sell their souls for glory. When you reach 6th level, you can achieve contact with the lower realms in less dramatic circumstances. For you, any significant liminal space—the threshold between one space and another, such as the edge of a forest, the entrance to a cave, or the doorway leading from a church to its graveyard—will do. In such a place, you can perform a ritual that summons a dark spirit from beyond, a shadowy form that will offer you power for power.

When you do so, you can expend a number of spell slots (equal to your wizard level or lower) in exchange for a pool of an equal number of dice that you can use in one of two ways. You can spend one or more dice as an action on your turn to heal yourself, regaining 1d8 hit points for every die you spend. Or you can spend one or more dice to boost the damage of a spell you cast. Each die you spend adds an additional die of damage to a spell you cast, of the same size used in the spell (d6s for *fireball*, for example).

Once you use this feature, you cannot use it again until you finish a long rest. Any unused dice in the pool are lost when you rest, and you regain your normal number of spell slots after the rest.

Planar Defense

When you reach 10th level, you have learned to enhance your magic to provide you with greater benefit against extraplanar threats. You are protected not only against attack or betrayal by fiends, but by celestials that would see you judged for your connection with darkness. You have advantage on any saving throws against spells and abilities of celestials or fiends that would cause you to become charmed, frightened, paralyzed, restrained, stunned, or possessed by such a creature.

In addition, if you have a 5th-level spell slot available and a celestial or fiend attacks you, you can expend that spell slot to cast the *dispel evil and good* spell as a reaction. Once you do so, you can't use this additional benefit again until you finish a long rest.

Master of Dark Conjuration
Starting at 14th level, when you cast a *magic circle* spell that affects fiends, such creatures have disadvantage on any Charisma saving throws made in an attempt to enter or leave the cylinder by teleportation or interplanar travel. In addition, any fiend you summon with a conjuration spell gains 13 temporary hit points.

NECROPHAGE
The practice of necrophagy is similar to that of necromancy—but with a more horrific flavor. Necrophages, sometimes called death eaters, consume the flesh of the recently deceased to steal those creatures' knowledge and power.

Wizard Specialty
Adherents of this specialty claim that it is the origin of all necromancy magic and necrotic energy. They view the Negative Plane as a cosmic necrophage all its own, devouring all matter, energy, and life and replacing it with necrotic energy and undead.

Except as noted, necrophages function as necromancers and use the wizard spell list. Instead of gaining the corresponding features of the School of Necromancy, a necrophage has the features described below.

Undead Familiar
Beginning when you select this school at 2nd level, you add the *find familiar* spell to your spellbook if it's not already there. When you conjure a familiar, the creature is undead instead of a celestial, fey, or fiend. The familiar gains the following trait.

Undead Fortitude. If damage reduces the familiar to 0 hit points, it makes a Constitution saving throw with a DC equal to 5 + the damage taken, unless the damage is radiant or from a critical hit. On a success, the familiar drops to 1 hit point instead.

Memory of Flesh
Starting when you reach 6th level, you can use an action to consume a bit of flesh from an undead or a recently slain (within 1 hour) creature with an Intelligence of 6 or higher. An unwilling target is allowed a DC 14 Constitution saving throw to resist the effect.

If the target is affected, you gain temporary hit points equal to your wizard level, and if the target was proficient in any Intelligence skills, you can pick one of them. You gain proficiency in that skill or, if already proficient, double your normal proficiency bonus when using that skill. The temporary hit points and absorbed skill proficiency last until you finish a long rest.

You can't target the same creature with this feature twice within 24 hours. If you use the feature on a different creature, the original effect ends.

Fruit of the Mind
Beginning at 10th level, you can use Memory of Flesh to gain information from the creature as if you had cast *speak with dead* instead of gaining temporary hit points and a skill proficiency. An unwilling target has disadvantage on its saving throw.

As with Memory of Flesh, you can't target the same creature with this feature twice within 24 hours. If you use the feature on a different creature, the original effect ends.

A particular creature can be affected by Fruit of the Mind a number of times equal to its Constitution modifier. Beyond that maximum, further attempts to target it yield no results.

Feed on Life
Starting at 14th level, you gain several benefits after using Memory of Flesh or Fruit of the Mind:

- You no longer require air, food, drink, or sleep.
- You gain immunity to disease, to being poisoned, and to poison and necrotic damage.
- You can't suffer a reduction in hit point maximum.

These benefits last until you finish a long rest.

RING WARDEN

The dwarves long ago discovered the means to infuse magic into rings, and the first ring wardens came into being soon after that discovery came to light.

Wizard Specialty

With a focus on the school of transmutation, ring wardens blend dwarven craftsmanship with arcane might. They are rarely encountered outside dwarven nations, but they are easy to recognize thanks to their signature ring-staves.

Except as noted below, ring wardens function as transmuters and use the wizard spell list.

Transmutation Savant

Beginning when you select this specialty at 2nd level, the gold and time you must spend to copy a transmutation spell into your spellbook is halved.

Ring Savant

In addition, the gold and time you must spend to copy a ring magic spell into your spellbook is halved.

Bonus Proficiency

Also at 2nd level, you gain proficiency in your choice of blacksmith's tools or jeweler's tools.

Bonded Ring-Staff

At 2nd level, you create a special quarterstaff with two special metal rings adorning it. When you roll damage for a spell attack while you hold your ring-staff, you can add your proficiency bonus to the result. If the spell allows for multiple damage rolls against multiple targets (such as with *scorching ray*), you must choose which roll gains the benefit before you roll the die. You can use this ability a number of times equal to the number of rings on your staff. You regain all expended uses when you finish a short or long rest.

Whenever you gain a new wizard level, you can attach a new ring to your staff by spending 8 hours of work with blacksmith's tools or jeweler's tools and paying a cost of 5 gp in raw materials.

Master Metalsmith

Beginning at 6th level, you can add twice your normal proficiency bonus when you use the tools you chose at 2nd level. When using your chosen tools to craft nonmagical or magical items, you make twice the normal amount of progress each day.

Additionally, you learn the method for crafting a single kind of magic ring chosen from the following list: *ring of jumping*, *ring of mind shielding*, *ring of protection*, *ring of the ram*, *ring of regeneration*, or *ring of resistance*. At the GM's discretion, you can choose a ring not listed here. You must meet all the standard prerequisites for crafting the ring and pay the required gold as normal, along with providing any special materials or meeting any conditions set by the GM.

Imbue Ring

Starting at 10th level, you can imbue magic into the special rings that decorate your ring-staff. When you cast a spell, instead of having it take effect normally, you can choose to store the spell in one of the rings. As long as the spell is stored, you can't regain the expended spell slot. You can remove an imbued ring from the staff and give it to another creature (or hold it yourself) as an action. A creature holding an imbued ring can release the stored spell as an action. Attack rolls, saving throws, and damage are based on the caster who imbued the ring, but the creature holding the ring counts as the spell's caster for all other purposes.

After you remove an imbued ring from the staff, you must create a new special ring and affix it to the staff by working for 8 hours and spending 5 gp in raw materials. An imbued ring is considered a magical effect for the purpose of *dispel magic*. You can have a number of rings imbued at one time equal to your proficiency bonus.

Ring Bond

At 14th level or higher, with 1 hour of work (which can be accomplished during a short rest), you can embed a single magic ring that you possess into your ring-staff. The ring's rarity must be common, uncommon, or rare. As long as you hold the ring-staff, you gain the effect of the embedded ring as if you were attuned to it and wearing it (including any negative effects of attuning to the item, such as curses). This embedded ring doesn't count as one of your three allowable attuned magic items.

With one hour of work, you can remove an embedded ring (along with its attunement) and replace it with a new one if desired.

TIMEKEEPER

For those who understand its secrets, the flow of time itself is a powerful source of magical power.

Wizard Specialty

Wizards who strive to master temporal magic view seconds and minutes not merely as a way to measure life span, but as a way of manifesting great and mysterious power.

How to Start. If you're a wizard who wants to become a timekeeper, you make that decision upon reaching 2nd level, when you are also entitled to choose an arcane tradition. If you decide to follow the path of the timekeeper exclusively, you can forego the selection of an arcane tradition and gain the features of the timekeeper specialty instead.

You can also pursue the timekeeper specialty in conjunction with one of the standard arcane traditions. If you choose to do this, you gain the Savant feature of your chosen school in addition to Temporal Magic Savant (described below). Also at 2nd level, you choose whether to gain the Temporal Points feature (see below) or the 2nd-level feature of your chosen school. Thereafter, at 6th, 10th, and 14th level, you choose between the lowest-level features still available. For instance, an abjurer might select Arcane Ward at 2nd level and Temporal Points at 6th level, followed by either Projected Ward or Extended Magic at 10th level.

Temporal Magic Savant

Beginning when you select this school at 2nd level, the gold and time you must spend to copy a temporal spell into your spellbook is halved.

Temporal Points

Starting at 2nd level, you gain access to temporal points, which you can spend to acquire benefits. You receive 2 temporal points at 2nd level, and you gain 1 additional point every time you gain a level, to a maximum of 20 points at 20th level. You regain all spent temporal points when you finish a long rest.

You can spend 1 temporal point as a reaction or a bonus action on your turn to gain one of the following effects for 1 round:

- You can use a bonus action on your next turn to take the Dash, Disengage, Hide, or Use an Object action.
- Your Armor Class increases by 2.
- You have advantage on the next Dexterity check you make.

Optionally, you can spend 2 temporal points as a bonus action on your turn to grant a creature you touch one of the listed effects for 1 round.

Extended Magic

Beginning at 6th level, when you cast a spell whose duration is 1 minute or longer, you can spend 1 temporal point to double the spell's duration, to a maximum of 24 hours.

Hastened

At 10th level, you add the *haste* spell to your spellbook, if you don't have it already. From now on, you never suffer the negative aftereffects of the *haste* spell and can act normally when the spell ends.

CHAPTER 1 CHARACTER OPTIONS | 29

Also, you can cast *haste* on yourself without expending a spell slot. Once you cast *haste* in this way, you can't do so again until you finish a short or long rest. You can still cast it normally using an available spell slot.

Time Mastery

Starting at 14th level, you can choose to ignore the effect of a temporal spell that would otherwise affect you. For instance, you can exempt yourself from the effect of a *slow* spell cast in the area you occupy. Or, if you would be affected by a *quick time* spell, you can choose to automatically succeed on the saving throw.

Also, you can spend temporal points in the following ways:

- When you cast a spell with a casting time of 1 action, you can spend 2 temporal points to change the casting time for this casting to 1 bonus action.
- When you must make a saving throw against a temporal spell, you can spend 2 temporal points to succeed on the saving throw automatically. You can make the decision to spend the points after rolling the d20 and seeing the result.
- As a reaction when another creature casts *time stop*, you can spend 5 temporal points to gain the ability to act during the spell's duration. You and the spell's caster alternate taking turns, with the caster acting first. You have the same restrictions as the caster. If the caster ends the spell, it ends for everyone; if you take an action that ends the spell, it ends only for you, not for the caster.

WHITE NECROMANCER

An enlightened few wizards know that true mastery of life and death requires understanding of the uneasy balance between life, death, and undeath—the necromantic triad.

Wizard Specialty

You don't walk the same path as traditional users of necromantic magic, which your order refers to as "dark necromancers." You have profound respect for life's eternal cycle and use the power you have accumulated to honor the dead and aid the living.

Restriction: Non-Evil. You can choose this wizard specialty only if you have an alignment that isn't evil.

Necromancy Savant

Beginning when you select this specialty at 2nd level, the gold and time you must spend to copy a necromancy spell into your spellbook is halved.

Lore of Life and Death

At 2nd level, you gain proficiency in Medicine and Religion if you don't already have it, your proficiency bonus is doubled for Wisdom (Medicine) checks, and you have advantage on Intelligence (Religion) checks to recall lore about deities of death, burial practices, and the afterlife. In addition, you learn the *spare the dying* cantrip, which is a wizard cantrip for you and doesn't count against the number of wizard cantrips you know.

Rebuke Death

Also starting at 2nd level, you can use an action to heal a creature you can touch. The creature regains hit points equal to your Intelligence modifier + your wizard level (minimum of 1). This feature can restore a creature to no more than half its hit point maximum. Once a creature has regained hit points from this feature, it can't do so again until it finishes a long rest.

White Necromancy

At 6th level, you add the *animate dead* spell to your spellbook if it is not there already. When you cast this spell, it has additional effects:

- If the undead creature has an Intelligence score of 5 or lower, its Intelligence becomes 6, and it gains the ability to understand and speak one language of your choice that you speak.
- The undead creature's alignment is the same as yours.
- At the end of the undead creature's first 24 hours of serving you, it might continue to serve you for another 24 hours or else return to its eternal rest. You can convince the undead creature to continue serving you with a successful Charisma (Persuasion) check against a DC equal to 8 + the creature's challenge rating. On a successful check, the creature remains under your control, and the DC of the next check you make to maintain control 24 hours later increases by 1. You have disadvantage on this check if you were disrespectful to the creature in the previous 24 hours. On a failed check, or if you choose not to maintain control, the undead creature immediately crumbles to dust.

When you reach 11th level, you add the *create undead* spell to your spellbook. All of the above effects also apply whenever you cast that spell.

Life Bond

At 10th level, you add the *warding bond* spell to your spellbook, and it is a wizard spell for you. You can cast *warding bond* without expending a spell slot or requiring the material component, and the spell's duration increases to 4 hours.

Once you cast *warding bond* in this way, you can't do so again until you finish a long rest. You can still cast *warding bond* normally using an available spell slot.

Protect Life

Once you reach 14th level, you can use an action to cause life-preserving magic to emit from you. When you do so, you and friendly creatures within 20 feet of you have resistance to necrotic damage for 1 minute. In addition, each creature affected by your use of Protect Life has advantage on saving throws against spells and effects that reduce its hit point maximum, such as a specter's Life Drain or the *harm* spell.

Once you use this feature, you can't use it again until you finish a short or long rest.

BARD COLLEGES

At 3rd level, a bard gains the Bard College feature, and the following new options become available.

COLLEGE OF WYRDSINGERS

Bards of the College of Wyrdsingers subscribe to the wyrd, or rather that which will be—that which inexorably ties us to our destiny or fate. Though some might consider the idea of a fixed destiny fatalistic, the bards of this college are inspired by this viewpoint. One may not choose the manner of one's death, but one can choose how to meet it, and that idea is at the heart of this college. An insect might be caught in a spider's web. Whether it lives or dies, its struggles ultimately shake the web in its entirety, and it might free itself through such effort. The struggle affects all things, however remotely connected they might be, whereas the insect that merely accepts its death leaves not even a ripple behind. To confront fate, to embrace the wyrd and whatever it brings, is to have the power to shake the world and make it take notice.

Braggart

When you join the College of Wyrdsingers at 3rd level, you are already a master of the art of bragging about your deeds. The fact that you exaggerate is of little importance. What matters is that boasting of your deeds makes people listen to you. Your proficiency bonus is doubled when you make a Charisma (Intimidation or Persuasion) check.

Inspire Greatness

Also beginning at 3rd level, you can use a bonus action to instill a sense of worth in a single ally within 60 feet who can hear you. Your ally gains a bonus equal to your Charisma modifier on ability checks, attack rolls, damage rolls, and saving throws for a number of rounds equal to your bard level. That ally cannot benefit from your Bardic Inspiration until the duration of this feature has run its course. You can use this feature once at 3rd level, twice at 8th level, and three times at 15th level. You regain all expended uses when you finish a long rest.

Additionally, you can use a bonus action to cast any abjuration spell you know that normally takes 1 action to cast (for example, *laugh in the face of fear*, described in **Chapter 5**, or *lesser restoration*). Once you use this feature, you must finish a long rest before you can use it again.

Not This Day

Starting at 6th level, if an ally of yours drops to 0 hit points, you can use a reaction to expend one of your uses of Bardic Inspiration. Your ally gains a number of temporary hit points equal to the die roll and remains conscious. If the attack that reduced the ally to 0 hit points would have been fatal, the ally will die if they lose all temporary hit points they currently possess unless their hit point total is raised to 1 or higher before that happens.

Make Your Own Fate
At 14th level and higher, you can use an action to sing a song of valor that enables you to remain courageous and fight fiercely in the face of the gravest danger. For 1 minute thereafter, you gain immunity to the frightened condition. Any ally you affect with your Bardic Inspiration feature also gains this immunity until they expend the Bardic Inspiration die or the duration expires.

In addition, while this feature is in effect, you add your Charisma modifier to your weapon damage and to the damage of any spell you cast.

GREENLEAF COLLEGE
The Greenleaf College was founded by half-elves who sought to celebrate their varied heritage. Drawing from elven lore for inspiration and power, Greenleaf bards strengthen their connection to nature. Through their magic and their tales, they convey the rejuvenating strength of the forests and rivers to their allies.

Bonus Proficiencies
When you join the Greenleaf College at 3rd level, you gain proficiency in Nature and two other skills of your choice.

Rejuvenating Inspiration
At 3rd level, you learn to infuse your Bardic Inspiration with a magical seed of healing energy. When a creature uses a Bardic Inspiration die from you to increase the result of one ability check, attack roll, or saving throw, it also gains temporary hit points equal to the number rolled on the Bardic Inspiration die plus your Charisma modifier.

Land's Stride
Beginning at 6th level, moving through nonmagical difficult terrain costs you no extra movement. You can also pass through nonmagical plants without being slowed by them and without taking damage from them if they have thorns, spines, or a similar feature. In addition, you have advantage on saving throws against plants that are magically created or manipulated to impede movement, such as those created by the *entangle* spell.

Vital Surge
Starting at 14th level, you can expend one use of Bardic Inspiration as an action to magically remove one disease or detrimental condition affecting a creature you can see within 60 feet. The condition can be blinded, charmed, deafened, frightened, paralyzed, or poisoned.

DIVINE DOMAINS
At 1st level, a cleric gains the Divine Domain feature, and the following new options become available.

ANGELIC SCRIBE
An angelic scribe studies angelic seals, which harness the power of celestial messengers through their names, and they shape that power into magical effects. Beyond the seals and wards themselves, you learn esoteric spells to call down the essence of the angelic host.

Wizard or Cleric Specialty
Most angelic scribes take up their craft out of reverence and the desire to protect the righteous, though a few tempt angelic wrath with their lust for a power that's otherwise beyond their grasp.

How to Start. If you're a wizard who wants to become an angelic scribe, you make that decision upon reaching 2nd level, when you are also entitled to choose an arcane tradition. If you decide to follow the path of the angelic scribe exclusively, you can forego the selection of an arcane tradition and gain the features of the angelic scribe specialty instead.

You can also pursue the angelic scribe specialty in conjunction with one of the standard arcane traditions. If you choose to do this, you gain the Savant feature of your chosen school in addition to Angelic Savant (described below). Also at 2nd level, you choose whether to gain Seal Scribe (see below) or the 2nd-level feature of your chosen school. Thereafter, at 6th, 10th, and 14th level, you choose between the lowest-level features still available. For instance, a conjurer might select Seal Scribe at 2nd level and Minor Conjuration at 6th level, followed by either Warding Seal or Benign Transposition at 10th level.

For a cleric, the process is much the same, except that it involves making choices between angelic scribe features and the features provided by your domain. These decisions occur at 2nd, 6th, 8th, and 17th level instead of at the levels indicated for wizards.

Paladins, though they can cast angelic spells and gain angelic feats, cannot become angelic scribes.

Angelic Savant

Beginning when you take up this specialty at 2nd level, the gold and time you must spend to copy an angelic spell into your spellbook is halved.

Seal Scribe

Also at 2nd level, you learn the language Celestial, if you don't already know it, and you gain the ability to scribe angelic seals.

Seals. You learn two angelic seals of your choice (see below). You can spend 10 minutes scribing an angelic seal you know on paper, canvas, stone tiles, or some other surface or object that can be carried or displayed. Alternatively, you can spend 8 hours using appropriate artisan tools to carve or etch a more permanent seal into harder material. Once you have scribed a seal, you can activate it as an action:

- You can have one seal active at a time. The number of active seals you can maintain increases by one at 6th level (two seals), 10th level (three seals), and 14th level (four seals).
- A seal's magic is suppressed while you are concentrating on maintaining a spell or similar effect. A suppressed seal still counts against the number of active seals you can maintain.
- As a bonus action, you can deactivate a seal prior to activating another one. A broken or defaced seal deactivates immediately and must be replaced.
- You can give an active seal to another creature, enabling it to gain the benefit of the seal while it holds or openly wears the seal, except when it is concentrating on maintaining a spell or similar effect.
- You learn one additional angelic seal of your choice at 6th, 10th, and 14th levels. Each time you learn a new seal, you can also replace one seal you know with a different one.

Warding Seal

Beginning at 6th level, you can place warding seals to protect areas. This follows the procedure for scribing an angelic seal, but a warding seal must be fashioned on the ground or on a similarly suitable portion of a structure, such as a floor, wall, column, or ceiling. As an action, you can touch the seal to activate it. You must maintain concentration on the effect as if concentrating on a spell.

Once activated, a warding seal creates a spherical "safe space" that extends out to 30 feet around it, large enough to surround a small building or series of rooms of appropriate dimensions (a 22-foot cube, for example, or any space of approximately 11,000 cubic feet). An aberration, fey, fiend, or undead cannot physically cross the boundary, cast spells through it, or project its abilities across the boundary unless it makes a successful Charisma saving throw against your spell save DC. A creature that fails the saving throw can try again on its next turn. A creature that makes a successful save and moves across the boundary into the protected area isn't affected by the boundary while it remains inside—the boundary impedes only incoming entities and effects, not outgoing ones—but it must contend with the ward again if it leaves the area and tries to reenter.

Greater Seal

Starting at 10th level (or 8th level for a cleric), you can use an action to empower one of your active angelic seals or warding seals to greater effect. If you choose an

CHAPTER 1 CHARACTER OPTIONS

angelic seal, its user typically gains the greater benefit of the seal for 1 minute (unless otherwise noted), replacing the normal benefit during that time. If you choose a warding seal, for the next hour, a creature that fails its saving throw against the ward takes 6d6 radiant damage and automatically fails additional saves against the ward during this time.

You can use this ability twice, and you regain expended uses when you finish a short or long rest.

Angelic Wrath

At 14th level (or 17th level for a cleric), you add *conjure celestial* to your spellbook or to your spells known if you don't already know it.

Additionally, you can use a bonus action to infuse your seals with angelic wrath. For 1 minute, you deal an additional 1d8 radiant damage with weapon attacks—and so does anyone within 30 feet of you that is in possession of one of your active seals.

You can't use this ability again until you finish a short or long rest.

Angelic Seals

Each angelic seal consists of the name of an angel, written in Celestial on a suitable surface, which resonates with a given seal's effect.

Amnayeth (Benevolence). You can reroll a failed ability check made to improve another creature's attitude. *Greater:* As an action, once during the next minute, you can cause a creature that can hear you to make a successful Wisdom saving throw against your spell save DC or be charmed for 10 minutes. This seal can't be used again on a check involving the same creature until you finish a short or long rest.

Barrateth (Fortune). You can add 1 to an ability check, attack roll, or saving throw. The addition is made after rolling the die but before the GM reveals whether it was a success or failure. *Greater:* After making an ability check, attack roll, or saving throw, you can roll another d20 and choose which result to use. The second roll is made after the initial roll but before the GM reveals whether that roll was a success or failure. This seal can't be used again until you finish a short or long rest.

Chamule (Judgment). When you hit a creature with an opportunity attack, you can move up to half your speed, provided you end the move no farther away from the creature you hit. *Greater:* As a reaction when hit by an attack, once during the next minute, you can cause the attacker to take radiant damage equal to your Intelligence modifier (minimum of 1) if the attacker is within 60 feet.

Iaothe (Temperance). When making a Wisdom saving throw, you can use your reaction to add your Intelligence modifier (minimum of 1) to the roll. The bonus is added after the die is rolled but before the GM reveals whether the saving throw succeeds or fails. *Greater:* You can't be charmed or frightened. This seal can't be used again until you finish a short or long rest.

Jelaal (Recovery). You automatically succeed on your first death saving throw and then regain 1 hit point. *Greater:* When regaining hit points, you regain an additional number of hit points equal to your Intelligence modifier (minimum of 1). This seal can't be used again until you finish a short or long rest.

Ophanim (Humility). You add half your Intelligence modifier (minimum of 1) to your Dexterity (Stealth) checks. You keep this benefit until the start of your next turn or when you take a hostile action (any action that could inflict intentional damage on a creature), whichever comes first. *Greater:* If you haven't taken a hostile action this turn, you can use your action to present an aura of humility. A creature that wants to attack you must succeed on a Wisdom saving throw against your spell save DC or choose another target. If there are no other targets it can attack, the creature spends its action doing nothing.

Rikbil (Fortitude). When hit by an attack, you can use your reaction to add 2 to your AC against that attack. You must be able to see the attacker to use this effect. *Greater:* You gain resistance to nonmagical bludgeoning, piercing, and slashing damage.

Simil (Clarity). You add half your Intelligence modifier (minimum of 1) to Wisdom (Insight or Perception) checks for 1 minute. *Greater:* You gain blindsight out to a range of 10 feet.

Vrechiel (Glory). When you reduce an enemy to 0 hit points, you gain temporary hit points equal to your Intelligence modifier (minimum of 1). *Greater:* At the start of your turn, once during the next minute, you gain temporary hit points equal to your caster level.

Xapanie (Wrath). Once on your turn, when making a weapon attack, the attack gains +1 to its damage. *Greater:* Your attacks are magical, and once on your turn, during the next minute, a hit with a weapon attack deals additional radiant damage equal to half your caster level (minimum of 1).

BEER DOMAIN

The heady brew of fortitude, courage, and companionship is your nectar, and you share its blessings with those who need it.

BEER DOMAIN SPELLS

Cleric Level	Spells
1st	*comprehend languages, heroism*
3rd	*blur, bolstering brew**
5th	*hypnotic pattern, mass healing word*
7th	*confusion, resilient sphere*
9th	*dream, modify memory*

* Described in **Chapter 5**

Disciple of the Draught

When you choose this domain at 1st level, you learn the *ale-dritch blast* cantrip (described in **Chapter 5**). You also gain proficiency in either Insight or Medicine (your choice), and you gain proficiency with brewer's supplies. Your proficiency bonus is doubled for any ability check you make that uses those supplies.

Channel Divinity: Blessed Brew

Starting at 2nd level, you can use your Channel Divinity to transform a container of nonmagical liquid into blessed brew. The number of doses equals 3 + your Wisdom modifier. Any special properties the liquid previously had are negated. Anyone who imbibes one dose of this brew can choose one of the following benefits:

- +1 bonus to AC.
- +1 increase to DC of saving throws for enchantment spells.
- Advantage on Charisma ability checks.

The benefit lasts for 1 hour, leaving behind a warm buzz when it fades. A creature must finish a short or long rest before it can benefit from another dose of blessed brew. Any blessed brew that is not consumed within an hour turns into ordinary beer.

Boot and Rally

Starting at 6th level, you can use an action to aid and rally your allies. Each friendly creature within 30 feet of you that is frightened, paralyzed, poisoned, or stunned can immediately repeat the saving throw that caused the condition. Each target has advantage on this saving throw. On a successful save, the condition ends on the target, and the target regains 2d6 hit points. Once you use this feature, you can't use it again until you finish a long rest.

Divine Strike

At 8th level, you gain the ability to infuse your weapon strikes with radiant energy. Once on each of your turns, when you hit a creature with a weapon attack, you can cause the attack to deal an extra 1d8 radiant damage to the target. When you reach 14th level, the extra damage increases to 2d8.

Fire in the Belly

At 17th level, you gain resistance to cold, poison, and psychic damage.

CAT DOMAIN

You embody the grace, strength, and resilience of felines. Eventually, you gain the ability to take the form of a lion or a tiger.

CAT DOMAIN SPELLS

Cleric Level	Spells
1st	*find familiar (feline only), speak with animals*
3rd	*animal messenger, pass without trace*
5th	*bestow curse, nondetection*
7th	*dimension door, locate creature*
9th	*commune with nature, mislead*

Silent Claws

When you choose this domain at 1st level, you learn the *true strike* cantrip, and you gain proficiency in Acrobatics and Stealth.

Channel Divinity: Feline Finesse

At 2nd level, you can use your Channel Divinity to add a +10 bonus to a single Dexterity ability check made by you or someone within 30 feet that you designate. Doing this requires no action. You simply make the choice after you see the roll but before the GM says whether the check succeeds or fails.

Eyes of the Cat

Beginning at 6th level, you gain darkvision out to a range of 60 feet. If you already have darkvision, the range becomes 90 feet.

Divine Strike

At 8th level, you gain the ability to infuse your weapon strikes with divine energy. Once on each of your turns, when you hit a creature with a weapon attack, you can cause the attack to deal an extra 1d8 damage of the same type dealt by the weapon to the target. When you reach 14th level, the extra damage increases to 2d8.

Emissary of the Cat

At 17th level, you become a natural lycanthrope. You use the statistics of a weretiger, though your form can be that of a werelion, werepanther, wereleopard, or other large cat, whichever is appropriate for your deity. Your alignment doesn't change as a result of this lycanthropy, and you can't spread the disease of lycanthropy.

DRAGON DOMAIN

Dragons are known for many things: mastery of the most unforgiving environments, sagacity, long life, and an eternal hunger for ever more wealth and power. Those who worship dragons, or the gods of dragons, might strive to emulate several or perhaps all of these qualities themselves.

DRAGON DOMAIN SPELLS

Cleric Level	Spells
1st	*detect magic, thunderwave*
3rd	*enthrall, lair sense**
5th	*catch the breath**, *fear*
7th	*blight, scale rot**
9th	*claws of the earth dragon**, *legend lore*

* Described in **Chapter 5**

Bonus Proficiency

When you choose this domain at 1st level, you gain proficiency in Arcana, and your proficiency bonus is doubled for any ability check you make that uses this skill. You also gain advantage on saving throws against being frightened.

Channel Divinity: Charmer of Reptiles

Starting at 2nd level, you can use your Channel Divinity to charm nonintelligent reptiles. As an action, you present your holy symbol and invoke the name of your deity. Each reptilian beast within 30 feet of you that can see you must make a successful Wisdom saving throw or be charmed by you for 1 minute or until it takes damage. While a reptile is charmed by you, it is friendly to you and to other creatures you designate.

Dragon's Resistance

Starting at 6th level, you can call on the might of draconic resilience to protect you. When you fail a saving throw, you can use a reaction to succeed on that saving throw instead. Once you use this feature, you can't use it again until you finish a long rest.

Divine Strike

At 8th level, you gain the ability to infuse your weapon strikes with divine energy. Once on each of your turns, when you hit a creature with a weapon attack, you can cause the attack to deal an extra 1d8 damage of the type dealt by the weapon to the target. When you reach 14th level, the extra damage increases to 2d8.

Frightful Presence

At 17th level, as an action, you can use a Frightful Presence like that of a dragon's. You must finish a short or long rest before using it again.

Frightful Presence. Each creature of your choice that is within 60 feet of you and aware of you must succeed on a DC 16 Wisdom saving throw or become frightened for 1 minute. A frightened creature repeats the saving throw at the end of each of its turns, ending the effect on itself on a success. If a creature's saving throw is successful or the effect ends for it, the creature is immune to your Frightful Presence for the next 24 hours.

FROST DOMAIN

Nearly every part of the world must deal with a change in temperature and the coming of winter. Nowhere is this more evident than in the extreme north and south, where winter is a pervasive part of life. As civilization expands into inhospitable terrain and environments, its reliance increases on divine providence to ensure survivability.

Good-aligned clerics appeal to winter deities such as Boreas to spare their people the worst of bitter cold, storms that last for days, and other calamities caused by weather. They couch the onset of winter as necessary for strengthening their people and as respite from toil, pointing to the peacefulness of the frozen, snow-draped landscape. Evil clerics embrace the storms and brutal conditions and even enhance them to advance their deities' agendas and to spread fear through their enemies.

FROST DOMAIN SPELLS

Cleric Level	Spells
1st	*breathtaking wind*, icicle daggers**
3rd	*creeping ice*, sheen of ice**
5th	*sleet storm, steal warmth**
7th	*fusillade of ice*, ice storm*
9th	*clash of glaciers*, cone of cold*

* Described in **Chapter 5**

A Cold Wind
At 1st level, you learn the *ray of frost* cantrip, and you gain proficiency in Nature and Survival.

Channel Divinity: Snow Walker
Starting at 2nd level, you can use your Channel Divinity to grant yourself the ability to walk on the surface of snow, ignoring any movement penalties that would normally apply. Ice supports your weight no matter how thin, and you can travel on it as if you're wearing ice skates. You still leave tracks in snow and ice.

Additionally, your vision is not impaired by snow, and you have advantage on Dexterity (Stealth) checks to hide in snowy environments.

Deep Cold
Beginning at 6th level, when you deal cold damage to a creature, it must succeed on a Constitution saving throw against your spell save DC or be stunned until the end of its next turn.

Divine Strike
At 8th level, you gain the ability to infuse your weapon strikes with divine energy. Once on each of your turns, when you hit a creature with a weapon attack, you can cause the attack to deal an extra 1d8 cold damage to the target. When you reach 14th level, the extra damage increases to 2d8.

Bringer of Winter's Wrath
Starting at 17th level, you gain resistance to cold.

Additionally, you can use your action to surround yourself with swirling snow that fills a 20-foot-radius sphere. All other creatures have disadvantage on Wisdom (Perception) checks and attack rolls against you. Creatures other than you within the area have disadvantage on saving throws against magic that deals cold damage. The swirling snow lasts for 1 minute or until you dismiss it as a bonus action.

HUNGER DOMAIN

You have dedicated your life to the satisfaction of your appetites, sometimes without regard for others' needs. You realize you can never be truly sated, but you also know that remaining hungry is the key to amassing power.

HUNGER DOMAIN SPELLS

Cleric Level	Spells
1st	*false life, goodberry*
3rd	*locate animals or plants, suggestion*
5th	*create food and water, vampiric touch*
7th	*blight, desiccating breath**
9th	*cloudkill, cone of cold*

* Described in **Chapter 5**

Unsated

When you choose this domain at 1st level, you learn the *poison spray* cantrip. You also gain proficiency in Survival and proficiency with cooking tools.

Bonus Proficiency

Also at 1st level, you gain proficiency with heavy armor.

Channel Divinity: Ferocious Feast

At 2nd level, you can use your Channel Divinity to gain a bite attack for 1 minute. The bite deals piercing damage equal to 1d6 + your Strength modifier. On a critical hit, you can also add your Wisdom modifier to the damage roll, in addition to the normal benefits of critical hits.

Revitalize

Beginning at 6th level, you can cure a disease, neutralize a poison, or remove either the poisoned condition or a level of exhaustion from yourself, as an action. You must finish a long rest before using this ability again.

Divine Strike

At 8th level, you gain the ability to infuse your weapon strikes with divine energy. Once on each of your turns, when you hit a creature with a weapon attack, you can cause the attack to deal an extra 1d8 necrotic damage to the target. When you reach 14th level, the extra damage increases to 2d8.

Ravening Horde

At 17th level, you can sacrifice the vitality of those around you by inspiring an insatiable and horrifying hunger within them. Each living creature within 60 feet of you must succeed on a Charisma saving throw or take 10d8 necrotic damage and succumb to a ravening hunger, dropping whatever it holds and attacking unaffected creatures with their hands and teeth or with whatever natural weapons they possess, in an attempt to devour them. This effect lasts for a number of rounds equal to 3 + your Wisdom modifier. An affected creature repeats the saving throw at the end of each of its turns, ending the effect on itself on a success. You can exclude up to 10 creatures from the effect, but this doesn't shield them against being attacked by those who do succumb. This ability doesn't affect constructs or the undead.

HUNTING DOMAIN

You are master of the hunt. The bounty of the land is yours for the taking.

HUNTING DOMAIN SPELLS

Cleric Level	Spells
1st	*hunter's mark, strength of an ox**
3rd	*locate animals or plants, pass without trace*
5th	*speak with plants, tracer**
7th	*heart-seeking arrow*, power word pain**
9th	*commune with nature, hold monster*

* Described in **Chapter 5**

Forest Master

When you choose this domain at 1st level, you gain proficiency with longbows and heavy crossbows. You also gain proficiency in Nature and Survival.

Channel Divinity: Undetected

At 2nd level, you can use your Channel Divinity to camouflage yourself in any environment, gaining advantage on Stealth checks made to move quietly or to hide. You also leave no scent. The effect lasts for a number of rounds equal to your cleric level + your Wisdom modifier.

Resolute Hunter

At 6th level, you can select a favored enemy as if you were a ranger. You gain all the benefits of the ranger's Favored Enemy feature with one exception: you choose additional favored enemies (and languages) at 10th and 16th level instead of at 6th and 14th level.

Divine Strike

At 8th level, you gain the ability to infuse your weapon strikes with divine energy. On your turn, you can cause one successful weapon attack against a creature to deal an extra 1d8 damage of the type dealt by the weapon to the target. When you reach 14th level, the extra damage increases to 2d8.

Deadly Stalker

At 17th level, you can use an action to describe or name a creature that is familiar to you or that you can see within 120 feet. For 24 hours or until the target is dead, whichever comes first, you have advantage on Wisdom (Survival) checks to track your target and on Wisdom (Perception) checks to detect your target. In addition, you have advantage on weapon attack rolls against the target.

You can't use this feature again until you finish a short or long rest.

JUSTICE DOMAIN

All seek some form of justice when they have been wronged, and many live under the promise of its protection—whether or not the promise is ultimately kept—but few take on the holy burden of delivering the justice of the gods. The mercy of the divine, when in evidence at all, is not the mercy of mortals, and meting out divine justice makes for a lonely life. Yet someone must make the sacrifice.

JUSTICE DOMAIN SPELLS

Cleric Level	Spells
1st	divine favor, longstrider
3rd	blade of wrath*, see invisibility
5th	call lightning, fear
7th	faithful hound, inspiring speech
9th	dominate person, hold monster

* Described in **Chapter 5**

Bonus Proficiency

When you choose this domain at 1st level, you gain proficiency with heavy armor and with martial weapons.

Channel Divinity: No Hiding Place

Starting at 2nd level, you can use your Channel Divinity to determine the general direction to the location of a creature that is guilty of an injustice or that is wanted for commission of a serious crime. At 7th level, you can determine the distance in miles to the creature as well as the direction.

Hand of Justice

At 6th level, you become immune to the frightened condition.

Divine Strike

At 8th level, you gain the ability to infuse your weapon strikes with divine energy. Once on each of your turns, when you hit a creature with a weapon attack, you can cause the attack to deal an extra 1d8 radiant damage to the target. When you reach 14th level, the extra damage increases to 2d8.

Channel Divinity: Holy Denunciation

At 17th level, you can use your Channel Divinity to persuade others that you hold divine authority to mete out justice. You must present your holy symbol and invoke the name of your deity. As long as your deity is worshiped openly in the land where you are asserting this authority, you have advantage on Wisdom and Charisma checks involving justice, judgment, and the law.

LUST DOMAIN

The Lust domain concerns itself with desire, sex, and awakening passion in others. Clerics of lust often seek to seduce others with their wiles, either for their own pleasure or to manipulate them into doing their bidding.

LUST DOMAIN SPELLS

Cleric Level	Spells
1st	charm person, command
3rd	alter self, suggestion
5th	hypnotic pattern, throes of ecstasy*
7th	compulsion, lovesick*
9th	dominate person, kiss of the succubus*

* Described in **Chapter 5**

Gifts of Lust

When you choose this domain at 1st level, you learn the *message* cantrip and gain proficiency in one of the following skills: Deception, Performance, or Persuasion.

Channel Divinity: Lustful Distraction

Starting at 2nd level, you can use Channel Divinity to instill fascination and desire in others. As an action, you speak and act seductively toward creatures of your choice within 30 feet who can see and hear you. Each target must make a DC 12 Wisdom saving throw. On a failed save, a target is compelled to devote its attention to you for 1 minute. While you command their attention, the targets have disadvantage on Wisdom (Perception) checks to perceive any creature other than you, and you have advantage on Charisma (Deception or Persuasion) checks to further influence their behavior.

Lingering Seduction

At 6th level, you can keep the targets of a Lustful Distraction spellbound for up to 10 minutes as long as you continue to speak to them.

Divine Strike

At 8th level, you have the ability to infuse your weapon strikes with divine energy. Once on each of your turns, when hitting a creature with a weapon attack, you can cause the attack to deal an extra 1d8 psychic damage to the target. When you reach 14th level, the extra psychic damage increases to 2d8.

Master of Seduction

At 17th level, you can command creatures that you have seduced. While creatures are enraptured by Lustful Distraction, you can take a bonus action on your turn to verbally command what each of those creatures will do on its next turn.

MOON DOMAIN

You are an initiate into the quiet mysteries of the moon and the subtleties of the night. Your faith illuminates any darkness you face.

MOON DOMAIN SPELLS

Cleric Level	Spells
1st	agonizing mark*, faerie fire
3rd	dome of silence*, moonbeam
5th	fear, hypnotic pattern
7th	compulsion, greater invisibility
9th	dream, hold monster

* Described in **Chapter 5**

Moon's Grace

When you select this domain at 1st level, you gain proficiency in Perception and Stealth, and you don't have disadvantage on Stealth checks when you wear medium armor.

Channel Divinity: Night's Chill

Starting at 2nd level, you can use your Channel Divinity to harness moonlight, which banishes magical light and deals cold damage to your foes. When you present your holy symbol as an action and use your Channel Divinity, any magical light within 30 feet of you is dispelled. Additionally, each hostile creature within 30 feet of you takes cold damage equal to 2d10 + your cleric level, or half as much damage with a successful Constitution saving throw. A creature that has total cover from you is not affected.

Luminescent Aura

At 6th level, you can use an action to emit a nimbus of light in a 30-foot radius for a number of rounds equal to your cleric level. This effect acts as a *light* spell but provides only dim light. All weapons and ammunition are treated as silvered while they're in the aura and for 1 round after leaving it. Opponents that end their turn in the aura must make a successful Dexterity saving throw or be limned in silver light, identical in effect to a *faerie fire* spell, until the end of their next turn.

You can use this feature three times, and you regain expended uses when you finish a long rest.

Divine Strike

At 8th level, you gain the ability to infuse your weapon strikes with divine energy. Once on each of your turns when you hit a creature with a weapon attack, you can cause the attack to deal an extra 1d8 cold damage to the target. When you reach 14th level, the extra damage increases to 2d8.

The Moonlit Way

Beginning at 17th level, whenever the moon is visible in the sky, you can use an action to detect magical pathways, portals, and gate effects. To be detected, a portal must be within your line of sight and no farther than 120 feet from you. Detected portals are visible only to you, but you can point out their locations to others. Once you use this feature, you can't use it again until you finish a short or long rest.

MOUNTAIN DOMAIN

Mountains signify strength, endurance, and hard-won wisdom. Many gods make their homes in the mountains, and so do many horrors. Those who would know themselves in full must embrace the ordeal of scaling the highest peaks, despite the thin, cold air, deprivation, and hardships that await.

MOUNTAIN DOMAIN SPELLS

Cleric Level	Spells
1st	*feather fall, jump*
3rd	*enhance ability, spider climb*
5th	*meld into stone, sleet storm*
7th	*stone shape, stoneskin*
9th	*commune with nature, cone of cold*

Bonus Proficiency

When you choose this domain at 1st level, you gain proficiency in Athletics, Nature, or Survival (your choice).

Tongues of the Mountains

Also at 1st level, you become fluent in Dwarvish or Giant (your choice).

Channel Divinity: Ever Upward

Starting at 2nd level, you can use your Channel Divinity to grant yourself and up to five other creatures advantage on skill or ability checks made to climb, avoid falling, or avoid the prone condition. The effect lasts for 1 hour.

Darkvision

Beginning at 6th level, you gain darkvision out to a range of 30 feet. If you already have darkvision, you can see in magical darkness out to a range of 30 feet as if it were dim light.

Divine Strike

At 8th level, you gain the ability to infuse your weapon strikes with divine energy. Once on each of your turns when you hit a creature with a weapon attack, you can cause the attack to deal an extra 1d8 cold damage to the target. When you reach 14th level, the extra damage increases to 2d8.

Avalanche

At 17th level, you can create an avalanche that crushes and buries everything in its path. A 60-foot cone of ice, snow, and rubble erupts from a point of your choosing within 20 feet of you, in a direction you select. Each creature in the cone takes 15d8 bludgeoning damage, or half as much damage with a successful Strength saving throw. A creature that fails the saving throw is also restrained. A restrained creature can be freed by spending an action to make a successful Strength check, either by itself or by an ally within 5 feet of it.

You must be outdoors to create the avalanche. The direction of the cone must be downhill or level; the avalanche can't flow uphill. Walls and other permanent structures block the avalanche. After using this feature, you must finish a long rest before using it again.

OCEAN DOMAIN

You invoke the power of salt and sea—the fountain of life—in all its chaotic glory. You are an emissary between sea and shore.

OCEAN DOMAIN SPELLS

Cleric Level	Spells
1st	*fog cloud, speak with animals*
3rd	*locate animals or plants, misty step*
5th	*gaseous form, water breathing*
7th	*black tentacles, conjure minor elementals* (excluding fire)
9th	*awaken, conjure elemental* (excluding fire)

Envoy to the Waves

When you choose this domain at 1st level, you learn the *chill touch* cantrip. You also learn the Aquan language, gain proficiency in the Survival skill, and gain proficiency with tridents and nets.

Channel Divinity: Sea Speaker

Beginning at 2nd level, you can use your Channel Divinity to communicate telepathically with aquatic creatures within 100 feet of you. This ability lasts for 1 hour.

At Home in the Waves

At 6th level, you gain a swimming speed of 30 feet and darkvision out to a range of 60 feet. If you already have darkvision, its range extends by 30 feet.

Divine Strike

At 8th level, you gain the ability to infuse your weapon strikes with divine energy. Once on each of your turns when you hit a creature with a weapon attack, you can cause the attack to deal an extra 1d8 cold damage to the target. When you reach 14th level, the extra damage increases to 2d8.

Scales of the Sea

At 17th level, you become able to breathe in water as easily as in air. You also gain the ability to transform your skin into fishlike scales at will. While covered in scales, you have resistance to bludgeoning, piercing, and slashing damage from nonmagical weapons, and you have advantage on Dexterity (Stealth) checks made in natural underwater environments. You must use an action to grow the scales or to transform back to your normal skin. The scales can be any color you choose. The scales need to be kept wet; you gain one level of exhaustion at the end of each hour when you have scales, and they haven't been thoroughly wetted for that length of time.

PROPHECY DOMAIN

You see the future, whether for good or ill. Eventually, you might become an oracle renowned across the region.

PROPHECY DOMAIN SPELLS

Cleric Level	Spells
1st	divine favor, insightful maneuver*
3rd	mirror image, see invisibility
5th	counterspell, slow
7th	arcane eye, compulsion
9th	contact other plane, modify memory

*Described in **Chapter 5**

A Path Foretold
When you choose this domain at 1st level, you gain proficiency in History and Insight. You also learn one exotic language of your choice, subject to GM approval.

Channel Divinity: One Move Ahead
Beginning at 2nd level, you can use your Channel Divinity to add 20 feet to your walking speed for a number of rounds equal to your cleric level.

Future Sight
At 6th level, you can manipulate fate to change the outcomes from decisions you make. When you take an action or move at least 5 feet, you can use a reaction to undo that action or movement. Any spells cast, resources expended, and similar outcomes don't happen, and you can choose a different action to take or to move differently. You can use this feature after the result of your activity is known, so long as the activity didn't result in you becoming incapacitated or didn't result in your death. Only a single action or movement up to your speed can be undone. The mixing of future and present is disorienting, and you gain one level of exhaustion after using this feature. Levels of exhaustion gained from using this feature can be reduced only by finishing a long rest, reducing your exhaustion level by one as normal with each long rest.

Divine Strike
At 8th level, you gain the ability to infuse your weapon strikes with divine energy. Once on each of your turns when you hit a creature with a weapon attack, you can cause the attack to deal an extra 1d8 damage of the same type dealt by the weapon to the target. When you reach 14th level, the extra damage increases to 2d8.

It Was Foretold
At 17th level, you gain advantage on Dexterity saving throws, Wisdom (Perception) checks, and Wisdom (Insight) checks. You also gain resistance to fire, poison, and psychic damage.

With the GM's consent, you can issue a prophecy from your deity once per month. You might become a renowned (and controversial) prophet, attracting both loyal followers and terrible enemies. Consult with your GM to find out what news, if any, your deity wants foretold.

SPEED DOMAIN

In speed and skill there is power, and you serve your faith by engaging in acts of incredible quickness and agility. Eventually you become able to control time itself.

SPEED DOMAIN SPELLS

Cleric Level	Spells
1st	expeditious retreat, feather fall
3rd	blur, web
5th	haste, slow
7th	conjure minor elementals, dimension door
9th	hold monster, teleportation circle

Celerity in Thought and Action
When you choose this domain at 1st level, your speed increases by 5 feet, and you gain proficiency in Acrobatics and Insight.

Channel Divinity: Burst of Speed
Beginning at 2nd level, you can use your Channel Divinity to grant yourself or another creature greater speed. When you use an action to touch a creature, the target adds 10 feet to its walking speed. It also gains the benefit of a *bless* spell, but only on attacks and saving throws that rely on Dexterity. This effect lasts for a number of rounds equal to 3 + your Wisdom modifier.

Quickness of the Gods
At 6th level, your speed increases by another 5 feet. Also, as a reaction or a bonus action, you can increase your Dexterity modifier by +5 until the end of your current turn. This benefit can be used for all purposes except attack rolls. Once you use this feature, you can't use it again until you finish a long rest.

Divine Strike
At 8th level, you gain the ability to infuse your weapon strikes with divine energy. Once on each of your turns when you hit a creature with a weapon attack, you can cause the attack to deal an extra 1d8 damage of the same type dealt by the weapon to the target. When you reach 14th level, the extra damage increases to 2d8.

Channel Divinity: Time Stop
At 17th level, you can use your Channel Divinity to stop the flow of time. The effect is identical to the *time stop* spell; you can take three turns in a row when the effect is triggered. You must finish a long rest before using this ability again.

TIME DOMAIN

The gods that deal with time are varied. Some see into the future and past; others deal with the cycles of life that mark the passage of time—birth and death, the seasons, or renewal and decay—or have some particular connection to the timeline, such as gods of creation or apocalypse do. The clerics of such gods are often granted powers that allow them to see through or manipulate time, emulating their deities and enabling them to alter events as their gods see fit.

TIME DOMAIN SPELLS

Cleric Level	Spells
1st	auspicious warning*, feather fall
3rd	decelerate*, gentle repose
5th	haste, slow
7th	flickering fate*, reset*
9th	modify memory, wall of time*

* Described in **Chapter 5**

Prescient Glimpses

When you choose this domain at 1st level, you gain proficiency in Insight and Perception, and your proficiency bonus is doubled for any ability check you make that uses either of those skills.

Additionally, whenever you might be surprised, you can make a Wisdom saving throw against a DC equal to the highest result among the enemy's initiative rolls. On a successful save, you are not surprised.

Channel Divinity: Time Shift

Starting at 2nd level, you can use your Channel Divinity to shift time and alter the order of initiative. As an action, you can move yourself in the initiative order to any point of your choosing.

Group Time Shift

Starting at 6th level, when you use your Channel Divinity to Time Shift, you can choose up to three friendly and willing creatures you can see within 30 feet of you to also be affected, moving each creature in the initiative order to any position of your choice.

Prescient Strike

Beginning at 8th level, you intuitively know where your enemies will be in the immediate future and how they will attack. You gain advantage on one attack roll each turn when you take the Attack action. Alternatively, you can take a reaction when a creature attacks you to give that creature disadvantage on its attack roll against you.

Master of Time

At 17th level, you add *foresight* and *time stop* to your spell list. You are never surprised, and whenever you and your allies might be surprised, you can grant up to six allies the ability to make Wisdom saving throws to avoid being surprised, as if they had your Prescient Glimpses feature.

TRAVEL DOMAIN

Voyages across oceans, over mountain ranges, through steaming jungles, and from one world to the next all have an aspect of the sacred to them. The wisdom, knowledge, and prosperity gained through furthering one's experience of the world also venerates the gods who made such places and those who watch over such journeys. An agent of one of these deities might be in some demand as a charm to help ensure safe travel, though the wise know that the gods often consider an easy journey to be less beneficial to the traveler's spirit.

TRAVEL DOMAIN SPELLS

Cleric Level	Spells
1st	comprehend languages, longstrider
3rd	find steed, pass without trace
5th	haste, water walk
7th	dimension door, freedom of movement
9th	passwall, teleportation circle

Born to the Road
When you choose this domain at 1st level, you gain proficiency in one of the following skills of your choice: Insight, Nature, or Survival. In addition, you learn two standard languages of your choice and gain proficiency with cartographer's tools.

Channel Divinity: Reinvigorate
Starting at 2nd level, you can use your Channel Divinity to remove one level of exhaustion from yourself or from someone else you touch.

Trailblazer
Beginning at 6th level, if you are planning to travel any distance longer than 5 days' travel and you have a map of the region to be traversed or firsthand knowledge of the area, you can find a shortcut. Using the alternate path can reduce your travel time by 50 percent.

Divine Strike
At 8th level, you gain the ability to infuse your weapon strikes with divine energy. Once on each of your turns when you hit a creature with a weapon attack, you can cause the attack to deal an extra 1d8 lightning damage to the target. When you reach 14th level, the extra damage increases to 2d8.

World Traveler
At 17th level, you ignore difficult terrain, and you gain resistance to cold and fire damage.

DRUID CIRCLES
At 2nd level, a druid gains the Druid Circle feature, and the following new options become available.

CIRCLE OF OAKS
There is power in the ancient trees of the world—a quiet, abiding power. Those who live among trees, like the elves, are aware of this power, and they treat it with respect, even reverence. Some druids learn to tap into this power. These are the members of the Circle of Oaks. By suffusing themselves with the vitality and strength of the ancient green, they can perform mighty feats. Although they commonly hail from the ancient forests of the world, Circle of Oaks druids can be found anywhere there are trees of sufficient age from which to draw power.

CIRCLE OF OAKS SPELLS

Druid Level	Spells
3rd	locate animals or plants, pass without trace
5th	plant growth, speak with plants
7th	conjure woodland beings, locate creature
9th	awaken, tree stride

Tree Step
Starting at 6th level, you can spend half your movement to magically step into a tree and transport yourself through it and out of another tree of the same kind within 60 feet, reappearing in a space of your choice within 5 feet of the destination tree. You can use this feature twice when you reach 10th level, and three times at 14th level, when the range becomes 120 feet. You regain all expended uses when you finish a long rest.

Might of the Oak
At 10th level, you can expend two uses of Wild Shape at the same time to transform into a tree-like humanoid, similar to a treant, though not as powerful. While in this form, you are a Large plant, and you have the following statistics:

AC 15   **HIT POINTS** 10d10 + 50   **SPEED** 30 ft.
STRENGTH 22 (+6); **DEXTERITY** 9 (−1); **CONSTITUTION** 20 (+5)
DAMAGE RESISTANCES bludgeoning, piercing
DAMAGE VULNERABILITIES fire

False Appearance. While you remain motionless, you are indistinguishable from a tree.

Multiattack. You make two Slam attacks.

Slam. Melee Weapon Attack: +9 to hit, reach 10 ft., one target. *Hit:* 14 (2d8 + 5) bludgeoning damage

Rock. Ranged Weapon Attack: +9 to hit, range 60/180 ft., one target. *Hit:* 21 (3d10 + 5) bludgeoning damage.

Rouse the Grove
At 14th level, you can use an action on your turn to stir the trees around you, bringing them to your aid. All trees within 60 feet of you become animated, their roots churning the earth and their branches whipping and slashing. All spaces within 15 feet of a tree are considered difficult terrain for your enemies, but not for you or your allies. A creature concentrating on a spell that starts its turn in one of the affected spaces must succeed on a Constitution saving throw against your spell save DC or lose concentration on the spell.

Also, you can use a bonus action on your turn to cause one affected tree to strike a creature within 15 feet of it with a branch. Make an attack roll, using your spellcasting ability modifier as a bonus to the roll. On a hit, the creature takes 4d6 bludgeoning damage. You can use this feature for a number of rounds equal to your druid level; these rounds need not be consecutive. You regain the full use of this feature when you finish a long rest.

If this feature is used underground, beneath an area where trees grow, the effect is the same, except it is the trees' roots that burst through walls into rooms or tunnels, producing the same effects. If the GM decides the area is too far underground or is otherwise unsuitable for this feature to be used, it has no effect.

CIRCLE OF OWLS

Druids of the Circle of Owls maintain their tradition of spying and gathering knowledge and, occasionally, of permanently silencing those who would misuse knowledge. The Circle of Owls druids draw on the power of their namesakes, moving about the world unnoticed as they see and hear what others try desperately to hide.

Circle Spells

The ever-present eyes and ears of the natural world impart magical knowledge to you. At 2nd level, you learn the *message* cantrip. At 3rd, 5th, 7th, and 9th levels, you gain access to the spells listed for those levels in the Circle of Owls Spells table.

Once you gain access to a circle spell, you always have it prepared, and it doesn't count against the number of spells you can prepare each day. If you gain access to a spell that doesn't appear on the druid spell list, the spell is nonetheless a druid spell for you.

CIRCLE OF OWLS SPELLS

Druid Level	Spells
3rd	*detect thoughts, invisibility*
5th	*nondetection, sending*
7th	*arcane eye, private sanctum*
9th	*modify memory, scrying*

Bonus Proficiency

When you choose this circle at 2nd level, you gain proficiency in either Deception or Stealth.

On Silent Wings

Starting at 2nd level, you can magically evade the notice of even those who watch you. You can take the Hide action even when other creatures can see you. If you hide successfully, you remain hidden in this way until the end of your next turn (or sooner, if you choose to stop hiding).

You can use this feature a number of times equal to your Wisdom modifier (minimum of once). You regain all expended uses when you finish a long rest.

Owl's Eyes

At 6th level, you can cast the *clairvoyance* spell. When you cast the spell in this way, you don't require components, and the casting time is 1 action. You can choose for the invisible sensor to instead be visible as the image of an owl.

Once you use this feature, you can't use it again until you finish a long rest.

Shadow Flight

At 10th level, you can slip partially into shadow for a short time. As an action, you can cast the *etherealness* spell. When you cast the spell in this way, its duration is concentration, up to 1 minute.

Once you use this feature, you can't use it again until you finish a short or long rest.

Parliament of Owls

When you reach 14th level, you can disperse your form into a swirling storm of owls. As an action, you can use your Wild Shape to become a swarm of owls, which uses the statistics of a swarm of ravens.

CIRCLE OF ROSES

Druids of the Circle of Roses use the power of nature to influence the minds and hearts of those around them, alleviating sorrow, spreading terror, and ensnaring hearts in equal measure. They create sweet and bitter perfumes that transmit their power to any who inhale the scent.

Circle Spells

Your bond with the ebb and flow of nature grants you knowledge of certain spells. At 2nd level, you learn the *poison spray* cantrip. At 3rd, 5th, 7th, and 9th levels, you gain access to the spells listed for those levels in the Circle of Roses Spells table.

Once you gain access to a circle spell, you always have it prepared, and it doesn't count against the number of spells you can prepare each day. If you gain access to a spell that doesn't appear on the druid spell list, the spell is nonetheless a druid spell for you.

CIRCLE OF ROSES SPELLS

Druid Level	Spells
3rd	calm emotions, suggestion
5th	hypnotic pattern, tongues
7th	confusion, phantasmal killer
9th	dominate person, geas

Bonus Proficiency
When you choose this circle at 2nd level, you gain proficiency in Deception, Intimidation, or Persuasion.

Bittersweet Perfume
Starting at 2nd level, you can expend one use of your Wild Shape as an action to create a floral perfume that manipulates the minds of those who breathe it. One creature of your choice within 10 feet of you must make a Charisma saving throw against your spell save DC. On each of your turns while the perfume lasts, you can use an action to choose a different creature within 10 feet of you to affect with your perfume.

On a failed save, the creature is charmed by you or frightened (your choice) for as long as it remains in the area of your perfume and for 1 minute after it leaves the area. If it ends its turn outside the area, the creature can repeat the saving throw, ending the effect on itself on a success. If you or your allies attack or harm a charmed creature, it is no longer charmed.

If the creature's saving throw is successful or if the effect ends for it, it is immune to your perfume for the next 24 hours. A creature that doesn't breathe or that is immune to poison is immune to your perfume.

The perfume lasts for 10 minutes or until you use your Wild Shape again.

Overpowering Remedy
At 6th level, your perfume can affect one creature of your choice within 20 feet of you, and you can use the scent to offset harmful effects. When you use your Bittersweet Perfume, you can choose to end one disease or one condition affecting a creature in your perfume instead of charming or frightening it. The condition removed can be charmed, frightened, or poisoned.

Rose's Thorns
At 10th level, you can stab thorns at the minds of those who dare to take you on. When a creature within 20 feet of you hits you with an attack, you can use your reaction to force the creature to make a Wisdom saving throw against your spell save DC. On a failed save, the creature takes 1d10 psychic damage.

Lingering Perfume
When you reach 14th level, a whiff of your perfume surrounds you at all times and lingers in your wake. You are immune to harmful gases and vapors, you have advantage on saving throws against becoming charmed or frightened, and your Bittersweet Perfume now lasts for 1 hour or until you use your Wild Shape again.

In addition, you can intensify the power of your perfume. When a creature becomes charmed or frightened from your Bittersweet Perfume, you can use a bonus action to wrap some of your perfume around it. That creature is considered to be in the area of your perfume, no matter how far it moves away from you, for 1 hour or until you use your Wild Shape again. Once you use this feature, you can't use it again until you finish a long rest.

MARTIAL ARCHETYPES

At 3rd level, a fighter gains the Martial Archetype feature, and the following new options become available.

PRESCIENT KNIGHT

The archetypal Prescient Knight is the culmination of long years of study and dedication to the craft of combat, supplemented by the use of magic that provides a glimpse of the future or makes it possible to turn back the hands of time.

Bonus Proficiency

When you choose this archetype at 3rd level, you gain proficiency in Arcana.

Reactive Echo

Also at 3rd level, you become able to innately anticipate the actions of your foes. You can take a second reaction during a round in which you use your Action Surge.

PRESCIENT KNIGHT FEATURES

Fighter Level	Feature
3rd	Bonus Proficiency, Martial Caster, Reactive Echo, Spellcasting
7th	Constant Vigilance
10th	Evasion
15th	Anticipatory Strike
18th	Action Free of Thought

Spellcasting

When you reach 3rd level, you augment your martial prowess with the ability to cast spells.

Cantrips. You learn two cantrips of your choice from among *guidance*, *quicken* (described in **Chapter 5**), and *true strike*. You learn the remaining cantrip of the three at 10th level.

Spell Slots. The Prescient Knight Spellcasting table indicates how many spell slots you have available for casting spells. You regain used spell slots when you finish a long rest.

Spells Known of 1st Level and Higher. You know three 1st-level spells of your choice, all of which you must choose from the divination and temporal spells on the wizard spell list.

The Spells Known column of the Prescient Knight Spellcasting table shows when you learn more wizard spells of 1st level or higher. You learn additional spells as you progress; newly learned spells have the same school and list restrictions as your original spells.

Whenever you gain a level, you can replace one spell you know with another from among those spells you are able to learn.

Spellcasting Ability. Intelligence is your spellcasting ability for your wizard spells. You use your Intelligence modifier when you make an attack roll with a spell and when setting the saving throw DC for a spell you cast.

PRESCIENT KNIGHT SPELLCASTING

Fighter Level	Cantrips Known	Spells Known	1	2	3	4
3rd	2	3	2	—	—	—
4th	2	4	3	—	—	—
5th	2	4	3	—	—	—
6th	2	4	3	—	—	—
7th	2	5	4	2	—	—
8th	2	6	4	2	—	—
9th	2	6	4	2	—	—
10th	3	7	4	3	—	—
11th	3	8	4	3	—	—
12th	3	8	4	3	—	—
13th	3	9	4	3	2	—
14th	3	10	4	3	2	—
15th	3	10	4	3	2	—
16th	3	11	4	3	3	—
17th	3	11	4	3	3	—
18th	3	11	4	3	3	—
19th	3	12	4	3	3	1
20th	3	13	4	3	3	1

Martial Caster
At 3rd level and higher, you can perform somatic components for your spells while you are wielding a weapon or a shield, as long as you have proficiency with those items.

Constant Vigilance
Beginning at 7th level, you have a preternatural awareness of your surroundings in times of duress. If you are surprised but not incapacitated at the start of combat, you can use your Action Surge to negate surprise for yourself and take a normal turn plus one additional action (from the Action Surge) in the first round of combat. Additionally, using your Action Surge in this way allows you to give sufficient warning to allies who are within 15 feet of you, so they can also start taking reactions after your turn.

Evasion
At 10th level, your foreknowledge of events to come allows you to position yourself in the most advantageous manner. When you are subjected to an effect that allows you to make a Dexterity saving throw to take only half damage, you instead take no damage if you succeed on the saving throw, and only half damage if you fail.

Anticipatory Strike
At 15th level, your innate connection to the threads of fate strengthens, providing greater insight into the movements and actions of your opponents. When you use your Action Surge, you have advantage on attack rolls and a +2 bonus to your AC until the end of your next turn.

Action Free of Thought
At 18th level, your mastery of divination and temporal effects is such that you are able to react to your opponents without conscious thought and with minimal physical effort. During combat, you can take one reaction every turn instead of one per round.

OTHERWORLDLY PATRONS
At 1st level, a warlock gains the Otherworldly Patron feature, and the following new options become available.

FROZEN ONE
This is typically a powerful entity of winter, such as the **avatar of Boreas** (see *Tome of Beasts*), but prominent **ice maidens** (see *Tome of Beasts*), ice devils, and other creatures associated with the cold can also serve as patrons.

Your patron seeks to immerse the world in eternal winter or bring about some similar fate. Though you might not share this goal, you have sworn fealty to this being, and you act as its agent to spread winter wherever you roam.

Expanded Spell List
The Frozen One lets you choose from an expanded list of spells when you learn a warlock spell. The following spells are added to the warlock spell list for you.

CHAPTER 1 CHARACTER OPTIONS | 49

EXPANDED SPELLS

Spell Level	Spells
1st	create or destroy water, snowy coat*
2nd	ice hammer*, sculpt snow*
3rd	protective ice*, sleet storm
4th	ice storm, wintry glide*
5th	cone of cold, ice fortress*

* Described in **Chapter 5**

Deflective Ice

Starting at 1st level, you can bring a small chunk of ice to your aid. As a reaction when a creature makes a weapon attack against you, the ice shields you from the attack. The creature has disadvantage on its attack roll. Regardless of the result of the attack, the ice melts away immediately afterward. Once you use this feature, you can't use it again until you finish a short or long rest.

Frozen Path

Beginning at 6th level, as part of your move, you can leave a layer of ice on the ground along your path. This ice persists for 1 minute. A creature other than you that enters a space of ice must make a successful Dexterity saving throw against your spell save DC or fall prone in that space. Once you use this feature, you can't use it again until you finish a short or long rest.

Icy Body

Beginning at 10th level, your skin takes on an icy sheen. You are immune to cold damage, and you have advantage on Strength and Dexterity checks you make to escape from being grappled.

Wintry Blast

Starting at 14th level, you can designate a creature you see within 60 feet of you. It must make a Constitution saving throw against your warlock spell save DC. On a failed save, the creature feels numbing cold emanating from your patron. The creature takes 10d10 cold damage and must make another Constitution saving throw. If the second saving throw is failed, the creature is also restrained for 1 minute. A creature restrained in this way repeats the saving throw at the end of each of its turns, ending the condition on a success. After using this feature, you must finish a short or long rest before using it again.

Pact Boons

At 3rd level, the Frozen One bestows a gift upon you for your loyal service. You gain one of the following features of your choice.

Pact of the Blade. Your pact weapon has a patina of ice, and small icicles dangle from it. When you create or summon your pact weapon, you can choose whether it deals its standard damage type or cold damage.

Pact of the Chain. When you conjure your familiar or change its form, you can choose the form of an ice mephit in addition to the usual options granted by the pact boon. When you use your action to command your mephit familiar to attack, it can use its breath or cast an innate spell instead.

Pact of the Tome. Your book is formed from rune-etched sheets of ice that are cold to the touch to everyone but you. The book is immune to cold damage.

Eldritch Invocations

The following invocations are available to Frozen One warlocks.

BOREAL AURA

Prerequisite: 3rd Level, Frozen One Patron

Ice and snow cascade around you. When you use an action, your melee attacks deal an extra 1d6 cold damage, and attackers within 5 feet of you who hit you in melee take 1d6 cold damage, for as long as you maintain concentration.

HORRIFIC WINTRY VISAGE

Prerequisite: 5th Level, Frozen One Patron

You can cast *sculpt snow* once using a warlock spell slot. Creatures that see your sculpture for the first time must make a successful Wisdom saving throw against your spell save DC or become frightened of the sculpture for 1 round. You must finish a long rest before using this invocation again.

GENIE LORD

You have made a pact with a powerful ruler of geniekind on one of the Elemental Planes. The Genie Lord's concerns encompass a myriad of topics, ranging from those inscrutable to the mortal mind to those that are simple and straightforward. Genie lords compete endlessly against each other, and rivalries between these elemental rulers can engulf entire nations. They aren't above bribing a rival's mortal agents to switch sides if they think it will gain them an advantage.

Expanded Spell List

The Genie Lord lets you choose from an expanded list of spells when you learn a warlock spell. The following spells are added to the warlock spell list for you.

GENIE LORD EXPANDED SPELLS

Spell Level	Spells
1st	thunderwave, wind tunnel*
2nd	gust of wind, sleet storm
3rd	protection from energy, water breathing
4th	conjure minor elementals, fire shield
5th	creation, wall of stone

* Described in **Chapter 5**

Genie Lord's Favor

Starting at 1st level, you can speak, read, and write Primordial. You can understand and be understood by any creature that speaks Auran, Ignan, Terran, or Aquan.

Additionally, your patron grants you a token that can absorb elemental power. You gain a magical gemstone with the following properties:

- You can use the gem as an arcane focus.
- The gem can capture elemental power. When you take acid, cold, fire, lighting, or thunder damage, you can choose to transfer some or all of the damage into the gem instead of taking the damage yourself. The gem can absorb damage equal to twice your warlock level + twice your Charisma modifier. The gem becomes empty again when you finish a long rest.
- While the gem holds any amount of elemental power, you can use an action to cause it to shed bright light out to 20 feet and dim light for an additional 20 feet, to shed dim light out to 5 feet, or to douse the light.

If you lose your token, you can perform a 1-hour ceremony to receive a replacement from your patron. This ceremony can be performed during a short or long rest, and it destroys the previous token. Your token shatters to slivers when you die.

Release Energy

Starting at 6th level, you can use the energy stored in your token against foes. When you damage a target with any kind of attack, you can spend stored points to deal extra damage of the same type equal to your Charisma bonus. If you deal damage to multiple targets with a single attack, choose which one takes the extra damage.

Additionally, you can extend the protection of your gem to other creatures. When an ally within 30 feet that you can see takes acid, cold, fire, lighting, or thunder damage, you can use your reaction to transfer some of the damage into your gem.

Minor Wish

Starting at 10th level, you can call upon your Genie Lord to twist fate in your favor. Immediately after you make an attack roll, saving throw, ability check, or damage roll, you can choose to reroll and take the better result.

Once you use this feature, you can't use it again until you finish a short or long rest.

Herald's Aspect

Starting at 14th level, you can channel the power of your patron into your flesh to magically transform into a herald of your Genie Lord. Your legs fade away into a swirl of elemental energy, and your skin and features take on a cast that resembles that of your patron. You can transform as a bonus action, and the transformation lasts for 1 minute, during which you gain the following benefits:

- You gain a flying speed of 60 feet.
- You have advantage on saving throws against spells and other magical effects.
- Choose one of the following damage types: acid, cold, fire, lightning, or thunder. You gain immunity to that damage type.
- Once on your turn when you hit with any attack, you can deal an extra 3d6 damage of one of the following types: acid, cold, fire, lightning, or thunder.

Once you use this feature, you can't use it again until you finish a short or long rest.

Pact Boons

The pact boons bestowed by the Genie Lord are modified or augmented as described below. Add these details to whichever pact boon you select.

Pact of the Blade. Your pact weapon takes on a sheen of elemental power. When you create or summon your pact weapon, you can choose its damage type to be one

CHAPTER 1 CHARACTER OPTIONS | **51**

of the following: acid, cold, fire, lightning, or thunder. You can select a different damage type each time you create the weapon.

Pact of the Chain. When you conjure your familiar or change its form, you can choose the form of a mephit in addition to the usual alternatives. When you use your action to command your mephit familiar to attack, it can use its breath or its Innate Spellcasting if you so desire.

Pact of the Tome. Your book is immune to damage or wear caused by the elements. This includes acid, cold, fire, lightning, or thunder damage, as well as simple effects such as being immersed in water or set aflame.

SIBYL

You have made a pact with the Sibyl, a divine being associated with prophecy, knowledge, and fate. Your patron guides you through visions, portents, and periods of ecstatic clarity to act on its behalf and to further its stratagems. Your relationship to your patron is different from that of its clergy. You are not asked for faith, worship, or adulation; instead, you serve solely through your actions and influence in the world. Because of that, you might have a strained relationship with the deity's most dedicated priests and other zealots.

Expanded Spell List

The Sibyl lets you choose from an expanded list of spells when you learn a warlock spell. The following spells are added to the warlock spell list for you.

SYBIL EXPANDED SPELLS

Spell Level	Spells
1st	alarm, seer's reaction*
2nd	augury, blindness/deafness
3rd	bestow curse, clairvoyance
4th	confusion, divination
5th	eidetic memory*, legend lore

*Described in **Chapter 5**

Touched by the Sybil

Starting at 1st level, you are driven to ecstatic gibbering and utterances because of your connection to your patron. Your prophetic commentary, startling insights, and frenetic appearance are unsettling, distracting, and psychically damaging to your target. Although the manifestation is different, this effect functions the same as the *vicious mockery* cantrip.

Additionally, you have proficiency in Performance, and your proficiency bonus is doubled on ability checks you make using that skill.

Disastrous Prognostication

Starting at 6th level, you can direct your patron to infiltrate and overwhelm your target's psyche with knowledge of failures in the target's immediate future. As an action, designate a creature within 60 feet that can see and hear you. It must make a successful Charisma saving throw or be stunned until the end of your next turn.

After using this feature, you can't use it again until you finish a short or long rest.

Whispered Warnings

When you reach 10th level, the voices in your mind become clearer and more focused. They bolster your mindfulness of your surroundings and grant you a preternatural awareness of creatures that mean you harm. While you are wearing light armor or no armor, you can add your Charisma modifier (minimum of 1) to your Armor Class.

Pierce the Veil

Starting at 14th level, when you deal psychic damage to a target, you can also inundate it with frenetic and discordant voices of doom. The awful truths revealed to the target cause it to take an extra 8d10 psychic damage, and it is affected as if by a *confusion* spell until the end of its next turn.

Once you use this feature, you can't use it again until you finish a long rest.

Pact Boons

The pact boons bestowed by the Sybil are modified or augmented as described below. Add these details to whichever pact boon you select.

Pact of the Blade. Your weapon is usually, but not always, the weapon favored by your patron. When you create or summon your pact weapon, you can choose whether it deals damage of its usual type or psychic damage.

Pact of the Chain. Your patron grants you a special familiar, a **giant moth** (see *Creature Codex*), to aid you.

Pact of the Tome. Your tome is an illuminated manuscript with depictions of prophets foretelling events to come. As your adventuring career progresses, new illuminations appear in the book's pages, recording your notable acts in the service of your patron. While this book is on your person, your passive Perception score is increased by 1 when being contested by an enemy's Stealth check.

RANGER ARCHETYPES

At 3rd level, a ranger gains the Ranger Archetype feature, and the following new options become available.

GRIFFON SCOUT

Elves of the forested woodlands and mountain foothills often uphold the tradition of taming and riding griffons, living on the same windswept crags where griffons nest, thus giving themselves the ability to command vast tracts of woodland territory. Trained by elf veterans and beast tamers, rangers of the Griffon Scout archetype learn to move swiftly and stealthily both on foot and while mounted, gathering information on their enemies and mounting devastating hit-and-run raids with precision and coordination.

Griffon Scout Magic

Starting at 3rd level, you learn an additional spell when you reach certain levels, as shown in the Griffon Scout Spells table. These spells count as ranger spells for you, but they don't count against the number of ranger spells you can know.

GRIFFON SCOUT SPELLS

Ranger Level	Spells
3rd	*feather fall*
5th	*find steed*
9th	*haste*
13th	*greater invisibility*
17th	*telepathic bond*

Mounted Scout

Also starting at 3rd level, you have advantage on Dexterity (Stealth) checks while mounted, and your Dexterity (Stealth) checks apply to both you and your mount.

Skirmisher's Step

Beginning at 3rd level, when you move at least 20 feet straight toward a creature and hit it with a melee weapon attack in the same turn, that attack deals an extra 1d8 damage of the same type dealt by the

weapon to the target. If you move out of the target's reach before the end of your next turn, whether you are mounted or not, you don't provoke an opportunity attack from the target.

Coordinated Strikes
Starting at 7th level, you can deliver punishing flurries of attacks in perfect coordination with your allies. When one of your allies hits a target within 30 feet of you with an attack, you can use your reaction to make one weapon attack against that target.

Griffon Wings
Beginning at 11th level, when you cast *find steed*, you can choose for your steed to take the form of a griffon, though it is a fey instead of a monstrosity.

Strike and Fade
Starting at 15th level, when you move at least 20 feet during your turn, whether you are mounted or not, you become an evasive blur. Until the start of your next turn, a creature that attacks you has disadvantage on the first attack roll it makes against you or your mount.

VAMPIRE SLAYER
Vampire slayers wander remote forests, haunted hills, and fog-bound moors, protecting the common folk at the edge of civilized lands from the creatures of the night. Moving unseen through woodlands, your specialized training allows you to hunt vampires, ghouls, werewolves, and other monsters that prey on the innocent. Although you are most at home in the wilderness, as your skills improve, your attention might turn to older vampires that rule entire baronies, or that command dark keeps and sprawling manors closer to civilization.

Favored Enemy
If you choose this archetype at 3rd level, your favored enemy becomes undead if you did not select undead at 1st level. When you choose additional favored enemies at 6th and 14th level, you can choose freely from the standard list, and you can also select hags or lycanthropes as an alternative.

Hunter's Prey
At 3rd level, you gain one of the following features of your choice: either Colossus Slayer, Giant Killer, or Horse Breaker from the Hunter archetype in the standard rules, or Empowered Strike, which is described below.

Empowered Strike. Your expertise in fighting undead and lycanthropes allows you to harm them even when you're not wielding a magic weapon. When you fight a creature that has resistance to bludgeoning, piercing, or slashing damage from nonmagical weapons, you can ignore this resistance once per turn when you score a hit with a nonmagical weapon. If you are wielding a magic weapon, the creature takes an extra 1d8 damage from one of your successful attacks on each of your turns.

Defensive Tactics
At 7th level, you gain one of the following features of your choice: either Escape the Horde, Multiattack Defense, or Steel Will from the Hunter archetype in the standard rules, or Ranger's Resilience, which is described below.

Ranger's Resilience. You have advantage on saving throws against paralysis and against effects that would reduce your hit point maximum.

Slayer's Strike
At 11th level, you gain one of the following features of your choice: either Volley or Whirlwind Attack from the Hunter archetype in the standard rules, or Straight Through the Heart, which is described below.

Straight Through the Heart. When you use an attack action, you can choose to make a single melee attack against a favored enemy in an effort to strike a vulnerable spot. If the attack hits, it deals an extra 6d6 damage.

Superior Hunter's Defense
At 15th level, you gain one of the following features of your choice: either Evasion, Stand Against the Tide, or Uncanny Dodge from the Hunter archetype in the standard rules, or Greater Resilience, which is described below.

Greater Resilience. You have advantage on saving throws against the spells and abilities of your favored enemies.

SACRED OATHS
At 3rd level, a paladin gains the Sacred Oath feature, and the following new options become available.

OATH OF RADIANCE
The Oath of Radiance is a beacon in the night, burning away the corruption of shadow and undeath. Radiant paladins are bold and brash, abhorring stealth and grandly striding into battle against the forces of darkness. Paladins of the Oath of Radiance are overwhelmingly good-aligned, and most are lawful. Some reject the rigid nature of knightly orders for the life of a knight errant. Though still nearly universally good, these wayward paladins are more neutral than lawful, and they use their relative freedom to bring their light to bear as they deem it necessary.

Tenets of Radiance
Paladins who swear the Oath of Radiance devote themselves to fighting the insidious powers that darken mortal hearts and against the undead that extinguish the light of life and replace it with hungry darkness. Most important, they take it upon themselves to rescue those corrupted by shadow or undead influence. They will spare mortal foes held in the thrall of darkness in the hope that such creatures can be redeemed.

Cleanse Corruption. I will burn out all creatures born of darkness, showing no pity or mercy. I will not suffer the company of dark creatures, save those taken in by darkness whom I might redeem.

Lead with Light. I stand open and courageous in the face of battle and will be the last of my companions to quit the field, just as the last ray of sun leaves the day.

Preserve the Righteous. I will defend those who labor and live in fear of shadow. I will shield them from harm and keep the light upon them.

Redeem the Beguiled. Those tempted into the service of darkness may yet be saved, and I will do everything in my power to bring them back to the light. I will be discerning in offering this mercy, but the redemption of the corrupted is paramount.

Remain Pure. I will never yield to the lies of darkness or suffer corruption to take me. I will cleanse myself of dark taint or die before threatening those I defend.

Oath Spells

You gain oath spells at the paladin levels listed.

OATH OF RADIANCE SPELLS

Paladin Level	Spells
3rd	*guiding bolt, protection from evil and good*
5th	*magic weapon, scorching ray*
9th	*beacon of hope, daylight*
13th	*fire shield, inspiring speech**
17th	*greater restoration, sun's bounty**

* Described in **Chapter 5**

Channel Divinity

When you take this oath at 3rd level, you gain the following two Channel Divinity options.

Dawn's Radiance. As an action, you present your holy symbol or a melee weapon, and it flares with the radiance of the newly risen sun. Magical darkness within 20 feet of you is dispelled. Thereafter, the object continues to shine for 1 hour or until you lose possession of it. The object sheds bright light out to 20 feet and dim light for an additional 20 feet.

An undead creature, a creature native to the Plane of Shadow, or any creature harmed by sunlight (such as a creature with the Sunlight Sensitivity feature) suffers pain and disorientation when bathed in this radiance. The creature has disadvantage on attack rolls and on Dexterity (Stealth) and Wisdom (Perception) checks while it, the target of its attack, or anything it is trying to perceive is in the bright light shed by the holy symbol or weapon.

Turn the Corrupted. As an action, you present your holy symbol and speak a prayer against the corruptive power of death and shadow, using your Channel Divinity. Each undead or creature native to the Plane of Shadow that is within 30 feet of you and that can see or hear you must make a successful Wisdom saving throw or be turned for 1 minute or until it takes damage.

Aura of Resolve

At 7th level, you and your allies within 10 feet of you have advantage on saving throws against spells and effects created by undead creatures and by creatures native to the Plane of Shadow. This benefit lasts until someone fails a saving throw that was made with advantage because of your Aura of Resolve. Once that happens, you must finish a short or long rest before you can use this feature again.

At 18th level, the range of this aura increases to 30 feet.

Soul of Light

Starting at 15th level, you have resistance to necrotic damage, and your ability scores and hit point maximum can't be reduced by any effect.

Radiant Champion

At 20th level, as an action, you can suffuse your being with divine radiance that brings life and burns away dark corruption. For 1 minute, you gain the following benefits:

- At the beginning of each of your turns, you regain 10 hit points.

- Once on your turn when you hit an undead creature or a creature native to the Plane of Shadow, it must make a successful Wisdom saving throw against your spell save DC or be incapacitated until the end of its next turn.
- An undead creature or a creature native to the Plane of Shadow that touches you or hits you with a melee attack from 5 feet away takes 2d8 radiant damage.

Once you use this feature, you can't use it again until you finish a long rest.

OATH OF THUNDER

Paladins who swear the Oath of Thunder are even more reserved and humble in daily life than other paladins. That veneer splits like a thunderclap in battle when they erupt as vicious hellions. Indeed, thundering paladins love to strike "thunder-wise," meaning suddenly and with surprise, appearing like a bolt of lightning in their enemies' midst before those enemies know what hit them. Paladins of the Oath of Thunder are often devoted to the cause of good but care little about the struggle between law and chaos.

Tenets of Thunder

The Oath of Thunder stresses moderation and clear purpose in daily life, along with crushing, decisive strikes on the battlefield. Paladins sworn to Thunder see aberrations and fiends as the ultimate forces of corruption in the world and strive tirelessly to thwart their designs.

Composure Is My Shield. My deeds are my armor, and I am not easily provoked. If anyone shall insult me, I shall laugh at their ignorance. If anyone shall insult my companions, I shall show them their error.

Crush the Abomination. Twisted creatures from beyond the world have no place in it. Aberrations and fiends will feel my blade and know death.

Decisiveness in Battle. When the time for words has passed, I will strike first to bring a swift end to my enemies.

Duty Above All. Though I drink with the gods and laugh with the valkyries, I will stand my watch. I will defend my nation. I will defend my companions.

Humility in Life. I am Thunder's servant, not its master. I will live without excess, assured in my own strength without ostentation. Charity and courage are twins.

Voice Like Thunder. My voice rings clear and true in defense of those who can't speak out for themselves. I will speak the truth because such words echo through the ages.

Oath Spells

You gain oath spells at the paladin levels listed.

OATH OF THUNDER SPELLS

Paladin Level	Spells
3rd	*heroism, thunderwave*
5th	*find steed, gust of wind*
9th	*call lightning, thunderclap**
13th	*freedom of movement, stoneskin*
17th	*not this day!**, *rain of blades**

* Described in **Chapter 5**

Bonus Proficiency

When you take this oath at 3rd level, you gain proficiency in the Stealth skill.

Channel Divinity

When you take this oath at 3rd level, you gain the following two Channel Divinity options.

Storm Strike. As an action, you can use your Channel Divinity to infuse a ranged or thrown weapon you are holding with the wrath of a storm god. Make a ranged weapon attack as normal. In addition to the weapon attack, you create a line of lightning 5 feet wide and 60 feet long that extends from you straight toward the target. If the target is less than 60 feet from you, the line of lightning continues beyond it. Each creature in the line takes lightning damage equal to 2d10 + your paladin level, or half the damage with a successful Dexterity saving throw. If your ranged or thrown weapon attack hits, the target has disadvantage on its saving throw.

Turn the Unclean. As an action, you present your holy symbol and utter a war cry, using your Channel Divinity. Each aberration or fiend within 30 feet of you that can see or hear you must make a successful Wisdom saving throw or be turned for 1 minute or until it takes damage.

Aura of Alacrity

Beginning at 7th level, you and any allies within 10 feet of you add your proficiency bonus to initiative rolls.

At 18th level, the range of this aura increases to 30 feet.

Strike like Lightning

Starting at 15th level, when your attack hits a creature that hasn't yet taken its first turn in this combat, or when you hit a creature you were hidden from when you attacked, that creature has disadvantage on attack rolls, ability checks, and saving throws until the start of your next turn.

Child of the Storm

At 20th level, you can take on the aspect of the thunder god. While at rest, you have the gloomy demeanor of a thundercloud. When you go into action, your clothing and hair blow wildly in a wind that arises suddenly, your eyes flare with lightning, and your voice booms like thunder.

By using an action, you undergo a transformation. For 1 hour, you gain the following benefits:

- You don't have disadvantage on Dexterity (Stealth) checks because of armor.
- You have advantage on Dexterity (Stealth) checks and initiative rolls.
- Your weapon attacks deal an extra 1d10 lightning or thunder damage (your choice when you hit).
- As an action, you can unleash a terrifying war cry. Every enemy creature in a 30-foot cone must make a successful Wisdom saving throw or become frightened of you for 1 minute. While frightened in this way, the creature must spend its turn trying to move as far away from you as it can. It can't take reactions. On this turn, the creature can do nothing other than take the Dash action or try to escape from an effect that prevents it from moving. If there's nowhere to move, the creature can use the Dodge action. A frightened creature that's more than 30 feet from you and can't see you repeats the saving throw at the start of its turn, ending the effect on itself on a success. A creature that succeeds on its saving throw can't be affected by your war cry for 24 hours.

Once you use this feature, you can't use it again until you finish a long rest.

SORCEROUS ORIGINS

At 1st level, a sorcerer gains the Sorcerous Origin feature, and the following new options become available.

BOREAL

Your magic comes from the power of divine or magical entities of winter, beings born to the ice and cold. You might trace your descent down a line of ancestry from a mighty sorcerer that bargained with the God of the North Wind for power or that formed a pact with powerful creatures of ice and snow. Or perhaps you are the product of a union between a parent of your own kind and some wintry being. You might even be the one to traffic with a powerful boreal being in order to master the icy might of winter magic.

Boreal Magic

Starting at 1st level, you learn additional spells when you reach certain levels in this class, as shown below. Each of these spells counts as a sorcerer spell for you, but it doesn't count against the number of sorcerer spells you know.

Whenever you gain a sorcerer level, you can replace one spell you gained from this feature with another spell of the same level. The new spell must be an abjuration or a transmutation spell from the sorcerer, warlock, or wizard spell list.

BOREAL SPELLS

Sorcerer Level	Spells
1st	*flurry**, *snowy coat**
3rd	*creeping ice**, *sculpt snow**
5th	*breeze compass**, *protective ice**
7th	*snow boulder**, *wintry glide**
9th	*ice fortress**, *see beyond**

* Described in **Chapter 5**

Numbing Cold

Starting when you choose this origin at 1st level, your affinity for winter means that your enemies suffer more than normal from the cold spells you cast. A creature that takes cold damage from one of your spells takes extra damage equal to your Charisma modifier.

Winter's Child

Your affinity with winter allows you to venture forth in the cold without harm. You never suffer the effects of extreme cold, even if you are not dressed for the weather. Additionally, you can move over snow and ice without taking penalties for difficult terrain.

Gelid Form

At 6th level, you gain resistance to cold damage. Also, when you use sorcery points to apply a Metamagic option to a spell that deals cold damage or that produces an effect that involves snow or ice (*sleet storm*, for example), you can reduce the cost by 1 sorcery point, to a minimum of 1 point.

Winter's Form

At 14th level, you can give your wintry power physical form. As a bonus action, you can spend 1 sorcery point to transform your body for 1 minute. When you use this feature, you can take one of two forms:

- Your body transforms into a swirling mass of sleet or snow. Your gear transforms with you or falls to the ground in the space you occupy, as you choose. While in this form, you cannot speak, manipulate objects, attack, or cast spells. You gain immunity to cold damage, resistance to nonmagical bludgeoning, piercing, and slashing damage, and vulnerability to fire damage. In this form, your only method of movement is a flying speed of 60 feet, and you can hover. You can pass through small holes and narrow openings at least 1 inch in width, but you treat liquids as if they were solid surfaces. You cannot fall, and you remain hovering even while stunned or incapacitated. You can enter the space of another creature and remain there. Any creature whose space you occupy takes cold damage equal to your Charisma modifier.
- Your body transforms into translucent, blue-white ice, and your hair becomes a crown of snow. You gain

immunity to cold damage, resistance to nonmagical bludgeoning damage, and vulnerability to fire damage, and your Armor Class is never lower than 15 + your Dexterity modifier. Any creature within 5 feet of you that hits you with a melee weapon attack or a touch attack takes cold damage equal to your Charisma modifier. While in this form, you gain a slam attack with your icy fists that deals 1d4 bludgeoning damage plus cold damage equal to your Charisma modifier.

Winter's Soul
At 18th level, you gain immunity to cold damage and resistance to fire damage. (You don't have this resistance when you use Winter's Form, but you also no longer gain vulnerability to fire damage when you use that feature.) When you cast a spell that deals cold damage, any creature that gets a failure on its saving throw against the spell is also encased in ice, becoming grappled until it or a creature allied with it within 5 feet succeeds on a Strength check against your spell save DC. If the spell does not normally allow a saving throw, the creature makes a saving throw to avoid being grappled. If the spell already causes the grappled condition, the creature has disadvantage on the saving throw.

ELEMENTAL ESSENCE
Your magic arises from elemental power suffused into your being. You might have an elemental creature, such as genie, in your ancestry. Perhaps you lived most of your life near a portal to one of the Elemental Planes, and the ambient magic of the plane saturated everything you ate and drank. Perhaps a magical conjuring went awry, and the essence of an elemental merged with your own. Whatever the ultimate source, you are a walking conduit to an elemental plane.

Elemental Magic
Starting at 1st level, you learn additional spells when you reach certain levels in this class, as shown below, based on your Elemental Heritage. Each of these spells counts as a sorcerer spell for you, but it doesn't count against the number of sorcerer spells you know.

Whenever you gain a sorcerer level, you can replace one spell you gained from this feature with another spell of the same level. The new spell must be an abjuration or an evocation spell from the sorcerer, warlock, or wizard spell list.

Elemental Heritage
At 1st level, choose one element from the Elemental Heritage table. You can speak, read, and write the language associated with your heritage, and its damage type is used by features you gain later.

ELEMENTAL HERITAGE

Element	Language	Damage Type
Air	Auran	Lightning or thunder (choose one)
Earth	Terran	Bludgeoning
Fire	Ignan	Fire
Water	Aquan	Cold

Manifest Aura
Starting when you choose this origin at 1st level, you are able to channel your elemental power into a swirling aura. As a bonus action, you can surround yourself in a magical aura of elemental material or energy appropriate to your heritage element for 1 minute. While the aura persists, you gain the following benefits:

- When you are attacked, you can use your reaction to impose disadvantage on the attack roll.
- When you cast a spell of 1st level or higher, the aura around you intensifies until the start of your next turn. During this time, any creature that ends its turn within 5 feet of you or that enters that area takes 1d6 damage of the type associated with your heritage element. This damage increases to 2d6 when you reach 7th level.

You can use this feature twice. You regain all expended uses when you finish a long rest.

ELEMENTAL SPELLS

Sorcerer Level	Air Spells	Earth Spells	Fire Spells	Water Spells
1st	flurry*, wind tunnel*	gliding step*, nourishing repast*	candle's insight*, fire under the tongue*	snowy coat*, tidal barrier*
3rd	feather travel*, wresting wind*	boulder toss*, lair sense*	ashen memories*, fire darts*	delay potion*, mud pack*
5th	breeze compass*, storm god's doom*	bones of stone*, mire*	blade of wrath*, ire of the mountain*	bolstering brew*, riptide*
7th	consult the storm*, deva's wings*	chains of torment*, lava stone*	searing sun*, torrent of fire*	snow boulder*, wintry glide*
9th	see beyond*, tongue tied*	earth wave*, instant fortification*	blazing chariot*, sun's bounty*	control ice*, frostbite*

* Described in **Chapter 5**

Infuse Elements

Starting at 6th level, you gain resistance to the damage type associated with your heritage.

Additionally, when you damage a creature with a spell, you can spend 1 sorcery point to enhance it with the power of your heritage element. The spell takes on a visual cast that reflects the elemental infusion (fire and embers dance in the area, wind swirls around a bolt of energy, and so forth) and delivers the following additional effects depending on your heritage:

- *Air.* The creature is buffeted by strong winds, arcs of lighting, and claps of thunder. It can't take reactions until the start of its next turn.
- *Earth.* The creature is restrained until the start of your next turn.
- *Fire.* The creature is seared by your fiery magic. It is frightened until the end of its next turn. Creatures that are immune to fire are unaffected.
- *Water.* The creature is disoriented as the world seems to roll and pitch in waves. It is poisoned until the end of its next turn.

Elemental Jaunt

At 14th level, you can teleport by skimming the outer boundary of the Elemental Planes. As a bonus action, you can magically teleport up to 60 feet to an unoccupied space you can see. When you appear, you can create one of the following effects, depending on your heritage element:

- *Air.* When you appear within 5 feet of an area of wind (whether natural or magical), you create a cyclonic burst of wind. All creatures within 10 feet of you must succeed on a Constitution saving throw or take 2d6 slashing damage and be blinded by dust and debris until the start of your next turn.
- *Earth.* When you appear within 5 feet of nonmagical, unworked stone filling at least one 5-foot square, you create tremors in the earth that ripple outward from you. Each creature within 10 feet of you that is touching the ground must succeed on a Strength saving throw or take 4d6 bludgeoning damage and fall prone.
- *Fire.* When you appear within 5 feet of a fire at least the size of a campfire, you create a burst of flame around yourself. Each creature within 10 feet must succeed on a Dexterity saving throw or take 2d6 fire damage and catch on fire. Until a creature takes an action to douse the fire, a creature on fire takes 1d6 fire damage at the start of each of its turns.
- *Water.* When you appear within 5 feet of at least 50 gallons of water, you create a torrent of water that assails the creatures around you. Each creature within 10 feet of you must succeed on a Constitution saving throw or take 2d6 bludgeoning damage and choke on the water that forces its way into the creature's throat. A choking creature can't speak and has disadvantage on attack rolls and ability checks until the start of your next turn. Creatures that don't have to breathe or that can breathe water aren't subject to choking.

Saving throws against these effects are made against your spell save DC. You can use this feature twice. You regain all expended uses when you finish a short or long rest.

Elemental Soul

At 18th level, you gain immunity to the damage type associated with your heritage element.

Depending on your elemental heritage, you also gain one of the following benefits:

- *Air.* You gain a magical flying speed equal to your current walking speed. Additionally, during your turn you can spend 1 sorcery point to become insubstantial wind and mist. Until the start of your next turn, you can enter a hostile creature's space, you can move through a space as narrow as 1 inch without squeezing, you are immune to the effects of strong wind, and you have resistance to bludgeoning, piercing, and slashing damage from nonmagical attacks.
- *Earth.* You gain a burrowing speed equal to your current walking speed, and you can burrow through nonmagical, unworked earth and stone. While doing so, you don't disturb the material you move through. Additionally, you can spend 1 sorcery point to become stony and unyielding until the start of your next turn. During this time, you have resistance to piercing and slashing damage, you are immune to poison damage, and you can't be petrified or poisoned.
- *Fire.* Your speed increases by 10 feet. Additionally, during your turn you can spend 1 sorcery point to become fiery and insubstantial. Until the start of your next turn, you can move through a hostile creature's space. The first time you enter a creature's space on a turn, that creature takes 1d10 fire damage and catches on fire. Until a creature takes an action to douse the fire, a creature on fire takes 1d10 fire damage at the start of each of its turns.
- *Water.* You gain a swimming speed equal to your current walking speed, and you can breathe both water and air. Additionally, during your turn you can spend 1 sorcery point to take on a watery form. Until the start of your next turn, you can enter a hostile creature's space and move through a space as narrow as 1 inch wide without squeezing. When you enter a hostile creature's space, the creature must succeed on a Strength saving throw against your spell save DC or fall prone.

FARSEER

Your magic comes from a god of prophecy and prognostication who imbued a sliver of their power in your ancestry. Farseers can trace their power through the generations to a single, powerful ancestor whose divine gift gave them access to the webs of fate. Some are plagued by visions and omens, having no knowledge of their august lineage. These unfortunate individuals might be driven to madness and ostracized because of their uncontrolled, forbidden knowledge. Regardless, the touch of the divine has forever changed you, and the skeins of fate unravel in your view.

Farseer Magic

Starting at 1st level, you learn additional spells when you reach certain levels in this class, as shown below. Each of these spells counts as a sorcerer spell for you, but it doesn't count against the number of sorcerer spells you know.

Whenever you gain a sorcerer level, you can replace one spell you gained from this feature with another spell of the same level. The new spell must be a conjuration or a divination spell from the sorcerer, warlock, or wizard spell list.

FARSEER SPELLS

Sorcerer Level	Spells
1st	candle's insight*, Voorish sign*
3rd	read object*, time step*
5th	mortal insight*, soul borrowing*
7th	flickering fate*, true light of revelation*
9th	battle mind*, cruor of visions*

*Described in **Chapter 5**

Blood of the Seer

When you choose this origin at 1st level, the blood of your ancestors signals your destiny. You gain proficiency in Insight and History. Your preternatural sense of what is to come also allows you to sense imminent danger, so you make initiative rolls with advantage.

Quickening

Starting at 1st level, you can take the Dodge action as a bonus action on your turn. You use this feature a number of times equal to your Constitution modifier (minimum of once). You regain all expended uses when you finish a short or long rest.

Commune with the Unknown

When you reach 6th level, your prophetic insight allows you to commune with otherworldly powers. By focusing all your attention on a single yes-or-no question for 1 minute, you can pose that question to the powers beyond. The entity that responds to your question has vast knowledge, but it isn't omniscient; it can predict only what might happen, not what's certain to occur. Questions about the future must be phrased in terms of what's possible or plausible to avoid nonanswers. You must finish a short or long rest before using this feature again.

Time Slip

When you reach 14th level, the skeins of time enshroud your body, distorting the fabric of reality around you. As an action, you can expend 3 sorcery points to step out of sync with the current timeline. You can be seen only as an indistinct, shimmery outline. Attacks against you are made with disadvantage, and you have resistance to bludgeoning, piercing, and slashing damage from nonmagical weapons. Additionally, you can move through other creatures and solid objects as if they were difficult terrain. If you end your turn inside a solid object, you take 1d10 force damage and are expelled into the nearest open space.

The effect lasts for up to 1 minute, provided you maintain concentration on it as on a spell.

Sharing the Dream

At 18th level, visions of likely futures constantly weave across your consciousness. You can share that foreknowledge with your companions. As an action, you can grant up to five creatures (which can include yourself) advantage on attack rolls or saving throws—each creature chooses for itself—for up to 1 minute, provided you maintain concentration on this effect as on a spell. You must expend 2 sorcery points per affected creature to trigger this effect.

SEROPHAGE

Your magic comes from blood, both your own and that of others. Serophages learn early in life that they can exercise some control over their own blood, and they harness that ability to awaken the magic that flows through their veins. The dark possibilities of this form of magic become apparent when a sorcerer discovers that they can control the blood flowing in the veins of other creatures as well. Thus is born the serophage, a sorcerer unlike all others.

Serophage Magic

Starting at 1st level, you learn additional spells when you reach certain levels in this class, as shown below, based on your Elemental Heritage. Each of these spells counts as a sorcerer spell for you, but it doesn't count against the number of sorcerer spells you know.

Whenever you gain a sorcerer level, you can replace one spell you gained from this feature with another spell of the same level. The new spell must be a necromancy or a transmutation spell from the sorcerer, warlock, or wizard spell list.

SEROPHAGE SPELLS

Sorcerer Level	Spells
1st	blood scarab*, bloody hands*
3rd	mephitic croak*, shared sacrifice*
5th	delayed healing*, vital mark*
7th	blood and steel*, blood puppet*
9th	exsanguinate*, sanguine horror*

* Described in **Chapter 5**

Strength Beneath the Skin

When you choose this origin at 1st level, you gain control over your blood flow, directing it away from a recent wound. When you take bludgeoning damage, you roll a d4 and subtract the result from the damage taken. When you reach 6th level, the die increases to a d6.

Blood Fuel

Starting at 6th level, instead of taking a move action, you can deal 1d4 slashing damage to yourself and regain a number of sorcery points equal to the slashing damage. Alternatively, you can choose to increase the save DC or the attack bonus of the next spell you cast by +1 instead of regaining sorcery points. When you reach 12th level, the die becomes a d8 and the increase to your attack bonus or save DC becomes +2.

Blood Barrier

At 14th level, you gain the ability to draw blood from a creature with Intelligence 5 or higher that has been killed within the last 30 minutes and form it into swirling rings that surround you. The number of rings is equal to your Charisma modifier.

The rings absorb physical damage. When you are struck by a melee or ranged weapon attack, one ring absorbs 1d10 damage from the attack and then disappears in a splash.

As an action, you can cause one ring to form into a magical spear of blood and launch itself at a target that you select within 60 feet. You make a ranged spell attack. On a hit, the target takes piercing damage equal to 1d6 + your Charisma modifier and must succeed on a Constitution saving throw or be stunned until the start of your next turn. The spear is considered a magic weapon. It evaporates after it's expended. Each ring remains until it either absorbs damage or is expended as a weapon.

Siphon Blood

At 18th level, you gain the ability to siphon a steady stream of blood from a living creature at a distance. As an action, you designate a creature within 40 feet, and that creature must make a Constitution saving throw. On a failed save, the creature takes 2d6 necrotic damage as blood oozes through its skin and flows through the air to you, where you absorb it through your own skin. For every 2 points of damage dealt to the target, you can choose to regain either 1 hit point or 1 sorcery point. The siphoning continues, dealing damage and restoring hit points or sorcery points at the start of your turn, until you end the effect (no action required) or until the target makes a successful Constitution saving throw at the end of its turn.

BACKGROUNDS

Many people come of age after being exposed to some form of arcane magic, or after being attracted to the study of supernatural forces. The arcane backgrounds presented below are examples of how to expand the concept, all designed to give players a wider range of choices when fleshing out their characters if the GM allows this material into the campaign. Optionally, the GM can use these backgrounds to add depth and complexity to NPCs that the player characters will come up against.

ARCHIVIST

Some of your earliest memories are of the library you called home while you learned to read and write under the tutelage of your mentor. The stacks comforted you, protected you, and took you to lands undreamed of. Now the time has come to turn that knowledge into practical experience, and to record your own journey for posterity.

Skill Proficiencies: Arcana, Investigation
Tool Proficiencies: Artisan's tools (calligrapher's supplies)
Languages: Two of your choice
Equipment: A leather-bound journal full of notes from past research projects, a set of robes, calligrapher's supplies, 5 sheets of loose paper, a pair of spectacles, and a pouch containing 15 gp

FEATURE: EXPERT RESEARCHER

Your familiarity with libraries and the tomes contained in them is unmatched. If you spend 1 hour studying the available books, grimoires, and codices in an archive, library, or similar collection while researching a specific subject, you can treat any Intelligence-based check result related to that subject of 9 or lower as a 10. Once you use this feature, you can't use it again to research the same subject in the same library.

SUGGESTED CHARACTERISTICS

Arcane archivists are most at home in their libraries. Their personalities and motivations reflect their focus, sometimes obsessive, on recorded knowledge and the search for it. Their motives for pursuing a life as an archivist are rarely so straightforward.

d8	Personality Trait
1	There is nothing more important than knowledge. It is neither good nor bad. To suggest otherwise is to be closed in mind and thought.
2	I would rather spend time with my nose in a book. I find interacting with people discomfiting.
3	I am fascinated by a specific area of esoteric knowledge. If I find someone who shares that interest, we might become fast friends.
4	My mind is my sanctum. I neglect the needs of my body as secondary, often forgoing meals and bathing, when I'm lost in contemplation and study.
5	I am an observer and chronicler of the journeys, experiences, trials, and tribulations of my companions as viewed from the outside looking in.
6	The path to knowledge is not solely traversed through books and study. To fully learn, you must experience!
7	I find the blind faith of religions, cults, and their ilk perturbing, and I ask endless questions of those who profess such beliefs.
8	Because I believe that a sound body is essential for a clear intellect, I relish physical activity and exercise.

d6	Ideal
1	*Purity.* The truth of a matter is subject to the whims of the historian. Facts are pure and incontrovertible. (Any)
2	*Focus.* Precision and concentration: These are the keys to successful completion of my objectives. (Lawful)
3	*Objectivity.* Action and inaction have consequences far beyond the immediate future. The appearance of one morality does not preclude the emergence of another as time goes on. (Neutral)
4	*Objectification.* I use resources—including companions, allies, and bystanders—as I need them to further my ends. (Evil)
5	*Preservation.* Life is knowledge, and knowledge is life. Preserving life in all its forms is paramount to a civilized culture. (Good)
6	*Observation.* I will participate only as a last resort. Events, to be true and accurate, must unfold without interference. (Neutral)

d6	Bond
1	I always keep a journal. It grounds me to my past and organizes my thoughts. Without it, I would be lost.
2	I carefully consider my options before making any decision of importance.
3	I am a student—in thoughts, actions, and words—ahead of all other roles and responsibilities.
4	A quill, given to me be my mentor during our first lessons, is precious to me above all other things.
5	I am bound to fulfill a sacred duty to a university or a tutor that started me on my path.
6	I stole a priceless grimoire from my patron, and they have learned of my theft.

d6	Flaw
1	I am protective of all that I have learned. I have sacrificed much for it, and it is mine to do with as I please.
2	I have found the one true way, the path to enlightenment. I share my teachings with all who can hear me, whether they want to follow the path or not.
3	I place my safety ahead of the welfare of all others. How else will my knowledge be recorded and shared with future generations?
4	I was once confined in a prison of my own making. Never again will I limit myself to learning without experiencing.
5	I will not destroy a book, tome, grimoire, or text of any kind. To lose knowledge is an abomination.
6	I share the knowledge I have worked so hard to attain with all who seek it. A question asked is a question that deserves to be answered.

FEY HOSTAGE

Years, possibly centuries, ago you were captured by the fey. Each host, as the fey called themselves, treated their "guest" differently. The relationship you forged with your captors defines you just as strongly as the circumstances of your abduction and of your escape or release. You have been indelibly marked—emotionally, psychically, and physically—by the fey and their special brand of hospitality.

Skill Proficiencies: Deception, Insight
Tool Proficiencies: One type of gaming set, one type of musical instrument
Languages: Elvish, Sylvan
Equipment: A flower with petals that will never wilt, a musical instrument (one of your choice), a set of fine clothes, and a pouch containing 10 gp

LIFE-CHANGING EVENT
The fey have a multitude of reasons for abducting—or rescuing—folk like you, and it's also possible that you or others did something to bring about your situation. Choose or randomly determine the reason behind your sojourn in the realm of the fey.

FEATURE: FIRST IMPRESSIONS
You were raised in a situation in which failing to adhere to the nuances, niceties, and intrigues of the fey court could have catastrophic repercussions. The first impressions one makes set the tone for future endeavors. You have learned that lesson well and continue to apply it. In your initial social interaction with an individual fey, you gain a +2 bonus to the first Charisma-based check you make.

CHAPTER 1 CHARACTER OPTIONS | 63

SUGGESTED CHARACTERISTICS

A fey hostage never forgets the circumstances that led to their capture, the treatment they experienced, or the events of their release. Their experiences with the unpredictable fey might range from whimsical to pathological.

d8	Event
1	My childhood was tithed to the fey by my family in return for prosperity for as long I remained in their care.
2	I made a bargain with a fox to play with its cubs in their den. The fox turned out to be an emissary of the Summer Court, and I was not released until the cubs came of age.
3	Centuries ago, my ancestors were rulers and made a political alliance with the fey in exchange for tribute to be paid every third generation. We are no longer rulers, but the fey still demand their tithe.
4	I have no memories of my past before I was taken by the fey.
5	I wandered into an ancient, primeval wood shortly after learning to walk and was found by the fey, who took me in.
6	A fey child befriended me and invited me to their home.
7	I am the only survivor of a fey raid. They killed my parents but spared me for their own unknowable reasons.
8	My parents could not care for me, and their choices were to abandon me in a forest or a city. They chose the forest.

d8	Personality Trait
1	I remain a child in thought, action, and deed.
2	I defer decisions to elves and fey that I encounter, always looking to them for guidance.
3	I long for the accommodations and sustenance I became accustomed to as a hostage of the Fair Folk.
4	I distrust any who display traits of fey heritage.
5	I tell others what I think they want to hear, whether I believe it not, to keep them happy.
6	I see danger in every shadow, enemies behind each door, and threats in the eyes of strangers.
7	I never speak unless spoken to, and never look people in the eyes.
8	I am fascinated, frightened, and uncomfortable in an urban environment.

d6	Bond
1	I left a friend behind when I escaped, and I am gathering resources to return and free them.
2	I did not escape from my fey captors. They allowed me my freedom in exchange for my continued clandestine service.
3	I earned my freedom by tricking another to take my place with the fey. My betrayal of that person's trust haunts me.
4	I am free because of the actions of an unknown benefactor. I wait for them to reveal why I was released.
5	I feel a constant, ever-tugging connection to the lands of the fey.
6	I was given my freedom after years of diligent, demeaning, and debauched servitude.

d6	Ideal
1	*Art.* Works of art are meant to question, challenge, and disturb. (Any)
2	*Pleasure.* There are no long-term rewards, only the enjoyments of the moment. (Chaotic)
3	*Independence.* Independence is the privilege of the few who are strong to assert it. (Any)
4	*Fellowship.* Lasting fellowship is born in shared suffering and teamwork when overcoming adversity. (Any)
5	*Self-Confidence.* There are no views, perspectives, or standards of any worth aside from my own. (Evil)
6	*Malice.* I feel nothing but spite, rancor, and envy for those that took me, and for those that let me be taken. (Evil)

d6	Flaw
1	I cannot lie outright, only by omission, because of my years with the fey.
2	I will never willingly make another promise to anyone or anything.
3	The fey creature that abducted me haunts me in my dreams.
4	I will never accept free food, drink, or gifts from strangers.
5	I speak in sing-song voice and in rhymes. I never answer questions directly.
6	I am certain that my freedom from the fey is only temporary and that any fey I meet want to recapture me.

SOUL CHANNELER

A quirk of fate, or a circumstance of birth, exposed you to the intoxicating power of arcane magic and changed you irrevocably. You spent your formative years learning about yourself, gauging your inner reserves and how much you are willing to sacrifice to achieve your goals.

Skill Proficiencies: Arcana and either Persuasion or Intimidation
Tool Proficiencies: Artisan's tools (alchemist's supplies), poisoner's kit
Languages: Infernal or Abyssal
Equipment: A set of alchemist's supplies, a pocketknife, a piece of chalk connected to a string, a chapbook of esoteric symbols, a set of common clothes, and a pouch containing 10 gp

FEATURE: CHANNEL ESSENCE

You can call upon your inner reserves to recover from debilitating, long-term injuries. As part of a short rest, you can offset a reduction to one of your ability scores by expending a number of Hit Dice equal to twice the amount of the reduction that you want to negate. When used in this manner, the Hit Dice do not confer other benefits, such as additional hit points.

SUGGESTED CHARACTERISTICS

Soul channelers are drawn to the dark arts and the manipulation of available resources to achieve their goals. For some this might include using their own capabilities, but an easier (and more common) method employs summoned creatures, undead servants, and duped allies. Not every soul channeler chooses to exploit such opportunities, but the temptation is there for all.

d8	Personality Trait
1	I realize that gaining power comes at a cost, and I am prepared to pay that cost, whatever it is.
2	My companions are useful for the abilities they contribute and the protection they provide me.
3	I am comfortable in places where the dead are gathered. I find solace and strength in the crypts, graveyards, and necropolises of the land.
4	I loathe any who profess faith, duty, and devotion to an entity or a cause without ensuring they will be compensated for their service.
5	I care nothing for the suffering, pain, and plight of others. Their concerns are not mine.
6	I will sacrifice my possessions, my needs, and my well-being for my trusted companions.
7	I detest myself for the depths of depravity I have plumbed to gain the power I now wield.
8	I mistrust any who have power over me or others.

d6	Ideal
1	*Will.* Embarking on the pursuit of greatness is not enough. I must have the will to do what others shy away from in order to accomplish my goals. (Any)
2	*Sacrifice.* I believe that sacrifice—personal, emotional, or otherwise—is necessary to achieve greatness. (Any)
3	*Abstinence.* I cleanse myself of distractions to achieve purity of purpose. (Lawful)
4	*Deception.* I never tell the whole truth, even if there is no apparent need to lie. The truth has been used against me too many times. (Evil)
5	*Lunacy.* I embrace the turmoil in my mind and soul that comes with manipulating eldritch energies. (Chaotic)
6	*Diabolic.* I inflict pain, suffering, and strife with zeal and gusto. (Evil)

d6	Bond
1	My spellcasting focus is a trinket I created. I cannot live without it.
2	My self-sufficiency provides me with comfort and confidence.
3	I am searching for an ancient text of esoteric, arcane knowledge. I try to make decisions and take actions that lead me to this goal.
4	I take advantage of any opportunities that crop up, regardless of the possible consequences.
5	I seek to harness living energies from plants, animals, and the magical world. I wish to see beyond flesh to the soul itself.
6	My loyalty is rather hard-won, but once earned it is unwavering.

d6	Flaw
1	I consider my companions and all those I meet as resources to be used and advantages to be gained.
2	I have no regard for my physical form. It is a tool and a source of energy, nothing more.
3	I prefer the company of gregarious, ebullient, and vociferous folk. They lift my somber spirits.
4	The easiest way is always the best way.
5	I allow myself to be driven by impulses. My first inclination is the course of action I pursue.
6	I distrust all who rely on fickle deities and unknowable patrons to acquire their spells, influence, and power.

d8	Event
1	My bond was severed, and my form irrevocably changed in a surge of wild, uncontrolled magic that claimed the life of the mage who called me their familiar.
2	The Pact of the Chain between my warlock and myself was dissolved unexpectedly with their passing. Their patron, not wanting to lose two advocates, granted me my current form as a reward for services rendered, and expects me to continue their works.
3	My service to, and partnership with, a mage of great power and cunning was rewarded with transmogrification into my new body.
4	I awoke in an unfamiliar body, with only dream-like memories of my prior service to a being of great arcane ability.
5	I broke my bond with my master, replacing it with a pledge of service to a higher power. Part of the bargain was providing me with a new form to hide from my past more easily.
6	I stood by my master's side as aide, ally, and advisor until an unknown enemy severed our connection, robbed me of my true body, and captured my master.
7	My master, infirm with age and senility, unintentionally released me and altered my body in an attempt to rejuvenate themselves.
8	I betrayed my master in a time of crisis, and their last act was to transform me into my current form, robbing me of my natural body forever.

TRANSFORMED FAMILIAR

Your connection to magic began with a term of service, or servitude, to a magician of power. Your partnership continued as expected for years, until the bond was abruptly broken. In the aftermath, you found yourself with a new body. Despite your new appearance, your actions often betray your origin. The struggle between what you have become and what you once were rages within you.

Skill Proficiencies: Perception, Survival
Tool Proficiencies: Artisan's tools (alchemist's kit)
Languages: One of your choice
Equipment: A trinket worn or carried by your previous form, a set of traveler's clothes, an alchemist's kit, an explorer's pack, and a pouch containing 5 gp

LIFE-CHANGING EVENT

You were previously a different kind of creature. How you became what you are, and what you know of your former existence, can vary greatly depending on the circumstances. Choose or randomly determine the life-changing event that brought about your transformation.

FEATURE: FAMILIAR INSIGHT
You are a transformed familiar, and although your physical form has changed, you will never forsake the instincts and insights you were born with. When interacting with creatures of your original type, you have a +2 bonus on Wisdom (Insight) checks to detect their motives and the veracity of their claims.

SUGGESTED CHARACTERISTICS
Transformed familiars often display personality traits and quirks that are holdovers from their prior lives. They might hold to these affectations consciously, or without realizing their behavior is unusual. Either way, every transformed familiar carries their past with them in some manner.

d8	Personality Trait
1	I am fiercely independent, and do not form strong emotional connections to others.
2	I seek the advice and guidance of others before acting.
3	I continue to behave as if I'm in my original body.
4	I am lost in social situations, and the behaviors expected of me confound me.
5	I punctuate my exclamations with a subtle growl of emphasis.
6	I keep my own counsel, sharing my thoughts reluctantly, if at all.
7	I am fascinated by seeing familiar places through the eyes of my new body.
8	I react instinctually to stress, problems, and challenges. My gut reaction is the right one.

d6	Ideal
1	*Loyalty.* Remaining steadfast when there are no witnesses to see it or accolades to celebrate it is the measure of a person. (Any)
2	*Service.* The path to enlightenment lies in serving a greater cause. (Any)
3	*Freedom.* Better to die free than to live in chains. (Chaotic)
4	*Duty.* A pact, entered into freely, can never be taken back and must be fulfilled. (Lawful).
5	*Atonement.* It is my lot in my new life to make up for the failings in my first one. (Good)
6	*Family.* My family is my port in the storm and my refuge from the world. (Any)

d6	Flaw
1	I prefer to sleep in the same fashion that I rested when I was a familiar.
2	Transmutation magic of all kinds frightens me to the core. I will not willingly use it or have it used on me.
3	In my heart of hearts, I long for the life I left behind.
4	I sometimes speak in the language of my old form or forget the speech of humanoids.
5	I still prefer the foods of my prior form, and sometimes refuse the foods commonly consumed by my new one.
6	Life was easier as a familiar, and I am wistful about those bygone times.

d6	Bond
1	I am still friendly and even loyal to arcane casters, especially wizards.
2	I swear no oaths and make no promises to anyone else. I stand alone.
3	I loathe slavery and enchantments, and work to free those trapped by chains or magic.
4	I have not forgot my former master, and I continue to honor my pledge to them.
5	I prefer to serve, aid, and protect my allies and friends.
6	I dislike disguises or changing my form further; I want the world to see me as I now am.

Styles of Magic

This chapter provides both an overview of how to use magic styles and details on existing styles commonly found in most magical settings.

What are Magic Styles?

Magic styles are subsets of magic, each distinguished by a strong theme. A style includes descriptive and mechanical information that allows a caster to create a specialized relationship with their spellcasting. Adopting a magic style allows a character to explore their special brand of magic, giving their spells unique flourishes, similar to the way artists approach their work. Weaving different styles of magic into a campaign transforms spellcasting from a basic mechanic into a living, breathing part of a magical world.

Magic styles are not limited to drawing from a single school, and they utilize many different mechanical elements, often encompassing spells from multiple schools and including magic items, feats, and more to weave together into a more complete magical toolkit.

How to Use This Section

Each magic style in this section contains the following core elements—and frequently more—to give players the means to create characters that incorporate the style's flavor.

Overview. Each magic style starts with a description of the style's core theme and provides ideas for how the particular style might fit into a fantasy world.

Recommended Spell List. Suggested lists are provided, containing new spells (further detailed in **Chapter 5**) and those from the core game that would work well for characters interested in adopting a particular magic style. You will note that these spells are not restricted to certain schools of magic, which is intentional in order to broaden the versatility of each magic style. The spells included on these lists are also not restricted by individual class spell lists. If you are interested in pursuing a particular style, consider asking your GM to allow access to all the spells presented on the recommended spell list—even if they wouldn't typically be available for your character class.

STYLE DESCRIPTIONS

This section presents an array of magic styles suitable for use in any fantasy setting. Quick descriptions of each style are listed here:

- **Alkemancy Magic** combines alchemical reagents and elixirs with spellcraft to create formidable magical effects.
- **Angelic Magic** draws upon the power of creation by invoking the sacred names of angelic beings.
- **Blood Magic** extracts and redirects life power from the blood of its practitioners—and their victims.
- **Chaos Magic** harnesses raw entropic forces to create random and often startling magical effects.
- **Dragon Magic** relies on ancient spells that were born of the world's first casters—dragons.
- **Fiendish Magic** distills the cruel powers of hell's denizens into blasphemous spell work.
- **Frost Magic** serves as a conduit for one aspect of the awesome elemental forces of the universe.
- **Hieroglyph Magic** allows creatures to leverage the universal power locked within symbols.
- **Illumination Magic** siphons energy from the cosmos, allowing its practitioners to shape light.
- **Mythos Magic** exacts a toll on the user's sanity in exchange for powers born of eldritch beings known as the Great Old Ones.
- **Ring Magic** uses metal rings to produce and enhance spellcasting.
- **Rune Magic** binds power into symbols that can later be unleashed.
- **Temporal Magic** manipulates and controls the flow of time.

ALKEMANCY MAGIC

Too many arcane spellcasters and scholars view alchemy as magic's poor second cousin—an academic pursuit with practical applications, but still nothing that wizards with real talent would devote serious time or effort to. While alchemy can achieve astounding, even nearly miraculous feats, it's always been overshadowed by the power and versatility of arcane magic. Because alchemy requires extensive preparation and forethought, adventurers tend to prefer the flexibility and immediacy of spellcasting.

In some areas, a branch of alchemy is practiced that surpasses the simple alchemy familiar to the rest of the world. Known as magical chemistry, or simply alkemancy, this discipline delves into the properties of common alchemical substances, such as brimstone and salt, and the means by which they can be used to achieve physical and metaphysical transformation in objects and creatures on levels unseen in most lands. Alkemancy practitioners combine their understanding of alchemical reagents and elixirs with their knowledge of spellcraft to create new and formidable magical effects.

Even more than this, though, alkemancy embodies a unique philosophy of life and nature. Alkemancers don't concoct useful potions and philters as an end in itself. Ultimately, they seek to expand their minds past mortal limits, or even to achieve true immortality, and alkemancy is simply the path they follow in pursuit of that goal.

Transmuters and alkemancers belong to similar schools of thought. But where transmuters have little use for alchemy and its secrets, preferring to rely on brute magical force to achieve their aims—at least, that's the opinion held by traditional alchemists—alkemancers combine extensive knowledge of alchemy with the many ways that the six fundamental essences can be applied to arcane magic.

MAGIC IN ALL THINGS

The power of alkemancy resides within the six fundamental essences: brimstone, lead, quicksilver, quintessence, salt, and void salt. These essences parallel the four standard elements, as well as the two more esoteric elements of metal and void, but are unique to alchemy.

CREATING YOUR OWN STYLE

If you don't see a magic style that perfectly fits your character concept, you can create your own using the following steps:

- Start by creating a clear concept and then make sure it fits the game world (though players should consult their GMs first).
- Think about where your unique style comes from and who else in the world might practice it. Laying foundations about its history and invention can help make your creation feel like an exciting new piece of a campaign setting.
- Create a signature spell list of "must have" spells or monstrous traits that will allow you to show off your concept at the table.

Brimstone. The yellow of brimstone (otherwise known as sulfur) represents activity, energy, and masculinity, and it's related to the sun, volcanoes, and elemental fire. Brimstone is a destructive essence present in small amounts in explosives, various acids, and in substances such as alchemist's fire.

Lead. Also erroneously referred to as antimony (a different metal that lead is sometimes combined with), lead represents coldness and heaviness, transformation, and the removal of impurities in objects and creatures. It is associated with broader elemental metals and is often called the oldest or first metal. Lead is reactive and can be toxic in various forms over long periods of exposure—useful qualities in lingering poisons and slow-acting corrosives. It's used as a component in many alchemical creations and supplies.

Quicksilver. Also known as mercury, this silvery metal represents passivity, femininity, and malleability. It's associated with elemental water and the moon. Quicksilver is seen as a creative essence despite its passive nature. It's also a lethal poison, much faster-acting than lead, for example. A fluid dram of refined quicksilver is occasionally used in vials of both alchemical poisons and antitoxins.

Quintessence. One of the rarest and most mysterious of the six fundamental essences, quintessence represents thought, life, and spirit. It is distantly related to elemental air; in its commonest form, it appears as a vaporous, silvery liquid. Quintessence is never used in common alchemical items, largely because it's one of the most difficult of the essences to obtain and it dissipates as soon as it's exposed to air. Alkemancers are always keen to find viable substitutes for quintessence in their concoctions.

Salt. The most common of the six fundamental essences is salt, which represents matter, physicality, and the human body. It is closely related to elemental earth. Purified salt is used in many common alchemical items, and solutions of salt are used widely in mundane and supernatural formulas and rituals.

Void Salt. Dull black crystals distilled from the blood of slain creatures of the Void, the substance known as void salt takes its name from its granular appearance. Void salt is associated with dissolution, entropy, and madness. It is a dangerous substance to work with, because merely touching it with bare skin deals 1 necrotic damage. Anyone intending to work with void salt should wear gloves of metal or thick leather, and even those substances corrode soon after coming in contact with void salt unless they're protected with an anti-necrotic energy coating. The use of void salt is reserved for rare alchemical concoctions, mainly acids, poisons, and explosives.

RECOMMENDED SPELL LIST

This section presents a sampling of spells in alignment with the alkemancy magic style. These spells are available to any spellcasting class with the GM's consent. Spells marked with an asterisk (*) appear in **Chapter 5**.

Cantrips (0 Level)
Acid splash (conjuration)
Brimstone infusion* (transmutation)
Poison spray (conjuration)

1st Level
Bottomless stomach* (transmutation)
Fog cloud (conjuration)
Grease (conjuration)

2nd Level
Acid arrow (evocation)
Boiling oil* (conjuration)
Delay potion* (transmutation)
Mephitic croak* (conjuration)

3rd Level
Gaseous form (transmutation)
Gluey globule* (conjuration)
Salt lash* (conjuration)
Stinking cloud (conjuration)

4th Level
Control water (transmutation)
Quicksilver mantle* (transmutation)
Ray of alchemical negation* (transmutation)
Stoneskin (abjuration)

5th Level
Acid rain* (conjuration)
Bottled arcana* (transmutation)
Cloudkill (conjuration)

6th Level
Alchemical form* (transmutation)
Flesh to stone (transmutation)

7th Level
Acid gate* (conjuration)

8th Level
Caustic torrent* (conjuration)
Life hack* (necromancy)

9th Level
Blood to acid* (transmutation)

ALKEMANCY MAGIC ITEMS

Alkemancers have devised countless magic items over the centuries. Their creations range from fairly standard items such as the *bubbling retort* and *scalehide cream* to uniquely alkemantic items such as *Anuraag's crucible*.

ALEMBIC OF UNMAKING

Wondrous Item, Very Rare

This large alembic is a glass retort supported by a bronze tripod and connected to a smaller glass container by a bronze spout. The bronze fittings are etched with arcane symbols, and the glass parts of the alembic sometimes emit bright, amethyst sparks.

If a magic item is placed inside the alembic and a fire lit beneath it, the magic item dissolves and its magical energy drains into the smaller container. Artifacts, legendary magic items, and any magic item that won't physically fit into the alembic (anything larger than a shortsword or a cloak) can't be dissolved in this way. Full dissolution and distillation of an item's magical energy takes 1 hour, but 10 minutes is enough time to render most items nonmagical.

If an item spends a full hour dissolving in the alembic, its magical energy coalesces in the smaller container as a lump of material resembling gray-purple, stiff dough known as arcanoplasm. This material is safe to handle and easy to incorporate into new magic items. Using arcanoplasm while creating a magic item reduces the cost of the new item by 10 percent per degree of rarity of the magic item that was distilled into the arcanoplasm.

An *alembic of unmaking* can distill or disenchant one item per 24 hours.

ANURAAG'S CRUCIBLE

Wondrous Item, Artifact

Thousands of years ago, a powerful alkemancer named Anuraag constructed an enormous crucible in his quest to create the perfect organism. He hoped it would bring forth an immortal being that could surpass the limitations imposed by human flesh and surpass even the gods. Anuraag used the crucible to create so many monstrosities that eventually the local deities had to take action against him. The alkemancer was destroyed for his impertinence, and his crucible was sealed away at the bottom of a mighty chasm.

Anuraag's crucible is an enormous object fashioned from white clay and engraved with mystical symbols chased with burnished copper and electrum. The crucible is large enough to hold a single Huge creature, two Large creatures, four Medium creatures, or eight Small ones.

If one or more creatures are placed in the crucible and the crucible is heated over an intense, magical flame, each creature must make a DC 20 Constitution saving throw against the crucible's powerful transmutation magic. If this saving throw fails, the creature's body liquefies and

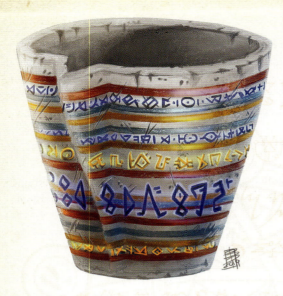

the creature is blinded, deafened, and paralyzed until the transformation is complete. The creature's equipment doesn't dissolve; as a result, most creatures are stripped naked before being placed in the crucible. Over the course of 10 minutes, the liquefied creature transforms into another creature.

If this transformation is interrupted, the transforming creature is slain. It can be brought back to life in its original form by a *resurrection* spell or similar magic.

If the process reaches completion, the creature transforms into another creature as if affected by a *shapechange* spell. The transformed creature must make a successful DC 20 Wisdom saving throw or lose its memory and all its previous abilities, traits, and features, which are replaced by the blank mind of a newly born version of the creature it transformed into. Whether or not a creature retains its mental faculties, the newly assumed form is permanent. At that point, the creature can regain its former form (and memories and abilities) only through a *wish* spell.

Constructs and undead are immune to the crucible's power, as is any creature that has the Shapechanger trait, such as a doppelganger.

To determine what a creature transforms into, roll a d20 and consult the following table.

d20	Creature	d20	Creature
01	Aboleth	11	Giant toad
02	Ape	12	Gibbering mouther
03	Basilisk	13	Griffon
04	Camel	14	Harpy
05	Cat	15	Lamia
06	Chimera	16	Manticore
07	Dire wolf	17	Mastiff
08	Gargoyle	18	Spirit naga
09	Giant fly	19	Tiger
10	Giant lizard	20	New life form (GM's choice)

Destroying the Crucible. *Anuraag's crucible* can be destroyed if a celestial and a fiend, both of at least challenge rating 15, willingly allow themselves to be transformed at the same time. If this happens, the crucible can't take the burden of transforming both creatures and shatters in a spectacular explosion that deals 20d6 piercing damage to all creatures in a 60-foot radius, or half as much damage with a successful DC 15 Dexterity saving throw.

BRAIN JUICE

Potion, Very Rare

This foul-smelling, murky, purple-gray liquid is created from the liquefied brains of spellcasting creatures, such as aboleths. Anyone consuming this repulsive mixture must make a DC 15 Intelligence saving throw. On a successful save, the drinker is infused with magical power and regains 1d6 + 4 expended spell slots. On a failed save, the drinker is afflicted with short-term madness for 1 day. If a creature consumes multiple doses of *brain juice* and fails three consecutive Intelligence saving throws, it is afflicted with long-term madness permanently and automatically fails all further saving throws brought about by drinking *brain juice*.

BUBBLING RETORT

Wondrous Item, Uncommon

This long, thin retort is fashioned from smoky yellow glass and is topped with an intricately carved brass stopper. You can unstopper the retort and fill it with liquid as an action. Once you do so, it spews out multicolored bubbles in a 20-foot radius. The bubbles last for 1d4 + 1 rounds. While they last, creatures within the radius are blinded and the area is heavily obscured to all creatures except those with tremorsense. The liquid in the retort is destroyed in the process with no harmful effect on its surroundings. If any bubbles are popped, they burst with a wet smacking sound but no other effect.

GIRDLE OF TRAVELING ALCHEMY

Wondrous Item, Very Rare (Requires Attunement)

This wide leather girdle has many sewn-in pouches and holsters that hold an assortment of empty beakers and vials. Once you have attuned to the girdle, these containers magically fill with the following liquids:

- 2 flasks of alchemist's fire
- 2 flasks of alchemist's ice*
- 2 vials of acid
- 2 jars of swarm repellent*
- 1 vial of assassin's blood poison
- 1 *potion of climbing*
- 1 *potion of healing*

(*) See Mundane Alkemical Items below.

Each container magically replenishes each day at dawn, if you are wearing the girdle. All the potions and alchemical substances produced by the girdle lose their properties if they're transferred to another container before being used.

OIL OF DEFOLIATION

Potion, Uncommon

Sometimes known as *weedkiller oil*, this greasy amber fluid contains the crushed husks of dozens of locusts. One vial of the oily substance can coat one weapon or up to 5 pieces of ammunition. Applying the oil takes 1 minute. For 1 hour, the coated item deals an extra 1d6 necrotic damage to plants or plant creatures on a successful hit.

The oil can also be applied directly to a willing, restrained, or immobile plant or plant creature. In this case, the substance deals 4d6 necrotic damage, which is enough to kill most ordinary plant life smaller than a large tree.

POTION, PILL FORM

Potion, Rarity Varies

Alkemancers have mastered the craft of condensing potions into pills. Potions in pill form have the same effect as regular potions and have the same color as the potions they're derived from, but an individual pill has effectively no weight and can be concealed very easily in a boot, pouch, hatband, or secret pocket. A pill can be swallowed as a bonus action. A potion in pill form costs five times as much as the regular version of the potion.

SCALEHIDE CREAM

Wondrous Item, Rare

As an action, you can rub this dull green cream over your skin. When you do, you sprout thick, olive-green scales like those of a giant lizard or green dragon that last for 1 hour. These scales give you a natural AC of 15 + your Constitution modifier. This natural AC doesn't combine with any worn armor or with a Dexterity bonus to AC.

A jar of *scalehide cream* contains 1d6 + 1 doses.

MUNDANE ALKEMICAL ITEMS

In addition to the many spells and magic items alkemancers have created, they are also responsible for scores of nonmagical items that are tremendously useful. A few of these are described here.

Alchemist's Ice

This blue-white flask is cool to the touch because it contains a volatile liquid that turns to ice when exposed to air. If the flask is poured over a surface, it creates a 5-foot patch of ice that functions as regular ice for movement purposes. The flask can be thrown at a creature like a flask of alchemist's fire; if it hits, it deals 1d8 cold damage and the creature must make a successful DC 10 Dexterity saving throw or its speed becomes 0 until the start of your next turn.

Alchemist's ice was invented by alkemancers in the tropics as a way of keeping their food and drinks cold, and many restaurants and taverns still use it for this purpose. A vial of alchemist's ice costs 50 gp.

Hypodermic Arrow

The head of this arrow is fitted with a syringe that can be filled with liquid. When it strikes a creature, the arrow deals 1d4 piercing damage plus the effect of whatever liquid the syringe injects into the creature. Poisons are commonly employed, as are acid, drugs, and various eclectic potions.

A hypodermic arrow is extremely fragile; it always breaks on impact, whether it hits the target or not. One hypodermic arrow costs 25 gp. They're always sold empty, but those found in treasure hoards or among monsters' gear might be already filled. Filling the syringe takes an action, but it can be done hours or days before the arrow is used.

Swarm Repellent

This slimy yellow paste can be smeared over exposed parts of the body to protect against attacks by insect swarms. A swarm of ants, beetles, biting flies, wasps, or similar insects that enters your space while you're protected by swarm repellent must make a successful DC 10 Constitution saving throw or be unable to attack you. A repelled swarm can repeat this saving throw at the start of its next turn; most swarms prefer to seek out an unprotected target.

A jar of swarm repellent costs 40 gp and holds enough paste to protect two Medium or four Small creatures. Applying the repellent takes 1 minute, so it's not a good option in the middle of combat, but it's effective for 1 hour or until you're immersed in water.

Tooth Capsule

A tooth capsule is a false tooth, or a cap that fits over a tooth, that contains a dose of a potion in pill form. (The pill loaded into a tooth capsule can't be changed.) To activate the tooth capsule, you simply bite down on it as a bonus action and make a DC 10 Strength check. On a successful check, the capsule shatters and releases the pill, which you can then swallow, hold in your mouth, or spit out.

Determining whether a tooth in someone else's mouth is a tooth capsule takes a successful DC 15 Intelligence (Investigation) or Wisdom (Medicine) check. Obviously, the creature must be restrained, unconscious, paralyzed, or cooperative in order for the tooth to be examined.

Tooth capsules containing poison are often used by spies and operatives of fanatical organizations who are willing to die rather than allow their secrets to be captured by their enemies.

Tooth capsules are usually priced at 100 gp plus the cost of whatever potion they're loaded with. The use of poison or other harmful potions in a tooth capsule is illegal in some places, and the black market price for one in such a place might be much higher.

ANGELIC MAGIC

The heavenly planes shine with light and power as deities both benevolent and stern look down from their thrones. Without question, the most powerful of those gods' servants are the angels. Angels carry the word of their creators to mortal ears and bring their righteous blades against creatures of darkness. These entities are mighty beyond mortal ken, and their very names seethe with the essence of creation. The secrets of harnessing the power of the angels are hidden within those names, and a select few mortals have learned how to realize that potential.

The first angelic seals and wards were passed to worthy mortals as rewards for their sacrifice and valor in the service of light, and as weapons to be used in the struggle against the fiendish hordes. An angelic seal is the written form of the true name of an angel, inscribed on an object or a surface in a particular way to draw on the essence of that angel's power. That power flows through the written representation and into the individual who carries it, or into a location that bears a ward. The angel isn't harmed or hindered when a fraction of its power is siphoned this way, but it does notice, and woe befalls any wicked soul who steals the secret of a seal and misuses its power.

ANGELIC SPELLS

Seals and wards aren't the only expressions of angelic power available to mortals. In the ages since the first angelic names were carved into earthly forms, the battles between light and darkness have tested the limits of the heavenly host. In the wake of these struggles, mortal practitioners experimented with variations on the seals and found ways to isolate the power of the angels and shape it into spells.

Knowledge of angelic spells is rare, and it's not possible for a spellcaster to develop or learn these esoteric spells without being trained in these specialized practices. Occasionally, the powers of light make a gift of a particular spell to a favored champion. Also, tomes containing the notes and experiments of the first angelic scribes still exist in hidden libraries and forgotten shrines.

A spellcaster fortunate enough to discover an angelic spell in written form can gain access to it through study. The usual method of gaining this access is through the pursuit of the angelic scribe wizard specialty. Angelic scribes preserve the knowledge embodied in the angels' names and pass those secrets to their apprentices so the forces of good will always be able to wield their mightiest weapons in times of need.

RECOMMENDED SPELL LIST

This section presents a sampling of spells in alignment with the angelic magic style. These spells are available to any spellcasting class with the GM's consent. Spells marked with an asterisk (*) appear in **Chapter 5**.

Cantrips (0 Level)
*Benediction** (abjuration)

1st Level
*Angelic guardian** (conjuration)

2nd Level
*Blessed halo** (evocation)

3rd Level
*Blade of wrath** (evocation)

4th Level
*Deva's wings** (transmutation)

5th Level
*Blazing chariot** (conjuration)

6th Level
*Celestial fanfare** (evocation)

7th Level
*Seal of sanctuary** (abjuration)

8th Level
*Quintessence** (transmutation)

9th Level
*Greater seal of sanctuary** (abjuration)

> ### VARIANT RULE: VIRTUOUS CASTERS
>
> Angelic spells are principally intended to be used by good-aligned spellcasters, though nothing prevents non-good casters from learning them. As an optional rule, the GM can declare that a non-good caster of angelic spells can gradually become more inclined toward a good alignment, provided that the caster uses such magic frequently for non-evil purposes.
>
> The alignment of a spellcaster who satisfies that condition while advancing through two levels of experience moves from evil to neutral or from neutral to good (at the player's option, for a player character). After gaining an additional four levels, a caster who started out evil can move from neutral to good.
>
> Angelic magic has no effect on the lawful or chaotic component of a caster's alignment.

BLOOD MAGIC

Blood is life, and blood magic is closely tied to the dark gods, blood sacrifices, and malevolent casters. Typically, this style of magic is found among vengeful druids, dark magical societies, cultists of forbidden gods, and lone arcane practitioners with a wanton disregard for others.

RECOMMENDED SPELL LIST

This section presents a sampling of spells in alignment with the blood magic style. These spells are available to any spellcasting class with the GM's consent. Spells marked with an asterisk (*) appear in **Chapter 5**.

Cantrips (0 Level)
*Blood tide** (necromancy)

1st Level
*Blood scarab** (necromancy)
*Bloody hands** (necromancy)
*Bloody smite** (necromancy)
*Stanch** (transmutation)
*Weapon of blood** (transmutation)

2nd Level
*Blood lure** (enchantment)
*Bloodshot** (conjuration)
*Caustic blood** (transmutation)

3rd Level
*Blood armor** (necromancy)
*Vital mark** (transmutation)

4th Level
*Blood and steel** (transmutation)
*Blood puppet** (transmutation)
*Blood spoor** (divination)
*Boiling blood** (necromancy)

5th Level
*Cruor of visions** (divination)
*Exsanguinate** (necromancy)
*Exsanguinating cloud** (necromancy)
*Sanguine horror** (conjuration)

CHAOS MAGIC

There exists a form of raw arcane power with no rules or structure—only an unthinking addiction to changing the reality with which it comes into contact. This force is known as chaos magic. Those who learn to channel this energy eventually expand and aid this magic in its chaos. To master it, though, chaos demands an emotional price of extreme highs and lows. An eccentric lifestyle or even full-on madness is common among chaos magic specialists, who are collectively known as chaos mages.

CHAOS MAGIC SURGES

The use of chaos magic sometimes causes a chaos magic surge. This phenomenon is similar to the wild magic surge caused by some sorcerers. When a chaos magic surge has a chance of occurring, the caster rolls a d20. On a 1, roll percentile dice and consult the Chaos Magic Surge table to determine the result.

CHAOS MAGIC SURGE

d100	Result
1	You cast *hypnotic pattern* centered on yourself.
2	You conjure a small hedge maze with a 30-foot radius centered on you. The hedge maze has 1d4 + 1 exits, provides partial cover for you and anyone else within it, and is permanent, though subject to light, soil, and water needs like normal plants. Anyone can spend an action using a slashing weapon to cut through a 5-foot square of the maze to create an opening.
3	The target of your spell or ability is also enlarged by an *enlarge/reduce* spell. If your spell or ability has no target, the enlargement affects you.
4	Any metal weapons, armor, or jewelry you are wearing immediately slides off you into a pile at your feet.
5	An angry **constrictor snake** controlled by the GM appears wrapped around your waist.
6	You cast *protection from good and evil* on yourself, but it only works against cats and dogs.
7	For 10 rounds, a *gust of wind* spell blows out from you in all directions.
8	Bright light shines from your eyes up to 20 feet and extends another 20 feet as dim light for the next hour.
9	Three targets you can see within 60 feet chosen by you are targeted by a *ray of frost* cantrip.
10	Six random targets you can see within 60 feet are targeted by a *mass healing word* spell.
11	You rise 30 feet into the air and hover there until the start of your next turn, during which you fall.
12	You become so heavy, until the start of your next turn, that you cannot stand, and you fall prone.
13	You grow a purple mustache 3d6 inches in length.
14	Your eyelashes grow 3d6 inches in length and extra bushy, making you effectively blind unless you hold them up or cut them.
15	You are cloaked in shadow and reek of brimstone for 1 hour. During this time, you have advantage on Charisma (Intimidation) checks and disadvantage on Charisma (Persuasion) checks.
16	Tiny songbirds fly in and out of your ears for the next 10 minutes, causing you to have disadvantage on concentration checks until the effect wears off.
17	You summon a mule 100 feet above the target of your spell or ability. If your spell or ability has no target, the mule appears above you. Both the mule and the creature it lands on take 10d6 bludgeoning damage from the inevitable fall, or the creature under the mule takes no damage with a successful Dexterity saving throw. The DC is equal to your spell save DC.
18	You summon a blood hound in a random unoccupied space within 30 feet of you. The blood hound is sleepy and refuses to obey any command unless it is fed treats and a successful Wisdom (Handle Animal) check is made.
19	You cast *contact other plane*.
20	You and five other random targets within 60 feet all take 1 piercing damage as your mouths are physically sewn shut. It takes an action to use a small blade to cut the threads open, dealing 1 slashing damage in the process.
21	Rum rains from the sky in a 30-foot radius centered on you for 10 rounds.
22	Small frogs rain down from the sky in a 30-foot radius centered on you for 10 rounds.
23	You cast a hemispherical *wall of force*, centered on you.

24	An armchair, an end table with an oil lamp, and your third favorite book all appear in an unoccupied space adjacent to you.
25	All your hair falls out. It grows back at the normal rate.
26	You gain resistance to one type of damage, determined randomly, for 1 hour.
27	Your clothes constrict, effectively grappling you (escape DC 14) and making it impossible to cast spells with somatic or material components requiring your hands.
28	Loud horns that can be heard for a mile sound for 1 hour. The sound moves with you.
29	Disembodied laughing and emphatic clapping follow your every move and action, and they are audible up to 120 feet away. This effect persists for 1 hour with three 2-minute breaks every 15 minutes.
30	Until you finish a long rest, every word you utter sounds normal to you but is heard by others as incomprehensible babbling. This effect doesn't impair your ability to cast spells.
31	One random target within 30 feet of you becomes incapacitated for the next minute as they spit up slugs. If there is no target within range, you are incapacitated instead.
32	Three random creatures within 30 feet of you that you can see are targeted by a ray of light. They must succeed on a Constitution saving throw or take 1d8 radiant damage.
33	Three random creatures within 30 feet of you that you can see are smacked with a disembodied hand in a white glove. They must succeed on a Dexterity saving throw or take 1d4 bludgeoning damage and fall prone.
34	Every creature within 60 feet of you, except you, teleports 10 feet in a random direction. If the destination is a solid object or hazardous terrain, the creature doesn't move.
35	The nearest piece of furniture within 100 feet of you turns entirely into aged cheese. If there is no furniture nearby, your shoes turn into cheese instead.
36	The sun (or the moon, at night) is eclipsed for 10 minutes.
37	You develop a weakness to all damage for 1 round.
38	You become immune to all damage for 1 round.
39	You cast *guiding bolt* on a suitable target within range. If no target exists, you cast it directed at yourself.
40	Until you finish a long rest, you leave burning footprints that smolder in your wake for 5 rounds. The flames are hot enough to ignite easily flammable material.
41	Until you finish a long rest, you leave icy footprints that slowly melt in your wake over 5 rounds. Each 5-foot space you pass through becomes difficult terrain for 1 minute.
42	You turn into a succulent, cooked ham for 10 rounds. While a ham, you are incapacitated and have vulnerability to all damage. The gold plate that you appear upon can be sold for 5 gp.
43	All difficult terrain within 300 feet of you immediately smoothes out and becomes even, normal terrain.
44	For 30 feet around you, the ground turns into broken, uneven, difficult terrain.
45	For 1 hour, your spellcasting modifier is chosen randomly every time you cast a spell. Roll a d6: 1 Strength, 2 Dexterity, 3 Constitution, 4 Intelligence, 5 Wisdom, 6 Charisma.
46	For 1 hour, you gain a bonus to weapon damage equal to your spellcasting ability modifier.
47	You open a portal to a random elemental plane that stays open for 10 rounds. Each round, there is a 1 in 20 chance that an elemental creature of the GM's choice emerges. Roll a d4: 1 Plane of Fire, 2 Plane of Water, 3 Plane of Air, 4 Plane of Earth.
48	You open a portal to the Abyss that stays open for 10 rounds. Each round there is a 1 in 20 chance that a fiend or similar creature of the GM's choice emerges.
49	You cast *vicious mockery* on a target of your choice.
50	You cast *healing word* on a target of your choice.
51	Your eyes turn into potatoes and fall from their sockets. You are blinded until you are the recipient of a *remove curse* or *regenerate* spell.
52	Your ears fill with baby carrots that are impossible to pull out. You are deafened until you are the recipient of a remove curse or regenerate spell.
53	A thunderous peal stuns you until the end of your next turn.

54	You hear a glorious bell ringing and gain a Bardic Inspiration die, as the 1st-level bard feature, that remains for the next 10 minutes or until you expend it.
55	You cast *moonbeam*.
56	You fly into a rage, as the 1st-level barbarian class feature.
57	An item you hold is covered in a *continual flame* effect. If you are not holding an item, the GM chooses an item within 30 feet of you to be the target.
58	You and two targets that you can see within 30 feet of you are affected by the *protection from poison* spell.
59	You and two targets that you can see within 30 feet of you are affected by a bane spell.
60	You cast *spiritual weapon*. The weapon manifests as a giant, roasted turkey leg.
61	You gain advantage on your next ability check, attack roll, or saving throw made within 24 hours.
62	You are unable to have advantage or disadvantage for the next 24 hours. A remove curse spell removes this effect.
63	You have disadvantage on your next ability check, attack roll, or saving throw made within 24 hours.
64	A random target within 30 feet of you polymorphs into a **dire wolf** for the next 10 minutes.
65	Choose a creature that you can see within 60 feet (other than yourself) to gain temporary hit points equal to your level.
66	A barrel of lima beans appears adjacent to you.
67	A barrel of lamp oil appears adjacent to you.
68	A barrel of freshly caught, assorted saltwater fish appears adjacent to you. You have made an enemy of a fisherman somewhere.
69	You are targeted by a *disguise self* spell, making you appear as a dirt-covered human child of another gender.
70	You are targeted by a *disguise self* spell, making you appear 5d10 years older.
71	Dim pink light fills an area 30 feet around your target. If your spell or ability has no target, the light is centered on you.
72	You summon a **brown bear** to a space you can see within 30 feet. The bear follows your commands for 1 minute and then disappears. It is wearing a top hat and vest.
73	You summon a **boar** to a space you can see within 30 feet. The boar follows your commands for 1 minute and then disappears. It is wearing a green dress.
74	You cast *awaken* on the nearest suitable beast or plant you can see within 30 feet.
75	You cast *flame strike* centered on yourself.
76	You gain 1d4 × 10 pounds of weight.
77	You lose 1d4 × 10 pounds of weight.
78	You gain +2 to your AC for a number of rounds equal to your spellcasting ability modifier.
79	You gain +2 to your initiative for a number of hours equal to your spellcasting ability modifier.
80	The ground beneath your target, or beneath you if your spell or ability has no target, sinks 1 foot. The target also falls prone unless it makes a successful Dexterity saving throw.
81	You and every creature within 60 feet of you are immediately suited up in sequined costumes, reducing everyone's AC to 11 + their Dexterity modifier for the next minute.
82	Red silk scarves and paper cranes swirl through the air within 500 feet of you, causing the area to be obscured. The scarves are worth a total of 100 gp if collected and sold.
83	A crushing vat (10 feet wide by 10 feet tall) appears beneath your feet, half filled with grapes.
84	A table with a *heroes' feast* effect on it appears 10 feet from you.
85	Three kobolds with musical instruments appear and proceed to play a lively soundtrack to your escapades until they are made to feel like they are not wanted.
86	Three skeletons under the control of the GM claw their way out of the ground and attack random living creatures until they are destroyed.
87	You cast *mage armor* on yourself. Your skin is imprinted with 1d4 sacred geometrical tattoos in random places that can only be removed if you are the recipient of a *remove curse* spell or comparable magic.

88	You cast *barkskin* on yourself. Your hair is permanently replaced with green leaves until you are the recipient of a *remove curse* spell or comparable magic.
89	Your tongue turns into a talking fish, which comments on everything you say. This does not affect your ability to cast spells.
90	Your teeth turn into moths and fly away.
91	Your legs turn into a centaur's lower half, increasing your speed to 40 feet. This alteration lasts for 1 minute.
92	You sprout insect wings, giving you a flying speed of 30 feet. This alteration lasts for 1 minute.
93	The bones in your fingers harmlessly dissolve, making them swollen and unable to articulate. You are unable to hold things or cast spells with a somatic component until you are the recipient of a *remove curse* or *regenerate* spell.
94	A random weapon you can see within 30 feet glows and becomes a *+1 weapon* for 1 minute.
95	A random weapon you can see within 30 feet breaks if it is non-magical. If it is magical, its enchantment is suppressed for 1 minute.
96	For the next 24 hours, anything you touch sprouts a soft blanket of harmless green moss.
97	You cast *gaseous form* on yourself.
98	You cast *heat metal* on a target within 60 feet. If there is no target within range, you cast it upon yourself instead.
99	Every held weapon within 30 feet of you reappears in its sheathe, belt loop, or container, and in their place, in the hands that wielded them, a pie appears.
100	Reroll twice and apply both results.

RECOMMENDED SPELL LIST

This section presents a sampling of spells in alignment with the chaos magic style. These spells are available to any spellcasting class with the GM's consent. Spells marked with an asterisk (*) appear in **Chapter 5**.

Cantrips (0 Level)
*Bewilderment** (enchantment)

1st Level
*Ill-fated word** (divination)
*Roaming pain** (necromancy)
*Undermine armor** (transmutation)
*Unruly item** (transmutation)

2nd Level
*Bad timing** (divination)
*Chaotic vitality** (conjuration)
*Elemental twist** (evocation)
*Frenzied bolt** (evocation)
*Mist of wonders** (conjuration)
*Shifting the odds** (divination)
*Timely distraction** (evocation)

3rd Level
*Calm of the storm** (abjuration)
*Entropic damage field** (transmutation)
*Surge dampener** (abjuration)

4th Level
*Chaotic form** (transmutation)
Confusion (enchantment)
*Fluctuating alignment** (enchantment)
*Wild shield** (abjuration)

5th Level
*Babble** (enchantment)
*Mass surge dampener** (abjuration)

6th Level
*Chaotic world** (illusion)
*Misfortune** (necromancy)

7th Level
Prismatic spray (evocation)
*Uncontrollable transformation** (transmutation)
*Wild trajectory** (transmutation)

8th Level
*Paragon of chaos** (transmutation)
*Roaring winds of Limbo** (conjuration)

9th Level
*Unshackled magic** (enchantment)

DRAGON MAGIC

Some scholars believe that true magic springs only from deep inside an individual creature, such as a dragon or a demon, and those possessing bloodlines from such terrible creatures can tap their personal magical stores. Others speculate that magic comes only from other planes of existence or from the gods themselves.

The truth is that magic comes from several sources, and powerful beings can utilize any wellspring of magic to craft spells and fuel seemingly miraculous effects. One of the first creatures to master all types of magic were the majestic and terrible dragons. Although they were capable of controlling the elements and inducing terrible fear, they also mastered more subtle magic. They wove a tapestry of magic into their homes, giving their lairs innate defenses. They taught their servants, from humans to kobolds to elves, how to make use of the magic that permeated the atmosphere. And they also passed on to their kin—both true dragons and lesser creatures—the kind of magic that roiled in blood and bone.

Dragon magic is a distinct branch of arcane study, founded in the Draconic language and in an elemental understanding of arcane forces.

RECOMMENDED SPELL LIST

This section presents a sampling of spells in alignment with the dragon magic style. These spells are available to any spellcasting class with the GM's consent. Spells marked with an asterisk (*) appear in **Chapter 5**.

Cantrips (0 Level)
*Dragon roar** (evocation)
*Puff of smoke** (evocation)
*Thunder bolt** (evocation)

1st Level
*Converse with dragon** (divination)
*Draconic smite** (evocation)
*Kobold's fury** (transmutation)
*Waft** (transmutation)

2nd Level
*Detect dragons** (divination)
*Enhance greed** (divination)
*Lair sense** (dragon)
*Shade** (abjuration)
*Treasure chasm** (enchantment)

3rd Level
*Catch the breath** (transmutation)
*Draconic majesty** (enchantment)
*Dragon's pride** (enchantment)
*Phantom dragon** (illusion)

4th Level
*Draconic senses** (divination)
*Overwhelming greed** (enchantment)
*Raid the lair** (abjuration)
*Scale rot** (necromancy)
*Scaly hide** (transmutation)
*Torrent of fire** (conjuration)

5th Level
*Claws of the earth dragon** (evocation)
*Dragon breath** (evocation)
*Thunderstorm** (transmutation)

6th Level
*Cave dragon's dominance** (transmutation)
*Claim lair** (abjuration)
*Fire dragon's fury** (transmutation)
*Mithral dragon's might** (transmutation)

7th Level
*Aspect of the dragon** (transmutation)
*Legend killer** (divination)

8th Level
*Deadly sting** (transmutation)

FIENDISH MAGIC

Any mortal in the world can be evil by choice or can be forced into performing evil acts. The same cannot be said for certain denizens of other planes, particularly demons and devils. These fiends are not only innately evil—no choice about it for them, no forcing needed—but also the very personification of evil.

Some spellcasters take up the practice of a certain kind of magic that enables them to emulate or interact with those fiends or to protect themselves from being annihilated by the evil creatures they revere. The largest repertoire of fiendish magic belongs to evil wizards, but like-minded clerics, sorcerers, and warlocks can also traffic in these spells.

RECOMMENDED SPELL LIST

This section presents a sampling of spells in alignment with the fiendish magic style. These spells are available to any spellcasting class with the GM's consent. Spells marked with an asterisk (*) appear in **Chapter 5**.

Cantrips (0 Level)
*Decay** (necromancy)

1st Level
Hellish rebuke (evocation)
*Mammon's avarice** (divination)
Protection from evil and good (abjuration)

2nd Level
*Cloak of fiendish menace** (transmutation)
Darkness (evocation)
Enthrall (enchantment)
Suggestion (enchantment)

3rd Level
*Chains of perdition** (conjuration)
*Demon within** (conjuration)
Magic circle (abjuration)
*Nest of infernal vipers** (conjuration)
*Wave of corruption** (necromancy)

4th Level
Banishment (abjuration)
*Conjure fiends** (conjuration)
Fire shield (evocation)
*Tome curse** (necromancy)

5th Level
*Channel fiendish power** (transmutation)
*Conjure nightmare** (conjuration)
Contact other plane (divination)
*Dark lord's mantle** (enchantment)
Dominate person (enchantment)
*Fiendish brand** (necromancy)
Planar binding (abjuration)

6th Level
*Aura of wrath** (enchantment)
Forbiddance (abjuration)
Mass suggestion (enchantment)
Planar ally (conjuration)

7th Level
Plane shift (conjuration)

8th Level
Dominate monster (enchantment)

9th Level
Imprisonment (abjuration)

FROST MAGIC

Winter has considerable power, regardless of how it presents itself. In its most obvious manifestation, it is snow and ice driven by howling wind that reduces visibility to zero and covers everything in a frozen shell. Just as dangerous as this overt display of power is winter's deceptively beautiful form, when an ineffective sun shines brightly on a serene tableau of glistening trees and smooth, powder-coated landscapes. Those who travel unprepared through this misleading peacefulness are liable to end up blinded or frozen.

RECOMMENDED SPELL LIST

This section presents a sampling of spells in alignment with the frost magic style. These spells are available to any spellcasting class with the GM's consent. Spells marked with an asterisk (*) appear in **Chapter 5**.

Cantrips (0 Level)
*Biting arrow** (evocation)
Ray of frost (evocation)
*Shiver** (evocation)

1st Level
*Boreas's kiss** (conjuration)
*Breathtaking wind** (evocation)
*Flurry** (transmutation)
*Freeze potion** (transmutation)
*Icicle daggers** (conjuration)
*Snowy coat** (transmutation)

2nd Level
*Creeping ice** (conjuration)
*Ice hammer** (conjuration)
*Sculpt snow** (transmutation)
*Sheen of ice** (evocation)
*Snow fort** (conjuration)

3rd Level
*Freeze blood** (transmutation)
*Ice burn** (conjuration)
*Protective ice** (abjuration)
Sleet storm (conjuration)
*Steal warmth** (necromancy)

4th Level
*Boreas's embrace** (conjuration)
*Brittling** (transmutation)
*Deep freeze** (evocation)
*Evercold** (necromancy)
*Fusillade of ice** (evocation)
Ice storm (evocation)
*Snow boulder** (transmutation)
*Wintry glide** (conjuration)

5th Level
*Clash of glaciers** (evocation)
Cone of cold (evocation)
*Control ice** (transmutation)
*Frostbite** (evocation)
*Ice fortress** (conjuration)

6th Level
*Curse of Boreas** (transmutation)
Freezing sphere (evocation)
Wall of ice (evocation)
*Winter's radiance** (evocation)
*Winterdark** (transmutation)

7th Level
*Blizzard** (conjuration)
*Glacial fog** (evocation)
*Triumph of ice** (transmutation)

8th Level
*Glacial cascade** (evocation)

9th Level
*Crystal confinement** (abjuration)

HIEROGLYPH MAGIC

For countless ages, the heat and shifting sands of the deserts have held many secrets that fascinate, delight, and terrify. Ancient knowledge can be found here by those who know how and where to look, unlocking a new world of power and possibility. But beware—this knowledge is difficult to learn and dangerous to the unschooled. Few of its masters are willing to teach their secrets to anyone outside their own sect. But perhaps as an astute linguist, a talented artist, or even a clever mason, you can tap into the secret script of magic from ancient times and unlock the power of hieroglyphs.

Accessing the magic of hieroglyphs requires the Script Carver and Script Sage feats. If the option to gain feats isn't used in your campaign, then Script Carver and Script Sage can be gained in place of level-based ability score improvement, if your GM approves. Alternatively, characters might need to accomplish other, story-related tasks determined by the GM to gain the abilities bestowed by the Script Carver and Script Sage feats. Once any obstacles are cleared, all characters who meet the prerequisites can gain these feats.

SCRIPT CARVER
Prerequisite: Intelligence 12 or Higher
You have learned how to expertly scribe two hieroglyphs of your choice, and you gain the benefit associated with each one. In addition, you can invoke one power of each hieroglyph you have learned, provided you meet any other requirements, such as a minimum level.

You can select this feat multiple times. Each time you do, you gain the benefit and powers of two additional hieroglyphs of your choice.

SCRIPT SAGE
Prerequisite: Script Carver

Through dedicated study, you have mastered one hieroglyph of your choice. Choose one hieroglyph that you have already learned through Script Carver. You can invoke one of its mastery powers, provided you meet any other requirements, such as a minimum level.

You can select this feat multiple times. Each time you do, you learn the mastery powers of a different hieroglyph from your repertoire.

Invoking hieroglyph Powers
Invoking one of a hieroglyph's powers requires an action and provokes opportunity attacks. Generally, you must either draw a physical representation of the glyph (in paint, in blood, in the dirt or snow, and so forth) or trace the shape of an existing carving of the glyph that was created to an exacting standard.

Each hieroglyph confers a benefit on someone who knows how to scribe it. A hieroglyph's benefit is always in effect for a character who knows that hieroglyph. In addition, that character can call upon one of the hieroglyph's powers when so desired. Unless otherwise noted, all hieroglyph powers can be used once, and that expended use is regained when you finish a long rest.

Some powers have a level requirement (given in parentheses); when a character attains that level, this power becomes an additional choice. Mastery powers are a separate category: only a character who has the Script Sage feat for a particular hieroglyph can use its mastery power. If a power or a mastery power has no level requirement, it becomes available to you as soon as you acquire the necessary feat.

If a hieroglyph power gives you the ability to cast a spell, you can do so without needing any components (aside from materials needed for the drawing of the glyph), and the spell is always cast as if using the lowest-level spell slot possible. It typically has the same duration as a normal casting of the spell and uses your character level as the caster level.

CHAPTER 2 STYLES OF MAGIC | 83

When a hieroglyph power calls for a saving throw, the DC equals 8 + your ability bonus + your proficiency bonus. The ability that applies to the DC calculation is the same as the ability used for the saving throw.

HIEROGLYPH DESCRIPTIONS

The hieroglyphs are presented below in alphabetical order.

AS DOES EVERY GOD, EVERY BIRD, EVERY FISH, AND EVERY CREEPING WORM

This symbol represents the fertility and abundance of animal life and every being's place in the chain of life.

Benefit: You gain advantage on ability checks or skill checks to identify creatures.

Power: You can use an action to quickly trace this glyph in the air and stare down a beast or a monstrosity. The targeted creature must make a Wisdom saving throw. On a failed save, the creature is frightened of you for as long as you continue staring at it. While frightened in this way, the creature must move at its full speed away from you on each of its turns until you can't see it or until it makes a successful saving throw. An affected creature repeats the saving throw at the end of each of its turns, ending the effect on itself with a successful save. When a creature's saving throw is successful (regardless of whether it failed previously), it has disadvantage on attack rolls against you until the end of its next turn.

Mastery Power: If you spend 1 minute tracing this glyph on the body of an animal, you can grant yourself a measure of the animal's ability. You gain one of the following: a climbing or swimming speed of 30 feet, or a flying or burrowing speed of 20 feet—whichever is most appropriate to the type of animal the bone came from. The effect lasts for as long as you maintain concentration, up to 1 hour.

DRESS THE AIR WITH THE CLOYING AND THE FAIR

This symbol represents sweet scents, perfumes, allure, and pleasant feelings. It can also be associated with influencing or changing the mind of another.

Benefit: You gain a +1 bonus on Charisma (Persuasion) checks.

Power: If you use an action to trace this glyph on your body in cologne or perfume, you have advantage on Charisma checks for the next hour.

Power (3rd Level): If you use an action to trace this hieroglyph on the ground with dust or ink made from the petals of flowers, every creature within 10 feet of you must make a successful Charisma saving throw or be charmed by you for 1 minute.

Power (5th Level): You use an action to contemplate flower petals as they drift in the breeze, enabling you to cast a *gust of wind* spell.

Mastery Power: When you use an action to anoint yourself with perfume, for the next 10 minutes you have advantage on Charisma checks to influence people within 50 feet of you.

DRINK DEEP OF THE RIVER'S POWER

This hieroglyph represents the flow of magic through the land, as well as the physical flow of rivers.

Benefit: You gain the ability to cast one cantrip of your choice from the wizard spell list. Your spellcasting ability is Intelligence when you cast this cantrip.

Power (2nd Level): You trace this hieroglyph over a creature's eyes in a ritual that takes 10 minutes to perform. When the ritual is complete, it produces a *detect magic* effect that works on the creature and on any items the creature is holding or carrying. The effect lasts for 1 minute while you maintain concentration.

Mastery Power: You trace this hieroglyph in dirt over the course of 1 hour. At the end of the hour, you dispel a magical effect of up to 4th level that is within 120 feet of you. If the effect is higher than 4th level, you dispel it if you make a successful Intelligence (Arcana) check against a DC equal to 10 + the level of the effect.

FLOURISH IN DEATH AS IN LIFE

This symbol represents the transition from the realm of the living to the realm of the dead. It is often engraved on the tombs of fallen heroes.

Benefit: You gain a +1 bonus on Constitution saving throws.

Power: When you drop to 0 hit points, you become stabilized immediately and automatically.

Mastery Power: You can see a distance of 60 feet into the Ethereal Plane for 1 hour. You also can determine whether anyone within 60 feet of you is possessed by a spirit; you see such a figure as having a vague, dim outline around it.

FLY AS THE FALCON, HOWL AS THE WOLF

This symbol represents hunting, tracking, stalking, and bringing prey to the ground.

Benefit: You gain a +1 bonus on Wisdom (Survival) checks.

Power (2nd Level): When you use an action to trace this symbol on the body of a willing creature, the creature gains darkvision out to a range of 20 feet, which lasts for 1 minute and works even in magical darkness.

Power (4th Level): You trace this hieroglyph on an item that belongs to a specific creature or clearly represents a creature you have encountered, then use an action to consume it. For the next hour, the tracks of that creature glow brightly in your sight. You can follow and track the creature automatically while moving at the speed of a forced march.

Mastery Power: By using an action to trace this glyph on your hand, you invoke the hunter's gift against a specific creature. The target must be a creature you have previously used one of this hieroglyph's powers against. The next time you hit the creature with an attack, it must make a successful Constitution saving throw or take an additional 1d10 necrotic damage from the attack.

GIFTS TAKEN FROM THE SILVER COFFER

This symbol represents gifts, knowledge, secrets, and things hidden.

Benefit: You gain a +1 bonus on Intelligence (Investigation) checks.

Power: By spending 1 minute in concentration while holding a papyrus reed, you can cast the *speak with inanimate object* spell (see page 107).

Power (4th Level): By taking an action to break open an egg, you create an extradimensional space (a "silver coffer") that is 5 cubic feet in volume and can hold up to 50 pounds of material. This space looks like a simple, empty hole in the ground, but when you reach inside it, you always find whatever you placed inside. The extradimensional space remains visible as a hole in the ground for 24 hours, then disappears, along with its contents. It can be reopened with another use of this hieroglyph power. The silver coffer's location on the Material Plane depends on your location when you trigger the hieroglyph. This power always opens the same extradimensional space no matter how much time passes or how far you travel between uses, so it's not a good way to dispose of, for example, unwanted or dangerous magic items. If the person who created the extradimensional space dies, any items in the silver coffer eventually reappear on their plane of origin at a random location, anytime from a day to several centuries after the creator's death.

Mastery Power (10th Level): By taking an action to rub a special brown paste over your eyes that costs 50 gp, you can cast *true seeing* on yourself.

GIVE SUCCOR TO THY PEOPLE

This symbol represents charity, healing, benevolent leadership, and sanctuary given to friends and kin as well as enemies.

Benefit: You have advantage on Wisdom (Medicine) checks.

Power: If you spend an hour in meditation while holding a mug of beer or a goblet of wine, your sincere wish to help someone transfers into the brew. When a creature drinks the brew, it gains all the benefits of finishing a short rest. This brew remains potent for 24 hours.

Mastery Power: If you spend an hour in meditation while holding a full waterskin, up to six creatures that drink from the waterskin recover from two levels of exhaustion and don't need any food or water until after finishing a long rest. The water remains potent for up to 24 hours, or until six creatures have drunk it.

GODS' COMPANY LIKE LIGHT

This symbol represents knowledge gained over an extended time through dedication and effort.

Benefit: You gain the ability to speak and read one additional language of your choice.

Power: After meditating on this hieroglyph for 10 minutes, you can cast *comprehend languages*.

Power (2nd Level): If you take an action to trace this symbol on your forehead or that of another creature, the recipient gains advantage on Intelligence checks for 1 minute.

Mastery Power: By inhaling incense and powders over the course of an hour, you call upon your ancestors to reveal a bit of knowledge from the past. This knowledge enables you to gain your ancestors' assistance with a problem immediately before you. The implementation of this benefit is up to the GM; you might receive a specific clue that helps you to solve the problem, or you might gain proficiency for 1 hour with a skill or a set of tools, or advantage on a single type of skill check for the same length of time.

GRASPING ARMS OF BALANCE

This symbol represents the judgment of the dead, ever watchful and weighing the actions of the living in expectation of the moment when they eventually pass on from the world.

Benefit: You gain a +1 bonus on Intelligence (Investigation) checks.

Power: You trace this hieroglyph in ash on the body of a willing creature, which requires an action. For the next hour, the creature has advantage on Wisdom ability checks.

Power (3rd Level): If you use an action to trace this hieroglyph in the air with your fingers, you force a creature you can see to make a Wisdom saving throw. On a failed save, you can immediately give the creature one command, either verbally or in writing, that can be completed in the next minute. The creature must try to obey the command to the best of its ability, provided that doing so won't directly harm it. If the task isn't completed within 1 minute, the glyph's power wears off and the creature is freed from the compulsion.

Mastery Power (9th Level): You spend 10 minutes decorating a piece of paper with this hieroglyph. If you then take an action to burn the paper, you can cast a *geas* spell on one target. As with a normal casting of the spell, you and the target must have a language in common for the effect to work.

HE HATH REPULSED THE FIENDS

This symbol represents the prevention of harm, usually through the protection of devoted soldiers or bodyguards.

Benefit: When you wear no armor, your Armor Class is equal to 10 + your Wisdom modifier + your Dexterity modifier.

Power (3rd Level): If you take an action to trace this hieroglyph on a creature, you grant that creature resistance to bludgeoning, piercing, or slashing damage (your choice) for 1 minute.

Power (5th Level): By taking an action to burn a bit of incense, you can conjure a squad of soldiers. These soldiers can appear different to different creatures; some might see a squad of orcs, others a group of the king's guards. The soldiers appear standing inside a 10-foot-square space within 10 feet of you, and they can't leave that space. Within that space, they behave like a swarm; other creatures can enter the space and end their turn there. Whenever one of your enemies enters the soldiers' space or starts its turn in the space or within 5 feet of it, the soldiers attack that creature. Their attack bonus is equal to your Wisdom modifier + your proficiency modifier, and a successful attack deals 2d6 force damage. The soldiers remain for 1 minute, provided you maintain concentration on them. They are immune to all forms of damage and can't be dispelled except by breaking your concentration.

Mastery Power (8th Level): If you take an action to trace this hieroglyph on the ground and then throw a handful of sand into the air, you can cast *banishment*.

HOLD THE STORM IN AN URN OF THE WIND

This symbol represents the power of storms and wind and the effect these phenomena can have on the world.

Benefit: You can resist any effect or attack that would move you, causing you to be moved 5 feet less than the effect's normal distance.

Power (3rd Level): By drawing this hieroglyph in the air for three consecutive turns (each one requiring an action), you gain the ability to cast *wind wall*.

Power (5th Level): After spending an hour in meditation with burning incense before tracing this hieroglyph in the air, you can cast a modified version of *control weather*. Unlike the spell, this power affects an area only a quarter mile in radius, and the change lasts no longer than 20 minutes.

Mastery Power: Immediately after performing a 10-minute ritual with special incense, you can cast a modified version of *wind walk*. Unlike the spell, this power affects up to five creatures, and the effect lasts for up to 2 hours and requires your concentration.

JACKAL MOVES ON TIRELESSLY

This symbol represents travel, persistence, and not giving up in the face of challenge.

Benefit: You gain a +1 bonus on saving throws to resist exhaustion.

Power (3rd Level): If you take an action to trace this symbol on the body of a willing creature, you increase that creature's speed by 15 feet for 1 hour. This power affects all forms of movement the creature can use.

Mastery Power: By drawing this hieroglyph on the ground over the course of 10 minutes, you create a temporary portal to another place within 1 mile that you're familiar with. You can step through the portal once, after which it disappears. You can bring along a number of other creatures equal to one-fourth your level (round up), provided all of them are your size or smaller and either willing or helpless.

ON THE DAY OF THE DESTRUCTION OF THE FIENDS

This symbol represents triumph over your enemies, victory, and celebration of those victories.

Benefit: You gain a +1 bonus on Charisma (Intimidation) checks.

Power (3rd Level): To trigger this power, you must use an action to trace the symbol on yourself with a knife or other sharp object (pressing hard enough to leave a mark on the skin but not hard enough to draw blood) and emit a loud battle cry. Each creature you designate within 10 feet of you that hears the battle cry must make a successful Charisma saving throw or be frightened for 1 minute.

Mastery Power: Once a week, you can host a feast for your companions and other allies. Each individual who partakes in the feast gains temporary hit points equal to your Charisma modifier (minimum of 2) and has advantage on the same number of its next attack rolls. The effect dissipates for each creature after 24 hours if the benefits have not been used by then.

OPEN THE HIDDEN SPRINGS AND UNBOLT THE SHRINE

This symbol represents casting off chains, putting down oppression, and opening pathways.

Benefit: You gain a +1 bonus on Dexterity (Sleight of Hand) checks.

Power: If you use an action to trace this hieroglyph on a rope, chain, or other implement that's holding you in place, you gain advantage on Dexterity checks made to free yourself. This benefit doesn't apply to checks made to escape a grapple, unless you're being grappled by an inanimate object.

Mastery Power: When you take an action to trace this hieroglyph on the body of a willing creature, you can impart to that creature the effect of a *blink* spell.

SAVOR THE DIVINE COMPANY OF THE GODS

This symbol represents robust and vigorous health and the favor of the gods.

Benefit: Your hit point maximum increases by 1 for each Hit Die you have.

Power: When you take an action to trace this hieroglyph on a creature's skin with blood, that creature gains a number of temporary hit points equal to your Hit Dice.

Mastery Power: If you spend 1 minute repeatedly tracing this hieroglyph on the body of an afflicted creature, you can cast *lesser restoration* on that creature.

SHINE AT THE MONUMENT OF THE MIGHTY

This symbol represents physical and mental strength, overcoming weakness, and surpassing limits.

Benefit: You count as one size larger for the purpose of determining your carrying capacity and the weight you can push, drag, or lift.

Power: By using an action to trace this hieroglyph on a creature, you double that creature's Strength bonus for the purpose of determining the damage from its next successful attack.

Power (3rd Level): If you take an action to crush a previously prepared clay semblance of this hieroglyph, you gain advantage on Strength checks for 1 minute. You can also give the clay hieroglyph to another creature, so that creature can gain the benefit from crushing it.

Mastery Power: If you use an action to trace this hieroglyph on a creature, it is freed from the need for sleep and immune to the effects of exhaustion for 24 hours.

STAND ABOVE ALL

This symbol represents moral rightness, dominance, rulership, and ego.

Benefit: You have advantage on Charisma saving throws.

Power (3rd Level): By tracing this hieroglyph on your clothing, you rally your allies and improve their morale. For the next minute, each of your allies gains a +1 bonus on attack rolls, saving throws against fear effects, and skill checks while within 10 feet of you.

Mastery Power: If you use an action to trace this hieroglyph on a willing creature, it gains the ability to overawe the mind of one other creature within 60 feet. The targeted creature must make a successful Charisma saving throw or prostrate itself before the creature that bears the hieroglyph. An awed creature repeats the saving throw at the end of each of its turns, ending the effect on itself with a success. The effect lasts for 1 minute or until the awed creature is attacked.

STARS AND BIRDS PERCEIVE ALL

This symbol represents vision, sight, and perceiving from great distances.

Benefit: You gain a +1 bonus on Wisdom (Perception) checks.

Power: If you use an action to trace this glyph on a creature, you can cast *enhance ability* on the target, which gains the benefit of the Owl's Wisdom effect.

Mastery Power: By tracing this glyph over and over in a 10-minute ritual, you can cast *clairvoyance*.

WATCHFUL EYES SEE WHAT IS HIDDEN

This symbol represents looking beneath the surface to see the world differently or to question the way things are done.

Benefit: You gain a +1 bonus on Wisdom (Insight) checks.

Power (3rd Level): By spending 5 minutes tracing the hieroglyph on a creature, you imbue that creature with the ability to cast *detect evil and good* once in the next 24 hours. The hieroglyph can also be created on a small object instead of directly on a creature; in that case, *detect evil and good* can be cast once by a creature holding the object.

Power (6th Level): After spending 10 minutes inking this hieroglyph in the middle of your forehead, you gain the benefits of casting *detect thoughts* for as long as you concentrate, up to 1 minute.

Mastery Power: By taking an action to draw this hieroglyph, you can cast *arcane eye*.

WITH ONE HEART AND VOICE, THE PEOPLE RAISE CRIES OF JOY

This symbol represents unity, community, common purpose and goals, and protecting one another.

Benefit: You have advantage on any saving throw that is also being made by at least one of your allies.

Power (3rd Level): By using an action to draw this hieroglyph on a rope that you use to bind your wrist to another creature, you can absorb the damage and other effects from the next attack that hits the other creature. The attack must hit the other creature, but it affects you instead; the other creature is unaffected. The rope can be no more than 30 feet long.

Mastery Power: By invoking this hieroglyph during a 10-minute ritual, you can grant telepathy to up to ten creatures that are within 60 feet of you. The telepathy lasts for 1 hour, and it works only among the affected creatures (including you); it can't be used to communicate with creatures outside the group.

WITH THE SIGHT AND TALONS OF THE HAWK

This symbol is associated with strength, speed, honor, and heroism.

Benefit: You gain a +1 bonus on initiative rolls.

Power (4th Level): As an action, you can trace this hieroglyph on a creature to grant it advantage on Strength checks and Constitution checks for as long as you maintain concentration, up to 1 hour.

Power (6th Level): By spending 1 round in concentration to summon power from the sky, you can target one creature that has this hieroglyph emblazoned on its forehead. The creature gains the effects of the *enlarge* spell, and its head takes on the appearance of a hawk for the duration of the effect.

Mastery Power (8th Level): When you use an action to trace this symbol in the air, you grant the speed of the air to an ally within 60 feet. The affected ally gains the effect of a *haste* spell for 1 minute.

ILLUMINATION MAGIC

Illumination magic concerns both the manipulation of light and the observation of the heavens. Its practitioners have been likened to elemental specialists who have an affinity for light instead of fire, earth, air, or water. Naturally, these individuals are anathema to creatures and spellcasters that lurk in places where darkness and shadow hold sway.

RECOMMENDED SPELL LIST

This section presents a sampling of spells in alignment with the illumination magic style. These spells are available to any spellcasting class with the GM's consent. Spells marked with an asterisk (*) appear in **Chapter 5**.

Mastery of illumination magic comes from long and dedicated study, and thus wizards have access to more of these spells than other spellcasting classes do.

Cantrips (0 Level)
Bright sparks* (evocation)
Light (evocation)
Luminous Bolt* (evocation)
Starburst* (evocation)

1st Level
Amplify light* (transmutation)
Faerie fire (evocation)
Guiding bolt (evocation)
Guiding star* (divination)

2nd Level
Continual flame (evocation)
Intensify light* (transmutation)
Orb of light* (evocation)
Phantom light (illusion)

3rd Level
Daylight (evocation)
Protective nimbus* (abjuration)
Shield of starlight* (abjuration)
Tracking beacon* (divination)

4th Level
Searing sun* (transmutation)

5th Level
Greater protective nimbus* (abjuration)
Radiant beacon* (evocation)
Starfall* (evocation)

6th Level
*Burning radiance** (evocation)

7th Level
*Last rays of the dying sun** (evocation)
*Soothing incandescence** (evocation)

8th Level
*Child of light and darkness** (transmutation)
*Summon star** (conjuration)
Sunburst (evocation)

9th Level
*Star's heart** (transmutation)

MYTHOS MAGIC

The works of author H.P. Lovecraft—the Cthulhu mythos—have been a cornerstone of RPG storytelling since E. Gary Gygax immortalized its influence in his "Inspirational and Educational Reading" list. Taking its name from Lovecraft's famous story, "The Call of Cthulhu," the mythos has become the backdrop for a subgenre of fiction sometimes called cosmic horror. At the foundation of cosmic horror are two ideas: that the human mind is too tiny and weak to comprehend more than the barest glimmer of the vastness of the universe and the alien mysteries it contains; and that among those mysteries are entities so ancient, powerful, and malevolent that they could extinguish Earth's insignificant civilization without caring or even noticing.

With that in mind, this section explores those "hidden and fathomless worlds of strange life which may pulsate in the gulfs beyond the stars" that Lovecraft and his contemporaries pioneered in their strange fiction. Herein you will find a host of forbidden secrets and eldritch lore; a clandestine sort of magic that is full of both cosmic potential and horrific consequences, and knowledge of which erodes the sanity of all who pursue it.

ESSENCE OF THE VOID

The spells in this category resemble void magic in that they harness the power of the Void, but they are not beholden to it. Mythos magic uses the Great Old Ones as a conduit for its power while void magic originates from the Void itself (a place of negation and emptiness that devours the cosmos, not an entity).

Mythos spells can be learned by anyone with magical aptitude—any character who has the ability to cast spells can add mythos spells to their spell list. All other characters can acquire a mythos spell only if they learn it from one of the forbidden and furtive tomes of the Cthulhu mythos or see the spell being cast.

But this power comes at great risk. Casters of mythos magic literally exchange their sanity for magical ability.

Unless a character is protected by great Wisdom or a bulwark of arcane wards, using these spells will certainly lead to madness.

RECOMMENDED SPELL LIST

This section presents a sampling of spells in alignment with the mythos magic style. These spells are available to any spellcasting class with the GM's consent. Spells marked with an asterisk (*) appear in **Chapter 5**.

Mythos magic is typically the province of wizards, though any spellcaster can learn these spells under the right circumstances.

Cantrips (0 Level)
*Black Goat's blessing** (enchantment)
*Semblance of dread** (illusion)

1st Level
*Voorish sign** (divination)

2nd Level
*Ectoplasm** (necromancy)

3rd Level
*Mind exchange** (transmutation)
*Sleep of the deep** (illusion)
*Unseen strangler** (conjuration)

4th Level
*Emanation of Yoth** (necromancy)
*Green decay** (necromancy)
*Hunger of Leng** (enchantment)
*Yellow sign** (enchantment)

5th Level
*Curse of Yig** (transmutation)
*Eldritch communion** (divination)
*Summon eldritch servitor** (conjuration)

6th Level
*Warp mind and matter** (transmutation)

7th Level
*Sign of Koth** (abjuration)

8th Level
*Seed of destruction** (enchantment)

9th Level
*Summon avatar** (conjuration)

GRIMOIRES OF THE CTHULHU MYTHOS

If antiquity looks upon the stories of Tolkien and dreams of fated rings or reflects upon the multiverse of Moorcock's White Wolf and thinks of cursed swords, then surely the Cthulhu mythos will be remembered for its magical tomes. Described here are three of the most infamous installments in the mythos atheneum: the accursed *Necronomicon*, Robert E. Howard's *Nameless Cults*, and the ubiquitous *Book of Eibon*. Mythos spells can be learned only from a mythos grimoire like these or through direct contact with a mythos spellcaster—and those grimoires and casters take many abhorrent forms.

With a multiverse-wide perspective in mind, these books are considered to be translations of the "real world" originals—which is to say, they come from the alternate-history Earth of Lovecraft's Cthulhu mythos setting, including elements of Howard's Hyborian Age. How they made their way through time and space to wind up on alien worlds or your own setting is the stuff of splendidly macabre speculation (and ultimately is up to you, the GM). One thing's for sure: these tomes are beyond precious to all who hunger for the eldritch knowledge of the Great Old Ones, and such longings aren't restricted to humanity and near-humanity. There also exist multitudes of odious aberrations, monstrosities, fiends, and worse entities who will stop at nothing to possess these tomes.

Book of Eibon
Wondrous Item, Legendary (Requires Attunement)
This fragmentary black book is reputed to descend from the realms of Hyperborea. It contains puzzling guidelines for frightful necromantic rituals and maddening interdimensional travel.

The book holds the following spells: *animate dead, astral projection, create undead, ectoplasm*, eldritch communion*, emanation of Yoth*, gate, green decay*, harm, semblance of dread*, speak with dead*, and *yellow sign**. Spells marked with an asterisk (*) can be found in **Chapter 5**. At the GM's discretion, the book can contain other spells similarly related to necromancy, madness, or interdimensional travel.

If you are attuned to this book, you can use it as a spellbook and as an arcane focus. In addition, while holding the book, you can use a bonus action to cast a necromancy spell that is written in this tome without expending a spell slot or using any verbal or somatic components. Once used, this property of the book can't be used again until the next dawn.

Nameless Cults
Wondrous Item, Legendary (Requires Attunement)
This dubious old book, bound in heavy leather with iron hasps, details the forbidden secrets and monstrous blasphemy of a multitude of nightmare cults that worship nameless and ghastly entities. It reads like the monologue of a maniac, illustrated with unsettling glyphs and filled with fluctuating moments of vagueness and clarity.

The tome contains all mythos magic spells (see Recommended Spell List above), plus any additional spells of the GM's choosing.

While attuned to the book, you can reference it whenever you make an Intelligence check to recall information about any aspect of evil or the occult, such as lore about Great Old Ones, mythos creatures, or the cults that worship them. When doing so, your proficiency bonus for that check is doubled.

Necronomicon
Wondrous Item, Artifact (Requires Attunement)
This monstrous-looking tome bound in humanoid skin has an almost palpable aura of dread. A grotesque and ghoulish face is stretched across its loathsome cover.

The *Necronomicon* is replete with fantastic legends of elder magic and abhorrent secrets from beyond. Its author, the mad poet-philosopher Alhazred, is said to have been seized by an invisible monster in broad daylight and devoured in front of a large number of horror-stricken witnesses. Throughout unknown centuries, the *Necronomicon* was rigidly suppressed by civil authorities and by all branches of organized ecclesiasticism. Reading this dreaded tome always leads to terrible consequences.

Among its hideous contents, the *Necronomicon* details abstract formulae on the properties of space and the linkage of dimensions both known and unknown. It describes the presence of forbidden cults among human beings who serve elder, primordial races and who worship unseen entities with alien-tongued names such as Yog-Sothoth and Cthulhu.

Despite centuries of repression, a handful of copies of this horrible artifact still exist. Each one is a closely guarded secret of its owner, and not all the owners are human or even humanoid.

To reap the "benefits" of the *Necronomicon*, a creature must become attuned to it and then spend another 19 hours reading and studying its blasphemous text. The

creature can then add to and copy the book's contents, provided any additions advance the cause of chaos or evil and expand upon the lore already inside. (Because of this, no two copies of the *Necronomicon* are identical, and no one knows what has been added to or excised from Alhazred's original text.)

When a non-evil creature becomes attuned to the *Necronomicon*, it must make a successful DC 18 Charisma saving throw, or its alignment changes to neutral evil.

Unseen forces of evil will pursue any owner of the book, hoping to steal it for themselves or for a more powerful master. Once every three days while a creature is attuned to the book, it has a 19 percent chance to encounter or be attacked by a mythos entity or occult adversary of the GM's choosing. If a creature dies while attuned to the book, a Great Old One claims its soul, and it can't be restored to life by any means.

Random Properties. The *Necronomicon* has the following random properties:

- 2 minor beneficial properties
- 1 major beneficial property
- 1 minor detrimental property
- 2 major detrimental properties

Adjusted Ability Scores. After a creature spends the requisite amount of time reading and studying the book, its Intelligence score increases by 2, to a maximum of 24, and its Wisdom score decreases by 2, to a minimum of 3. The book can't adjust the same creature's ability scores more than once.

Abstract Formulae. The *Necronomicon* contains a multitude of mind-shattering evil magic, including all mythos spells and void spells in this section, all standard necromancy spells, and any additional spells of the GM's design or choosing.

Eldritch Magic. Once a creature has read and studied the book, any spell slot it expends to cast an arcane spell counts as a spell slot one level higher when determining the spell's effect.

Eldritch Lore. The book's bearer can reference the *Necronomicon* whenever it makes an Intelligence check to recall information about any aspect of evil or secrets of the multidimensional universe, such as lore about Great Old Ones or the properties of disquieting technology. When doing so, the proficiency bonus for that check is doubled.

Eldritch Guise. While a creature carries the *Necronomicon* and is attuned to it, the creature can speak, read, and write Void Speech, and it can cast *semblance of dread* (described in **Chapter 5**) as a bonus action.

Voidmarked. After a creature spends the requisite amount of time reading and studying the book, it acquires mental and physical disfigurements as hideous signs of its devotion to the Great Old Ones. The creature gains one flesh warp and one form of indefinite madness. The voidmark grants you advantage on Persuasion checks made to interact with aberrations and on Intimidation checks made to interact with non-aberrations.

Thought Control. A creature that is attuned to the book and holding it can use an action to cast *dominate monster* on a creature within range (save DC 18). This property can't be used again for 19 hours.

Destroying the Book. Pages can be torn from the *Necronomicon*, but any eldritch lore contained on those pages finds its way back into the book eventually, usually when a new author or translator adds pages to the tome. It is rumored that the *Necronomicon* can't be destroyed as long as a spawn of the Great Old One Azathoth exists in the multiverse. A short-term solution exists, however: casting the book into the fire of a dying star scorches all the writing and imagery from its pages and renders the book useless for 6d6 + 6 years.

RING MAGIC

Dwarves are renowned as shapers of the physical world. Earth, stone, and metal bend to the will of dwarven hammers. It's easy to assume that because dwarves have such great skill at shaping material, they must lack the time and energy to become masters of the arcane, too—but that assumption is wrong. Taking unformed matter and shaping it to conform to one's will is an effective way of blending the physical and arcane arts. The dwarves' greatest magic has come from this effort, as evidenced by the legendary weapons, armor, and implements of war that emerge from their mountain strongholds. Few dwarves pursue the study of magic aside from devotion to their deities, but one discipline bridges the gap between creation and spellcasting: ring magic.

Ring magic is the dwarven art of forging metal into rings, often with runes inscribed on their surface, and using those rings to produce or bring about magical effects. Dedicated practitioners known as ring wardens channel their magic through specially prepared rings, increasing the devastation wreaked upon their foes, and they can even imbue spells into rings that they or someone else can unleash later.

Rings created for the purpose of invoking ring magic are more than decorative hand jewelry. They often take the form of circlets of precious metal large enough to adorn a weapon, a staff, or a suit of armor. Wizards who devote themselves to ring magic are rare outside the dwarves' lands, but they're instantly recognizable by the ring-adorned staffs they carry.

Although ring magic spells often require a ring of some form as a material component, the effects they produce are quite distinct and variable, from illusions to transmutations and evocations. What they have in common is that dwarves have uncovered a way to bind the effects into rings; the deeper arcane connection between the rings and the spells is sometimes elusive.

RING MAGIC FEATS

The ring is a powerful shape, with no beginning or end, and potent ties to life. These feats allow any character to experience the distinctive power of ring magic.

CIRCLE SPELLCASTER

Prerequisite: Ability to Cast at Least One Spell

You have learned to create a circular flow of magic between yourself and an allied spellcaster to bolster your spells. You gain the following benefits:

- Increase your Intelligence, Wisdom, or Charisma score by 1, to a maximum of 20.
- You can spend 2 hours (which can be during a long rest) creating a mystical bond with another spellcaster. Both of you must spend this time in meditation, and you must remain within 10 feet of each other. The bond goes into effect when the meditation is over (or when you finish your long rest). Once the bond is formed, the two of you can bolster one another's magic. When one of you must make a Constitution saving throw to maintain concentration on a spell, the other can use his or her reaction to help maintain the effect. Both of you make the saving throw. If either save is successful, the caster maintains concentration. If both saves are failed, both of you lose concentration on any spells you are maintaining and each of you takes 2d6 psychic damage from the strain. You can maintain this bond with only one spellcaster at a time. If you create a new bond, the previous one breaks. Otherwise, the bond lasts until you finish your next long rest.

RING-BOUND

Prerequisite: Ability to Cast at Least One Spell

You have acquired a magic-imbued ring as a token of respect. You gain the following benefits from the ring:

- You have advantage on saving throws against transmutation spells.
- You can physically bind your ring to a weapon with 1 hour of work that can be completed during a short rest. While the ring is attached to the weapon, you can use a bonus action to make the weapon magical until

the start of your next turn. After activating this ability twice, you must finish a short or long rest before using it again.
- Ring wardens and others who respect the traditions of ring magic are favorably disposed toward you. Their starting attitude toward you automatically improves by one step, and you have advantage on Charisma checks related to social interaction with such individuals.

RECOMMENDED SPELL LIST

This section presents a sampling of spells in alignment with the ring magic style. These spells are available to any spellcasting class with the GM's consent. Spells marked with an asterisk (*) appear in **Chapter 5**.

The following spells are available to ring wardens in addition to those on the wizard spell list, and also to sorcerers and warlocks who have a ring magic feat (Circle Spellcaster or Ring-bound).

SORCERER RING SPELLS

Cantrips (0 Level)
Hoarfrost* (evocation)

1st Level
Circle of wind* (abjuration)
Ring strike* (transmutation)

2nd Level
Bitter chains* (transmutation)
Reverberate* (evocation)

3rd Level
Innocuous aspect* (illusion)

4th Level
Spinning axes* (evocation)

5th Level
Curse ring* (necromancy)

6th Level
Enchant ring* (enchantment)

7th Level
Ring ward* (abjuration)

8th Level
Create ring servant* (transmutation)

9th Level
Circle of devastation* (evocation)

WARLOCK RING SPELLS

Cantrips (0 Level)
Hoarfrost* (evocation)

1st Level
Circle of wind* (abjuration)
Ring strike* (transmutation)

2nd Level
Bitter chains* (transmutation)
Reverberate* (evocation)

3rd Level
Innocuous aspect* (illusion)

4th Level
Spinning axes* (evocation)

5th Level
Curse ring* (necromancy)

9th Level
Circle of devastation* (evocation)

WIZARD RING SPELLS

Cantrips (0 Level)
Hoarfrost* (evocation)

1st Level
Circle of wind* (abjuration)
Ring strike* (transmutation)

2nd Level
Bitter chains* (transmutation)
Reverberate* (evocation)

3rd Level
Innocuous aspect* (illusion)

4th Level
Spinning axes* (evocation)

5th Level
Curse ring* (necromancy)

6th Level
Enchant ring* (enchantment)

7th Level
Ring ward* (abjuration)

8th Level
Create ring servant* (transmutation)

9th Level
Circle of devastation* (evocation)

RUNE MAGIC

Writing can be an expression of magic and a way to trap and focus arcane energy. This precept is the foundation of rune magic, which requires carving, writing, or otherwise generating glyphs, sigils, signs, and runes of many kinds. This practice is quite common among many different people, from dwarves and druids to northlanders and even some goblin tribes. The rune magic presented here is somewhat northern-flavored, but it could easily serve for dwarven runes, druidic ogham, or goblin graffiti magic. The deeper understanding is that shapes bind power, and that magic can be made tangible. That tangible magic can be a stone rune, a silvery sigil, or even a bloody scrawl—its power functions regardless of how it was made.

RUNE POWERS

Accessing the magic inherent within runes requires the Rune Knowledge feat. If the option to gain feats isn't used in your campaign, then Rune Knowledge can be gained in place of level-based ability score improvement, if your GM approves. Alternatively, characters might need to accomplish other, story-related tasks determined by the GM to gain Rune Knowledge. Once those obstacles are cleared, all characters who meet the prerequisites can gain Rune Knowledge and Rune Mastery. A character who acquires the Rune Knowledge feat can begin making use of the runes described here.

When one of your rune powers calls for a saving throw, the DC is equal to 8 + your ability modifier + your proficiency bonus. Your applicable ability modifier is the same one being used for the saving throw unless a different ability is specified; for example, if a rune calls for a Charisma saving throw, your Charisma modifier is used to set the DC.

RUNE KNOWLEDGE
Prerequisite: Wisdom 12 or Higher

You are wise in the lore of two runes of your choice. You always have access to the benefit that a rune provides. In addition, you can invoke one rune power of each rune you have learned, provided you meet any other requirements such as a minimum level.

You can select this feat multiple times. Each time you do, you gain the benefit and powers of two additional runes of your choice.

RUNE MASTERY
Prerequisite: Rune Mastery

You have mastered the special powers of one rune. Choose one rune that you have already learned through Rune Knowledge. You can invoke one of its mastery powers, provided you meet any other requirements such as a minimum level.

You can select this feat multiple times. Each time you do, you learn the mastery powers of a different rune from your repertoire.

INVOKING RUNE POWERS

Invoking one of a rune's powers requires an action and provokes opportunity attacks. Generally, you must either create a physical representation of the rune (in paint, in blood, drawn in the dirt or snow, and so forth) or trace the shape of an existing carving of the rune that was created to an exacting standard.

Each rune confers a benefit on someone who knows how to scribe it. A rune's benefit is always in effect for a character who knows that rune. In addition, that character can call upon one of the rune's powers when so desired. Unless otherwise noted, any rune power can be used once, and that expended use is regained when you finish a long rest.

Some powers have a level requirement (given in parentheses); when a character attains that level, this power becomes an additional choice. Mastery powers are a separate category: only a character who has the Rune Mastery feat for a particular rune can use its mastery power. If a power or a mastery power has no level requirement, it becomes available to you as soon as you acquire the necessary feat.

If a rune's power gives you the ability to cast a spell, you can do so without needing any components (aside from materials needed for the drawing of the rune), and the spell is always cast as if using the lowest-level spell slot possible. It typically has the same duration as a normal casting of the spell and uses your character level as the caster level.

When a rune power calls for a saving throw, the DC equals 8 + your ability bonus + your proficiency bonus. Typically, the ability that applies to the DC calculation is the same as the ability used for the saving throw.

RUNE DESCRIPTIONS
The following runes are presented in alphabetical order.

ALGIZ
Elk and Reindeer, Evading Danger; the God Heimdall

Benefit: You gain a +1 bonus on initiative rolls.

Power (5th level): Living creatures that are within 10 feet of an algiz rune when you draw it on the ground or on a wall gain a +2 bonus on Wisdom (Perception) checks and have advantage on saving throws against *sleep* spells and other magical effects that cause unconsciousness. Both effects last for 8 hours. Scribing the rune takes 15 minutes.

Mastery Power (8th level): Marking a willing creature with the algiz rune transforms the creature into an elk, as if by a *polymorph* spell. Drawing the rune on the creature takes an action, and the change lasts while you concentrate, for up to 1 hour.

ANSUZ
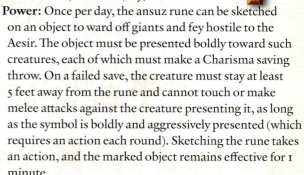

Gods and Outsiders

Benefit: You gain a +1 bonus on Intelligence (Arcana) checks to identify the type, powers, or weaknesses of aberrations, celestials, fey, or fiends.

Power: Once per day, the ansuz rune can be sketched on an object to ward off giants and fey hostile to the Aesir. The object must be presented boldly toward such creatures, each of which must make a Charisma saving throw. On a failed save, the creature must stay at least 5 feet away from the rune and cannot touch or make melee attacks against the creature presenting it, as long as the symbol is boldly and aggressively presented (which requires an action each round). Sketching the rune takes an action, and the marked object remains effective for 1 minute.

Power (7th level): If you sketch ansuz on a floor or a wall, each of your allies within 10 feet of it can roll a d4 and add the result to each of its attack rolls, similar to the effect of a *bless* spell. Sketching the rune takes two actions, and it remains effective thereafter for as long as you concentrate, for up to 1 minute.

Mastery Power (11th level): When you trace ansuz on the forehead of a willing creature, the creature falls into a trance, during which it receives a message from the gods (identical in effect to a *divination* spell). A creature can experience only one such trance per week. Tracing the rune takes 10 minutes, and the trance lasts for 1 round.

BERKANAN

Birch Tree, Love, New Beginnings; the Bear Maiden

Benefit: You gain a +1 bonus on Charisma (Persuasion) checks.

Power: When you trace berkanan on a living creature, the rune grants the creature advantage on a single Charisma (Persuasion) check of its choosing. Tracing the rune takes 10 minutes, and it remains effective for up to 1 hour.

When you trace this rune on a living plant, an effect identical to a *spike growth* spell erupts in a 20-foot radius around the rune. Tracing the rune on a plant takes an action, and the effect lasts while you concentrate, for up to 10 minutes.

Mastery Power (8th level): You can create a *philter of love* once a week.

DAGAZ

Day and Laying the Dead to Rest

Benefit: You can always tell whether a creature you can see within 10 feet of you is alive or dead.

Power (4th level): If you use an action to trace dagaz on a creature that is blinded, deafened, paralyzed, poisoned, or diseased, the creature's affliction is cured as if by a *lesser restoration* spell.

Power (6th level): Tracing dagaz on an object makes it give off bright light in a 60-foot radius and dim light for 60 feet beyond that. Magical darkness of 3rd level or lower is dispelled in an area where this light overlaps it. The light is blocked as normal by opaque objects or structures. Tracing the rune for this purpose takes an action, and the light lasts while you concentrate, for up to 1 hour.

Mastery Power (13th level): Once a week, you can sketch dagaz on the ground or a wall to create an instantaneous effect identical to a cleric's Turn Undead class feature. Sketching the rune takes an action, and it affects undead within 30 feet that can see it at the moment of completion.

EHWAZ

Horses, Freedom, the Nithing Pole

Benefit: You gain a +1 bonus to Wisdom (Animal Handling) checks made to control a mount, and to Dexterity checks made to wriggle free of bonds.

Power (5th level): Using an action to trace ehwaz on a lock or a set of shackles has the same effect as casting a *knock* spell but makes no sound.

Mastery Power (8th level): When you sketch ehwaz on the ground, you can produce the effect of a *phantom steed* spell. Sketching the rune takes 5 minutes, and the illusory steed remains for 1 hour or until it takes damage.

Mastery Power (9th level): You can create a *nithing pole* once per month. The process can be performed only during a new moon, takes 12 hours, and requires bloodletting that leaves a permanent scar in the shape of the ehwaz rune on the rune maker's left hand. Each new use of this power creates a new scar; those after the first don't need to be on the hand, but they must be on the hands or arms.

EIWAZ

Yew Tree, Yggdrasil

Benefit: You have proficiency on Intelligence (Arcana) checks.

Power (4th level): Spending an action to trace eiwaz onto a suitably sized piece of wood subjects it to the effect of a *shillelagh* spell for 1 minute. This power is usable at will.

Mastery Power (8th level): If you take 1 minute to write out three questions on a piece of paper or parchment and trace eiwaz on the bottom of the sheet, you can later produce an effect similar to a *contact other plane* spell

NITHING POLE

Wondrous Item, Rare

A *nithing pole* is crafted to exact retribution for an act of cowardice or dishonor. It is a sturdy wooden staff, 6 to 10 feet long, carved with runes that name the dishonored target of the staff's curse. The carved shaft is draped in horsehide, topped with a horse's skull, and placed where its target is expected to pass by; typically, the pole is driven into the ground or wedged into a rocky cleft in a remote spot, where the victim won't see it until it's too late.

A pole is created to punish a certain person for a specific crime. The target must be named on the pole; a description such as "the person who blinded Lars Gustafson" isn't precise enough. The moment the target approaches within 60 feet, the pole casts *bestow curse* (with a range of 60 feet instead of touch) on the target. The DC for the target's Wisdom saving throw is 15. On a successful save, the pole recasts the spell every round until the target's saving throw is a failure, the target retreats out of range, or the *nithing pole* is destroyed. Anyone other than the pole's creator who tries to destroy or knock down a *nithing pole* is also targeted by a *bestow curse* spell, but only once.

You determine the effect of the curse when the pole is created. The pole becomes nonmagical only after it has laid its curse on its intended target; an untriggered and forgotten *nithing pole* remains dangerous for centuries. The curse, once activated, lasts for 8 hours and doesn't require concentration.

CHAPTER 2 STYLES OF MAGIC

(including the possible negative consequences). If you later sleep for at least 10 minutes while holding the sheet, your dreams yield answers to those questions that you can receive when you awaken if you make a successful Intelligence saving throw.

Mastery Power (11th level): When carved on the bark of a living tree, eiwaz allows you to travel between that tree and another tree within 500 feet that you have previously marked with eiwaz, as if both were under the effect of a *tree stride* spell. Each carving takes an action, and the effect lasts while you concentrate, for up to 1 minute after the second carving is finished.

FEHU

Cattle, Livestock, and Wealth

Benefit: You have advantage on Wisdom (Animal Handling) checks concerning domesticated animals that aren't used as riding mounts.

Power: Sketching fehu on an object makes that item easier to lift or drag, as if it were only half its actual weight. Sketching the rune takes 1 minute, and the effect lasts while you concentrate, for up to 1 hour. This power works equally well on a single object, such as a block of stone, or on a collection of objects that are bundled together, such as a large chest stuffed with coins.

Mastery Power (8th level): By spending 1 minute tracing fehu on your skin, you can cast *dominate beast* as though from a 6th-level spell slot. The effect must be used within 10 minutes of completing the tracing, or the rune's power dissipates.

GEBU

Generosity and Hospitality, Gifts

Benefit: You have advantage on Intelligence checks to estimate an item's value.

Power: When you spend 1 minute carefully examining an item while tracing gebu on it, you learn the item's name and magical properties, as if you had cast an *identify* spell. Alternatively, if you use an action to trace gebu on a willing creature, that creature gains the effect of a *sanctuary* spell. (You can't use this power on yourself.) The effect lasts while you concentrate, for up to 1 minute.

Mastery Power (8th level): To use this power, you take an action to scratch or sketch gebu on a wall, floor, or other surface of an enclosed space, in a place where it is clearly visible. For up to 1 minute thereafter, you can activate the rune with a command word, provided you are within 20 feet of it. When you do so, each creature within 20 feet of the rune and with a clear line of sight to it (regardless of whether the creature can actually see it) must make a Charisma saving throw. On a failed save, a creature is affected as if by a *calm emotions* spell that lasts while you concentrate, for up to 1 minute.

HAGALAZ

Hail, Winter Weather

Benefit: You have advantage on Wisdom (Survival) checks to predict weather conditions for the next 24 hours in your vicinity.

Power: If you take an action to trace hagalaz on a willing creature, it receives the benefit of a *protection from energy (cold)* spell while you concentrate, for up to 1 hour.

Mastery Power (9th level): When you sketch hagalaz on the ground under the open sky, you produce the effect of a *sleet storm* centered on a point you choose within 150 feet. Sketching the rune takes 4 rounds, and the storm lasts while you concentrate, for up to 2 minutes.

Mastery Power (14th level): When hagalaz is sketched on the ground inside the area of an effect caused by *sleet storm*, *ice storm*, *control weather* (hail or blizzard only), or a similar spell, the rune brings about a *dispel magic* effect as if that spell had been cast with a 7th-level slot. If the effect being dispelled is from 8th- or 9th-level magic, you use Charisma for the ability check to determine the rune's effectiveness. Sketching the rune takes 2 rounds.

Mastery Power (14th level): When hagalaz is sketched on the ground inside the area of a natural (nonmagical) storm, the rune brings about the effect of a *control weather* spell. Sketching the rune takes 1 hour, and the control lasts while you concentrate, for up to 8 hours.

INGWAZ

Ancestors, Major Deities

Benefit: You have proficiency on Intelligence (History) checks.

Power (4th level): When you use an action to trace ingwaz on a spear, the first character who uses the spear against an enemy adds 1d4 radiant damage to attacks made with the spear. The first attack must be made within 8 hours after the rune is traced, and the benefit lasts for 1 minute after it is triggered.

Power (5th level): When you trace ingwaz on the face of a willing creature, the creature gains the benefit of the barbarian's Rage class feature, as though it were a barbarian of your character level. Tracing the rune takes two actions, and the effect lasts for 1 minute.

Mastery Power (8th level): When ingwaz is traced on the flesh of a corpse, the rune creates the effect of a *speak with dead* spell on that corpse. Tracing the rune takes 1 minute, and the effect lasts while you concentrate, for up to 10 minutes.

ISAZ

Ice, Imprisonment, Paralysis

Benefit: Whenever you take cold damage, that damage is reduced by 1.

Power (4th level): When you take an action to sketch isaz on the ground, slick ice spreads out from that point to cover an area of 225 square feet. The iced area can have any shape you want, as long as every square of ice has at least one side in common with another square of ice; on a grid of 5-foot squares, the ice can cover as many as 9 squares. Ice-filled squares are difficult terrain, and the DC of Dexterity (Acrobatics) checks made in the area increases by 5. The ice is nonmagical and melts normally.

Power (5th level): When isaz is traced on a weapon, the weapon sheds bright light in a 10-foot radius and dim light for 10 feet beyond that, and it deals an extra 1d4 cold damage on a hit. Tracing the rune takes an action, and the effect lasts while you concentrate, for up to 1 hour.

Mastery Power (8th level): A shield marked with this rune glitters like frost in the morning sun. As an action, a wielder of the shield who is in direct sunlight can use it to focus reflected light on a single creature within 30 feet. The target must make a successful Constitution saving throw or become blinded. The DC for the saving throw equals 8 + your Dexterity bonus + your proficiency bonus. Marking the shield takes an action, and the rune remains effective while you concentrate, for up to 1 hour.

JERA

Abundant Harvest; the Gods Frey and Freya

Benefit: You have proficiency on Intelligence (Nature) checks.

Power (4th level): When jera is traced on the belly of a living creature, the rune guarantees that any sexual union involving that creature in the next 24 hours proves fruitful. If the rune is traced on a pregnant creature at least once per month during its pregnancy, the act guarantees a successful birth and healthy offspring. Tracing the rune takes an action.

Power (6th level): When jera is traced on a wooden table, plate, or platter, all food and drink that's spoiled, rotten, diseased, poisonous, or otherwise contaminated within 20 feet of that object becomes pure and safe for consumption. Tracing the rune takes an action.

Mastery Power (8th level): When jera is drawn in the earth among living plants, the effect of a *plant growth* spell arises in a 100-foot radius around the rune. Sketching the rune takes an action.

KAUNEN

Flaming Torch, Enlightenment, Ulcers

Benefit: You gain darkvision to a range of 30 feet. If you already have darkvision, you gain proficiency on Wisdom (Perception) checks.

Power (4th level): When you spend 1 minute tracing kaunen on the ground, that spot burns like a campfire for up to 8 hours. The fire is 2 feet in diameter, and the flames deal 2d6 fire damage to any creature that ends its turn in the fire. It provides warmth as a campfire, but the flame cannot be transported or used to set other objects afire.

Power (5th level): Tracing kaunen onto a weapon causes it to shed bright light in a 10-foot radius and dim light for 10 feet beyond that, and the weapon deals an extra 1d6 fire damage on a hit. Tracing the rune takes an action, and the effect lasts while you concentrate, for up to 1 hour.

Mastery Power (8th level): When you use an action to trace the rune on a living creature, kaunen produces the effect of a *lesser restoration* spell on that creature.

LAUKAZ

Water, the Sea, the God Njord

Benefit: You gain Aquan as a bonus language. If you already know this language, you have advantage on Charisma (Persuasion) checks involving creatures from the Elemental Plane of Water.

Power (4th level): When you take an action to trace laukaz on an object, it becomes more buoyant for 24 hours. Anyone grasping the object has advantage on Strength (Athletics) checks to swim or to stay afloat.

Power (7th level): When you trace laukaz on a living creature's chest, the creature gains the benefit of a *water breathing* spell. Tracing the rune takes an action, and the effect lasts for 24 hours.

Mastery Power (11th level): When you draw the rune on the surface of a lakebed, riverbed, or sea bottom, you can manipulate a 100-foot cube of the nearby water as if by a *control water* spell. Sketching the rune takes an action, and the effect lasts while you concentrate, up to 10 minutes.

MANNAZ

Humanoids, Especially Humans and Dwarves

Benefit: You gain a +1 bonus on saving throws against petrification and against effects that alter your form, such as lycanthropy, *polymorph*, or *flesh to stone*.

Power (5th level): When mannaz is traced on the ground, a boulder, or a wall, it produces the effect of a *calm emotions* spell on all living creatures within 20 feet of the rune. Tracing the rune takes an action, and the effect lasts while you concentrate, for up to 1 minute.

CHAPTER 2 STYLES OF MAGIC | 99

- **Mastery Power (8th level):** When you use an action to trace mannaz on the flesh of a creature, the act returns a lycanthrope to its humanoid form or dispels (as if by *dispel magic*) a polymorph effect the target is currently under. An unwilling creature can resist this change with a successful Charisma saving throw (using your Wisdom modifier to set the DC).
- **Mastery Power (9th level):** Tracing mannaz on a plant or animal causes it to be affected as if by the *awaken* spell. Drawing the rune in this way takes 8 hours, and the effect is permanent.

NAUDIZ

Necessity and Filling Needs

- **Benefit:** Once a day, you can cast *spare the dying*.
- **Power (4th level):** By spending an action to trace naudiz on an item, you grant a creature that touches the item the benefit of a *guidance* or *resistance* spell (creature's choice). A number of creatures equal to your proficiency bonus can benefit from this effect. Both the rune and the effect last while you concentrate, for up to 1 minute.
- **Power (5th level):** You can trace naudiz in the air in such a way that five creatures within 10 feet of you have their hit point maximums increased by 5, and each gains 5 hit points. Tracing the rune takes an action, and the effect lasts for 8 hours.
- **Mastery Power (15th level):** When you use an action to trace naudiz on an object weighing no more than 20 pounds, you can call that item to you once during the next 24 hours if it is anywhere within 400 feet. The item teleports into your hand instantly when you use an action to call it. If another creature is holding the object, that creature prevents it from teleporting with a successful Charisma saving throw (using your Wisdom modifier to set the DC).

NYKÖPING

Passage of Time, the Seasons, Phases of the Moon

- **Benefit:** You gain proficiency on Wisdom (Survival) checks.
- **Power (5th level):** When nyköping is sketched on the ground, up to six creatures of your choice can each regain hit points equal to 2d8 + your Wisdom modifier. You must be able to see the creatures, and they must be within 30 feet of you. Sketching the rune in this way takes 10 minutes.
- **Power (6th level):** When you take an action to trace the rune on the ground under an open sky, nyköping creates the effect of a *gust of wind* spell. The wind lasts while you concentrate, for up to 1 minute.
- **Mastery Power (9th level):** Tracing nyköping on a creature grants it the benefit of a *haste* spell. Drawing the rune takes an action, and the effect lasts while you concentrate, for up to 1 minute.
- **Mastery Power (13th level):** When you sketch nyköping on the ground beneath the open sky, the weather in the area improves toward clear skies, as if you had cast *control weather*. The rune can only improve the weather, not make it more severe. Sketching the rune takes 1 hour, and the effect lasts for 8 hours.

OTALAN

Property, Inheritance, Family

- **Benefit:** You gain proficiency on Charisma (Persuasion) checks.
- **Power (7th level):** When this rune is traced on a reflective surface (for example, a mirror, a polished shield, or even still water), otalan lets you scry on an object that you have possessed for at least one week, or on any member of your immediate family within three generations of you, as if subjected to the *scrying* spell. Tracing the rune takes 10 minutes, and the effect lasts while you concentrate, for up to 10 minutes.
- **Mastery Power (13th level):** When otalan is invoked on an object, the rune's power lingers harmlessly in the item until the death of the item's owner. The moment that creature dies, the object teleports into the hands of another individual whose identity is specified when the rune is created. This person can be described by name, by title, or by relationship (for example, "the king of Noatun" or "my firstborn son"). This power functions over any range as long as the object and the individual are on the same plane. If another creature is holding the object when its owner dies, that creature can prevent the object from teleporting by making a successful Charisma saving throw (using your Wisdom modifier to set the DC). The rune remains effective until it is triggered or until you use this power to invoke the rune on a different object. Preparing the object takes 10 minutes.

PERTO

Things Not as They Seem, the God Loki

- **Benefit:** You gain a +1 bonus on Wisdom ability checks to solve riddles or puzzles, and on Wisdom saving throws against illusions.
- **Power (4th level):** When you take an action to trace perto on a creature, you can change the creature's appearance as if by a *disguise self* spell. If the creature has Intelligence 3 or higher, it decides how to change its appearance. The effect persists for 1 hour.
- **Mastery Power (8th level):** Spending an action to trace perto on the ground causes all objects within 10 feet of the rune to be undetectable by divination magic or scrying sensors. The effect lasts for 8 hours.

RAIDO

Travel

Benefit: Your speed is 5 feet faster than the norm for your race, and you always know which way is north.

Power (4th level): The possessor of an object that has had raido sketched on it has advantage on Dexterity (Acrobatics) checks to ski, skate, or control a sled. Sketching the rune in this way takes 1 minute, and the effect lasts while you concentrate, up to 1 hour.

Power (5th level): By using an action to trace raido on your skin, you bestow the benefit of a *water walk* spell on yourself and up to five other creatures of your choice that you can see.

Power (7th level): If you take 1 minute to sketch raido on the sole of your foot or boot, you gain the ability to engage in a forced march for 12 hours instead of the usual 8 hours before risking exhaustion. You can impart this ability on up to five other creatures of your choice that you can see, but all of you must travel together for the entire period. The effect ends 12 hours after your forced march begins, regardless of whether you are traveling at that time.

SOWILO

The Sun, the God Balder

Benefit: You gain immunity to the blinded condition.

Power (5th level): When traced on a creature, sowilo grants it magical confidence and magnetism, enabling it to use an *enthrall* effect on an audience, as with the spell. Tracing the rune takes an action, and the effect lasts for 1 minute.

Power (7th level): Spending an action tracing sowilo on an object makes it glow, as if by the *daylight* spell, for 1 hour.

Mastery Power (13th level): Spending an action drawing sowilo on the brow of a creature causes its eyes to emit a brilliant light, as a *sunbeam* spell. The creature is immune to the blinded condition for the duration of the effect, which lasts while you concentrate, for up to 1 minute.

TEWAZ

Fearlessness, Assemblies or Councils, the God Tyr

Benefit: You gain advantage on saving throws against the frightened condition.

Power (4th level): Tewaz can be sketched on an object to ward off wolves, worgs, werewolves, and other lupine creatures. The object must be presented boldly toward such creatures, each of which makes a Charisma saving throw. On a failed save, the creature must stay at least 5 feet away from the rune and cannot touch or make melee attacks against the creature presenting it, as long as the symbol is boldly and aggressively presented (which requires an action each round). Sketching the rune takes an action, and the marked object remains effective for 1 hour.

Power (5th level): When tewaz is sketched somewhere clearly visible, it produces the effect of a *calm emotions* spell on all creatures that can see it within a 20-foot radius. Sketching the rune takes an action, and the effect lasts while you concentrate, for up to 1 minute.

TURISAZ

Giants, Thunder and Lightning

Benefit: You gain Giant as a bonus language. If you already know this language, you gain advantage on Wisdom (Insight) checks involving giants.

Power (4th level): A weapon marked with turisaz deals an extra 1d4 lightning damage on each of the next five times it hits its target within the next hour. Marking the weapon takes an action.

Power (5th level): Armor marked with turisaz has resistance to lightning damage and grants a +2 bonus to the wearer's Strength score. Marking the armor takes an action, and the effect lasts while you concentrate, for up to 1 hour.

Mastery Power (8th level): When inscribed on a surface, the turisaz rune acts as a *glyph of warding* that deals 6d8 lightning damage if triggered. Sketching the rune takes 1 hour, and the effect lasts for up to 24 hours, or until the glyph is triggered or dispelled.

URUZ

Wild Oxen, Sacrifice to the Gods, Strength

Benefit: You gain a +2 bonus to your Strength score for the purpose of determining carrying capacity.

Power (4th level): When the wielder of a shield that's been inscribed with the uruz rune uses an action to Dash, the wielder can shove or make one melee weapon attack as a bonus action. Tracing the rune takes 1 minute, and the effect lasts for 1 hour.

Power (5th level): When uruz is traced on the flesh of a living creature, the creature's carrying capacity doubles, and the creature has advantage on Strength checks. Tracing the rune takes an action, and the effect lasts while you concentrate, for up to 1 hour.

Mastery Power (8th level): When you trace this rune on an appropriate sacrifice (food, a symbolic weapon, an animal), any offenses the sacrifice giver has committed against the gods are forgiven (treat as a *remove curse* effect). Tracing the rune in this way takes 1 hour, and the sacrifice must be offered no more than 1 hour later.

WUNJO

Happiness and Joy

Benefit: After using inspiration or gifting it to another player, you have a 20 percent chance to retain it. If you use inspiration that was retained in this way, it can't be retained again.

Power (4th level): Tracing the wunjo rune on the ground or on a boulder creates the effect of an *animal friendship* spell on one beast within 30 feet. Tracing the rune takes an action, and the effect lasts for 24 hours.

Mastery Power (8th level): If you use an action to sketch wunjo on an object that you then hold aloft, your allies that can see you have advantage on saving throws against fear, charm, and domination effects. The effect lasts while you concentrate, for up to 10 minutes.

TEMPORAL MAGIC

The control and manipulation of time is an esoteric and mysterious branch of magic. Spellcasters who seek to alter its flow have the potential to perform incredible deeds. That potential is tempered by the great danger of intervening with time though, which resists mortal interference. Many gods also look unfavorably on those who try to divert or dam its currents, and their disfavor should never be taken lightly.

VARIANT: CLOCKWORK MAGIC

Clockwork magic is a style of magic from the Midgard Campaign Setting, divinely granted to humans and dwarves by the goddess Rava, patron of industry and mistress of time.

If you play in Midgard, or if you want to add clockwork magic to your game, this category of magic includes several temporal magic spells and some of the spells described in **Chapter 5**. (For more on clockwork magic, see also *Midgard Heroes Handbook*.)

RECOMMENDED SPELL LIST

This section presents a sampling of spells in alignment with the temporal magic style. These spells are available to any spellcasting class with the GM's consent. Spells marked with an asterisk (*) appear in **Chapter 5**.

Esoteric though it may be, the knowledge of how to manipulate time through magic is not restricted to only certain types of spellcasters. Anyone, even paladins, can amass a repertoire of these spells sufficient to attract the attention of a higher power.

Cantrip (0 Level)
*Clockwork bolt** (evocation)
*Fist of iron** (transmutation)
Guidance (divination)
Mending (transmutation)
*Quicken** (transmutation)

1st Level
*Analyze device** (divination)
*Anticipate weakness** (divination)
*Auspicious warning** (enchantment)
*Chronal lance** (transmutation)
Feather fall (transmutation)
*Foretell distraction** (divination)
Grease (conjuration)
*Pendulum** (enchantment)
*Seer's reaction** (divination)
*Tireless** (transmutation)

2nd Level
*Anticipate attack** (divination)
Arcane lock (abjuration)
*Decelerate** (transmutation)
*Gear barrage** (conjuration)
Gentle repose (necromancy)
*Greater analyze device** (divination)
*Heartstop** (necromancy)
Knock (transmutation)
Locate object (divination)
*Lock armor** (transmutation)
*Spin** (enchantment)
*Time step** (conjuration)

3rd Level
*Accelerate** (transmutation)
*Anticipate arcana** (divination)
Haste (transmutation)
Slow (transmutation)
*Thousand darts** (evocation)

4th Level
*Flickering fate** (divination)
*Quick time** (conjuration)
*Reset** (transmutation)
*Scry ambush** (divination)
*Steam blast** (evocation)
*Time vortex** (evocation)

5th Level
*Chains of the goddess** (enchantment)
*Clockwork bodyguard** (conjuration)
Modify memory (enchantment)
*Wall of time** (abjuration)

6th Level
*Catapult** (transmutation)
*Time loop** (transmutation)

7th Level
*Alter time flow** (transmutation)
*Ravages of time** (transmutation)
*Right the stars** (divination)
*Time jaunt** (transmutation)

8th Level
*Steam whistle** (evocation)
*Time jump** (transmutation)
*Time slippage** (enchantment)

9th Level
*Time in a bottle** (transmutation)
Time stop (transmutation)

Spellcasting Allies

The brooding archmage alone in their tower is a staple of fantasy literature. The more powerful a wizard becomes, the more distant they seem from the common folk, and the greatest are often the most misunderstood or feared. Some wizards try to alleviate this loneliness by passing on their knowledge to those around them, taking on one or more apprentices. Others create magical constructs to guard their homes—or simply to keep them company—and summon familiars for much the same reason.

This chapter describes various companions and accoutrements that a powerful spellcaster, particularly a wizard, might have. These creatures and features help to flesh out a wizard's home and are often encountered in the wizard's stead. They also provide opportunities for adventure, whether independent of the wizard or linked to them.

Apprentices

Every archmage needs someone to clean dishes, tend to meals, and wash bedpans. Although some wizards use spells or servants to perform these duties, others give these jobs to their apprentices, budding wizards they have taken under their wings to learn the esteemed art of magic. Many wizards also rely on their apprentices to deal with the riffraff who wander into their towers looking for help; for many player characters, the wizard's apprentice is their first point of contact.

Below are presented five apprentices that can be inserted into a new or ongoing campaign. These apprentices are more than just collections of numbers; each has their own history and motivations that can impact the lives of the characters who deal with them.

ARN OF ROWAN

"I was a warrior before I became a wizard, a sword for hire who traveled the world looking for adventure. I made a name for myself as well. Perhaps you've heard of me? Arn's the name—Arn of Rowan."

Arn of Rowan (CN human) is a strapping man in his mid-thirties with long brown hair, a thick beard, and piercing black eyes. Tall and full of vigor, Arn seems like an odd choice for a wizard's apprentice, and his master, Jainara Meadowwands (LN human), seems more like a harried wife than a teacher. Indeed, most people find their pairing to be odd, especially given that Arn is much more famous than his master.

Background. Arn began his career as a soldier in the army of a self-righteous duke who waged war against his neighbors under the pretense of dispensing justice. It was during this bloody time that Arn solidified his reputation as a vicious fighter with axe and shield, and once the duke had his fill of warfare, Arn forged his own career as a mercenary for hire, basing himself in the small town of Rowan, which he soon put on the map with his legendary exploits.

It was after one particularly harrowing mission that Arn drank too much ale at the local tavern and lost a bet to one of his companions, a bard who claimed that Arn could never master any trade but that of the blade. Haughtily, Arn took up the challenge and availed himself of the talents of Jainara Meadowwands, a mousy-haired woman and capable illusionist, agreeing to pay off her debts in exchange for becoming her pupil. Jainara accepted the deal, believing that Arn would quickly grow bored and leave—but much to her amazement, he not only stayed but quickly excelled as her student.

Personality. Arn is a boisterous and carefree individual who has many scars and tales from his past. Naturally charismatic and with an unusually keen intellect, he would probably have been a lord by now if it were not for his chaotic nature. The fact that he is good at magecraft does not surprise Arn, since he is good at whatever he puts his mind to. What does surprise him, however, is that he actually enjoys the work. He has also grown quite fond of Jainara, and finds her presence strangely calming.

Plot Hook. The characters are passing through the area when Rowan is attacked by a flight of wyvern-riding hobgoblins. Arn and Jainara are also present, and through their combined efforts they and the characters manage to turn back the attack. Jainara is injured during the fight, and it is at this stage that Arn decides to turn his back on the blade and try being a wizard full-time. Of course, being Arn of Rowan, he cannot let the culprits get away with hurting his master, so he offers the PCs his magic battleaxe if they track the hobgoblins back to their base and finish them off.

EROLIMAR

"Master Taramind took me on as his apprentice even though there were more suitable candidates. I'll be forever grateful to him."

Erolimar (LG elf) is a young elf with sweeping silvery locks and amethyst eyes. Stout of limb, graceful and handsome, Erolimar seems almost like the perfect elf—yet despite these qualities, he has been cursed with only middling intelligence and wisdom, making him a poor choice as a wizard's apprentice. Nevertheless, he has been taken on by Taramind the Scorched (NE elf), a mysterious elf with hideously burned features who is known for his dealings with elementals and fiends.

Background. Erolimar comes from a long line of accomplished spellcasters. Indeed, it was expected that young Erolimar would enroll at an esteemed college of magic when he came of age so he could follow in his forebears' footsteps. This would have been the case, had he passed the entrance exam. Soon, it became clear that Erolimar was not the paragon of wizardry his father and mother thought he would be. Dejected, he turned his back on magic to pursue the meaningful but far less prestigious role of hunter for his village.

Just when it seemed that magic had left Erolimar behind, he was saved by Taramind, who approached the

CHAPTER 3 SPELLCASTING ALLIES

young elf to be his apprentice. At first fearful of the wizard's reputation, Erolimar finally accepted the offer and has taken to his new position with gusto, unaware that his master has taken him on to prepare Erolimar's soul for sacrifice to a fiend, whose life force he will then transfer into the young elf's body.

Personality. Erolimar is a kind-hearted, generous, and naive individual who does not see a bad bone in anyone around him. Even Taramind, with his menacing demeanor and harsh teaching methods, does not set off Erolimar's alarm bells; he prefers to focus on his master's strengths, rather than worry about his flaws. Erolimar is envied by many in his village for his good looks and natural agility, but they are also aware of his failings, and there are few who can hold a bad thought in their hearts for the elf for too long.

Plot Hook. The characters are hired by the local elf population to investigate a spate of bizarre animal attacks in the vicinity of Taramind's mansion. The attacks have been violent and erratic, the animals in question extremely vicious and difficult to kill. During their investigation, the characters run into Erolimar, and the elf proves to be helpful on more than one occasion. Eventually (perhaps with Erolimar's help), they realize that the animals have become possessed by lesser fiends and that some sort of conjuration magic is responsible. It is at this point when Taramind begins to prepare the young elf for sacrifice, and it is up to the characters to save him. How this plays out is up to the GM, but Taramind is no pushover—his mansion is home to magic traps, bound fiends, and terrible golems.

LEREILEL CLOUDWOOD

"Magic never judges you based on your appearance. It doesn't care what you look like. Magic accepts you the way you are."

Lereilel Cloudwood (NG human) is a young woman in her early twenties with dark reddish-brown hair, pale green eyes, and numerous freckles. Overweight and lacking confidence, Lereilel has always been anxious about her appearance and is frequently tongue-tied, particularly when dealing with members of the opposite sex. She has a real passion for magic, however, and was taken in as an apprentice by Ravin Wyrdstone (LN human), who has great faith in Lereilel's abilities.

Background. Lereilel was born into an affluent family and displayed an affinity for magic when she came of age—much to the chagrin of her socialite mother, who constantly expressed her disappointment that Lereilel had taken after her father's looks and whims. Although she was discouraged by her mother's disapproval and the mirthful stares of the men her mother brought to woo her, Lereilel eventually convinced her father to let her study magic under the tutelage of Ravin Wyrdstone. Since then, Lereilel has worked hard to prove herself but still thinks that her appearance holds her back. She has faith that the transmutation magic she is studying might hold the key to "correcting" her unsightly looks and finally make her mother proud of her.

Recently, Lereilel has been seeing Thaliydor Brightcrest, a handsome half-elf and a local carpenter who seems to think the world of her despite her homeliness. Unfortunately for her, Lereilel does not realize she is being duped and that Thaliydor is actually an assassin (CE half-elf) who is using her to get closer to her master.

Personality. Lereilel is highly intelligent and well versed in arcane lore, but finds it difficult to speak with people and has been something of a wallflower throughout her life. As such, she can easily be taken advantage of by someone who gives her any attention, particularly if that person is both attractive and charming. If Lereilel realizes that Thaliydor's feelings are false, the last shreds of her confidence might finally break, leading her to do something potentially self-destructive unless someone steps in to save her.

Plot Hook. One easy way for the characters to become involved with Lereilel is to have them hired by her master as guards. Ravin is concerned that he might be the target of an assassination attempt by an old enemy and wants the characters to protect him and his apprentice until he can track down the villain. Strangely, the archmage is more concerned about Lereilel than he is about himself and tells the characters to watch her carefully. Alternatively, they could be hired by Lereilel's father to check on his daughter and see how she is doing. Regardless of how the characters become involved, their arrival puts a major chink in Thaliydor's plans and forces the assassin's hand, as the half-elf hires a band of evil brigands to deal with the characters while he uses Lereilel as bait to make an attempt on the life of her master.

TERINDOR GRAYVEIL

"Ever since my sister was forced to marry that horrible noble, I've been looking for a way to free her. You lot might be just the heroes I need."

Terindor Grayveil (CG human) is a wiry lad of fifteen with unruly orange hair and deep blue eyes. An earnest and helpful soul, Terindor is also far smarter than most of the adults around him and has taken to the study of magic with natural aplomb. His master is Elgretta Mathelzor (LG human), a famous war wizard who is often away on military campaigns, leaving Terindor to fend for himself.

Background. Terindor was born to hard-working but luckless mercantile parents who gave everything they had to make the lives of their children better, even teaching them letters and history to help them establish themselves in the world. The family became crippled by debt, and rather than seeing her parents cast out onto the streets, Terindor's sister, Ileena, agreed to marry a lecherous noble in order to save the family business. Shortly thereafter, Terindor sought out the war wizard and begged to become her apprentice—a move that shocked his mother and father, even more so when Elgretta agreed. Since then, Terindor has worked hard at his training, moving forward in leaps and bounds even though his master is frequently absent.

Personality. Terindor is a determined lad who consistently pushes himself to become a better wizard. While maintaining this focus, he frequently pauses his studies to help those in need, whether by fixing the roof of a spinster's cottage or driving out giant rats from the local brewery. Well-liked by those in his community, he is also the only one not awestruck by his mistress, who is renowned for her success in single-handedly destroying a horde of goblins and felling a mighty white dragon with a barrage of spells.

Terindor's main reason for wanting to become stronger is to free Ileena from her forced marriage. Although he knows that Elgretta sympathizes with him, she has told him quite bluntly that seeking retribution against the noble is wrong and not something she can be part of.

Plot Hook. While he is training, Terindor keeps his ear to the ground in the community for talk of passing adventurers, particularly those who don't care about breaking the rules but are still fundamentally good at heart. If he hears of the characters' deeds, he approaches them at his first opportunity and expresses his desire to help his sister out of her predicament. Terindor has nothing to give the characters in payment but promises to help them enchant their gear when he becomes a more powerful wizard. If the characters seem about to refuse his request, he offers them the services of Elgretta—a promise that he knows might cause him a lot of trouble in the future.

XELASORA

"Master Dramothir will be with you shortly. Just be sure to mind your manners and don't put any dirt on the furniture."

Xelasora (LN dragonborn) is a graceful dragonborn in her late teens with mottled blue and green scales, four short horns that sweep back from her brow, and large amber eyes. She also has a large, reddish birthmark on her left shoulder that she normally keeps hidden under her robes. Xelasora is serious and humble and possesses a razor-sharp mind. Her master is Dramothir Galefnir (LG dwarf), who in addition to being a learned mage is also a renowned artisan and jeweler.

Background. The youngest of seven siblings, Xelasora lived a happy childhood, until the disastrous day when a red dragon attacked her community and killed the rest of her family. Mentally and emotionally scarred by the experience, Xelasora withdrew into herself after she was placed in an orphanage. She was ostracized by the other children in the orphanage, who were mostly human and considered her little more than a monster. Eventually, her pent-up emotions boiled over, and she unleashed some of her latent magic, setting fire to the clothing of one of her tormentors. This act led to her being expelled from the orphanage and forced to live on the streets, where she barely managed to stay alive by using her powers. Finally, when all hope seemed lost, Xelasora was taken in by the mage Dramothir, a dwarf who was intrigued by her intelligence and wit, and who was a natural sucker for a damsel in distress. Since then, Xelasora has done her best to be a dutiful apprentice and astutely handles Dramothir's busy schedule.

Personality. Xelasora is the best student that any wizard could hope for. She pursues both her magical studies and her mundane duties with the same rigorous attention to detail and is faultless in her execution. Her poised exterior, however, conceals a tormented soul. She constantly doubts herself and is worried that she could lose control of her sorcerous abilities if she becomes flustered or upset. The deaths of her family and the trouble she faced at the orphanage also still weigh on her heavily, and lately she has been plagued with dreams of fire and shadowy flying shapes, causing her to suddenly awaken in terror.

Plot Hook. Xelasora's magic comes from a bit of theft: in her younger days, she stole a set of scrolls from an ancient red dragon. The dragon still exists in the form of a terrible undead monstrosity, and it shares a strange link with the young dragonborn that allows the two of them to share dreams and images of their lives. By the time the characters enter the picture, the dragon is close to discovering Xelasora's location—and when it does so, it plans to slay her and recover its scrolls. Before this event comes to pass, the characters have a chance to stop it, either by destroying the dragon or somehow trapping it. Of course, defeating an undead dragon is no easy feat; depending on the characters' level, the GM might want to lead them up to the event with battles against the dragon's servants in the form of ghouls, trolls, vampires, and lesser evil dragons.

Magic Constructs

Golems and similar constructs are common features in a wizard's home. The most powerful mages have access to even more dangerous and complex automatons. Although golems are the most common of these constructs, they seldom have any individuality or personality, making them little more than defensive window-dressing.

Described below are several unique magic constructs, each with its own history and personality. Some of them are presented along with ready-made adventure scenarios.

Bzeldruin's Hundred

Spread out across the ground before you is an impressive collection of close to a hundred wooden miniatures. Most seem to be human, but you can see elves, dwarves, halflings, and even a few centaurs and other creatures scattered among them. As soon as you notice them, the figures begin to mimic your every movement.

Bzeldruin's Hundred is a group of one hundred wooden miniature figures created by the gnomish transmuter Bzeldruin Tiwaskar to represent his friends and family. Bzeldruin created them in celebration of his life's many achievements, but their creation was flawed, and they became inhabited by an evil spirit that sought to slay the very people they were modeled after. Unable to bring himself to destroy them, Bzeldruin tried to seal them away in the depths of his tower—and although he succeeded, the effort cost him his life. Now his tower lies deserted, enticing explorers with the promise of powerful magic if they can overcome the horrors within.

BZELDRUIN'S HUNDRED

Medium Swarm of Tiny Constructs, Neutral Evil

ARMOR CLASS 17 (natural armor)
HIT POINTS 88 (16d4 + 48)
SPEED 10 ft.

STR	DEX	CON	INT	WIS	CHA
1 (–5)	20 (+5)	16 (+3)	5 (–3)	10 (+0)	1 (–5)

DAMAGE IMMUNITIES cold, poison, psychic; bludgeoning, piercing, and slashing damage from nonmagical attacks
DAMAGE RESISTANCES fire, lightning, necrotic, radiant
CONDITION IMMUNITIES charmed, exhaustion, grappled, paralyzed, petrified, poisoned, stunned, restrained
SENSES darkvision 60 ft., passive Perception 10
LANGUAGES understands all languages but can't speak
CHALLENGE 7 (2,900 XP) **PROFICIENCY BONUS** +3

Immutable Form. Bzeldruin's Hundred is immune to any spell or effect that would alter its form.

Magic Resistance. Bzeldruin's Hundred has advantage on saving throws against spells and other magical effects.

Magic Weapons. Weapon attacks made by Bzeldruin's Hundred are magical.

Perfect Mimicry. The scores of individual figures that make up the swarm can perfectly mimic the actions of a single humanoid creature within 30 feet as an action. The swarm can mimic only one creature at a time, and the act of doing so grants the construct advantage on attack rolls and saving throws it makes involving the mimicked creature until the start of the construct's next turn.

Swarm. The swarm can occupy another creature's space and vice versa, and the swarm can move through any opening large enough for a Tiny figurine. The swarm can't regain hit points or gain temporary hit points.

Rejuvenation. If Bzeldruin's Hundred is reduced to 0 hit points, it collapses and disintegrates into dust, then re-forms 24 hours later in the same location with its full hit points. There is no way to stop this rejuvenation from happening, short of a carefully worded *wish* spell or divine intervention.

ACTIONS

Slam. *Melee Weapon Attack:* +8 to hit, reach 0 ft., one target in the swarm's space. *Hit:* 33 (8d6 + 5) bludgeoning damage. If the swarm is reduced to half its hit points or fewer, the bludgeoning damage from its slam attack is 19 (4d6 + 5).

Hindering Strike. Any Medium or smaller creature damaged by the swarm must make a DC 15 Strength saving throw. On a failed save, several of the figures cling to its body, reducing its speed by 10 feet and giving it disadvantage on Dexterity saving throws and Dexterity checks. A creature can repeat the save at the end of each of its turns, ending the effect on itself on a success.

LEOTHAR'S BUST

Floating before you is an exquisitely-crafted bust of a middle-aged man with a balding pate and a well-cropped beard. The bust appears to be constructed out of white marble. Its features are animated, and the entity is watching you with an expectant expression. Close behind the bust are two maids' uniforms, suspended in the air as though being worn by unseen creatures.

The archmage Leothar Wickerfrost is a noted explorer and adventurer, and as such is often away from home for long periods of time. During some of these absences, thieves raided his tower, and after he surprised them on his return, he ended up spending a lot of time cleaning up their corpses. To rid himself of this chore, the wizard decided to create the perfect servant, a bust in his own magnificent image endowed with magical power.

Leothar's bust shares many traits with its creator. It has the same haughty and egomaniacal attitude and looks down on those who cannot wield magic. The construct is scrupulous in its duties and is in command of the tower's many servants, including a pair of modified unseen servants wearing maid outfits. Leothar's bust welcomes visitors with the same abrasive manner its creator displays, whether they are legitimate guests or intruders, but will not take hostile action against creatures until it can discern the details of their intentions.

LEOTHAR'S BUST

Tiny Construct, Lawful Neutral

ARMOR CLASS 16 (natural armor)
HIT POINTS 42 (12d4 + 12)
SPEED 5 ft., fly 40 ft. (hover)

STR	DEX	CON	INT	WIS	CHA
8 (−1)	16 (+3)	12 (+1)	18 (+4)	10 (+0)	8 (−1)

SAVING THROWS Dex +5, Int +6
SKILLS Arcana +6, History +6, Investigation +6
DAMAGE IMMUNITIES poison, psychic
DAMAGE RESISTANCES cold, fire, lightning; bludgeoning, piercing, and slashing damage from nonmagical attacks
CONDITION IMMUNITIES charmed, exhaustion, frightened, paralyzed, petrified, poisoned, stunned
SENSES darkvision 60 ft., passive Perception 10
LANGUAGES Common, Draconic, Elvish
CHALLENGE 3 (700 XP)   **PROFICIENCY BONUS** +2

Magic Resistance. The bust has advantage on saving throws against spells and other magical effects.

ACTIONS

Multiattack. The bust makes two Arcane Ray or Paralysis Ray attacks or a single Slam attack.

Slam. *Melee Weapon Attack:* +1 to hit, reach 5 ft., one target. *Hit:* 4 (1d4 + 2) bludgeoning damage.

Arcane Ray. *Ranged Weapon Attack:* +5 to hit, range 120 ft., one target. *Hit:* 14 (4d4 + 4) force damage.

Paralysis Ray. *Ranged Weapon Attack:* +5 to hit, range 60 ft., one target. *Hit:* The target must succeed on a DC 15 Constitution saving throw or be paralyzed for 1 minute. A creature can repeat this save at the end of each of its turns, ending the effect on itself on a success.

Spellcasting. The bust casts one of the following spells, using Intelligence as the spellcasting ability (spell save DC 14):

At will: *light, mending, prestidigitation*
5/day each: *detect magic, floating disk*
3/day each: *knock, suggestion*
1/day each: *fear, sending*

NISRUEL'S COACHFLY

This long, narrow contraption resembles a clockwork dragonfly that's larger than a horse. It is fashioned from silver and lapis lazuli, with panes of delicate-looking multicolored stained glass for wings. The back of the construct contains a hollow that looks like it could hold one or more occupants.

Decades ago, the noble half-elf wizard Nisruel created a beautiful clockwork construct fashioned after the enormous dragonflies of her marshy homeland. Though she was usually content to teleport when she wanted to go somewhere, sometimes Nisruel wanted to travel in style—so she crafted this construct to impress her friends and others in the elven court. Word of her wondrous carriage spread throughout the land shortly after she revealed it, and Nisruel enjoyed receiving recognition for her work.

Sadly, her fame also drew the ire of her rival, the sorceress Ymelda, who lured Nisruel and her construct into the web of a gargantuan spider before ambushing the wizard with foul magic. Both Nisruel and Ymelda died in this struggle, but Nisruel's construct survived intact, and it still lies caught up in the webs of the great arachnid, awaiting rescue.

NISRUEL'S COACHFLY

Large Construct, Unaligned

ARMOR CLASS 15 (natural armor)
HIT POINTS 60 (8d10 + 16)
SPEED 20 ft., fly 80 ft.

STR	DEX	CON	INT	WIS	CHA
12 (+1)	18 (+4)	14 (+2)	3 (−4)	10 (+0)	1 (−5)

SKILLS Perception +4
DAMAGE IMMUNITIES poison, psychic, radiant
CONDITION IMMUNITIES charmed, exhaustion, frightened, paralyzed, petrified, poisoned, stunned
SENSES darkvision 90 ft., passive Perception 14
LANGUAGES understands Common and Elvish but can't speak
CHALLENGE 2 (450 XP)   **PROFICIENCY BONUS** +2

Compartment. One Medium creature, two Small creatures, or four Tiny creatures can comfortably fit inside the compartment at the rear of the coachfly. A creature inside the compartment is protected from the effects of wind, rain, and snow, and can share any spell it casts on itself with the coachfly if the spell also affects constructs. A creature can enter or leave the compartment as an action but cannot fall out even if the coachfly is upside down and has advantage on grapple checks to avoid being dragged out. Creatures in the compartment also have total cover against all attacks, though if the coachfly fails a saving throw against an area attack that deals damage, those in the compartment take half as much damage. If the coachfly is destroyed, occupants are ejected into an unoccupied space within 5 feet of it.

An occupant of the compartment can direct the coachfly to move and to make attacks against a target within range. Only one occupant can direct the coachfly in each round, even if it has multiple occupants. If the coachfly is not being controlled, it moves and attacks only to defend itself.

Immutable Form. The coachfly is immune to any spell or effect that would alter its form.

Magic Resistance. The coachfly has advantage on saving throws against spells and other magical effects.

ACTIONS

Multiattack. The coachfly makes two Light Ray attacks.

Light Ray. *Ranged Spell Attack:* +6 to hit, range 120 ft., one target. *Hit:* 13 (2d8 + 4) radiant damage. A creature struck by the ray must also make a successful DC 14 Constitution saving throw or be blinded until the end of its next turn.

SIVVAR'S WRITING DESK

This large ebony writing table has glossy brass fittings and a broad, flat top, dangling from which is a thin brass chain. Carved at the end of the desk's wooden legs are the claws of some sort of beast. As you approach, these claws animate and paw menacingly at the ground.

Over a century ago, the wizard Sivvar was counted among the most learned historians of his age. So respected was he that people came from miles around to ask him for help in tracking down lost relics, forgotten tombs, and ancient ruins. The knowledge he amassed came with a price, though, and Sivvar eventually gathered many secrets that were too dangerous to be shared openly. To protect himself and his works, Sivvar fashioned a construct out of his writing desk. Not only would this piece of simple furniture store the knowledge he had gathered, but it would also protect itself from harm if someone tried to take the contents by force.

Recently, after years of foiling or dodging enemy attacks, Sivvar suddenly vanished, leaving his desk and other worldly possessions in the care of his sister's granddaughter, Emelia Nightmace. Emelia knows that her great-uncle's mansion and possessions are potentially dangerous and seeks the help of adventurers to enter the place and catalogue its contents. What she doesn't know is that Sivvar is still alive somewhere inside the mansion, and his desk holds the key to contacting him.

SIVVAR'S WRITING DESK

Medium Construct, Unaligned

ARMOR CLASS 14 (natural armor)
HIT POINTS 47 (5d8 + 25)
SPEED 40 ft.

STR	DEX	CON	INT	WIS	CHA
18 (+4)	12 (+1)	20 (+5)	2 (–4)	8 (–1)	1 (–5)

SAVING THROWS Str +7
DAMAGE IMMUNITIES poison, psychic
DAMAGE RESISTANCES cold, necrotic; bludgeoning, piercing, and slashing damage from nonmagical attacks
CONDITION IMMUNITIES blinded, charmed, deafened, exhaustion, frightened, paralyzed, petrified, poisoned, stunned
SENSES tremorsense 60 ft. (blind beyond this radius), passive Perception 9
LANGUAGES understands Common but can't speak
CHALLENGE 1 (200 XP)   **PROFICIENCY BONUS** +2

Antimagic Susceptibility. The desk is incapacitated while in the area of an *antimagic field*. If targeted by *dispel magic*, the desk must succeed on a Constitution saving throw against the caster's spell save DC or become inanimate for 1 minute.

False Appearance. While the desk remains motionless, it is indistinguishable from a normal writing desk.

Immutable Form. The desk is immune to any spell or effect that would alter its form.

Locked Drawers. The drawers of the desk are locked by a modified version of the *arcane lock* spell. The desk opens its drawers when someone speaks the appropriate command word. If someone tries to open the drawers without the correct password, the desk animates and attacks.

ACTIONS

Multiattack. The desk makes two Claw attacks. If the desk hits the same target with both claw attacks, it rakes the victim for an extra 10 (3d6) slashing damage.

Claw. *Melee Weapon Attack:* +7 to hit, reach 5 ft., one target. *Hit:* 14 (3d6 + 4) slashing damage.

REACTIONS

Desperate Escape (1/day). The desk can use *dimension door* as a bonus action. It uses this ability only when reduced to 10 hit points or fewer.

FAMILIAR TERRITORY

Although the list of available familiars in the standard rules is sufficient for most campaigns, some players and GMs might enjoy using an unusual creature that has features not found in other familiars.

To determine what familiar an NPC spellcaster might have, the GM can roll on one of the tables in this section or select a creature. Players can also use these tables to choose familiars for their characters, with the GM's approval. (Of course, any creature that can be a familiar must also exist in the world on its own.)

The familiars presented here are of two basic kinds: standard familiars, which function the same as other beasts that serve the caster of the *find familiar* spell, and variant familiars, each of which is an intelligent creature that offers a special benefit to its master.

Common Traits

As stated in the *find familiar* spell, each of these creatures gains the celestial, fey, or fiend type (spellcaster's choice) when it becomes a familiar. Also, as noted in the spell, a familiar can't attack (though it can deliver a touch spell on behalf of its master). The stat blocks in this section include information on attacks because it might come into play if any of these creatures are encountered as monsters in their own right, or perhaps as allies of the player characters.

STANDARD FAMILIARS

With the GM's consent, any of the beasts described in this section can be chosen by a character who casts the *find familiar* spell. These creatures might also be encountered as the familiars of NPC spellcasters.

STANDARD FAMILIARS

d12	Standard Familiar	d12	Standard Familiar
1	Archaeopteryx	7	Parrot
2	Carrion crow	8	Platypus
3	Catfish shark	9	Shocker lizard
4	Goldbug	10	Tortoise
5	Hedgehog	11	Tsuchinoko
6	Mongoose	12	Wharfling

Archaeopteryx

A prehistoric bird native to warm climates the archaeopteryx makes a faithful familiar.

ARCHAEOPTERYX

Tiny Beast, Unaligned

ARMOR CLASS 12 (natural armor)
HIT POINTS 7 (3d4)
SPEED 5 ft., fly 50 ft.

STR	DEX	CON	INT	WIS	CHA
6 (−2)	13 (+1)	10 (+0)	2 (−4)	14 (+2)	6 (−2)

SENSES passive Perception 12
LANGUAGES —
CHALLENGE 1/4 (50 XP)   **PROFICIENCY BONUS** +2

Flyby. The archaeopteryx doesn't provoke opportunity attacks when it flies out of an enemy's reach.

ACTIONS

Multiattack. The archaeopteryx makes two attacks: one with its Beak and one with its Talons.

Beak. *Melee Weapon Attack:* +3 to hit, reach 5 ft., one target. *Hit:* 3 (1d4 + 1) piercing damage.

Talons. *Melee Weapon Attack:* +3 to hit, reach 5 ft., one target. *Hit:* 3 (1d4 + 1) slashing damage.

Carrion Crow

Feasting on the hearts of fallen evil warriors on battlefields has corrupted these crows. They resemble normal crows, but they are easily distinguished by their rust-colored, barbed beaks and a patch of feathers on their breasts of the same color. Sometimes, carrion crows use their mimicry to lure animals and people into danger, in hopes of having more dead meat on which to feast.

Evil spellcasters find carrion crows to be capable familiars. The creatures are happy to serve a master if they are provided with a steady supply of dead flesh and blood.

CARRION CROW

Tiny Beast, Unaligned

ARMOR CLASS 13
HIT POINTS 21 (6d4 + 6)
SPEED 10 ft., fly 50 ft.

STR	DEX	CON	INT	WIS	CHA
5 (−3)	16 (+3)	13 (+1)	2 (−4)	13 (+1)	10 (+0)

SKILLS Perception +3, Stealth +5
DAMAGE RESISTANCES poison
CONDITION IMMUNITIES poisoned
SENSES passive Perception 13
LANGUAGES understands Common but can't speak
CHALLENGE 1/2 (100 XP)   **PROFICIENCY BONUS** +2

Mimicry. The carrion crow can mimic complex sounds it has heard, such as a specific person speaking, a bugle call, or various animal calls. A creature that hears the sounds can tell they are imitations with a successful DC 13 Wisdom (Insight) check.

ACTIONS

Beak. *Melee Weapon Attack:* +5 to hit, reach 5 ft., one target. *Hit:* 1 piercing damage and the target must succeed on a DC 13 Constitution saving throw or lose 1 hit point each round from blood loss until it receives magical healing or until the target or an ally succeeds on a DC 10 Wisdom check to stop the bleeding.

Shriek. As an action, the carrion crow emits a raucous caw. Any creature other than a carrion crow within 10 feet of the carrion crow must succeed on a DC 13 Wisdom saving throw or be frightened until the start of the creature's next turn. On a successful saving throw, a creature is immune to the shriek of any carrion crow for 1 hour.

Catfish Shark

The catfish shark lives in deep water. Most species are less than 1 foot long and range from pale orange to silvery white in color. Some are also bioluminescent. The catfish shark is an ideal familiar for a spellcaster who operates underwater.

CATFISH SHARK

Tiny Beast, Unaligned

ARMOR CLASS 11
HIT POINTS 2 (1d4)
SPEED 0 ft., swim 40 ft.

STR	DEX	CON	INT	WIS	CHA
3 (–4)	12 (+1)	10 (+0)	1 (–5)	8 (–1)	2 (–4)

SKILLS Stealth +3
SENSES darkvision 90 ft., passive Perception 9
LANGUAGES —
CHALLENGE 0 (10 XP) **PROFICIENCY BONUS** +2

Bioluminescent. The catfish shark can cause its body to glow with orange light, providing dim light in a 5-foot radius.

Water Breathing. The catfish shark can breathe only underwater.

ACTIONS

Bite. *Melee Weapon Attack:* +0 to hit, reach 5 ft., one target. *Hit:* 1 piercing damage.

Goldbug

The goldbug is a strange sort of insect, a creature whose round, flat body resembles a gold coin. This "disguise" helps goldbugs get close to their prized food source: gold. When placed in a pouch or chest along with the gold coins it resembles, a goldbug will happily devour the coins at the rate of one per day.

Goldbugs live underground near veins of gold and are common in areas where gold is used as coinage and in art objects.

GOLDBUG

Tiny Beast, Unaligned

ARMOR CLASS 15 (natural armor)
HIT POINTS 18 (4d4 + 8)
SPEED 10 ft., climb 10 ft.

STR	DEX	CON	INT	WIS	CHA
3 (–4)	14 (+2)	15 (+2)	1 (–5)	10 (+0)	6 (–2)

SENSES blindsight 20 ft., passive Perception 13
LANGUAGES understands Common but can't speak
CHALLENGE 0 (10 XP) **PROFICIENCY BONUS** +2

False Appearance. While the goldbug remains motionless, it is indistinguishable from a gold coin.

Scent Gold. The goldbug can pinpoint, by scent, the location of gold within 60 feet of it.

ACTIONS

Bite. *Melee Weapon Attack:* +4 to hit, reach 5 ft., one target. *Hit:* 1 piercing and 1 poison damage, and the target must succeed on a DC 11 Constitution saving throw or be poisoned for 1 hour.

Hedgehog

The hedgehog is a small terrestrial mammal that eats insects and worms. Its body is covered in hollow spines that it can extend as a defense mechanism. Hedgehogs are often used as familiars by gnomes and halflings.

HEDGEHOG

Tiny Beast, Unaligned

ARMOR CLASS 11 (natural armor)
HIT POINTS 1 (1d4 – 1)
SPEED 20 ft., burrow 5 ft.

STR	DEX	CON	INT	WIS	CHA
3 (–4)	10 (+0)	8 (–1)	2 (–4)	12 (+1)	5 (–3)

SKILLS Stealth +2
SENSES darkvision 60 ft., passive Perception 11
LANGUAGES —
CHALLENGE 0 (10 XP) **PROFICIENCY BONUS** +2

Keen Hearing and Smell. The hedgehog has advantage on Wisdom (Perception) checks that rely on hearing or smell.

REACTIONS

Spiked Roll. As a reaction, a hedgehog can roll into a spiny ball to protect its body from harm. The hedgehog uses this reaction whenever a creature makes an attack roll against it but before the roll takes place. A creature that attacks the hedgehog must succeed on a DC 10 Dexterity check or take 1 piercing damage. A creature that uses a reach weapon or a ranged weapon against the hedgehog is unaffected by this ability.

Mongoose

The mongoose is a sleek mammal with tiny, sharp teeth that lives in forests and deserts and eats insects, eggs, and small lizards. The mongoose is a fierce familiar and has even been known to kill snakes.

MONGOOSE

Tiny Beast, Unaligned

ARMOR CLASS 13
HIT POINTS 2 (1d4)
SPEED 30 ft., burrow 5 ft.

STR	DEX	CON	INT	WIS	CHA
4 (–3)	14 (+2)	10 (+0)	2 (–4)	10 (+0)	6 (–2)

SKILLS Perception +2, Stealth +4
SENSES darkvision 60 ft., passive Perception 10
LANGUAGES —
CHALLENGE 0 (10 XP)   **PROFICIENCY BONUS** +2

Keen Hearing and Smell. The mongoose has advantage on Wisdom (Perception) checks that rely on hearing or smell.

Venom Resistance. The mongoose has advantage on saving throws against the poison of snakes and snakelike monsters.

ACTIONS

Bite. *Melee Weapon Attack:* +1 to hit, reach 5 ft., one target. *Hit:* 1 piercing damage.

Parrot

This bird is noted for its colorful plumage and boisterous disposition. Parrots are favored as familiars by spellcasters who like bright and flashy magic.

PARROT

Tiny Beast, Unaligned

ARMOR CLASS 12
HIT POINTS 1 (1d4 – 1)
SPEED 10 ft., fly 50 ft.

STR	DEX	CON	INT	WIS	CHA
2 (–4)	14 (+2)	8 (–1)	2 (–4)	12 (+1)	6 (–2)

SKILLS Perception +3
SENSES passive Perception 13
LANGUAGES —
CHALLENGE 0 (10 XP)   **PROFICIENCY BONUS** +2

Mimicry. The parrot can mimic simple sounds it has heard, such as a person whispering, a baby crying, or an animal chittering. A creature that hears the sounds can tell they are imitations with a successful DC 10 Wisdom (Insight) check.

ACTIONS

Beak. *Melee Weapon Attack:* +4 to hit, reach 5 ft., one target. *Hit:* 1 piercing damage.

Platypus

The platypus is a water-dwelling mammal that feeds on worms and other creatures living in the mud of streams and rivers. Because of its odd appearance, the platypus is often taken as a familiar by transmuters.

PLATYPUS

Tiny Beast, Unaligned

ARMOR CLASS 11
HIT POINTS 1 (1d4 – 1)
SPEED 10 ft., swim 40 ft.

STR	DEX	CON	INT	WIS	CHA
3 (–4)	12 (+1)	8 (–1)	2 (–4)	12 (+1)	5 (–3)

SENSES blindsight 90 ft., passive Perception 11
LANGUAGES —
CHALLENGE 1/8 (25 XP)   **PROFICIENCY BONUS** +2

ACTIONS

Spur. *Melee Weapon Attack:* +0 to hit, reach 5 ft., one target. *Hit:* 1 piercing damage. A creature struck by the spur must succeed on a DC 11 Constitution saving throw or be poisoned for 1 minute. The creature can repeat the saving throw at the end of each of its turns, ending the effect on a success.

Shocker Lizard

A social beast that dwells in swamps and forests, the shocker lizard can be a suitable familiar for a wizard who specializes in lightning or storm magic. Taking a shocker lizard as a familiar requires an additional material component of 50 gp worth of fulgurite when the *find familiar* spell is cast.

SHOCKER LIZARD

Small Beast, Unaligned

ARMOR CLASS 14 (natural armor)
HIT POINTS 16 (3d8 + 3)
SPEED 40 ft., climb 20 ft., swim 20 ft.

STR	DEX	CON	INT	WIS	CHA
8 (–1)	15 (+2)	13 (+1)	2 (–4)	8 (–1)	3 (–4)

SENSES darkvision 30 ft., passive Perception 13

CHAPTER 3 SPELLCASTING ALLIES

LANGUAGES —

CHALLENGE 1/2 (100 XP)   **PROFICIENCY BONUS** +2

Electricity Sense. The shocker lizard automatically detects any electrical discharge within 100 feet.

Shock. A shocker lizard's body generates a potent charge of electricity. A creature that touches the lizard or makes a successful melee attack against it must make a DC 10 Dexterity saving throw, taking 3 (1d4) lightning damage on a failed save, or half as much damage on a successful one. If other shocker lizards are within 20 feet, the fields augment each other to a maximum of 24 (8d4) lightning damage.

ACTIONS

Bite. *Melee Weapon Attack:* +4 to hit, reach 5 ft., one target. *Hit:* 4 (1d4 + 2) piercing damage and the target must make a DC 10 Dexterity saving throw, taking 2 (1d4) lightning damage on a failed save, or half as much damage on a successful one.

Tortoise

The tortoise is a reptile with a thick shell on its back that grants it superior armor at the expense of speed. The tortoise is a popular familiar among abjurers, dragonborn, and lizardfolk wizards, despite its ponderous movement.

TORTOISE

Tiny Beast, Unaligned

ARMOR CLASS 15 (natural armor)

HIT POINTS 1 (1d4 − 1)

SPEED 5 ft.

STR	DEX	CON	INT	WIS	CHA
3 (−4)	7 (−2)	8 (−1)	2 (−4)	10 (+0)	4 (−3)

SENSES darkvision 60 ft., passive Perception 10

LANGUAGES —

CHALLENGE 0 (10 XP)   **PROFICIENCY BONUS** +2

Keen Smell. The tortoise has advantage on Wisdom (Perception) checks that rely on smell.

Tsuchinoko

A snakelike creature with a fondness for alcohol that lurks in forests, the tsuchinoko is more capable than a typical standard familiar, and as such at least 50 gp worth of wine or spirits must be expended as part of the casting of the *find familiar* spell.

TSUCHINOKO

Tiny Beast, Unaligned

ARMOR CLASS 14

HIT POINTS 14 (4d4 + 4)

SPEED 30 ft.

STR	DEX	CON	INT	WIS	CHA
5 (−3)	18 (+4)	12 (+1)	2 (−4)	12 (+1)	5 (−3)

SKILLS Perception +3, Stealth +6

DAMAGE IMMUNITIES poison

CONDITION IMMUNITIES poisoned

SENSES blindsight 10 ft., passive Perception 13

LANGUAGES —

CHALLENGE 1/2 (100 XP)   **PROFICIENCY BONUS** +2

Keen Smell. The tsuchinoko has advantage on Wisdom (Perception) checks that rely on smell.

Plant Camouflage. The tsuchinoko has advantage on Dexterity (Stealth) checks it makes in any terrain with ample obscuring plant life.

Standing Leap. The tsuchinoko's long jump is up to 15 feet and its high jump is up to 5 feet, with or without a running start.

ACTIONS

Multiattack. The tsuchinoko makes two Leaping Bite attacks. The second attack is made with disadvantage and must be against the same target as the first.

Leaping Bite. *Melee Weapon Attack:* +6 to hit, reach 10 ft., one target. *Hit:* 1 piercing damage plus 5 (2d4) poison damage.

Hoop Formation. The tsuchinoko bites its tail, forming a hoop with its body. While in hoop formation, it has a walking speed of 60 feet and can't use its Leaping Bite. The tsuchinoko can end its Hoop Formation as a bonus action.

Wharfling

Tiny, doglike creatures with slippery, hairless skin and webbed claws, wharflings are occasionally chosen as familiars by spellcasters who are unconcerned about their personal appearance, who frequently engage in acts of larceny, or who dwell in watery conditions.

WHARFLING

Tiny Beast, Unaligned

ARMOR CLASS 13
HIT POINTS 6 (4d4 – 4)
SPEED 30 ft., climb 30 ft., swim 20 ft.

STR	DEX	CON	INT	WIS	CHA
4 (–3)	16 (+3)	8 (–1)	2 (–4)	12 (+1)	8 (–1)

SKILLS Perception +3, Sleight of Hand +5
SENSES darkvision 60 ft., passive Perception 13
LANGUAGES —
CHALLENGE 1/8 (25 XP) **PROFICIENCY BONUS** +2

ACTIONS

Bite. *Melee Weapon Attack:* +5 to hit, reach 5 ft., one target. *Hit:* 5 (1d4 + 3) piercing damage, and the target is grappled (escape DC 10). Until this grapple ends, the wharfling can't use its bite on another target. While the target is grappled, the wharfling's bite attack hits it automatically.

Pilfer. A wharfling that has an opponent grappled at the start of its turn can make a Dexterity (Sleight of Hand) check as a bonus action against a DC equal to 10 + the grappled target's Dexterity modifier. On a successful check, the wharfling steals a small metallic object from the target, and the theft is unnoticed if the check result equals or exceeds the target's passive Perception. A wharfling flees with its treasure.

VARIANT FAMILIARS

This section expands the roster of potential familiars to include several intelligent creatures with supernatural abilities. The relationship between the familiar and its master, and the benefits the master receives, resembles how the imp, the quasit, and the pseudodragon are presented as variant familiars in the standard rules.

If the GM allows the use of any of these variant familiars by player characters, it might or might not be necessary for the would-be master to start the process by casting *find familiar*. Either way, a variant familiar is an actual creature (not a spirit) that serves at its own discretion, obeying its master's commands only when doing so does not immediately bring it harm, and it will not hesitate to end the link with its master as a matter of self-preservation. Unlike standard familiars, a variant familiar does not disappear if it drops to 0 hit points; it simply dies or falls unconscious (GM's choice).

VARIANT FAMILIARS

d12	Variant Familiar	d12	Variant Familiar
1	Abyssal worm	7	Library automaton
2	Alkonost	8	Living shade
3	Crimson drake	9	Stryx
4	Infernal viper	10	Witchlight
5	Kuunganisha	11	Wolpertinger
6	Leonino	12	Zoog

Abyssal Worm

These creatures can be found in vast numbers in the lower planes, mostly providing fodder for demons and other denizens. Typically, an abyssal worm measures a foot to a foot and a half in length, its body gray in color, with mossy green and mustard yellow mottling. The worm's mouth is a round orifice ringed with sharp, needle-like teeth. The worm's skin exudes a slime that leaves a glistening trail in its path.

Evil spellcasters often choose the abyssal worm as a familiar as an intimidation tactic. The creature's disgusting appearance makes it an excellent tool for unnerving

VARIANT: CLOCKWORK FAMILIARS

A wizard who embraces clockwork magic can use the *find familiar* spell in a special way. A small clockwork device in the form of an animal (worth 10 gp) is substituted for the spell's usual material component. The device must resemble one of the allowable animals listed in the spell. When the casting is complete, the clockwork animates. It has the statistics of the chosen animal form, but is a construct, rather than a beast.

A clockwork familiar's form can be changed by rebuilding the clockwork device into a new form of animal and casting the spell again. If the familiar is destroyed, it can be rebuilt (in the same form or a new one) with the same components, if they are recovered; otherwise, 10 gp must be spent on replacement parts.

others, especially if they aren't hardened adventurers. Abyssal worms are happy to serve as familiars, so long as they get a steady diet of flesh and the chance to torment the living.

Familiar. If an abyssal worm agrees to serve another creature as a familiar, it forms a telepathic bond with its master. While the two are bonded, the master can sense what the abyssal worm senses, as long as they are within 1 mile of each other. While the abyssal worm is within 10 feet of its master, the master gains the worm's immunity to poison damage and the poisoned condition. If its master causes it physical harm, or if it simply chooses to do so, the abyssal worm will abandon its service as a familiar, breaking the telepathic bond.

ABYSSAL WORM

Tiny Monstrosity, Neutral Evil

ARMOR CLASS 13
HIT POINTS 21 (6d4 + 6)
SPEED 20 ft., burrow 20 ft.

STR	DEX	CON	INT	WIS	CHA
7 (−2)	16 (+3)	13 (+1)	4 (−3)	12 (+1)	7 (−2)

SKILLS Perception +3, Stealth +5
DAMAGE RESISTANCES cold, fire, bludgeoning from nonmagical weapons
DAMAGE IMMUNITIES poison
CONDITION IMMUNITIES poisoned
SENSES blindsight 30 ft., passive Perception 13
LANGUAGES —
CHALLENGE 1/4 (50 XP)   **PROFICIENCY BONUS** +2

Stench. Any creature other than an abyssal worm that starts its turn within 5 feet of the abyssal worm must succeed on a DC 13 Constitution saving throw or be poisoned until the start of the creature's next turn. On a successful saving throw, the creature is immune to the stench of all abyssal worms for 1 hour.

ACTIONS

Bite. *Melee Weapon Attack:* +5 to hit, 5 ft. reach, one target. *Hit:* 5 (1d4 + 3) piercing damage plus 1 poison damage, and the abyssal worm attaches to the target. While attached, the abyssal worm doesn't attack. Instead, at the start of the abyssal worm's turn, the target loses 5 (1d4 + 3) hit points due to blood loss and also takes 1 poison damage.

The abyssal worm can detach itself by spending 5 feet of movement. It does so after draining 10 hit points of blood from its target or when the target dies. A creature, including the target, can use an action to detach the abyssal worm.

Alkonost

The alkonost is a graceful bird that has the face of a beautiful man or woman. Flocks of these creatures lurk on the edges of dark clouds. Their plumage is the color of storms, ranging from light gray to dark slate with a shimmer of green or violet hue on the eldest.

Familiar. If an alkonost agrees to serve another creature as a familiar, it forms a telepathic bond with its master. While the two are bonded, the master can sense what the alkonost senses, as long as they are within 1 mile of each other. While the alkonost is within 10 feet of its master, the master shares the alkonost's One with Wind trait. If its master causes it physical harm, or if it simply chooses to do so, the alkonost will abandon its service as a familiar, ending the telepathic bond.

ALKONOST

Small Monstrosity, Neutral

ARMOR CLASS 12
HIT POINTS 17 (5d6)
SPEED 20 ft., fly 40 ft.

STR	DEX	CON	INT	WIS	CHA
11 (+0)	14 (+2)	10 (+0)	7 (−2)	14 (+2)	13 (+1)

SENSES darkvision 60 ft., passive Perception 12
DAMAGE RESISTANCES lightning
LANGUAGES Common
CHALLENGE 1/2 (100 XP)   **PROFICIENCY BONUS** +2

One with Wind. An alkonost is immune to the effects of magical and natural wind, including effects that would force it to move, would impose disadvantage on Wisdom (Perception) checks, or would force it to land when flying.

ACTIONS

Claws. *Melee Weapon Attack:* +4 to hit, reach 5 ft., one creature. *Hit:* 4 (1d4 + 2) slashing damage. The alkonost's weapon attacks deal an extra 2 (1d4) lightning damage if it is within 1 mile of a lightning storm.

Charged Melody (Recharge 6). The alkonost sings a beautiful melody. Each creature within 30 feet of it that can hear the melody must succeed on a DC 12 Charisma saving throw or take 7 (2d6) lightning damage the next time it moves.

Crimson Drake

An evil drake that resembles a pseudodragon, the crimson drake is a popular familiar among evil evokers, particularly those who favor fire magic. An evil warlock who has the Pact of the Chain can acquire a crimson drake companion in place of a quasit, while an evil wizard can procure the services of one through treats and sacrifices worth at least 150 gp.

Familiar. If a crimson drake agrees to serve as a familiar, it forms a telepathic bond with its master. While the two are bonded, the master can sense what the crimson drake senses, as long as they are within 1 mile of each other. While the crimson drake is within 10 feet of its master, the master shares the drake's Magic Resistance trait. At any time and for any reason, the drake can abandon its service as a familiar, ending the telepathic bond.

CRIMSON DRAKE

Tiny Dragon, Chaotic Evil

ARMOR CLASS 14 (natural armor)
HIT POINTS 54 (12d4 + 24)
SPEED 15 ft., fly 80 ft.

STR	DEX	CON	INT	WIS	CHA
10 (+0)	14 (+2)	14 (+2)	8 (–1)	9 (–1)	14 (+2)

SAVING THROWS Dex +4
SKILLS Acrobatics +4, Perception +1
DAMAGE IMMUNITIES fire
CONDITION IMMUNITIES paralyzed, unconscious
SENSES darkvision 60 ft., passive Perception 11
LANGUAGES Common, Draconic, telepathy 60 ft.
CHALLENGE 1 (200 XP)   **PROFICIENCY BONUS** +2

Magic Resistance. The drake has advantage on saving throws against spells and other magical effects.

ACTIONS

Multiattack. The crimson drake makes one bite attack and one stinger attack.

Bite. *Melee Weapon Attack:* +4 to hit, reach 5 ft., one target. *Hit:* 5 (1d6 + 2) piercing damage plus 4 (1d8) fire damage.

Stinger. *Melee Weapon Attack:* +4 to hit, reach 5 ft., one target. *Hit:* 4 (1d4 + 2) piercing damage, and the target must succeed on a DC 13 Constitution saving throw or become poisoned for 1 hour. If the saving throw fails by 5 or more, the target takes 2 (1d4) poison damage at the start of each of its turns for 3 rounds. A target poisoned in this way can the saving throw at the end of each of its turns, ending the condition on a success.

Breath Weapon (Recharge 6). The drake exhales fire in a 15-foot cone. Each target in that cone takes 18 (4d8) fire damage, or half as much damage with a successful DC 12 Dexterity saving throw.

Infernal Viper

Infernal vipers resemble earthly vipers, but for the red and black patterns of their scales. They roam the Hells, tormenting the damned souls with their painful bites and burning venom. They have a dim intelligence that makes them more dangerous than common snakes.

Familiar. If an infernal viper agrees to serve another creature as a familiar, it forms a telepathic bond with its master. While the two are bonded, the master can sense what the infernal viper senses, as long as they are within 1 mile of each other. While the infernal viper is within 10 feet of its master, the master gains the viper's resistance to fire damage. If its master causes it physical harm, or if it simply chooses to do so, the viper will abandon its service as a familiar, breaking the telepathic bond.

INFERNAL VIPER

Tiny Fiend, Neutral Evil

ARMOR CLASS 13
HIT POINTS 28 (8d4 + 8)
SPEED 30 ft., swim 30 ft.

STR	DEX	CON	INT	WIS	CHA
5 (–3)	17 (+3)	13 (+1)	3 (–4)	12 (+1)	6 (–2)

SKILLS Perception +3, Stealth +5
DAMAGE RESISTANCES fire
SENSES blindsight 10 ft., passive Perception 13
LANGUAGES understands Infernal but can't speak
CHALLENGE 1/2 (100 XP)   **PROFICIENCY BONUS** +2

ACTIONS

Bite. *Melee Weapon Attack:* +5 to hit, reach 5 ft., one target. *Hit:* 5 (1d4 + 3) piercing damage; target must make a DC 13 Constitution saving throw, taking 5 (2d4) poison damage on a failed save, or half as much damage on a successful one.

CHAPTER 3 SPELLCASTING ALLIES

Kuunganisha

The kuunganisha is a type of fiend that appears to have been specifically created by the powers of villainy to serve as a familiar. An evil warlock who has the Pact of the Chain can summon a kuunganisha in place of a quasit or an imp, while a wizard can acquire one only by casting a *planar binding* spell (though the kuunganisha serves the wizard permanently in this case, rather than for just 24 hours).

Familiar. If a kuunganisha agrees to serve another creature as a familiar, it forms a telepathic bond with its master. While the two are bonded, the master can sense what the kuunganisha senses, as long as they are within 1 mile of each other. While the kuunganisha is within 10 feet of its master, the master gains the kuunganisha's Magic Resistance trait. If its master causes it physical harm, or if it simply chooses to do so, the kuunganisha will abandon its service as a familiar, breaking the telepathic bond.

KUUNGANISHA

Small Fiend, Any Evil

ARMOR CLASS 13
HIT POINTS 17 (5d6)
SPEED 20 ft., fly 40 ft.

STR	DEX	CON	INT	WIS	CHA
6 (–2)	17 (+3)	11 (+0)	10 (+0)	12 (+1)	13 (+1)

SKILLS Insight +3, Stealth +5
DAMAGE RESISTANCES fire, lightning; bludgeoning, piercing, and slashing from nonmagical attacks not made with silver
DAMAGE IMMUNITIES poison
CONDITION IMMUNITIES poisoned
SENSES darkvision 120 ft., passive Perception 11
LANGUAGES Abyssal, Common, Infernal
CHALLENGE 2 (450 XP)   **PROFICIENCY BONUS** +2

Fiend Sight. Magical darkness doesn't impede the fiend's darkvision.

Magic Resistance. The kuunganisha has advantage on saving throws against spells and other magical effects.

Regeneration. The kuunganisha regains 1 hp at the start of its turn if it has at least 1 hp.

Will of the Master. The master of a kuunganisha familiar can cast a spell through the creature, using the fiend's senses to target the spell. The range limitations are treated as if the spell originated from the kuunganisha, not the master. The spell effect occurs on the kuunganisha's turn, though the master must cast the spell during the master's turn. Concentration spells must still be maintained by the master.

ACTIONS

Multiattack. The kuunganisha makes one Claw attack and one Bite attack.

Bite. *Melee Weapon Attack:* +5 to hit, reach 5 ft., one target. *Hit:* 5 (1d4 + 3) piercing damage, and the target must succeed on a DC 13 Constitution saving throw or take 5 (2d4) poison damage and become poisoned for 1 minute. The target can repeat the saving throw at the end of each of its turns, ending the effect on itself on a success.

Claw. *Melee Weapon Attack:* +5 to hit, reach 5 ft., one target. *Hit:* 8 (2d4 + 3) slashing damage.

Invisibility. The kuunganisha magically turns invisible until it attacks or until its concentration ends (as if concentrating on a spell). Any equipment the fiend wears or carries becomes invisible with it.

Leonino

Appearing as a wild cat with hawk-like wings, the leonino is a much sought-after familiar by elf wizards, particularly those who have an affinity for air or wind. Acquiring a leonino familiar requires the casting of the *find familiar* spell, with an additional offering of fine fish and at least 200 feet of dyed red yarn. Once the spell is cast, the wizard makes a Charisma check contested by the leonino's Charisma check. If the leonino wins the contest, the creature flies off and the wizard is hated and distrusted by all feline creatures for at least a month.

Familiar. If a leonino agrees to serve another creature as a familiar, it forms a telepathic bond with its master. While the two are bonded, the master can sense what the leonino senses, as long as they are within 1 mile of each other. While the leonino is within 10 feet of its master, the master gains the leonino's Evasion trait. If its master causes it physical harm, or if it simply chooses to do so, the leonino will abandon its service as a familiar, breaking the telepathic bond.

LEONINO

Tiny Beast, Unaligned

ARMOR CLASS 13
HIT POINTS 13 (3d4 + 6)
SPEED 30 ft., fly 40 ft.

STR	DEX	CON	INT	WIS	CHA
10 (+0)	16 (+3)	14 (+2)	8 (−1)	8 (−1)	12 (+1)

SAVING THROWS Wis +1, Dex +5
SKILLS Perception +1, Persuasion +3, Stealth +5
SENSES darkvision 30 ft., passive Perception 11
LANGUAGES Elvish
CHALLENGE 1/8 (25 XP) **PROFICIENCY BONUS** +2

Evasion. If the leonino is subjected to an effect that allows it to make a Dexterity saving throw to take only half damage, the leonino instead takes no damage if it succeeds on the saving throw, and only half damage if it fails.

Flyby. The leonino doesn't provoke opportunity attacks when it flies out of an enemy's reach.

Silent Wings. The flight of a leonino is especially silent and difficult to notice in forests and urban settings. It has advantage on Dexterity (Stealth) checks made while flying in these areas.

ACTIONS

Bite. *Melee Weapon Attack:* +5 to hit, reach 5 ft., one target. *Hit:* 5 (1d4 + 3) slashing damage. If this is the first time the leonino has hit the target within the past 24 hours, the target must succeed on a DC 10 Wisdom saving throw or be charmed by the leonino for 1 hour.

Library Automaton

These strange-looking constructs are unusually intelligent for creatures of their type and will sometimes serve a lawful or neutral spellcaster (though never a chaotic one) as a familiar.

Familiar. If a library automaton agrees to serve another creature as a familiar, it forms a telepathic bond with its master. While the two are bonded, the master can sense what the library automaton senses, as long as they are within 1 mile of each other. While the automaton is within 10 feet of its master, the master gains the automaton's immunity to poison damage and the poisoned condition. If its master causes it physical harm, or if it simply chooses to do so, the automaton will abandon its service as a familiar, breaking the telepathic bond.

LIBRARY AUTOMATON

Small Construct, Lawful Neutral

ARMOR CLASS 13 (natural armor)
HIT POINTS 7 (2d6)
SPEED 30 ft.

STR	DEX	CON	INT	WIS	CHA
8 (−1)	13 (+1)	10 (+0)	14 (+2)	12 (+1)	8 (−1)

SKILLS History +4, Investigation +4
DAMAGE IMMUNITIES poison
CONDITION IMMUNITIES charmed, poisoned
SENSES blindsight 60 ft., truesight 10 ft., passive Perception 11
LANGUAGES Common
CHALLENGE 1/2 (100 XP) **PROFICIENCY BONUS** +2

Extradimensional Book Repository. A small door on the chest of the library automaton opens into an extradimensional bookcase. This bookcase functions exactly as a *bag of holding*, except that it can store only written materials, such as books, scrolls, tomes, parchment, folders, notebooks, spellbooks, and the like.

CHAPTER 3 SPELLCASTING ALLIES

ACTIONS

Gaze of Confusion. The library automaton chooses one creature it can see within 40 feet. The target must succeed on a DC 12 Intelligence saving throw or take 9 (3d4 + 2) psychic damage and have disadvantage on Intelligence checks, saving throws, and attack rolls until the end of its next turn. On a successful save, the target takes half as much damage and suffers no other effect.

Bibliotelekinesis. This ability functions as the *mage hand* cantrip but can be used only on books, scrolls, maps, and other printed or written materials.

Living Shade

One of the rarer and more bizarre options for a familiar is the living shade, a fey creature often confused with undead creatures such as the shadow. Illusionists, wizards who specialize in shadow, and Pact of the Archfey warlocks are the most common masters of these creatures. Obtaining a living shade by casting the *find familiar* spell requires an additional material component: 50 gp worth of powdered jet.

Familiar. If a living shade agrees to serve another creature as a familiar, it forms a telepathic bond with its master. While the two are bonded, the master can sense what the living shade senses, as long as they are within 1 mile of each other. While the living shade is within 10 feet of its master, the master gains the living shade's Shadow Stealth trait. If its master causes it physical harm, or if it simply chooses to do so, the shade will abandon its service as a familiar, breaking the telepathic bond.

LIVING SHADE

Medium Fey, Neutral

ARMOR CLASS 12
HIT POINTS 18 (4d8)
SPEED 40 ft.

STR	DEX	CON	INT	WIS	CHA
6 (–2)	14 (+2)	10 (+0)	9 (–1)	10 (+0)	12 (+1)

SKILLS Stealth +6
DAMAGE VULNERABILITIES radiant
DAMAGE RESISTANCES acid, cold, fire, lightning, thunder; bludgeoning, piercing, and slashing from nonmagical attacks
DAMAGE IMMUNITIES necrotic, poison
CONDITION IMMUNITIES exhaustion, frightened, grappled, paralyzed, petrified, poisoned, prone, restrained
SENSES darkvision 60 ft., passive Perception 10
LANGUAGES understands Common but can't speak
CHALLENGE 1/4 (100 XP)   **PROFICIENCY BONUS** +2

Amorphous. The living shade can move through a space as narrow as 1 inch wide without squeezing.

Shadow Stealth. While in dim light or darkness, the living shade can take the Hide action as a bonus action.

Sunlight Sensitivity. While in sunlight, the living shade has disadvantage on attack rolls, as well as on Wisdom (Perception) checks that rely on sight.

ACTIONS

Shadow Touch. *Melee Weapon Attack:* +4 to hit, reach 5 ft., one target. *Hit:* 2 (1d4) cold damage.

Stryx

Owl-like monstrosities with vaguely human-like heads, stryx sometimes serve mortal spellcasters, particularly one of elven blood or one who has some tie to the fey, such as a half-elf enchanter or a warlock whose patron is the Archfey.

Familiar. If a stryx agrees to serve another creature as a familiar, it forms a telepathic bond with its master. While the two are bonded, the master can sense what the stryx senses, as long as they are within 1 mile of each other. While the stryx is within 10 feet of its master, the master senses, the benefit of the spell whenever the stryx casts *comprehend languages*. If its master causes it physical harm, or if it simply chooses to do so, the stryx will abandon its service as a familiar, breaking the telepathic bond.

STRYX

Tiny Monstrosity, Neutral

ARMOR CLASS 13
HIT POINTS 10 (4d4)
SPEED 10 ft., fly 60 ft.

STR	DEX	CON	INT	WIS	CHA
3 (–4)	17 (+3)	11 (+0)	8 (–1)	15 (+2)	6 (–2)

SKILLS Perception +4, Stealth +5
SENSES darkvision 120 ft., passive Perception 14
LANGUAGES Common, Elvish
CHALLENGE 1/8 (25 XP)   **PROFICIENCY BONUS** +2

False Appearance. Until a stryx speaks or opens its mouth, it is indistinguishable from a normal owl.

Flyby. The stryx doesn't provoke opportunity attacks when it flies out of an enemy's reach.

Innate Spellcasting. The stryx's innate spellcasting ability is Wisdom. It can cast the following spell, requiring no components:

3/day: *comprehend languages*

Keen Hearing and Sight. The stryx has advantage on Wisdom (Perception) checks that rely on hearing or sight.

ACTIONS

Talons. *Melee Weapon Attack:* +5 to hit, reach 5 ft., one target. *Hit:* 1 slashing damage.

Witchlight

These tiny constructs that resemble will-o-wisps are similar to homunculi, in that they are created (from pieces of quartz) and animated by their creators rather than brought into being by the spell. Conjurers and spellcasters who concentrate on illumination and light magic are the most common masters of these constructs.

Familiar. If a witchlight agrees to serve another creature as a familiar, it forms a telepathic bond with its master. While the two are bonded, the master can sense what the witchlight senses, as long as they are within 1 mile of each other. While the witchlight is within 10 feet of its master, the master gains the witchlight's immunity to poison damage and the poisoned condition. If its master causes it physical harm, or if it simply chooses to do so, the witchlight will abandon its service as a familiar, breaking the telepathic bond.

WITCHLIGHT

Tiny Construct, Neutral

ARMOR CLASS 14
HIT POINTS 10 (4d4)
SPEED fly 50 ft.

STR	DEX	CON	INT	WIS	CHA
1 (−5)	18 (+4)	10 (+0)	10 (+0)	13 (+1)	7 (−2)

SKILLS Perception +3
DAMAGE IMMUNITIES poison, radiant
CONDITION IMMUNITIES charmed, exhaustion, frightened, paralyzed, petrified, poisoned
SENSES darkvision 60 ft., passive Perception 13
LANGUAGES understands the language of its creator but can't speak
CHALLENGE 1/4 (50 XP)   **PROFICIENCY BONUS** +2

Dispel Magic Weakness. Casting *dispel magic* on a witchlight paralyzes it for 1d10 rounds.

Luminance. A witchlight normally glows as brightly as a torch. The creature can dim itself to the luminosity of a candle, but it cannot extinguish its light. Because of its glow, the witchlight has disadvantage on Dexterity (Stealth) checks.

Thin as Light. Although a witchlight is not incorporeal, it can pass through any opening that light can.

ACTIONS

Light Ray. *Ranged Weapon Attack:* +6 to hit, range 30 ft., one target. *Hit:* 6 (1d4 + 4) radiant damage.

Flash (Recharge 5–6). The witchlight emits a bright burst of light that causes any sighted creature within 30 feet to be blinded for 1d4 rounds unless it succeeds on a DC 10 Constitution saving throw.

Wolpertinger

Woodland-dwelling monstrosities, wolpertingers are popular familiars among gnomish wizards but will serve just about any spellcaster if they are treated with care and respect. Since these creatures are more powerful than a standard familiar, 25 gp worth of holly berries must also be expended as part of the casting of the *find familiar* spell.

Familiar. If a wolpertinger agrees to serve another creature as a familiar, it forms a telepathic bond with its master. While the two are bonded, the master can sense what the wolpertinger senses, as long as they are within 1 mile of each other. While the wolpertinger is within 10 feet of its master, the master gains the wolpertinger's Standing Leap trait. If its master causes it physical harm, or if it simply chooses to do so, the wolpertinger will abandon its service as a familiar, breaking the telepathic bond.

WOLPERTINGER

Tiny Monstrosity, Unaligned

ARMOR CLASS 13
HIT POINTS 9 (2d4 + 4)
SPEED 30 ft., burrow 10 ft., fly 30 ft.

STR	DEX	CON	INT	WIS	CHA
6 (−2)	16 (+3)	14 (+2)	5 (−3)	12 (+1)	6 (−2)

SENSES darkvision 60 ft., passive Perception 11
LANGUAGES —
CHALLENGE 1/4 (50 XP) **PROFICIENCY BONUS** +2

Charge. If the wolpertinger moves at least 10 feet straight toward a target and then hits it with a gore attack on the same turn, the target takes an extra 2 (1d4) piercing damage.

Flyby. The wolpertinger doesn't provoke an opportunity attack when it flies out of an enemy's reach.

Standing Leap. The wolpertinger's long jump is up to 20 feet and its high jump is up to 10 feet, with or without a running start.

ACTIONS

Bite. *Melee Weapon Attack:* +5 to hit, reach 5 ft., one target. *Hit:* 5 (1d4 + 3) piercing damage.

Gore. *Melee Weapon Attack:* +5 to hit, reach 5 ft., one target. *Hit:* 5 (1d4 + 3) piercing damage.

Keening (Recharge 6). The wolpertinger emits a piercing shriek. Each creature within 30 feet that can hear the wolpertinger must succeed on a DC 13 Constitution saving throw or be deafened for 1 minute. A beast with an Intelligence of 4 or lower that is in the area must also succeed on a DC 13 Wisdom saving throw or be frightened until the start of its next turn.

Zoog

Alien-looking creatures, zoogs are intelligent and will serve an evil-aligned spellcaster as a familiar with the correct sort of inducement (normally the sacrifice of a cat or other feline creature).

Familiar. If a zoog agrees to serve another creature as a familiar, it forms a telepathic bond with its master. While the two are bonded, the master can sense what the zoog senses, as long as they are within 1 mile of each other. If its master causes it physical harm, or if it simply chooses to do so, the zoog will abandon its service as a familiar, breaking the telepathic bond.

ZOOG

Tiny Aberration, Chaotic Evil

ARMOR CLASS 13
HIT POINTS 3 (1d4 + 1)
SPEED 30 ft., climb 30 ft.

STR	DEX	CON	INT	WIS	CHA
3 (−4)	16 (+3)	12 (+1)	11 (+0)	10 (+0)	8 (−1)

SKILLS Perception +2, Stealth +5
SENSES darkvision 60 ft., passive Perception 12
LANGUAGES Deep Speech, Void Speech
CHALLENGE 0 (10 XP) **PROFICIENCY BONUS** +2

ACTIONS

Bite. *Melee Weapon Attack:* +5 to hit, reach 5 ft., one target. *Hit:* 1 piercing damage.

SPELL LISTS

The spells in this book are all listed in this chapter, broken out by class, and the individual spell descriptions can be found in **Chapter 5**.

BARD SPELLS

Cantrips (0 Level)
Abhorrence (enchantment)
Acumen (transmutation)
Ale-dritch blast (conjuration)
Allure (transmutation)
Bewilderment (enchantment)
Brawn boost (transmutation)
Bright sparks (evocation)
Clockwork bolt (evocation)
Clumsiness (necromancy)
Dragon roar (evocation)
Encrypt / decrypt (alteration)
Enumerate (divination)
Exceptional wit (transmutation)
Fortitude (transmutation)
Frailty (necromancy)
Hamstring (evocation)
Hobble (evocation)
Impotence (necromancy)
Iron hand (abjuration)
Nimbleness (transmutation)
Obtuse (enchantment)
Quicken (transmutation)
Scribe (transmutation)
Telekinetic trip (transmutation)
Uncanny avoidance (divination)

1st Level
Adjust position (transmutation)
Agonizing mark (evocation)
Alter arrow's fortune (divination)
Anchoring rope (evocation)
Anticipate weakness (divination)
Auspicious warning (enchantment)
Avoid grievous injury (divination)
Blinding pain (enchantment)
Boreas's kiss (conjuration)
Candle's insight (divination)
Converse with dragon (divination)
Earworm melody (enchantment)
Fey glamor (illusion)
Foretell distraction (divination)

CHAPTER 4 SPELL LISTS | 125

Glamor of mundanity (illusion)
Gordolay's pleasant aroma (transmutation)
Hard heart (enchantment)
Heart to heart (necromancy)
Ill-fated word (divination)
Kobold's fury (transmutation)
Liar's gift (enchantment)
Nourishing repast (transmutation)
Pendulum (enchantment)
Screaming ray (evocation)
Seer's reaction (divination)
Slippery fingers (enchantment)
Telekinetic parry (evocation)
Tireless (transmutation)
Trick question (enchantment)
Undermine armor (transmutation)
Unluck on that (enchantment)
Unruly item (transmutation)
Withered sight (necromancy)

2nd Level

Anticipate attack (divination)
Ashen memories (divination)
Bad timing (divination)
Batsense (transmutation)
Beguiling bet (enchantment)
Bleating call (enchantment)
Chaotic vitality (conjuration)
Convoluted dictum (enchantment)
Detect dragons (divination)
Discern weakness (divination)
Distracting divination (divination)
Distraction cascade (divination)
Dome of silence (abjuration)
Enhance greed (divination)
Frenzied bolt (evocation)
Gift of resilience (enchantment)
Gift of luck (divination)
Glyph of shifting (conjuration)
Grain of truth (divination)
Heartache (enchantment)
Heartstop (necromancy)
Holy warding (abjuration)
Hypnotic missive (enchantment)
Indecision (enchantment)
Lacerate (evocation)
Power word kneel (enchantment)
Read object (divination)
Shade (abjuration)
Shifting the odds (divination)
Timely distraction (evocation)
Time step (conjuration)
Trench (transmutation)
Warning shout (divination)

3rd Level

Accelerate (transmutation)
Aura of listlessness (enchantment)
Calm of the storm (abjuration)
Catch the breath (transmutation)
Closing in (illusion)
Compelled movement (enchantment)
Curse of incompetence (necromancy)
Draconic majesty (transmutation)
Dragon's pride (enchantment)
Entropic damage field (transmutation)
Hero's steel (transmutation)
Illusory trap (illusion)
Iron mind (abjuration)
Laugh in the face of fear (abjuration)
Legion of rabid squirrels (conjuration)
Life sense (divination)
Opportunistic foresight (divination)
Outflanking boon (illusion)
Sidestep arrow (divination)
Sir Mittinz's move curse (transmutation)
Soothing chant (abjuration)
Soul borrowing (necromancy)
Surge dampener (abjuration)
Targeting foreknowledge (divination)
Throes of ecstasy (transmutation)
Tongue of sand (illusion)

4th Level

Abhorrent apparition (illusion)
Binding oath (necromancy)
Boreas's embrace (conjuration)
Chaotic form (transmutation)
Cursed gift (abjuration)
Distressing resonance (evocation)
Draconic senses (divination)
Energy foreknowledge (divination)
Fluctuating alignment (enchantment)
Fog of war (illusion)
Giant's jest (transmutation)
Harry (enchantment)
Inspiring speech (enchantment)
Keening wail (necromancy)
Lovesick (enchantment)
Raid the lair (abjuration)
Reposition (conjuration)
Reset (transmutation)
Sacrificial healing (necromancy)
Scale rot (necromancy)
Scry ambush (divination)
Sudden stampede (conjuration)
Wild shield (abjuration)

5th Level

Animated object swarm (conjuration)
Babble (enchantment)
Battle mind (divination)
Claws of the earth dragon (evocation)
Eidetic memory (transmutation)
Fey crown (abjuration)
Kiss of the succubus (necromancy)
Maim (necromancy)
Mass surge dampener (abjuration)
Recharge (evocation)
See beyond (divination)
Tongue tied (enchantment)

6th Level

Ally aegis (abjuration)
Chaotic world (illusion)
Claim lair (abjuration)
Extract knowledge (necromancy)
Misfortune (necromancy)
Time loop (transmutation)

7th Level

Alter time flow (transmutation)
Time jaunt (transmutation)
Uncontrollable transformation (transmutation)

8th Level

Paragon of chaos (transmutation)
Time jump (transmutation)

9th Level

Time in a bottle (transmutation)

CLERIC SPELLS

Cantrips (0 Level)

Abhorrence (enchantment)
Acumen (transmutation)
Allure (transmutation)
Benediction (abjuration)
Bewilderment (enchantment)
Bless the dead (abjuration)
Brawn boost (transmutation)
Bright sparks (evocation)
Caustic touch (evocation)
Clockwork bolt (evocation)
Clumsiness (necromancy)
Dark maw (necromancy)
Decay (necromancy)
Encrypt / decrypt (alteration)
Exceptional wit (transmutation)
Fist of iron (transmutation)
Fortitude (transmutation)
Frailty (necromancy)

Hobble (evocation)
Impotence (necromancy)
Iron hand (abjuration)
Luminous bolt (evocation)
Nimbleness (transmutation)
Obtuse (enchantment)
Quicken (transmutation)
Scribe (transmutation)
Shiver (evocation)

1st Level

Adjust position (transmutation)
Agonizing mark (evocation)
Alter arrow's fortune (divination)
Ancestor's strength (transmutation)
Angelic guardian (conjuration)
Anticipate weakness (divination)
Avoid grievous injury (divination)
Blood scarab (necromancy)
Bloody smite (necromancy)
Bolster undead (necromancy)
Converse with dragon (divination)
Deep breath (transmutation)
Find kin (divination)
Flurry (transmutation)
Foretell distraction (divination)
Freeze potion (transmutation)
Gird the spirit (abjuration)
Hobble mount (necromancy)
Hone blade (transmutation)
Insightful maneuver (divination)
Kareef's entreaty (abjuration)
Kobold's fury (transmutation)
Liar's gift (enchantment)
Life transference arrow (necromancy)
Mammon's avarice (divination)
Nourishing repast (transmutation)
Pendulum (enchantment)
Seer's reaction (divination)
Slippery fingers (enchantment)
Speak with inanimate object (divination)
Stanch (transmutation)
Strength of an ox (transmutation)
Twist the skein (enchantment)
Unluck on that (enchantment)
Withered sight (necromancy)

2nd Level

Animate ghoul (necromancy)
Anticipate attack (divination)
As you were (necromancy)
Ashen memories (divination)
Blessed halo (evocation)
Blessed rest (enchantment)
Blood lure (enchantment)
Cloak of fiendish menace (transmutation)
Conjure scarab swarm (conjuration)
Conjure spectral dead (conjuration)
Crushing trample (transmutation)
Distracting divination (divination)
Distraction cascade (divination)
Dome of silence (abjuration)
Enhance greed (divination)
Fire darts (evocation)
Furious hooves (transmutation)
Gift of luck (divination)
Grain of truth (divination)
Holy warding (abjuration)
Ice hammer (conjuration)
Intensify light (transmutation)
Lacerate (evocation)
Mantle of the brave (abjuration)
Power word kneel (enchantment)
Rotting corpse (necromancy)
Shade (abjuration)
Shared sacrifice (evocation)
Snow fort (conjuration)
Time step (conjuration)
Trench (transmutation)

Unholy defiance (necromancy)
Warning shout (divination)

3rd Level
Accelerate (transmutation)
Alone (enchantment)
Anticipate arcana (divination)
Aura of protection or destruction (abjuration)
Blade of wrath (evocation)
Bolstering brew (conjuration)
Bones of stone (transmutation)
Catch the breath (transmutation)
Command undead (necromancy)
Conjure undead (conjuration)
Curse of incompetence (necromancy)
Delayed healing (evocation)
Gloomwrought barrier (conjuration)
Hematomancy (divination)
Hero's steel (transmutation)
Invested champion (evocation)
Iron mind (abjuration)
Lance of the sun god (evocation)
Life from death (necromancy)
Life sense (divination)
Mass hobble mount (necromancy)
Mire (transmutation)
Mortal insight (divination)
Nest of infernal vipers (conjuration)
Nightfall (evocation)
Protective ice (abjuration)
Reaver spirit (enchantment)
Sidestep arrow (divination)
Soothing chant (abjuration)
Soul borrowing (necromancy)
Spiteful weapon (necromancy)
Sting of the scorpion goddess (transmutation)
Sudden dawn (evocation)
Targeting foreknowledge (divination)
Throes of ecstasy (transmutation)
Thunderclap (evocation)
Tongue of sand (illusion)
Touch of the unliving (necromancy)
Vital mark (transmutation)
Wave of corruption (necromancy)

4th Level
Binding oath (necromancy)
Blade of my brother (transmutation)
Blood and steel (transmutation)
Blood puppet (transmutation)
Brittling (transmutation)
Cherub's burning blade (evocation)
Consult the storm (divination)
Desiccating breath (evocation)
Deva's wings (transmutation)
Energy foreknowledge (divination)
Evercold (necromancy)
Inspiring speech (enchantment)
Keening wail (necromancy)
Lovesick (enchantment)
Not dead yet (necromancy)
Power word pain (enchantment)
Reset (transmutation)
Scale rot (necromancy)
Scry ambush (divination)
Shocking shroud (evocation)
Shroud of death (necromancy)
Spectral herd (conjuration)
Staff of violet fire (evocation)
True light of revelation (abjuration)

5th Level
Ancient shade (necromancy)
Blazing chariot (conjuration)
Chains of the goddess (enchantment)
Claws of the earth dragon (evocation)
Clockwork bodyguard (conjuration)
Cruor of visions (divination)
Eidetic memory (transmutation)
Exsanguinate (necromancy)
Exsanguinating cloud (necromancy)
Fiendish brand (necromancy)
Grasp of the tupilak (necromancy)
Holy ground (evocation)
Ice fortress (conjuration)
Kiss of the succubus (necromancy)
Lay to rest (evocation)
Not this day! (abjuration)
Rain of blades (conjuration)
Recharge (evocation)
Sanguine horror (conjuration)
Surprise blessing (abjuration)
Tongue tied (enchantment)
Wall of time (abjuration)

6th Level
Ally aegis (abjuration)
Animate greater undead (necromancy)
Aspect of the firebird (transmutation)
Burning radiance (evocation)
Celestial fanfare (evocation)
Curse of Boreas (transmutation)
Extract knowledge (necromancy)
Fault line (evocation)
Firewalk (transmutation)
Heavenly crown (enchantment)
Smiting arrow (evocation)
Time loop (transmutation)
Tolling doom (necromancy)
Winter's radiance (evocation)

7th Level
Alter time flow (transmutation)
Conjure greater spectral dead (conjuration)
Curse of dust (necromancy)
Curse of the grave (necromancy)
Death god's touch (necromancy)
Glacial fog (evocation)
Ice soldiers (conjuration)
Ravages of time (transmutation)
Seal of sanctuary (abjuration)
Soothing incandescence (evocation)
Time jaunt (transmutation)

8th Level
Child of light and darkness (transmutation)
Costly victory (evocation)
Ghoul king's cloak (transmutation)
Lower the veil (divination)
Quintessence (transmutation)
Wind of the hereafter (conjuration)

9th Level
Form of the gods (transmutation)
Greater seal of sanctuary (abjuration)
Mammon's due (conjuration)
Time in a bottle (transmutation)

DRUID SPELLS

Cantrips (0 Level)
Abhorrence (enchantment)
Acumen (transmutation)
Ale-dritch blast (conjuration)
Allure (transmutation)
Animated scroll (transmutation)
Bewilderment (enchantment)
Biting arrow (evocation)
Bless the dead (abjuration)
Brawn boost (transmutation)
Caustic touch (evocation)
Clumsiness (necromancy)
Decay (necromancy)
Exceptional wit (transmutation)
Fortitude (transmutation)
Frailty (necromancy)
Hobble (evocation)
Impotence (necromancy)
Iron hand (abjuration)
Luminous bolt (evocation)
Obtuse (enchantment)
Shiver (evocation)

Starburst (evocation)
Tree heal (evocation)

1st Level
Agonizing mark (evocation)
Alter arrow's fortune (divination)
Ancestor's strength (transmutation)
Anchoring rope (evocation)
Anticipate weakness (divination)
Avoid grievous injury (divination)
Bloodhound (transmutation)
Bloody smite (necromancy)
Breathtaking wind (evocation)
Conjure mock animals (conjuration)
Cure beast (evocation)
Deep breath (transmutation)
Draconic smite (evocation)
Feather field (abjuration)
Fire under the tongue (transmutation)
Flurry (transmutation)
Forest affinity (illusion)
Forest native (transmutation)
Freeze potion (transmutation)
Gird the spirit (abjuration)
Gliding step (abjuration)
Goat's hoof charm (transmutation)

Gordolay's pleasant aroma (transmutation)
Green mantle (transmutation)
Hobble mount (necromancy)
Hone blade (transmutation)
Illuminate spoor (divination)
Maw of needles (transmutation)
Mosquito bane (necromancy)
Mud pack (conjuration)
Nature's aegis (abjuration)
Scentless (transmutation)
Seer's reaction (divination)
Slippery fingers (enchantment)
Snowy coat (transmutation)
Stanch (transmutation)
Thin the ice (transmutation)
Tree speak (divination)
Trick question (enchantment)
Withered sight (necromancy)
Wolfsong (transmutation)

2nd Level
Animal spy (divination)
Anticipate attack (divination)
Aspect of the ape (transmutation)
Aspect of the ram (transmutation)

Batsense (transmutation)
Boulder toss (transmutation)
Carmello-Volta's irksome preserves (conjuration)
Caustic blood (transmutation)
Comprehend wild shape (divination)
Conjure scarab swarm (conjuration)
Creeping ice (conjuration)
Crushing trample (transmutation)
Decelerate (transmutation)
Detect dragons (divination)
Distraction cascade (divination)
Elemental horns (evocation)
Feather travel (transmutation)
Fire darts (evocation)
Furious hooves (transmutation)
Heartstrike (divination)
Hunter's cunning (divination)
Intensify light (transmutation)
Iron stomach (transmutation)
Mark prey (divination)
Nip at the heels (illusion)
Phantom light (illusion)
Poisoned volley (conjuration)
Revive beast (necromancy)
Sculpt snow (transmutation)

Snap the leash (enchantment)
Thorn cage (conjuration)
Tree running (transmutation)
Trench (transmutation)
Weiler's ward (conjuration)
Wresting wind (evocation)

3rd Level
Accelerate (transmutation)
Aspect of the serpent (transmutation)
Blood offering (necromancy)
Bones of stone (transmutation)
Breeze compass (divination)
Conjure undead (conjuration)
Cynophobia (enchantment)
Dark heraldry (necromancy)
Deep focus (evocation)
Defensive quills (transmutation)
Drown (evocation)
Dryad's kiss (conjuration)
Ears of the bat (transmutation)
Freezing fog (conjuration)
Going in circles (illusion)
Hedren's birds of clay (conjuration)
Ice burn (conjuration)
Legion of rabid squirrels (conjuration)
Life sense (divination)
Mass hobble mount (necromancy)
Mire (transmutation)
Monstrous empathy (enchantment)
Mortal insight (divination)
Nightfall (evocation)
Phantom dragon (illusion)
Phase bolt (evocation)
Potency of the pack (transmutation)
Quench (transmutation)
Reaver spirit (enchantment)
Remove scent (transmutation)
Sidestep arrow (divination)
Sir Mittinz's move curse
  (transmutation)
Soul borrowing (necromancy)
Storm god's doom (evocation)
Sudden dawn (evocation)
Targeting foreknowledge (divination)
Thunderous wave (evocation)
Tongue of sand (illusion)
Tracer (divination)

4th Level
Brittling (transmutation)
Consult the storm (divination)
Desiccating breath (evocation)
Energy foreknowledge (divination)
Harry (enchantment)

Hunting stand (conjuration)
Looping trail (transmutation)
Quick time (conjuration)
Ray of life suppression (necromancy)
Reset (transmutation)
Scry ambush (divination)
Shocking shroud (evocation)
Snow boulder (transmutation)
Storm of wings (conjuration)
Sudden stampede (conjuration)
Wintry glide (conjuration)

5th Level
Clash of glaciers (evocation)
Conjure fey hound (conjuration)
Control ice (transmutation)
Earth wave (transmutation)
Eidetic memory (transmutation)
Energy absorption (abjuration)
Fey crown (abjuration)
Forest of spears (evocation)
Harrying hounds (enchantment)
Maim (necromancy)
Necrotic leech (necromancy)
Radiant beacon (evocation)
Recharge (evocation)
See beyond (divination)
Starfall (evocation)
Sun's bounty (transmutation)

6th Level
Conjure forest defender (conjuration)
Fault line (evocation)
Firewalk (transmutation)
Storm form (transmutation)
Time loop (transmutation)
Winterdark (transmutation)
Winter's radiance (evocation)

7th Level
Arcane parasite (transmutation)
Curse of dust (necromancy)
Glacial fog (evocation)
Ice soldiers (conjuration)
Triumph of ice (transmutation)
Volley shield (abjuration)

8th Level
Awaken object (transmutation)
Disruptive aura (evocation)
Harsh light of summer's glare
  (enchantment)

9th Level
Forest sanctuary (abjuration)

PALADIN SPELLS

1st Level
Ancestor's strength (transmutation)
Angelic guardian (conjuration)
Draconic smite (evocation)
Find kin (divination)
Gird the spirit (abjuration)
Heart to heart (necromancy)
Hobble mount (necromancy)
Insightful maneuver (divination)
Life transference arrow (necromancy)
Litany of sure hands (divination)
Pendulum (enchantment)
Spur mount (transmutation)
Strength of an ox (transmutation)

2nd Level
Anticipate attack (divination)
Blessed halo (evocation)
Blessed rest (enchantment)
Champion's weapon (conjuration)
Decelerate (transmutation)
Holy warding (abjuration)
Intensify light (transmutation)
Mantle of the brave (abjuration)
Shared sacrifice (evocation)
Trench (transmutation)
Warning shout (divination)

3rd Level
Anticipate arcana (divination)
Aura of protection or destruction
  (abjuration)
Blade of wrath (evocation)
Hero's steel (transmutation)
Holy vow (abjuration)
Invested champion (evocation)
Iron mind (abjuration)
Lance of the sun god (evocation)
Life from death (necromancy)
Life sense (divination)
Mass hobble mount (necromancy)
Sir Mittinz's move curse
  (transmutation)

4th Level
Binding oath (necromancy)
Blade of my brother (transmutation)
Cherub's burning blade (evocation)
Deva's wings (transmutation)
Echoes of steel (evocation)
Inspiring speech (enchantment)
Reset (transmutation)
Spectral herd (conjuration)
True light of revelation (abjuration)

5th Level
Battle mind (divination)
Blazing chariot (conjuration)
Holy ground (evocation)
Lay to rest (evocation)
Rain of blades (conjuration)
Surprise blessing (abjuration)

RANGER SPELLS

1st Level
Agonizing mark (evocation)
Alter arrow's fortune (divination)
Anchoring rope (evocation)
Anticipate weakness (divination)
Biting arrow (evocation)
Bleed (necromancy)
Bloodhound (transmutation)
Bloody smite (necromancy)
Breathtaking wind (evocation)
Cobra fangs (transmutation)
Conjure mock animals (conjuration)
Converse with dragon (divination)
Cure beast (evocation)
Feather field (abjuration)
Fire under the tongue (transmutation)
Flurry (transmutation)
Forest affinity (illusion)
Foretell distraction (divination)
Gliding step (abjuration)
Goat's hoof charm (transmutation)
Green mantle (transmutation)
Hobble mount (necromancy)
Hone blade (transmutation)
Hunter's endurance (enchantment)
Illuminate spoor (divination)
Insightful maneuver (divination)
Maw of needles (transmutation)
Mud pack (conjuration)
Nature's aegis (abjuration)
Scentless (transmutation)
Seer's reaction (divination)
Snowy coat (transmutation)
Spur mount (transmutation)
Stanch (transmutation)
Step like me (transmutation)
Thin the ice (transmutation)
Thunderous charge (transmutation)
Withered sight (necromancy)
Wolfsong (transmutation)

2nd Level
Animal spy (divination)
Anticipate attack (divination)
Aspect of the ape (transmutation)
Aspect of the ram (transmutation)
Batsense (transmutation)
Bestial fury (enchantment)
Bleating call (enchantment)
Caustic blood (transmutation)
Conjure mantelet (abjuration)
Creeping ice (conjuration)
Crushing trample (transmutation)
Dead walking (illusion)
Decelerate (transmutation)
Distraction cascade (divination)
Elemental horns (evocation)
Grudge match (evocation)
Heartstrike (divination)
Hunter's cunning (divination)
Ice hammer (conjuration)
Instant snare (abjuration)
Intensify light (transmutation)
Mark prey (divination)
Nip at the heels (illusion)
Poisoned volley (conjuration)
Revive beast (necromancy)
Time step (conjuration)
Tree running (transmutation)
Wresting wind (evocation)

3rd Level
Blood offering (necromancy)
Bones of stone (transmutation)
Booster shot (evocation)
Conjure undead (conjuration)
Cynophobia (enchantment)
Defensive quills (transmutation)
Going in circles (illusion)
Hedren's birds of clay (conjuration)
Hero's steel (transmutation)
Legion of rabid squirrels (conjuration)
Life sense (divination)
Mass hobble mount (necromancy)
Monstrous empathy (enchantment)
Mortal insight (divination)
Potency of the pack (transmutation)
Quench (transmutation)
Reaver spirit (enchantment)
Remove scent (transmutation)
Sidestep arrow (divination)
Spiteful weapon (necromancy)
Targeting foreknowledge (divination)
Tracer (divination)

4th Level
Blood spoor (divination)
Fusillade of ice (evocation)
Harry (enchantment)
Heart-seeking arrow (transmutation)
Hunting stand (conjuration)
Looping trail (transmutation)
Raid the lair (abjuration)
Scale rot (necromancy)
Scry ambush (divination)
Snow boulder (transmutation)
Storm of wings (conjuration)
Sudden stampede (conjuration)
Wintry glide (conjuration)

5th Level
Conjure fey hound (conjuration)
Fey crown (abjuration)
Harrying hounds (enchantment)
Killing fields (transmutation)
Primal infusion (transmutation)
See beyond (divination)
Sun's bounty (transmutation)

SORCERER SPELLS

Cantrips (0 Level)
Abhorrence (enchantment)
Acumen (transmutation)
Allure (transmutation)
Animated scroll (transmutation)
Bewilderment (enchantment)
Biting arrow (evocation)
Blood tide (necromancy)
Brawn boost (transmutation)
Bright sparks (evocation)
Caustic touch (evocation)
Clumsiness (necromancy)
Dark maw (necromancy)
Dragon roar (evocation)
Encrypt / decrypt (alteration)
Enumerate (divination)
Exceptional wit (transmutation)
Fist of iron (transmutation)
Fortitude (transmutation)
Frailty (necromancy)
Hamstring (evocation)
Hoarfrost (evocation)
Hobble (evocation)
Impotence (necromancy)
Luminous bolt (evocation)
Nimbleness (transmutation)
Obtuse (enchantment)
Puff of smoke (evocation)
Pummelstone (conjuration)
Quicken (transmutation)
Shiver (evocation)
Telekinetic trip (transmutation)
Thunder bolt (evocation)
Uncanny avoidance (divination)
Wind lash (evocation)

1st Level
Agonizing mark (evocation)
Anticipate weakness (divination)
Alter arrow's fortune (divination)
Analyze device (divination)
Auspicious warning (enchantment)
Avoid grievous injury (divination)
Blinding pain (enchantment)
Bloodhound (transmutation)
Bloody hands (necromancy)
Bolster undead (necromancy)
Boreas's kiss (conjuration)
Breathtaking wind (evocation)
Chronal lance (transmutation)
Circle of wind (abjuration)
Converse with dragon (divination)
Deep breath (transmutation)
Disquieting gaze (necromancy)
Fey glamor (illusion)
Forest affinity (illusion)
Foretell distraction (divination)
Freeze potion (transmutation)
Glamor of mundanity (illusion)
Goat's hoof charm (transmutation)
Gordolay's pleasant aroma (transmutation)
Heart to heart (necromancy)
Icicle daggers (conjuration)
Ill-fated word (divination)
Insightful maneuver (divination)
Kobold's fury (transmutation)
Mosquito bane (necromancy)
Mud pack (conjuration)
Pendulum (enchantment)
Ring strike (transmutation)
Scentless (transmutation)
Screaming ray (evocation)
Seer's reaction (divination)
Slippery fingers (enchantment)
Stanch (transmutation)
Step like me (transmutation)
Strength of an ox (transmutation)
Telekinetic parry (evocation)
Thin the ice (transmutation)
Thunderous charge (transmutation)
Tidal barrier (abjuration)
Tireless (transmutation)
Trick question (enchantment)
Twist the skein (enchantment)
Undermine armor (transmutation)
Unluck on that (enchantment)
Unruly item (transmutation)
Waft (transmutation)
Weapon of blood (transmutation)
Wind tunnel (evocation)
Writhing arms (transmutation)

2nd Level
Althea's travel tent (conjuration)
Animate ghoul (necromancy)
Anticipate attack (divination)
Bad timing (divination)
Batsense (transmutation)
Bitter chains (transmutation)
Black swan storm (evocation)
Bleating call (enchantment)
Blood lure (enchantment)
Bloodshot (conjuration)
Boiling oil (conjuration)
Caustic blood (transmutation)
Chaotic vitality (conjuration)
Cloak of fiendish menace (transmutation)
Convoluted dictum (enchantment)
Creeping ice (conjuration)
Crushing trample (transmutation)
Dead walking (illusion)
Decelerate (transmutation)
Detect dragons (divination)
Discern weakness (divination)
Distracting divination (divination)
Distraction cascade (divination)
Dome of silence (abjuration)
Elemental horns (evocation)
Elemental twist (evocation)
Enhance greed (divination)
Exude acid (transmutation)
Frenzied bolt (evocation)
Furious hooves (transmutation)
Gear barrage (conjuration)
Gift of resilience (enchantment)
Greater analyze device (divination)
Heartache (enchantment)
Indecision (enchantment)
Lacerate (evocation)
Lock armor (transmutation)
Mist of wonders (conjuration)
Power word kneel (enchantment)
Reverberate (evocation)
Rolling thunder (evocation)
Sculpt snow (transmutation)
Shade (abjuration)
Sheen of ice (evocation)
Shifting the odds (divination)
Snap the leash (enchantment)
Snow fort (conjuration)
Spin (enchantment)
Spy my shadow (transmutation)
Thunderous stampede (transmutation)
Timely distraction (evocation)
Treasure chasm (enchantment)
Trench (transmutation)
Vomit tentacles (transmutation)
Weiler's ward (conjuration)
Wresting wind (evocation)

3rd Level
Accelerate (transmutation)
Alone (enchantment)
Anticipate arcana (divination)
Aspect of the serpent (transmutation)
Aura of listlessness (enchantment)
Blood armor (necromancy)
Blood offering (necromancy)
Booster shot (evocation)
Chains of perdition (conjuration)
Chilling words (enchantment)
Compelled movement (enchantment)
Cynophobia (enchantment)
Deep focus (evocation)
Draconic majesty (enchantment)
Dragon's pride (enchantment)
Drown (evocation)
Entropic damage field (transmutation)
Flesh to paper (transmutation)
Freeze blood (transmutation)
Freezing fog (conjuration)
Frozen razors (evocation)
Gloomwrought barrier (conjuration)
Going in circles (illusion)
Hematomancy (divination)
Ice burn (conjuration)
Illusory trap (illusion)
Impending ally (conjuration)
Innocuous aspect (illusion)
Ire of the mountain (transmutation)
Jeweled fissure (conjuration)
Life sense (divination)
Opportunistic foresight (divination)
Outflanking boon (illusion)
Phantom dragon (illusion)
Phase bolt (evocation)
Portal jaunt (conjuration)
Riptide (conjuration)
Rune of imprisonment (abjuration)
Shield of starlight (abjuration)
Sidestep arrow (divination)
Spiteful weapon (necromancy)
Steal warmth (necromancy)
Storm god's doom (evocation)
Targeting foreknowledge (divination)
Thousand darts (evocation)
Throes of ecstasy (transmutation)
Thunderclap (evocation)
Thunderous wave (evocation)
Touch of the unliving (necromancy)
Vital mark (transmutation)

4th Level
Abhorrent apparition (illusion)
Blood puppet (transmutation)
Boiling blood (necromancy)
Boreas's embrace (conjuration)
Chaotic form (transmutation)
Cursed gift (abjuration)
Deep freeze (evocation)
Desiccating breath (evocation)
Distressing resonance (evocation)
Draconic senses (divination)
Drain item (evocation)
Dread wings (necromancy)
Earthskimmer (transmutation)
Endow attribute (transmutation)
Energy foreknowledge (divination)
Evercold (necromancy)
Flame wave (evocation)
Fluctuating alignment (enchantment)
Fog of war (illusion)
Fusillade of ice (evocation)
Giant's jest (transmutation)
Harry (enchantment)
Looping trail (transmutation)
Lovesick (enchantment)
Night terrors (illusion)
Not dead yet (necromancy)
Overwhelming greed (enchantment)
Pitfall (transmutation)
Power word pain (enchantment)
Ray of life suppression (necromancy)
Reposition (conjuration)
Sacrificial healing (necromancy)
Scale rot (necromancy)
Scaly hide (transmutation)
Scry ambush (divination)
Searing sun (transmutation)
Shocking shroud (evocation)
Spinning axes (evocation)
Steam blast (evocation)
Time vortex (evocation)
Torrent of fire (conjuration)
Visage of the dead (necromancy)
Wayward strike (transmutation)

5th Level
Acid rain (conjuration)
Animated object swarm (conjuration)
Babble (enchantment)
Battle mind (divination)
Channel fiendish power (transmutation)
Clash of glaciers (evocation)
Claws of the earth dragon (evocation)
Clockwork bodyguard (conjuration)
Conjure fey hound (conjuration)
Control ice (transmutation)
Cruor of visions (divination)
Curse ring (necromancy)
Dark lord's mantle (enchantment)
Dragon breath (evocation)
Energy absorption (abjuration)
Essence instability (transmutation)
Exsanguinating cloud (necromancy)
Frostbite (evocation)
Grasp of the tupilak (necromancy)
Harrying hounds (enchantment)
Ice fortress (conjuration)
Kiss of the succubus (necromancy)
Labyrinthine howl (illusion)
Magnetize (evocation)
Maim (necromancy)
Necrotic leech (necromancy)
Prismatic ray (evocation)
Radiant beacon (evocation)
Recharge (evocation)
Sanguine horror (conjuration)

Starfall (evocation)
Swift exchange (conjuration)
Thunderstorm (transmutation)
Wall of time (abjuration)

6th Level
Absorbing field (abjuration)
Ally aegis (abjuration)
Aspect of the firebird (transmutation)
Catapult (transmutation)
Cave dragon's dominance (transmutation)
Chaotic world (illusion)
Claim lair (abjuration)
Curse of Boreas (transmutation)
Enchant ring (enchantment)
Entomb (transmutation)
Fault line (evocation)
Fire dragon's fury (transmutation)
Firewalk (transmutation)
Icy manipulation (transmutation)
Misfortune (necromancy)
Mithral dragon's might (transmutation)
Time loop (transmutation)
Walk the twisted path (conjuration)
Winterdark (transmutation)
Winter's radiance (evocation)

7th Level
Amplify gravity (transmutation)
Arcane parasite (transmutation)
Aspect of the dragon (transmutation)
Blizzard (conjuration)
Curse of the grave (necromancy)
Death god's touch (necromancy)
Glacial fog (evocation)
Ice soldiers (conjuration)
Last rays of the dying sun (evocation)
Legend killer (divination)
Ravages of time (transmutation)
Ring ward (abjuration)
Symbol of sorcery (evocation)
Talons of a hungry land (evocation)
Triumph of ice (transmutation)
Uncontrollable transformation (transmutation)
Volley shield (abjuration)
Walking wall (transmutation)
Wild trajectory (transmutation)

8th Level
Arcane sight (divination)
Black sunshine (illusion)
Caustic torrent (conjuration)
Child of light and darkness (transmutation)
Create ring servant (transmutation)
Deadly sting (transmutation)
Disruptive aura (evocation)
Glacial cascade (evocation)
Harsh light of summer's glare (enchantment)
Malevolent waves (abjuration)
Roaring winds of Limbo (conjuration)
Steam whistle (evocation)
Time jump (transmutation)

9th Level
Circle of devastation (evocation)
Pyroclasm (evocation)
Star's heart (transmutation)
Time in a bottle (transmutation)
Unshackled magic (enchantment)

WARLOCK SPELLS

Cantrips (0 Level)
Bless the dead (abjuration)
Dark maw (necromancy)
Decay (necromancy)
Encrypt / decrypt (alteration)
Fist of iron (transmutation)
Hamstring (evocation)
Hoarfrost (evocation)
Hobble (evocation)
Pummelstone (conjuration)
Starburst (evocation)
Uncanny avoidance (divination)
Wind lash (evocation)

1st Level
Adjust position (transmutation)
Anticipate weakness (divination)
Avoid grievous injury (divination)
Bleed (necromancy)
Blinding pain (enchantment)
Blood scarab (necromancy)
Bloody hands (necromancy)
Bolster undead (necromancy)
Boreas's kiss (conjuration)
Breathtaking wind (evocation)
Candle's insight (divination)
Circle of wind (abjuration)
Disquieting gaze (necromancy)
Feather field (abjuration)
Fire under the tongue (transmutation)
Flurry (transmutation)
Foretell distraction (divination)
Freeze potion (transmutation)
Hobble mount (necromancy)
Hunter's endurance (enchantment)
Icicle daggers (conjuration)
Insightful maneuver (divination)
Kobold's fury (transmutation)
Liar's gift (enchantment)
Mammon's avarice (divination)
Mosquito bane (necromancy)
Ring strike (transmutation)
Slippery fingers (enchantment)
Stanch (transmutation)
Strength of an ox (transmutation)
Thin the ice (transmutation)
Thunderous charge (transmutation)
Tidal barrier (abjuration)
Trick question (enchantment)
Twist the skein (enchantment)
Unluck on that (enchantment)
Wind tunnel (evocation)
Withered sight (necromancy)
Writhing arms (transmutation)

2nd Level
Bitter chains (transmutation)
Black swan storm (evocation)
Bloodshot (conjuration)
Caustic blood (transmutation)
Conjure spectral dead (conjuration)
Convoluted dictum (enchantment)
Creeping ice (conjuration)
Dead walking (illusion)
Decelerate (transmutation)
Distracting divination (divination)
Distraction cascade (divination)
Enhance greed (divination)
Exude acid (transmutation)
Gear barrage (conjuration)
Gift of luck (divination)
Grain of truth (divination)
Grudge match (evocation)
Heartache (enchantment)
Heartstop (necromancy)
Lock armor (transmutation)
Orb of light (evocation)
Power word kneel (enchantment)
Read object (divination)
Reverberate (evocation)
Rolling thunder (evocation)
Rotting corpse (necromancy)
Shade (abjuration)
Sheen of ice (evocation)
Spin (enchantment)
Spy my shadow (transmutation)
Thorn cage (conjuration)
Thunderous stampede (transmutation)
Time step (conjuration)
Vomit tentacles (transmutation)

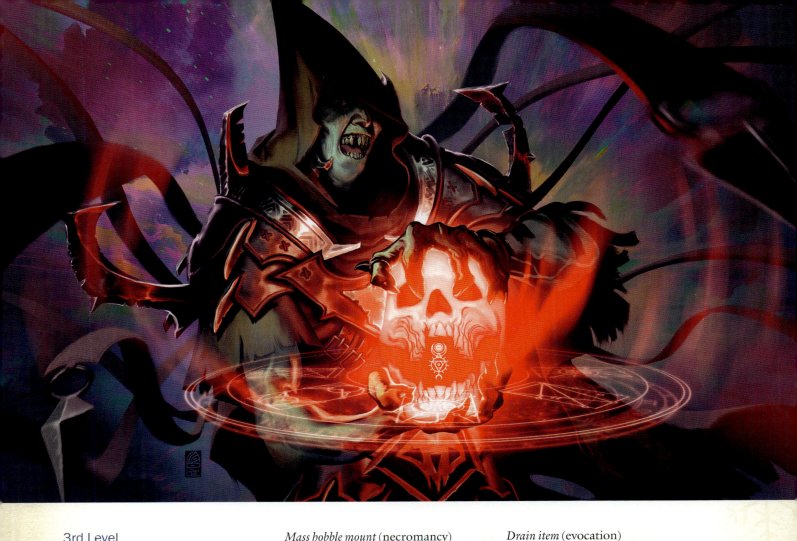

3rd Level
Alone (enchantment)
Anticipate arcana (divination)
Blood armor (necromancy)
Blood offering (necromancy)
Booster shot (evocation)
Catch the breath (transmutation)
Chains of perdition (conjuration)
Chilling words (enchantment)
Closing in (illusion)
Curse of hostility (necromancy)
Curse of incompetence (necromancy)
Cynophobia (enchantment)
Dark heraldry (necromancy)
Deep focus (evocation)
Demon within (conjuration)
Ears of the bat (transmutation)
Freeze blood (transmutation)
Frozen razors (evocation)
Gloomwrought barrier (conjuration)
Going in circles (illusion)
Ice burn (conjuration)
Impending ally (conjuration)
Innocuous aspect (illusion)
Ire of the mountain (transmutation)
Life sense (divination)
Mass hobble mount (necromancy)
Mire (transmutation)
Mortal insight (divination)
Nightfall (evocation)
Opportunistic foresight (divination)
Outflanking boon (illusion)
Phase bolt (evocation)
Potency of the pack (transmutation)
Riptide (conjuration)
Sidestep arrow (divination)
Sir Mittinz's move curse (transmutation)
Spiteful weapon (necromancy)
Steal warmth (necromancy)
Sudden dawn (evocation)
Terrifying lash (conjuration)
Thousand darts (evocation)
Throes of ecstasy (transmutation)
Touch of the unliving (necromancy)

4th Level
Boiling blood (necromancy)
Boreas's embrace (conjuration)
Chains of torment (conjuration)
Cloak of serpents (abjuration)
Conjure fiends (conjuration)
Drain item (evocation)
Dread wings (necromancy)
Earthskimmer (transmutation)
Endow attribute (transmutation)
Evercold (necromancy)
Flame wave (evocation)
Fog of war (illusion)
Fusillade of ice (evocation)
Giant's jest (transmutation)
Keening wail (necromancy)
Looping trail (transmutation)
Lovesick (enchantment)
Night terrors (illusion)
Not dead yet (necromancy)
Overwhelming greed (enchantment)
Power word pain (enchantment)
Ray of life suppression (necromancy)
Reposition (conjuration)
Scale rot (necromancy)
Scry ambush (divination)
Spinning axes (evocation)
Steam blast (evocation)
Time vortex (evocation)
Visage of madness (enchantment)
Visage of the dead (necromancy)
Wayward strike (transmutation)

5th Level
Acid rain (conjuration)
Channel fiendish power (transmutation)
Clash of glaciers (evocation)
Conjure nightmare (conjuration)
Cruor of visions (divination)
Curse ring (necromancy)
Dark lord's mantle (enchantment)
Dark web of the spider monarch (conjuration)
Dragon breath (evocation)
Energy absorption (abjuration)
Exsanguinate (necromancy)
Fey crown (abjuration)
Fiendish brand (necromancy)
Frostbite (evocation)
Grasp of the tupilak (necromancy)
Harrying hounds (enchantment)
Kiss of the succubus (necromancy)
Necrotic leech (necromancy)
Not this day! (abjuration)
Recharge (evocation)
Sanguine horror (conjuration)
Tongue tied (enchantment)

6th Level
Aura of wrath (enchantment)
Avronin's astral assembly (necromancy)
Catapult (transmutation)
Entomb (transmutation)
Extract knowledge (necromancy)
Time loop (transmutation)
Tolling doom (necromancy)
Winterdark (transmutation)

7th Level
Amplify gravity (transmutation)
Blizzard (conjuration)
Conjure greater spectral dead (conjuration)
Curse of dust (necromancy)
Curse of the grave (necromancy)
Death god's touch (necromancy)
Symbol of sorcery (evocation)
Talons of a hungry land (evocation)

8th Level
Arcane sight (divination)
Caustic torrent (conjuration)
Disruptive aura (evocation)
Ghoul king's cloak (transmutation)
Malevolent waves (abjuration)
Time slippage (enchantment)

9th Level
Circle of devastation (evocation)
Crystal confinement (abjuration)
Mammon's due (conjuration)
Pyroclasm (evocation)

WIZARD SPELLS

Cantrips (0 Level)
Abhorrence (enchantment)
Acumen (transmutation)
Ale-dritch blast (conjuration)
Allure (transmutation)
Animated scroll (transmutation)
Benediction (abjuration)
Bewilderment (enchantment)
Biting arrow (evocation)
Black Goat's blessing (enchantment)
Blood tide (necromancy)
Brawn boost (transmutation)
Bright sparks (evocation)
Brimstone infusion (transmutation)
Caustic touch (evocation)
Clockwork bolt (evocation)
Clumsiness (necromancy)
Dark maw (necromancy)
Decay (necromancy)
Dragon roar (evocation)
Encrypt / decrypt (alteration)
Enumerate (divination)
Exceptional wit (transmutation)
Fist of iron (transmutation)
Fortitude (transmutation)
Frailty (necromancy)
Hamstring (evocation)
Hoarfrost (evocation)
Hobble (evocation)
Impotence (necromancy)
Luminous bolt (evocation)
Nimbleness (transmutation)
Obtuse (enchantment)
Pummelstone (conjuration)
Quicken (transmutation)
Scribe (transmutation)
Semblance of dread (illusion)
Shiver (evocation)
Starburst (evocation)
Telekinetic trip (transmutation)
Uncanny avoidance (divination)
Wind lash (evocation)

1st Level
Adjust position (transmutation)
Agonizing mark (evocation)
Alter arrow's fortune (divination)
Amplify light (transmutation)
Analyze device (divination)
Angelic guardian (conjuration)
Anticipate weakness (divination)
Auspicious warning (enchantment)
Avoid grievous injury (divination)
Bloodhound (transmutation)
Bloody hands (necromancy)
Bloody smite (necromancy)
Bolster undead (necromancy)
Boreas's kiss (conjuration)
Bottomless stomach (transmutation)
Breathtaking wind (evocation)
Candle's insight (divination)
Chronal lance (transmutation)
Circle of wind (abjuration)
Converse with dragon (divination)
Deep breath (transmutation)
Disquieting gaze (necromancy)
Feather field (abjuration)
Forest affinity (illusion)
Foretell distraction (divination)
Freeze potion (transmutation)
Goat's hoof charm (transmutation)
Gordolay's pleasant aroma (transmutation)
Guiding star (divination)
Hard heart (enchantment)
Heart to heart (necromancy)
Hobble mount (necromancy)
Icicle daggers (conjuration)
Ill-fated word (divination)
Insightful maneuver (divination)
Kobold's fury (transmutation)
Mammon's avarice (divination)
Mosquito bane (necromancy)
Mud pack (conjuration)
Pendulum (enchantment)
Ring strike (transmutation)
Roaming pain (necromancy)
Scentless (transmutation)
Screaming ray (evocation)
Seer's reaction (divination)
Slippery fingers (enchantment)
Speak with inanimate object (divination)
Stanch (transmutation)
Step like me (transmutation)
Strength of an ox (transmutation)
Telekinetic parry (evocation)
Thin the ice (transmutation)
Thunderous charge (transmutation)
Tidal barrier (abjuration)
Tireless (transmutation)
Trick question (enchantment)
Twist the skein (enchantment)

Undermine armor (transmutation)
Unluck on that (enchantment)
Unruly item (transmutation)
Voorish sign (divination)
Weapon of blood (transmutation)
Wind tunnel (evocation)
Withered sight (necromancy)
Writhing arms (transmutation)

2nd Level

Althea's travel tent (conjuration)
Animate ghoul (necromancy)
Anticipate attack (divination)
As you were (necromancy)
Asher memories (divination)
Bad timing (divination)
Bitter chains (transmutation)
Black swan storm (evocation)
Bleating call (enchantment)
Blessed halo (evocation)
Blood lure (enchantment)
Bloodshot (conjuration)
Boiling oil (conjuration)
Caustic blood (transmutation)
Chaotic vitality (conjuration)
Cloak of fiendish menace (transmutation)
Conjure scarab swarm (conjuration)
Conjure spectral dead (conjuration)
Convoluted dictum (enchantment)
Creeping ice (conjuration)
Daggerhawk (transmutation)
Dead walking (illusion)
Decelerate (transmutation)
Delay potion (transmutation)
Detect dragons (divination)
Discern weakness (divination)
Distracting divination (divination)
Distraction cascade (divination)
Ectoplasm (necromancy)
Elemental horns (evocation)
Elemental twist (evocation)
Enhance familiar (transmutation)
Enhance greed (divination)
Exude acid (transmutation)
Feather travel (transmutation)
Fire darts (evocation)
Frenzied bolt (evocation)
Furious hooves (transmutation)
Gear barrage (conjuration)
Gift of resilience (enchantment)
Glyph of shifting (conjuration)
Greater analyze device (divination)
Heartache (enchantment)
Heartstop (necromancy)
Holy warding (abjuration)
Hypnotic missive (enchantment)
Indecision (enchantment)
Kavelin's instant aerosol (transmutation)
Lacerate (evocation)
Lair sense (divination)
Lock armor (transmutation)
Mephitic croak (conjuration)
Mist of wonders (conjuration)
Orb of light (evocation)
Phantom light (illusion)
Poisoned volley (conjuration)
Power word kneel (enchantment)
Read object (divination)
Reverberate (evocation)
Rolling thunder (evocation)
Rotting corpse (necromancy)

Sculpt snow (transmutation)
Shade (abjuration)
Sheen of ice (evocation)
Shifting the odds (divination)
Snap the leash (enchantment)
Snow fort (conjuration)
Spin (enchantment)
Spy my shadow (transmutation)
Thunderous stampede (transmutation)
Timely distraction (evocation)
Time step (conjuration)
Trench (transmutation)
Vomit tentacles (transmutation)
Warning shout (divination)
Weiler's ward (conjuration)
Unholy defiance (necromancy)

3rd Level
Accelerate (transmutation)
Alone (enchantment)
Anticipate arcana (divination)
Aspect of the serpent (transmutation)
Aura of listlessness (enchantment)
Blade of wrath (evocation)
Blood armor (necromancy)
Blood offering (necromancy)
Breeze compass (divination)
Calm of the storm (abjuration)
Catch the breath (transmutation)
Chains of perdition (conjuration)
Chilling words (enchantment)
Closing in (illusion)
Command undead (necromancy)
Compelled movement (enchantment)
Compelling fate (divination)
Curse of hostility (necromancy)
Curse of incompetence (necromancy)
Cynophobia (enchantment)
Deep focus (evocation)
Demon within (conjuration)
Draconic majesty (enchantment)
Dragon's pride (enchantment)
Drown (evocation)
Entropic damage field (transmutation)
Flesh to paper (transmutation)
Freeze blood (transmutation)
Freezing fog (conjuration)
Frozen razors (evocation)
Gloomwrought barrier (conjuration)
Gluey globule (conjuration)
Going in circles (illusion)
Hedren's birds of clay (conjuration)
Hematomancy (divination)
Ice burn (conjuration)
Illusory trap (illusion)
Impending ally (conjuration)
Innocuous aspect (illusion)
Ire of the mountain (transmutation)
Jeweled fissure (conjuration)
Life sense (divination)
Mass hobble mount (necromancy)
Mind exchange (transmutation)
Mire (transmutation)
Nest of infernal vipers (conjuration)
Opportunistic foresight (divination)
Outflanking boon (illusion)
Phantom dragon (illusion)
Phase bolt (evocation)
Portal jaunt (conjuration)
Protective nimbus (abjuration)
Riptide (conjuration)
Rune of imprisonment (abjuration)
Salt lash (conjuration)
Shield of starlight (abjuration)
Sidestep arrow (divination)
Sir Mittinz's move curse (transmutation)
Sleep of the deep (illusion)
Spiteful weapon (necromancy)
Steal warmth (necromancy)
Storm god's doom (evocation)
Sudden dawn (evocation)
Surge dampener (abjuration)
Targeting foreknowledge (divination)
Thousand darts (evocation)
Throes of ecstasy (transmutation)
Tongue of sand (illusion)
Thunderclap (evocation)
Thunderous wave (evocation)
Touch of the unliving (necromancy)
Tracking beacon (divination)
Unseen strangler (conjuration)
Vital mark (transmutation)
Wave of corruption (necromancy)

4th Level
Abhorrent apparition (illusion)
Blood and steel (transmutation)
Blood puppet (transmutation)
Boiling blood (necromancy)
Boreas's embrace (conjuration)
Brittling (transmutation)
Chains of torment (conjuration)
Chaotic form (transmutation)
Conjure fiends (conjuration)
Cursed gift (abjuration)
Deep freeze (evocation)
Desiccating breath (evocation)
Deva's wings (transmutation)
Distressing resonance (evocation)
Draconic senses (divination)
Drain item (evocation)
Dread wings (necromancy)
Earthskimmer (transmutation)
Emanation of Yoth (necromancy)
Endow attribute (transmutation)
Energy foreknowledge (divination)
Evercold (necromancy)
Flame wave (evocation)
Flickering fate (divination)
Fluctuating alignment (enchantment)
Fog of war (illusion)
Fusillade of ice (evocation)
Giant's jest (transmutation)
Green decay (necromancy)
Harry (enchantment)
Heart-seeking arrow (transmutation)
Hunger of Leng (enchantment)
Instant siege weapon (transmutation)
Lava stone (transmutation)
Looping trail (transmutation)
Lovesick (enchantment)
Night terrors (illusion)
Not dead yet (necromancy)
Overwhelming greed (enchantment)
Pitfall (transmutation)
Power word pain (enchantment)
Quicksilver mantle (transmutation)
Raid the lair (abjuration)
Ray of alchemical negation (transmutation)
Ray of life suppression (necromancy)
Reposition (conjuration)
Reset (transmutation)
Sacrificial healing (necromancy)
Sand ship (transmutation)
Scale rot (necromancy)
Scry ambush (divination)
Searing sun (transmutation)
Shocking shroud (evocation)
Shroud of death (necromancy)
Spinning axes (evocation)
Staff of violet fire (evocation)
Steam blast (evocation)
Time vortex (evocation)
Tome curse (necromancy)
Visage of madness (enchantment)
Visage of the dead (necromancy)
Wild shield (abjuration)
Wintry glide (conjuration)
Yellow sign (enchantment)

5th Level
Acid rain (conjuration)
Ancient shade (necromancy)

Animated object swarm (conjuration)
Babble (enchantment)
Battle mind (divination)
Blazing chariot (conjuration)
Bottled arcana (transmutation)
Channel fiendish power (transmutation)
Clash of glaciers (evocation)
Claws of the earth dragon (evocation)
Clockwork bodyguard (conjuration)
Conjure fey hound (conjuration)
Conjure nightmare (conjuration)
Control ice (transmutation)
Cruor of visions (divination)
Curse of Yig (transmutation)
Curse ring (necromancy)
Dark lord's mantle (enchantment)
Dragon breath (evocation)
Eidetic memory (transmutation)
Eldritch communion (divination)
Energy absorption (abjuration)
Essence instability (transmutation)
Exsanguinate (necromancy)
Exsanguinating cloud (necromancy)
Fiendish brand (necromancy)

Forest of spears (evocation)
Frostbite (evocation)
Grasp of the tupilak (necromancy)
Greater protective nimbus (abjuration)
Harrying hounds (enchantment)
Ice fortress (conjuration)
Instant fortification (transmutation)
Kiss of the succubus (necromancy)
Labyrinthine howl (illusion)
Magnetize (evocation)
Maim (necromancy)
Mass surge dampener (abjuration)
Necrotic leech (necromancy)
Prismatic ray (evocation)
Radiant beacon (evocation)
Recharge (evocation)
Sanguine horror (conjuration)
See beyond (divination)
Starfall (evocation)
Summon eldritch servitor (conjuration)
Swift exchange (conjuration)
Tongue tied (enchantment)
Wall of time (abjuration)

6TH LEVEL
Absorbing field (abjuration)
Alchemical form (transmutation)
Ally aegis (abjuration)
Animate greater undead (necromancy)
Aura of wrath (enchantment)
Avronin's astral assembly (necromancy)
Burning radiance (evocation)
Catapult (transmutation)
Cave dragon's dominance (transmutation)
Celestial fanfare (evocation)
Chaotic world (illusion)
Claim lair (abjuration)
Curse of Boreas (transmutation)
Enchant ring (enchantment)
Entomb (transmutation)
Extract knowledge (necromancy)
Fault line (evocation)
Fire dragon's fury (transmutation)
Firewalk (transmutation)
Heavenly crown (enchantment)
Icy manipulation (transmutation)
Misfortune (necromancy)

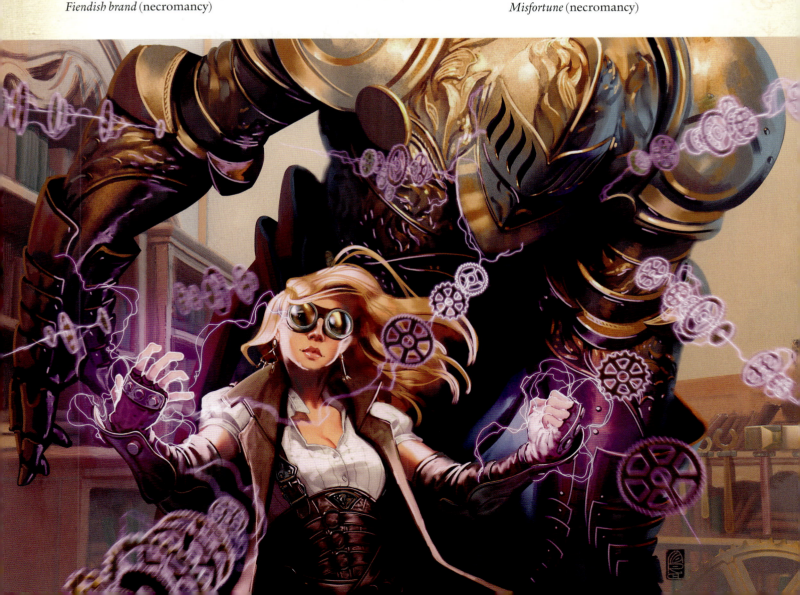

Mithral dragon's might (transmutation)
Time loop (transmutation)
Walk the twisted path (conjuration)
Warp mind and matter (transmutation)
Winterdark (transmutation)
Winter's radiance (evocation)

7th Level

Acid gate (conjuration)
Amplify gravity (transmutation)
Arcane parasite (transmutation)
Blizzard (conjuration)
Conjure greater spectral dead (conjuration)
Curse of the grave (necromancy)
Create thunderstaff (transmutation)
Death god's touch (necromancy)
Glacial fog (evocation)
Ice soldiers (conjuration)
Last rays of the dying sun (evocation)
Legend killer (divination)
Ravages of time (transmutation)
Right the stars (divination)
Ring ward (abjuration)
Seal of sanctuary (abjuration)
Sign of Koth (abjuration)
Soothing incandescence (evocation)
Starry vision (divination)
Symbol of sorcery (evocation)
Talons of a hungry land (evocation)
Triumph of ice (transmutation)
Uncontrollable transformation (transmutation)
Volley shield (abjuration)
Walking wall (transmutation)
Wild trajectory (transmutation)

8th Level

Arcane sight (divination)
Black sunshine (illusion)
Caustic torrent (conjuration)
Child of light and darkness (transmutation)
Create ring servant (transmutation)
Deadly sting (transmutation)
Disruptive aura (evocation)
Glacial cascade (evocation)
Harsh light of summer's glare (enchantment)
Life hack (necromancy)
Lower the veil (divination)
Malevolent waves (abjuration)
Paragon of chaos (transmutation)
Quintessence (transmutation)
Roaring winds of Limbo (conjuration)
Seed of destruction (enchantment)
Steam whistle (evocation)
Summon star (conjuration)
Time jump (transmutation)
Time slippage (enchantment)
Wind of the hereafter (conjuration)

9th Level

Blood to acid (transmutation)
Circle of devastation (evocation)
Crystal confinement (abjuration)
Greater seal of sanctuary (abjuration)
Mammon's due (conjuration)
Pyroclasm (evocation)
Star's heart (transmutation)
Summon avatar (conjuration)
Time in a bottle (transmutation)
Unleash effigy (transmutation)
Unshackled magic (enchantment)

SPELL DESCRIPTIONS

This chapter contains more than six hundred spells designed for use by player characters and NPCs. The spell descriptions are presented in alphabetical order.

ABHORRENCE

Enchantment Cantrip

Casting Time: 1 action
Range: 30 feet
Components: V, S
Duration: 1 minute

You temporarily make a creature within range less appealing to others. The target makes a Wisdom saving throw against your spell. On a successful save, the spell is ineffective. On a failed save, the next time the creature makes a Charisma check before the spell ends, roll a d6 and subtract the result from the roll. The spell then ends.

ABHORRENT APPARITION

4th-Level Illusion

Casting Time: 1 action
Range: 60 feet
Components: M (a gourd with a face carved on it)
Duration: Instantaneous

You imbue a terrifying visage onto a gourd and toss it ahead of you to a spot of your choosing within range. Each creature within 15 feet of that spot takes 6d8 psychic damage and becomes frightened of you for 1 minute; a successful Wisdom saving throw halves the damage and negates the fright. A creature frightened in this way repeats the saving throw at the end of each of its turns, ending the effect on itself on a success.

At Higher Levels. If you cast this spell using a spell slot of 5th level or higher, the damage increases by 1d8 for each slot level above 4th.

ABSORBING FIELD

6th-Level Abjuration

Casting Time: 1 action
Range: Self
Components: V, S
Duration: Concentration, up to 1 minute

You cloak yourself in a protective field that absorbs incoming magic, rejuvenating your spell slots. When you are the target of a spell (including spells that affect multiple targets, but not area spells such as *fireball*), make an ability check using your spellcasting ability. The DC equals 10 + the spell's level. On a successful check, the spell has no effect on you and is absorbed by the field. You regain a spell slot of the same level as the spell that was cast against you. If you have no expended spell slots of that level, you don't regain a spell slot, but this spell remains in effect.

Even if the spell manages to bypass the field, you gain advantage on your saving throw.

ACCELERATE

3rd-Level Transmutation

Casting Time: 1 action
Range: Touch
Components: V, S, M (a toy top)
Duration: Concentration, up to 1 minute

Choose up to three willing creatures within range, which can include you. For the duration of the spell, each target's walking speed is doubled. Each target can also use a bonus action on each of its turns to take the Dash action, and it has advantage on Dexterity saving throws.

At Higher Levels. When you cast this spell using a spell slot of 4th level or higher, you can affect one additional creature for each slot level above 3rd.

ACID GATE

7th-Level Conjuration

Casting Time: 1 action
Range: 60 feet
Components: V, S, M (a vial of acid and a polished silver mirror worth 125 gp)
Duration: Concentration, up to 1 minute

You create a portal of swirling, acidic green vapor in an unoccupied space you can see. This portal connects with a target destination within 100 miles that you are personally familiar with and have seen with your own eyes, such as your wizard's tower or an inn you have stayed at. You and up to three creatures of your choice can enter the portal and pass through it, arriving at the target destination (or within 10 feet of it, if it is currently occupied). If the target destination doesn't exist or is inaccessible, the spell automatically fails and the gate doesn't form.

ACID RAIN

5th-Level Conjuration

Casting Time: 1 action
Range: 150 feet
Components: V, S, M (a drop of acid)
Duration: Concentration, up to 1 minute

You unleash a storm of swirling acid in a cylinder 20 feet wide and 30 feet high, centered on a point you can see. The area is heavily obscured by the driving acid fall. A creature that starts its turn in the area or that enters the area for the first time on its turn takes 6d6 acid damage, or half as much damage if it makes a successful Dexterity saving throw. A creature takes half as much damage from the acid (as if it had made a successful saving throw) at the start of its first turn after leaving the affected area.

At Higher Levels. When you cast this spell using a spell slot of 6th level or higher, the damage increases by 1d6 for each slot level above 5th.

ACUMEN

Transmutation Cantrip

Casting Time: 1 action
Range: Touch
Components: V, S
Duration: Concentration, up to 1 minute

You touch a willing creature. Once before the spell ends, the target can roll a d6 and add the result to one Wisdom check of its choice. It can roll the die before or after making the check. The spell then ends.

ADJUST POSITION

1st-Level Transmutation

Casting Time: 1 bonus action
Range: 30 feet
Components: V
Duration: Instantaneous

You adjust the location of an ally to a better tactical position. You move one willing creature within range 5 feet. This movement does not provoke opportunity attacks. The creature moves bodily through the intervening space (as opposed to teleporting), so there can be no physical obstacle (such as a wall or a door) in the path.

At Higher Levels. When you cast this spell using a spell slot of 2nd level or higher, you can target an additional willing creature for each slot level above 1st.

AGONIZING MARK

1st-Level Evocation

Casting Time: 1 action

Range: 90 feet

Components: S

Duration: Concentration, up to 1 minute

You choose a creature you can see within range to mark as your prey, and a ray of black energy issues forth from you. Until the spell ends, each time you deal damage to the target it must make a Charisma saving throw. On a failed save, it falls prone as its body is filled with torturous agony.

ALCHEMICAL FORM

6th-Level Transmutation

Casting Time: 1 action

Range: Self

Components: V, S, M (a vial of acid, poison, or alchemist's fire)

Duration: 1 minute

You transform into an amoebic form composed of highly acidic and poisonous alchemical jelly. While in this form:

- You are immune to acid and poison damage and to the poisoned and stunned conditions.
- You have resistance to nonmagical fire, piercing, and slashing damage.
- You can't speak, cast spells, use items or weapons, or manipulate objects.
- Your gear melds into your body and reappears when the spell ends.
- You don't need to breathe.
- Your speed is 20 feet.
- Your size doesn't change, but you can move through and between obstructions as if you were two size categories smaller.
- You gain the following action: *Melee Weapon Attack*: spellcasting ability modifier + proficiency bonus to hit, range 5 ft., one target; *Hit*: 4d6 acid or poison damage (your choice), and the target must make a successful Constitution saving throw or be poisoned until the start of your next turn.

ALE-DRITCH BLAST

Conjuration Cantrip

Casting Time: 1 action

Range: 60 feet

Components: V, S

Duration: Instantaneous

A stream of ice-cold ale blasts from your outstretched hands toward a creature or object within range. Make a ranged spell attack against the target. On a hit, it takes 1d8 cold damage and it must make a successful Constitution saving throw or be poisoned until the end of its next turn. A targeted creature has disadvantage on the saving throw if it has drunk any alcohol within the last hour.

The damage increases when you reach higher levels: 2d8 at 5th level, 3d8 at 11th level, and 4d8 at 17th level.

ALLURE

Transmutation Cantrip

Casting Time: 1 action

Range: Touch

Components: V, S

Duration: Concentration, up to 1 minute

You touch a willing creature. Once before the spell ends, the target can roll a d6 and add the result to one Charisma check of its choice. It can roll the die before or after making the check. The spell then ends.

ALLY AEGIS

6th-Level Abjuration

Casting Time: 1 reaction, which you take when your ally is hit by an attack or is targeted by a spell that deals damage other than psychic damage

Range: 60 feet

Components: V, S

Duration: 1 round

When you see an ally within range in imminent danger, you can use your reaction to protect that creature with a shield of magical force. Until the start of your next turn, your ally has a +5 bonus to AC and is immune to force damage. In addition, if your ally must make a saving throw against an enemy's spell that deals damage, the ally takes half as much damage on a failed saving throw and no damage on a successful save. *Ally aegis* offers no protection, however, against psychic damage from any source.

At Higher Levels. When you cast this spell using a spell slot of 7th level or higher, you can target one additional ally for each slot level above 6th.

ALONE

3rd-Level Enchantment

Casting Time: 1 action

Range: 30 feet

Components: V, S

Duration: Concentration, up to 1 minute

You cause a creature within range to believe its allies have been banished to a different realm. The target must succeed on a Wisdom saving throw, or it treats its allies as if they were invisible and silenced. The affected creature cannot target, perceive, or otherwise interact with its allies for the duration of the spell. If one of its allies hits it with a melee attack, the affected creature can make another Wisdom saving throw. On a successful save, the spell ends.

ALTER ARROW'S FORTUNE

1st-Level Divination

Casting Time: 1 reaction, which you take when an enemy makes a ranged attack that hits
Range: 100 feet
Components: S
Duration: Instantaneous

You clap your hands, setting off a chain of tiny events that culminate in throwing off an enemy's aim. When an enemy makes a ranged attack with a weapon or a spell that hits one of your allies, this spell causes the enemy to reroll the attack roll unless the enemy makes a successful Charisma saving throw. The attack is resolved using the lower of the two rolls (effectively giving the enemy disadvantage on the attack).

ALTER TIME FLOW

7th-Level Transmutation

Casting Time: 1 action
Range: Self (30-foot radius)
Components: V, S, M (an hourglass)
Duration: Concentration, up to 1 minute

You control the currents of time, affecting all creatures within 30 feet of yourself. You can choose to deliver either a *haste* or *slow* effect (as the spell) to each creature in the area. An unwilling creature makes a Constitution saving throw, avoiding the effect on a success. Each unwilling creature must make a new saving throw if it remains in the affected area at the end of its turn. Any affected creature returns to normal if it exits the area, but if a creature reenters the area while the spell is still active, it is subject to the effect of the spell (and receives another saving throw, if unwilling).

ALTHEA'S TRAVEL TENT

2nd-Level Conjuration (Ritual)

Casting Time: 5 minutes
Range: Touch
Components: V, S, M (a canvas tent)
Duration: 8 hours

You touch an ordinary, properly pitched canvas tent to create a space where you and a companion can sleep in comfort. From the outside, the tent appears normal, but inside it has a small foyer and a larger bedchamber. The foyer contains a writing desk with a chair; the bedchamber holds a soft bed large enough to sleep two, a small nightstand with a candle, and a small clothes rack. The floor of both rooms is a clean, dry, hard-packed version of the local ground. When the spell ends, the tent and the ground return to normal, and any creatures inside the tent are expelled to the nearest unoccupied spaces.

At Higher Levels. When the spell is cast using a 3rd-level slot, the foyer becomes a dining area with seats for six and enough floor space for six people to sleep, if they bring their own bedding. The sleeping room is unchanged. With a 4th-level slot, the temperature inside the tent is comfortable regardless of the outside temperature, and the dining area includes a small kitchen. With a 5th-level slot, an unseen servant is conjured to prepare and serve food (from your supplies). With a 6th-level slot, a third room is added that has three two-person beds. With a slot of 7th level or higher, the dining area and second sleeping area can each accommodate eight persons.

AMPLIFY GRAVITY

7th-Level Transmutation

Casting Time: 1 action
Range: 100 feet
Components: V, S, M (a piece of lead)
Duration: Concentration, up to 1 minute

This spell intensifies gravity in a 50-foot-radius area within range. Inside the area, damage from falling is quadrupled (2d6 per 5 feet fallen) and maximum damage from falling is 40d6. Any creature on the ground in the area when the spell is cast must make a successful Strength saving throw or be knocked prone; the same applies to a creature that enters the area or ends its turn in the area. A prone creature in the area must make a successful Strength saving throw to stand up. A creature on the ground in the area moves at half speed and has disadvantage on Dexterity checks and ranged attack rolls.

AMPLIFY LIGHT

1st-Level Transmutation

Casting Time: 1 action
Range: Touch
Components: V, S, M (a nonmagical light source)
Duration: Special

You touch a nonmagical light source and increase its brightness. While the spell is in effect, the radius of the bright light around the source is doubled, and dim light extends for the same distance beyond that area. The light source's duration is halved, however, so that a torch affected by *amplify light* would burn out in half an hour, or a hooded lantern would burn through its fuel in 3 hours. Adding new fuel to a light source while it is under the effect of *amplify light* will end the spell and return it to its normal brightness.

ANALYZE DEVICE

1st-Level Divination

Casting Time: 1 hour
Range: Touch
Components: V, S, M (a set of clockworker's tools)
Duration: Instantaneous

You discover all mechanical properties, mechanisms, and functions of a single construct or clockwork device, including how to activate or deactivate those functions, if appropriate.

ANCESTOR'S STRENGTH

1st-Level Transmutation

Casting Time: 1 action
Range: Touch
Components: V, S
Duration: Concentration, up to 8 hours

Choose a willing creature you can see and touch. Its muscles bulge and become invigorated. For the duration, the target is considered one size category larger for determining its carrying capacity, the maximum weight it can lift, push, or pull, and its ability to break objects. It also has advantage on Strength checks.

ANCHORING ROPE

1st-Level Evocation

Casting Time: 1 action, or 1 reaction that you take while falling
Range: 30 feet
Components: V, S
Duration: 5 minutes

You create a spectral lanyard. One end is tied around your waist, and the other end is magically anchored in the air at a point you select within range. You can choose to make the rope from 5 to 30 feet long, and it can support up to 800 pounds. The point where the end of the rope is anchored in midair can't be moved after the spell is cast. If this spell is cast as a reaction while you are falling, you stop at a point of your choosing in midair and take no falling damage. You can dismiss the rope as a bonus action.

At Higher Levels. When you cast this spell using a spell slot of 3rd level or higher, you can create one additional rope for every two slot levels above 1st. Each rope must be attached to a different creature.

ANCIENT SHADE

5th-Level Necromancy

Casting Time: 1 action
Range: 10 feet
Components: V, S, M (burning candles of planar origin worth 500 gp)
Duration: 10 minutes

You grant the semblance of life and intelligence to a pile of bones (or even bone dust) of your choice within range, allowing the ancient spirit to answer the questions you pose. These remains can be the remnants of undead, including animated but unintelligent undead, such as skeletons and zombies. (Intelligent undead are not affected.) Though it can have died centuries ago, the older the spirit called, the less it remembers of its mortal life.

Until the spell ends, you can ask the ancient spirit up to five questions if it died within the past year, four questions if it died within ten years, three within one hundred years, two within one thousand years, and but a single question for spirits more than one thousand years dead. The ancient shade knows only what it knew in life, including languages. Answers are usually brief, cryptic, or repetitive, and the corpse is under no compulsion to offer a truthful

answer if you are hostile to it, or it recognizes you as an enemy. This spell doesn't return the creature's soul to its body, only its animating spirit. Thus, the corpse can't learn new information, doesn't comprehend anything that has happened since it died, and can't speculate about future events.

ANGELIC GUARDIAN

1st-Level Conjuration

Casting Time: 1 action
Range: 30 feet
Components: V, S
Duration: Concentration, up to 1 minute

You conjure a minor celestial manifestation to protect a creature you can see within range. A faintly glowing image resembling a human head and shoulders hovers within 5 feet of the target for the duration. The manifestation moves to interpose itself between the target and any incoming attacks, granting the target a +2 bonus to AC.

Also, the first time the target gets a failure on a Dexterity saving throw while the spell is active, it can use its reaction to reroll the save. The spell then ends.

ANIMAL SPY

2nd-Level Divination

Casting Time: 1 action
Range: 30 feet
Components: V, S
Duration: 1 hour

You create a mental link between you and a beast within range. Until the spell ends, you can use a bonus action to transfer your awareness to the beast—using its vision, hearing, smell, taste, and touch—and another bonus action on any subsequent turn to return your awareness to your body. You can use an action to dismiss the spell entirely.

This spell affects normal beasts, including giant versions of animals, but not conjured animals or familiars. The spell does not allow you to control the beast or make it friendly to you. While you experience the world through the beast's senses, your body is motionless, unaware of the outside world and effectively unconscious.

The spell ends if the distance between you and the beast is ever greater than 1 mile, or if the beast is killed. If you are using the beast's senses when it is killed, you must succeed on a DC 14 Wisdom saving throw or be stunned for 1d4 rounds from the shock of experiencing its death.

ANIMATE GHOUL

2nd-Level Necromancy

Casting Time: 1 action
Range: Touch
Components: V, S, M (piece of rotting flesh and an onyx gemstone worth 100 gp)
Duration: Instantaneous

You raise one Medium or Small humanoid corpse as a ghoul under your control. Any class levels or abilities the creature had in life are gone, replaced by the standard ghoul stat block.

At Higher Levels. When you cast this spell using a 3rd-level spell slot, it can be used on the corpse of a Large humanoid to create a Large ghoul. When you cast this spell using a spell slot of 4th level or higher, this spell creates a ghast, but the material component changes to an onyx gemstone worth at least 200 gp.

ANIMATE GREATER UNDEAD

6th-Level Necromancy

Casting Time: 1 hour
Range: 15 feet
Components: V, S, M (a pint of blood, a pound of flesh, and an ounce of bone dust, all of which the spell consumes)
Duration: Instantaneous

Animate greater undead creates an undead servant from a pile of bones or from the corpse of a Large or Huge humanoid within range. The spell imbues the target with a foul mimicry of life, raising it as an undead skeleton or zombie. A skeleton uses the stat block of a minotaur skeleton, or a zombie uses the stat block of an ogre zombie, unless a more appropriate stat block is available.

The creature is under your control for 24 hours, after which it stops obeying your commands. To maintain control of the creature for another 24 hours, you must cast this spell on it again while you have it controlled. Casting the spell for this purpose reasserts your control over up to four creatures you have previously animated rather than animating a new one.

At Higher Levels. When you cast this spell using a spell slot of 7th level or higher, you can reanimate one additional creature for each slot level above 6th.

ANIMATED OBJECT SWARM

5th-Level Conjuration

Casting Time: 1 action
Range: 120 feet
Components: V, S
Duration: Concentration, up to 1 minute

Myriad Tiny objects animate at your command, forming a swarm. The objects' abilities conform to the rules stated in the *animate objects* spell, except that you animate only Tiny objects, which gather together into a Medium swarm. The area of the swarm is considered difficult terrain, and creatures in it are lightly obscured. The swarm has the following statistics:

- **Armor Class:** 18
- **Hit Points:** 20
- **STR** 4; **DEX** 18
- **Damage Resistances:** bludgeoning, piercing, slashing
- **Condition Immunities:** charmed, frightened, grappled, paralyzed, petrified, prone, restrained, stunned
- **Melee Weapon Attack:** +8 to hit, reach 0 ft., one target in the swarm's space. Hit: 6 (1d4 + 4) damage.

ANIMATED SCROLL

Transmutation Cantrip

Casting Time: 1 action
Range: Touch
Components: V, S, M (intricately folded paper or parchment)
Duration: 24 hours

The paper or parchment must be folded into the shape of an animal before casting the spell. It then becomes an animated paper animal of the kind the folded paper most closely resembles. The creature uses the stat block of any beast that has a challenge rating of 0. It is made of paper, not flesh and bone, but it can do anything the real creature can do: a paper owl can fly and attack with its talons, a paper frog can swim without disintegrating in water, and so forth. It follows your commands to the best of its ability, including carrying messages to a recipient whose location you know.

You can't have more than one animated paper animal at a time. If you cast this spell while you already have an animated paper animal, you instead cause it to adopt a new form. Choose any beast that has a challenge rating of 0. Your animated paper animal transforms into the chosen creature.

The duration increases by 24 hours at 5th level (48 hours), 11th level (72 hours), and 17th level (96 hours).

ANTICIPATE ARCANA

3rd-Level Divination

Casting Time: 1 reaction, which you take when an enemy you can see casts a spell
Range: Self
Components: V, S
Duration: Instantaneous

Your foresight gives you an instant to ready your defenses against a magical attack. When you cast *anticipate arcana*, you have advantage on saving throws against spells and other magical effects until the start of your next turn.

ANTICIPATE ATTACK

2nd-Level Divination

Casting Time: 1 reaction, which you take when you are attacked but before the attack roll is made
Range: Self
Components: V, S
Duration: Instantaneous

In a flash of foreknowledge, you spot an oncoming attack with enough time to avoid it. Upon casting this spell, you can move up to half your speed without provoking opportunity attacks. The oncoming attack still occurs but misses automatically if you are no longer within the attack's range, are in a space that's impossible for the attack to hit, or can't be targeted by that attack in your new position. If none of those circumstances apply but the situation has changed—you have moved into a position where you have cover, for example—then the attack is made after taking the new situation into account.

ANTICIPATE WEAKNESS

1st-Level Divination

Casting Time: 1 bonus action
Range: Self
Components: V, S
Duration: Instantaneous

With a quick glance into the future, you pinpoint where a gap is about to open in your foe's defense, and then you strike. After casting *anticipate weakness*, you have advantage on attack rolls until the end of your turn.

ARCANE PARASITE

7th-Level Transmutation (Ritual)

Casting Time: 1 action
Range: Self
Components: V, S
Duration: 2 hours

This spell creates a link between you and a nearby source of arcane power, allowing you to draw on its strength to bolster your spellcasting ability. When you cast a spell, you can use a bonus action to draw on the link. Doing so means you expend no spell slots to cast the spell, the energy instead comes from the external power.

The more you draw on the link, the harder it is to maintain. Each spell you cast in this manner decreases the duration of the *arcane parasite* spell by 10 minutes per level of the spell you cast using the link. For example, if you cast a *fireball* spell using the link, you would not expend a spell slot in the casting, but the duration of this spell would decrease by 30 minutes. If you cast a spell using the link and your remaining duration is equal to or less than the spell's level × 10 minutes, then this spell ends as soon as that spell is cast.

ARCANE SIGHT

8th-Level Divination

Casting Time: 1 action
Range: Touch
Components: V, S, M (a piece of clear quartz)
Duration: Concentration, up to 1 hour

The recipient of this spell gains the benefits of both *true seeing* and *detect magic* until the spell ends, and they also know the name and effect of every spell they witness during the spell's duration.

AS YOU WERE

2nd-Level Necromancy

Casting Time: 1 minute
Range: Touch
Components: V, S, M (a piece of flesh from a creature of the target's race)
Duration: Instantaneous

When cast on a dead or undead body, *as you were* returns that creature to the appearance it had in life while it was healthy and uninjured. The target must have a physical body; the spell fails if the target is normally noncorporeal.

If *as you were* is cast on a corpse, its effect is identical to that of *gentle repose*, except that the corpse's appearance is restored to that of a healthy, uninjured (albeit dead) person.

If the target is an undead creature, it also is restored to the appearance it had in life, even if it died from disease or from severe wounds, or centuries ago. The target looks, smells, and sounds (if it can speak) as it did in life. Friends and family can tell something is wrong only with a successful Wisdom (Insight) check against your spell save DC, and only if they have reason to be suspicious. (Knowing that the person should be dead is sufficient reason.) Spells and abilities that detect undead are also fooled, but the creature remains susceptible to Turn Undead as normal.

This spell doesn't confer the ability to speak on undead that normally can't speak. The creature eats, drinks, and breathes as a living creature does; it can mimic sleep, but it has no more need for it than it had before.

The effect lasts for a number of hours equal to your caster level. You can use an action to end the spell early. Any amount of radiant or necrotic damage dealt to the creature, or any effect that reduces its Constitution, also ends the spell.

If this spell is cast on an undead creature that isn't your ally or under your control, it makes a Charisma saving throw to resist the effect.

ASHEN MEMORIES

2nd-Level Divination (Ritual)

Casting Time: 1 minute
Range: Touch
Components: V, S
Duration: Instantaneous

You touch the ashes, embers, or soot left behind by a fire and receive a vision of one significant event that occurred in the area while the fire was burning. For example, if you were to touch the cold embers of a campfire, you might witness a snippet of a conversation that occurred around the fire. Similarly, touching the ashes of a burned letter might grant you a vision of the person who destroyed the letter or the contents of the letter. You have no control over what information the spell reveals, but your vision usually is tied to the most meaningful event related to the fire. The GM determines the details of what is revealed.

ASPECT OF THE APE

2nd-Level Transmutation

Casting Time: 1 action
Range: Touch
Components: V, S
Duration: Concentration, up to 1 hour

You alter the appearance of a creature you touch, giving it a more simian form. While this spell is in effect, the subject gains a climbing speed equal to its normal walking speed, and gains advantage on Strength (Athletics) checks made when jumping or climbing. When up in a tree's branches (or in a similar area, at the GM's discretion) the target can move up to its climbing speed as a bonus action, using brachiation to reach a nearby tree if the branches are close enough together. This bonus action can be taken only if the subject has at least two hands free, or one hand free if the subject is barefoot.

ASPECT OF THE DRAGON

7th-Level Transmutation

Casting Time: 1 action
Range: Self
Components: V, S, M (a dragon scale)
Duration: Concentration, up to 1 minute

This spell draws out the ancient nature within your blood, allowing you to assume the form of any dragon-type creature of challenge 10 or less.

You assume the hit points and Hit Dice of the new form. When you revert to your normal form, you return to the number of hit points you had before you transformed. If you revert as a result of dropping to 0 hit points, any excess damage carries over to your normal form. As long as the excess damage doesn't reduce your normal form to 0 hit points, you aren't knocked unconscious.

You retain the benefits of any features from your class, race, or other source and can use them, provided that your new form is physically capable of doing so. You can speak only if the dragon can normally speak.

When you transform, you choose whether your equipment falls to the ground, merges into the new form, or is worn by it. Worn equipment functions normally, but equipment doesn't change shape or size to match the new form. Any equipment that the new form can't wear must either fall to the ground or merge into the new form. The GM has final say on whether the new form can wear or use a particular piece of equipment. Equipment that merges has no effect in that state.

ASPECT OF THE FIREBIRD

6th-Level Transmutation

Casting Time: 1 action
Range: Self
Components: V, S, M (a lit candle and the tail feather of a bird)
Duration: Concentration, up to 8 hours

You take on the aspect of a **firebird** (see *Tome of Beasts*), including some physical attributes. A fiery mantle descends upon you, resembling feathery wings and an expansive tail. You gain immunity to fire and a flying speed of 60 feet. Any creatures within 5 feet of you gain immunity to natural, environmental cold.

As an action, you can emit a blast of light 5 feet wide and 50 feet long. All creatures in its path take 6d6 fire damage and are blinded for 1d4 rounds. A successful Dexterity saving throw reduces the damage by half and negates the blindness. Each time you use this feature of the spell, its duration is reduced by 1 hour. When you expend the last hour of the duration, the spell ends at the start of your next turn.

ASPECT OF THE RAM

2nd-Level Transmutation

Casting Time: 1 action
Range: Self
Components: V, S
Duration: Concentration, up to 10 minutes

You take on the aspect of a ram, including some physical attributes. Your body hair grows thick and woolly, and a curling pair of horns sprouts from your head. You can make a ram attack with these horns as an action, and you are proficient with this attack. You deal 1d6 bludgeoning damage on a hit.

If you move at least 20 feet straight toward a target and hit with a ram attack on the same turn, the target takes an extra 1d6 bludgeoning damage. If the target is a creature, it must succeed on a Strength check against your spell save DC or be knocked prone.

You ignore difficult terrain caused by rubble, ice sheets, scree, or steep slopes. You also gain advantage on Strength (Athletics) checks made while climbing or jumping, and Dexterity (Acrobatics) checks made for balance or to stay on your feet.

ASPECT OF THE SERPENT

3rd-Level Transmutation

Casting Time: 1 action
Range: Touch
Components: V, S, M (a dried snakeskin)
Duration: Concentration, up to 1 minute

A creature you touch takes on snakelike aspects for the duration of the spell. Its tongue becomes long and forked, its canine teeth become fangs with venom sacs, and its pupils become sharply vertical. The target gains darkvision with a range of 60 feet and blindsight with a range of 30 feet. As a bonus action when you cast the spell, the target can make a ranged weapon attack with a normal range of 60 feet that deals 2d6 poison damage on a hit.

   As an action, the target can make a bite attack using either Strength or Dexterity (*Melee Weapon Attack:* range 5 ft., one creature; *Hit:* 2d6 piercing damage), and the creature must make a successful DC 14 Constitution saving throw or be paralyzed for 1 minute. A creature paralyzed in this way repeats the saving throw at the end of each of its turns, ending the effect on itself on a success).

   At Higher Levels. When you cast this spell using a spell slot of 4th level or higher, both the ranged attack and bite attack damage increase by 1d6 for each slot level above 3rd.

AURA OF LISTLESSNESS

3rd-Level Enchantment

Casting Time: 1 action
Range: Self (20-foot radius)
Components: V, S, M (a lump of clay or a piece of wet paper)
Duration: Concentration, up to 1 minute

You create an aura of power around you that saps the will and determination from creatures, making them unable to act. Any creature within 20 feet of you must succeed on a Wisdom saving throw or be unable to take actions, reactions, or bonus actions on its turn, except for the Disengage action. Affected creatures can move, but only to distance themselves from harmful conditions, such as attacks by other creatures or hazardous effects that damage or cause ill effects. A creature that moves out of the area can act normally in the following round. Any creature that remains in the area must make another successful saving throw on its turn or continue to be affected by the spell.

AURA OF PROTECTION OR DESTRUCTION

3rd-Level Abjuration

Casting Time: 1 action
Range: Self (30-foot radius)
Components: V, S
Duration: Instantaneous

When you cast this spell, you radiate an otherworldly energy that warps the fate of all creatures within 30 feet of you. Decide whether to call upon either a celestial or a fiend for aid. Choosing a celestial charges a 30-foot-radius around you with an aura of nonviolence; until the start of your next turn, every attack roll made by or against a creature inside the aura is treated as a natural 1. Choosing a fiend charges the area with an aura of violence; until the start of your next turn, every attack roll made by or against a creature inside the aura, including you, is treated as a natural 20.

   At Higher Levels. When you cast this spell using a spell slot of 4th level or higher, you can extend the duration by 1 round for each slot level above 3rd.

AURA OF WRATH

6th-Level Enchantment

Casting Time: 1 action
Range: Self (20-foot radius)
Components: V, S
Duration: Concentration, up to 1 minute

You surround yourself with a psychic aura that drives creatures within 20 feet of you into a violent frenzy. A creature inside the aura or that enters the aura must succeed on a Wisdom saving throw or be overcome with rage. A creature overcome with rage must take its next action to attack the nearest possible target —if more than one target is available, choose randomly. The creature uses a melee weapon if it has one; otherwise, it attacks with any other offensive ability it possesses. If an affected creature leaves the aura, the aura's effect persists for 1 round afterward. A creature affected by the aura makes a new saving throw at the start of each of its turns, ending the effect on itself on a success. Once a creature makes a successful save, that creature cannot be affected again by the same aura.

   If a creature affected by your aura hits you with an attack that targets you, the creature takes 4d8 psychic damage.

   At Higher Levels. When you cast this spell using a spell slot of 7th level or higher, creatures that leave the aura remain under the effect of the spell for 1 additional round for each slot level above 6th. Also, the damage an affected creature takes from striking you increases by 2d8 for each slot level above 6th.

AUSPICIOUS WARNING

1st-Level Enchantment

Casting Time: 1 reaction, which you take when an ally makes an attack roll, ability check, or saving throw

Range: 30 feet

Components: V

Duration: Instantaneous

Just in time, you call out a fortunate warning to a creature within range. The target rolls a d4 and adds the number rolled to an attack roll, ability check, or saving throw that it has just made and uses the new result for determining success or failure.

AVOID GRIEVOUS INJURY

1st-Level Divination

Casting Time: 1 reaction, which you take when you are struck by a critical hit

Range: Self

Components: V, S

Duration: Instantaneous

You cast this spell when a foe strikes you with a critical hit but before damage dice are rolled. The critical hit against you becomes a normal hit.

AVRONIN'S ASTRAL ASSEMBLY

6th-Level Necromancy (Ritual)

Casting Time: 10 minutes

Range: Unlimited

Components: V, M (a spool of fine copper wire and a gem worth at least 100 gp for each target)

Duration: Concentration, up to 1 hour

You alert a number of creatures that you are familiar with, up to your spellcasting ability modifier (minimum of 1), of your intent to communicate with them through spiritual projection. The invitation can extend any distance and even cross to other planes of existence. Once notified, the creatures can choose to accept this communication at any time during the duration of the spell.

When a creature accepts, its spirit is projected into one of the gems used in casting the spell. The material body it leaves behind falls unconscious and doesn't need food or air. The creature's consciousness is present in the room with you, and its normal form appears as an astral projection within 5 feet of the gem its spirit occupies. You can see and hear all the creatures who have joined in the assembly, and they can see and hear you and each other as if they were present (which they are, astrally). They can't interact with anything physically.

A creature can end the spell's effect on itself voluntarily at any time, as can you. When the effect ends or the duration expires, a creature's spirit returns to its body, and it regains consciousness. A creature that withdraws voluntarily from the assembly can't rejoin it even if the spell is still active. If a gem is broken while occupied by a creature's astral self, the spirit in the gem returns to its body and the creature suffers two levels of exhaustion.

AWAKEN OBJECT

8th-Level Transmutation

Casting Time: 8 hours

Range: Touch

Components: V, S, M (a ruby worth at least 1,000 gp, which the spell consumes)

Duration: Permanent

After spending the casting time enchanting a ruby along with a Large or smaller nonmagical object in humanoid form, you touch the ruby to the object. The ruby dissolves into the object, which becomes a living construct imbued with sentience. If the object has no face, a humanoid face appears on it in an appropriate location. The awakened object's statistics are determined by its size, as shown on the table below. An awakened object can use an action to make a melee weapon attack against a target within 5 feet of it. It has free will, acts independently, and speaks one language you know. It is initially friendly to anyone who assisted in its creation.

An awakened object's speed is 30 feet. If it has no apparent legs or other means of moving, it gains a flying speed of 30 feet and it can hover. Its sight and hearing are equivalent to a typical human's senses. Intelligence, Wisdom, and Charisma can be adjusted up or down by the GM to fit unusual circumstances. A beautiful statue might awaken with increased Charisma, for example, or the bust of a great philosopher could have surprisingly high Wisdom.

AWAKENED OBJECTS

Size	HP	AC	Attack	Str	Dex	Con	Int	Wis	Cha
T	20	18	+8 to hit, 1d4 + 4 damage	4	18	10	2d6	2d6	2d6
S	25	16	+6 to hit, 1d8 + 2 damage	6	14	10	3d6	2d6	2d6
M	40	13	+5 to hit, 2d6 + 1 damage	10	12	10	3d6	3d6	2d6
L	50	10	+6 to hit, 2d10 + 2 damage	14	10	10	3d6	3d6	2d6 + 2

An awakened object needs no air, food, water, or sleep. Damage to an awakened object can be healed or mechanically repaired.

BABBLE

5th-Level Enchantment

Casting Time: 1 action

Range: 60 feet

Components: V, S

Duration: Concentration, up to 1 hour

This spell causes the speech of affected creatures to sound like nonsense. Each creature in a 30-foot-radius sphere centered on a point you choose within range must succeed on an Intelligence saving throw when you cast this spell or be affected by it.

An affected creature cannot communicate in any spoken language that it knows. When it speaks, the words come out as gibberish. Spells with verbal components cannot be cast. The spell does not affect telepathic communication, nonverbal communication, or sounds emitted by any creature that does not have a spoken language. As an action, a creature under the effect of this spell can attempt another Intelligence saving throw against the effect. On a successful save, the spell ends.

BAD TIMING

2nd-Level Divination

Casting Time: 1 action

Range: 60 feet

Components: V

Duration: Instantaneous

You point toward a creature that you can see and twist strands of chaotic energy around its fate. If the target gets a failure on a Charisma saving throw, the next attack roll or ability check the creature attempts within 10 minutes is made with disadvantage.

BATSENSE

2nd-Level Transmutation

Casting Time: 1 action

Range: Touch

Components: V, S, M (a bit of fur from a bat's ear)

Duration: 1 hour

For the duration of the spell, a creature you touch can produce and interpret squeaking sounds used for echolocation, giving it blindsight out to a range of 60 feet. The target cannot use its blindsight while deafened, and its blindsight doesn't penetrate areas of magical silence. While using blindsight, the target has disadvantage on Dexterity (Stealth) checks that rely on being silent. Additionally, the target has advantage on Wisdom (Perception) checks that rely on hearing.

BATTLE MIND

5th-Level Divination (Ritual)

Casting Time: 1 action

Range: Self

Components: V, S, M (a bit of spiderweb or a small crystal orb)

Duration: Concentration, up to 10 minutes

You gain a preternatural sense of the surrounding area, allowing you insights you can share with comrades to provide them with an edge in combat. You gain advantage on Wisdom (Perception) checks made when determining surprise at the beginning of a combat encounter. If you are not surprised, then neither are your allies. When you are engaged in combat while the spell is active, you can use a bonus action on your turn to produce one of the following effects (allies must be able to see or hear you in order to benefit):

- One ally gains advantage on its next attack roll, saving throw, or ability check.
- An enemy has disadvantage on the next attack roll it makes against you or an ally.
- You divine the location of an invisible or hidden creature and impart that knowledge to any allies who can see or hear you. This knowledge does not negate any advantages the creature has, it only allows your allies to be aware of its location at the time. If the creature moves after being detected, its new location is not imparted to your allies.
- Three allies who can see and hear you on your turn are given the benefit of a *bless*, *guidance*, or *resistance* spell on their turns; you choose the benefit individually for each ally. An ally must use the benefit on its turn, or the benefit is lost.

BEGUILING BET

2nd-Level Enchantment

Casting Time: 1 action

Range: 30 feet

Components: V, S

Duration: 1 minute

You issue a challenge against one creature you can see within range, which must make a successful Wisdom saving throw or become charmed. On a failed save, you can make an ability check as a bonus action. For example, you could make a Strength (Athletics) check to climb a difficult surface or to jump as high as possible; you could make a Dexterity (Acrobatics) check to perform a backflip; or you could make a Charisma (Performance) check to sing a high note or to extemporize a clever rhyme. You can choose to use your spellcasting ability modifier in place of the usual ability modifier for this check, and you add your proficiency bonus if you're proficient in the skill being used.

The charmed creature must use its next action (which can be a legendary action) to make the same ability check in a contest against your check. Even if the creature can't perform the action—it may not be close enough to a wall to climb it, or it might not have appendages suitable for strumming a lute—it must still attempt the action to the best of its capability. If you win the contest, the spell (and the contest) continues, with you making a new ability check as a bonus action on your turn. The spell ends when it expires or when the creature wins the contest.

At Higher Levels. When you cast this spell using a spell slot of 4th level or higher, you can target one additional creature for every two slot levels above 2nd. Each creature must be within 30 feet of another creature when you cast the spell.

BENEDICTION

Abjuration Cantrip

Casting Time: 1 action
Range: 60 feet
Components: V, S
Duration: Concentration, up to 1 minute

You call down a blessing in the name of an angel of protection. A creature you can see within range shimmers with a faint white light. The next time the creature takes damage, it rolls a d4 and reduces the damage by the result. The spell then ends.

BESTIAL FURY

2nd-Level Enchantment

Casting Time: 1 action
Range: 30 feet
Components: V, S
Duration: Concentration, up to 1 minute

You instill primal fury into a creature you can see within range. The target must make a Charisma saving throw; a creature can choose to fail this saving throw. On a failure, the target must use its action to attack its nearest enemy it can see with unarmed strikes or natural weapons. For the duration, the target's attacks deal an extra 1d6 damage of the same type dealt by its weapon, and the target can't be charmed or frightened. If there are no enemies within reach, the target can use its action to repeat the saving throw, ending the effect on a success.

This spell has no effect on undead or constructs.

At Higher Levels. When you cast this spell using a spell slot of 3rd level or higher, you can target one additional creature for each slot level above 2nd.

BEWILDERMENT

Enchantment Cantrip

Casting Time: 1 action
Range: 30 feet
Components: V, S
Duration: 1 minute

You temporarily inhibit the cognitive ability of a creature within range. If the target makes a successful Wisdom saving throw, the spell is ineffective. On a failed save, the next time the creature makes an Intelligence check before the spell ends, roll a d6 and subtract the result from the roll. The spell then ends.

BINDING OATH

4th-Level Necromancy

Casting Time: 10 minutes
Range: 30 feet
Components: V, S
Duration: Until dispelled

You seal an agreement between two or more willing creatures with an oath in the name of the god of justice, using ceremonial blessings during which both the oath and the consequences of breaking it are set: if any of the sworn break this vow, they are struck by a curse. For each individual that does so, you choose one of the options given in the *bestow curse* spell. When the oath is broken, all participants are immediately aware that this has occurred, but they know no other details.

The curse effect of *binding oath* can't be dismissed by *dispel magic*, but it can be removed with *dispel evil and good*, *remove curse*, or *wish*. *Remove curse* functions only if the spell slot used to cast it is equal to or higher than the spell slot used to cast *binding oath*. Depending on the nature of the oath, one creature's breaking it may or may not invalidate the oath for the other targets. If the oath is completely broken, the spell ends for every affected creature, but curse effects already bestowed remain until dispelled.

BITING ARROW

Evocation Cantrip

Casting Time: 1 action
Range: Self
Components: V, M (an arrow or a thrown weapon)
Duration: 1 round

As part of the action used to cast this spell, you make a ranged weapon attack with a bow, a crossbow, or a thrown weapon. The effect is limited to a range of 120 feet despite the weapon's range, and the attack is made with disadvantage if the target is in the weapon's long range.

If the weapon attack hits, it deals damage as usual. In addition, the target becomes coated in thin frost until the start of your next turn. If the target uses its reaction before the start of your next turn, it immediately takes 1d6 cold damage and the spell ends.

The spell's damage, for both the ranged attack and the cold damage, increases by 1d6 when you reach 5th level (+1d6 and 2d6), 11th level (+2d6 and 3d6), and 17th level (+3d6 and 4d6).

BITTER CHAINS

2nd-Level Transmutation

Casting Time: 1 action
Range: Touch
Components: V, S, M (a spiked metal ring)
Duration: 1 minute

The spiked ring in your hand expands into a long, barbed chain to ensnare a creature you touch. Make a melee spell attack against the target. On a hit, the target is bound in metal chains for the duration. While bound, the target can move only at half speed and has disadvantage on attack rolls, saving throws, and Dexterity checks. If it moves more than 5 feet during a turn, it takes 3d6 piercing damage from the barbs.

The creature can escape from the chains by using an action and making a successful Strength or Dexterity check against your spell save DC, or if the chains are destroyed. The chains have AC 18 and 20 hit points.

BLACK GOAT'S BLESSING

Enchantment Cantrip

Casting Time: 1 action
Range: 30 feet
Components: V, S
Duration: 1 round

You raise your hand with fingers splayed and utter an incantation of the Black Goat with a Thousand Young. Your magic is blessed with the eldritch virility of the All-Mother. The target has disadvantage on saving throws against spells you cast until the end of your next turn.

BLACK SUNSHINE

8th-Level Illusion

Casting Time: 1 action
Range: Self (60-foot radius)
Components: V, M (a discolored pearl, which the spell consumes)
Duration: Concentration, up to 1 minute

You hold up a flawed pearl and it disappears, leaving behind a magic orb in your hand that pulses with dim purple light. Allies that you designate become invisible if they're within 60 feet of you and if light from the orb can reach the space they occupy. An invisible creature still casts a faint, purple shadow.

The orb can be used as a thrown weapon to attack an enemy. On a hit, the orb explodes in a flash of light and the spell ends. The targeted enemy and each creature within 10 feet of it must make a successful Dexterity saving throw or be blinded for 1 minute. A creature blinded in this way repeats the saving throw at the end of each of its turns, ending the effect on itself on a success.

BLACK SWAN STORM

2nd-Level Evocation

Casting Time: 1 action
Range: 30 feet
Components: V, S, M (a feather from a black swan)
Duration: Concentration, up to 1 minute

You call forth a whirlwind of black feathers that fills a 5-foot cube within range. The feathers deal 2d8 force damage to creatures in the cube's area and radiate darkness, causing the illumination level within 20 feet of the cube to drop by one step (from bright light to dim light, and from dim light to darkness). Creatures that make a successful Dexterity saving throw take half the damage and are still affected by the change in light.

At Higher Levels. When you cast this spell using a spell slot of 3rd level or higher, the feathers deal an extra 1d8 force damage for each slot level above 2nd.

BLADE OF MY BROTHER

4th-Level Transmutation

Casting Time: 1 action
Range: Touch
Components: V, S, M (melee weapon owned by a dead ally of the target)
Duration: Concentration, up to 4 rounds

You touch a melee weapon that was used by an ally who is now dead, and it leaps into the air and flies to another ally (chosen by you) within 15 feet of you. The weapon enters that ally's space and moves when the ally moves. If the weapon or the ally is forced to move more than 5 feet from the other, the spell ends.

The weapon acts on your turn by making an attack if a target presents itself. Its attack modifier equals your spellcasting level + the weapon's inherent magical bonus, if any; it receives only its own inherent magical bonus to damage. The weapon fights for up to 4 rounds or until your concentration is broken, after which the spell ends, and it falls to the ground.

BLADE OF WRATH

3rd-Level Evocation

Casting Time: 1 bonus action
Range: Self
Components: V, S, M (a rebuke of evil, written in Celestial)
Duration: Concentration, up to 10 minutes

You create a sword of pure white fire in your free hand. The blade is similar in size and shape to a longsword, and it lasts for the duration. The blade disappears if you let go of it, but you can call it forth again as a bonus action.

You can use your action to make a melee spell attack with the blade. On a hit, the target takes 2d8 fire damage and 2d8 radiant damage. An aberration, fey, fiend, or undead creature damaged by the blade must succeed on a Wisdom saving throw or be frightened until the start of your next turn.

The blade sheds bright light in a 20-foot radius and dim light for an additional 20 feet.

At Higher Levels. When you cast this spell using a spell slot of 4th level or higher, either the fire damage or the radiant damage (your choice) increases by 1d8 for each slot level above 3rd.

BLAZING CHARIOT

5th-Level Conjuration

Casting Time: 1 action
Range: 30 feet
Components: V, S, M (small golden wheel worth 250 gp)
Duration: 1 hour

Calling upon the might of the angels, you conjure a flaming chariot made of gold and mithral in an unoccupied 10-foot-square space you can see within range. Two horses made of fire and light pull the chariot. You and up to three other Medium or smaller creatures you designate can board the chariot (at the cost of 5 feet of movement) and are unharmed by the flames. Any other creature that touches the chariot or hits it (or a creature riding in it) with a melee attack while within 5 feet of the chariot takes 3d6 fire damage and 3d6 radiant damage. The chariot has AC 18 and 50 hit points, is immune to fire, poison, psychic, and radiant damage, and has resistance to all other nonmagical damage. The horses are not separate creatures but are part of the chariot. The chariot vanishes if it is reduced to 0 hit points, and any creature riding it falls out. The chariot has a speed of 50 feet and a flying speed of 40 feet.

On your turn, you can guide the chariot in place of your own movement. You can use a bonus action to direct it to take the Dash, Disengage, or Dodge action. As an action, you can use the chariot to overrun creatures in its path. On this turn, the chariot can enter a hostile creature's space. The creature takes damage as if it had touched the chariot, is shunted to the nearest unoccupied space that it can occupy, and must make a successful Strength saving throw or fall prone in that space.

BLEATING CALL

2nd-Level Enchantment

Casting Time: 1 action

Range: 90 feet

Components: S, M (a bit of fur or hair from a young beast or humanoid)

Duration: 1 minute

You create a sound on a point within range. The sound's volume can range from a whisper to a scream, and it can be any sound you choose. The sound continues unabated throughout the duration, or you can make discrete sounds at different times before the spell ends.

Each creature that starts its turn within 30 feet of the sound and can hear it must make a Wisdom saving throw. On a failed save, the target must take the Dash or Disengage action and move toward the sound by the safest available route on each of its turns. When it arrives to the source of the sound, the target must use its action to examine the sound. Once it has examined the sound, the target determines the sound is illusory and can no longer hear it, ending the spell's effects on that target and preventing the target from being affected by the sound again for the duration of the spell. If a target takes damage from you or a creature friendly to you, it is no longer under the effects of this spell.

Creatures that can't be charmed are immune to this spell.

BLEED

1st-Level Necromancy

Casting Time: 1 bonus action

Range: Self

Components: V, S, M (a drop of blood)

Duration: Concentration, up to 1 minute

Crackling energy coats the blade of one weapon you are carrying that deals slashing damage. Until the spell ends, when you hit a creature with the weapon, the weapon deals an extra 1d4 necrotic damage and the creature must make a Constitution saving throw. On a failed save, the creature suffers a bleeding wound. Each time you hit a creature with this weapon while it suffers from a bleeding wound, your weapon deals an extra 1 necrotic damage for each time you have previously hit the creature with this weapon (to a maximum of 10 necrotic damage).

Any creature can take an action to stanch the bleeding wound by succeeding on a Wisdom (Medicine) check against your spell save DC. The wound also closes if the target receives magical healing. This spell has no effect on undead or constructs.

BLESS THE DEAD

Abjuration Cantrip

Casting Time: 1 action

Range: Touch

Components: V, S

Duration: Instantaneous

You grant a blessing to one deceased creature, enabling it to cross over to the realm of the dead in peace. A creature that benefits from *bless the dead* can't become undead. The spell has no effect on living creatures or the undead.

BLESSED HALO

2nd-Level Evocation

Casting Time: 1 action

Range: Self

Components: V, S

Duration: Concentration, up to 1 minute

A nimbus of golden light surrounds your head for the duration. The halo sheds bright light in a 20-foot radius and dim light for an additional 20 feet.

This spell grants you a pool of 10 points of healing. When you cast the spell and as an action on subsequent turns during the spell's duration, you can expend points from this pool to restore an equal number of hit points to one creature within 20 feet that you can see.

Additionally, you have advantage on Charisma checks made against good creatures within 20 feet.

If any of the light created by this spell overlaps an area of magical darkness created by a spell of 2nd level or lower, the spell that created the darkness is dispelled.

At Higher Levels. When you cast this spell using a spell slot of 3rd level or higher, the spell's pool of healing points increases by 5 for each spell slot above 2nd, and the spell dispels magical darkness created by a spell of a level equal to the slot used to cast this spell.

BLESSED REST

2nd-Level Enchantment

Casting Time: 1 action

Range: Touch

Components: V, S, M (a sprinkling of holy water)

Duration: 8 hours

You place a benediction upon a creature, ensuring it a healthy rest. If the target takes a short rest, it can reroll any Hit Die spent for regaining hit points and take the higher roll.

If the target takes a long rest, it regains up to two extra Hit Dice when resting, up to its maximum Hit Dice. For example, if the target has eight Hit Dice, it can regain six spent Hit Dice upon finishing a long rest.

Once the target has taken one rest (long or short), the spell ends.

At Higher Levels. When you cast this spell using a spell slot of 4th level or higher, you can target one additional humanoid for every two slot levels above 2nd.

BLINDING PAIN

1st-Level Enchantment

Casting Time: 1 action
Range: 30 feet
Components: V, S, M (an ice pick)
Duration: 1 minute

You cause a creature within range to suffer severe pain in its head. At the start of its turn, the target takes 1d4 psychic damage and is blinded for 1 round. On a successful Wisdom saving throw, the creature takes half as much damage and is not blinded. A *cure wounds* or *healing word* spell cast on the target ends this spell, in addition to its regular effects.

At Higher Levels. When you cast this spell using a spell slot of 2nd level or higher, you can affect one additional creature for each slot level above 1st.

BLIZZARD

7th-Level Conjuration

Casting Time: 1 action
Range: 100 feet
Components: V, S
Duration: Concentration, up to 1 minute

A howling storm of thick snow and ice crystals appears in a cylinder 40 feet high and 40 feet in diameter within range. The area is heavily obscured by the swirling snow. When the storm appears, each creature in the area takes 8d8 cold damage, or half as much damage with a successful Constitution saving throw. A creature also makes this saving throw and takes damage when it enters the area for the first time on a turn or ends its turn there. In addition, a creature that takes cold damage from this spell has disadvantage on Constitution saving throws to maintain concentration until the start of its next turn.

BLOOD AND STEEL

4th-Level Transmutation

Casting Time: 1 action
Range: Touch
Components: V, S
Duration: Concentration, up to 1 minute

When you cast this spell, you cut your hand and take 1d4 slashing damage that can't be healed until you take a long rest. You then touch a construct; it must make a successful Constitution saving throw or be charmed by you for the duration. If you or your allies are fighting the construct, it has advantage on the saving throw. Even constructs that are immune to charm effects can be affected by this spell.

While the construct is charmed, you have a telepathic link with it as long as the two of you are on the same plane of existence. You can use this telepathic link to issue commands to the creature while you are conscious (no action required), which it does its best to obey. You can specify a simple and general course of action, such as, "Attack the ghouls," "Block the bridge," or, "Fetch that bucket." If the construct completes the order and doesn't receive further direction from you, it defends itself.

You can use your action to take total and precise control of the target. Until the end of your next turn, the construct takes only the actions you specify and does nothing you haven't ordered it to do. During this time, you can also cause the construct to use a reaction, but doing this requires you to use your own reaction as well.

Each time the construct takes damage, it makes a new Constitution saving throw against the spell. If the saving throw succeeds, the spell ends.

If the construct is already under your control when the spell is cast, it gains an Intelligence of 10 (unless its own Intelligence is higher, in which case it retains the higher score) for 4 hours. The construct is capable of acting independently, though it remains loyal to you for the spell's duration. You can also grant the target a bonus equal to your Intelligence modifier on one skill in which you have proficiency.

At Higher Levels. When you cast this spell using a 5th-level spell slot, the duration is concentration, up to 10 minutes. When you use a 6th-level spell slot, the duration is concentration, up to 1 hour. When you use a spell slot of 7th level or higher, the duration is concentration, up to 8 hours.

BLOOD ARMOR

3rd-Level Necromancy

Casting Time: 1 bonus action

Range: Self

Components: V, S (you must have just struck a foe with a melee weapon)

Duration: 1 hour

When you strike a foe with a melee weapon attack, you can immediately cast *blood armor* as a bonus action. The foe you struck must contain blood; if the target doesn't bleed, the spell ends without effect. The blood flowing from your foe magically increases in volume and forms a suit of armor around you, granting you an Armor Class of 18 – your Dexterity modifier for the spell's duration. This armor has no Strength requirement, doesn't hinder spellcasting, and doesn't incur disadvantage on Dexterity (Stealth) checks.

If the creature you struck was a celestial, *blood armor* also grants you advantage on Charisma saving throws for the duration of the spell.

BLOOD LURE

2nd-Level Enchantment

Casting Time: 1 action

Range: 10 feet

Components: V, S, M (a container or pool of blood)

Duration: 1 minute

You point at any location (a jar, a bowl, even a puddle) within range that contains at least a pint of blood. Each creature that feeds on blood and is within 60 feet of that location must make a Charisma saving throw. (This includes undead, such as vampires.) A creature that has Keen Smell or any similar scent-boosting ability has disadvantage on the saving throw, while undead have advantage on the saving throw. On a failed save, the creature is attracted to the blood and must move toward it unless impeded.

Once an affected creature reaches the blood, it tries to consume it, foregoing all other actions while the blood is present. A successful attack against an affected creature ends the effect, as does the consumption of the blood, which requires an action by an affected creature.

BLOOD OFFERING

3rd-Level Necromancy

Casting Time: 1 minute

Range: Touch

Components: V, S

Duration: Instantaneous

You touch the corpse of a creature that isn't undead or a construct and consume its life force. You must have dealt damage to the creature before it died, and it must have been dead for no more than 1 hour. You regain a number of hit points equal to 1d4 × the creature's challenge rating (minimum of 1d4). The creature can be restored to life only by means of a *true resurrection* or a *wish* spell.

BLOOD PUPPET

4th-Level Transmutation

Casting Time: 1 action

Range: 100 feet

Components: V, M (a drop of blood from the target)

Duration: Concentration, up to 1 minute

With a sample of its blood, you are able to magically control a creature's actions, like a marionette on magical strings. Choose a creature you can see within range whose blood you hold. The target must succeed on a Constitution saving throw, or you gain control over its physical activity (as long as you interact with the blood material component each round). As a bonus action on your turn, you can direct the creature to perform various

CHAPTER 5 SPELL DESCRIPTIONS | 159

activities. You can specify a simple and general course of action, such as, "Attack that creature," "Run over there," or, "Fetch that object." If the creature completes the order and doesn't receive further direction from you, it defends and preserves itself to the best of its ability. The target is aware of being controlled. At the end of each of its turns, the target can make another Constitution saving throw. On a success, the spell ends.

BLOOD SCARAB

1st-Level Necromancy

Casting Time: 1 action
Range: 30 feet
Components: V, M (a drop of the caster's blood, and the exoskeleton of a scarab beetle)
Duration: Instantaneous

Your blood is absorbed into the beetle's exoskeleton to form a beautiful, rubylike scarab that flies toward a creature of your choice within range. The target must make a successful Constitution saving throw or take 1d6 necrotic damage. You gain temporary hit points equal to the necrotic damage dealt.

At Higher Levels. When you cast this spell using a spell slot of 2nd level or higher, the number of scarabs increases by one for each slot level above 1st. You can direct the scarabs at the same target or at different targets. Each target makes a single saving throw, regardless of the number of scarabs targeting it.

BLOOD SPOOR

4th-Level Divination

Casting Time: 1 action
Range: Self
Components: V, S, M (a drop of the quarry's blood)
Duration: Concentration, up to 10 minutes

By touching a drop of your quarry's blood (spilled or drawn within the past hour), you can follow the creature's trail unerringly across any surface or under water, no matter how fast you are moving. If your quarry takes flight, you can follow its trail along the ground—or through the air, if you have the means to fly.

If your quarry moves magically (such as by way of a *dimension door* or a *teleport* spell), you sense its trail as a straight path leading from where the magical movement started to where it ended. Such a route might lead through lethal or impassable barriers. This spell even reveals the route of a creature using *pass without trace*, but it fails to locate a creature protected by *nondetection* or by other effects that prevent *scrying* spells or cause *divination* spells to fail. If your quarry moves to another plane, its trail ends without trace, but *blood spoor* picks up the trail again if the caster moves to the same plane as the quarry before the spell's duration expires.

BLOOD TIDE

Necromancy Cantrip

Casting Time: 1 action
Range: 25 feet
Components: V
Duration: 4 rounds

When you cast this spell, a creature you designate within range must succeed on a Constitution saving throw or bleed from its nose, eyes, ears, and mouth. This bleeding deals no damage but imposes a −2 penalty on the creature's Intelligence, Charisma, and Wisdom checks. *Blood tide* has no effect on undead or constructs.

A bleeding creature might attract the attention of creatures such as stirges, sharks, or giant mosquitoes, depending on the circumstances.

A *cure wounds* spell stops the bleeding before the duration of *blood tide* expires, as does a successful DC 10 Wisdom (Medicine) check.

The spell's duration increases to 2 minutes when you reach 5th level, to 10 minutes when you reach 11th level, and to 1 hour when you reach 17th level.

BLOOD TO ACID

9th-Level Transmutation

Casting Time: 1 action
Range: 60 feet
Components: V, S
Duration: Instantaneous

You designate a creature within range and convert its blood into virulent acid. The target must make a Constitution saving throw. On a failed save, it takes 10d12 acid damage and is stunned by the pain for 1d4 rounds. On a successful save, it takes half the damage and isn't stunned.

Creatures without blood, such as constructs and plants, are not affected by this spell. If *blood to acid* is cast on a creature composed mainly of blood, such as a blood elemental or a **blood zombie** (see *Creature Codex*), the creature is slain by the spell if its saving throw fails.

BLOODHOUND

1st-Level Transmutation

Casting Time: 1 action

Range: Touch

Components: V, S, M (a drop of ammonia)

Duration: 8 hours

You touch a willing creature to grant it an enhanced sense of smell. For the duration, that creature has advantage on Wisdom (Perception) checks that rely on smell and on Wisdom (Survival) checks to follow tracks.

At Higher Levels. When you cast this spell using a spell slot of 3rd level or higher, you also grant the target blindsight out to a range of 30 feet for the duration.

BLOODSHOT

2nd-Level Conjuration

Casting Time: 1 action

Range: 30 feet

Components: V, S

Duration: Instantaneous

You launch a jet of boiling blood from your eyes at a creature within range. You take 1d6 necrotic damage and make a ranged spell attack against the target. If the attack hits, the target takes 2d10 fire damage plus 2d8 psychic damage.

At Higher Levels. When you cast this spell using a spell slot of 3rd level or higher, the fire damage increases by 1d10 for each slot level above 2nd.

BLOODY HANDS

1st-Level Necromancy

Casting Time: 1 action

Range: 30 feet

Components: V, S

Duration: Concentration, up to 1 minute

You cause the hands (or other appropriate body parts, such as claws or tentacles) of a creature within range to bleed profusely. The target must succeed on a Constitution saving throw or take 1 necrotic damage each round and suffer disadvantage on all melee and ranged attack rolls that require the use of its hands for the spell's duration.

Casting any spell that has somatic or material components while under the influence of this spell requires a DC 10 Constitution saving throw. On a failed save, the spell is not cast but it is not lost; the casting can be attempted again in the next round.

BLOODY SMITE

1st-Level Necromancy

Casting Time: 1 bonus action

Range: Self

Components: V

Duration: Concentration, up to 1 minute

The next time during the spell's duration that you hit a creature with a melee weapon attack, your weapon pulses with a dull red light, and the attack deals an extra 1d6 necrotic damage to the target. Until the spell ends, the target must make a Constitution saving throw at the start of each of its turns. On a failed save, it takes 1d6 necrotic damage, it bleeds profusely from the mouth, and it can't speak intelligibly or cast spells that have a verbal component. On a successful save, the spell ends. If the target or an ally within 5 feet of it uses an action to tend the wound and makes a successful Wisdom (Medicine) check against your spell save DC, or if the target receives magical healing, the spell ends.

BOILING BLOOD

4th-Level Necromancy

Casting Time: 1 action

Range: 30 feet

Components: V, S, M (a vial of blood)

Duration: Concentration, up to 1 minute

You cause the blood within a creature's body to boil with supernatural heat. Choose one creature that you can see within range that isn't a construct or an undead. The target must make a Constitution saving throw. On a successful save, it takes 2d6 fire damage and the spell ends. On a failed save, the creature takes 4d6 fire damage and is blinded. At the end of each of its turns, the target can make another Constitution saving throw. On a success, the spell ends. On a failure, the creature takes an additional 2d6 fire damage and remains blinded.

At Higher Levels. When you cast this spell using a spell slot of 5th level or higher, you can target one additional creature for each slot level above 4th. The creatures must be within 30 feet of each other when you target them.

BOILING OIL

2nd-Level Conjuration

Casting Time: 1 action

Range: 60 feet

Components: V, S, M (a vial of oil)

Duration: Concentration, up to 1 minute

You conjure a shallow, 15-foot-radius pool of boiling oil centered on a point within range. The pool is difficult terrain, and any creature that enters the pool or starts its turn there must make a Dexterity saving throw. On a failed save, the creature takes 3d8 fire damage and falls prone. On a successful save, a creature takes half as much damage and doesn't fall prone.

At Higher Levels. When you cast this spell using a spell slot of 3rd level or higher, the damage increases by 1d8 for each slot level above 2nd.

BOLSTER UNDEAD

1st-Level Necromancy

Casting Time: 1 action
Range: 60 feet
Components: V, S, M (a sprinkle of unholy water)
Duration: 1 hour

You suffuse an area with negative energy to increase the difficulty of harming or affecting undead creatures.

Choose up to three undead creatures within range. When a targeted creature makes a saving throw against being turned or against spells or effects that deal radiant damage, the target has advantage on the saving throw.

At Higher Levels. When you cast this spell using a spell slot of 2nd level or higher, you can affect one additional undead creature for each slot level above 1st.

BOLSTERING BREW

3rd-Level Conjuration (Ritual)

Casting Time: 1 action
Range: 30 feet
Components: V, S, M (a silver tankard worth 100 gp, which the spell consumes)
Duration: Instantaneous

Calling upon the patron deity of brewers, you bring forth a vibrant brew of beer or ale. Up to six other creatures within range can partake of this drink with you and share in its magical benefits, each drawing a mug from the small keg of magical brew that appears. A creature that downs a mug of magical beer gains advantage on either all Strength checks or all Charisma checks (chosen when it drinks), is immune to being frightened, and makes all Constitution saving throws with advantage. These benefits last for 8 hours.

BONES OF STONE

3rd-Level Transmutation

Casting Time: 1 action
Range: Touch
Components: V, S, M (a pebble and a sliver of bone)
Duration: Concentration, up to 1 minute

The bones of a creature you touch gain the strength and density of stone. Until the spell ends, the target has resistance to slashing damage and bludgeoning damage, and it gains advantage on Strength checks against effects that would move the target against its will.

BOOSTER SHOT

3rd-Level Evocation

Casting Time: 1 action
Range: Touch
Components: V, S
Duration: Concentration, up to 1 minute

You imbue a two-handed ranged weapon (typically a shortbow, longbow, light crossbow, or heavy crossbow) that you touch with a random magical benefit. While the spell lasts, a projectile fired from the weapon has an effect that occurs on a hit in addition to its normal damage. Roll a d6 to determine the additional effect for each casting of this spell.

d6	Effect
1	2d10 acid damage to all creatures within 10 feet of the target
2	2d10 lightning damage to the target and 1d10 lightning damage to all creatures in a 5-foot-wide line between the weapon and the target
3	2d10 necrotic damage to the target, and the target has disadvantage on its first attack roll before the start of the weapon user's next turn
4	2d10 cold damage to the target and 1d10 cold damage to all other creatures in a 60-foot cone in front of the weapon
5	2d10 force damage to the target, and the target is pushed 20 feet
6	2d10 psychic damage to the target, and the target is stunned until the start of the weapon user's next turn

At Higher Levels. When you cast this spell using a spell slot of 4th level or higher, all damage increases by 1d10 for each slot level above 3rd.

BOREAS'S EMBRACE

4th-Level Conjuration

Casting Time: 1 action
Range: 120 feet
Components: V, S
Duration: Instantaneous and 1 minute (see text)

You cause a downburst of freezing cold wind and rain with a 15-foot radius, which freezes in moments into a sheet of slick, encasing ice. All fires in the area are extinguished. Creatures in the area must make a Strength saving throw, taking 6d6 cold damage and being restrained on a failed save or half as much damage and no additional effects on a successful one. Anyone entering or moving through the affected area for 1 minute afterward must succeed on a Dexterity saving throw or fall prone.

At Higher Levels. When you cast this spell using a spell slot of 5th level or higher, you may either inflict an additional 1d6 cold damage or increase the duration of the ice slick by 1 minute for each slot level above 4th.

BOREAS'S KISS

1st-Level Conjuration

Casting Time: 1 action
Range: 30 feet
Components: V, S
Duration: 1 minute

You encapsulate a creature within range in a pocket of fiercely cold air. The target must succeed on a Constitution saving throw or drop any object in hand. They also have disadvantage on any cold-based saving throws until they make a successful Constitution saving throw.

At Higher Levels. When you cast this spell using a spell slot of 2nd level or higher, you may extend the duration by 1 minute. Alternatively, for every two levels above 1st level, you may instead choose to have the target suffer a level of exhaustion on the first failed saving throw, up to a maximum of three levels of exhaustion.

BOTTLED ARCANA

5th-Level Transmutation

Casting Time: 1 action
Range: Touch
Components: V, S, M (an empty glass container)
Duration: See below

By touching an empty, stoppered glass container such as a vial or flask, you magically enable it to hold a single spell. To be captured, the spell must be cast within 1 round of casting *bottled arcana* and it must be intentionally cast into the container. The container can hold one spell of 3rd level or lower. The spell can be held in the container for as much as 24 hours, after which the container reverts to a mundane vessel and any magic inside it dissipates harmlessly.

As an action, any creature can unstop the container, thereby releasing the spell. If the spell has a range of self, the creature opening the container is affected; otherwise, the creature opening the container designates the target according to the captured spell's description. If a creature opens the container unwittingly (not knowing that the container holds a spell), the spell targets the creature opening the container or is centered on its space instead (whichever is more appropriate). *Dispel magic* cast on the container targets *bottled arcana*, not the spell inside. If *bottled arcana* is dispelled, the container becomes mundane and the spell inside dissipates harmlessly.

Until the spell in the container is released, its caster can't regain the spell slot used to cast that spell. Once the spell is released, its caster regains the use of that slot normally.

At Higher Levels. When you cast this spell using a spell slot of 6th level or higher, the level of the spell the container can hold increases by one for every slot level above 5th.

BOTTOMLESS STOMACH

1st-Level Transmutation

Casting Time: 1 action
Range: Self
Components: V
Duration: Concentration, up to 1 hour

When you cast this spell, you gain the ability to consume dangerous substances and contain them in an extradimensional reservoir in your stomach. The spell allows you to swallow most liquids, such as acids, alcohol, poison, and even quicksilver, and hold them safely in your stomach. You are unaffected by swallowing the substance, but the spell doesn't give you resistance or immunity to the substance in general; for example, you could safely drink a bucket of a black dragon's acidic spittle, but you'd still be burned if you were caught in the dragon's breath attack or if that bucket of acid were dumped over your head.

The spell allows you to store up to 10 gallons of liquid at one time. The liquid doesn't need to all be of the same type, and different types don't mix while in your stomach. Any liquid in excess of 10 gallons has its normal effect when you try to swallow it.

At any time before you stop concentrating on the spell, you can regurgitate up to 1 gallon of liquid stored in your stomach as a bonus action. The liquid is vomited into an adjacent 5-foot square. A target in that square must succeed on a DC 15 Dexterity saving throw or be affected by the liquid. The GM determines the exact effect based on the type of liquid regurgitated, using 1d6 damage of the appropriate type as the baseline.

When you stop concentrating on the spell, its duration expires, or it's dispelled, the extradimensional reservoir and the liquid it contains cease to exist.

BOULDER TOSS

2nd-Level Transmutation

Casting Time: 1 action
Range: Self
Components: V, S
Duration: Concentration, up to 1 minute

You draw the power of the mountains into you, gaining a surge of strength that allows you to take an action to hurl a rock (or similar object) as a giant does. Your Strength is considered to be 19 for the purpose of determining damage from objects that you hurl.

Your hurled rock has a range of 60/240 feet and deals 2d10 bludgeoning damage on a hit. If the target is a creature, it must succeed on a Strength check against your spell save DC or be knocked prone.

At Higher Levels. If you cast this spell using a spell slot of 4th or 5th level, your Strength is considered to be 21, and the bludgeoning damage increases to 3d10. If you cast this spell using a spell slot of 6th level or higher, your Strength is considered to be 23, and the bludgeoning damage increases to 4d10.

BRAWN BOOST

Transmutation Cantrip

Casting Time: 1 action
Range: Touch
Components: V, S
Duration: Concentration, up to 1 minute

You touch a willing creature. Once before the spell ends, the target can roll a d6 and add the result to one Strength check of its choice. It can roll the die before or after making the check. The spell then ends.

BREATHTAKING WIND

1st-Level Evocation

Casting Time: 1 action
Range: 30 feet
Components: V, S
Duration: Concentration, up to 1 minute

You target a creature with a blast of wintry air. That creature must make a successful Constitution saving throw or become unable to speak or cast spells with a vocal component for the duration of the spell.

BREEZE COMPASS

3rd-Level Divination

Casting Time: 1 action
Range: Self
Components: V, S, M (a magnetized needle)
Duration: Concentration, up to 1 hour

When you cast *breeze compass*, you must clearly imagine or mentally describe a location. It doesn't need to be a location you've been to as long as you know it exists on the Material Plane. Within moments, a gentle breeze arises and blows along the most efficient path toward that destination. Only you can sense this breeze, and whenever it brings you to a decision point (a fork in a passageway, for example), you must make a successful DC 8 Intelligence (Arcana) check to deduce which way the breeze indicates you should go. On a failed check, the spell ends. The breeze guides you around cliffs, lava pools, and other natural obstacles, but it doesn't avoid enemies or hostile creatures.

BRIGHT SPARKS

Evocation Cantrip

Casting Time: 1 action
Range: Self
Components: V, M (flint and steel)
Duration: 1 round

Sparks fly from your fingers for a moment, generating bright blue light. This illuminates the region around you to a distance of 60 feet until the start of your next turn. Wisdom (Perception) checks have advantage to spot creatures hidden in shadows.

BRIMSTONE INFUSION

Transmutation Cantrip

Casting Time: 1 action
Range: Touch
Components: V, S, M (a flask of alchemist's fire and 5 gp worth of brimstone)
Duration: 24 hours

You infuse an ordinary flask of alchemist's fire with magical brimstone. While so enchanted, the alchemist's fire can be thrown 40 feet instead of 20, and it does 2d6 fire damage instead of 1d4. The Dexterity saving throw to extinguish the flames uses your spell save DC instead of DC 10. Infused alchemist's fire returns to its normal properties after 24 hours.

BRITTLING

4th-Level Transmutation

Casting Time: 1 action
Range: Touch
Components: V, S, M (an icicle)
Duration: Instantaneous

This spell uses biting cold to make a metal or stone object you touch become brittle and more easily shattered. The object's hit points are reduced by a number equal to your level as a spellcaster, and Strength checks to shatter or break the object are made with advantage if they occur within 1 minute of the spell's casting. If the object isn't shattered during this time, it reverts to the state it was in before the spell was cast.

BURNING RADIANCE

6th-Level Evocation

Casting Time: 1 action
Range: Self (60-foot line)
Components: V, S
Duration: Instantaneous

A line of light 60 feet long and 5 feet wide emanates from you in a direction of your choice. Each creature in the line must make a Dexterity saving throw. On a failed save, a creature takes 10d8 radiant damage and catches fire; until someone takes an action to douse the fire, the creature takes 1d10 fire damage at the start of each of its turns. A successful saving throw halves the damage and prevents a creature from catching fire.

The burning radiance ignites flammable objects in the area that aren't being worn or carried.

CALM OF THE STORM

3rd-Level Abjuration

Casting Time: 1 action

Range: Touch

Components: V, S, M (an amethyst worth 250 gp, which the spell consumes)

Duration: Instantaneous

While visualizing the world as you wish it was, you lay your hands upon a creature other than yourself and undo the effect of a chaos magic surge that affected the creature within the last minute. Reality reshapes itself as if the surge never happened, but only for that creature.

At Higher Levels. When you cast this spell using a spell slot of 4th level or higher, the time since the chaos magic surge can be 1 minute longer for each slot level above 3rd.

CANDLE'S INSIGHT

1st-Level Divination

Casting Time: 1 action

Range: 10 feet

Components: V, S, M (a blessed candle)

Duration: 10 minutes

Candle's insight is cast on its target as the component candle is lit. The candle burns for up to 10 minutes unless it's extinguished normally or by the spell's effect. While the candle burns, the caster can question the spell's target, and the candle reveals whether the target speaks truthfully. An intentionally misleading or partial answer causes the flame to flicker and dim. An outright lie causes the flame to flare and then go out, ending the spell. The candle judges honesty, not absolute truth; the flame burns steadily through even an outrageously false statement, as long as the target believes it's true.

Candle's insight is used across society: by merchants while negotiating deals, by inquisitors investigating heresy, and by monarchs as they interview foreign diplomats. In some societies, casting *candle's insight* without the consent of the spell's target is considered a serious breach of hospitality.

CARMELLO-VOLTA'S IRKSOME PRESERVES

2nd-Level Conjuration

Casting Time: 1 action

Range: 30 feet

Components: V, S, M (a small berry or a piece of fruit)

Duration: Concentration, up to 1 minute

At your command, delicious fruit jam oozes from a small mechanical device (such as a crossbow trigger, a lock, or a clockwork toy), rendering the device inoperable until the spell ends, and the device is cleaned with a damp cloth. Cleaning away the jam takes an action, but doing so has no effect until the spell ends. One serving of the jam can be collected in a suitable container. If it's eaten (as a bonus action) within 24 hours, the jam restores 1d4 hit points. The jam's flavor is determined by the material component.

The spell can affect constructs, with two limitations. First, the target creature negates the effect with a successful Dexterity saving throw. Second, unless the construct is Tiny, only one component (an eye, a knee, an elbow, and so forth) can be disabled. The affected construct has disadvantage on attack rolls and ability checks that depend on the disabled component until the spell ends and the jam is removed.

CATAPULT

6th-Level Transmutation

Casting Time: 1 action

Range: 400 feet

Components: V, S, M (a small platinum lever and fulcrum worth 400 gp)

Duration: Instantaneous

You magically hurl an object or creature weighing 500 pounds or less 40 feet through the air in a direction of your choosing (including straight up). Objects hurled at specific targets require a spell attack roll to hit. A thrown creature takes 6d10 bludgeoning damage from the force of the throw, plus any appropriate falling damage, and lands prone. If the target of the spell is thrown against another creature, the total damage is divided evenly between them and both creatures are knocked prone.

At Higher Levels. When you cast this spell using a spell slot of 7th level or higher, the damage increases by 1d10, the distance thrown increases by 10 feet, and the weight thrown increases by 100 pounds for each slot level above 6th.

CATCH THE BREATH

3rd-Level Transmutation

Casting Time: 1 reaction, which you take when you make a saving throw against a breath weapon attack
Range: Self
Components: V
Duration: Instantaneous

You can cast this spell as a reaction when you're targeted by a breath weapon. Doing so gives you advantage on your saving throw against the breath weapon. If your saving throw succeeds, you take no damage from the attack even if a successful save normally only halves the damage.

Whether your saving throw succeeded or failed, you absorb and store energy from the attack. On your next turn, you can make a ranged spell attack against a target within 60 feet. On a hit, the target takes 3d10 force damage. If you opt not to make this attack, the stored energy dissipates harmlessly.

At Higher Levels. When you cast this spell using a spell slot of 4th level or higher, the damage done by your attack increases by 1d10 for each slot level above 3rd.

CAUSTIC BLOOD

2nd-Level Transmutation

Casting Time: 1 reaction, which you take when an enemy's attack deals piercing or slashing damage to you
Range: Self (30-foot radius)
Components: V, S
Duration: Instantaneous

Your blood becomes caustic when exposed to the air. When you take piercing or slashing damage, you can use your reaction to select up to three creatures within 30 feet of you. Each target takes 1d10 acid damage unless it makes a successful Dexterity saving throw.

At Higher Levels. When you cast this spell using a spell slot of 3rd level or higher, the number of targets increases by one for each slot level above 2nd, to a maximum of six targets.

CAUSTIC TORRENT

8th-Level Conjuration

Casting Time: 1 action
Range: Self (60-foot line)
Components: V, S, M (a chip of bone pitted by acid)
Duration: Instantaneous

A swirling jet of acid sprays from you in a direction you choose. The acid fills a line 60 feet long and 5 feet wide. Each creature in the line takes 14d6 acid damage, or half as much damage if it makes a successful Dexterity saving throw. A creature reduced to 0 hit points by this spell is killed, and its body is liquefied. In addition, each creature other than you that's in the line or within 5 feet of it is poisoned for 1 minute by toxic fumes. Creatures that don't breathe or that are immune to acid damage aren't poisoned. A poisoned creature can repeat the Constitution saving throw at the end of each of its turns, ending the effect on itself on a success.

CAUSTIC TOUCH

Evocation Cantrip

Casting Time: 1 action
Range: Touch
Components: V, S
Duration: Instantaneous

Your hand sweats profusely and becomes coated in a film of caustic slime. Make a melee spell attack against a creature you touch. On a hit, the target takes 1d8 acid damage. If the target was concentrating on a spell, it has disadvantage on its Constitution saving throw to maintain concentration.

This spell's damage increases by 1d8 when you reach 5th level (2d8), 11th level (3d8), and 17th level (4d8).

CAVE DRAGON'S DOMINANCE

6th-Level Transmutation

Casting Time: 1 action
Range: Self
Components: V, S
Duration: Concentration, up to 1 minute

You take on some of the physical characteristics and abilities of the cave dragon, growing protective scales and claws. Until the spell ends, your AC can't be lower than 16, regardless of what kind of armor you are wearing. You gain blindsight out to a range of 60 feet. You can take two actions on your turn to attack with your claws, dealing 1d6 slashing damage on a hit. You have resistance to poison damage. Up to three times while the spell is active, as an action, you can breathe a 20-foot cone of poison gas, dealing 6d8 poison damage to each creature in the cone and making it poisoned until it finishes a long or short rest. A creature that succeeds on a Constitution saving throw takes half as much damage from your breath weapon and is not poisoned. Finally, you gain a climbing speed of 40 feet.

CELESTIAL FANFARE

6th-Level Evocation

Casting Time: 1 action
Range: 100 feet
Components: V, S, M (miniature trumpet worth 100 gp)
Duration: Instantaneous

A great blaring of trumpets from on high blasts down upon an area you designate. All evil creatures in a 30-foot radius take 4d6 thunder damage and 4d6 radiant damage and are blinded and deafened for 2d4 rounds. A successful Constitution saving throw reduces the damage and the duration of the blinded and deafened conditions by half.

Neutral or unaligned creatures take half as much damage and are blinded and deafened for 1d4 rounds. A successful save reduces the damage to one-quarter and negates the blinding and deafening effects.

Good-aligned creatures are not harmed by this spell.

CHAINS OF PERDITION

3rd-Level Conjuration

Casting Time: 1 action
Range: 60 feet
Components: V, S, M (a few links of iron chain)
Duration: Concentration, up to 1 minute

Lengths of iron chain appear near a creature you choose within range, possibly ensnaring the target and causing it physical and mental suffering. The targeted creature must succeed on a Dexterity saving throw or be restrained by the chains and take 2d8 bludgeoning damage and 2d8 psychic damage. The creature takes this damage on your turn every round that it remains restrained by the chains. On its turn, a restrained creature can make a Strength or Dexterity check (its choice) against your spell save DC. On a success, it frees itself.

The chains remain until the spell ends. If they are not restraining a creature, you can use a bonus action to direct the chains to target the same creature or another one, moving the chains up to 20 feet (within the range of the spell) if necessary to do so. If the chains move beyond the maximum range, the spell ends. The chains can be destroyed; treat them as an object with AC 18, 15 hit points, resistance to piercing damage, and immunity to poison damage and psychic damage.

At Higher Levels. When you cast this spell using a spell slot of 4th level or higher, the spell deals an extra 1d8 bludgeoning damage and 1d8 psychic damage for every two slot levels above 3rd.

CHAINS OF THE GODDESS

5th-Level Enchantment

Casting Time: 1 action
Range: 90 feet
Components: V, S, M (1 foot of iron chain)
Duration: Concentration, up to 1 minute

Choose a creature you can see within 90 feet. The target must make a successful Wisdom saving throw or be restrained by chains of psychic force and take 6d8 bludgeoning damage. A restrained creature can repeat the saving throw at the end of each of its turns, ending the effect on itself on a successful save. While restrained in this way, the creature also takes 6d8 bludgeoning damage at the start of each of your turns.

CHAINS OF TORMENT

4th-Level Conjuration

Casting Time: 1 action
Range: Self
Components: V, S, M (an iron chain link dipped in blood)
Duration: Concentration, up to 1 minute

You are surrounded by dim light in a 10-foot radius as you conjure an iron chain that extends out to a creature you can see within 30 feet. The creature must make a successful Dexterity saving throw or be grappled (escape DC equal to your spell save DC). While grappled in this way, the creature is also restrained. A creature that's restrained at the start of its turn takes 4d6 psychic damage. You can have only one creature restrained in this way at a time.

As an action, you can scan the mind of the creature that's restrained by your chain. If the creature gets a failure on a Wisdom saving throw, you learn one discrete piece of information of your choosing known by the creature (such as a name, a password, or an important number). The effect is otherwise harmless.

At Higher Levels. When you cast this spell using a spell slot of 5th level or higher, the psychic damage increases by 1d6 for each slot level above 4th.

CHAMPION'S WEAPON

2nd-Level Conjuration

Casting Time: 1 bonus action
Range: Self
Components: V, S
Duration: Concentration, up to 10 minutes

A spectral version of a melee weapon of your choice materializes in your hand. It has standard statistics for a weapon of its kind, but it deals force damage instead of its normal damage type and it sheds dim light in a 10-foot radius. You have proficiency with this weapon for the spell's duration. The weapon can be wielded only by the caster; the spell ends if the weapon is held by a creature other than you or if you start your turn more than 10 feet from the weapon.

At Higher Levels. When you cast this spell using a spell slot of 3rd level or higher, the weapon deals an extra 1d8 force damage for each slot level above 2nd.

CHANNEL FIENDISH POWER

5th-Level Transmutation

Casting Time: 1 action
Range: Self
Components: V, S, M (an amulet inscribed with a demonic or diabolic symbol)
Duration: 10 minutes

You infuse yourself with dark power from the Lower Planes, which grants you magical gifts for a short time. While this spell is in effect, your body takes on minor fiendish characteristics: scales, a reddish or greenish hue to your skin, small horns protruding from your forehead, or other such features. While the spell is in effect, you gain two of the following abilities:

- Darkvision with a range of 120 feet, unimpeded by magical darkness.
- Immunity to fire damage.
- Immunity to poison damage and the poisoned condition.
- Advantage on saving throws against spells and other magical effects.
- Resistance to one of the following damage types: cold, fire, or lightning.
- Resistance to bludgeoning, piercing, and slashing damage from weapons that aren't silvered.
- Resistance to bludgeoning, piercing, and slashing damage from nonmagical weapons.
- Claws that grant you a melee weapon attack that deals 1d8 slashing damage.
- Wings that grant you a flying speed of 60 feet.

At Higher Levels. When you cast this spell using a spell slot of 6th level or higher, you can choose one additional benefit to be granted by the spell for each slot level above 5th.

CHAOTIC FORM

4th-Level Transmutation

Casting Time: 1 action
Range: Touch
Components: V, S
Duration: 10 minutes

You cause the form of a willing creature to become malleable, dripping and flowing according to the target's will as if the creature were a vaguely humanoid-shaped ooze. The creature is not affected by difficult terrain, it has advantage on Dexterity (Acrobatics) checks made to escape a grapple, and it suffers no penalties when squeezing through spaces one size smaller than itself. The target's movement is halved while it is affected by *chaotic form*.

At Higher Levels. When you cast this spell using a spell slot of 5th level or higher, the duration increases by 10 minutes for each slot level above 4th.

CHAOTIC VITALITY

2nd-Level Conjuration

Casting Time: 1 action
Range: Touch
Components: V, S
Duration: Instantaneous

Make a melee spell attack against a creature that has a number of Hit Dice no greater than your level and has at least 1 hit point. On a hit, you conjure pulsating waves of chaotic energy within the creature and yourself. After a brief moment that seems to last forever, your hit point total changes, as does the creature's. Roll a d100 and increase or decrease the number rolled by any number up to your spellcasting level, then find the result on the Hit Point Flux table. Apply that result both to yourself and the target creature. Any hit points gained beyond a creature's normal maximum are temporary hit points that last for 1 round per caster level.

For example, a 3rd-level spellcaster who currently has 17 of her maximum 30 hit points casts *chaotic vitality* on a creature with 54 hit points and rolls a 75 on the Hit Point Flux table. The two creatures have a combined total of 71 hit points. A result of 75 indicates that both creatures get 50 percent of the total, so the spellcaster and the target end up with 35 hit points each. In the spellcaster's case, 5 of those hit points are temporary and will last for 3 rounds.

At Higher Levels. When you cast this spell using a spell slot of 3rd level or higher, the maximum Hit Dice of the affected creature increases by 2 for each slot level above 2nd.

HIT POINT FLUX

Size	HP
01–09	0
10–39	1
40–69	25 percent of total
70–84	50 percent of total
85–94	75 percent of total
95–99	100 percent of total
100	200 percent of total, and both creatures gain the effect of a *haste* spell that lasts for 1 round per caster level

CHAOTIC WORLD

6th-Level Illusion

Casting Time: 1 action
Range: 60 feet
Components: V, M (seven irregular pieces of colored cloth that you throw into the air)
Duration: Concentration, up to 1 minute

You throw a handful of colored cloth into the air while screaming a litany of disjointed phrases. A moment later, a 30-foot cube centered on a point within range fills with multicolored light, cacophonous sound, overpowering scents, and other confusing sensory information. The effect is dizzying and overwhelming. Each enemy within the cube must make a successful Intelligence saving throw or become blinded and deafened and fall prone. An affected enemy cannot stand up or recover from the blindness or deafness while within the area, but all three conditions end immediately for a creature that leaves the spell's area.

CHERUB'S BURNING BLADE

4th-Level Evocation

Casting Time: 1 action
Range: Self
Components: V, S
Duration: Concentration, up to 10 minutes

A sword made of holy fire blazes to life in your hand. The size and shape of the blade conforms to your will, but it is never larger than a one-handed weapon sized for a Medium creature. If you let go of the blade, it disappears, but if you maintain concentration on the spell, you can evoke the blade again as a bonus action.

You can use your action to make a melee attack with the burning blade. On a hit, the target takes 2d6 fire and 2d6 radiant damage. On a critical hit, the target catches fire; until someone takes an action to douse the fire, the target takes 2d6 fire damage at the start of each of its turns. The burning blade sheds bright light in a 10-foot radius and dim light for an additional 10 feet.

At Higher Levels. When you cast this spell using a spell slot of 6th level or higher, both the fire damage and radiant damage increase by 1d6 for every two slot levels above 4th.

CHILD OF LIGHT AND DARKNESS

8th-Level Transmutation

Casting Time: 1 action
Range: Self
Components: V, S, M (a pebble from the Shadow Realm that has been left in the sun)
Duration: 1 minute

Roll a d20 at the end of each of your turns for the duration of the spell. On a roll of 1–10, you take the form of a humanoid made of pure, searing light. On a roll of 11–20, you take the form of a humanoid made of bone-chilling darkness. In both forms, you have immunity to bludgeoning, piercing, and slashing damage from nonmagical attacks, and a creature that attacks you has disadvantage on the attack roll. You gain additional benefits while in either form.

In Light Form. You shed bright light in a 60-foot radius and dim light for an additional 60 feet, you are immune to fire damage, and you have resistance to radiant damage. Once per turn as a bonus action, you can teleport to a space you can see within the light you shed.

In Darkness Form. You are immune to cold damage, and you have resistance to necrotic damage. Once per turn as a bonus action, you can target up to three Large or smaller creatures within 30 feet of you. Each target must succeed on a Strength saving throw or be pulled or pushed (your choice) up to 20 feet straight toward or away from you.

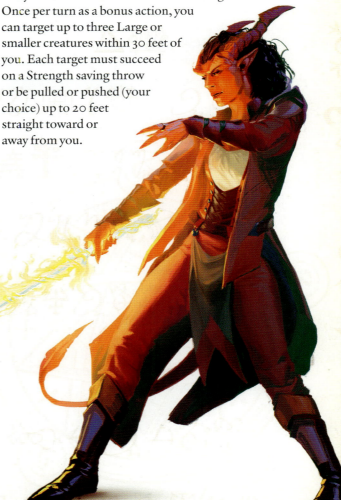

CHILLING WORDS

3rd-Level Enchantment

Casting Time: 1 action
Range: 30 feet
Components: V, S, M (a strip of paper with writing on it)
Duration: Concentration, up to 1 hour

You utter a short phrase and designate a creature within range to be affected by it. The target must make a Wisdom saving throw to avoid the spell. On a failed save, the target is susceptible to the phrase for the duration of the spell. At any later time while the spell is in effect, you and any of your allies within range when you cast the spell can use an action to utter the phrase, which causes the target to freeze in fear. Each of you can use the phrase against the target once only, and the target must be within 30 feet of the speaker for the phrase to be effective.

When the target hears the phrase, it must make a successful Constitution saving throw or take 1d6 psychic damage and become restrained for 1 round. Whether this saving throw succeeds or fails, the target can't be affected by the phrase for 1 minute afterward.

You can end the spell early by making a final utterance of the phrase (even if you've used the phrase on this target previously). On hearing this final utterance, the target takes 4d6 psychic damage and is restrained for 1 minute or, with a successful Constitution saving throw, it takes half the damage and is restrained for 1 round.

CHRONAL LANCE

1st-Level Transmutation

Casting Time: 1 action
Range: 60 feet
Components: V, S
Duration: 1 minute

You inflict the ravages of aging on up to three creatures within range, temporarily discomfiting them and making them appear elderly for a time. Each target must make a successful Wisdom saving throw, or its walking speed is halved (round up to the nearest 5-foot increment) and it has disadvantage on Dexterity checks (but not saving throws). An affected creature can repeat the saving throw at the end of each of its turns, ending the effect on itself on a success.

At Higher Levels. When you cast this spell using a spell slot of 2nd level or higher, you can target one additional creature for each slot level above 1st.

CIRCLE OF DEVASTATION

9th-Level Evocation

Casting Time: 1 action
Range: 1 mile
Components: V, S, M (a metal ring)
Duration: Concentration, up to 1 minute

You create a 10-foot-tall, 20-foot-radius cylinder of destructive energy around a point you can see within range. The area is difficult terrain. When you cast the spell and as a bonus action on each of your turns, you can choose one of the following damage types: cold, fire, lightning, necrotic, or radiant. Each creature or object that is inside the cylinder when it's created or ends its turn inside the cylinder takes 6d6 damage of the chosen type, or half the damage with a successful Constitution saving throw. A creature or object dropped to 0 hit points by the spell is reduced to fine ash.

The cylinder's radius expands by 20 feet at the start of each of your turns after the spell is cast. Any creatures or objects enveloped in the enlarged area are subject to its effects immediately.

CIRCLE OF WIND

1st-Level Abjuration

Casting Time: 1 action
Range: Self
Components: V, S, M (a crystal ring)
Duration: 8 hours

Light wind encircles you, leaving you in the center of a mild vortex. For the duration, you gain a +2 bonus to your AC against ranged attacks. You also have advantage on saving throws against extreme environmental heat and against harmful gases, vapors, and inhaled poisons.

CLAIM LAIR

6th-Level Abjuration

Casting Time: 10 minutes
Range: Touch
Components: V, S, M (material goods and wealth worth at least 2,000 gp)
Duration: 24 hours

By placing your personal wealth within an area and invoking the dragon's territorial nature, you claim the area as your lair, imbuing you with extra power within its confines. You can claim an area of up to 2,500 square feet (a space 50 feet square, or one hundred 5-foot squares, or twenty-five 10-foot squares). The claimed area can be up to 20 feet tall and shaped as you desire. While within these confines, you can take one of the following lair actions once per round on initiative count 20:

- Magical darkness spreads from a point you choose within 30 feet, filling a 15-foot-radius sphere until you dismiss it as an action, use this lair action again, or die. The darkness spreads around corners. A creature with darkvision can't see through this darkness, and nonmagical light can't illuminate it, but you can see in the area as if it were brightly lit. If any of the effect's area overlaps with an area of light created by a spell of 2nd level or lower, the spell that created the light is dispelled.
- Part of the ceiling collapses above one creature you can see within 60 feet of you. The creature must succeed on a Dexterity saving throw against your spell save DC or take 3d6 bludgeoning damage and be knocked prone and buried. A buried target is restrained and unable to breathe or stand up. A creature can take an action to make a DC 10 Strength check, ending the buried state with a success.
- A tremor shakes the lair in a 30-foot radius around you. Each creature on the ground in that area other than you must succeed on a Dexterity saving throw against your spell save DC or be knocked prone.

You can take an action to dismiss this spell.

CLASH OF GLACIERS

5th-Level Evocation

Casting Time: 1 action
Range: Self (100-foot line)
Components: V, S, M (a piece of cracked glass)
Duration: Instantaneous

You conjure several icy boulders in a line 100 feet long, which crush anything beneath them. Each creature in the area must make a Dexterity saving throw, taking 5d6 bludgeoning damage and 5d6 cold damage on a failed save or half as much damage on a successful one.

At Higher Levels. When you cast this spell using a spell slot of 6th level or higher, the damage increases by 1d6 for each slot level above 5th. You decide whether each extra die deals bludgeoning or cold damage.

CLAWS OF THE EARTH DRAGON

5th-Level Evocation

Casting Time: 1 action
Range: 60 feet
Components: V
Duration: Instantaneous

You summon the power of the earth dragon and shoot a ray at one target within 60 feet. The target falls prone and takes 6d8 bludgeoning damage from being slammed to the ground. If the target was flying or levitating, it takes an additional 1d6 bludgeoning damage per 10 feet it falls. If the target makes a successful Strength saving throw, damage is halved, it doesn't fall, and it isn't knocked prone.

At Higher Levels. When you cast this spell using a spell slot of 6th level or higher, the damage done by the attack increases by 1d8 and the range increases by 10 feet for each slot level above 5th.

CLOAK OF FIENDISH MENACE

2nd-Level Transmutation

Casting Time: 1 action
Range: Personal
Components: V, S
Duration: Concentration, up to 1 minute

You wrap yourself in an aura of fiendish power, intimidating those that face you. When a creature is within 5 feet of you, it must make a Wisdom saving throw. On a failed save, the creature becomes frightened. A frightened creature can make another saving throw at the start of each of its turns. On a successful saving throw, the creature is no longer frightened and cannot again be affected by this particular casting of the spell.

If you deal damage to a creature that is frightened by this spell, it must take the Dash action and move away from you by the safest available route on its next turn, unless there is nowhere to move. The creature is unable to move toward you again while the spell is in effect, unless it makes a successful saving throw against the spell.

CLOAK OF SERPENTS

4th-Level Abjuration

Casting Time: 1 action
Range: Self
Components: V, S, M (a snake scale)
Duration: 10 minutes

A mass of writhing, translucent snakes drapes your body, protecting you from harm and fending off enemies. You can end the spell early by using an action to dismiss it.

For the duration of the spell, you gain resistance to poison damage and immunity to the poisoned condition. In addition, whenever a creature within 5 feet hits you with a melee attack, that creature is struck by one of the serpents. The attacker takes 2d8 poison damage and must succeed on a Constitution saving throw or be poisoned for 1 minute. A successful saving throw halves the damage and negates the poisoned effect.

CLOCKWORK BODYGUARD

5th-Level Conjuration

Casting Time: 1 action
Range: 60 feet
Components: V, S
Duration: Concentration, up to 1 hour

You summon clockwork minions to fight for you. Choose one of the following options for what appears (see *Tome of Beasts*):

- One **clockwork huntsman**
- Two **clockwork hounds**
- Four **clockwork watchmen**

The clockwork creatures are friendly to you and your companions for the duration. Roll initiative for the creatures, which have their own turns. They obey any verbal commands you issue to them (no action required by you). If you don't issue commands, the clockwork creatures defend themselves or you from hostile creatures but otherwise take no actions. The clockwork creatures disappear when they drop to 0 hit points or when the spell ends.

At Higher Levels. When you cast this spell using certain higher-level spell slots, more creatures of your choice appear: twice as many with a 6th-level slot, three times as many with a 7th-level slot, and four times as many with an 8th-level slot.

CLOCKWORK BOLT

Evocation Cantrip

Casting Time: 1 action
Range: 60 feet
Components: V, S, M (an arrow or crossbow bolt)
Duration: 1 round

You imbue an arrow or crossbow bolt with clockwork magic just as you fire it at your target; spinning blades materialize on the missile after it strikes to further mutilate your enemy.

As part of the action used to cast this spell, you make a ranged weapon attack with a bow or a crossbow against one creature within range. If the attack hits, the missile embeds in the target. Unless the target (or an ally of it within 5 feet) uses an action to remove the projectile (which deals no additional damage), the target takes an additional 1d8 slashing damage at the end of its next turn from spinning blades that briefly sprout from the missile's shaft. Afterward, the projectile reverts to normal.

This spell deals more damage when you reach higher levels. At 5th level, the ranged attack deals an extra 1d8 slashing damage to the target, and the target takes an additional 1d8 slashing damage (2d8 total) if the embedded ammunition isn't removed. Both damage amounts increase by 1d8 again at 11th level and at 17th level.

CLOSING IN

3rd-Level Illusion

Casting Time: 1 action
Range: 30 feet
Components: V, S
Duration: Concentration, up to 1 minute

Choose a creature you can see within range. The target must succeed on a Wisdom saving throw, which it makes with disadvantage if it's in an enclosed space. On a failed save, the creature believes the world around it is closing in and threatening to crush it. Even in open or clear terrain, the creature feels as though it is sinking into a pit, or that the land is rising around it. The creature has disadvantage on ability checks and attack rolls for the duration, and it takes 2d6 psychic damage at the end of each of its turns. An affected creature repeats the saving throw at the end of each of its turns, ending the effect on itself on a success.

At Higher Levels. When you cast this spell using a spell slot of 4th level or higher, you can target one additional creature for each slot level above 3rd.

CLUMSINESS

Necromancy Cantrip

Casting Time: 1 action

Range: 30 feet

Components: V, S

Duration: 1 minute

You temporarily make a creature within range less dexterous. If the target makes a successful Constitution saving throw, the spell is ineffective. On a failed save, the next time the creature makes a Dexterity check before the spell ends, roll a d6 and subtract the result from the roll. The spell then ends.

COBRA FANGS

1st-Level Transmutation

Casting Time: 1 action

Range: Touch

Components: V, S, M (a drop of snake venom or a patch of snakeskin)

Duration: 1 minute

The spell causes the target to grow great, snake-like fangs. An unwilling creature must make a Wisdom saving throw to avoid the effect. The spell fails if the target already has a bite attack that deals poison damage.

If the target doesn't have a bite attack, it gains one. The target is proficient with the bite, and it adds its Strength modifier to the attack and damage rolls. The damage is piercing and the damage die is a d4.

When the target hits a creature with its bite attack, the creature must make a Constitution saving throw, taking 3d6 poison damage on a failed save, or half as much damage on a successful one.

At Higher Levels. When you cast this spell using a spell slot of 3rd level or higher, the target's bite counts as magical for the purpose of overcoming resistance and immunity to nonmagical attacks and damage.

COMMAND UNDEAD

3rd-Level Necromancy

Casting Time: 1 action

Range: 60 feet

Components: V

Duration: Concentration

You speak a one-word command to all undead creatures you can see within range. Any target must succeed on a Wisdom saving throw or follow the command on its next turn. The spell has no effect if the target is living, if it doesn't understand your language, or if your command is directly harmful to it.

COMPELLED MOVEMENT

3rd-Level Enchantment

Casting Time: 1 action

Range: 60 feet

Components: V, S, M (the embalmed body of a millipede with its right legs removed, worth at least 50 gp)

Duration: Concentration, up to 1 minute

Choose two living creatures (not constructs or undead) you can see within range. Each must make a Charisma saving throw. On a failed save, a creature is compelled to use its movement to move toward the other creature. Its route must be as direct as possible, but it avoids dangerous terrain and enemies. If the creatures are within 5 feet of each other at the end of either one's turn, their bodies fuse together. Fused creatures still take their own turns, but they can't move, can't use reactions, and have disadvantage on attack rolls, Dexterity saving throws, and Constitution checks to maintain concentration.

A fused creature can use its action to make a Charisma saving throw. On a success, the creature breaks free and can move as it wants. It can become fused again, however, if it's within 5 feet of a creature that's still under the spell's effect at the end of either creature's turn.

Compelled movement doesn't affect a creature that can't be charmed or that is incorporeal.

At Higher Levels. When you cast this spell using a spell slot of 5th level or higher, the number of creatures you can affect increases by one for every two slot levels above 3rd.

COMPELLING FATE

3rd-Level Divination

Casting Time: 1 action

Range: 30 feet

Components: V, M (a sprinkling of silver dust worth 20 gp)

Duration: 1 round

You view the actions of a single creature you can see through the influence of the stars, and you read what is written there. If the target fails a Charisma saving throw, you can predict that creature's actions. This has the following effects:

- You have advantage on attack rolls against the target.
- For every 5 feet the target moves, you can move 5 feet (up to your normal movement) on the target's turn when it has completed its movement. This is deducted from your next turn's movement.
- As a reaction at the start of the target's turn, you can warn yourself and allies that can hear you of the target's offensive intentions; any creature targeted by the target's next attack gains a +2 bonus to AC or to its saving throw against that attack.

CHAPTER 5 SPELL DESCRIPTIONS | 173

At Higher Levels. When you cast this spell using a spell slot of 4th level or higher, the duration is extended by 1 round for each slot level above 3rd.

COMPREHEND WILD SHAPE

2nd-Level Divination

Casting Time: 1 action
Range: Touch
Components: V, S, M (two or more matching carved totems)
Duration: 1 hour

Give one of the carved totems to an ally while keeping the other yourself. For the duration of the spell, you and whoever holds the other totem can communicate while either of you is in a beast shape. This isn't a telepathic link; you simply understand each other's verbal communication, similar to the effect of a *speak with animals* spell. This effect doesn't allow a druid in beast shape to cast spells.

At Higher Levels. When you cast this spell using a spell slot of 3rd level or higher, you can increase the number of target creatures by two for each slot level above 2nd. Each creature must receive a matching carved totem.

CONJURE FEY HOUND

5th-Level Conjuration

Casting Time: 1 action
Range: 60 feet
Components: V, S, M (a wooden or metal whistle)
Duration: Concentration, up to 1 hour

You summon a fey hound to fight by your side. A **hound of the night** (see *Tome of Beasts*) appears in an unoccupied space that you can see within range. The hound disappears when it drops to 0 hit points or when the spell ends.

The summoned hound is friendly to you and your companions. Roll initiative for the summoned hound, which has its own turns. It obeys any verbal commands that you issue to it (no action required by you). If you don't issue any commands to the hound, it stands by your side and attacks nearby creatures that are hostile to you but otherwise takes no actions.

At Higher Levels. When you cast this spell using a spell slot of 7th level or higher, you summon two hounds. When you cast this spell using a 9th-level spell slot, you summon three hounds.

CONJURE FIENDS

4th-Level Conjuration

Casting Time: 1 minute
Range: 90 feet
Components: V, S
Duration: Concentration, up to 1 hour

You summon fiends that appear in unoccupied spaces that you can see within range. You choose one of the following options for what appears:

- One fiend of challenge rating 2 or lower
- Two fiends of challenge rating 1 or lower
- Four fiends of challenge rating 1/2 or lower
- Eight fiends of challenge rating 1/4 or lower

A fiend summoned by this spell disappears when it drops to 0 hit points or when the spell ends.

The summoned creatures are friendly to you and your companions. Roll initiative for the summoned creatures as a group, which has its own turns. They obey any verbal commands that you issue to them (no action required by you). If you don't issue any commands to them, they defend themselves from hostile creatures, but otherwise take no actions.

The GM has the creatures' statistics.

At Higher Levels. When you cast this spell using certain higher-level spell slots, you choose one of the summoning options above, and more creatures appear: twice as many with a 6th-level spell slot and three times as many with an 8th-level spell slot.

CONJURE FOREST DEFENDER

6th-Level Conjuration

Casting Time: 1 hour
Range: 30 feet
Components: V, S, M (one humanoid body, which the spell consumes)
Duration: Until destroyed

When you cast this spell in a forest, you fasten sticks and twigs around a body. The body comes to life as a forest defender (see below). The forest defender is friendly to you and your companions. Roll initiative for the forest defender, which has its own turns. It obeys any verbal or mental commands that you issue to it (no action required by you), as long as you remain within its line of sight. If you don't issue any commands to the forest defender, if you are out of its line of sight, or if you are unconscious, it defends itself from hostile creatures but otherwise takes no actions. A body sacrificed to form the forest defender is permanently destroyed and can be restored to life only by means of a *true resurrection* or a *wish* spell. You can have only one forest defender under your control at a time. If you cast this spell again, the previous forest defender crumbles to dust.

At Higher Levels. When you cast this spell using a 9th-level spell slot, you summon two forest defenders instead of one, and you can control up to two forest defenders at a time.

Forest Defender

Medium Construct, Neutral

ARMOR CLASS 14
HIT POINTS 67 (9d8 + 27)
SPEED 30 ft., climb 30 ft.

STR	DEX	CON	INT	WIS	CHA
12 (+1)	18 (+4)	17 (+3)	6 (−2)	10 (+0)	5 (−3)

SKILLS Perception +2, Stealth +6
DAMAGE VULNERABILITIES slashing
DAMAGE RESISTANCES bludgeoning and piercing from nonmagical attacks not made with adamantine weapons
DAMAGE IMMUNITIES poison
CONDITION IMMUNITIES charmed, exhaustion, frightened, paralyzed, poisoned
SENSES darkvision 60 ft., passive Perception 12
LANGUAGES understands the languages of its creator but can't speak
CHALLENGE 3 (700 XP)   **PROFICIENCY BONUS** +2

Immutable Form. The forest defender is immune to any spell or effect that would alter its form.

Magic Resistance. The forest defender has advantage on saving throws against spells and other magical effects.

Plant Camouflage. The forest defender has advantage on Dexterity (Stealth) checks it makes in any terrain with ample obscuring plant life.

ACTIONS

Multiattack. The forest defender makes two thorned vine attacks.

Thorned Vine. *Melee Weapon Attack*: +6 to hit, reach 15 ft., one creature. *Hit:* 8 (1d8 + 4) piercing damage, and the target must succeed on a DC 14 Strength saving throw or be pulled 10 feet toward the forest defender.

Thorned Embrace. *Melee Weapon Attack*: +6 to hit, reach 5 ft., one Medium or smaller creature. *Hit:* 13 (2d8 + 4) piercing damage, and the target is grappled (escape DC 11). Until the grapple ends, the target is restrained, and the forest defender can't embrace another target.

CONJURE GREATER SPECTRAL DEAD

7th-Level Conjuration

Casting Time: 1 minute
Range: 60 feet
Components: V, S, M (a handful of bone dust, a crystal prism worth at least 100 gp, and a platinum coin)
Duration: Concentration, up to 1 hour

You summon an incorporeal undead creature that appears in an unoccupied space you can see within range. You choose one of the following options for what appears:

- One wraith
- One **spectral guardian** (see *Tome of Beasts*)
- One **swarm of wolf spirits** (see *Tome of Beasts*)

Summoned creatures disappear when they drop to 0 hit points or when the spell ends.

The summoned creature doesn't attack you or your companions for the duration. Roll initiative for the summoned creature, which has its own turns. The creature attacks your enemies and tries to stay within 60 feet of you, but it otherwise controls its own actions. The summoned creature despises being bound and might harm or impede you and your companions by any means at its disposal other than direct attacks if the opportunity arises. At the beginning of the creature's turn, you can use your reaction to verbally command it. The creature obeys your commands for that turn, and you take 1d6 psychic damage at the end of the turn. If your concentration is broken, the creature doesn't disappear. Instead, you can no longer command it, it becomes hostile to you and your companions, and it attacks you and your allies if it believes it has a chance to win the fight or to inflict meaningful harm; otherwise it flees. You can't dismiss the uncontrolled creature, but it disappears 1 hour after you summoned it.

At Higher Levels. When you cast this spell using a 9th-level spell slot, you summon a **deathwisp** (see *Tome of Beasts*) or two **ghosts** instead.

CONJURE MANTELET

2nd-Level Abjuration

Casting Time: 1 action
Range: Self
Components: V, S
Duration: Concentration, up to 1 minute

You summon a transparent, faintly luminous barrier with a single arrow slit. The magical mantelet provides you with three-quarters cover for the duration of the spell. If you move on your turn, the mantelet moves with you.

CONJURE MOCK ANIMALS

1st-Level Conjuration

Casting Time: 1 action
Range: 30 feet
Components: V, S
Duration: Concentration, up to 10 minutes

You summon fey spirits that take the outward appearance of animals, but merely to serve as a distraction and trap for the unwary. The spell functions as *conjure animals*, but each mock animal has only 1 hit point and deals only 1 damage on a hit regardless of its appearance.

When a mock animal is dropped to 0 hit points, it explodes in a flash of light, dealing 2d4 radiant damage to all creatures within 5 feet of it. Each creature that takes damage must make a Dexterity saving throw. On a failed save, the creature is blinded for 1 round.

CONJURE NIGHTMARE

5th-Level Conjuration

Casting Time: 1 action
Range: 60 feet
Components: V, S, M (brimstone and a torch)
Duration: Concentration, up to 1 hour

You call forth a nightmare to serve you. The creature appears in an unoccupied space you choose within range. The nightmare will serve you as a mount, in combat and out. The nightmare is friendly to you and your companions for the duration and follows any commands you issue to it. If your concentration is broken, the nightmare is no longer bound by the spell. It might leave immediately, especially if it has been wounded or threatened, but it is just as likely to attack you or an ally, or otherwise gain retribution for being summoned and bound to your service. If you provide the nightmare with a sacrifice it can devour when it is first summoned, it will be appeased enough to simply return home once the spell ends, without causing harm to you or your companions.

At Higher Levels. When you cast this spell using a spell slot of 6th level or higher, the duration increases by 1 hour for each slot level above 5th.

CONJURE SCARAB SWARM

2nd-Level Conjuration

Casting Time: 1 action
Range: 60 feet
Components: V, S, M (a beetle carapace)
Duration: Concentration, up to 10 minutes

You summon swarms of scarab beetles to attack your foes. Two swarms of insects (beetles) appear in unoccupied spaces that you can see within range.

Each swarm disappears when it drops to 0 hit points or when the spell ends. The swarms are friendly to you and your allies. Make one initiative roll for both swarms, which have their own turns. They obey verbal commands that you issue to them (no action required by you). If you don't issue any commands to them, they defend themselves from hostile creatures but otherwise take no actions.

CONJURE SPECTRAL DEAD

2nd-Level Conjuration

Casting Time: 1 minute
Range: 60 feet
Components: V, S, M (a handful of bone dust, a crystal prism, and a silver coin)
Duration: Concentration, up to 1 hour

You summon a **shroud** (see *Tome of Beasts*) to do your bidding. The creature appears in an unoccupied space that you can see within range. The creature is friendly to you and your allies for the duration. Roll initiative for the creature, which has its own turns. It obeys any verbal commands that you issue to it (no action required by

you). If you don't issue any commands to the creature, it defends itself from hostile creatures but otherwise takes no actions. The creature disappears when it drops to 0 hit points or when the spell ends.

At Higher Levels. When you cast this spell using a 3rd-level spell slot, you can choose to summon two shrouds or one specter. When you cast this spell with a spell slot of 4th level or higher, you can choose to summon four shrouds or one will-o'-wisp.

CONJURE UNDEAD

3rd-Level Conjuration

Casting Time: 1 minute
Range: 30 feet
Components: V, S, M (a humanoid skull)
Duration: Concentration, up to 1 hour

You summon a shadow to do your bidding. The creature appears in an unoccupied space that you can see within range. The creature is friendly to you and your allies for the duration. Roll initiative for the shadow, which has its own turns. It obeys any verbal commands that you issue to it (no action required by you). If you don't issue any commands to the creature, it defends itself from hostile creatures but otherwise takes no actions. The shadow disappears when the spell ends.

At Higher Levels. When you cast this spell using a 4th-level spell slot, you can choose to summon a wight or a shadow. When you cast this spell with a spell slot of 5th level or higher, you can choose to summon a ghost, a shadow, or a wight.

CONSULT THE STORM

4th-Level Divination

Casting Time: 1 action
Range: 90 feet
Components: V
Duration: Instantaneous

You ask a question of an entity connected to storms, such as an elemental, a deity, or a primal spirit, and the entity replies with destructive fury.

As part of the casting of the spell, you must speak a question consisting of fifteen words or fewer. Choose a point within range. A short, truthful answer to your question booms from that point. It can be heard clearly by any creature within 600 feet. Each creature within 15 feet of the point takes 7d6 thunder damage, or half as much damage with a successful Constitution saving throw.

At Higher Levels. When you cast this spell using a spell slot of 5th level or higher, the damage increases by 1d6 for each slot level above 4th.

CONTROL ICE

5th-Level Transmutation

Casting Time: 1 action
Range: 300 feet
Components: V, S, M (a cube of white wax)
Duration: Concentration, up to 1 minute

Until the spell ends, you control any ice inside an area you choose within range that can be as large as a cube 100 feet on a side. You choose one of the following three effects when you cast this spell. As an action on each of your turns thereafter, you can use the same effect or choose a different one. Any alterations made to the ice remain after the spell ends, but can be altered by other effects (temperature, seismic action, or another application of this spell, for example).

Crack. You cause ice in the area to crack and splinter. On level terrain, this effect turns the ice into difficult terrain, possibly producing other hazards, depending on the terrain and the nature of the ice—ice over a deep chasm might open onto a pit, while ice over water can break into individual floes, for example. Using this effect on cliffs, walls, or ceilings made of ice can cause collapse, dealing 4d10 bludgeoning damage to creatures in the area below the collapse, or half the damage with a successful Dexterity saving throw. After such a collapse, the area where the fallen ice collects becomes difficult terrain.

Reshape. You cause ice in a portion of the area to rapidly melt, move, and re-form into whatever shape you command. You can block holes, open tunnels, form bridges, remove difficult terrain, or otherwise alter the form of the ice in the area. You can cause ice to become slippery, making it difficult terrain, or dry to remove difficult terrain. You can fill a hole up to a 20-foot cube or create 20 feet (up to 20 feet wide) of a bridge across a chasm or raise a 20-foot-tall pillar of ice (up to 20 feet square). You can continue this action on consecutive rounds to increase the size of the affected area while you maintain concentration on the spell.

Thicken/Thin. You cause existing ice to increase or decrease in thickness, up to 1 inch per round over some or all of the total area, either making the surface stronger or creating thin ice that is hazardous to walk on.

CONVERSE WITH DRAGON

1st-Level Divination

Casting Time: 1 action
Range: Self
Components: V
Duration: Concentration, up to 10 minutes

You gain limited telepathy, allowing you to communicate with any creature within 120 feet of you that has the dragon type, regardless of the creature's languages. A

CHAPTER 5 SPELL DESCRIPTIONS | 177

dragon can choose to make a Charisma saving throw to prevent telepathic contact with itself.

This spell doesn't change a dragon's disposition toward you or your allies, it only opens a channel of communication. In some cases, unwanted telepathic contact can worsen the dragon's attitude toward you.

CONVOLUTED DICTUM

2nd-Level Enchantment

Casting Time: 1 action
Range: 60 feet
Components: V, S, M (a long, twisted piece of red ribbon)
Duration: Concentration, up to 1 minute

You manipulate the thinking of a creature within range, compelling it to take longer, more elaborate means to complete actions. The target must succeed on a Wisdom saving throw or take only one action or bonus action on its turn until the spell ends.

If the target tries to cast a spell with a casting time of 1 action, roll a d20. On an 11 or higher, the spell doesn't take effect until the creature's next turn, and the creature must use its action on that turn to complete the spell. If it can't do so, the spell is wasted. If the target interacts with an object while taking its action, such as drawing a sword as part of an attack, it must also roll a d20. On an 11 or higher, it must make the interaction with the object its sole action on that round, taking the Use An Object action. In the example given, the target would take its action drawing the sword with an extensive amount of flourish or drama and be unable to attack with it until its next turn.

At the end of each of its turns, the target can make another Wisdom saving throw. On a successful save, the spell ends.

COSTLY VICTORY

8th-Level Evocation

Casting Time: 1 action
Range: 90 feet
Components: V, S
Duration: 1 hour

You select up to ten enemies you can see that are within range. Each target must make a Wisdom saving throw. On a failed save, that creature is cursed to burst into flame if it reduces one of your allies to 0 hit points before this spell's duration expires. The affected creature takes 6d8 fire damage and 6d8 radiant damage when it bursts into flame.

If the affected creature is wearing flammable material (or is made of flammable material, such as a plant creature), it catches on fire and continues burning; the creature takes fire damage equal to your spellcasting ability modifier at the end of each of its turns until the creature or one of its allies within 5 feet of it uses an action to extinguish the fire.

CREATE RING SERVANT

8th-Level Transmutation

Casting Time: 1 minute
Range: Touch
Components: V, S, M (two metal rings)
Duration: Concentration, up to 1 hour

You touch two metal rings and infuse them with life, creating a short-lived but sentient construct known as a **ring servant** (see *Creature Codex*). The ring servant appears adjacent to you. It reverts form, changing back into the rings used to cast the spell, when it drops to 0 hit points or when the spell ends.

The ring servant is friendly to you and your companions for the duration. Roll initiative for the ring servant, which acts on its own turns. It obeys any verbal commands that you issue to it (no action required by you). If you don't issue any commands to the ring servant, it defends itself and you from hostile creatures but otherwise takes no actions.

CREATE THUNDERSTAFF

7th-Level Transmutation

Casting Time: 10 minutes
Range: Touch
Components: V, S, M (a quarterstaff)
Duration: Instantaneous

After you cast *create thunderstaff* on a normal quarterstaff, the staff must then be mounted in a noisy location, such as a busy marketplace, and left there for 60 days. During that time, the staff gradually absorbs ambient sound.

After 60 days, the staff is fully charged and can't absorb any more sound. At that point, it becomes a *thunderstaff*, a +1 *quarterstaff* that has 10 charges. When you hit on a melee attack with the staff and expend 1 charge, the target takes an extra 1d8 thunder damage. You can cast a *thunderwave* spell from the staff as a bonus action by expending 2 charges. The staff cannot be recharged.

If the final charge is not expended within 60 days, the staff becomes nonmagical again.

CREEPING ICE

2nd-Level Conjuration

Casting Time: 1 action
Range: 60 feet
Components: V, S
Duration: Concentration, up to 1 minute

You create a sheet of ice that covers a 5-foot square within range and lasts for the spell's duration. The iced area is difficult terrain.

A creature in the area where you cast the spell must make a successful Strength saving throw or be restrained

by ice that rapidly encases it. A creature restrained by the ice takes 2d6 cold damage at the start of its turn. A restrained creature can use an action to make a Strength check against your spell save DC, freeing itself on a success, but it has disadvantage on this check. The creature can also be freed (and the spell ended) by dealing at least 20 damage to the ice. The restrained creature takes half the damage from any attacks against the ice.

At Higher Levels. When you cast this spell using a spell slot of 4th to 6th level, the area increases to a 10-foot square, the ice deals 4d6 cold damage, and 40 damage is needed to melt each 5-foot square. When you cast this spell using a spell slot of 7th level or higher, the area increases to a 20-foot square, the ice deals 6d6 cold damage, and 60 damage is needed to melt each 5-foot square.

CRUOR OF VISIONS

5th-Level Divination

Casting Time: 1 minute
Range: Self
Components: V, S, M (a bone needle and a catch basin)
Duration: Concentration, up to 5 minutes

You prick your finger with a bone needle as you cast this spell, taking 1 necrotic damage. This drop of blood must be caught in a container, such as a platter or a bowl, where it grows into a pool 1 foot in diameter. This pool acts as a crystal ball for the purpose of scrying.

If you place a drop (or dried flakes) of another creature's blood in the container, the creature has disadvantage on any Wisdom saving throw to resist scrying. Additionally, you can treat the pool of blood as a *crystal ball of telepathy*.

At Higher Levels. When you cast this spell using a spell slot of 7th level or higher, the pool of blood acts as either a *crystal ball of mind reading* or a *crystal ball of true seeing* (your choice when the spell is cast).

CRUSHING TRAMPLE

2nd-Level Transmutation

Casting Time: 1 action
Range: Self
Components: V, S
Duration: 1 round

Upon casting this spell, you are filled with a desire to overrun your foes. You immediately move up to twice your speed in a straight line, trampling every foe in your path that is of your size category or smaller. If you try to move through the space of an enemy whose size is larger than yours, your movement (and the spell) ends. Each enemy whose space you move through must make a successful Strength saving throw or be knocked prone and take 4d6 bludgeoning damage. If you have hooves, add your Strength modifier (minimum of +1) to the damage.

You move through the spaces of foes whether or not they succeed on their Strength saving throws. You do not provoke opportunity attacks while moving under the effect of *crushing trample*.

CRYSTAL CONFINEMENT

9th-Level Abjuration

Casting Time: 1 action
Range: Sight
Components: V, S
Duration: Concentration, up to 1 minute

You attempt to preserve a number of creatures in a shell of ice. When you first cast this spell, you can choose up to 20 creatures that you can see: Medium targets count as two creatures, Large targets count as four creatures, Huge targets count as eight creatures, and Gargantuan targets count as 20 creatures.

Each target must make a Constitution saving throw or choose to automatically fail the save. On a successful save, nothing happens to the target this round, but it must repeat the save at the start of your next turn—provided you maintain concentration on the spell. On a failed save, a creature is coated in a creeping rime of ice and is restrained. If the saving throw fails by 5 or more, the target is instantly petrified as it becomes encased in ice. A restrained creature can repeat the saving throw at the end of its next turn, becoming petrified on a failure or ending the restrained effect on a success.

A creature petrified by this spell remains petrified until you either die or choose to end the effect. No other magic can free it. When a creature becomes petrified, you can choose for it to remain aware of its surroundings, though its senses are limited to what it could perceive while motionless and through a thick coating of clear ice. While coated in ice, the creature is immune to all damage and to the effects of aging.

CURE BEAST

1st-Level Evocation

Casting Time: 1 bonus action
Range: 60 feet
Components: V, S
Duration: Instantaneous

A beast of your choice that you can see within range regains a number of hit points equal to 1d6 + your spellcasting modifier.

At Higher Levels. When you cast this spell using a spell slot of 2nd level or higher, the healing increases by 1d6 for each slot level above 1st.

CURSE OF BOREAS

6th-Level Transmutation

Casting Time: 1 action
Range: Self (60-foot cone)
Components: V, S
Duration: Concentration, up to 1 minute

A whisper of freezing wind wafts from your lips in a 60-foot cone. Each creature in the area must make a Charisma saving throw, taking 4d8 cold damage and being restrained on a failed save or half as much damage with no additional effect on a successful one.

A creature restrained by this spell takes 2d8 cold damage at the end of each of its turns and then must make another Charisma saving throw. It has advantage on this saving throw if it has taken any fire damage since the end of its last turn. If it successfully saves against this spell three times, the spell ends for it. If it fails its save three times, it is shrouded in ice and restrained for 10 minutes. The successes and failures don't need to be consecutive; keep track of both until the target collects three of a kind.

Another creature can free a restrained creature in 1 minute using fire or weapons to chip away the ice.

At Higher Levels. When you cast this spell using a spell slot of 7th level or higher, the initial damage increases by 1d8 for each slot level above 6th.

CURSE OF DUST

7th-Level Necromancy

Casting Time: 10 minutes
Range: 500 feet
Components: V, S, M (a piece of spoiled food)
Duration: 5 days

You cast a curse on a creature within range that you're familiar with, causing it to be unsatiated by food no matter how much it eats. This effect isn't merely an issue of perception; the target physically can't draw sustenance from food. Within minutes after the spell is cast, the target feels constant hunger no matter how much food it consumes. The target must make a Constitution saving throw 24 hours after the spell is cast and every 24 hours thereafter. On a failed save, the target gains one level of exhaustion. The effect ends when the duration expires or when the target makes two consecutive successful saves.

CURSE OF HOSTILITY

3rd-Level Necromancy

Casting Time: 1 action
Range: Touch
Components: V, S
Duration: Concentration, up to 1 minute

You touch a creature, and that creature must succeed on a Wisdom saving throw or become cursed with the antipathy of a certain type of creature, chosen you when you cast the spell. Choose one of the following: aberrations, beasts, celestials, dragons, elementals, fey, fiends, giants, humanoids, monstrosities, plants, or undead. In situations involving creatures of the selected type, the following effects apply:

- In encounters with creatures of the selected type when the creatures are already hostile, they will attack the target of this spell in preference to other targets.
- A creature of the selected type gains advantage on any attack rolls made against the target if the target has attacked and hit that creature at least once during the encounter.
- The target has disadvantage on any Charisma-based checks made against creatures of the chosen type.

A *remove curse* spell ends this effect.

At Higher Levels. If you cast this spell using a spell slot of 4th level, the duration is concentration, up to

10 minutes. If you use a spell slot of 5th or 6th level, the duration is 8 hours. If you use a spell slot of 7th or 8th level, the duration is 24 hours. If you use a 9th-level spell slot, the spell lasts until dispelled.

CURSE OF INCOMPETENCE

3rd-Level Necromancy

Casting Time: 1 action
Range: 60 feet
Components: V, S
Duration: Concentration, up to 1 minute

By making mocking gestures toward one creature within range that can see you, you leave the creature incapable of performing at its best. If the target fails on an Intelligence saving throw, roll a d4 and refer to the following table to determine what the target does on its turn.

d4	Result
1	Target spends its turn shouting mocking words at caster and takes a –5 penalty to its initiative roll.
2	Target stands transfixed and blinking, taking no action.
3	Target flees or fights (50 percent chance of each).
4	Target charges directly at caster, enraged.

An affected target repeats the saving throw at the end of each of its turns, ending the effect on itself on a success or applying the result of another roll on the table on a failure.

CURSE OF THE GRAVE

7th-Level Necromancy

Casting Time: 1 action
Range: 120 feet
Components: V, S, M (dirt from a freshly dug grave)
Duration: Until dispelled

You tap your connection to death to curse a humanoid, making the grim pull of the grave stronger on that creature's soul.

Choose one humanoid you can see within range. The target must succeed on a Constitution saving throw or become cursed. A *remove curse* spell or similar magic ends this curse. While cursed in this way, the target suffers the following effects:

- The target fails death saving throws on any roll but a 20.
- If the target dies, it rises 1 round later as a vampire spawn under your control and is no longer cursed.
- The target, as a vampire spawn, seeks you out in an attempt to serve its new master. You can have only one vampire spawn under your control at a time through this spell. If you create another, the existing one turns to dust. If you or your companions do anything harmful to the target, it can make a Wisdom saving throw. On a success, it is no longer under your control.

CURSE OF YIG

5th-Level Transmutation (Ritual)

Casting Time: 1 minute
Range: 60 feet
Components: V, S, M (a drop of snake venom)
Duration: Concentration, up to 10 minutes

This spell transforms a Small, Medium, or Large creature that you can see within range into a **servant of Yig** (see *Creature Codex*). An unwilling creature can attempt a Wisdom saving throw, negating the effect with a success. A willing creature is automatically affected and remains so for as long as you maintain concentration on the spell.

The transformation lasts for the duration or until the target drops to 0 hit points or dies. The target's statistics, including mental ability scores, are replaced by the statistics of a servant of Yig. The transformed creature's alignment becomes neutral evil, and it is both friendly to you and reverent toward the Father of Serpents. Its equipment is unchanged. If the transformed creature was unwilling, it makes a Wisdom saving throw at the end of each of its turns. On a successful save, the spell ends, the creature's alignment and personality return to normal, and it regains its former attitude toward you and toward Yig.

When it reverts to its normal form, the creature has the number of hit points it had before it transformed. If it reverts as a result of dropping to 0 hit points, any excess damage carries over to its normal form.

CURSE RING

5th-Level Necromancy

Casting Time: 1 action
Range: Touch
Components: V, S, M (250 gp worth of diamond dust, which the spell consumes)
Duration: Permanent until discharged

You lay a curse upon a ring you touch that isn't being worn or carried. When you cast this spell, select one of the possible effects of *bestow curse*. The next creature that willingly wears the ring suffers the chosen effect with no saving throw. The curse transfers from the ring to the wearer once the ring is put on; the ring becomes a mundane ring that can be taken off, but the curse remains on the creature that wore the ring until the curse is removed or dispelled. An *identify* spell cast on the cursed ring reveals the fact that it is cursed.

CURSED GIFT

4th-Level Abjuration

Casting Time: 1 action
Range: Touch
Components: V, S, M (an object worth at least 75 gp)
Duration: 24 hours

Cursed gift imbues an object with a harmful magical effect that you or another creature in physical contact with you is currently suffering from. If you give this object to a creature that freely accepts it during the duration of the spell, the recipient must make a Charisma saving throw. On a failed save, the harmful effect is transferred to the recipient for the duration of the spell (or until the effect ends). Returning the object to you, destroying it, or giving it to someone else has no effect. *Remove curse* and comparable magic can relieve the individual who received the item, but the harmful effect still returns to the previous victim when this spell ends if the effect's duration has not expired.

At Higher Levels. When you cast this spell using a spell slot of 5th level or higher, the duration increases by 24 hours for each slot level above 4th.

CYNOPHOBIA

3rd-Level Enchantment

Casting Time: 1 action
Range: 30 feet
Components: V, S, M (a dog's tooth)
Duration: 8 hours

Choose a creature that you can see within range. The target must succeed on a Wisdom saving throw or develop an overriding fear of canids, such as dogs, wolves, foxes, and worgs. For the duration, the first time the target sees a canid, the target must succeed on a Wisdom saving throw or become frightened of that canid until the end of its next turn. Each time the target sees a different canid, it must make the saving throw. In addition, the target has disadvantage on ability checks and attack rolls while a canid is within 10 feet of it.

At Higher Levels. When you cast this spell using a 5th-level spell slot, the duration is 24 hours. When you use a 7th-level spell slot, the duration is 1 month. When you use a spell slot of 8th or 9th level, the spell lasts until it is dispelled.

DAGGERHAWK

2nd-Level Transmutation

Casting Time: 1 action
Range: Self
Components: V, S, M (a dagger)
Duration: 1 minute

When *daggerhawk* is cast on a nonmagical dagger, a ghostly hawk appears around the weapon. The hawk and dagger fly into the air and make a melee attack against one creature you select within 60 feet, using your spell attack modifier and dealing piercing damage equal to 1d4 + your Intelligence modifier on a hit. On your subsequent turns, you can use an action to cause the daggerhawk to attack the same target. The daggerhawk has AC 14 and, although it's invulnerable to all damage, a successful attack against it that deals bludgeoning, force, or slashing damage sends the daggerhawk tumbling, so it can't attack again until after your next turn.

DARK HERALDRY

3rd-Level Necromancy

Casting Time: 1 action
Range: 60 feet
Components: V
Duration: Concentration, up to 1 minute

Dark entities herald your entry into combat, instilling a dread in your enemies. Designate a number of creatures up to your spellcasting ability modifier (minimum of one) that you can see within range and that have an alignment different from yours. Each of those creatures takes 5d8 psychic damage and becomes frightened of you; a creature that makes a successful Wisdom saving throw takes half as much damage and is not frightened.

A creature frightened in this way repeats the saving throw at the end of each of its turns, ending the effect on itself on a success. The creature makes this saving throw with disadvantage if you can see it.

At Higher Levels. When you cast this spell using a spell slot of 4th level or higher, you can target one additional creature for each slot level above 3rd.

DARK LORD'S MANTLE

5th-Level Enchantment

Casting Time: 1 action
Range: Self (30-foot radius)
Components: V, S
Duration: Concentration, up to 10 minutes

You infuse yourself with fiendish power, which inspires your allies and intimidates your foes. While the spell lasts, you exude confidence. You gain advantage on saving throws against all enchantment spells and effects. In addition, each ally within 30 feet of you can roll a d4 once per round and add the result to an attack roll as a bonus action, or to a saving throw as a reaction.

An enemy that starts its turn within 30 feet of you, or that moves within 30 feet of you on its turn, must succeed on a Wisdom saving throw or become frightened of you. If a creature moves out of the spell's radius, it remains frightened until the start of its next turn, and then the spell ends for that creature. While frightened in this way, the creature repeats the saving throw at the end of each of its turns. On a success, the creature is no longer frightened, and it cannot be affected again by your casting of this spell for 24 hours.

DARK MAW

Necromancy Cantrip

Casting Time: 1 action
Range: Touch
Components: V, S
Duration: 1 round

Penumbral ichor drips from your shadow-stained mouth, filling your mouth with giant shadow fangs. Make a melee spell attack against the target. On a hit, the target takes 1d8 necrotic damage as your shadowy fangs sink into it. If you have a bite attack (such as from a racial trait or a spell like *alter self*), you can add your spellcasting ability modifier to the damage roll but not to your temporary hit points.

If you hit a humanoid target, you gain 1d4 temporary hit points until the start of your next turn.

This spell's damage increases by 1d8 when you reach 5th level (2d8), 11th level (3d8), and 17th level (4d8).

DARK WEB OF THE SPIDER MONARCH

5th-Level Conjuration

Casting Time: 1 action
Range: Self (30-foot cube)
Components: V, S, M (a thread of black silk)
Duration: Concentration, up to 1 hour

A 30-foot cube centered on you, fills with sticky, night-black webbing. The webs are difficult terrain and lightly obscure the area. You are unaffected by the aforementioned effects of the webs and gain a climbing speed of 30 feet when moving on the webs.

If the webs aren't anchored between two solid masses (such as walls or trees) or layered across a floor, wall, or ceiling, the web collapses on itself, and the spell ends at the start of your next turn. Webs layered over a flat surface have a depth of 5 feet.

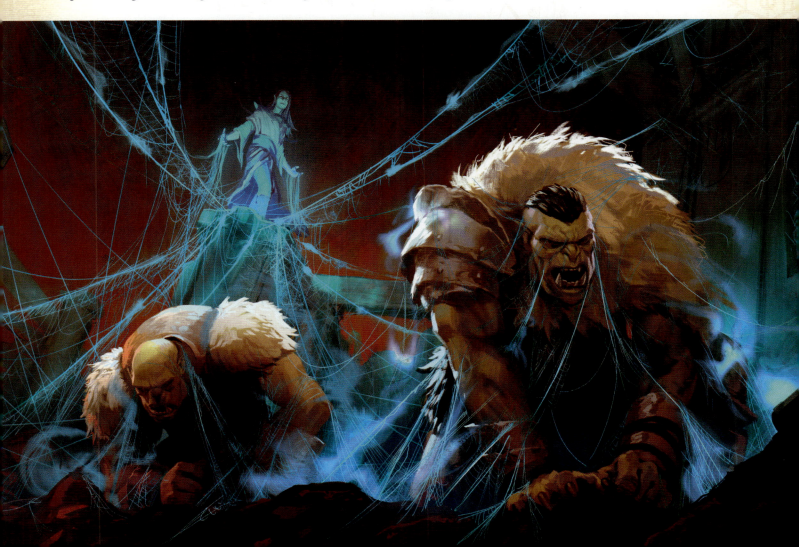

Each creature that starts its turn in the webs or that enters the webs during its turn must make a Dexterity saving throw. On a failed save, the creature is restrained for as long as it remains in the webs or until it breaks free.

Each turn that you are in the webs, you can use a bonus action to siphon life force from every creature restrained by the webs. Each creature takes 3d6 necrotic damage, and you regain hit points equal to half the damage dealt.

A creature restrained by the webs can use its action to make a Strength check against your spell save DC. On a successful check, it is no longer restrained.

The webs are not flammable, but are susceptible to radiant damage. Any 5-foot cube of webs exposed to radiant damage dissipates to nothing in 1 round.

DEAD WALKING

2nd-Level Illusion

Casting Time: 1 action
Range: 10 feet
Components: V, S, M (a copper piece)
Duration: Concentration, up to 1 hour

As part of the casting of this spell, you place a copper piece under your tongue. This spell makes up to six willing creatures you can see within range invisible to undead for the duration. Anything a target is wearing or carrying is invisible as long as it is on the target's person. The spell ends for all targets if one target attacks or casts a spell.

At Higher Levels. When you cast this spell using a 3rd-level spell slot, it lasts for 1 hour without requiring your concentration. When you cast this spell using a spell slot of 4th level or higher, the duration increases by 1 hour for each slot level above 3rd.

DEADLY STING

8th-Level Transmutation

Casting Time: 1 action
Range: Self
Components: V, S, M (a thorn)
Duration: Concentration, up to 1 minute

You grow a 10-foot-long tail as supple as a whip, tipped with a horrible stinger. During the spell's duration, you can use the stinger to make a melee spell attack with a reach of 10 feet. On a hit, the target takes 1d4 piercing damage plus 4d10 poison damage, and a creature must make a successful Constitution saving throw or become vulnerable to poison damage for the duration of the spell.

DEATH GOD'S TOUCH

7th-Level Necromancy

Casting Time: 1 action
Range: Touch
Components: V, S
Duration: Instantaneous

This spell allows you to shred the life force of a creature you touch. You become invisible and make a melee spell attack against the target. On a hit, the target takes 10d10 necrotic damage. If this damage reduces the target to 0 hit points, the target dies. Whether the attack hits or misses, you remain invisible until the start of your next turn.

At Higher Levels. When you cast this spell using a spell slot of 8th level or higher, the damage increases by 2d10 for each slot level above 7th.

DECAY

Necromancy Cantrip

Casting Time: 1 action
Range: Touch
Components: V, S, M (a handful of ash)
Duration: Instantaneous

Make a melee spell attack against a creature you touch. On a hit, the target takes 1d10 necrotic damage. If the target is a Tiny or Small nonmagical object that isn't being worn or carried by a creature, it automatically takes maximum damage from the spell.

This spell's damage increases by 1d10 when you reach 5th level (2d10), 11th level (3d10), and 17th level (4d10).

DECELERATE

2nd-Level Transmutation

Casting Time: 1 action
Range: 60 feet
Components: V, S, M (a toy top)
Duration: 1 minute

You slow the flow of time around a creature within range that you can see. The creature must make a successful Wisdom saving throw, or its walking speed is halved (round up to the nearest 5-foot increment). The creature can repeat the saving throw at the end of each of its turns, ending the effect on a success. Until the spell ends, on a failed save the target's speed is halved again at the start of each of your turns. For example, if a creature with a speed of 30 feet fails its initial saving throw, its speed drops to 15 feet. At the start of your next turn, the creature's speed drops to 10 feet on a failed save, then to 5 feet on the following round on another failed save. *Decelerate* can't reduce a creature's speed to less than 5 feet.

At Higher Levels. When you cast this spell using a spell slot of 3rd level or higher, you can affect an additional creature for each slot level above 2nd.

DEEP BREATH

1st-Level Transmutation

Casting Time: 1 action
Range: Touch
Components: V, S
Duration: 2 hours

The recipient of this spell can breathe and function normally in thin atmosphere, suffering no ill effect at altitudes of up to 20,000 feet. If more than one creature is touched during the casting, the duration is divided evenly among all creatures touched.

At Higher Levels. When you cast this spell using a spell slot of 2nd level or higher, the duration increases by 2 hours for each slot level above 1st.

DEEP FOCUS

3rd-Level Evocation (Ritual)

Casting Time: 1 action
Range: Self
Components: V, S
Duration: Special

You tap into ambient magical energy to stabilize and maintain a spell. The next spell you cast that normally requires concentration will last its full normal duration without the need for concentration, as long as it is cast within 1 minute of your casting of this spell, and the spell to be affected is of 4th level or lower. At the end of the duration, or if 1 minute goes by without your casting a spell that requires concentration, the spell ends.

At Higher Levels. When you cast this spell using a spell slot of 4th level or higher, you can affect any spell you can cast that requires concentration and is up to one level higher than the spell slot you used to cast *deep focus*.

DEEP FREEZE

4th-Level Evocation

Casting Time: 1 action
Range: 60 feet
Components: V, S, M (a piece of ice or quartz)
Duration: Concentration, up to 1 minute

You send a blast of deep cold at a creature, dealing 4d8 cold damage to it and encasing it in ice. An encased creature is grappled and takes an extra 2d8 cold damage at the start of its turn every round it remains encased. If the target of this spell makes a successful Dexterity saving throw, it takes half the damage and none of the extra damage and is not encased in ice, but the ice that clings to its body reduces its speed by 15 feet (to a minimum speed of 5 feet) until it takes an action to remove the ice.

A grappled target can take an action to make a Strength check against your spell save DC, breaking free of the ice on a success. Alternatively, another creature within 5 feet of the target can make a Strength check on its turn, freeing the creature on a success. The ice can also be attacked. It has AC 12, 10 hit points, and vulnerability to fire damage.

At Higher Levels. When you cast this spell using a spell slot of 5th level or higher, you can target one additional creature for each slot level above 4th.

DEFENSIVE QUILLS

3rd-Level Transmutation

Casting Time: 1 action
Range: Self
Components: V, S, M (a porcupine's quill)
Duration: 10 minutes

Sharp quills grow from your skin. You can end the spell early by using an action to dismiss it. You gain a +1 bonus to AC for the duration. If a creature hits you with an attack made by a light weapon, a natural attack, or an unarmed strike, it takes 2d8 piercing damage from your quills. A creature that grapples you takes damage from the quills at the beginning of each of its turns in which it is grappling you. If a creature swallows you, it takes damage from the quills each round at the start of your turn.

DELAY POTION

2nd-Level Transmutation

Casting Time: 1 action
Range: Touch
Components: V, S
Duration: 1 hour (see below)

Upon casting this spell, you delay the next potion you consume from taking effect for up to 1 hour. You must consume the potion within 1 round of casting *delay potion*; otherwise, the spell has no effect. At any point during *delay potion*'s duration, you can use a bonus action to cause the potion to go into effect. When the potion is activated, it works as if you had just drunk it. While the potion is delayed, it has no effect at all, and you can consume and benefit from other potions normally.

You can delay only one potion at a time. If you try to delay the effect of a second potion, the spell fails, the first potion has no effect, and the second potion has its normal effect when you drink it.

DELAYED HEALING

3rd-Level Evocation

Casting Time: 1 minute
Range: Touch
Components: V, M (a bloodstone worth 100 gp, which the spell consumes)
Duration: Instantaneous

Touch a living creature (not a construct or undead) as you cast the spell. The next time that creature takes damage, it immediately regains hit points equal to 1d4 + your spellcasting ability modifier (minimum of 1).

At Higher Levels. When you cast this spell using a spell slot of 4th level or higher, the healing increases by 1d4 for each slot level above 3rd.

DEMON WITHIN

3rd-Level Conjuration

Casting Time: 1 action
Range: 30 feet
Components: V, S, M (a vial of blood from a humanoid killed within the previous 24 hours)
Duration: Concentration, up to 1 minute

One humanoid of your choice within range becomes a gateway for a demon to enter the plane of existence you are on. You choose the demon's type from among those of challenge rating of 4 or lower. The target must make a Wisdom saving throw. On a success, the gateway fails to open, and the spell has no effect. On a failed save, the target takes 4d6 force damage from the demon's attempt to claw its way through the gate. For the spell's duration, you can use a bonus action to further agitate the demon, dealing an additional 2d6 force damage to the target each time.

If the target drops to 0 hit points while affected by this spell, the demon tears through the body and appears in the same space as its now incapacitated or dead victim. You do not control this demon; it is free to either attack or leave the area as it chooses. The demon disappears after 24 hours or when it drops to 0 hit points.

DESICCATING BREATH

4th-Level Evocation

Casting Time: 1 action
Range: Self (30-foot cone)
Components: V, S, M (a clump of dried clay)
Duration: Instantaneous

You spew forth a cloud of black dust that draws all moisture from a 30-foot cone. Each animal in the cone takes 4d10 necrotic damage, or half as much damage if it makes a successful Constitution saving throw. The damage is 6d10 for plants and plant creatures, also halved on a successful Constitution saving throw.

DETECT DRAGONS

2nd-Level Divination

Casting Time: 1 action
Range: Self
Components: V, S
Duration: Concentration, up to 10 minutes

You can detect the presence of dragons and other draconic creatures within your line of sight and 120 feet, regardless of disguises, illusions, and alteration magic such as polymorph. The information you uncover depends on the number of consecutive rounds you spend an action studying a subject or area. On the first round of examination, you detect whether any draconic creatures are present, but not their number, location, identity, or type. On the second round, you learn the number of such creatures as well as the general condition of the most powerful one. On the third and subsequent rounds, you make a DC 15 Intelligence (Arcana) check; if it succeeds, you learn the age, type, and location of one draconic creature. Note that the spell provides no information on the turn in which it is cast, unless you have the means to take a second action that turn.

DEVA'S WINGS

4th-Level Transmutation

Casting Time: 1 action
Range: Touch
Components: V, S, M (a wing feather from any bird)
Duration: Concentration, up to 10 minutes

You touch a willing creature. The target grows feathery white wings that grant it a flying speed of 60 feet and the ability to hover. When the target takes the Attack action, it can use a bonus action to make a melee weapon attack with the wings, with a reach of 10 feet. If the wing attack hits, the target takes bludgeoning damage equal to 1d6 + your spellcasting ability modifier and must make a successful Strength saving throw or fall prone. When the spell ends, the wings disappear, and the target falls if it was aloft.

At Higher Levels. When you cast this spell using a spell slot of 5th level or higher, you can target one additional target for each slot level above 4th.

DISCERN WEAKNESS

2nd-Level Divination

Casting Time: 1 action
Range: Self
Components: V, S, M (a glass lens)
Duration: Concentration, up to 1 minute

You divine the weak points in your foes' defenses, allowing you to strike with deadly effect. If you score a critical hit or a successful sneak attack on an opponent, roll damage twice and take the better result.

DISQUIETING GAZE

1st-Level Necromancy

Casting Time: 1 action
Range: Self
Components: V, S
Duration: 1 minute

Your eyes burn with scintillating motes of unholy crimson light. Until the spell ends, you have advantage on Charisma (Intimidation) checks made against creatures that can see you, and you have advantage on spell attack rolls that deal necrotic damage to creatures that can see your eyes.

DISRUPTIVE AURA

8th-Level Evocation

Casting Time: 1 action
Range: 150 feet
Components: V, S
Duration: Concentration, up to 1 minute

A warping, prismatic aura surrounds and outlines each creature inside a 10-foot cube within range. The aura sheds dim light out to 10 feet, and the locations of hidden or invisible creatures are outlined. If a creature in the area tries to cast a spell or use a magic item, it must make a Wisdom saving throw. On a successful save, the spell or item functions normally. On a failed save, the effect of the spell or the item is suppressed for the duration of the aura. Time spent suppressed counts against the duration of the spell's or item's effect.

At Higher Levels. When you cast this spell using a 9th-level spell slot, the cube is 20 feet on a side.

DISTRACTING DIVINATION

2nd-Level Divination

Casting Time: 1 reaction, which you take when an enemy tries to cast a spell
Range: Touch
Components: V, S
Duration: Instantaneous

Foresight tells you when and how to be just distracting enough to foil an enemy spellcaster. When an adjacent enemy tries to cast a spell, make a melee spell attack against that enemy. On a hit, the enemy's spell fails and has no effect; the enemy's action is used up, but the spell slot isn't expended.

DISTRACTION CASCADE

2nd-Level Divination

Casting Time: 1 reaction, which you take when an ally declares an attack against an enemy you can see
Range: 30 feet
Components: V, S
Duration: Instantaneous

With a flash of foresight, you throw a foe off balance. Choose one creature you can see that your ally has just declared as the target of an attack. Unless that creature makes a successful Charisma saving throw, attacks against it are made with advantage until the end of this turn.

DISTRESSING RESONANCE

4th-Level Evocation

Casting Time: 1 action
Range: 30 feet
Components: V, S
Duration: Concentration, up to 1 minute

You create a field of subsonic vibrations in a 30-foot-radius sphere, centered on a point you choose within range, which causes physical distress and extreme discomfort. A creature in this area or that enters it after you cast the spell must succeed on a Constitution saving throw or be incapacitated until the beginning of its next turn. On a successful save, the creature can act normally. If a creature begins its turn in the area, it must make another successful save to avoid being incapacitated. Constructs, deafened creatures, oozes, plants, and undead are not affected by this spell.

The vibrations from the distressing resonance interfere with tremorsense, negating any use of that ability in the spell's area.

DOME OF SILENCE

2nd-Level Abjuration

Casting Time: 1 action
Range: Self
Components: V, S
Duration: Concentration, up to 10 minutes

An invisible dome encompasses a 10-foot-radius around you, creating a damper for any sound traveling into or out of the area. Creatures can pass through the dome normally, but sound does not. You and any creatures in the dome can hear one another, but nothing outside. Likewise, any noise made in the dome of silence cannot be heard outside it.

Any attack that deals thunder damage dispels the dome, but the dome reduces that damage to any creatures inside it by half.

DRACONIC MAJESTY

3rd-Level Enchantment

Casting Time: 1 action
Range: Self (30-foot radius)
Components: V, S
Duration: Concentration, up to 1 minute

You exude the powerful presence of a dragon, frightening your enemies. For the duration of the spell, all creatures who are aware of your presence and within 30 feet of you must succeed on a Wisdom saving throw or become frightened for 1 minute. A creature can repeat the saving throw at the end of each of its turns, ending the effect on itself on a success.

At Higher Levels. When you cast this spell using a spell slot of 4th level or higher, the radius increases by 30 feet for each slot level above 3rd, to a maximum of 120 feet for a slot of 6th level or higher.

DRACONIC SENSES

4th-Level Divination

Casting Time: 1 action
Range: Self
Components: V, S
Duration: 8 hours

You enhance your senses, granting yourself the keen perception of a dragon. For the duration of the spell, you gain darkvision out to a range of 60 feet. If you already have darkvision, its range increases by 60 feet. You also gain blindsight out to a range of 60 feet.

DRACONIC SMITE

1st-Level Evocation

Casting Time: 1 bonus action
Range: Self
Components: V
Duration: Concentration, up to 1 minute

The next time you hit a creature with a melee weapon attack during the spell's duration, your weapon takes on the form of a silver dragon's head. Your attack deals an extra 1d6 cold damage, and up to four other creatures of your choosing within 30 feet of the attack's target must each make a successful Constitution saving throw or take 1d6 cold damage.

At Higher Levels. When you cast this spell using a spell slot of 2nd level or higher, the extra cold damage and the cold damage dealt to the secondary creatures increases by 1d6 for each slot level above 1st.

DRAGON BREATH

5th-Level Evocation

Casting Time: 1 action
Range: Self (15-foot cone or 30-foot line)
Components: V, S, M (a piece of a dragon's tooth)
Duration: Concentration, up to 1 minute

You summon draconic power to gain a breath weapon. When you cast dragon breath, you can immediately exhale a cone or line of elemental energy, depending on the type of dragon you select. While the spell remains active, roll a d6 at the start of your turn. On a roll of 5 or 6, you can take a bonus action that turn to use the breath weapon again.

When you cast the spell, choose one of the dragon types listed below. Your choice determines the affected area and the damage of the breath attack for the spell's duration.

Dragon Type	Area	Damage
Black	30-foot line, 5 feet wide	6d6 acid damage
Blue	30-foot line, 5 feet wide	6d6 lightning damage
Green	15-foot cone	6d6 poison damage
Red	15-foot cone	6d6 fire damage
White	15-foot cone	6d6 cold damage

At Higher Levels. When you cast this spell using a spell slot of 6th level or higher, the damage increases by 2d6 for each slot level above 5th.

DRAGON ROAR

Evocation Cantrip

Casting Time: 1 action
Range: 30 feet
Components: V
Duration: Instantaneous

Your voice is amplified to assault the mind of one creature. The target must make a Charisma saving throw. If it fails, the target takes 1d4 psychic damage and is frightened until the start of your next turn. A target can be affected by your dragon roar only once per 24 hours.

This spell's damage increases by 1d4 when you reach 5th level (2d4), 11th level (3d4), and 17th level (4d4).

DRAGON'S PRIDE

3rd-Level Enchantment

Casting Time: 1 action
Range: Self
Components: V, S
Duration: Concentration, up to 1 hour

Your sense of self grows to draconic proportions. Until the spell ends, you gain advantage on all Charisma checks and on all saving throws against being charmed or frightened.

DRAIN ITEM

4th-Level Evocation

Casting Time: 1 action
Range: Touch
Components: V, S
Duration: Instantaneous

You touch a magic item and cause its magical energies to drain away. If the item is currently carried or held by another creature, you must make a melee spell attack to touch the item, against the wielder's AC. On a hit, the item loses 1d3 charges. If this reduction drops the item's charges to 0, any effects that occur when the item loses all its charges immediately take effect.

At Higher Levels. When you cast this spell using a spell slot of 5th level or higher, you can drain more charges from an item: 1d4 for a 5th-level slot, 1d6 for a 6th-level slot, 1d8 for a 7th-level slot, or 2d6 for an 8th- or 9th-level slot.

DREAD WINGS

4th-Level Necromancy

Casting Time: 1 action
Range: 60 feet
Components: V, S
Duration: Concentration, up to 1 minute

A swarm of flying, bat-like shapes swirl into existence in a 20-foot-radius cloud around the point you target your spell. Each round a creature begins its turn in the swarm, it takes 4d8 necrotic damage and must succeed on a Wisdom saving throw or become frightened for 1d4 rounds. Creatures that are immune to necrotic damage are not susceptible to the frightened effect.

You can use an action on your turn to move the swarm up to 40 feet in any direction.

DROWN

3rd-Level Evocation

Casting Time: 1 action
Range: 90 feet
Components: V, S, M (a small piece of flotsam or seaweed)
Duration: Instantaneous

You cause a creature's lungs to fill with seawater. Unless the target makes a successful Constitution saving throw, it immediately begins suffocating. A suffocating creature can't speak or perform verbal spell components. It can hold its breath, and thereafter can survive for a number of rounds equal to its Constitution modifier (minimum of 1 round), after which it drops to 0 hit points and is dying. Huge or larger creatures are unaffected, as are creatures that can breathe water or that don't require air.

A suffocating (not dying) creature can repeat the saving throw at the end of each of its turns, ending the effect on a success.

At Higher Levels. When you cast this spell using a spell slot of 4th level or higher, you can target one additional creature for each slot level above 3rd.

DRYAD'S KISS

3rd-Level Conjuration

Casting Time: 1 action
Range: 120 feet
Components: V, M (a flower petal or a drop of blood)
Duration: Concentration, up to 1 minute

You perform an ancient incantation that summons flora from the fey realm. A creature you can see within range is covered with small, purple buds and takes 3d8 necrotic damage; a successful Wisdom saving throw negates the damage but doesn't prevent the plant growth. The buds can be removed by the target or an ally of the target within 5 feet who uses an action to make a successful Intelligence (Nature) or Wisdom (Medicine) check against your spell save DC, or by a *greater restoration* or *blight* spell. While the buds remain, whenever the target takes damage from a source other than this spell, one bud blossoms into a purple and yellow flower that deals an extra 1d8 necrotic damage to the target. Once four blossoms have formed in this way, the buds can no longer be removed by nonmagical means. The buds and blossoms wilt and fall away when the spell ends, provided the creature is still alive.

If a creature affected by this spell dies, sweet-smelling blossoms quickly cover its body. The flowers wilt and die after one month.

At Higher Levels. If this spell is cast using a spell slot of 5th level or higher, the number of targets increases by one for every two slot levels above 3rd.

EARS OF THE BAT

3rd-Level Transmutation

Casting Time: 1 action
Range: Self
Components: V, S, M (a bit of bat fur)
Duration: Concentration, up to 1 hour

You gain the keen hearing and echolocation abilities of a bat. For the duration of the spell, you have advantage on Wisdom (Perception) checks that rely on hearing, and you gain blindsight out to a range of 60 feet.

You cannot use the blindsight ability while deafened. While the spell is in effect, you have disadvantage on saving throws against spells and effects that deal thunder damage.

EARTH WAVE

5th-Level Transmutation

Casting Time: 1 action
Range: Self (15-foot radius)
Components: V, S
Duration: Concentration, up to 8 hours

You command the earth beneath your feet to rise and surge forward, carrying you and your companions where you bid while rolling over enemies and obstacles in your path. The earth rises in a 15-foot-high, 15-foot-radius swell that can carry you and up to eight other Medium creatures, propelling you in whatever direction you choose at a rate of up to 90 feet per round. You use a bonus action to direct the wave each round. Your movement is limited to the surface of the wave to maintain control. If you move off the wave, it continues on the same course you directed it, then the spell ends at the beginning of your next turn.

Natural obstacles do not impede the spell's movement; trees, rocks, and other natural obstacles simply rise up and around the swell and settle back into place behind it. The wave can travel up or down natural slopes with angles as great as 60 degrees.

You can direct the wave to surge over man-made obstacles and creatures in its path. The swell washes over walls and other manufactured obstacles up to 15 feet high and 10 feet thick with no loss of movement, dealing 6d6 bludgeoning damage to an object as it passes. Resolve this damage against larger, rigid objects, such as walls, vehicles, or other similar structures; smaller or malleable objects such as unsecured ropes or cloth are simply buried by the swell's passing. Larger objects are subject to the damage, but the wave cannot move over them unless the damage is enough to destroy the object.

Creatures of Large size or smaller in the path of the wave take 6d6 bludgeoning damage and are buried. Buried creatures are considered restrained and must hold their breath or begin to suffocate. A creature in the path of the wave can make a Dexterity saving throw against your spell save DC. On a successful save, the creature takes half as much damage and avoids being buried. Each round, a buried creature can use an action to make a Strength check against your spell save DC to dig itself out.

You can cast *earth wave* only when standing on natural earth or stone. The spell can be cast underground, but not inside buildings unless they have no floor.

EARTHSKIMMER

4th-Level Transmutation

Casting Time: 1 action
Range: Self
Components: V, S, M (a piece of shale or slate)
Duration: Concentration, up to 1 minute

You cause earth and stone to rise up beneath your feet, lifting you up to 5 feet. For the duration, you can use your movement to cause the slab to skim along the ground or other solid, horizontal surface at a speed of 60 feet. This movement ignores difficult terrain. If you are pushed or moved against your will by any means other than teleporting, the slab moves with you.

Until the end of your turn, you can enter the space of a creature up to one size larger than yourself when you take the Dash action. The creature must make a Strength saving throw. It takes 4d6 bludgeoning damage and is knocked prone on a failed save, or it takes half as much damage and isn't knocked prone on a successful one.

EARWORM MELODY

1st-Level Enchantment

Casting Time: 1 action
Range: 30 feet
Components: V, S
Duration: Concentration, up to 1 minute

You sing or play a catchy tune that only one creature of your choice within range can hear. Unless the creature makes a successful Wisdom saving throw, the verse becomes ingrained in its head. If the target is concentrating on a spell, it must make a Constitution check with disadvantage against your spell save DC in order to maintain concentration.

For the spell's duration, the target takes 2d4 psychic damage at the start of each of its turns as the melody plays over and over in its mind. The target repeats the saving throw at the end of each of its turns, ending the effect on a success. On a failed save, the target must also repeat the Constitution check with disadvantage if it is concentrating on a spell.

At Higher Levels. If you cast this spell using a spell slot of 2nd level or higher, the damage increases by 1d4 for each slot level above 1st.

ECHOES OF STEEL

4th-Level Evocation

Casting Time: 1 bonus action
Range: Self (30-foot radius)
Components: S
Duration: Concentration, up to 1 minute

When you hit a creature with a melee weapon attack, you can use a bonus action to cast *echoes of steel*. All creatures you designate within 30 feet of you take thunder damage equal to the damage from the melee attack, or half as much damage with a successful Constitution saving throw.

ECTOPLASM

2nd-Level Necromancy

Casting Time: 1 action
Range: 60 feet
Components: V, S, M (a pinch of bone dust)
Duration: Concentration, up to 1 minute

You call forth an ectoplasmic manifestation of Medium size that appears in an unoccupied space of your choice within range that you can see. The manifestation lasts for the spell's duration. Any creature that ends its turn within 5 feet of the manifestation takes 2d6 psychic damage, or half the damage with a successful Wisdom saving throw.

As a bonus action, you can move the manifestation up to 30 feet. It can move through a creature's space but can't remain in the same space as that creature. If it enters a creature's space, that creature takes 2d6 psychic damage, or half the damage with a successful Wisdom saving throw. On a failed save, the creature also has disadvantage on Dexterity checks until the end of its next turn.

When you move the manifestation, it can flow through a gap as small as 1 square inch, over barriers up to 5 feet tall, and across pits up to 10 feet wide. The manifestation sheds dim light in a 10-foot radius. It also leaves a thin film of ectoplasmic residue on everything it touches or moves through. This residue doesn't illuminate the surroundings but does glow dimly enough to show the manifestation's path. The residue dissipates 1 round after it is deposited.

At Higher Levels. When you cast this spell using a spell slot of 3rd level or higher, the damage increases by 1d6 for each slot level above 2nd.

EIDETIC MEMORY

5th-Level Transmutation (Ritual)

Casting Time: 1 action
Range: Self
Components: V, S, M (a string tied in a knot)
Duration: Concentration, up to 1 hour

When you cast this spell, you can recall any piece of information you've ever read or heard in the past. This ability translates into a +10 bonus on Intelligence checks for the duration of the spell.

ELDRITCH COMMUNION

5th-Level Divination (Ritual)

Casting Time: 1 minute
Range: Self
Components: V, S, M (corvid entrails, a dried opium poppy, and a glass dagger)
Duration: 1 minute

You contact a Great Old One and ask one question that can be answered with a one-sentence reply no more than twenty words long. You must ask your question before the spell ends. There is a 25 percent chance that the answer contains a falsehood or is misleading in some way. (The GM determines this secretly.)

Great Old Ones have vast knowledge, but they aren't omniscient, so if your question pertains to information beyond the Old One's knowledge, the answer might be vacuous, gibberish, or an angry, "I don't know."

This also reveals the presence of all aberrations within 300 feet of you. There is a 1-in-6 chance that each aberration you become aware of also becomes aware of you.

If you cast *eldritch communion* two or more times before taking a long rest, there is a cumulative 25 percent chance for each casting after the first that you receive no answer and become afflicted with short-term madness.

ELEMENTAL HORNS

2nd-Level Evocation

Casting Time: 1 action
Range: Touch
Components: V, S, M (a brass wand)
Duration: Concentration, up to 1 minute

The target of this spell must be a creature that has horns, or the spell fails. *Elemental horns* causes the touched creature's horns to crackle with elemental energy. Select one of the following energy types when casting this spell: acid, cold, fire, lightning, or radiant. The creature's gore attack deals 3d6 damage of the chosen type in addition to any other damage the attack normally deals.

Although commonly seen among tieflings and minotaurs, this spell is rarely employed by other races.

At Higher Levels. When you cast this spell using a spell slot of 3rd level or higher, the damage increases by 2d6 for each slot level above 2nd.

ELEMENTAL TWIST

2nd-Level Evocation

Casting Time: 1 action
Range: Self
Components: V, S, M (a thin piece of copper twisted around itself)
Duration: Concentration, up to 1 minute

During this spell's duration, reality shifts around you whenever you cast a spell that deals acid, cold, fire, lightning, poison, or thunder damage. Assign each damage type a number and roll a d6 to determine the type of damage this casting of the spell deals. In addition, the spell's damage increases by 1d6. All other properties or effects of the spell are unchanged.

EMANATION OF YOTH

4th-Level Necromancy (Ritual)

Casting Time: 1 minute
Range: 90 feet
Components: V, S, M (a fistful of grave earth and a vial of child's blood)
Duration: Concentration, up to 1 hour

You call forth a ghost that takes the form of a spectral, serpentlike assassin. It appears in an unoccupied space that you can see within range. The ghost disappears when it's reduced to 0 hit points or when the spell ends.

The ghost is friendly to you and your companions for the duration of the spell. Roll initiative for the ghost, which takes its own turns. It obeys verbal commands that you issue to it (no action required by you). If you don't issue a command to it, the ghost defends itself from hostile creatures but doesn't move or take other actions.

You are immune to the ghost's Horrifying Visage action but can willingly become the target of the ghost's Possession ability. You can end this effect on yourself as a bonus action.

At Higher Levels. When you cast this spell using a spell slot of 6th or 7th level, you call forth two ghosts. If you cast it using a spell slot of 8th or 9th level, you call forth three ghosts.

ENCHANT RING

6th-Level Enchantment

Casting Time: 1 action
Range: Touch
Components: V, S, M (500 gp worth of diamond dust, which the spell consumes)
Duration: Permanent until discharged

You enchant a ring you touch that isn't being worn or carried. The next creature that willingly wears the ring becomes charmed by you for 1 week or until it is harmed by you or one of your allies. If the creature dons the ring while directly threatened by you or one of your allies, the spell fails.

The charmed creature regards you as a friend. When the spell ends, it doesn't know it was charmed by you, but it does realize that its attitude toward you has changed (possibly greatly) in a short time. How the creature reacts to you and regards you in the future is up to the GM.

ENCRYPT / DECRYPT

Transmutation Cantrip

Casting Time: 1 action
Range: Touch
Components: V, S
Duration: Instantaneous

By touching a page of written information, you can encode its contents. All creatures that try to read the information when its contents are encoded see the markings on the page as nothing but gibberish. The effect ends when either *encrypt / decrypt* or *dispel magic* is cast on the encoded writing, which turns it back into its normal state.

ENDOW ATTRIBUTE

4th-Level Transmutation

Casting Time: 1 action
Range: Touch
Components: V, S, M (a ring worth at least 200 gp, which the spell consumes)
Duration: Concentration, up to 1 hour

You touch a creature with a ring that has been etched with symbols representing a particular ability (Strength, Dexterity, and so forth). The creature must make a successful Constitution saving throw or lose one-fifth (rounded down) of its points from that ability score. Those points are absorbed into the ring and stored there for the spell's duration. If you then use an action to touch the ring to another creature on a later turn, the absorbed ability score points transfer to that creature. Once the points are transferred to another creature, you don't need to maintain concentration on the spell; the recipient creature retains the transferred ability score points for the remainder of the hour.

The spell ends if you lose concentration before the transfer takes place, if either the target or the recipient dies, or if either the target or the recipient is affected by a successful *dispel magic* spell. When the spell ends, the ability score points return to the original owner. Before then, that creature can't regain the stolen attribute points, even with *greater restoration* or comparable magic.

At Higher Levels. If you cast this spell using a spell slot of 7th or 8th level, the duration is 8 hours. If you use a 9th-level spell slot, the duration is 24 hours.

ENERGY ABSORPTION

5th-Level Abjuration

Casting Time: 1 action
Range: Touch
Components: V, S
Duration: Concentration, up to 1 minute

A creature you touch has resistance to acid, cold, fire, force, lightning, and thunder damage until the spell ends.

If the spell is used against an unwilling creature, you must make a melee spell attack with a reach of 5 feet. If the attack hits, for the duration of the spell the affected creature must make a saving throw using its spellcasting ability whenever it casts a spell that deals one of the given damage types. On a failed save, the spell is not cast but its slot is expended; on a successful save, the spell is cast but its damage is halved before applying the effects of saving throws, resistance, and other factors.

ENERGY FOREKNOWLEDGE

4th-Level Divination

Casting Time: 1 reaction, which you take when you are the target of a spell that deals cold, fire, force, lightning, necrotic, psychic, radiant, or thunder damage
Range: Self
Components: V, S
Duration: Instantaneous

When you cast this spell, you gain resistance to every type of energy listed above that is dealt by the spell hitting you. This resistance lasts until the end of your next turn.

At Higher Levels. When you cast this spell using a spell slot of 5th level or higher, you can include one additional ally in its effect for each slot level above 4th. Affected allies must be within 15 feet of you.

ENHANCE FAMILIAR

2nd-Level Transmutation (Ritual)

Casting Time: 1 action
Range: 30 feet
Components: V, S, M (a pinch of powdered iron)
Duration: Concentration, up to 1 hour

You temporarily imbue your familiar with power, making it larger, tougher, and more vicious. While the spell lasts, your familiar has all the statistics of the giant version of its type, except for the fish (**quipper**), which has the statistics of a **reef shark**. Your familiar retains all its special abilities as described in the *find familiar* spell.

If your familiar drops to 0 hit points and disappears, or you dismiss your familiar, the spell ends, and your familiar is returned to its normal form when you next summon it.

At Higher Levels. When you cast this spell using a spell slot of 4th level or higher, its duration is 1 hour and does not require concentration. When you cast this spell using a spell slot of 6th level or higher, the duration increases to 24 hours.

ENHANCE GREED

2nd-Level Divination

Casting Time: 1 action
Range: Self
Components: V, S
Duration: Concentration, up to 10 minutes

You detect precious metals, gems, and jewelry within 60 feet. You do not discern their exact location, only their presence and direction. Their exact location is revealed if you are within 10 feet of the spot.

Enhance greed penetrates barriers but is blocked by 1 foot of stone, 1 inch of common metal, a thin sheet of lead, or 3 feet of dirt or wood.

At Higher Levels. When you cast this spell using a spell slot of 3rd level or higher, the duration of the spell increases by 1 minute, and another 10 feet can be added to its range, for each slot level above 2nd.

ENTOMB

6th-Level Transmutation

Casting Time: 1 action
Range: 90 feet
Components: V, S, M (a chip of granite)
Duration: 8 hours

You cause slabs of rock to burst out of the ground or other stone surface to form a hollow, 10-foot cube within range. A creature inside the cube when it forms must make a successful Dexterity saving throw or be trapped inside the stone tomb. The tomb is airtight, with enough air for a single Medium or Small creature to breathe for 8 hours. If more than one creature is trapped inside, divide the time evenly between all the occupants. A Large creature counts as four Medium creatures. If the creature is still trapped inside when the air runs out, it begins to suffocate.

The tomb has AC 18 and 50 hit points. It is resistant to fire, cold, lightning, bludgeoning, and slashing damage, is immune to poison and psychic damage, and is vulnerable to thunder damage. When reduced to 0 hit points, the tomb crumbles into harmless powder.

ENTROPIC DAMAGE FIELD

3rd-Level Transmutation

Casting Time: 1 action
Range: 60 feet
Components: V, S, M (a silver wire)
Duration: Concentration, up to 1 minute

By twisting a length of silver wire around your finger, you tie your fate to those around you. When you take damage, that damage is divided equally between you and all creatures in range who get a failure on a Charisma saving throw. Any leftover damage that can't be divided equally is taken by you. Creatures that approach to within 60 feet of you after the spell was cast are also affected. A creature is allowed a new saving throw against this spell each time you take damage, and a successful save ends the spell's effect on that creature.

ENUMERATE

Divination Cantrip

Casting Time: 1 action
Range: 30 feet
Components: V
Duration: Instantaneous

You are able to divine the exact amount of a number of like objects in a 10-foot-cube centered on a point within range. You can be general ("How many coins in this chest?") or specific ("How many silver coins in this chest?") but can receive only one number as a response from the casting of this spell. If, for example, you want to know the number of coins of each denomination in a chest, you must cast the spell anew for each type of coin to be counted (copper, silver, gold, and so forth).

ESSENCE INSTABILITY

5th-Level Transmutation

Casting Time: 1 action
Range: 120 feet
Components: V, S
Duration: 1 minute

You cause the target to radiate a harmful aura. Both the target and every creature beginning or ending its turn within 20 feet of the target suffer 2d6 poison damage per round. The target can make a Constitution saving throw each round to negate the damage and end the affliction. Success means the target no longer takes damage from the aura, but the aura still persists around the target for the full duration.

Creatures affected by the aura must make a successful Constitution saving throw each round to negate the damage. The aura moves with the original target and is unaffected by *gust of wind* and similar spells.

The aura does not detect as magical or poison, and is invisible, odorless, and intangible (though the spell's presence can be detected on the original target). *Protection from poison* negates the spell's effects on targets but will not dispel the aura. A foot of metal or stone, two inches of lead, or a force effect such as *mage armor* or *wall of force* will block it.

At Higher Levels. When you cast this spell using a spell slot of 6th level or higher, the aura lasts 1 minute longer, and the poison damage increases by 1d6 for each slot level above 5th.

EVERCOLD

4th-Level Necromancy

Casting Time: 1 action
Range: 30 feet
Components: V, S, M (an insect that froze to death)
Duration: Until dispelled

You target a creature within the spell's range, and that creature must make a successful Wisdom saving throw or take 1d6 cold damage. In addition, the target is cursed to feel as if it's exposed to extreme cold. For the duration of *evercold*, the target must make a successful DC 10 Constitution saving throw at the end of each hour or gain one level of exhaustion. The target has advantage on the hourly saving throws if wearing suitable cold-weather clothing, but it has disadvantage on saving throws against other spells and magic that deal cold damage (regardless of its clothing) for the spell's duration.

The spell can be ended by its caster or by *dispel magic* or *remove curse*.

EXCEPTIONAL WIT

Transmutation Cantrip

Casting Time: 1 action
Range: Touch
Components: V, S
Duration: Concentration, up to 1 minute

You touch a willing creature. Once before the spell ends, the target can roll a d6 and add the result to one Intelligence check of its choice. It can roll the die before or after making the check. The spell then ends.

EXSANGUINATE

5th-Level Necromancy

Casting Time: 1 action
Range: 30 feet
Components: V, S, M (a desiccated horse heart)
Duration: Concentration, up to 1 minute

You cause the body of a creature within range to become engorged with blood or ichor. The target must make a Constitution saving throw. On a successful save, it takes 2d6 bludgeoning damage. On a failed save, it takes 4d6 bludgeoning damage each round, it is incapacitated, and it cannot speak, as it vomits up torrents of blood or ichor. In addition, its hit point maximum is reduced by an amount equal to the damage taken. The target dies if this effect reduces its hit point maximum to 0.

At the end of each of its turns, a creature can make a Constitution saving throw, ending the effect on a success—except for the reduction of its hit point maximum, which lasts until the creature finishes a long rest.

At Higher Levels. When you cast this spell using a spell slot of 6th level or higher, you can target one additional creature for each slot level above 5th.

EXSANGUINATING CLOUD

5th-Level Necromancy

Casting Time: 1 action
Range: 100 feet
Components: V, S
Duration: Concentration, up to 5 minutes

When you cast this spell, a rose-colored mist billows up in a 20-foot radius, centered on a point you indicate within range, making the area heavily obscured and draining blood from living creatures in the cloud. The cloud spreads around corners. It lasts for the duration or until strong wind disperses it, ending the spell.

This cloud leaches the blood or similar fluid from creatures in the area. It doesn't affect undead or constructs. Any creature in the cloud when it's created or at the start of your turn takes 6d6 necrotic damage and gains one level of exhaustion; a successful Constitution saving throw halves the damage and prevents the exhaustion.

EXTRACT KNOWLEDGE

6th-Level Necromancy (Ritual)

Casting Time: 1 action
Range: Touch
Components: V, S, M (a blank page)
Duration: Instantaneous

By touching a recently deceased corpse, you gain one specific bit of knowledge from it that was known to the creature in life. You must form a question in your mind as part of casting the spell; if the corpse has an answer to your question, it reveals the information to you telepathically. The answer is always brief—no more than a sentence—and very specific to the framed question. It doesn't matter whether the creature was your friend or enemy; the spell compels it to answer in any case.

EXUDE ACID

2nd-Level Transmutation

Casting Time: 1 action
Range: Self
Components: V
Duration: Concentration, up to 10 minutes

You cause your body to produce a caustic acid. You and anything you were holding or carrying when the spell is cast is immune to the acid. While the spell is active, you can make a melee attack roll against a target, dealing 4d4 acid damage on a hit. If you are grappling a creature, it takes the acid damage every round on your turn, as if you had made a successful attack. If you are grappled by a creature, or restrained or immobilized by physical means (ropes, chains, or similar restraints), the creature or the restraints takes the acid damage each round.

FAULT LINE

6th-Level Evocation

Casting Time: 1 action
Range: Self (60-foot line)
Components: V, S
Duration: Permanent

The ground thrusts sharply upward along a 5-foot-wide, 60-foot-long line that you designate. All spaces affected by the spell become difficult terrain. In addition, all creatures in the affected area are knocked prone and take 8d6 bludgeoning damage. Creatures that make a successful Dexterity saving throw take half as much damage and are not knocked prone. This spell doesn't damage permanent structures.

FEATHER FIELD

1st-Level Abjuration

Casting Time: 1 reaction, which you take when you are targeted by a ranged attack from a magic weapon but before the attack roll is made
Range: Self
Components: V, S, M (fletching from an arrow)
Duration: 1 round

A magical barrier of chaff in the form of feathers appears and protects you. Until the start of your next turn, you have a +5 bonus to AC against ranged attacks by magic weapons.

At Higher Levels. When you cast *feather field* using a spell slot of 2nd level or higher, the duration is increased by 1 round for each slot level above 1st.

FEATHER TRAVEL

2nd-Level Transmutation

Casting Time: 1 action
Range: Touch
Components: V, M (a feather)
Duration: Concentration, up to 1 hour

The target of *feather travel* (along with its clothing and other gear) transforms into a feather and drifts on the wind. The drifting creature has a limited ability to control its travel. It can move only in the direction the wind is blowing and at the speed of the wind. It can, however, shift up, down, or sideways 5 feet per round as if caught by a gust, allowing the creature to aim for an open window or doorway, to avoid a flame, or to steer around an animal or another creature. When the spell ends, the feather settles gently to the ground and transforms back into the original creature.

At Higher Levels. When you cast this spell using a spell slot of 3rd level or higher, two additional creatures can be transformed per slot level above 2nd.

FEY CROWN

5th-Level Abjuration

Casting Time: 1 action
Range: Self
Components: V, S, M (five flowers of different colors)
Duration: 1 hour

By channeling the ancient wards of the Seelie Court, you create a crown of five flowers on your head. While wearing this crown, you have advantage on saving throws against spells and other magical effects and are immune to being charmed. As a bonus action, you can choose a creature within 30 feet of you (including yourself). Until the end of its next turn, the chosen creature is invisible and has advantage on saving throws against spells and other magical effects. Each time a chosen creature becomes invisible, one of the blossoms in the crown closes. After the last of the blossoms closes, the spell ends at the start of your next turn and the crown disappears.

At Higher Levels. When you cast this spell using a spell slot of 6th level or higher, the crown can have one additional flower for each slot level above 5th. One additional flower is required as a material component for each additional flower in the crown.

FEY GLAMOR

1st-Level Illusion

Casting Time: 1 action
Range: Touch
Components: V, S, M (a pinch of powdered mica)
Duration: Concentration, up to 10 minutes

You lay a glamor upon a touched creature that makes it more interesting, attractive, and compelling. For the duration of the spell, the target has advantage on all Charisma checks.

FIENDISH BRAND

5th-Level Necromancy

Casting Time: 1 action
Range: Touch
Components: V, S, M (a branding iron)
Duration: 7 days

You infuse a branding iron (typically one bearing the mark of a demon lord or a lord of Hell) with the bone-chilling cold of the Lower Planes and a promise of damnation. To mark a creature with the brand, you make a melee spell attack. On a hit, you deal 2d8 cold damage to the target and cause it to become branded. The damage can be healed normally, but the brand remains until a remove curse spell is cast on the target, the duration expires, or you use an action to remove the brand. You can remove the brand from any distance, as long as the branded creature is on the same plane of existence as you.

While the creature wears the brand, it has disadvantage on any saving throws it makes against spells you cast on it. If you try to locate the creature with a *scrying* spell, it takes the −10 penalty to its saving throw as if you possessed a lock of its hair or other body part.

FIND KIN

1st-Level Divination (Ritual)

Casting Time: 1 action
Range: touch
Components: V, S, M (a freshly dug up tree root that is consumed by the spell)
Duration: Instantaneous

You touch one willing creature or make a melee spell attack against an unwilling creature, which is entitled to a Wisdom saving throw. On a failed save, or automatically if the target is willing, you learn the identity, appearance, and location of one randomly selected living relative of the target.

FIRE DARTS

2nd-Level Evocation

Casting Time: 1 action

Range: 20 feet

Components: V, S, M (a fire the size of a small campfire or larger)

Duration: Instantaneous

When this spell is cast on any fire that's at least as large as a small campfire or cooking fire, three darts of flame shoot out from the fire toward creatures within 30 feet of the fire. Darts can be directed against the same or separate targets as the caster chooses. Each dart deals 4d6 fire damage, or half as much damage if its target makes a successful Dexterity saving throw.

At Higher Levels. When you cast this spell using a spell slot of 3rd level or higher, the damage increases by 1d6 for each slot level above 2nd.

FIRE DRAGON'S FURY

6th-Level Transmutation

Casting Time: 1 action

Range: Self

Components: V, S

Duration: Concentration, up to 1 minute

You take on some of the physical characteristics and abilities of the fire dragon, growing protective scales, wings, and claws. Until the spell ends, your AC can't be less than 16, regardless of what kind of armor you are wearing. You can take two actions on your turn to attack with your claws, dealing 1d6 slashing damage on a hit. You are resistant to fire. Up to three times while the spell is active, as an action, you can breathe a 20-foot cone of flames, dealing 6d8 fire damage to all creatures in the cone. A creature that succeeds on a Dexterity saving throw takes half as much damage from your breath weapon. Finally, the wings grant you a flying speed of 40 feet.

FIRE UNDER THE TONGUE

1st-Level Transmutation

Casting Time: 1 action

Range: 5 feet

Components: V, S

Duration: 24 hours

You can ingest a nonmagical fire up to the size of a normal campfire that is within range. The fire is stored harmlessly in your mouth and dissipates without effect if it is not used before the spell ends. You can spit out the stored fire as an action. If you try to hit a particular target, then treat this as a ranged attack with a range of 5 feet. Campfire-sized flames deal 2d6 fire damage, while torch-sized flames deal 1d6 fire damage. Once you have spit it out, the fire goes out immediately unless it hits flammable material that can keep it fed.

FIREWALK

6th-Level Transmutation

Casting Time: 1 action

Range: Touch

Components: V, S

Duration: Concentration, up to 10 minutes

The creature you cast *firewalk* on becomes immune to fire damage. In addition, that creature can walk along any burning surface, such as a burning wall or burning oil spread on water, as if it were solid and horizontal. Even if there is no other surface to walk on, the creature can walk along the tops of the flames.

At Higher Levels. When you cast this spell using a spell slot of 7th level or higher, two additional creatures can be affected for each slot level above 6th.

FIST OF IRON

Transmutation Cantrip

Casting Time: 1 action
Range: Self
Components: V, S
Duration: Concentration, up to 1 minute

You transform your hand into iron. Your unarmed attacks deal 1d6 bludgeoning damage and are considered magical.

FLAME WAVE

4th-Level Evocation

Casting Time: 1 action
Range: Self (40-foot cone)
Components: V, S, M (a drop of tar, pitch, or oil)
Duration: Instantaneous

A rushing burst of fire rips out from you in a rolling wave, filling a 40-foot cone. Each creature in the area must make a Dexterity saving throw. A creature takes 6d8 fire damage and is pushed 20 feet away from you on a failed save; on a successful save, the creature takes half as much damage and isn't pushed.

At Higher Levels. When you cast this spell using a spell slot of 5th level or higher, the damage increases by 1d8 for each slot level above 3rd.

FLESH TO PAPER

3rd-Level Transmutation

Casting Time: 1 action
Range: Touch
Components: V, S
Duration: Concentration, up to 1 hour

A willing creature you touch becomes as thin as a sheet of paper until the spell ends. Anything the target is wearing or carrying is also flattened. The target can't cast spells or attack, and attack rolls against it are made with disadvantage. It has advantage on Dexterity (Stealth) checks while next to a wall or similar flat surface. The target can move through a space as narrow as 1 inch without squeezing. If it occupies the same space as an object or a creature when the spell ends, the creature is shunted to the nearest unoccupied space and takes force damage equal to twice the number of feet it was moved.

At Higher Levels. When you cast this spell using a spell slot of 4th level or higher, you can target one additional creature for each slot level above 3rd.

FLICKERING FATE

4th-Level Divination

Casting Time: 1 action
Range: Touch
Components: V, S
Duration: 1 round

You or a creature that you touch can see a few seconds into the future. When the spell is cast, each other creature within 30 feet of the target must make a Wisdom saving throw. Those that fail must declare, in initiative order, what their next action will be. The target of the spell declares his or her action last, after hearing what all other creatures will do. Each creature that declared an action must follow its declaration as closely as possible when its turn comes. For the duration of the spell, the target has advantage on attack rolls, ability checks, and saving throws, and creatures that declared their actions have disadvantage on attack rolls against the target.

FLUCTUATING ALIGNMENT

4th-Level Enchantment

Casting Time: 1 action
Range: 120 feet
Components: V, S
Duration: Concentration, up to 10 minutes

You channel the force of chaos to taint your target's mind. A target that gets a failure on a Wisdom saving throw must roll 1d20 and consult the Alignment Fluctuation table to find its new alignment, and it must roll again after every minute of the spell's duration. The target's alignment stops fluctuating and returns to normal when the spell ends. These changes do not make the affected creature friendly or hostile toward the caster, but they can cause creatures to behave in unpredictable ways.

ALIGNMENT FLUCTUATION

d20	Alignment
1–2	Chaotic good
3–4	Chaotic neutral
5–7	Chaotic evil
8–9	Neutral evil
10–11	Lawful evil
12–14	Lawful good
15–16	Lawful neutral
17–18	Neutral good
19–20	Neutral

FLURRY

1st-Level Transmutation

Casting Time: 1 bonus action
Range: Self
Components: V, S, M (a fleck of quartz)
Duration: 1 round

A flurry of snow surrounds you and extends to a 5-foot radius around you. While it lasts, anyone trying to see into, out of, or through the affected area (including you) has disadvantage on Wisdom (Perception) checks and attack rolls.

FOG OF WAR

4th-Level Illusion

Casting Time: 1 action
Range: 60 feet
Components: V, S
Duration: Concentration, up to 1 minute

You cloud the minds of your opponents, hindering their perception of the battlefield and veiling reality with twisted illusions. You can affect up to six creatures within range. While the spell is in effect, targeted creatures in the area have disadvantage on Wisdom (Perception) checks made to locate enemies.

If a targeted creature makes an attack against a creature that has at least one other creature adjacent to it—friend or foe—the targeted creature must roll a d20. On an 11 or higher, its attack is applied to the adjacent creature instead (roll randomly to determine the new target if there is more than one adjacent creature) and deals damage as normal if it hits. Each round, a targeted creature can make a Wisdom saving throw. On a successful save, the creature is unhindered by the spell for that round.

FOREST AFFINITY

1st-Level Illusion

Casting Time: 1 action
Range: Self
Components: S, M (a raven's feather or a bit of panther fur)
Duration: Concentration, up to 1 hour

The forest floor swirls and shifts around you, welcoming you into its embrace. While in a forest, you have advantage on Dexterity (Stealth) checks to hide. While hidden in a forest, you have advantage on your next initiative roll. The spell ends if you attack or cast a spell.

At Higher Levels. When you cast this spell using a spell slot of 2nd level or higher, you can affect one additional creature for each slot level above 1st. The spell ends if you or any other target of this spell attacks or casts a spell.

FOREST NATIVE

1st-Level Transmutation

Casting Time: 1 action
Range: Touch
Components: V, S, M (a clump of soil from a forest)
Duration: 1 hour

While in a forest, you touch a willing creature and infuse it with the forest's energy, creating a bond between the creature and the environment. For the duration of the spell, as long as the creature remains within the forest, its movement is not hindered by difficult terrain composed of natural vegetation. In addition, the creature has advantage on saving throws against environmental effects such as excessive heat or cold or high altitude.

FOREST OF SPEARS

5th-Level Evocation

Casting Time: 1 action
Range: 120 feet
Components: V, S, M (a sliver of stone)
Duration: Concentration, up to 1 minute

A forest of stone spears rises up from the ground in a 30-foot radius around a point you designate within range. Creatures in the area take 5d8 piercing damage and are restrained. A successful Dexterity saving throw reduces the damage by half and negates the restrained condition. A creature that starts its turn in the area and is already restrained by the spears takes an extra 2d8 damage from the pain of being held aloft as well as bleeding from its wounds. A creature restrained by the spears can use its action to make a Strength or Dexterity check (its choice) against your spell save DC. On a successful save, it frees itself.

For the duration of the spell, the area is difficult terrain. The spears (AC 14) can be damaged; they are immune to piercing damage and have resistance to bludgeoning and slashing damage from nonmagical attacks. If a 5-foot-square section of spears takes 15 damage, that's enough to free a restrained creature or clear the section of spears.

FOREST SANCTUARY

9th-Level Abjuration

Casting Time: 1 minute
Range: 300 feet
Components: V, S, M (a bowl of fresh rainwater and a tree branch)
Duration: 24 hours

While in a forest, you create a protective, 200-foot cube centered on a point you can see within range. The atmosphere inside the cube has the lighting, temperature, and moisture that is most ideal for the forest, regardless of the lighting or weather outside the area. The cube is transparent, and creatures and objects can move freely through it. The cube protects the area inside it from storms, strong winds, and floods, including those created by magic such as *control weather*, *control water*, or *meteor swarm*. Such spells can't be cast while the spellcaster is in the cube.

You can create a permanently protected area by casting this spell at the same location every day for one year.

FORETELL DISTRACTION

1st-Level Divination

Casting Time: 1 bonus action
Range: Self
Components: S
Duration: Instantaneous

Thanks to your foreknowledge, you know exactly when your foe will take his or her eyes off you. Casting this spell has the same effect as making a successful Dexterity (Stealth) check, provided cover or concealment is available within 10 feet of you. It doesn't matter whether enemies can see you when you cast the spell; they glance away at just the right moment. You can move up to 10 feet as part of casting the spell, provided you're able to move (not restrained or grappled or reduced to a speed of less than 10 feet for any other reason). This move doesn't count as part of your normal movement. After the spell is cast, you must be in a position where you can remain hidden: a lightly obscured space, for example, or a space where you have total cover. Otherwise, enemies see you again immediately and you're not hidden.

FORM OF THE GODS

9th-Level Transmutation

Casting Time: 1 action
Range: Self
Components: V, S, M (a holy symbol)
Duration: Concentration, up to 1 hour

By drawing on the energy of the gods, you can temporarily assume the form of your patron's avatar. *Form of the gods* transforms you into an entirely new shape and brings about the following changes (summarized below and in the avatar form stat block):

- Your size becomes Large, unless you were already at least that big.
- You gain resistance to nonmagical bludgeoning, piercing, and slashing damage and to one other damage type of your choice.
- You gain a Multiattack action option, allowing you to make two slam attacks and a bite.
- Your ability scores change to reflect your new form, as shown in the stat block.

You remain in this form until you stop concentrating on the spell or until you drop to 0 hit points, at which time you revert to your natural form.

AVATAR FORM

Large

ARMOR CLASS 17
HIT POINTS 189 (18d10 + 90)
SPEED 30 ft.

STR	DEX	CON	INT	WIS	CHA
20 (+5)	18 (+4)	20 (+5)	18 (+4)	16 (+3)	20 (+5)

DAMAGE RESISTANCES bludgeoning, piercing, and slashing from nonmagical attacks, plus one additional type
SENSES darkvision 60 ft., passive Perception 13
LANGUAGES speaks all languages known in previous form
CHALLENGE 18 (20,000 XP)   **PROFICIENCY BONUS** +6

Awesome Presence. Each creature of your choice within 60 feet of you must succeed on a DC 17 Wisdom saving throw or become frightened for 1 minute. A frightened creature repeats the saving throw at the end of each of its turns, ending the effect on itself on a successful save. Once a creature makes a successful saving throw, that creature is immune to your Awesome Presence for 24 hours.

ACTIONS

Multiattack. You make two slam attacks and one bite attack.

Bite. *Melee Weapon Attack:* +11 to hit, reach 5 ft., one creature. *Hit:* 14 (2d8 + 5) piercing damage.

Slam. *Melee Weapon Attack:* +11 to hit, reach 5 ft., one creature. *Hit:* 16 (2d10 + 5) bludgeoning damage.

FORTITUDE

Transmutation Cantrip

Casting Time: 1 action

Range: Touch

Components: V, S

Duration: Concentration, up to 1 minute

You touch a willing creature. Once before the spell ends, the target can roll a d6 and add the result to one Constitution check of its choice. It can roll the die before or after making the check. The spell then ends.

FRAILTY

Necromancy Cantrip

Casting Time: 1 action

Range: 30 feet

Components: V, S

Duration: 1 minute

You temporarily inhibit the vital force of a creature within range. If the target makes a successful Constitution saving throw, the spell is ineffective. On a failed save, the next time the creature makes a Constitution check before the spell ends, roll a d6 and subtract the result from the roll. The spell then ends.

FREEZE BLOOD

3rd-Level Transmutation

Casting Time: 1 action

Range: Touch

Components: V, S

Duration: Concentration, up to 1 minute

You freeze a creature's blood with a successful melee spell attack. The target must be a living creature with a circulatory system. For the duration, the target's speed is halved, and it takes 2d6 cold damage at the start of each of its turns. In addition, if it takes bludgeoning damage from a critical hit, the attack's damage dice are rolled three times instead of twice. At the end of each of its turns, the creature can make a Constitution saving throw, ending the effect on a success.

FREEZE POTION

1st-Level Transmutation

Casting Time: 1 reaction, which you take when you see a creature within range about to consume a liquid

Range: 25 feet

Components: V, S

Duration: Instantaneous

A blue spark flies from your hand and strikes a potion vial, drinking horn, waterskin, or similar container, instantly freezing the contents. The substance melts normally thereafter and is not otherwise harmed, but it can't be consumed while it's frozen.

At Higher Levels. When you cast this spell using a spell slot of 2nd level or higher, the range increases by 5 feet for each slot level above 1st.

FREEZING FOG

3rd-Level Conjuration

Casting Time: 1 action

Range: 100 feet

Components: V, S

Duration: Concentration, up to 5 minutes

The spell creates a 20-foot-radius sphere of mist similar to a *fog cloud* spell centered on a point you can see within range. The cloud spreads around corners, and the area it occupies is heavily obscured. A wind of moderate or greater velocity (at least 10 miles per hour) disperses it in 1 round. The fog is freezing cold; any creature that ends its turn in the area must make a Constitution saving throw. It takes 2d6 cold damage and gains one level of exhaustion on a failed save, or takes half as much damage and no exhaustion on a successful one.

At Higher Levels. When you cast this spell using a spell slot of 4th level or higher, the damage increases by 1d6 for each slot level above 3rd.

FRENZIED BOLT

2nd-Level Evocation

Casting Time: 1 action

Range: 120 feet

Components: V, S

Duration: Instantaneous

You direct a bolt of rainbow colors toward a creature of your choice within range. If the bolt hits, the target takes 3d8 damage, of a type determined by rolling on the Random Damage Type table. If your attack roll (not the adjusted result) was odd, the bolt leaps to a new target of your choice within range that has not already been targeted by *frenzied bolt*, requiring a new spell attack roll to hit. The bolt continues leaping to new targets until you roll an even number on your spell attack roll, miss a target, or run out of potential targets. You and your allies are legal targets for this spell, if you are particularly lucky—or unlucky.

RANDOM DAMAGE TYPE

d10	Damage Type	d10	Damage Type
1	Acid	6	Necrotic
2	Cold	7	Poison
3	Fire	8	Psychic
4	Force	9	Radiant
5	Lightning	10	Thunder

At Higher Levels. When you cast this spell using a spell slot of 3rd level or higher, you create an additional bolt for each slot level above 2nd. Each potential target can be hit only once by each casting of the spell, not once per bolt.

FROSTBITE

5th-Level Evocation

Casting Time: 1 action
Range: 90 feet
Components: V, S, M (a strip of dried flesh that has been frozen at least once)
Duration: Concentration, up to 1 minute

Biting cold settles onto a creature you can see. The creature must make a Constitution saving throw. On a failed save, the creature takes 4d8 cold damage. In addition, for the duration of the spell, the creature's speed is halved, it has disadvantage on attack rolls and ability checks, and it takes another 4d8 cold damage at the start of each of its turns.

An affected creature can repeat the saving throw at the start of each of its turns. The effect ends when the creature makes its third successful save.

Creatures that are immune to cold damage are unaffected by *frostbite*.

At Higher Levels. When you cast this spell using a spell slot of 6th level or higher, you can target two additional creatures for each slot level above 5th.

FROZEN RAZORS

3rd-Level Evocation

Casting Time: 1 action
Range: 90 feet
Components: V, S, M (water from a melted icicle)
Duration: Concentration, up to 1 minute

Razor-sharp blades of ice erupt from the ground or other surface, filling a 20-foot cube centered on a point you can see within range. For the duration, the area is lightly obscured and is difficult terrain. A creature that moves more than 5 feet into or inside the area on a turn takes 2d6 slashing damage and 3d6 cold damage, or half as much damage if it makes a successful Dexterity saving throw. A creature that takes cold damage from frozen razors is reduced to half speed until the start of its next turn.

At Higher Levels. When you cast this spell using a spell slot of 4th level or higher, the damage increases by 1d6 for each slot level above 3rd.

FURIOUS HOOVES

2nd-Level Transmutation

Casting Time: 1 action
Range: Touch
Components: V, S, M (a nail)
Duration: Concentration, up to 1 minute

You enhance the feet or hooves of a creature you touch, imbuing it with power and swiftness. The target doubles its walking speed or increases it by 30 feet, whichever addition is smaller. In addition to any attacks the creature can normally make, this spell grants two hoof attacks, each of which deals bludgeoning damage equal to 1d6 + plus the target's Strength modifier (or 1d8 if the target of the spell is Large). For the duration of the spell, the affected creature automatically deals this bludgeoning damage to the target of its successful shove attack.

FUSILLADE OF ICE

4th-Level Evocation

Casting Time: 1 action
Range: Self (30-foot cone)
Components: V, S, M (a dagger shaped like an icicle)
Duration: Instantaneous

You unleash a spray of razor-sharp ice shards. Each creature in the 30-foot cone takes 4d6 cold damage and 3d6 piercing damage, or half as much damage with a successful Dexterity saving throw.

At Higher Levels. When you cast this spell using a spell slot of 5th level or higher, the damage increases by your choice of 1d6 cold damage or 1d6 piercing damage for each slot level above 4th. You can make a different choice (cold damage or piercing damage) for each slot level above 4th. Casting this spell with a spell slot of 6th level or higher increases the range to a 60-foot cone.

GEAR BARRAGE

2nd-Level Conjuration

Casting Time: 1 action
Range: Self (60-foot cone)
Components: V, S, M (a handful of gears and sprockets worth 5 gp)
Duration: Instantaneous

You create a burst of magically propelled gears. Each creature within a 60-foot cone takes 3d8 slashing damage, or half as much damage with a successful Dexterity saving throw. Constructs have disadvantage on the saving throw.

GHOUL KING'S CLOAK

8th-Level Transmutation

Casting Time: 1 action
Range: Touch
Components: V
Duration: Concentration, up to 1 minute

You touch a creature, giving it some of the power of a ghoul king. The target gains the following benefits for the duration:

- Its Armor Class increases by 2, to a maximum of 20.
- When it uses the Attack action to make a melee weapon attack or a ranged weapon attack, it can make one additional attack of the same kind.
- It is immune to necrotic damage and radiant damage.
- It can't be reduced to less than 1 hit point.

At Higher Levels. When you cast this spell using a 9th-level spell slot, the spell lasts for 10 minutes and doesn't require concentration.

GIANT'S JEST

4th-Level Transmutation

Casting Time: 1 action
Range: 25 feet
Components: V, S
Duration: 1 minute

This spell enlarges a weapon or other object that you can see within range, temporarily making it sized for a Gargantuan creature. The object is twelve times heavier than its original weight and in most circumstances cannot be used effectively by Huge or smaller creatures. The object retains its usual qualities (including magical powers and effects) and returns to normal size when the spell ends.

CHAPTER 5 SPELL DESCRIPTIONS | 203

GIFT OF LUCK

2nd-Level Divination (Ritual)

Casting Time: 1 action

Range: Touch

Components: V, S, M (a four-leaf clover, a pair of dice, or a silver coin)

Duration: 24 hours

You grant a touched creature a limited gift of luck. While the spell lasts, the target can gain advantage on any three rolls of its choice. Once three rolls have been affected by the *gift of luck*, the spell ends.

At Higher Levels. When you cast this spell using a spell slot of 3rd level or higher, you can target one additional creature for each slot level above 2nd.

GIFT OF RESILIENCE

2nd-Level Enchantment

Casting Time: 1 action

Range: Touch

Components: V, S

Duration: 24 hours, or until the target attempts a third death saving throw

A willing creature you touch has advantage on the first three death saving throws it attempts before the duration of the spell expires.

At Higher Levels. When you cast this spell using a spell slot of 5th, 6th, or 7th level, the maximum duration increases to 48 hours. When you cast this spell using a spell slot of 8th or 9th level, the maximum duration increases to 72 hours.

GIRD THE SPIRIT

1st-Level Abjuration

Casting Time: 1 reaction, which you take when you or a creature within 30 feet of you is hit by an attack from an undead creature

Range: 30 feet

Components: V, S

Duration: 1 minute

Your magic protects the target creature from the life-sapping energies of the undead. For the duration, the target has immunity to effects from undead creatures that reduce its ability scores, such as a shadow's Strength Drain, or its hit point maximum, such as a specter's Life Drain. This spell doesn't prevent damage from those attacks; it prevents only the reduction in ability score or hit point maximum.

GLACIAL CASCADE

8th-Level Evocation

Casting Time: 1 action

Range: Self (30-foot-radius sphere)

Components: V, S, M (a piece of alexandrite)

Duration: Instantaneous

By harnessing the power of ice and frost, you emanate pure cold, filling a 30-foot-radius sphere. Creatures other than you in the sphere take 10d8 cold damage, or half as much damage with a successful Constitution saving throw. A creature killed by this spell is transformed into ice, leaving behind no trace of its original body.

GLACIAL FOG

7th-Level Evocation

Casting Time: 1 action

Range: 100 feet

Components: V, S, M (crystalline statue of a polar bear worth at least 25 gp)

Duration: Concentration, up to 1 minute

As you cast this spell, a 30-foot-radius sphere centered on a point within range becomes covered in a frigid fog. Each creature that is in the area at the start of its turn while the spell remains in effect must make a Constitution saving throw. On a failed save, a creature takes 12d6 cold damage and gains one level of exhaustion, and it has disadvantage on Perception checks until the start of its next turn. On a successful save, the creature takes half the damage and ignores the other effects.

Stored devices and tools are all frozen by the fog: crossbow mechanisms become sluggish, weapons are stuck in scabbards, potions turn to ice, bag cords freeze together, and so forth. Such items require the application of heat for 1 round or longer in order to become useful again.

At Higher Levels. When you cast this spell using a spell slot of 8th level or higher, the damage increases by 1d6 for each slot level above 7th.

GLAMOR OF MUNDANITY

1st-Level Illusion

Casting Time: 1 action

Range: Touch

Components: V, S, M (a pinch of powdered iron)

Duration: Concentration, up to 10 minutes

You lay a glamor upon a touched creature that makes it easily overlooked and forgettable. For the duration of the spell, any Wisdom (Perception) checks to notice the target, or any ability checks made to recall details about the target or any interactions with it, are made with disadvantage. The target gains advantage on Dexterity (Stealth) checks but has disadvantage on any Charisma checks made while under the glamor.

GLIDING STEP

1st-Level Abjuration

Casting Time: 1 action
Range: Self
Components: V, S
Duration: 10 minutes

Provided you're not carrying more of a load than your carrying capacity permits, you can walk on the surface of snow rather than wading through it, and you ignore its effect on movement. Ice supports your weight no matter how thin it is, and you can travel on ice as if you were wearing ice skates. You still leave tracks normally while under these effects.

At Higher Levels. When you cast this spell using a spell slot of 2nd level or higher, the duration increases by 10 minutes for each slot level above 1st.

GLOOMWROUGHT BARRIER

3rd-Level Conjuration

Casting Time: 1 action
Range: 100 feet
Components: V, S, M (a piece of obsidian)
Duration: Concentration, up to 1 minute

When you cast this spell, you erect a barrier of energy drawn from the realm of death and shadow. This barrier is a wall 20 feet high and 60 feet long, or a ring 20 feet high and 20 feet in diameter. The wall is transparent when viewed from one side of your choice and translucent—lightly obscuring the area beyond it—from the other. A creature that tries to move through the wall must make a successful Wisdom saving throw or stop in front of the wall and become frightened until the start of the creature's next turn, when it can try again to move through. Once a creature makes a successful saving throw against the wall, it is immune to the effect of this barrier.

GLUEY GLOBULE

3rd-Level Conjuration

Casting Time: 1 action
Range: 120 feet
Components: V, S, M (a drop of glue)
Duration: 1 minute or 1 hour

You make a ranged spell attack to hurl a large globule of sticky, magical glue at a creature within 120 feet. If the attack hits, the target creature is restrained. A restrained creature can break free by using an action to make a successful Strength saving throw. When the creature breaks free, it takes 2d6 slashing damage from the glue tearing its skin. If your ranged spell attack roll was a critical hit or exceeded the target's AC by 5 or more, the Strength saving throw is made with disadvantage. The target can also be freed by an application of *universal solvent* or by taking 20 acid damage. The glue dissolves when the creature breaks free or at the end of 1 minute.

Alternatively, *gluey globule* can also be used to glue an object to a solid surface or to another object. In this case, the spell works like a single application of *sovereign glue* and lasts for 1 hour.

GLYPH OF SHIFTING

2nd-Level Conjuration

Casting Time: 10 minutes
Range: Touch
Components: V, S, M (powdered diamond worth at least 50 gp, which the spell consumes)
Duration: 24 hours

You create a hidden glyph by tracing it on a surface or object that you touch. When you cast the spell, you can also choose a location that's known to you, within 5 miles, and on the same plane of existence, to serve as the destination for the glyph's shifting effect.

The glyph is triggered when it's touched by a creature that's not aware of its presence. The triggering creature must make a successful Wisdom saving throw or be teleported to the glyph's destination. If no destination was set, the creature takes 4d4 force damage and is knocked prone.

The glyph disappears after being triggered or when the spell's duration expires.

At Higher Levels. When you cast this spell using a spell slot of 3rd level or higher, its duration increases by 24 hours and the maximum distance to the destination increases by 5 miles for each slot level above 2nd.

GOAT'S HOOF CHARM

1st-Level Transmutation

Casting Time: 1 action
Range: Touch
Components: V, S, M (a goat's hoof)
Duration: 1 minute

A creature you touch traverses craggy slopes with the surefootedness of a mountain goat. When ascending a slope that would normally be difficult terrain for it, the target can move at its full speed instead. The target also gains a +2 bonus on Dexterity checks and saving throws to prevent falling, to catch a ledge or otherwise stop a fall, or to move along a narrow ledge.

At Higher Levels. When you cast this spell using a spell slot of 2nd level or higher, you can increase the duration by 1 minute, or you can affect one additional creature, for each slot level above 1st.

GOING IN CIRCLES

3rd-Level Illusion

Casting Time: 10 minutes
Range: Sight
Components: V, S, M (a piece of the target terrain)
Duration: 24 hours

You make natural terrain in a 1-mile cube difficult to traverse. A creature in the affected area has disadvantage on Wisdom (Survival) checks to follow tracks or travel safely through the area, as paths through the terrain seem to twist and turn nonsensically. The terrain itself isn't changed, only the perception of those inside it. A creature that succeeds on two Wisdom (Survival) checks while in the terrain discerns the illusion for what it is and sees the illusory twists and turns superimposed on the terrain. A creature that reenters the area after exiting it before the spell ends is affected by the spell even if it previously succeeded in traversing the terrain. A creature with truesight can see through the illusion and is unaffected by the spell. A creature that casts *find the path* automatically succeeds in discovering a way out of the terrain.

When you cast this spell, you can designate a password. A creature that speaks the word as it enters the area automatically sees the illusion and is unaffected by the spell.

If you cast this spell on the same spot every day for one year, the illusion lasts until it is dispelled.

GORDOLAY'S PLEASANT AROMA

1st-Level Transmutation

Casting Time: 1 action
Range: 120 feet
Components: S, M (a few flower petals or a piece of fruit, which the spell consumes)
Duration: Concentration, up to 1 minute

You create an intoxicating aroma that fills the area within 30 feet of a point you can see within range. Creatures in this area smell something they find so pleasing that it's distracting. Each creature in the area that makes an attack roll must first make a Wisdom saving throw; on a failed save, the attack is made with disadvantage. Only a creature's first attack in a round is affected this way; subsequent attacks are resolved normally. On a successful save, a creature becomes immune to the effect of this particular scent, but they can be affected again by a new casting of the spell.

GRAIN OF TRUTH

2nd-Level Divination (Ritual)

Casting Time: 1 action
Range: Self
Components: V, S
Duration: Instantaneous

You gain a bit of supernatural insight or advice. The first Intelligence or Charisma ability check you make within 1 minute is made with advantage, and you can include twice your proficiency bonus. At the GM's discretion, this spell can instead provide a piece of general advice equivalent to the benefit of an *augury* spell.

At Higher Levels. At the GM's discretion, casting *grain of truth* using a 4th-level spell slot can provide advice equivalent to a *divination* spell; a 5th-level spell slot can provide advice equivalent to a single answer from a *commune* spell; and a 6th-level spell slot can provide advice equivalent to three answers from a *contact other plane* spell.

GRASP OF THE TUPILAK

5th-Level Necromancy

Casting Time: 1 action
Range: Self
Components: V, S, M (tupilak idol)
Duration: 1 hour or until triggered

This spell functions only against an arcane or divine spellcaster that prepares spells in advance and that has at least one unexpended spell slot of 6th level or lower. If you make a successful melee attack against such a creature before the spell ends, in addition to the usual effect of that attack, the target takes 2d4 necrotic damage and one or more of the victim's available spell slots are transferred to you, to be used as your own. Roll a d6; the result equals the total levels of the slots transferred. Spell slots of the highest possible level are transferred before lower-level slots.

For example, if you roll a 5 and the target has at least one 5th-level spell slot available, that slot transfers to you. If the target's highest available spell slot is 3rd level, then you might receive a 3rd-level slot and a 2nd-level slot, or a 3rd-level slot and two 1st-level slots if no 2nd-level slot is available.

If the target has no available spell slots of an appropriate level—for example, if you roll a 2 and the target has expended all of its 1st- and 2nd-level spell slots—then *grasp of the tupilak* has no effect, including causing no necrotic damage. If a stolen spell slot is of a higher level than you're able to use, treat it as of the highest level you can use.

Unused stolen spell slots disappear, returning whence they came, when you take a long rest or when the creature you stole them from receives the benefit of *remove curse*, *greater restoration*, or comparable magic.

GREATER ANALYZE DEVICE

2nd-Level Divination

Casting Time: 1 hour

Range: Touch

Components: V, S, M (a set of clockworker's tools)

Duration: Instantaneous

You discover all mechanical properties, mechanisms, and functions of a single construct, clockwork device, mechanical trap, or magic item, including how to activate or deactivate those functions, if appropriate.

GREATER PROTECTIVE NIMBUS

5th-Level Abjuration

Casting Time: 1 action

Range: Self

Components: V, S, M (a transparent gemstone worth at least 50 gp)

Duration: 10 minutes

You wrap yourself in a powerful corona that sheds bright light in a 30-foot radius and dim light for an additional 30 feet. Until the spell ends, you have resistance to necrotic damage and radiant damage. You can end the spell early by using an action to dismiss it, which creates a blast of light in a 30-foot radius. The blast deals 4d8 radiant damage to each creature in the area while simultaneously healing yourself of an equal amount of damage.

GREATER SEAL OF SANCTUARY

9th-Level Abjuration (Ritual)

Casting Time: 1 minute

Range: Touch

Components: V, S, M (incense and special inks worth 500 gp, which the spell consumes)

Duration: 24 hours

You inscribe an angelic seal on the ground, the floor, or other solid surface of a structure. The seal creates a spherical sanctuary with a radius of 100 feet, centered on the seal. For the duration, aberrations, elementals, fey, fiends, and undead that approach to within 5 feet of the boundary know they are about to come into contact with a deadly barrier. If such a creature moves so as to touch the boundary, or tries to cross the boundary by any means, including teleportation and extradimensional travel, it must make a Charisma saving throw. On a failed save, it takes 15d8 radiant damage, is repelled to 5 feet outside the boundary, and can't target anything inside the boundary with attacks, spells, or abilities until the spell ends. On a successful save, the creature takes half as much radiant damage and can cross the boundary. If the creature is a fiend that isn't on its home plane, it is immediately destroyed (no saving throw) instead of taking damage.

Aberrations, elementals, fey, and undead that are within 100 feet of the seal (inside the boundary) have disadvantage on ability checks, attack rolls, and saving throws, and each such creature takes 4d8 radiant damage at the start of its turn.

Creatures other than aberrations, elementals, fey, fiends, and undead can't be charmed or frightened while within 100 feet of the seal.

The seal has AC 18, 75 hit points, resistance to bludgeoning, piercing, and slashing damage, and immunity to psychic and poison damage. Ranged attacks against the seal are made with disadvantage. If it is scribed on the surface of an object that is later destroyed (such as a wooden door), the seal is not damaged and remains in place, perhaps suspended in midair. The spell ends only if the seal itself is reduced to 0 hit points.

GREEN DECAY

4th-Level Necromancy (Ritual)

Casting Time: 1 action

Range: Touch

Components: V, S

Duration: Concentration, up to 1 hour

Your touch inflicts a nauseating, alien rot. Make a melee spell attack against a creature within your reach. On a hit, you afflict the creature with the supernatural disease green decay (see below), and creatures within 15 feet of the target who can see it must make a successful Constitution saving throw or become poisoned until the end of their next turn.

You lose concentration on this spell if you can't see the target at the end of your turn.

Green Decay. The flesh of a creature that has this disease is slowly consumed by a virulent extraterrestrial fungus. While the disease persists, the creature has disadvantage on Charisma and Wisdom checks and on Wisdom saving throws, and it has vulnerability to acid, fire, and necrotic damage. An affected creature must make a Constitution saving throw at the end of each of its turns. On a failed save, the creature takes 1d6 necrotic damage, and its hit point maximum is reduced by an amount equal to the necrotic damage taken. If the creature gets three successes on these saving throws before it gets three failures, the disease ends immediately (but the damage and the hit point maximum reduction remain in effect). If the creature gets three failures on these saving throws before it gets three successes, the disease lasts for the duration of the spell, and no further saving throws are allowed.

GREEN MANTLE

1st-Level Transmutation

Casting Time: 1 action

Range: Touch

Components: V, S, M (a plant from the surrounding terrain)

Duration: 1 hour

You take on the physical characteristics of the terrain around you. In a forest, grass and tiny mushrooms sprout in your hair, moss beards your chin, and your flesh takes on the mottled hue of leaf green and bark brown. In an arctic grassland, gray lichens and the various shades of boreal grasses cloak your presence. This effect provides a +2 bonus to Stealth checks in the appropriate terrain.

At Higher Levels. When you cast this spell using a spell slot of 2nd level or higher, one additional creature is affected for each slot level above 1st.

GRUDGE MATCH

2nd-Level Evocation

Casting Time: 1 action

Range: 100 feet

Components: V, S

Duration: 1 round

This spell affects any creatures you designate within range, as long as the group contains an equal number of allies and enemies. If the number of allies and enemies targeted isn't the same, the spell fails. For the duration of the spell, each target gains a +2 bonus on saving throws, attack rolls, ability checks, skill checks, and weapon damage rolls made involving other targets of the spell. All affected creatures can identify fellow targets of the spell by sight. If an affected creature makes any of the above rolls against a non-target, it takes a –2 penalty on that roll.

At Higher Levels. When you cast this spell using a spell slot of 3rd level or higher, the duration increases by 1 round for each slot level above 2nd.

GUIDING STAR

1st-Level Divination (Ritual)

Casting Time: 10 minutes

Range: Self

Components: V, S

Duration: 8 hours

By observing the stars or the position of the sun, you are able to determine the cardinal directions, as well as the direction and distance to a stated destination. You can't become directionally disoriented or lose track of the destination. The spell doesn't, however, reveal the best route to your destination or warn you about deep gorges, flooded rivers, or other impassable or treacherous terrain.

HAMSTRING

Evocation Cantrip

Casting Time: 1 action

Range: 60 feet

Components: S

Duration: Instantaneous

You send an arrow of eldritch energy at a target you can see within range. Make a ranged spell attack against the target. On a hit, the target takes 1d4 force damage, and it can't take reactions until the end of its next turn.

The spell's damage increases by 1d4 when you reach 5th level (2d4), 11th level (3d4), and 17th level (4d4).

HARD HEART

1st-Level Enchantment

Casting Time: 1 action

Range: Touch

Components: V, S, M (an iron key)

Duration: 10 minutes

You imbue your touch with the power to make a creature aloof, hardhearted, and unfeeling. The creature you touch as part of casting this spell must make a Wisdom saving throw; a creature can choose to fail this saving throw unless it's currently charmed. On a successful save, this spell fails. On a failed save, the target becomes immune to being charmed for the duration; if it's currently charmed, that effect ends. In addition, Charisma checks against the target are made with disadvantage for the spell's duration.

At Higher Levels. When you cast this spell using a spell slot of 3rd or 4th level, the duration increases to 1 hour. If you use a spell slot of 5th level or higher, the duration is 8 hours.

HARRY

4th-Level Enchantment

Casting Time: 1 action

Range: 120 feet

Components: V, S, M (a bit of fur from a game animal)

Duration: Concentration, up to 1 hour

You instill an irresistible sense of insecurity and terror in the target. The target must make a Wisdom saving throw. On a failed save, the target has disadvantage on Dexterity (Stealth) checks to avoid your notice and is frightened of you while you are within its line of sight. While you are within 1 mile of the target, you have advantage on Wisdom (Survival) checks to track the target, and the target can't take a long rest, terrified that you are just around the corner. The target can repeat the saving throw once every 10 minutes, ending the spell on a success.

On a successful save, the target isn't affected, and you can't use this spell against it again for 24 hours.

At Higher Levels. When you cast this spell using a 6th-level spell slot, the duration is concentration, up to 8 hours, and the target can repeat the saving throw once each hour. When you use a spell slot of 8th level or higher, the duration is concentration, up to 24 hours, and the target can repeat the saving throw every 8 hours.

HARRYING HOUNDS

5th-Level Enchantment

Casting Time: 1 action
Range: 180 feet
Components: V, S, M (a tuft of fur from a hunting dog)
Duration: 8 hours

When you cast this spell, choose a direction (north, south, northeast, or the like). Each creature in a 20-foot-radius sphere centered on a point you choose within range must succeed on a Wisdom saving throw when you cast this spell or be affected by it.

When an affected creature travels, it travels at a fast pace in the opposite direction of the one you chose, as it believes a pack of dogs or wolves follows it from the chosen direction. When an affected creature isn't traveling, it is frightened of your chosen direction. The affected creature occasionally hears howls or sees glowing eyes in the darkness at the edge of its vision in that direction. An affected creature will not stop at a destination, instead pacing half-circles around the destination until the effect ends, terrified that the pack will overcome it if it stops moving. An affected creature can make a Wisdom saving throw at the end of each 4-hour period, ending the effect on itself on a success.

An affected creature moves along the safest available route unless it has nowhere to move, such as if it arrives at the edge of a cliff. When an affected creature can't safely move in the opposite direction from your chosen direction, it cowers in place, defending itself from hostile creatures, but otherwise takes no actions. In such circumstances, the affected creature can repeat the saving throw every minute, ending the effect on itself on a success. The spell's effect is suspended when an affected creature is engaged in combat, enabling it to move as necessary to face hostile creatures.

At Higher Levels. When you cast this spell using a spell slot of 6th level or higher, the duration increases by 4 hours for each slot level above 5th. If an affected creature travels for more than 8 hours, it risks exhaustion as if on a forced march.

HARSH LIGHT OF SUMMER'S GLARE

8th-Level Enchantment

Casting Time: 1 action
Range: 90 feet
Components: V, S
Duration: 1 round

You emit a burst of brilliant light, which bears down oppressively upon all creatures within range that can see you. Creatures with darkvision that fail a Constitution saving throw are blinded and stunned. Creatures without darkvision that fail a Constitution saving throw are blinded. This is not a gaze attack, and it cannot be avoided by averting one's eyes or wearing a blindfold.

HEART TO HEART

1st-Level Necromancy

Casting Time: 1 action
Range: Touch
Components: V, S, M (a drop of your blood)
Duration: 1 hour

For the duration, you and the creature you touch remain stable and unconscious if one of you is reduced to 0 hit points while the other has 1 or more hit points. If you touch a dying creature, it becomes stable but remains unconscious while it has 0 hit points. If both of you are reduced to 0 hit points, you must both make death saving throws, as normal. If you or the target regain hit points, either of you can choose to split those hit points between the two of you if both of you are within 60 feet of each other.

HEARTACHE

2nd-Level Enchantment

Casting Time: 1 action
Range: 30 feet
Components: V, S, M (a silver locket)
Duration: Instantaneous

You force an enemy to experience pangs of unrequited love and emotional distress. These feelings manifest with such intensity that the creature takes 5d6 psychic damage on a failed Charisma saving throw, or half the damage on a successful save.

At Higher Levels. When you cast this spell using a spell slot of 3rd level or higher, you can target an additional enemy for each slot level above 2nd.

HEART-SEEKING ARROW

4th-Level Transmutation

Casting Time: 1 bonus action

Range: Self

Components: V

Duration: Concentration, up to 1 minute

The next time you make a ranged weapon attack during the spell's duration, the weapon's ammunition—or the weapon itself, if it's a thrown weapon—seeks its target's vital organs. Make the attack roll as normal. On a hit, the weapon deals an extra 6d6 damage of the same type dealt by the weapon, or half as much damage on a miss, as it streaks unerringly toward its target. If this attack reduces the target to 0 hit points, the target has disadvantage on its next death saving throw, and, if it dies, it can be restored to life only by means of a *true resurrection* or a *wish* spell. This spell has no effect on undead or constructs.

At Higher Levels. When you cast this spell using a spell slot of 5th level or higher, the extra damage on a hit increases by 1d6 for each slot level above 4th.

HEARTSTOP

2nd-Level Necromancy

Casting Time: 1 action

Range: Touch

Components: V, S

Duration: Concentration, up to 10 minutes

You slow the beating of a willing target's heart to the rate of one beat per minute. The creature's breathing almost stops. To a casual or brief observer, the subject appears dead. At the end of the spell, the creature returns to normal with no ill effects.

HEARTSTRIKE

2nd-Level Divination

Casting Time: 1 bonus action

Range: Self

Components: V, S, M (an arrow, bolt, or other missile)

Duration: Instantaneous

The spirits of ancient archers carry your missiles straight to their targets. You have advantage on ranged weapon attacks until the start of your next turn, and you can ignore penalties for your enemies having half cover or three-quarters cover, and for an area being lightly obscured, when making those attacks.

HEAVENLY CROWN

6th-Level Enchantment

Casting Time: 1 action

Range: Self (30-foot radius)

Components: V, S, M (a small golden crown worth 50 gp)

Duration: Concentration, up to 1 minute

A glowing, golden crown appears on your head and sheds dim light in a 30-foot radius. When you cast the spell (and as a bonus action on subsequent turns, until the spell ends), you can target one willing creature within 30 feet of you that you can see. If the target can hear you, it can use its reaction to make one melee weapon attack and then move up to half its speed, or vice versa.

HEDREN'S BIRDS OF CLAY

3rd-Level Conjuration

Casting Time: 1 action

Range: Self

Components: V, M (a clay figurine shaped like a bird)

Duration: Concentration, up to 5 minutes

You create a number of clay pigeons equal to 1d4 + your spellcasting modifier (minimum of one) that swirl around you. When you are the target of a ranged weapon attack or a ranged spell attack and before the attack roll is made, you can use your reaction to shout "Pull!" When you do, one clay pigeon maneuvers to block the incoming attack. If the attack roll is less than 10 + your proficiency bonus, the attack misses. Otherwise, make a check with your spellcasting ability modifier and compare it to the attack roll. If your roll is higher, the attack is intercepted and has no effect. Regardless of whether the attack is intercepted, one clay pigeon is expended. The spell ends when the last clay pigeon is used.

At Higher Levels. When you cast this spell using a spell slot of 4th level or higher, add 1 to your roll for each slot level above 3rd when determining if an attack misses or when making a check to intercept the attack.

HEMATOMANCY

3rd-Level Divination

Casting Time: 1 minute

Range: Touch

Components: V, S, M (a drop of a creature's blood)

Duration: Instantaneous

You can learn information about a creature whose blood you possess. The target must make a Wisdom saving throw. If the target knows you're casting the spell, it can fail the saving throw voluntarily if it wants you to learn the information. On a successful save, the target isn't affected, and you can't use this spell against it again for 24 hours.

On a failed save, or if the blood belongs to a dead creature, you learn the following information:

- The target's most common name (if any).
- The target's creature type (and subtype, if any), gender, and which of its ability scores is highest (though not the exact numerical score).
- The target's current status (alive, dead, sick, wounded, healthy, etc.).
- The circumstances of the target shedding the blood you're holding (bleeding wound, splatter from an attack, how long ago it was shed, etc.).

Alternatively, you can forgo all of the above information and instead use the blood as a beacon to track the target. For 1 hour, as long as you are on the same plane of existence as the creature, you know the direction and distance to the target's location at the time you cast this spell. While moving toward the location, if you are presented with a choice of paths, the spell automatically indicates which path provides the shortest and most direct route to the location.

HERO'S STEEL

3rd-Level Transmutation

Casting Time: 1 action
Range: Touch
Components: V, S, M (a warrior's amulet worth 5 gp)
Duration: 1 minute

You infuse the metal of a melee weapon you touch with the fearsome aura of a mighty hero. The weapon's wielder has advantage on Charisma (Intimidation) checks made while aggressively brandishing the weapon. In addition, an opponent that currently has 30 or fewer hit points and is struck by the weapon must make a successful Charisma saving throw or be stunned for 1 round. If the creature has more than 30 hit points but fewer than the weapon's wielder currently has, it becomes frightened instead; a frightened creature repeats the saving throw at the end of each of its turns, ending the effect on itself on a successful save. A creature that succeeds on the saving throw is immune to castings of this spell on the same weapon for 24 hours.

HOARFROST

Evocation Cantrip

Casting Time: 1 bonus action
Range: Touch
Components: V, S, M (a melee weapon)
Duration: 1 minute

A melee weapon you are holding is imbued with cold. For the duration, a rime of frost covers the weapon and light vapor rises from it if the temperature is above freezing. The weapon becomes magical and deals an extra 1d4 cold damage on a successful hit. The spell ends after 1 minute, or earlier if you make a successful attack with the weapon or let go of it.

The spell's damage increases by 1d4 when you reach 5th level (2d4), 11th level (3d4), and 17th level (4d4).

HOBBLE

Evocation Cantrip

Casting Time: 1 bonus action
Range: 30 feet
Components: V, S, M (a broken rabbit's foot)
Duration: Instantaneous

You create an ethereal trap in the space of a creature you can see within range. The target must succeed on a Dexterity saving throw or its speed is halved until the end of its next turn.

HOBBLE MOUNT

1st-Level Necromancy

Casting Time: 1 action
Range: Touch
Components: V, S
Duration: Concentration, up to 1 hour

When you cast *hobble mount* as a successful melee spell attack against a horse, wolf, or other four-legged or two-legged beast being ridden as a mount, that beast is disabled so that it can't move at its normal speed without incurring injury. An affected creature that moves more than half its base speed in a turn takes 2d6 bludgeoning damage.

HOLY GROUND

5th-Level Evocation

Casting Time: 1 action
Range: Self
Components: V, S, M (a vial of holy water that is consumed in the casting)
Duration: Concentration, up to 10 minutes

You invoke divine powers to bless the ground within 60 feet of you. Creatures slain in the affected area cannot be raised as undead by magic or by the abilities of monsters, even if the corpse is later removed from the area. Any spell of 4th level or lower that would summon or animate undead within the area fails automatically. Such spells cast with spell slots of 5th level or higher function normally.

At Higher Levels. When you cast this spell using a spell slot of 6th level or higher, the level of spells that are prevented from functioning increases by 1 for each slot level above 5th.

HOLY VOW

3rd-Level Abjuration (Ritual)

Casting Time: 1 action
Range: Self
Components: V, S, M (a vial of holy water)
Duration: 24 hours

You willingly take a vow to complete a task or carry out a service. This task or service cannot conflict with your alignment or your sacred oath. While you serve under the vow, for as long as the spell lasts, your hit point maximum and current hit points increase by 10. Whenever you make an attack roll or a saving throw, roll a d4 and add the result to the attack roll or saving throw. These benefits apply only when you are involved in activities that directly relate to your avowed task, or to situations you encounter that interfere with your ability to carry out that task (such as random encounters while traveling).

If you willingly forsake your vow, the spell ends, and you take 4d10 psychic damage. At the GM's discretion, you might suffer other penalties and need to atone for your decision. See the "Breaking Your Oath" sidebar in the paladin class description for more details. Failing to complete the task does not incur any penalties as long as you remain true to your vow, nor are you penalized if some form of outside coercion, magical or otherwise, leads you to forsake your vow (being charmed, for instance, or if a villain threatens the lives of innocents if you do not break the vow).

HOLY WARDING

2nd-Level Abjuration

Casting Time: 1 action
Range: 30 feet
Components: V, S
Duration: 1 round

You make a protective gesture toward your allies. Choose three creatures that you can see within range. Until the end of your next turn, the allies you have chosen have resistance to normal weapon attacks, including bludgeoning, piercing, and slashing damage. If a target moves farther than 30 feet from you, the effect ends for that creature.

HONE BLADE

1st-Level Transmutation

Casting Time: 1 action
Range: Touch
Components: V, S, M (a chip of whetstone or lodestone)
Duration: Instantaneous

You magically sharpen the edge of any bladed weapon or object you are touching. The target weapon gets a +1 bonus to damage on its next successful hit.

HUNGER OF LENG

4th-Level Enchantment

Casting Time: 1 action
Range: 90 feet
Components: V, S, M (a pinch of salt and a drop of the caster's blood)
Duration: 1 minute

You curse a creature that you can see in range with an insatiable, ghoulish appetite. If it has a digestive system, the creature must make a successful Wisdom saving throw or be compelled to consume the flesh of living creatures for the duration.

The target gains a bite attack and moves to and attacks the closest creature that isn't an undead or a construct. The target is proficient with the bite, and it adds its Strength modifier to the attack and damage rolls. The damage is piercing and the damage die is a d4. If the target is larger than Medium, its damage die increases by 1d4 for each size category it is above Medium. In addition, the target has advantage on melee attack rolls against any creature that doesn't have all of its hit points.

If there isn't a viable creature within range for the target to attack, it deals piercing damage to itself equal to 2d4 + its Strength modifier. The target can repeat the saving throw at the end of each of its turns, ending the effect on a success. If the target has two consecutive failures, *hunger of Leng* lasts its full duration with no further saving throws allowed.

HUNTER'S CUNNING

2nd-Level Divination

Casting Time: 1 action
Range: Touch
Components: V, S
Duration: 1 hour

You grant a creature you touch preternatural senses and insight into its immediate environment. Until the spell ends, the target gains advantage on Wisdom (Perception) and Wisdom (Survival) checks and ignores the effect of natural (nonmagical) difficult terrain.

HUNTER'S ENDURANCE

1st-Level Enchantment

Casting Time: 1 minute
Range: Self
Components: V, S, M (a fingernail, lock of hair, bit of fur, or drop of blood from the target, if unfamiliar)
Duration: 24 hours

You call on the land to sustain you as you hunt your quarry. Describe or name a creature that is familiar to you. If you aren't familiar with the target creature, you must use a fingernail, lock of hair, bit of fur, or drop of blood from it as a material component to target that creature with this spell.

Until the spell ends, you have advantage on all Wisdom (Perception) and Wisdom (Survival) checks to find and track the target, and you must actively pursue the target as if under a *geas*. In addition, you don't suffer from exhaustion levels you gain from pursuing your quarry, such as from lack of rest or environmental hazards between you and the target, while the spell is active. When the spell ends, you suffer from all levels of exhaustion that were suspended by the spell. The spell ends only after 24 hours, when the target is dead, when the target is on a different plane, or when the target is restrained in your line of sight.

HUNTING STAND

4th-Level Conjuration

Casting Time: 1 minute

Range: 120 feet

Components: V, S, M (a crude model of the stand)

Duration: 8 hours

You make a camouflaged shelter nestled in the branches of a tree or among a collection of stones. The shelter is a 10-foot cube centered on a point within range. It can hold as many as nine Medium or smaller creatures. The atmosphere inside the shelter is comfortable and dry, regardless of the weather outside. The shelter's camouflage provides a modicum of concealment to its inhabitants; a creature outside the shelter has disadvantage on Wisdom (Perception) and Intelligence (Investigation) checks to detect or locate a creature within the shelter.

HYPNOTIC MISSIVE

2nd-Level Enchantment (Ritual)

Casting Time: 1 minute

Range: Touch

Components: V, S, M (ink made with powdered amber, worth at least 50 gp)

Duration: 14 days

You write on parchment, paper, or some other suitable writing material and imbue it with a powerful enchantment that lasts for the duration. What is actually written is unimportant; the enchantment laid upon the words works on the mind of a creature that reads it, convincing the creature that there is some importance to the message that must be discovered. A creature that reads the message must succeed on a Wisdom saving throw or be compelled to continue reading and rereading the writing, attempting to glean its meaning and importance. During combat, a creature so enthralled can take no actions or reactions on its turn, but can move if it chooses or needs to do so (to remove itself from danger, for example). A creature under the influence of the hypnotic missive can make a new saving throw against the effects at the beginning of its turn if in a combat situation. In nonthreatening conditions, the creature can make a new saving throw against the effects every hour.

Once a creature has made a successful save, it recognizes the magical compulsion that has affected it. This does not provide immunity from the spell, however, and if the creature reads the words again, it must make another save or fall under the spell's effects once more.

ICE BURN

3rd-Level Conjuration

Casting Time: 1 action

Range: 60 feet

Components: V, S

Duration: Instantaneous

You instill deep cold into the body of a creature within range, damaging it and impairing joints and muscles. Make a ranged spell attack. On a hit, the target takes 3d10 cold damage and has disadvantage on all Dexterity checks and Dexterity saving throws until this damage is healed.

At Higher Levels. When you cast this spell using a spell slot of 4th level or higher, you can target one additional creature within range for each slot level above 3rd. Each additional target must be within 30 feet of at least one other target.

ICE FORTRESS

5th-Level Conjuration

Casting Time: 1 minute

Range: 60 feet

Components: V, S, M (a miniature keep carved from ice or glass that is consumed in the casting)

Duration: Until dispelled or destroyed

A gleaming fortress of ice springs from a square area of ground that you can see within range. It is a 10-foot cube (including floor and roof). The fortress can't overlap any other structures, but any creatures in its space are harmlessly lifted up as the ice rises into position. The walls are made of ice (AC 13), have 120 hit points each, and are immune to cold, necrotic, poison, and psychic damage. Reducing a wall to 0 hit points destroys it and has a 50 percent chance to cause the roof to collapse. A damaged wall can be repaired by casting a spell that deals cold damage on it, on a point-for-point basis.

Each wall has two arrow slits. One wall also includes an ice door with an *arcane lock*. You designate at the time of the fort's creation which creatures can enter the fortification. The door has AC 18 and 60 hit points, or it can be broken open with a successful DC 25 Strength (Athletics) check (DC 15 if the *arcane lock* is dispelled).

The fortress catches and reflects light, so that creatures outside the fortress who rely on sight have disadvantage on Perception checks and attack rolls made against those within the fortress if it's in an area of bright sunlight.

At Higher Levels. When you cast this spell using a spell slot of 6th level or higher, you can increase the length or width of the fortification by 5 feet for every slot level above 5th. You can make a different choice (width or length) for each slot level above 5th.

ICE HAMMER

2nd-Level Conjuration

Casting Time: 1 action
Range: Self
Components: V, S, M (a miniature hammer carved from ice or glass)
Duration: Concentration, up to 1 hour

When you cast *ice hammer*, a warhammer fashioned from ice appears in your hands. This weapon functions as a standard warhammer in all ways, and it deals an extra 1d10 cold damage on a hit. You can drop the warhammer or give it to another creature.

The warhammer melts and is destroyed when it or its user accumulates 20 or more fire damage, or when the spell ends.

At Higher Levels. When you cast this spell using a spell slot of 3rd level or higher, you can create one additional hammer for each slot level above 2nd. Alternatively, you can create half as many hammers (round down), but each is oversized (1d10 bludgeoning damage, or 1d12 if wielded with two hands, plus 2d8 cold damage). Medium or smaller creatures have disadvantage when using oversized weapons, even if they are proficient with them.

ICE SOLDIERS

7th-Level Conjuration

Casting Time: 1 action
Range: 30 feet
Components: V, M (vial of water)
Duration: 1 minute

You pour water from the vial and cause two ice soldiers to appear within range. The ice soldiers cannot form if there is no space available for them. The soldiers act immediately on your turn. You can mentally command them (no action required by you) to move and act where and how you wish. If you command an ice soldier to attack, it attacks that creature exclusively until the target is dead, at which time

the soldier melts into a puddle of water. If an ice soldier moves farther than 30 feet from you, it immediately melts. Ice soldiers have the statistics shown below.

At Higher Levels. When you cast this spell using a spell slot of 8th level or higher, you create one additional ice soldier.

Ice Soldier
Medium Construct, Unaligned

ARMOR CLASS 13
HIT POINTS 72 (16d8)
SPEED 30 ft.

STR	DEX	CON	INT	WIS	CHA
21 (+5)	9 (-1)	10 (+0)	7 (-2)	12 (+1)	7 (-2)

DAMAGE VULNERABILITIES fire
DAMAGE RESISTANCES bludgeoning, piercing, and slashing damage from nonmagical attacks
DAMAGE IMMUNITIES cold
CONDITION IMMUNITIES charmed, exhaustion, frightened
SENSES passive Perception 13
LANGUAGES None
CHALLENGE 2 (450 XP)   **PROFICIENCY BONUS** +2

Heavy Blows. Creatures struck by two slam attacks from an ice soldier in the same round must make a DC 13 Strength save or be knocked prone.

ACTIONS

Multiattack. The ice soldier makes two slam attacks.

Slam. *Melee Weapon Attack:* +7 to hit, reach 5ft., one target, *Hit:* 10 (2d6+5) cold damage.

ICICLE DAGGERS

1st-Level Conjuration

Casting Time: 1 action
Range: Self
Components: V, S, M (a miniature dagger shaped like an icicle)
Duration: Instantaneous or special

When you cast this spell, three icicles appear in your hand. Each icicle has the same properties as a dagger but deals an extra 1d4 cold damage on a hit.

The icicle daggers melt a few seconds after leaving your hand, making it impossible for other creatures to wield them. If the surrounding temperature is at or below freezing, the daggers last for 1 hour. They melt instantly if you take 10 or more fire damage.

At Higher Levels. If you cast this spell using a spell slot of 2nd level or higher, you can create two additional daggers for each slot level above 1st. If you cast this spell using a spell slot of 4th level or higher, daggers that leave your hand don't melt until the start of your next turn.

ICY MANIPULATION

6th-Level Transmutation

Casting Time: 1 action
Range: 60 feet
Components: V, S, M (a piece of ice preserved from the plane of elemental ice)
Duration: Concentration, up to 1 minute

One creature you can see within range must make a Constitution saving throw. On a failed save, the creature is petrified (frozen solid). A petrified creature can repeat the saving throw at the end of each of its turns, ending the effect on itself if it makes two successful saves. If a petrified creature gets two failures on the saving throw (not counting the original failure that caused the petrification), the petrification becomes permanent.

The petrification also becomes permanent if you maintain concentration on this spell for a full minute. A permanently petrified/frozen creature can be restored to normal with *greater restoration* or comparable magic, or by casting this spell on the creature again and maintaining concentration for a full minute.

If the frozen creature is damaged or broken before it recovers from being petrified, the injury carries over to its normal state.

ILL-FATED WORD

1st-Level Divination

Casting Time: 1 reaction, which you take when an enemy makes an attack roll, ability check, or saving throw
Range: 30 feet
Components: V
Duration: Instantaneous

You call out a distracting epithet to a creature, worsening its chance to succeed at whatever it's doing. Roll a d4 and subtract the number rolled from an attack roll, ability check, or saving throw that the target has just made; the target uses the lowered result to determine the outcome of its roll.

ILLUMINATE SPOOR

1st-Level Divination

Casting Time: 1 action
Range: Touch
Components: V, S, M (a firefly)
Duration: Concentration, up to 1 hour

You touch a set of tracks created by a single creature. That set of tracks and all other tracks made by the same creature give off a faint glow. You and up to three creatures you designate when you cast this spell can see the glow. A creature that can see the glow automatically succeeds on Wisdom (Survival) checks to track that creature. If the tracks are covered by obscuring objects such as leaves or mud, you and the creatures you designate have advantage on Wisdom (Survival) checks to follow the tracks.

If the creature leaving the tracks changes its tracks, such as by adding or removing footwear, the glow stops where the tracks change. Until the spell ends, you can use an action to touch and illuminate a new set of tracks.

At Higher Levels. When you cast this spell using a spell slot of 3rd level or higher, the duration is concentration, up to 8 hours. When you use a spell slot of 5th level or higher, the duration is concentration, up to 24 hours.

ILLUSORY TRAP

3rd-Level Illusion

Casting Time: 1 action
Range: Touch
Components: V, S, M (a needle and a mirror)
Duration: 24 hours

You create the illusion of a trap upon an object you touch, such as a door, a chest, or a 5-foot-square area of floor. A creature specifically looking for traps that examines the object must make a Wisdom saving throw. On a successful save, the creature takes 1d10 psychic damage, the spell ends, and the creature realizes that the trap was not real.

On a failed save, the creature believes the object contains a trap. If the creature then tries to disarm or otherwise interact with the trap in order to set it off, it must make a Dexterity check against your spell save DC. On a successful check, the creature takes 1d10 psychic damage and realizes the trap is not real. On a failed check, the creature takes 5d10 psychic damage and is stunned for 1 round, believing that it accidentally set off the trap and was injured by it.

IMPENDING ALLY

3rd-Level Conjuration

Casting Time: 1 action
Range: 40 feet
Components: V, S, M (a broken chain link)
Duration: Concentration, up to 2 rounds

You summon a duplicate of yourself as an ally who appears in an unoccupied space you can see within range. You control this ally, whose turn comes immediately after yours. When you or the ally uses a class feature, spell slot, or other expendable resource, it's considered expended for both of you. When the spell ends, or if you are killed, the ally disappears immediately.

At Higher Levels. When you cast this spell using a spell slot of 5th level or higher, the duration is extended by 1 round for every two slot levels above 3rd.

IMPOTENCE

Necromancy Cantrip

Casting Time: 1 action
Range: 30 feet
Components: V, S
Duration: 1 minute

You temporarily weaken a creature within range. If the target makes a successful Constitution saving throw, the spell is ineffective. On a failed save, the next time the target makes a Strength check before the spell ends, roll a d6 and subtract the result from the roll. The spell then ends.

INDECISION

2nd-Level Enchantment

Casting Time: 1 action
Range: 30 feet
Components: V, S
Duration: Concentration, up to 1 minute

Choose a creature you can see within range. The target must succeed on a Charisma saving throw or be overcome with indecision. On a failed save, the target takes its entire turn to perform its next action due to the creature's hesitation. If the creature fails the saving throw by 5 or more, it takes no action that round. If the creature has moved before taking an action, its action does not occur until the start of its next turn. Each round, the creature can attempt another saving throw at the start of its turn. On a successful save, the spell ends.

This spell has no effect on a creature with an Intelligence score of 5 or lower.

At Higher Levels. When you cast this spell using a spell slot of 3rd level or higher, you can target one additional creature for each slot level above 2nd. The creatures must be within 30 feet of each other when you target them.

INNOCUOUS ASPECT

3rd-Level Illusion

Casting Time: 1 action
Range: Self (20-foot radius)
Components: V, S, M (a paper ring)
Duration: Concentration, up to 10 minutes

An area of false vision encompasses all creatures within 20 feet of you. You and each creature in the area that you choose to affect take on the appearance of a harmless creature or object, chosen by you. Each image is identical, and only appearance is affected. Sound, movement, or physical inspection can reveal the ruse.

A creature that uses its action to study the image visually can determine that it is an illusion with a successful Intelligence (Investigation) check against your spell save DC. If a creature discerns the illusion for what it is, that creature sees through the image.

INSIGHTFUL MANEUVER

1st-Level Divination

Casting Time: 1 bonus action

Range: Touch

Components: V, S

Duration: Instantaneous

With a flash of insight, you know how to take advantage of your foe's vulnerabilities. Until the end of your turn, the target has vulnerability to one type of damage (your choice). Additionally, if the target has any other vulnerabilities, you learn them.

INSPIRING SPEECH

4th-Level Enchantment

Casting Time: 10 minutes

Range: 60 feet

Components: V

Duration: 1 hour

The verbal component of this spell is a 10-minute-long, rousing speech. At the end of the speech, all your allies within the affected area who heard the speech gain a +1 bonus on attack rolls and advantage on saving throws for 1 hour against effects that cause the charmed or frightened condition. Additionally, each recipient gains temporary hit points equal to your spellcasting ability modifier. If you move farther than 1 mile from your allies or you die, this spell ends. A character can be affected by only one casting of this spell at a time; subsequent, overlapping castings have no additional effect and don't extend the spell's duration.

INSTANT FORTIFICATION

5th-Level Transmutation (Ritual)

Casting Time: 1 action

Range: 60 feet

Components: V, S, M (a statuette of a keep worth 250 gp, which is consumed in the casting)

Duration: Permanent

Through this spell, you transform a miniature statuette of a keep into an actual fort. The fortification springs from the ground in an unoccupied space within range. It is a 10-foot cube (including floor and roof).

Each wall has two arrow slits. One wall also includes a metal door with an *arcane lock* effect on it. You designate at the time of the fort's creation which creatures can ignore the lock and enter the fortification. The door has AC 20 and 60 hit points, and it can be broken open with a successful DC 25 Strength (Athletics) check. The walls are made of stone (AC 15) and are immune to necrotic, poison, and psychic damage. Each 5-foot-square section of wall has 90 hit points. Reducing a section of wall to 0 hit points destroys it, allowing access to the inside of the fortification.

At Higher Levels. When you cast this spell using a spell slot of 6th level or higher, you can increase the length or width of the fortification by 5 feet for each slot level above 5th. You can make a different choice (width or length) for each slot level above 5th.

INSTANT SIEGE WEAPON

4th-Level Transmutation (Ritual)

Casting Time: 1 action

Range: 60 feet

Components: V, S, M (raw materials with a value in gp equal to the hit points of the siege weapon to be created)

Duration: Permanent

With this spell, you instantly transform raw materials into a siege engine of Large size or smaller (the GM has information on this topic). The raw materials for the spell don't need to be the actual components a siege weapon is normally built from; they just need to be manufactured goods made of the appropriate substances (typically including some form of finished wood and a few bits of worked metal) and have a gold piece value of no less than the weapon's hit points.

For example, a mangonel has 100 hit points. *Instant siege weapon* will fashion any collection of raw materials worth at least 100 gp into a mangonel. Those materials might be lumber and fittings salvaged from a small house, or 100 gp worth of finished goods such as three wagons or two heavy crossbows. The spell also creates enough ammunition for ten shots, if the siege engine uses ammunition.

At Higher Levels. When you cast this spell using a spell slot of 6th level, a Huge siege engine can be made; at 8th level, a Gargantuan siege engine can be made. In addition, for each slot level above 4th, the spell creates another ten shots' worth of ammunition.

INSTANT SNARE

2nd-Level Abjuration

Casting Time: 1 action
Range: 120 feet
Components: V, S, M (a loop of twine)
Duration: 24 hours

You create a snare on a point you can see within range. You can leave the snare as a magical trap, or you can use your reaction to trigger the trap when a Large or smaller creature you can see moves within 10 feet of the snare. If you leave the snare as a trap, a creature must succeed on an Intelligence (Investigation) or Wisdom (Perception) check against your spell save DC to find the trap.

When a Large or smaller creature moves within 5 feet of the snare, the trap triggers. The creature must succeed on a Dexterity saving throw or be magically pulled into the air. The creature is restrained and hangs upside down 5 feet above the snare's location for 1 minute. A restrained creature can repeat the saving throw at the end of each of its turns, escaping the snare on a success. Alternatively, a creature, including the restrained target, can use its action to make an Intelligence (Arcana) check against your spell save DC. On a success, the restrained creature is freed, and the snare resets itself 1 minute later. If the creature succeeds on the check by 5 or more, the snare is destroyed instead.

This spell alerts you with a ping in your mind when the trap is triggered if you are within 1 mile of the snare. This ping awakens you if you are sleeping.

At Higher Levels. When you cast this spell using a spell slot of 3rd level or higher, you can create one additional snare for each slot level above 2nd. When you receive the mental ping that a trap was triggered, you know which snare was triggered if you have more than one.

INTENSIFY LIGHT

2nd-Level Transmutation

Casting Time: 1 action
Range: Self (15-foot radius)
Components V, S, M (scale from a light drake)
Duration: Concentration, up to 1 minute

When you are within range of a light source, that source of light sheds bright light and dim light for an additional 10 feet. If the object sheds light from the *daylight* spell, the light within 10 feet of the object is considered sunlight. If you move out of range of the light source, it immediately reverts to its normal illumination.

INVESTED CHAMPION

3rd-Level Evocation (Ritual)

Casting Time: 1 action
Range: Touch
Components: V, S, M (a vial of holy water)
Duration: Concentration, up to 1 hour

You touch one creature and choose either to become its champion, or for it to become yours. If you choose a creature to become your champion, it fights on your behalf. While this spell is in effect, you can cast any spell with a range of touch on your champion as if the spell had a range of 60 feet. Your champion's attacks are considered magical, and you can use a bonus action on your turn to encourage your champion, granting it advantage on its next attack roll.

If you become the champion of another creature, you gain advantage on all attack rolls against creatures that have attacked your charge within the last round. If you are wielding a shield, and a creature within 5 feet of you attacks your charge, you can use your reaction to impose disadvantage on the attack roll, as if you had the Protection fighting style. If you already have the Protection fighting style, then in addition to imposing disadvantage, you can also push an enemy 5 feet in any direction away from your charge when you take your reaction. You can use a bonus action on your turn to reroll the damage for any successful attack against a creature that is threatening your charge.

Whichever version of the spell is cast, if the distance between the champion and its designated ally increases to more than 60 feet, the spell ends.

IRE OF THE MOUNTAIN

3rd-Level Transmutation

Casting Time: 1 action
Range: 30 feet
Components: V, S, M (a piece of coal)
Duration: Instantaneous

An *ire of the mountain* spell melts nonmagical objects that are made primarily of metal. Choose one metal object weighing 10 pounds or less that you can see within range. Tendrils of blistering air writhe toward the target. A creature holding or wearing the item must make a Dexterity saving throw. On a successful save, the creature takes 1d8 fire damage and the spell has no further effect. On a failed save, the targeted object melts and is destroyed, and the creature takes 4d8 fire damage if it is wearing the object, or 2d8 fire damage if it is holding the object. If the object is not being held or worn by a creature, it is automatically melted and rendered useless. This spell cannot affect magic items.

At Higher Levels. When you cast this spell using a spell slot of 4th level or higher, you can target one additional object for each slot level above 3rd.

IRON HAND

Abjuration Cantrip

Casting Time: 1 bonus action
Range: Self
Components: V, S
Duration: Concentration, up to 1 hour

Iron hand is a common spell among metalsmiths and other crafters who work with heat. When you use this spell, one of your arms becomes immune to fire damage, allowing you to grasp red-hot metal, scoop up molten glass with your fingers, or reach deep into a roaring fire to pick up an object. In addition, if you take the Dodge action while you're protected by *iron hand*, you have resistance to fire damage until the start of your next turn.

IRON MIND

3rd-Level Abjuration

Casting Time: 1 action
Range: Touch
Components: V, S
Duration: Concentration, up to 1 hour

One willing creature you touch becomes immune to psychic damage and mind-altering effects for the spell's duration.

IRON STOMACH

2nd-Level Transmutation

Casting Time: 1 action
Range: Touch
Components: V, S
Duration: 24 hours

You subtly alter the digestive system of the creature you touch, allowing it to safely eat and extract nutrition from any organic matter it eats. As long as the creature eats at least 1 pound of organic matter per day, it does not suffer from hunger. If it eats organic matter that is poisonous, or that has been poisoned with an organic substance (serpent venom, for example), it has advantage on the saving throw.

At Higher Levels. When you cast this spell using a spell slot of 3rd level or higher, you can affect one additional creature for each slot level above 2nd.

JEWELED FISSURE

3rd-Level Conjuration

Casting Time: 1 action
Range: 100 feet
Components: V, S, M (a shard of jasper)
Duration: Instantaneous

With a sweeping gesture, you cause jagged crystals to burst from the ground and hurtle directly upward. Choose an origin point within the spell's range that you can see. Starting from that point, the crystals burst out of the ground along a 30-foot line that is 5 feet wide. Each creature in that line and up to 100 feet above it takes 2d8 thunder damage plus 2d8 piercing damage; a successful Dexterity saving throw negates the piercing damage.

On a failed save, a creature is impaled by a chunk of crystal that halves the creature's speed, prevents it from flying, and causes it to fall to the ground if it was flying. To remove a crystal, the creature or an ally within 5 feet of it must use an action and make a DC 13 Strength check. On a successful check, the impaled creature takes 1d8 piercing damage and its speed and flying ability are restored to normal.

KAREEF'S ENTREATY

1st-Level Abjuration

Casting Time: 1 reaction, which you take just before a creature makes a death saving throw
Range: 60 feet
Components: V
Duration: Instantaneous

Your kind words offer hope and support to a fallen comrade. Choose a willing creature you can see within range that is about to make a death saving throw. The creature gains advantage on the saving throw, and if the result of the saving throw is 18 or higher, the creature regains 3d4 hit points immediately.

At Higher Levels. When you cast this spell using a spell slot of 2nd level or higher, the creature adds 1 to its death saving throw for every two slot levels above 1st and regains an additional 1d4 hit points for each slot level above 1st if its saving throw result is 18 or higher.

KAVELIN'S INSTANT AEROSOL

2nd-Level Transmutation

Casting Time: 1 action
Range: 5 feet
Components: V, S, M (powdered gemstones worth 50 gp)
Duration: Instantaneous

You light a candle and place it beneath an open potion as you cast this spell. The potion is vaporized into a cloud that extends five feet from you in all directions. All creatures in range, including yourself, that breathe the magical vapors can benefit from the effects of the potion. The duration is divided equally among those partaking, rounding down any fractions. If the spell is used with a *potion of healing*, all creatures in the area receive the average number of hit points that would be healed by a potion of that type.

KEENING WAIL

4th-Level Necromancy

Casting Time: 1 action
Range: Self (15-foot cone)
Components: V, S, M (a ringed lock of hair from an undead creature)
Duration: Instantaneous

You emit an unholy shriek from beyond the grave. Each creature in a 15-foot cone must make a Constitution saving throw. A creature takes 6d6 necrotic damage on a failed save, or half as much damage on a successful one. If a creature with 50 hit points or fewer fails the saving throw by 5 or more, it is instead reduced to 0 hit points. This wail has no effect on constructs and undead.

At Higher Levels. When you cast this spell using a spell slot of 5th level or higher, the damage increases by 1d6 for each slot level above 4th.

KILLING FIELDS

5th-Level Transmutation

Casting Time: 10 minutes
Range: 300 feet
Components: V, S, M (a game animal, which must be sacrificed as part of casting the spell)
Duration: 24 hours

You invoke primal spirits of nature to transform natural terrain in a 100-foot cube in range into a private hunting preserve. The area can't include manufactured structures and if such a structure exists in the area, the spell ends.

While you are conscious and within the area, you are aware of the presence and direction, though not exact location, of each beast and monstrosity with an Intelligence of 3 or lower in the area. When a beast or monstrosity with an Intelligence of 3 or lower tries to leave the area, it must make a Wisdom saving throw. On a failure, it is disoriented, uncertain of its surroundings or direction, and remains within the area for 1 hour. On a success, it leaves the area.

When you cast this spell, you can specify individuals that are helped by the area's effects. All other creatures in the area are hindered by the area's effects. You can also specify a password that, when spoken aloud, gives the speaker the benefits of being helped by the area's effects.

Killing fields creates the following effects within the area.

Pack Hunters. A helped creature has advantage on attack rolls against a hindered creature if at least one helped ally is within 5 feet of the hindered creature and the helped ally isn't incapacitated.

Slaying. Once per turn, when a helped creature hits with any weapon, the weapon deals an extra 1d6 damage of the same type dealt by its weapon to a hindered creature.

Tracking. A helped creature has advantage on Wisdom (Survival) and Dexterity (Stealth) checks against a hindered creature.

You can create a permanent killing field by casting this spell in the same location every day for one year. Structures built in the area after the killing field is permanent don't end the spell.

KISS OF THE SUCCUBUS

5th-Level Necromancy

Casting Time: 1 action
Range: Touch
Components: S
Duration: Instantaneous

You kiss a willing creature or one you have charmed or held spellbound through spells or abilities such as *dominate person*. The target must make a Constitution saving throw. A creature takes 5d10 psychic damage on a failed save, or half as much damage on a successful one. The target's hit point maximum is reduced by an amount equal to the damage taken; this reduction lasts until the target finishes a long rest. The target dies if this effect reduces its hit point maximum to 0.

At Higher Levels. When you cast this spell using a spell slot of 6th level or higher, the damage increases by 1d10 for each slot level above 5th.

KOBOLD'S FURY

1st-Level Transmutation

Casting Time: 1 action
Range: Touch
Components: V, S, M (a kobold scale)
Duration: 1 round

Your touch infuses the rage of a threatened kobold into the target. The target has advantage on melee weapon attacks until the end of its next turn. In addition, its next successful melee weapon attack against a creature larger than itself does an additional 2d8 damage.

L

LABYRINTHINE HOWL

5th-Level Illusion

Casting Time: 1 action

Range: 60 feet

Components: V, S, M (a dead mouse)

Duration: 1 round

You let loose the howl of a ravenous beast, causing each enemy within range that can hear you to make a Wisdom saving throw. On a failed save, a creature believes it has been transported into a labyrinth and is under attack by savage beasts. An affected creature must choose either to face the beasts or to curl into a ball for protection. A creature that faces the beasts takes 7d8 psychic damage, and then the spell ends on it. A creature that curls into a ball falls prone and is stunned until the end of your next turn.

At Higher Levels. When you cast this spell using a spell slot of 6th level or higher, the damage increases by 2d8 for each slot level above 5th.

LACERATE

2nd-Level Evocation

Casting Time: 1 action

Range: 60 feet

Components: V, S, M (a shard of bone or crystal)

Duration: Instantaneous

You make a swift cutting motion through the air to lacerate a creature you can see within range. The target must make a Constitution saving throw. It takes 4d8 slashing damage on a failed save, or half as much damage on a successful one. If the saving throw fails by 5 or more, the wound erupts with a violent spray of blood, and the target gains one level of exhaustion.

At Higher Levels. When you cast this spell using a spell slot of 3rd level or higher, the damage increases by 1d8 for each slot level above 2nd.

LAIR SENSE

2nd-Level Divination (Ritual)

Casting Time: 1 minute

Range: 120 feet

Components: V, S, M (treasure worth at least 500 gp, which is not consumed in casting)

Duration: 24 hours

You set up a magical boundary around your lair. The boundary can't exceed the dimensions of a 100-foot cube, but within that maximum, you can shape it as you like—to follow the walls of a building or cave, for example. While the spell lasts, you instantly become aware of any Tiny or larger creature that enters the enclosed area. You know the creature's type but nothing else about it. You are also aware when creatures leave the area.

This awareness is enough to wake you from sleep, and you receive the knowledge as long as you're on the same plane of existence as your lair.

At Higher Levels. When you cast this spell using a spell slot of 3rd level or higher, add 50 feet to the maximum dimensions of the cube and add 12 hours to the spell's duration for each slot level above 2nd.

LANCE OF THE SUN GOD

3rd-Level Evocation

Casting Time: 1 action

Range: Self

Components: V, S

Duration: Concentration, up to 1 minute

You invoke a lance made of force and light. The lance glows brightly, providing light as a lantern. You are considered proficient with this weapon, and it has

the same weapon properties as a nonmagical lance. On a successful melee attack with the lance, you deal 1d12 force damage and 2d8 radiant damage.

You can perform a charge attack with the lance. If you move at least 20 feet straight toward a target and hit with the lance on the same turn, you double the damage of the attack.

LAST RAYS OF THE DYING SUN

7th-Level Evocation

Casting Time: 1 action
Range: 40 feet
Components: V, S
Duration: Instantaneous

A burst of searing heat explodes from you, dealing 6d6 fire damage to all enemies within range. Immediately afterward, a wave of frigid cold rolls across the same area, dealing 6d6 cold damage to enemies. A creature that makes a successful Dexterity saving throw takes half the damage.

At Higher Levels. When you cast this spell using a spell slot of 8th or 9th level, the damage from both waves increases by 1d6 for each slot level above 7th.

LAUGH IN THE FACE OF FEAR

3rd-Level Abjuration

Casting Time: 1 action
Range: 30 feet
Components: V, S
Duration: Concentration, up to 1 minute

You instill up to six creatures within range with the ability to laugh at something that would normally frighten them. An affected creature has advantage on saving throws against any spell or effect that causes the frightened condition. When a creature protected by this spell succeeds on such a saving throw, it can—if it has the mentality and capability to do so—laugh at the creature that caused the frightened condition. That creature must succeed on a Wisdom saving throw against your spell save DC or become frightened of the one who laughed. The frightened condition lasts as long as that creature can see or hear the creature who laughed, or until the spell's duration expires.

LAVA STONE

4th-Level Transmutation

Casting Time: 1 action
Range: Touch
Components: V, M (a sling stone)
Duration: Instantaneous

When you cast *lava stone* on a piece of sling ammo, the stone or bullet becomes intensely hot. As a bonus action, you can launch the heated stone with a sling: the stone increases in size and melts into a glob of lava while in flight. Make a ranged spell attack against the target. If it hits, the target takes 1d8 bludgeoning damage plus 6d6 fire damage. The target takes additional fire damage at the start of each of your next three turns, starting with 4d6, then 2d6, and then 1d6. The additional damage can be avoided if the target or an ally within 5 feet of the target scrapes off the lava. This is done by using an action to make a successful Wisdom (Medicine) check against your spellcasting save DC. The spell ends if the heated sling stone isn't used immediately.

LAY TO REST

5th-Level Evocation

Casting Time: 1 action
Range: Self (15-foot-radius sphere)
Components: V, S, M (a pinch of grave dirt)
Duration: Instantaneous

A pulse of searing light rushes out from you. Each undead creature within 15 feet of you must make a Constitution saving throw. A target takes 8d6 radiant damage on a failed save, or half as much damage on a successful one.

An undead creature reduced to 0 hit points by this spell disintegrates in a burst of radiant motes, leaving anything it was wearing or carrying in the space it formerly occupied.

LEGEND KILLER

7th-Level Divination

Casting Time: 1 action
Range: 60 feet
Components: V, S, M (a silver scroll describing the spell's target worth at least 1,000 gp, which the spell consumes)
Duration: Concentration, up to 1 minute

You tap into the life force of a creature that is capable of performing legendary actions. When you cast the spell, the target must make a successful Constitution saving throw or lose the ability to take legendary actions for the spell's duration. A creature can't use legendary resistance to automatically succeed on the saving throw against this spell. An affected creature can repeat the saving throw at the end of each of its turns, regaining 1 legendary action on a successful save. The target continues repeating the saving throw until the spell ends or it regains all its legendary actions.

LEGION OF RABID SQUIRRELS

3rd-Level Conjuration

Casting Time: 1 action
Range: 60 feet
Components: V, S, M (an acorn or nut)
Duration: Concentration, up to 1 minute

While in a forest, you call a legion of rabid squirrels to descend from the nearby trees at a point you can see within range. The squirrels form into a swarm that uses the statistics of a swarm of poisonous snakes, except it has a climbing speed of 30 feet rather than a swimming speed. The legion of squirrels is friendly to you and your companions. Roll initiative for the legion, which has its own turns. The legion of squirrels obeys your verbal commands (no action required by you). If you don't issue any commands to the legion, it defends itself from hostile creatures but otherwise takes no actions. If you command it to move farther than 60 feet from you, the spell ends and the legion disperses back into the forest. A canid, such as a dog, wolf, fox, or worg, has disadvantage on attack rolls against targets other than the legion of rabid squirrels while the swarm is within 60 feet of the creature. When the spell ends, the squirrels disperse back into the forest.

At Higher Levels. When you cast this spell using a spell slot of 4th level or higher, the legion's poison damage increases by 1d6 for each slot level above 3rd.

LIAR'S GIFT

1st-Level Enchantment

Casting Time: 1 action
Range: Self
Components: V, S
Duration: 1 minute

Liar's gift makes even the most barefaced untruth seem plausible: you gain advantage on Charisma (Deception) checks to convince another creature of the truth of whatever you're saying. On a failed check, the creature knows that you tried to manipulate it with magic. If you successfully lie to a creature that has a friendly attitude toward you, it must make a Charisma saving throw. On a failed save, you can also coax the creature to reveal a potentially embarrassing secret. The verbal component of this spell is the lie you are telling.

LIFE FROM DEATH

3rd-Level Necromancy

Casting Time: 1 action
Range: Self
Components: V, S
Duration: Concentration, up to 1 minute

The touch of your hand can siphon energy from the undead to heal your wounds. Make a melee spell attack against an undead creature within your reach. On a hit, the target takes 2d6 radiant damage, and you or an ally within 30 feet of you regains hit points equal to half the amount of radiant damage dealt. If used on an ally, this effect can restore the ally to no more than half of its hit point maximum. This effect can't heal an undead or a construct. Until the spell ends, you can make the attack again on each of your turns as an action.

At Higher Levels. When you cast this spell using a spell slot of 4th level or higher, the damage increases by 1d6 for each slot level above 3rd.

LIFE HACK

8th-Level Necromancy

Casting Time: 1 action
Range: 30 feet
Components: V, S, M (a ruby worth 500 gp, which is consumed during the casting)
Duration: 1 hour

Choose up to five creatures that you can see within range. Each of the creatures gains access to a pool of temporary hit points that it can draw upon over the spell's duration or until the pool is used up. The pool contains 120 temporary hit points. The number of temporary hit points each individual creature can draw is determined by dividing 120 by the number of creatures with access to the pool. Hit points are drawn as a bonus action by the creature gaining the temporary hit points. Any number can be drawn at once, up to the maximum allowed.

A creature can't draw temporary hit points from the pool while it has temporary hit points from any source, including a previous casting of this spell.

LIFE SENSE

3rd-Level Divination

Casting Time: 1 action
Range: Self
Components: V, S, M (a clear piece of quartz)
Duration: Concentration, up to 10 minutes

For the duration, you can sense the location of any creature that isn't a construct or an undead within 30 feet of you, regardless of impediments to your other senses. This spell doesn't sense creatures that are dead. A creature trying to hide its life force from you can make a Charisma saving throw. On a success, you can't sense the creature with this casting of the spell. If you cast the spell again, the creature must make the saving throw again to remain hidden from your senses.

LIFE TRANSFERENCE ARROW

1st-Level Necromancy

Casting Time: 1 action
Range: 120 feet
Components: V, S
Duration: Instantaneous

You create a glowing arrow of necrotic magic and command it to strike a creature you can see within range. The arrow can have one of two effects; you choose which at the moment of casting. If you make a successful ranged spell attack, you and the target experience the desired effect. If the attack misses, the spell fails:

- The arrow deals 2d6 necrotic damage to the target, and you heal the same amount of hit points.
- You take 2d6 necrotic damage, and the target heals the same amount of hit points.

At Higher Levels. When you cast this spell using a spell slot of 2nd level or higher, the spell's damage and hit points healed increase by 1d6 for each slot level above 1st.

LITANY OF SURE HANDS

1st-Level Divination

Casting Time: 1 bonus action
Range: 30 feet
Components: V, S
Duration: 1 minute

This spell allows a creature within range to quickly perform a simple task (other than attacking or casting a spell) as a bonus action on its turn. Examples include finding an item in a backpack, drinking a potion, and pulling a rope. Other actions may also fall into this category, depending on the GM's ruling. The target also ignores the loading property of weapons.

LOCK ARMOR

2nd-Level Transmutation

Casting Time: 1 action
Range: 60 feet
Components: V, S, M (a pinch of rust and metal shavings)
Duration: Concentration, up to 1 minute

You target a piece of metal equipment or a metal construct. If the target is a creature wearing metal armor or is a construct, it makes a Wisdom saving throw to negate the effect. On a failed save, the spell causes metal to cling to metal, making it impossible to move pieces

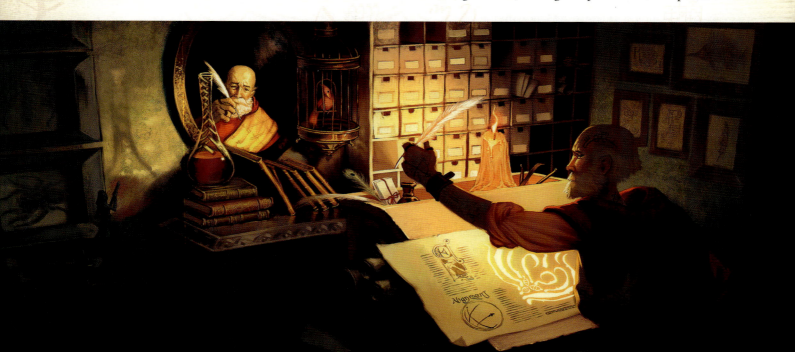

against each other. This effectively paralyzes a creature that is made of metal or that is wearing metal armor with moving pieces; for example, scale mail would lock up because the scales must slide across each other, but a breastplate would be unaffected. Limited movement might still be possible, depending on how extensive the armor is, and speech is usually not affected. Metal constructs are paralyzed. An affected creature or construct can repeat the saving throw at the end of each of its turns, ending the effect on itself on a success. A *grease* spell dispels *lock armor* on everything in its area.

At Higher Levels. When you cast this spell using a spell slot of 3rd level or higher, you can target one additional creature for each slot level above 2nd.

LOOPING TRAIL

4th-Level Transmutation

Casting Time: 1 minute
Range: Touch
Components: V, S, M (a piece of rope twisted into a loop)
Duration: 8 hours

You touch a trail no more than 1 mile in length, reconfiguring it to give it switchbacks and curves that make the trail loop back on itself. For the duration, the trail makes subtle changes in its configuration and in the surrounding environment to give the impression of forward progression along a continuous path. A creature on the trail must succeed on a Wisdom (Survival) check to notice that the trail is leading it in a closed loop.

LOVESICK

4th-Level Enchantment

Casting Time: 1 action
Range: 90 feet
Components: V, S, M (a handful of red rose petals)
Duration: Concentration, up to 1 minute

This spell causes creatures to behave unpredictably, as they randomly experience the full gamut of emotions of someone who has fallen head over heels in love. Each creature in a 10-foot-radius sphere centered on a point you choose within range must succeed on a Wisdom saving throw when you cast this spell or be affected by it.

An affected target can't take reactions and must roll a d10 at the start of each of its turns and consult the table below to determine its behavior for that turn.

At the end of each of its turns, an affected target can make a Wisdom saving throw, ending the effect on itself on a successful save.

At Higher Levels. When you cast this spell using a spell slot of 5th level or higher, the radius of the sphere increases by 5 feet for each slot level above 4th.

LOWER THE VEIL

8th-Level Divination

Casting Time: 1 action
Range: 60 feet
Components: V, S, M (a strip of thin gauze)
Duration: Instantaneous

You drop the veil of reality for selected targets, allowing a brief glimpse into the deep nothing beyond this realm to shatter their minds. Each creature you choose within 60 feet of you must succeed on a Wisdom saving throw or take 8d10 psychic damage and be driven insane for 10 minutes, per the *symbol* spell. On a successful saving throw, a creature takes half the damage and is stunned for 1 round. Creatures already suffering from insanity are immune to this spell. Blindness, however, is not a defense, since the experience is not sight-based, but an internal awareness.

LUMINOUS BOLT

Evocation Cantrip

Casting Time: 1 action
Range: 60 feet
Components: V, S
Duration: Instantaneous

A ray of sunlight shoots out at a creature within range. Make a ranged spell attack against the target. On a hit, it takes 1d6 radiant damage, and it must succeed on a Constitution saving throw or become blinded until the end of its next turn.

The spell's damage increases by 1d6 when you reach 5th level (2d6), 11th level (3d6), and 17th level (4d6).

d10	Behavior
1–3	The creature spends its turn moping like a lovelorn teenager; it doesn't move or take actions.
4–5	The creature bursts into tears, takes the Dash action, and uses all its movement to run off in a random direction. To determine the direction, roll a d8 and assign a direction to each die face.
6	The creature uses its action to remove one item of clothing or piece of armor. Each round spent removing pieces of armor reduces its AC by 1.
7–8	The creature drops anything it is holding in its hands and passionately embraces a randomly determined creature. Treat this as a grapple attempt which uses the Attack action.
9	The creature flies into a jealous rage and uses its action to attack a randomly determined creature.
10	The creature can act and move normally.

MAGNETIZE

5th-Level Evocation

Casting Time: 1 action
Range: Touch
Components: V, S, M (a lodestone)
Duration: Concentration, up to 10 minutes

You magnetize a large piece of metal or stone (such as a door, a stone pillar, or a 5-foot-square section of floor) that you touch, giving it a powerful attraction to ferrous metal. Any iron objects within 50 feet of the target that are not fastened down or being held or worn are pulled toward it, moving against or up to the target and remaining there. Any creature located between such an object and the magnet might be struck; roll a ranged spell attack against the target's AC. On a hit, the target takes 2d10 damage of the appropriate type (bludgeoning for a hammer, slashing or piercing for a sword, and so forth).

Objects held by or in the possession of a creature are also attracted. The creature must succeed on a Strength saving throw to retain a grip on any held or worn objects. On a successful save, the creature retains possession of the object, but is dragged 5 feet closer to the magnet. A creature can voluntarily release a metal object in its possession and forgo a save.

Creatures garbed in mostly metal armor, or made of metal, are also attracted to the magnet, and have disadvantage on their saving throws to avoid being pulled toward it. If such a creature succeeds on its saving throw, it can move away from the magnet on its turn, but the area within 50 feet of the magnet is considered difficult terrain. If the creature is still in this area at the start of its next turn, it must make another successful saving throw to avoid being drawn toward the magnet. A creature that comes into contact with the magnet is restrained. It can negate this condition by using an action and succeeding on a Strength check against your spell save DC to remove itself from the magnet.

MAIM

5th-Level Necromancy

Casting Time: 1 action
Range: Self
Components: V, S
Duration: Instantaneous

Your hands become black claws bathed in necrotic energy. Make a melee spell attack against a creature you can reach. On a hit, the target takes 4d6 necrotic damage and a section of its body of your choosing withers:

Upper Limb. The target has disadvantage on Strength ability checks, and, if it has the Multiattack action, it has disadvantage on its first attack roll each round.

Lower Limb. The target's speed is reduced by 10 feet, and it has disadvantage on Dexterity ability checks.

Body. Choose one damage type: bludgeoning, piercing, or slashing. The target loses its resistance to that damage type. If the target doesn't have resistance to the chosen damage type, it is vulnerable to that damage type instead.

The effect is permanent until removed by *remove curse*, *greater restoration*, or similar magic.

MALEVOLENT WAVES

8th-Level Abjuration

Casting Time: 1 action
Range: Self
Components: V, S, M (a profane object that has been bathed in blood)
Duration: Concentration, up to 1 minute

You create an invisible miasma that fills the area within 30 feet of you. All your allies have advantage on Dexterity (Stealth) checks they make within 30 feet of you, and all your enemies are poisoned while within that radius.

MAMMON'S AVARICE

1st-Level Divination

Casting Time: 1 action
Range: Self (30-foot radius)
Components: V, S
Duration: Concentration, up to 10 minutes

By casting this spell, you tap into the power of greed that is Mammon's sphere of influence, which manifests as a heightened olfactory sense. You can pinpoint, by smell, the location of any precious metals or gemstones within 30 feet of you. If you find anything, you can use an action to determine the exact types and amounts of any such materials. If materials of this sort are completely enclosed by, or separated from you by, more than 6 feet of earth or wood, 2 feet of stone, or 2 inches of common metal, you cannot detect them even if they are in range.

MAMMON'S DUE

9th-Level Conjuration (Ritual)

Casting Time: 1 hour
Range: 500 feet
Components: V, S, M (11 gilded human skulls worth 150 gp each, which are consumed by the spell)
Duration: Concentration, up to 1 minute

You summon a cylindrical sinkhole filled with burning ash and grasping arms made of molten metal at a point on the ground you can see within range. The sinkhole is 20 feet deep, 50 feet in diameter, and is difficult terrain. A creature that's in the area when the spell is cast, or that begins its turn in the area or enters it during its turn, takes

10d6 fire damage and must make a Strength or Dexterity (creature's choice) saving throw. On a failed save, the creature is restrained by the molten arms, which try to drag it below the surface of the ash.

A creature that's restrained by the arms at the start of your turn must make a successful Strength saving throw or be pulled 5 feet farther down into the ash. A creature pulled below the surface is blinded, deafened, and can't breathe. To escape, a creature must use an action to make a successful Strength or Dexterity check against your spell save DC. On a successful check, the creature is no longer restrained and can move through the difficult terrain of the ash pit. It doesn't need to make a Strength or Dexterity saving throw this turn to not be grabbed by the arms again, but it must make the saving throw as normal if it's still in the ash pit at the start of its next turn.

The diameter of the ash pit increases by 10 feet at the start of each of your turns for the duration of the spell. The ash pit remains after the spell ends, but the grasping arms disappear and restrained creatures are freed automatically. As the ash slowly cools, it deals 1d6 less fire damage for each hour that passes after the spell ends.

MANTLE OF THE BRAVE

2nd-Level Abjuration

Casting Time: 1 action
Range: Touch
Components: V, S
Duration: 1 hour

You touch up to four individuals, bolstering their courage. The next time a creature affected by this spell must make a saving throw against a spell or effect that would cause the frightened condition, it has advantage on the roll. Once a creature has received this benefit, the spell ends for that creature.

MARK PREY

2nd-Level Divination

Casting Time: 1 bonus action
Range: 120 feet
Components: V
Duration: Concentration, up to 1 hour

You choose a creature you can see within range as your prey. Until the spell ends, you have advantage on Wisdom (Perception) and Wisdom (Survival) checks to find or track your prey. In addition, the target is outlined in light that only you can see. Any attack roll you make against your prey has advantage if you can see it, and your prey can't benefit from being invisible against you. If the target drops to 0 hit points before this spell ends, you can use a bonus action on a subsequent turn to mark a new target as your prey.

At Higher Levels. When you cast this spell using a spell slot of 4th level, you can maintain your concentration on the spell for up to 8 hours. When you use a spell slot of 5th level or higher, you can maintain your concentration on the spell for up to 24 hours.

MASS HOBBLE MOUNT

3rd-Level Necromancy

Casting Time: 1 action
Range: 60 feet
Components: V, S
Duration: Concentration, up to 1 hour

When you cast *mass hobble mount*, you make separate ranged spell attacks against up to six horses, wolves, or other four-legged or two-legged beasts being ridden as mounts within 60 feet of you. The targets can be different types of beasts and can have different numbers of legs. Each beast hit by your spell is disabled so that it can't move at its normal speed without incurring injury. An affected creature that moves more than half its base speed in a turn takes 4d6 bludgeoning damage.

MASS SURGE DAMPENER

5th-Level Abjuration (Ritual)

Casting Time: 1 action
Range: 30 feet
Components: V, S
Duration: 1 minute, or until expended

Using your strength of will, you protect up to three creatures other than yourself from the effect of a chaos magic surge. A protected creature can make a DC 13 Charisma saving throw to negate the effect of a chaos magic surge that does not normally allow a saving throw, or it gains advantage on a saving throw that is normally allowed. Once a protected creature makes a successful saving throw allowed by *mass surge dampener*, the spell's effect ends for that creature.

MAW OF NEEDLES

1st-Level Transmutation

Casting Time: 1 bonus action
Range: Self
Components: V, S
Duration: 1 minute

A spiny array of needle-like fangs protrudes from your gums, giving you a spiny bite. For the duration, you can use your action to make a melee spell attack with the bite. On a hit, the target takes 2d6 piercing damage and must succeed on a Dexterity saving throw or some of the spines in your mouth break off, sticking in the target. Until this spell ends, the target must succeed on a Constitution saving throw at the start of each of its turns or take 1d6 piercing damage from the spines. If you hit a target that has your spines stuck in it, your attack deals extra damage equal to your spellcasting ability modifier, and more spines don't break off in the target. Your spines can stick in only one target at a time. If your spines stick into another target, the spines on the previous target crumble to dust, ending the effect on that target.

At Higher Levels. When you cast this spell using a spell slot of 3rd level or higher, the damage of the spiny bite and the spines increases by 1d6 for every two slot levels above 1st.

MEPHITIC CROAK

2nd-Level Conjuration

Casting Time: 1 action
Range: Self (15-foot cone)
Components: V, S, M (a dead toad and a dram of arsenic worth 10 gp)
Duration: Instantaneous

You release an intensely loud burp of acidic gas in a 15-foot cone. Creatures in the area take 2d6 acid damage plus 2d6 thunder damage, or half as much damage with a successful Dexterity saving throw. A creature whose Dexterity saving throw fails must also make a successful Constitution saving throw or be stunned and poisoned until the start of your next turn.

At Higher Levels. When you cast this spell using a spell slot of 3rd level or higher, both acid and thunder damage increase by 1d6 for each slot level above 2nd.

MIND EXCHANGE

3rd-Level Transmutation (Ritual)

Casting Time: 1 minute
Range: 60 feet
Components: V, S, M (a prism and silver coin)
Duration: Concentration, up to 8 hours

One humanoid of your choice that you can see within range must make a Charisma saving throw. On a failed save, you project your mind into the body of the target. You use the target's statistics but don't gain access to its knowledge, class features, or proficiencies, retaining your own instead. Meanwhile, the target's mind is shunted into your body, where it uses your statistics but likewise retains its own knowledge, class features, and proficiencies.

The exchange lasts until either of the two bodies drops to 0 hit points, until you end it as a bonus action, or until you are forced out of the target body by an effect such as a *dispel magic* or *dispel evil and good* spell (the latter spell defeats *mind exchange* even though possession by a humanoid isn't usually affected by that spell). When the effect of this spell ends, both switched minds return to their original bodies. The target of the spell is immune to *mind exchange* for 24 hours after succeeding on the saving throw or after the exchange ends.

The effects of the exchange can be made permanent with a *wish* spell or comparable magic.

MIRE

3rd-Level Transmutation

Casting Time: 1 action
Range: 100 feet
Components: V, S, M (a vial of sand mixed with water)
Duration: 1 hour

When you cast *mire*, you create a 10-foot-diameter pit of quicksand, sticky mud, or a similar dangerous natural hazard suited to the region. A creature that's in the area when the spell is cast or that enters the affected area must make a successful Strength saving throw or sink up to its waist and be restrained by the mire. From that point on, the mire acts as quicksand, but the DC for Strength checks to escape from the quicksand is equal to your spell save DC. A creature outside the mire trying to pull another creature free receives a +5 bonus on its Strength check.

MISFORTUNE

6th-Level Necromancy

Casting Time: 1 action
Range: 60 feet
Components: V, S, M (a broken mirror)
Duration: Concentration, up to 1 minute

You cast a pall of bad luck over all creatures in a 15-foot radius centered on a point within range. Each creature in that area must succeed on a Wisdom saving throw or be cursed with bad luck for the duration of the spell. A creature under the effect of this spell has disadvantage on all ability checks, saving throws, and attack rolls. A *remove curse* spell ends this effect.

Special. If a targeted creature is carrying a *stone of good luck*, the creature is unaffected by the spell, but the item ceases to function for 24 hours. Likewise, if a targeted creature is carrying a *luck blade*, the creature is unaffected by the spell, but the sword's Luck ability and saving throw bonuses cease to function for 24 hours.

MIST OF WONDERS

2nd-Level Conjuration

Casting Time: 1 action
Range: Self (30-foot radius)
Components: V, S
Duration: 1 minute

A colorful mist surrounds you out to a radius of 30 feet. Creatures inside the mist see odd shapes in it and hear random sounds that don't make sense. The very concepts of order and logic don't seem to exist inside the mist.

Any 1st-level spell that's cast in the mist by another caster or that travels through the mist is affected by its strange nature. The caster must make a Constitution saving throw when casting the spell. On a failed save, the spell transforms into another 1st-level spell the caster knows (chosen by the GM from those available), even if that spell is not currently prepared. The altered spell's slot level or its original target or targeted area can't be changed. Cantrips are unaffected. If (in the GM's judgment) none of the caster's spells known of that level can be transformed, the spell being cast simply fails.

At Higher Levels. When you cast this spell using a spell slot of 3rd level or higher, it affects any spell cast using a spell slot of any lower level. For instance, using a 6th-level slot enables you to transform a spell of 5th level or lower into another spell of the same level.

MITHRAL DRAGON'S MIGHT

6th-Level Transmutation

Casting Time: 1 action
Range: Self
Components: V, S
Duration: Concentration, up to 1 minute

You take on some of the physical characteristics and abilities of the mithral dragon, growing protective scales, wings, and claws. Until the spell ends, your AC can't be lower than 16, regardless of what armor you are wearing. You can take two actions on your turn to attack with your claws, dealing 1d6 slashing damage on a hit. You have resistance to acid and thunder damage. Up to three times while the spell is active, as an action, you can breathe a 20-foot cone of metal shards, dealing 6d8 slashing damage to all creatures in the cone. A creature that succeeds on a Dexterity saving throw takes half as much damage from your breath weapon. Finally, the wings grant you a flying speed of 40 feet.

MONSTROUS EMPATHY

3rd-Level Enchantment

Casting Time: 1 action
Range: 30 feet
Components: V, S, M (a morsel of food)
Duration: 24 hours

This spell lets you forge a connection with a monstrosity. Choose a monstrosity that you can see within range. It must see and hear you. If the monstrosity's Intelligence is 4 or higher, the spell fails. Otherwise, the monstrosity must succeed on a Wisdom saving throw or be charmed by you for the spell's duration. If you or one of your companions harms the target, the spell ends.

At Higher Levels. When you cast this spell using a spell slot of 4th level or higher, you can affect one additional monstrosity for each slot level above 3rd.

MORTAL INSIGHT

3rd-Level Divination

Casting Time: 1 action
Range: Self
Components: V, S
Duration: Concentration, up to 10 minutes

A supernatural olfactory sense allows you to smell wounded living creatures. Until the spell ends, you can pinpoint a creature that doesn't have all of its hit points within 30 feet of you, and you have advantage on Wisdom (Perception) and Wisdom (Survival) checks to track a creature that doesn't have all of its hit points. In addition, you have advantage on melee attack rolls against any creature that doesn't have all of its hit points. The spell has no effect on creatures that don't have blood.

MOSQUITO BANE

1st-Level Necromancy

Casting Time: 1 action
Range: 50 feet
Components: V, S
Duration: Instantaneous

This spell kills any insects or swarms of insects within range that have a total of 25 hit points or fewer.

At Higher Levels. When you cast this spell using a spell slot of 2nd level or higher, the number of hit points affected increases by 15 for each slot level above 1st. Thus, a 2nd-level spell kills insects or swarms that have up to 40 hit points, a 3rd-level spell kills those with 55 hit points or fewer, and so forth, up to a maximum of 100 hit points for a slot of 6th level or higher.

MUD PACK

1st-Level Conjuration (Ritual)

Casting Time: 1 action
Range: Touch
Components: V, S, M (a clump of mud)
Duration: 1 hour

This spell covers you or a willing creature you touch in mud consistent with the surrounding terrain. For the duration, the spell protects the target from extreme cold and heat, allowing the target to automatically succeed on Constitution saving throws against environmental hazards related to temperature. In addition, the target has advantage on Dexterity (Stealth) checks while traveling at a slow pace in the terrain related to the component for this spell.

If the target is subject to heavy precipitation for 1 minute, the precipitation removes the mud, ending the spell.

At Higher Levels. When you cast this spell using a spell slot of 3rd level or higher, the duration is 8 hours, and you can target up to ten willing creatures within 30 feet of you.

NATURE'S AEGIS

1st-Level Abjuration

Casting Time: 1 action
Range: Self
Components: V, S, M (an area of natural vegetation)
Duration: 1 hour

Grass, vines, branches, and other vegetation weave themselves over your body into a temporary suit of armor. You can use an action to dismiss this spell. *Nature's aegis* gives you an Armor Class of 14 + your Dexterity modifier. The armor weighs 8 pounds and provides you with advantage on Dexterity (Stealth) checks made to hide in the terrain from which you used the vegetation.

NECROTIC LEECH

5th-Level Necromancy

Casting Time: 1 action
Range: Touch
Components: V, S
Duration: Instantaneous

You channel destructive energy through your touch. Make a melee spell attack against a creature within your reach. The target takes 8d10 necrotic damage and must succeed on a Constitution saving throw or have disadvantage on attack rolls, saving throws, and ability checks for a number of rounds equal to the spell slot you expended. An affected creature can repeat the saving throw at the end of each of its turns, ending the effect on itself on a success.

This spell has no effect on constructs or undead.

At Higher Levels. When you cast this spell using a spell slot of 6th level or higher, the spell's damage increases by 1d10 for each slot level above 5th.

NEST OF INFERNAL VIPERS

3rd-Level Conjuration

Casting Time: 1 action
Range: 60 feet
Components: V, S
Duration: Concentration, up to 1 hour

You summon evil spirits that take the form of a swarm of poisonous snakes and appear in an unoccupied space you can see within range. The swarm of snakes is considered a fiend as well as a beast. It has resistance to fire damage and lasts until it drops to 0 hit points or the spell ends.

The summoned swarm is friendly to you and your companions. Roll initiative for the swarm, which takes its own turns. It obeys any verbal commands you issue to it (no action required by you). If you don't issue any commands to the swarm, it moves to attack the nearest creature that is not your ally.

The GM has the creature's statistics.

At Higher Levels. When you cast this spell using certain higher-level spell slots, you can summon additional swarms. You summon two swarms with a 5th-level spell slot, three swarms with a 7th-level spell slot, or four swarms with a 9th-level spell slot.

NIGHT TERRORS

4th-Level Illusion

Casting Time: 1 action
Range: 120 feet
Components: V, S, M (a crow's eye)
Duration: Concentration, up to 1 minute

You amplify the fear that lurks in the heart of all creatures. Select a target point you can see within the spell's range. Every creature within 20 feet of that point becomes frightened until the start of your next turn and must make a successful Wisdom saving throw or become paralyzed. A paralyzed creature can repeat the saving throw at the end of each of its turns, ending the effect on itself on a success. Creatures immune to being frightened are not affected by *night terrors*.

NIGHTFALL

3rd-Level Evocation (Ritual)

Casting Time: 1 action
Range: 100 feet
Components: V, S
Duration: Concentration, up to 10 minutes

You call upon night to arrive ahead of schedule. With a sharp word, you create a 30-foot-radius cylinder of night centered on a point on the ground within range. The cylinder extends vertically for 100 feet or until it reaches an obstruction, such as a ceiling. The area inside the cylinder is normal darkness, and thus heavily obscured. Creatures inside the darkened cylinder can see illuminated areas outside the cylinder normally.

NIMBLENESS

Transmutation Cantrip

Casting Time: 1 action
Range: Touch
Components: V, S
Duration: Concentration, up to 1 minute

You touch a willing subject. Once before the spell ends, the target can roll a d6 and add the result to one Dexterity check of its choice. It can roll the die before or after making the check. The spell then ends.

NIP AT THE HEELS

2nd-Level Illusion

Casting Time: 1 action
Range: 30 feet
Components: V, S, M (a dog's tooth)
Duration: 1 minute

You create an illusory pack of wild dogs that bark and nip at one creature you can see within range, which must make a Wisdom saving throw. On a failed save, the target has disadvantage on ability checks and attack rolls for the duration as it is distracted by the dogs. At the end of each of its turns, the target can make a Wisdom saving throw, ending the effect on itself on a successful save. A target that is at least 10 feet off the ground (in a tree, flying, and so forth) has advantage on the saving throw, staying just out of reach of the jumping and barking dogs.

At Higher Levels. When you cast this spell using a spell slot of 3rd level or higher, you can target one additional creature for each slot level above 2nd.

NOT DEAD YET

4th-Level Necromancy (Ritual)

Casting Time: 1 minute
Range: Touch
Components: V, S, M (a cloth doll filled with herbs and diamond dust worth 100 gp)
Duration: Concentration, up to 1 hour

You cast this spell while touching the cloth doll against the intact corpse of a Medium or smaller humanoid that died within the last hour. At the end of the casting, the body reanimates as an undead creature under your control. While the spell lasts, your consciousness resides in the animated body. You can use an action to manipulate the body's limbs in order to make it move, and you can see and hear through the body's eyes and ears, but your own body becomes unconscious. The animated body can neither attack nor defend itself. This spell doesn't change the appearance of the corpse, so further measures might be needed if the body is to be used in a way that involves fooling observers into believing it's still alive. The spell ends instantly, and your consciousness returns to your body, if either your real body or the animated body takes any damage.

You can't use any of the target's abilities except for nonmagical movement and darkvision. You don't have access to its knowledge, proficiencies, or anything else that was held in its now dead mind, and you can't make it speak.

NOT THIS DAY!

5th-Level Abjuration

Casting Time: 1 action
Range: Touch
Components: V, S
Duration: 24 hours

The creature you touch gains protection against either a specific damage type (slashing, poison, fire, radiant, and the like) or a category of creature (giant, beast, elemental, monstrosity, and so forth) that you name when the spell is cast. For the next 24 hours, the target has advantage on saving throws involving that type of damage or kind of creature, including death saving throws if the attack that dropped the target to 0 hit points is affected by this spell.

A character can be under the effect of only a single *not this day!* spell at one time; a second casting on the same target cancels the preexisting protection.

NOURISHING REPAST

1st-Level Transmutation (Ritual)

Casting Time: 1 minute
Range: Touch
Components: V, S
Duration: 24 hours

You touch a supply of food and turn it into a magical substance that promotes healing and health. Enough food for up to six creatures can be transformed by the spell. The effects of the spell last for 24 hours or until the food is eaten. If the food is eaten during a short rest, it provides a +1 bonus to each Hit Die spent to regain hit points.

If eaten as part of a long rest instead, then each creature partaking in the meal gains advantage on saving throws against disease or poison for the next 8 hours.

OBTUSE

Enchantment Cantrip

Casting Time: 1 action
Range: 30 feet
Components: V, S
Duration: 1 minute

You temporarily cloud the mind of a creature within range, inhibiting its decision-making skills. If the target succeeds on a Wisdom saving throw, the spell is ineffective. On a failed save, the next time the creature makes a Wisdom check before the spell ends, roll a d6 and subtract the result from the roll. The spell then ends.

OPPORTUNISTIC FORESIGHT

3rd-Level Divination

Casting Time: 1 action
Range: Touch
Components: V, S
Duration: Concentration, up to 1 minute

You instill a creature you touch with the ability to predict and react to advantages in combat. For the duration of the spell, the target gains a bonus action each turn that it can use to make an opportunity attack against a provoking opponent. The target gains advantage on any opportunity attacks it takes while the spell is in effect.

ORB OF LIGHT

2nd-Level Evocation

Casting Time: 1 action
Range: 60 feet
Components: V, S
Duration: 1 round

An orb of light the size of your hand shoots from your fingertips toward a creature within range, which takes 3d8 radiant damage and is blinded for 1 round. A target that makes a successful Dexterity saving throw takes half the damage and is not blinded.

At Higher Levels. When you cast this spell using a spell slot of 3rd level or higher, the damage increases by 1d8 for each slot level above 2nd.

OUTFLANKING BOON

3rd-Level Illusion

Casting Time: 1 action
Range: 30 feet
Components: V, S
Duration: Concentration, up to 1 minute

This spell targets one enemy, which must make a Wisdom saving throw. On a failed save, an illusory ally of yours appears in a space from which it threatens to make a melee attack against the target. Your allies gain advantage on melee attacks against the target for the duration because of the distracting effect of the illusion. An affected target repeats the saving throw at the end of each of its turns, ending the effect on itself on a success.

At Higher Levels. When you cast this spell using a spell slot of 4th level or higher, the spell targets one additional enemy for each slot level above 3rd.

OVERWHELMING GREED

4th-Level Enchantment

Casting Time: 1 action
Range: 60 feet
Components: V, S, M (a gold piece)
Duration: 1 hour

You fill the target with a dragon's greed for wealth. The target must succeed on a Wisdom saving throw or be overcome with greed, coveting any coins, jewelry, or art objects it can see that have a value of at least 1 gold piece, as well as jealously guarding any wealth it already owns. The target fixates on the most valuable-looking item or items, or the largest concentration of valuables in sight. It will not willingly let the wealth out of its sight. If the target sees an opportunity, it will take the valuables it has fixated on, gaining them by whatever means necessary. If doing so provokes a situation where it takes damage or is otherwise harmed, the affected creature can make another

Wisdom saving throw to end the effect. If the creature fails the save, it will continue to try to acquire the wealth, fighting back if necessary.

Ending the Effect. If the affected creature ends its turn in an area where it cannot see any obviously valuable objects to covet, nor any creatures that might conceivably attempt to take its own property (a horse, for example, would not be considered such a creature), then it can make another Wisdom saving throw. A successful save ends the spell, and the creature recognizes its feelings of greed as magically induced.

At Higher Levels. When you cast this spell using a spell slot of 5th level or higher, you can affect one additional creature for each slot level above 4th.

PARAGON OF CHAOS

8th-Level Transmutation

Casting Time: 1 action
Range: Self
Components: V
Duration: Concentration, up to 1 minute

You become a humanoid-shaped swirling mass of color and sound. You gain resistance to bludgeoning, piercing, and slashing damage, and immunity to poison and psychic damage. You are also immune to the following conditions: exhaustion, paralyzed, petrified, poisoned, and unconscious. Finally, you gain truesight to 30 feet and can teleport 30 feet as a move.

Each round, as a bonus action, you can cause an automatic chaos magic surge, choosing either yourself or another creature you can see within 60 feet as the caster for the purpose of resolving the effect. You must choose the target before rolling percentile dice to determine the nature of the surge. The DC of any required saving throw is calculated as if you were the caster.

PENDULUM

1st-Level Enchantment

Casting Time: 1 action
Range: Touch
Components: V, S, M (a small pendulum or metronome made of brass and rosewood worth 10 gp)
Duration: Concentration, up to 1 minute

You give the touched creature an aspect of regularity in its motions and fortunes. If the target gets a failure on a Wisdom saving throw, then for the duration of the spell it doesn't make d20 rolls—to determine the results of attack rolls, ability checks, and saving throws it instead follows the sequence 20, 1, 19, 2, 18, 3, 17, 4, and so on.

PHANTOM DRAGON

3rd-Level Illusion

Casting Time: 1 action
Range: Touch
Components: V, S, M (a piece of dragon egg shell)
Duration: Concentration, up to 1 hour

You tap your dragon magic to make an ally appear as a draconic beast. The target of the spell appears to be a dragon of size Large or smaller. When seeing this illusion, observers make a Wisdom saving throw to see through it.

You can use an action to make the illusory dragon seem ferocious. Choose one creature within 30 feet of the illusory dragon to make a Wisdom saving throw. If it fails, the creature is frightened. The creature remains frightened until it uses an action to make a successful Wisdom saving throw or the spell's duration expires.

At Higher Levels. When you cast this spell using a spell slot of 4th level or higher, increase the number of targets the illusion can affect by one for each slot level above 3rd.

PHANTOM LIGHT

2nd-Level Illusion

Casting Time: 1 action
Range: Touch
Components: V, S, M (a small sketch of a candle)
Duration: 1 hour

You touch one object that measures less than 10 feet in every dimension. Until the spell ends, the object sheds bright light in a 20-foot radius and dim light for an additional 20 feet. The light can be colored as you like. At the time of the casting, you designate up to six creatures. Only those creatures are able to see and gain benefit from the phantom light.

The object can be covered with something opaque to block the light. You can use an action to dismiss this spell.

PHASE BOLT

3rd-Level Evocation

Casting Time: 1 action
Range: Self (100-foot line)
Components: S, M (a bit of colored glass)
Duration: Instantaneous

You focus ambient energy into a crackling bolt 100 feet long and 5 feet wide. Each creature in the line takes 5d8 force damage, or half as much damage if it makes a successful Dexterity saving throw.

The bolt passes through the first inanimate object in its path, and creatures on the other side of it receive no benefit from cover. The bolt stops if it strikes a second object.

At Higher Levels. When you cast this spell using a spell slot of 4th level or higher, the bolt's damage increases by 1d8 for each slot level above 3rd.

CHAPTER 5 SPELL DESCRIPTIONS

PITFALL

4th-Level Transmutation

Casting Time: 1 action
Range: 60 feet
Components: V, S
Duration: 1 minute

A pit opens under a Huge or smaller creature you can see within range that does not have a flying speed. This pit isn't a simple hole in the floor or ground, but a passage to an extradimensional space. The target must succeed on a Dexterity saving throw or fall into the pit, which closes over it. At the end of your next turn, a new portal opens 20 feet above where the pit was located, and the creature falls out. It lands prone and takes 6d6 bludgeoning damage.

If the original target makes a successful saving throw, you can use a bonus action on your turn to reopen the pit in any location within range that you can see. The spell ends when a creature has fallen through the pit and taken damage, or when the duration expires.

POISONED VOLLEY

2nd-Level Conjuration

Casting Time: 1 action
Range: 60 feet
Components: V, S
Duration: Instantaneous

By drawing back and releasing an imaginary bowstring, you summon forth dozens of glowing green arrows. The arrows dissipate when they hit, but all creatures in a 20-foot square within range take 3d8 poison damage and become poisoned. A creature that makes a successful Constitution saving throw takes half as much damage and is not poisoned.

At Higher Levels. When you cast this spell using a spell slot of 3rd level or higher, the damage increases by 1d8 for each slot level above 2nd.

PORTAL JAUNT

3rd-Level Conjuration (Ritual)

Casting Time: 1 action
Range: 300 feet
Components: V, S, M (a small brass key)
Duration: 1 round

You touch a specially prepared key to a door or gate, turning it into a one-way portal to another such door within range. This spell works with any crafted door, doorway, archway, or any other artificial opening, but not natural or accidental openings such as cave entrances or cracks in walls. You must be aware of your destination or be able to see it from where you cast the spell.

On completing the spell, the touched door opens, revealing a shimmering image of the location beyond the destination door. You can move through the door, emerging instantly out of the destination door. You can also allow one other willing creature to pass through the portal instead. Anything you carry moves through the door with you, including other creatures, willing or unwilling.

For the purpose of this spell, any locks, bars, or magical effects such as *arcane lock* are ineffectual for the spell's duration. You can travel only to a side of the door you can see or have physically visited in the past (divinations such as *clairvoyance* count as seeing). Once you or a willing creature passes through, both doors shut, ending the spell. If you or another creature does not move through the portal within 1 round, the spell ends.

At Higher Levels. When you cast this spell using a spell slot of 4th level or higher, the range increases by 100 feet and the duration increases by 1 round for each slot level above 3rd. Each round added to the duration allows one additional creature to move through the portal before the spell ends.

POTENCY OF THE PACK

3rd-Level Transmutation

Casting Time: 1 action
Range: 25 feet
Components: V, S, M (a few hairs from a wolf)
Duration: 1 minute

You bestow lupine traits on a group of living creatures that you designate within range. Choose one of the following benefits to be gained by all targets for the duration:

- *Thick Fur.* Each target sprouts fur over its entire body, giving it a +2 bonus to Armor Class.
- *Keen Hearing and Smell.* Each target has advantage on Wisdom (Perception) checks that rely on hearing or smell.
- *Pack Tactics.* Each affected creature has advantage on an attack roll against a target if at least one of the attacker's allies (also under the effect of this spell) is within 5 feet of the target of the attack and the ally isn't incapacitated.

At Higher Levels. When you cast this spell using a spell slot of 4th level or higher, the duration increases by 1 minute for each slot level above 3rd.

POWER WORD KNEEL

2nd-Level Enchantment

Casting Time: 1 action
Range: 60 feet
Components: V, S, M (an emerald worth at least 100 gp)
Duration: Instantaneous

When you shout this word of power, creatures within 20 feet of a point you specify are compelled to kneel down facing you. A kneeling creature is treated as prone. Up to 55 hit points of creatures are affected, beginning with those that have the fewest hit points. A kneeling creature makes a Wisdom saving throw at the end of its turn, ending the effect on itself on a successful save. The effect ends immediately on any creature that takes damage while kneeling.

POWER WORD PAIN

4th-Level Enchantment

Casting Time: 1 action
Range: 60 feet
Components: V, S, M (a quill jabbed into your own body)
Duration: Instantaneous

When you utter this word of power, one creature within 60 feet of you takes 4d10 force damage. At the start of each of its turns, the creature must make a successful Constitution saving throw or take an extra 4d10 force damage. The effect ends on a successful save.

PRIMAL INFUSION

5th-Level Transmutation

Casting Time: 1 action
Range: Self
Components: V, S, M (a bit of fur from a carnivorous animal)
Duration: Concentration, up to 1 minute

You channel the fury of nature, drawing on its power. Until the spell ends, you gain the following benefits:

- You gain 30 temporary hit points. If any of these remain when the spell ends, they are lost.
- You have advantage on attack rolls when one of your allies is within 5 feet of the target and the ally isn't incapacitated.
- Your weapon attacks deal an extra 1d10 damage of the same type dealt by the weapon on a hit.
- You gain a +2 bonus to AC.
- You have proficiency on Constitution saving throws.

PRISMATIC RAY

5th-Level Evocation

Casting Time: 1 action
Range: 100 feet
Components: V, S
Duration: Instantaneous

A ray of shifting color springs from your hand. Make a ranged spell attack against a single creature you can see within range. The ray's effect and the saving throw that applies to it depend on which color is dominant when the beam strikes its target, determined by rolling a d8.

d8	Color	Effect	Saving Throw
1	Red	8d10 fire damage	Dexterity
2	Orange	8d10 acid damage	Dexterity
3	Yellow	8d10 lightning damage	Dexterity
4	Green	Target poisoned	Constitution
5	Blue	Target deafened	Constitution
6	Indigo	Target frightened	Wisdom
7	Violet	Target stunned	Constitution
8	Shifting ray	Target blinded	Constitution

A target takes half as much damage on a successful Dexterity saving throw. A successful Constitution or Wisdom saving throw negates the effect of a ray that inflicts a condition on the target; on a failed save, the target is affected for 5 rounds or until the effect is negated. If the result of your attack roll is a critical hit, you can choose the color of the beam that hits the target, but the attack does not deal additional damage.

PROTECTIVE ICE

3rd-Level Abjuration

Casting Time: 1 action
Range: Touch
Components: V, S, M (a seed encased in ice or glass)
Duration: Concentration, up to 1 hour

When you cast *protective ice*, you encase a willing target in icy, medium armor equivalent to a breastplate (AC 14). A creature without the appropriate armor proficiency has the usual penalties. If the target is already wearing armor, it only uses the better of the two armor classes.

A creature striking a target encased in *protective ice* with a melee attack while within 5 feet of it takes 1d6 cold damage.

If the armor's wearer takes fire damage, an equal amount of damage is done to the armor, which has 30 hit points and is damaged only when its wearer takes fire damage. Damaged ice can be repaired by casting a spell that deals cold damage on it, on a point-for-point basis, but the armor can't have more than 30 points repaired.

At Higher Levels. When you cast this spell using a 4th-level spell slot, it creates splint armor (AC 17, 40 hit points). If you cast this spell using a 5th-level spell slot, it creates plate armor (AC 18, 50 hit points). The armor's hit points increase by 10 for each spell slot above 5th, but the AC remains 18. Additionally, if you cast this spell using a spell slot of 4th level or higher, the armor deals an extra +2 cold damage for each spell slot above 3rd.

PROTECTIVE NIMBUS

3rd-Level Abjuration

Casting Time: 1 action
Range: Self
Components: V, S, M (a crystal or glass bead)
Duration: 10 minutes

You wrap yourself in a corona that sheds bright light in a 20-foot radius and dim light for an additional 20 feet. Until the spell ends, you have resistance to necrotic damage. You can end the spell early by using an action to dismiss it.

PUFF OF SMOKE

Evocation Cantrip

Casting Time: 1 bonus action
Range: 30 feet
Components: V, S
Duration: Instantaneous

By harnessing the elemental power of fire, you warp nearby air into obscuring smoke. One creature you can see within range must make a Dexterity saving throw. If it fails, the creature is blinded until the start of your next turn. *Puff of smoke* has no effect on creatures that have tremorsense or blindsight.

PUMMELSTONE

Conjuration Cantrip

Casting Time: 1 action
Range: 60 feet
Components: V, S, M (a pebble)
Duration: Instantaneous

You cause a fist-sized chunk of stone to appear and hurl itself against the spell's target. Make a ranged spell attack. On a hit, the target takes 1d6 bludgeoning damage and must roll a d4 when it makes an attack roll or ability check during its next turn, subtracting the result of the d4 from the attack or check roll.

The spell's damage increases by 1d6 when you reach 5th level (2d6), 11th level (3d6), and 17th level (4d6).

PYROCLASM

9th-Level Evocation

Casting Time: 1 action
Range: 500 feet
Components: V, S, M (a shard of obsidian)
Duration: Concentration, up to 1 minute

You point toward an area of ground or a similar surface within range. A geyser of lava erupts from the chosen spot. The geyser is 5 feet in diameter and 40 feet high. Each creature in the cylinder when it erupts or at the start of your turn takes 10d8 fire damage, or half as much damage if it makes a successful Dexterity saving throw.

The geyser also forms a pool of lava at its base. Initially, the pool is the same size as the geyser, but at the start of each of your turns for the duration, the pool's radius increases by 5 feet. A creature in the pool of lava (but not in the geyser) at the start of your turn takes 5d8 fire damage.

When a creature leaves the pool of lava, its speed is reduced by half and it has disadvantage on Dexterity saving throws, caused by a hardening layer of lava. These penalties last until the creature uses an action to break the hardened stone away from itself.

If you maintain concentration on *pyroclasm* for a full minute, the lava geyser and pool harden into permanent, nonmagical stone. A creature in either area when the stone hardens is restrained until the stone is broken away.

QUENCH

3rd-Level Transmutation

Casting Time: 1 action
Range: 120 feet
Components: V, S, M (a cloth soaked in water)
Duration: Instantaneous

You extinguish all nonmagical fires in a 30-foot-radius area centered on the point at which you cast the spell. You can extinguish fire spells in the area as well. For each fire spell in the area, make a Wisdom check. The DC equals 10 + the spell's level. On a successful check, the spell ends.

Fire elementals in the area take 8d6 cold damage. A successful Constitution saving throw reduces the damage by half.

At Higher Levels. When you cast this spell using a spell slot of 4th level or higher, the radius of the area increases by 10 feet, and the damage against fire elementals increases by 1d6, for each slot level above 3rd.

QUICK TIME

4th-Level Conjuration

Casting Time: 1 action
Range: 30 feet
Components: V, S, M (any seed)
Duration: Instantaneous

You make one living creature or plant within range move rapidly in time compared to you. The target becomes one year older. For example, you could cast this spell on a seedling, which causes the plant to sprout from the soil, or you could cast this spell on a newly hatched duckling, causing it to become a full-grown duck. If the target is a creature with an Intelligence of 3 or higher, it must succeed on a Constitution saving throw to resist the aging. It can choose to fail the saving throw.

At Higher Levels. When you cast this spell using a spell slot of 5th level or higher, you increase the target's age by one additional year for each slot level above 4th.

QUICKEN

Transmutation Cantrip

Casting Time: 1 action
Range: Touch
Components: V, S
Duration: Concentration, up to 1 minute

You touch one willing creature. Once before the duration of the spell expires, the target can roll a d4 and add the number rolled to an initiative roll or Dexterity saving throw it has just made. The spell then ends.

QUICKSILVER MANTLE

4th-Level Transmutation

Casting Time: 1 action
Range: Self
Components: V, S, M (a nonmagical cloak and a dram of quicksilver worth 10 gp)
Duration: 1 hour

You transform an ordinary cloak into a highly reflective, silvery garment. This mantle increases your AC by 2 and grants advantage on saving throws against gaze attacks. In addition, whenever you are struck by a ray such as a *ray of enfeeblement*, *scorching ray*, or even *disintegrate*, roll 1d4. On a result of 4, the cloak deflects the ray, which instead strikes a randomly selected target within 10 feet of you. The cloak deflects only the first ray that strikes it each round; rays after the first affect you as normal.

QUINTESSENCE

8th-Level Transmutation

Casting Time: 1 action
Range: Self (120-foot radius)
Components: V, S
Duration: Concentration, up to 1 minute

By calling upon an archangel, you become infused with celestial essence and take on angelic features such as golden skin, glowing eyes, and ethereal wings. For the duration of the spell, your Armor Class can't be lower than 20, you can't be frightened, and you are immune to necrotic damage.

In addition, each hostile creature that starts its turn within 120 feet of you or enters that area for the first time on a turn must succeed on a Wisdom saving throw or be frightened for 1 minute. A creature frightened in this way is restrained. A frightened creature can repeat the saving throw at the end of each of its turns, ending the effect on itself on a success. If a creature's saving throw is successful or if the effect ends for it, the creature is immune to the frightening effect of the spell until you cast *quintessence* again.

RADIANT BEACON

5th-Level Evocation

Casting Time: 1 action
Range: Self (5-foot radius)
Components: V, S, M (a piece of amber)
Duration: Concentration, up to 1 minute

A pillar of brilliant light falls from the air, filling the square you are in and the area within 5 feet of you. Each other creature in the area must make a Constitution saving throw. On a failed save, a creature takes 4d8 radiant damage and is blinded until the start of your next turn. On a successful save, it takes half as much damage and isn't blinded by this spell. Undead and oozes have disadvantage on this saving throw.

For the duration, a pillar of brilliant radiance shines around you and moves with you. It sheds bright light in a 10-foot radius and dim light for an additional 20 feet. The light is sunlight.

This spell's light can be seen from a distance of up to 10 miles outdoors at night or 5 miles during twilight.

RAID THE LAIR

4th-Level Abjuration

Casting Time: 10 minutes
Range: Self
Components: V, S, M (a piece of the dragon whose lair you are raiding)
Duration: Concentration, up to 1 hour

You create an invisible circle of protective energy centered on yourself with a radius of 10 feet. This field moves with you. The caster and all allies within the energy field are protected against dragons' lair actions:

- Attack rolls resulting directly from lair actions are made with disadvantage.
- Saving throws resulting directly from lair actions are made with advantage, and damage done by these lair actions is halved.
- Lair actions occur on an initiative count 10 lower than normal.

The caster has advantage on Constitution saving throws to maintain concentration on this spell.

RAIN OF BLADES

5th-Level Conjuration

Casting Time: 1 action
Range: 25 feet
Components: V, S, M (shard of metal from a weapon)
Duration: 4 rounds

You call down a rain of swords, spears, and axes. The blades fill 150 square feet (six 5-foot squares, a circle 15 feet in diameter, or any other pattern you want as long as it forms one contiguous space at least 5 feet wide in all places. The blades deal 6d6 slashing damage to each creature in the area at the moment the spell is cast, or half as much damage on a successful Dexterity saving throw. An intelligent undead injured by the blades is frightened for 1d4 rounds if it fails a Charisma saving throw. Most of the blades break or are driven into the ground on impact, but enough survive intact that any single piercing or slashing melee weapon can be salvaged from the affected area and used normally if it is claimed before the spell ends. When the duration expires, all the blades (including the one that was salvaged) disappear.

At Higher Levels. When you cast this spell using a spell slot of 6th level or higher, an unbroken blade can be picked up and used as a magical +1 *weapon* until it disappears.

RAVAGES OF TIME

7th-Level Transmutation

Casting Time: 1 action
Range: 60 feet
Components: V, S, M (a wilted flower)
Duration: 24 hours

You accelerate the aging of one creature within range, causing it to take on the state of a decrepit version of its type. The target suffers three levels of exhaustion that cannot be removed by normal means. A *greater restoration* spell partially reverses the effect of this spell, removing one level of exhaustion. Constructs and undead are unaffected by this spell, and creatures who live to great age without negative effects, such as dragons, are also unaffected.

RAY OF ALCHEMICAL NEGATION

4th-Level Transmutation

Casting Time: 1 action
Range: 60 feet
Components: V, S
Duration: Instantaneous

You launch a ray of blazing, polychromatic energy from your fingertips. Make a ranged spell attack against an alchemical item or a trap that uses alchemy to achieve its ends, such as a trap that sprays acid, releases poisonous gas, or triggers an explosion of alchemist's fire. A hit destroys the alchemical reagents, rendering them harmless. The attack is made against the most suitable object Armor Class.

This spell can also be used against a creature within range that is wholly or partially composed of acidic, poisonous, or alchemical components, such as an alchemical golem or an ochre jelly. In that case, a hit deals 6d6 force damage, and the target must make a successful Constitution saving throw or it deals only half as much damage with its acidic, poisonous, or alchemical attacks for 1 minute. A creature whose damage is halved can repeat the saving throw at the end of each of its turns, ending the effect on a success.

RAY OF LIFE SUPPRESSION

4th-Level Necromancy

Casting Time: 1 action
Range: 60 feet
Components: V, S
Duration: Instantaneous

You launch a swirling ray of disruptive energy at a creature within range. Make a ranged spell attack. On a hit, the creature takes 6d8 necrotic damage and its maximum hit points are reduced by an equal amount. This reduction lasts until the creature finishes a short or long rest, or until it receives the benefit of a *greater restoration* spell or comparable magic.

This spell has no effect on constructs or undead.

READ OBJECT

2nd-Level Divination (Ritual)

Casting Time: 1 minute
Range: Touch
Components: V, S
Duration: Concentration, up to 1 minute

By handling an object and reading the psychic residue on it, you can divine information about the item's history. After you cast the spell, you continue to handle the object, reading any impressions that might be left upon it. Each round, the GM may give you one piece of information related to the item's ownership and handling. The GM might determine that a particular item does not have enough psychic residue to provide any clear impressions. The following are examples of information you can obtain through use of this spell:

- The item's name, if it has one.
- A visual image of the last creature to handle the item.
- An impression of the emotional state of the creature that last used the item.
- If the item is a weapon, or has been used as a weapon, an image of the last creature injured or killed by it.
- A visual image of the item's owner or crafter.
- Information regarding the item's historical significance, if any.

REAVER SPIRIT

3rd-Level Enchantment

Casting Time: 1 action
Range: 30 feet
Components: V, S
Duration: Concentration, up to 1 minute

You inspire allies to fight with the savagery of berserkers. You and any allies you can see within range have advantage on Strength checks and Strength saving throws; resistance to bludgeoning, piercing, and slashing damage from nonmagical attacks; and a +2 bonus to damage with melee weapons.

When the spell ends, each affected creature must succeed on a Constitution saving throw or gain 1d4 levels of exhaustion.

At Higher Levels. When you cast this spell using a spell slot of 4th level or higher, the bonus to damage increases by 1 for each slot level above 2nd.

RECHARGE

5th-Level Evocation (Ritual)

Casting Time: 1 action
Range: Touch
Components: V, S, M (a diamond worth at least 250 gp, which is consumed during the casting)
Duration: Instantaneous

You draw magical energy through yourself as a conduit to recharge a magic item. A single magic item that uses charges and that you are touching at the time of the casting immediately regains 1d3 charges. An item cannot receive more than its maximum number of charges, and any excess energy dissipates harmlessly, unless the item in question is capable of a retributive strike. If such an item is charged past its capacity, it explodes as if you had used an action to enact the retributive strike, with all the resulting effects.

At Higher Levels. When you cast this spell using a spell slot of 6th level or higher, you restore 1 additional charge for each slot level above 5th.

REMOVE SCENT

3rd-Level Transmutation

Casting Time: 1 action
Range: 30 feet
Components: V, S, M (a pinch of charcoal dust)
Duration: Instantaneous

You magically remove strong odors from an area, person, or object. Up to a 40-foot cube or a single creature or object of up to Large size can be affected. A room full of garbage or carrion ceases to smell, for example, or someone sprayed by a skunk no longer bears the odor. If there is still material producing odors in the area, however, the smell will return within an hour. If cast upon the area of a *stinking cloud* spell, it removes the odor and the spell's nauseating qualities, but not the obscuring fog itself.

This spell can also be cast on a single creature of up to Large size, except for one that already gives off a strong odor (such as a troglodyte). For the next hour, the creature has no scent, and it cannot be detected by Wisdom (Perception) checks relying on scent.

REPOSITION

4th-Level Conjuration

Casting Time: 1 bonus action
Range: 30 feet
Components: V
Duration: Instantaneous

You designate up to three friendly creatures (one of which can be yourself) within range. Each target teleports to an unoccupied space of its choosing that it can see within 30 feet of itself.

At Higher Levels. When you cast this spell using a spell slot of 5th level or higher, the spell targets one additional friendly creature for each slot level above 4th.

RESET

4th-Level Transmutation

Casting Time: 1 action
Range: 60 feet
Components: V, S
Duration: Instantaneous

Choose up to four creatures within range. If a target is your ally, it can reroll initiative, keeping whichever of the two results it prefers. If a target is your enemy, it must make a successful Wisdom saving throw or reroll initiative, keeping whichever of the two results you prefer. Changes to the initiative order go into effect at the start of the next round.

At Higher Levels. When you cast this spell using a spell slot of 5th level or higher, you can affect one additional creature for each slot level above 4th.

REVERBERATE

2nd-Level Evocation

Casting Time: 1 action
Range: Self (15-foot cone)
Components: V, S, M (a metal ring)
Duration: Instantaneous

You touch the ground at your feet with the metal ring, creating an impact that shakes the earth ahead of you. Creatures and unattended objects touching the ground in a 15-foot cone emanating from you take 4d6 thunder damage, and creatures fall prone; a creature that makes a successful Dexterity saving throw takes half the damage and does not fall prone.

At Higher Levels. When you cast this spell using a spell slot of 3rd level or higher, the damage increases by 1d6 for each slot level above 2nd.

REVIVE BEAST

2nd-Level Necromancy

Casting Time: 1 action
Range: Touch
Components: V, S, M (emeralds worth 100 gp, which the spell consumes)
Duration: Instantaneous

You touch a beast that has died within the last minute. That beast returns to life with 1 hit point. This spell can't return to life a beast that has died of old age, nor can it restore any missing body parts.

RIGHT THE STARS

7th-Level Divination

Casting Time: 10 minutes
Range: Self
Components: V, S, M (seven black candles and a circle of powdered charred bone or basalt)
Duration: 1 hour

You subtly warp the flow of space and time to enhance your conjurations with cosmic potency. Until the spell ends, the maximum duration of any conjuration spell you cast that requires concentration is doubled, any creature that you summon or create with a conjuration spell has 30 temporary hit points, and you have advantage on Charisma checks and Charisma saving throws.

RING STRIKE

1st-Level Transmutation

Casting Time: 1 action
Range: Self
Components: V, S, M (two metal rings)
Duration: 1 hour

You infuse two metal rings with magic, causing them to revolve in a slow orbit around your head or hand. For the duration, when you hit a target within 60 feet of you with an attack, you can launch one of the rings to strike the target as well. The target takes 1d10 bludgeoning damage and must succeed on a Strength saving throw or be pushed 5 feet directly away from you. The ring is destroyed when it strikes.

At Higher Levels. When you cast this spell using a spell slot of 2nd level or higher, you can affect up to two additional rings for each spell slot level above 1st.

RING WARD

7th-Level Abjuration

Casting Time: 1 action
Range: Self
Components: V, S, M (an iron ring worth 200 gp, which the spell consumes)
Duration: Concentration, up to 1 hour

The iron ring you use to cast the spell becomes a faintly shimmering circlet of energy that spins slowly around you at a radius of 15 feet. For the duration, you and your allies inside the protected area have advantage on saving throws against spells, and all affected creatures gain resistance to one type of damage of your choice.

RIPTIDE

3rd-Level Conjuration

Casting Time: 1 action
Range: 60 feet
Components: V, S
Duration: 1 round

With a sweeping gesture, you cause water to swell up into a 20-foot tall, 20-foot radius cylinder centered on a point on the ground that you can see. Each creature in the cylinder must make a Strength saving throw. On a failed save, the creature is restrained and suspended in the cylinder; on a successful save, the creature moves to just outside the nearest edge of the cylinder.

At the start of your next turn, you can direct the current of the swell as it dissipates. Choose one of the following options:

- ***Riptide.*** The water in the cylinder flows in a direction you choose, sweeping along each creature in the cylinder. An affected creature takes 3d8 bludgeoning damage and is pushed 40 feet in the chosen direction, landing prone.
- ***Undertow.*** The water rushes downward, pulling each creature in the cylinder into an unoccupied space at the center. Each creature is knocked prone and must make a successful Constitution saving throw or be stunned until the start of your next turn.

ROAMING PAIN

1st-Level Necromancy

Casting Time: 1 action
Range: 30 feet
Components: V, S
Duration: Concentration, up to 1 minute

You afflict a single humanoid within range with severe pain in a random part of its body. Roll a d6 and consult the table to determine the spell's initial effect.

d6	Body Part	Effect
1	Head	Incapacitated
2	Throat	Unable to speak coherently or cast spells with verbal components
3	Chest	Cannot take reactions or bonus actions
4	Abdomen	Disadvantage on Constitution saving throws
5	Arm	Disadvantage on attack rolls, Strength and Dexterity skill checks
6	Leg	Movement halved

The target must make a Constitution saving throw. On a successful save, it is able to function despite the pain and ignore the effects. At the start of the target's turn each round for the duration of the spell, roll again on the table to see where the pain affects the target in that round.

ROARING WINDS OF LIMBO

8th-Level Conjuration

Casting Time: 1 action

Range: 150 feet

Components: V, S

Duration: Concentration, up to 1 minute

You tear open a breach to the planes of chaos, and the act of doing so fills an area with a dangerous windstorm. The area consists of twelve 10-foot cubes, which you can arrange as you wish. Each cube must have at least one face in common with a face of another cube. Each creature in the area is deafened, and any sound it makes cannot be heard outside the area. The wind disperses all gases and vapors and extinguishes all unprotected flames in the area, and has a 75 percent chance of extinguishing protected flames, such as lanterns. All Wisdom (Perception) checks that rely on sight made by a creature in the area have disadvantage due to the dust, grit, and debris being cast about.

Each creature in the area must make a Strength saving throw at the start of its turn. On a failed save, the creature is pushed 15 feet in a random direction. (Roll a d8, designating 1 as north, 2 as northeast, 3 as east, and so on around the points of the compass.) The wind also hampers movement; a creature in the area must spend 2 feet of movement for every 1 foot it moves.

As a bonus action on each of your turns, you can bombard up to twelve creatures in the area with flying debris, dealing 2d10 bludgeoning, 2d10 piercing, and 2d10 slashing damage. A creature that makes a successful Dexterity saving throw takes half the damage.

ROLLING THUNDER

2nd-Level Evocation

Casting Time: 1 action

Range: Self (30-foot line)

Components: V, S, M (a sliver of metal from a gong)

Duration: Instantaneous

A tremendous bell note explodes from your outstretched hand and rolls forward in a line 30 feet long and 5 feet wide. Each creature in the line must make a successful Constitution saving throw or be deafened for 1 minute. A creature made of material such as stone, crystal, or metal has disadvantage on its saving throw against this spell.

While a creature is deafened in this way, it is wreathed in thundering energy; it takes 2d8 thunder damage at the start of its turn, and its speed is halved. A deafened creature can repeat the saving throw at the end of each of its turns, ending the effect on itself on a success.

At Higher Levels. When you cast this spell using a spell slot of 3rd level or higher, the damage increases by 1d8 for each slot level above 2nd.

ROTTING CORPSE

2nd-Level Necromancy

Casting Time: 10 minutes

Range: Touch

Components: V, M (a rotting piece of flesh from an undead creature)

Duration: 3 days

Your familiarity with the foul effects of death allows you to prevent a dead body from being returned to life using anything but the most powerful forms of magic.

You cast this spell by touching a creature that died within the last 24 hours. The body immediately decomposes to a state that prevents the body from being returned to life by the *raise dead* spell (though a *resurrection* spell still works). At the end of this spell's duration, the body decomposes to a rancid slime, and it can't be returned to life except through a *true resurrection* spell.

At Higher Levels. When you cast this spell using a spell slot of 3rd level or higher, you can affect one additional corpse for each slot level above 2nd.

RUNE OF IMPRISONMENT

3rd-Level Abjuration

Casting Time: 1 action

Range: 30 feet

Components: V, S, M (ink)

Duration: Concentration, up to 1 minute

You trace a glowing black rune in the air which streaks toward and envelops its target. Make a ranged spell attack against the target. On a successful hit, the rune absorbs the target creature, leaving only the glowing rune hanging in the space the target occupied. The subject can take no actions while imprisoned, nor can the subject be targeted or affected by any means. Any spell durations or conditions affecting the creature are postponed until the creature is freed. A dying creature does not lose hit points or stabilize until freed.

A creature adjacent to the rune can use a move action to attempt to disrupt its energies; doing so allows the imprisoned creature to make a Wisdom saving throw. On a success, this disruption negates the imprisonment and ends the effect. Disruption can be attempted only once per round.

SACRIFICIAL HEALING

4th-Level Necromancy (Ritual)

Casting Time: 1 action
Range: Touch
Components: V, S, M (a silver knife)
Duration: Instantaneous

You heal another creature's wounds by taking them upon yourself or transferring them to another willing creature in range. Roll 4d8. The number rolled is the amount of damage healed by the target and the damage you take, as its wounds close and similar damage appears on your body (or the body of the other willing target of the spell).

SALT LASH

3rd-Level Conjuration

Casting Time: 1 action
Range: Self
Components: V, S, M (a pinch of salt worth 1 sp, which is consumed during the casting)
Duration: Concentration, up to 10 minutes

You create a long, thin blade of razor-sharp salt crystals. You can wield it as a longsword, using your spellcasting ability to modify your weapon attack rolls. The sword deals 2d8 slashing damage on a hit, and any creature struck by the blade must make a successful Constitution saving throw or be stunned by searing pain until the start of your next turn. Constructs and undead are immune to the blade's secondary (stun) effect; plants and creatures composed mostly of water, such as water elementals, also take an additional 2d8 necrotic damage if they fail the saving throw.

The spell lasts until you stop concentrating on it, the duration expires, or you let go of the blade for any reason.

SAND SHIP

4th-Level Transmutation (Ritual)

Casting Time: 1 minute
Range: 30 feet
Components: V, S, M (a boat or ship of 10,000 gp value or less)
Duration: 24 hours

Casting *sand ship* on a water vessel up to the size of a small sailing ship transforms it into a vessel capable of sailing on sand as easily as water. The vessel still needs a trained crew and relies on wind or oars for propulsion, but it moves at its normal speed across sand instead of water for the duration of the spell. It can sail only over sand, not soil or solid rock. For the duration of the spell, the vessel doesn't float; it must be beached or resting on the bottom of a body of water (partially drawn up onto a beach, for example) when the spell is cast, or it sinks into the water.

SANGUINE HORROR

5th-Level Conjuration

Casting Time: 1 action
Range: 5 feet
Components: V, S, M (a miniature dagger)
Duration: Concentration, up to 1 hour

When you cast this spell, you prick yourself with the material component, taking 1 piercing damage. The spell fails if this damage is prevented or negated in any way. From the drop of blood, you conjure a **blood elemental** (see *Creature Codex*). The blood elemental is friendly to you and your companions for the duration. It disappears when it's reduced to 0 hit points or when the spell ends.

Roll initiative for the elemental, which has its own turns. It obeys verbal commands from you (no action required by you). If you don't issue any commands to the blood elemental, it defends itself but otherwise takes no actions. If your concentration is broken, the blood elemental doesn't disappear, but you lose control of it and it becomes hostile to you and your companions. An uncontrolled blood elemental cannot be dismissed by you, and it disappears 1 hour after you summoned it.

SCALE ROT

4th-Level Necromancy

Casting Time: 1 action
Range: 30 feet
Components: V, S, M (a piece of rotten meat)
Duration: Concentration, up to 1 minute

You summon death and decay to plague your enemies. For dragons, this act often takes the form of attacking a foe's armor and scales, as a way of weakening an enemy dragon and leaving it plagued by self-doubt and fear. (This enchantment is useful against any armored creature, not just dragons.)

One creature of your choice within range that has natural armor must make a Constitution saving throw. If it fails, attacks against that creature's Armor Class are made with advantage, and the creature can't regain hit points through any means while the spell remains in effect. An affected creature can end the spell by making a successful Constitution saving throw, which also makes the creature immune to further castings of *scale rot* for 24 hours.

At Higher Levels. When you cast this spell using a spell slot of 5th level or higher, the number of affected targets increases by one for each slot level above 4th.

SCALY HIDE

4th-Level Transmutation

Casting Time: 1 action
Range: Touch
Components: V, S, M (a dragon scale)
Duration: Concentration, up to 10 minutes

A creature you touch grows a protective layer of scales that resembles that of a dragon. Until the spell ends, the target's AC can't be lower than 16, regardless of the type of armor it is wearing. Additionally, the target gains resistance to either acid, cold, fire, lightning, or poison damage for the duration of the spell.

SCENTLESS

1st-Level Transmutation

Casting Time: 1 action
Range: Touch
Components: V, S, M (1 ounce of pure water)
Duration: 1 hour

You touch a willing creature or object that is not being worn or carried. For the duration, the target gives off no odor. A creature that relies on smell has disadvantage on Wisdom (Perception) checks to detect the target and Wisdom (Survival) checks to track the target. The target is invisible to a creature that relies solely on smell to sense its surroundings. This spell has no effect on targets with unusually strong scents, such as ghasts.

SCREAMING RAY

1st-Level Evocation

Casting Time: 1 action
Range: 30 feet
Components: V, S
Duration: Instantaneous

You create a ray of psychic energy to attack your enemies. Make a ranged spell attack against a creature. On a hit, the target takes 1d4 psychic damage and is deafened until the end of your next turn. If the target succeeds on a Constitution saving throw, it is not deafened.

At Higher Levels. When you cast this spell using a spell slot of 2nd level or higher, you create one additional ray for each slot level above 1st. You can direct the rays at one target or several.

SCRIBE

Transmutation Cantrip

Casting Time: 1 action
Range: Touch
Components: V, S
Duration: Instantaneous

This spell enables you to create a copy of a one-page written work by placing a blank piece of paper or parchment near the work that you are copying. All the writing, illustrations, and other elements in the original are reproduced in the new document, in your handwriting

or drawing style. The new medium must be large enough to accommodate the original source. Any magical properties of the original aren't reproduced, so you can't use *scribe* to make copies of spell scrolls or magic books.

SCRY AMBUSH

4th-Level Divination

Casting Time: 1 reaction, which you take when an enemy tries to make a surprise attack against you
Range: Self
Components: V, S
Duration: Instantaneous

You foresee your foe's strike a split second before it occurs. When you cast this spell successfully, you also designate a number of your allies that can see or hear you equal to your spellcasting ability modifier + your proficiency bonus. Those allies are also not surprised by the attack and can act normally in the first round of combat.

If you would be surprised, you must make a check using your spellcasting ability at the moment your reaction would be triggered. The check DC is equal to the current initiative count. On a failed check, you are surprised and can't use your reaction to cast this spell until after your next turn. On a successful check, you can use your reaction to cast this spell immediately.

SCULPT SNOW

2nd-Level Transmutation

Casting Time: 1 action
Range: 60 feet
Components: V, S
Duration: Instantaneous

When targeting an area filled with snow, you can create one Large object, two Medium objects, or four smaller objects from snow. With a casting time of 1 action, your sculptures bear only a crude resemblance to generic creatures or objects. If you increase the casting time to 1 minute, your creations take on a more realistic appearance and can even vaguely resemble specific creatures; the resemblance isn't strong enough to fool anyone, but the creature can be recognized. The sculptures are as durable as a typical snowman.

Sculptures created by this spell can be animated with *animate objects* or comparable magic. Animated sculptures gain the AC, hit points, and other attributes provided by that spell. When they attack, they deal normal damage plus a similar amount of cold damage; an animated Medium sculpture, for example, deals 2d6 + 1 bludgeoning damage plus 2d6 + 1 cold damage.

At Higher Levels. When you cast this spell using a spell slot of 3rd level or higher, you can sculpt one additional Large object for each slot level above 2nd. Two Large objects can be replaced with one Huge object.

SEAL OF SANCTUARY

7th-Level Abjuration (Ritual)

Casting Time: 1 minute
Range: Touch
Components: V, S, M (incense and special inks worth 250 gp, which the spell consumes)
Duration: 24 hours

You inscribe an angelic seal on the ground, the floor, or other solid surface of a structure. The seal creates a spherical sanctuary with a radius of 50 feet, centered on the seal. For the duration, aberrations, elementals, fey, fiends, and undead that approach to within 5 feet of the boundary know they are about to come into contact with a deadly barrier. If such a creature moves so as to touch the boundary, or tries to cross the boundary by any means, including teleportation and extradimensional travel, it must make a Charisma saving throw. On a failed save, it takes 10d8 radiant damage, is repelled to 5 feet outside the boundary, and can't target anything inside the boundary with attacks, spells, or abilities until the spell ends. On a successful save, the creature takes half as much radiant damage and can cross the boundary. If the creature is a fiend that isn't on its home plane, it is immediately destroyed (no saving throw) instead of taking damage.

Aberrations, elementals, fey, and undead that are within 50 feet of the seal (inside the boundary) have disadvantage on ability checks, attack rolls, and saving throws, and each such creature takes 2d8 radiant damage at the start of its turn.

Creatures other than aberrations, elementals, fiends, and undead can't be charmed or frightened while within 50 feet of the seal.

The seal has AC 18, 50 hit points, resistance to bludgeoning, piercing, and slashing damage, and immunity to psychic and poison damage. Ranged attacks against the seal are made with disadvantage. If it is scribed on the surface of an object that is later destroyed (such as a wooden door), the seal is not damaged and remains in place, perhaps suspended in midair. The spell ends only if the seal is reduced to 0 hit points.

SEARING SUN

4th-Level Transmutation

Casting Time: 1 action
Range: 200 feet
Components: V, S, M (a magnifying lens)
Duration: Concentration, up to 1 minute

This spell intensifies the light and heat of the sun, so that it burns exposed flesh. You must be able to see the sun when you cast the spell. The searing sunlight affects a cylindrical area 50 feet in radius and 200 feet high, centered on a point within range. Each creature that starts its turn in that area takes 5d8 fire damage, or half the damage with a successful Constitution saving throw. A creature that's shaded by a solid object —such as an awning, a building, or an overhanging boulder— has advantage on the saving throw. On your turn, you can use an action to move the center of the cylinder up to 20 feet along the ground in any direction.

SEE BEYOND

5th-Level Divination

Casting Time: 1 action
Range: Touch
Components: V, S, M (a transparent crystal)
Duration: Concentration, up to 1 hour

This spell enables a willing creature you touch to see through any obstructions as if they were transparent. For the duration, the target can see into and through opaque objects, creatures, spells, and effects that obstruct line of sight to a range of 30 feet. Inside that distance, the creature can choose what it perceives as opaque and what it perceives as transparent as freely and as naturally as it can shift its focus from nearby to distant objects.

Although the creature can see any target within 30 feet of itself, all other requirements must still be satisfied before casting a spell or making an attack against that target. For example, the creature can see an enemy that has total cover but can't shoot that enemy with an arrow because the cover physically prevents it. That enemy could be targeted by a *geas* spell, however, because *geas* needs only a visible target.

SEED OF DESTRUCTION

8th-Level Enchantment (Ritual)

Casting Time: 1 action
Range: 60 feet
Components: V, S, M (five teeth from a still-living humanoid and a vial of the caster's blood)
Duration: 1 hour

This spell impregnates a living creature with a rapidly gestating hydra that consumes the target from within before emerging to wreak havoc on the world. Make a ranged spell attack against a living creature within range that you can see. On a hit, you implant a five-headed embryonic growth into the creature. Roll 1d3 + 1 to determine how many rounds it takes the embryo to mature.

During the rounds when the embryo is gestating, the affected creature takes 5d4 slashing damage at the start of its turn, or half the damage with a successful Constitution saving throw.

When the gestation period has elapsed, a tiny hydra erupts from the target's abdomen at the start of your turn. The hydra appears in an unoccupied space adjacent to the target and immediately grows into a full-size Huge aberration. Nearby creatures are pushed away to clear a sufficient space as the hydra grows. This creature is a standard hydra, but with the ability to cast *bane* as an action (spell save DC 11) requiring no spell components. Roll initiative for the hydra, which takes its own turns. It obeys verbal commands that you issue to it (no action required by you). If you don't give it a command or it can't follow your command, the hydra attacks the nearest living creature.

At the end of each of the hydra's turns, you must make a DC 15 Charisma saving throw. On a successful save, the hydra remains under your control and friendly to you and your companions. On a failed save, your control ends, the hydra becomes hostile to all creatures, and it attacks the nearest creature to the best of its ability.

The hydra disappears at the end of the spell's duration, or its existence can be cut short with a *wish* spell or comparable magic, but nothing less. The embryo can be destroyed before it reaches maturity by using a *dispel magic* spell under the normal rules for dispelling high-level magic.

SEER'S REACTION

1st-Level Divination

Casting Time: 1 reaction, which you take at the start of another creature's turn
Range: Self
Components: V, S
Duration: Instantaneous

Your foreknowledge allows you to act before others, because you knew what was going to happen. When you cast this spell, make a new initiative roll with a +5 bonus. If the result is higher than your current initiative, your place in the initiative order changes accordingly. If the result is also higher than the current place in the initiative order, you take your next turn immediately and then use the higher number starting in the next round.

SEMBLANCE OF DREAD

Illusion Cantrip

Casting Time: 1 action
Range: Self (10-foot radius)
Components: V, S
Duration: Concentration, up to 1 minute

You adopt the visage of the faceless god Nyarlathotep. For the duration, any creature within 10 feet of you and able to see you can't willingly move closer to you unless it makes a successful Wisdom saving throw at the start of its turn. Constructs and undead are immune to this effect.

For the duration of the spell, you also gain vulnerability to radiant damage and have advantage on saving throws against effects that cause the frightened condition.

SHADE

2nd-Level Abjuration

Casting Time: 1 action
Range: Self
Components: V, S
Duration: Concentration, up to 10 minutes

You create a magical screen across your eyes. While the screen remains, you are immune to blindness caused by visible effects, such as *color spray*. The spell doesn't alleviate blindness that's already been inflicted on you. If you normally suffer penalties on attacks or ability checks while in sunlight, those penalties don't apply while you're under the effect of this spell.

At Higher Levels. When you cast this spell using a spell slot of 3rd level or higher, the duration of the spell increases by 10 minutes for each slot level above 2nd.

SHARED SACRIFICE

2nd-Level Evocation

Casting Time: 1 minute
Range: 60 feet
Components: V, S
Duration: 1 hour

You and up to five of your allies within range contribute part of your life force to create a pool that can be used for healing. Each target takes 5 necrotic damage (which can't be reduced but can be healed normally), and those donated hit points are channeled into a reservoir of life essence. As an action, any creature who contributed to the pool of hit points can heal another creature by touching it and drawing hit points from the pool into the injured creature. The injured creature heals a number of hit points equal to your spellcasting ability modifier, and the hit points in the pool decrease by the same amount. This process can be repeated until the pool is exhausted or the spell ends.

SHEEN OF ICE

2nd-Level Evocation

Casting Time: 1 action
Range: 60 feet
Components: V, S, M (water within a glass globe)
Duration: 1 minute

An icy globe shoots from your finger to a point within range and then explodes in a spray of ice. Each creature within 20 feet of that point must make a successful Dexterity saving throw or become coated in ice for 1 minute. Ice-coated creatures move at half speed. An invisible creature becomes outlined by the ice so that it loses the benefits of invisibility while the ice remains. The spell ends for a specific creature if that creature takes 5 or more fire damage.

SHIELD OF STARLIGHT

3rd-Level Abjuration

Casting Time: 1 action
Range: Self
Components: V, S, M (a star chart)
Duration: 10 minutes

You wrap yourself in a protective shroud of the night sky made from swirling shadows and punctuated by twinkling motes of light. The shroud grants you resistance against either radiant or necrotic damage (your choice when the spell is cast). You also shed dim light in a 10-foot radius. You can end the spell early by using an action to dismiss it.

SHIFTING THE ODDS

2nd-Level Divination

Casting Time: 1 bonus action
Range: Self
Components: V
Duration: Instantaneous

By wrapping yourself in strands of chaotic energy, you gain advantage on the next attack roll or ability check that you make. Fate is a cruel mistress, however, and her scales must always be balanced. The second attack roll or ability check (whichever occurs first) that you make after casting *shifting the odds* is made with disadvantage.

SHIVER

Evocation Cantrip

Casting Time: 1 action
Range: 30 ft.
Components: V, S, M (humanoid tooth)
Duration: 1 round

You fill a humanoid creature with such cold that its teeth begin to chatter and its body shakes uncontrollably. Roll 5d8; the total is the maximum hit points of a creature this spell can affect. The affected creature must succeed on a Constitution saving throw, or it cannot cast a spell or load a missile weapon until the end of your next turn. Once a creature has been affected by this spell, it is immune to further castings of this spell for 24 hours.

The maximum hit points you can affect increases by 4d8 when you reach 5th level (9d8), 11th level (13d8), and 17th level (17d8).

SHOCKING SHROUD

4th-Level Evocation

Casting Time: 1 action
Range: Self
Components: V, S, M (a bit of fur and a bead of amber, crystal, or glass)
Duration: 10 minutes

Arcs of electricity dance over your body for the duration, granting you resistance to lightning damage. You can end the spell early by using an action to dismiss it.

In addition, whenever a creature within 5 feet of you hits you with a melee attack, arcs of electricity strike your attacker, who takes 2d8 lightning damage.

SHROUD OF DEATH

4th-Level Necromancy

Casting Time: 1 action
Range: Self (30-foot radius)
Components: V, S, M (a piece of ice)
Duration: Concentration, up to 10 rounds

You call up a black veil of necrotic energy that devours the living. You draw on the life energy of all living creatures within 30 feet of you that you can see. When you cast the spell, every living creature within 30 feet of you that you can see takes 1 necrotic damage, and all those hit points transfer to you as temporary hit points. The damage and the temporary hit points increase to 2 per creature at the start of your second turn concentrating on the spell, 3 per creature at the start of your third turn, and so on. All living creatures you can see within 30 feet of you at the start of each of your turns are affected. A creature can avoid the effect by moving more than 30 feet away from you or by getting out of your line of sight, but it becomes susceptible again if the necessary conditions are met. The temporary hit points last until the spell ends.

SIDESTEP ARROW

3rd-Level Divination

Casting Time: 1 reaction, which you take when an enemy targets you with a ranged attack
Range: Self
Components: V, S
Duration: Instantaneous

With a few perfectly timed steps, you interpose a foe between you and danger. You cast this spell when an enemy makes a ranged attack or a ranged spell attack against you but before the attack is resolved. At least one other foe must be within 10 feet of you when you cast *sidestep arrow*. As part of casting the spell, you can move up to 15 feet to a place where an enemy lies between you and the attacker. If no such location is available, the spell has no effect. You must be able to move (not restrained or grappled or prevented from moving for any other reason), and this move does not provoke opportunity attacks. After you move, the ranged attack is resolved with the intervening foe as the target instead of you.

SIGN OF KOTH

7th-Level Abjuration

Casting Time: 1 turn
Range: Self (60-foot radius)
Components: V, S, M (a platinum dagger and a powdered black pearl worth 500 gp, which the spell consumes)
Duration: Until dispelled

You invoke the twilight citadels of Koth to create a field of magical energy in the shape of a 60-foot-radius, 60-foot-tall cylinder centered on you. The only visible evidence of this field is a black rune that appears on every doorway, window, or other portal inside the area.

Choose one of the following creature types: aberration, beast, celestial, dragon, elemental, fey, fiend, giant, humanoid, monstrosity, ooze, plant, or undead. The sign affects creatures of the chosen type (including you, if applicable) in the following ways:

- The creatures can't willingly enter the cylinder's area by nonmagical means; the cylinder acts as an invisible, impenetrable wall of force. If an affected creature tries to enter the cylinder's area by using teleportation, a dimensional shortcut, or other magical means, it must make a successful Charisma saving throw or the attempt fails.
- They cannot hear any sounds that originate inside the cylinder.
- They have disadvantage on attack rolls against targets inside the cylinder.
- They can't charm, frighten, or possess creatures inside the cylinder.

Creatures that aren't affected by the field and that take a short rest inside it regain twice the usual number of hit points for each Hit Die spent at the end of the rest.

When you cast this spell, you can choose to reverse its magic; doing this will prevent affected creatures from leaving the area instead of from entering it, make them unable to hear sounds that originate outside the cylinder, and so forth. In this case, the field provides no benefit for taking a short rest.

At Higher Levels. When you cast this spell using a spell slot of 8th level or higher, the radius increases by 30 feet for each slot level above 7th.

SIR MITTINZ'S MOVE CURSE

3rd-Level Transmutation (Ritual)

Casting Time: 1 hour
Range: 20 feet
Components: V, S, M (a finely crafted hollow glass sphere and incense worth 50 gp, which the spell consumes)
Duration: Instantaneous

When you are within range of a cursed creature or object, you can transfer the curse to a different creature or object that's also within range. The curse must be transferred from object to object or from creature to creature.

SLEEP OF THE DEEP

3rd-Level Illusion (Ritual)

Casting Time: 1 action
Range: 60-foot radius
Components: V, S, M (a pinch of black sand, a tallow candle, and a drop of cephalopod ink)
Duration: 8 hours

Your magic haunts the dreams of others. Choose a sleeping creature that you are aware of within range. Creatures that don't sleep, such as elves, can't be targeted. The creature must succeed on a Wisdom saving throw or it garners no benefit from the rest, and when it awakens, it gains one level of exhaustion and is afflicted with short-term madness.

At Higher Levels. When you cast this spell using a spell slot of 4th level or higher, you can affect one additional creature for each slot level above 3rd.

SLIPPERY FINGERS

1st-Level Enchantment

Casting Time: 1 bonus action
Range: 30 feet
Components: V, S
Duration: Instantaneous

You set a series of small events in motion that cause the targeted creature to drop one nonmagical item of your choice that it's currently holding, unless it makes a successful Charisma saving throw.

SMITING ARROW

6th-Level Evocation (Ritual)

Casting Time: 1 action
Range: Touch
Components: V, S, M (an arrow and a drop of blood, strand of hair, or small personal item)
Duration: 24 hours

By casting this spell, you imbue a piece of ammunition to have greater effect on a specific target. To this end, you need something directly associated with the creature for which the arrow is intended—a drop of its blood, a strand of its hair, an item of clothing it recently wore, or something similar—which is consumed in the casting of the spell. For the next 24 hours, if the ammunition is used to make a ranged attack against the specific target and it hits, it deals an extra 6d10 radiant damage to the target and stuns it for 1 round. If the target makes a successful Constitution saving throw, it takes half as much radiant damage and is not stunned. If the attack is a critical hit, the creature has disadvantage on its saving throw.

SNAP THE LEASH

2nd-Level Enchantment

Casting Time: 1 action
Range: 30 feet
Components: V, S, M (a used leash or similar object)
Duration: Instantaneous

Choose a beast that you can see within range. If the beast's Intelligence is 4 or higher, the spell fails. The beast must make a Wisdom saving throw; on a failed save, you remove the shackles of domestication from the creature's mind, causing it to entirely forget being broken or trained. Mounts refuse to be ridden, and other animals forget any tricks learned and obedience taught. Other memories are not affected, so creatures might remain drawn to those who have treated them kindly and aggressive toward those who have harmed them. The animal can be domesticated again, but the trainer must start from scratch.

This spell is only partly effective against animal companions, familiars, and paladin mounts. Although the spell removes any tricks such creatures know, the bond between creature and master is otherwise unaffected.

SNOW BOULDER

4th-Level Transmutation

Casting Time: 1 action
Range: 90 feet
Components: V, S, M (a handful of snow)
Duration: Concentration, up to 4 rounds

A ball of snow forms 5 feet away from you and rolls in the direction you point at a speed of 30 feet, growing larger as it moves. To roll the boulder into a creature, you must make a successful ranged spell attack. If the boulder hits, the creature must make a successful Dexterity saving throw or be knocked prone and take the damage indicated below. Hitting a creature doesn't stop the snow boulder's movement or impede its growth, as long as you continue to maintain concentration on the effect. When the spell ends, the boulder stops moving.

Round	Size	Damage
1	Small	1d6 bludgeoning
2	Medium	2d6 bludgeoning
3	Large	4d6 bludgeoning
4	Huge	6d6 bludgeoning

SNOW FORT

2nd-Level Conjuration

Casting Time: 1 action
Range: 120 feet
Components: V, S, M (a ring carved from chalk)
Duration: Instantaneous

This spell creates a simple "fort" from packed snow. The snow fort springs from the ground in an unoccupied space within range. It encircles a 10-foot area with sloping walls 4 feet high. The fort provides half cover (+2 AC) against ranged and melee attacks coming from outside the fort. The walls have AC 12, 30 hit points per side, are immune to cold, necrotic, poison, and psychic damage, and are vulnerable to fire damage. A damaged wall can be repaired by casting a spell that deals cold damage on it, on a point-for-point basis, up to a maximum of 30 points.

The spell also creates a dozen snowballs that can be thrown (range 20/60) and that deal 1d4 bludgeoning damage plus 1d4 cold damage on a hit.

SNOWY COAT

1st-Level Transmutation

Casting Time: 1 action
Range: Touch
Components: V, S
Duration: Concentration, up to 1 hour

This spell makes a slight alteration to a target creature's appearance that gives it advantage on Dexterity (Stealth) checks to hide in snowy terrain. In addition, the target can use a bonus action to make itself invisible in snowy terrain for 1 minute. The spell ends at the end of the minute or when the creature attacks or casts a spell.

At Higher Levels. When you cast this spell using a spell slot of 2nd level or higher, you can target one additional creature for each slot level above 1st.

SOOTHING CHANT

3rd-Level Abjuration

Casting Time: 1 action
Range: Self
Components: V
Duration: Concentration, up to 1 minute

Intoning a lulling drone, you convince creatures not to do you harm. At the beginning of its turn, any creature that can hear you must make a Wisdom saving throw. On a failed save, the creature is charmed. A creature charmed by *soothing chant* can still act aggressively toward your allies. If it uses area attacks, the creature will position them so as not to include you in the area. On a successful save, a creature can act against you normally, but it must make another saving throw in every round when you continue to chant, and it can hear you.

On your turn, you can use a bonus action to designate up to six other creatures that the charmed creatures will not attack.

The effects last for the duration or until you (or any other designated creatures) engage in hostile action against a charmed creature or in its presence. Any creature that you attack or target with a harmful spell, or that sees you attack or cast a harmful spell against another charmed creature, is no longer affected by this spell and can act normally against you (or against any creature you designated).

SOOTHING INCANDESCENCE

7th-Level Evocation

Casting Time: 1 action
Range: Self (30-foot radius)
Components: V, S
Duration: Concentration, up to 1 hour

A soft, white radiance spreads out from a point just above your head, creating bright light in a 30-foot radius around your present location. If you move from your present location, the area of light remains fixed. A creature in the area other than a fiend or an undead regains 1 hit point at the start of each of its turns while within the bright light. Each fiend or undead in the area takes 2d4 radiant damage at the start of each of its turns.

SOUL BORROWING

3rd-Level Necromancy

Casting Time: 1 action
Range: Touch
Components: V, S, M (a polished vampire's fang)
Duration: 1 minute

By touching a creature, you gain one sense, movement mode and speed, feat, language, immunity, or other nonmagical ability of the target for the duration of the spell. The target also retains the use of the borrowed ability. An unwilling target prevents the effect with a successful Constitution saving throw. The target can be a living creature or one that has been dead no longer than 1 minute; a corpse automatically fails the saving throw. You can possess only one borrowed ability at a time.

At Higher Levels. When you cast this spell using a spell slot of 5th level or higher, its duration increases to 1 hour and the target loses the stolen power for the duration of the spell.

SPEAK WITH INANIMATE OBJECT

1st-Level Divination (Ritual)

Casting Time: 1 action
Range: Touch
Components: V, S
Duration: 10 minutes

You awaken a spirit that resides inside an inanimate object such as a rock, a sign, or a table, and can ask it up to three yes-or-no questions. The spirit is indifferent toward you unless you have done something to harm or help it. The spirit can give you information about its environment and about things it has observed (with its limited senses), and it can act as a spy for you in certain situations. The spell ends when its duration expires or after you have received answers to three questions.

SPECTRAL HERD

4th-Level Conjuration

Casting Time: 1 action
Range: 30 feet
Components: V, S
Duration: 1 minute

You summon a spectral herd of ponies to drag off a creature that you can see within range. The target must be Large or smaller. If it gets a failure on a Dexterity saving throw, a spectral rope wraps around the target, which falls prone and is restrained. It is immediately pulled 60 feet behind the galloping herd, in a direction of your choosing. The target also takes 3d6 bludgeoning damage from being dragged across the ground.

While the target is restrained in this way, it is dragged another 60 feet and takes another 3d6 bludgeoning damage at the start of each of your turns. The ponies continue running in the chosen direction for the duration of the spell. Once the direction is chosen, you can't change it, but the ponies do swerve around impassable obstacles. They ignore difficult terrain and are immune to damage.

The restrained creature can escape by using its action to make a successful Strength or Dexterity check against your spell DC. The spectral rope can't be severed.

At Higher Levels. When you cast this spell using a spell slot of 5th level or higher, one additional creature can be targeted for each slot level above 4th.

SPIN

2nd-Level Enchantment

Casting Time: 1 action
Range: 60 feet
Components: V, S
Duration: 1 minute

You designate a creature you can see within range and tell it to spin. The creature can resist this command with a successful Wisdom saving throw. On a failed save, the creature spins in place for the duration of the spell. A spinning creature can repeat the saving throw at the end of each of its turns, ending the effect on itself on a success. A creature that has spun for 1 round or longer becomes dizzy and has disadvantage on attack rolls and ability checks until 1 round after it stops spinning.

SPINNING AXES

4th-Level Evocation

Casting Time: 1 action
Range: Self
Components: V, S, M (an iron ring)
Duration: Instantaneous

Spinning axes made of luminous force burst out from you to strike all creatures within 10 feet of you. Each of those creatures takes 5d8 force damage, or half the damage with a successful Dexterity saving throw. Creatures damaged by this spell that aren't undead or constructs begin bleeding. A bleeding creature takes 2d6 necrotic damage at the end of each of its turns for 1 minute. A creature can stop the bleeding for itself or another creature by using an action to make a successful Wisdom (Medicine) check against your spell save DC or by applying any amount of magical healing.

At Higher Levels. When you cast this spell using a spell slot of 5th level or higher, the damage increases by 1d8 for each slot level above 4th.

SPITEFUL WEAPON

3rd-Level Necromancy

Casting Time: 1 action
Range: 25 feet
Components: V, S, M (a melee weapon that has been used to injure the target)
Duration: Concentration, up to 5 rounds

You create a connection between the target of the spell, an attacker that injured the target during the last 24 hours, and the melee weapon that caused the injury, all of which must be within range when the spell is cast.

For the duration of the spell, whenever the attacker takes damage while holding the weapon, the target must make a Charisma saving throw. On a failed save, the target takes the same amount and type of damage, or half as much damage on a successful one. The attacker can use the weapon on itself and thus cause the target to take identical damage. A self-inflicted wound hits automatically, but damage is still rolled randomly.

Once the connection is established, it lasts for the duration of the spell regardless of range, so long as all three elements remain on the same plane. The spell ends immediately if the attacker receives any healing.

At Higher Levels. The target has disadvantage on its Charisma saving throws if *spiteful weapon* is cast using a spell slot of 5th level or higher.

SPUR MOUNT

1st-Level Transmutation

Casting Time: 1 bonus action
Range: Touch
Components: V, S, M (an apple or a sugar cube)
Duration: 1 round

You urge your mount to a sudden burst of speed. Until the end of your next turn, you can direct your mount to use the Dash or Disengage action as a bonus action. This spell has no effect on a creature that you are not riding.

SPY MY SHADOW

2nd-Level Transmutation

Casting Time: 1 action
Range: Self
Components: V
Duration: Concentration, up to 1 minute

You bring your shadow to life as a tenebrous spy that can slip under doors, between shutters, and through the narrowest of cracks. You can stretch your shadow up to ten times your height and move it as you desire. It remains two-dimensional and cannot interact with physical objects.

You can spy through your shadow's eyes and ears as if they were your own, but magically enhanced senses do not work through this spell. You can utilize the Stealth skill normally if trying to keep your shadow's presence a secret: it gains advantage on Dexterity (Stealth) checks in dim lighting but disadvantage on Dexterity (Stealth) checks in brightly lit areas.

STAFF OF VIOLET FIRE

4th-Level Evocation

Casting Time: 1 bonus action
Range: Self
Components: V, S, M (mummy dust)
Duration: Concentration, but see description

You create a quarterstaff of pure necrotic energy that blazes with intense purple light; it appears in your chosen hand. If you let it go, it disappears, though you can evoke it again as a bonus action if you have maintained concentration on the spell.

This staff is an extremely unstable and impermanent magic item; it has 10 charges and does not require attunement. The wielder can use one of three effects:

- By using your action to make a melee attack and expending 1 charge, you can attack with it. On a hit, the target takes 5d10 necrotic damage.
- By expending 2 charges, you can release bolts of necrotic fire against up to 3 targets as ranged attacks for 1d8+4 necrotic damage each.

The staff disappears and the spell ends when all the staff's charges have been expended or if you stop concentrating on the spell.

At Higher Levels. When you cast this spell using a spell slot of 6th level or higher, the melee damage increases by 1d10 for every two slot levels above 4th, or you add one additional ranged bolt for every two slot levels above 4th.

STANCH

1st-Level Transmutation

Casting Time: 1 action
Range: Touch
Components: V, S
Duration: 1 hour

The target's blood coagulates rapidly, so that a dying target stabilizes and any ongoing bleeding or wounding effect on the target ends. The target can't be the source of blood for any spell or effect that requires even a drop of blood.

STAR'S HEART

9th-Level Transmutation

Casting Time: 1 action
Range: 50 feet
Components: V, S, M (an *ioun stone*)
Duration: 1 minute

This spell increases gravity tenfold in a 50-foot radius centered on you. Each creature in the area other than you drops whatever it's holding, falls prone, becomes incapacitated, and can't move. If a solid object (such as the ground) is encountered when a flying or levitating creature falls, the creature takes three times the normal falling damage. Any creature except you that enters the area or starts its turn there must make a successful Strength saving throw or fall prone and become incapacitated and unable to move. A creature that starts its turn prone and incapacitated makes a Strength saving throw. On a failed save, the creature takes 8d6 bludgeoning damage; on a successful save, it takes 4d6 bludgeoning damage, it's no longer incapacitated, and it can move at half speed.

All ranged weapon attacks inside the area have a normal range of 5 feet and a maximum range of 10 feet. The same applies to spells that create missiles that have mass, such as *flaming sphere*. A creature under the influence of a *freedom of movement* spell or comparable magic has advantage on the Strength saving throws required by this spell, and its speed isn't reduced once it recovers from being incapacitated.

STARBURST

Evocation Cantrip

Casting Time: 1 action
Range: 60 feet
Components: V, S
Duration: Instantaneous

You cause a mote of starlight to appear and explode in a 5-foot cube you can see within range. If a creature is in the cube, it must succeed on a Charisma saving throw or take 1d8 radiant damage.

This spell's damage increases to 2d8 when you reach 5th level, 3d8 when you reach 11th level, and 4d8 when you reach 17th level.

STARFALL

5th-Level Evocation

Casting Time: 1 action
Range: 60 feet
Components: V, S
Duration: Instantaneous

You cause bolts of shimmering starlight to fall from the heavens, striking up to five creatures that you can see within range. Each bolt strikes one target, dealing 6d6 radiant damage, knocking the target prone, and blinding it until the start of your next turn. A creature that makes a successful Dexterity saving throw takes half the damage, is not knocked prone, and is not blinded. If you name fewer than five targets, excess bolts strike the ground harmlessly.

At Higher Levels. When you cast this spell using a spell slot of 6th level or higher, you can create one additional bolt for each slot level above 5th.

STARRY VISION

7th-Level Divination

Casting Time: 1 reaction, which you take when an enemy starts its turn
Range: 100 feet
Components: V, M (sprinkle of gold dust worth 400 gp)
Duration: Concentration, up to 1 minute

This spell acts as *compelling fate*, except as noted above (*starry vision* can be cast as a reaction, has twice the range of *compelling fate*, and lasts up to 1 minute). At the end of each of its turns, the target repeats the Charisma saving throw, ending the effect on a success.

At Higher Levels. When you cast this spell using a spell slot of 8th level or higher, the bonus to AC increases by 1 for each slot level above 7th.

STEAL WARMTH

3rd-Level Necromancy

Casting Time: 1 reaction, which you take when you take cold damage from magic
Range: Self
Components: V, S
Duration: Instantaneous

When you cast *steal warmth* after taking cold damage, you select a living creature within 5 feet of you. That creature takes the cold damage instead, or half the damage with a successful Constitution saving throw. You regain hit points equal to the amount of cold damage taken by the target.

At Higher Levels. When you cast this spell using a spell slot of 4th level or higher, the distance to the target you can affect with this spell increases by 5 feet for each slot level above 3rd.

STEAM BLAST

4th-Level Evocation

Casting Time: 1 action
Range: Self (15-foot radius)
Components: V, S, M (a tiny copper kettle or boiler)
Duration: Instantaneous

You unleash a burst of superheated steam in a 15-foot radius around you. All other creatures in the area take 5d8 fire damage, or half as much damage on a successful Dexterity saving throw. Nonmagical fires smaller than a bonfire are extinguished, and everything becomes wet.

At Higher Levels. When you cast this spell using a spell slot of 5th level or higher, the damage increases by 1d8 for each slot level above 4th.

STEAM WHISTLE

8th-Level Evocation

Casting Time: 1 action
Range: Self (30-foot radius)
Components: V, S, M (a small brass whistle)
Duration: Instantaneous

You open your mouth and unleash a shattering scream. All other creatures in a 30-foot radius around you take 10d10 thunder damage and are deafened for 1d8 hours. A successful Constitution saving throw halves the damage and reduces the deafness to 1 round.

STEP LIKE ME

1st-Level Transmutation

Casting Time: 1 action
Range: 60 feet
Components: V, S, M (blood, hair, or a personal item of target)
Duration: 24 hours

Choose a creature within one size category of yourself that you can see within range. The target must succeed on a Constitution saving throw or you steal its footsteps. For the duration of the spell, you leave the tracks of the target, while it leaves tracks as if it were you. In addition, those capable of identifying creatures through tremorsense mistake you for a creature of the target's kind.

STING OF THE SCORPION GODDESS

3rd-Level Transmutation

Casting Time: 1 action
Range: Self
Components: V, S, M (a live scorpion)
Duration: 10 minutes

You grow a large scorpion's tail, complete with venomous stinger. While the spell is in effect, you can use a bonus action to make a melee attack with the stinger against an opponent within 5 feet. On a hit, you deal 1d6 piercing damage and 2d8 poison damage, and the target is poisoned for 1 minute. A creature hit by your stinger attack makes a Constitution saving throw. On a successful save, it takes just half the poison damage and is not poisoned.

STORM FORM

6th-Level Transmutation

Casting Time: 1 action
Range: Self
Components: V, S, M (a piece of wet wool)
Duration: Concentration, up to 10 minutes

You transform into a living storm cloud, becoming a swirling mass of black clouds illuminated from within by flickers of lightning.

While in this form, your only method of movement is a flying speed of 60 feet. You can enter and occupy the space of another creature. You have resistance to nonmagical damage, immunity to lightning damage, and advantage on Strength, Dexterity, and Constitution saving throws. If a creature strikes you with a melee weapon attack, it takes 3d8 lightning damage. You can pass through small holes, narrow openings, and even mere cracks, but you treat liquids as if they were solid surfaces. You can't fall, and you remain hovering in the air even if stunned or otherwise incapacitated. You cannot talk or manipulate objects in storm cloud form, and any objects you were carrying or holding can't be used, dropped, or interacted with in any way. You cannot cast spells while in this form.

As an action, you can attack an opponent up to 30 feet away, dealing 3d8 lightning damage on a hit. You can also use an action to bring down rain upon a 5-foot square within your reach, drenching it and putting out any nonmagical fires in that area.

Finally, you can use an action to expand your form to encompass a 20-foot-radius area, unleashing the storm's full fury in a burst of rain, wind, lightning, and thunder. Each creature in the area is drenched with rain, takes 3d8 lightning and 3d8 thunder damage, is deafened for 1d4 rounds, and is knocked prone. A successful Constitution saving throw halves the damage and negates the deafened and prone conditions. Taking this action uses up any remaining duration of the spell, and you resume your normal form at the end of your turn.

STORM GOD'S DOOM

3rd-Level Evocation

Casting Time: 1 action
Range: 60 feet
Components: V, S
Duration: Instantaneous

A powerful wind swirls from your outstretched hand toward a point you choose within range, where it explodes with a low roar into vortex of air. Each creature in a 20-foot-radius cylinder centered on that point must make a Strength saving throw. On a failed save, the creature takes 3d8 bludgeoning damage, is pulled to the center of the cylinder, and is thrown 50 feet upward into the air. If a creature hits a solid obstruction when it's thrown upward (such as a stone ceiling), it takes bludgeoning damage as if it had fallen 50 feet, minus the distance it traveled upward. For example, if a creature hits the ceiling after rising only 10 feet, it takes bludgeoning damage as if it had fallen 40 feet, or 4d6 bludgeoning damage.

 At Higher Levels. When you cast this spell using a spell slot of 4th level or higher, increase the distance affected creatures are thrown into the air by 10 feet for each slot level above 3rd.

STORM OF WINGS

4th-Level Conjuration

Casting Time: 1 action
Range: 60 feet
Components: V, S, M (a drop of honey)
Duration: Concentration, up to 1 minute

You create a storm of spectral birds, bats, or flying insects in a 15-foot-radius sphere on a point you can see within range. The storm spreads around corners, and its area is lightly obscured. Each creature in the storm when it appears and each a creature that starts its turn in the storm is affected by the storm.

 As a bonus action on your turn, you can move the storm up to 30 feet. As an action on your turn, you can change the storm from one type to another, such as from a storm of bats to a storm of insects.

 Bats. The creature takes 4d6 necrotic damage, and its speed is halved while within the storm as the bats cling to it and drain its blood.

 Birds. The creature takes 4d6 slashing damage, and it has disadvantage on attack rolls while within the storm as the birds fly in the way of the creature's attacks.

 Insects. The creature takes 4d6 poison damage, and it must make a Constitution saving throw each time it casts a spell while within the storm. On a failed save, the creature fails to cast the spell, losing the action but not the spell slot.

STRENGTH OF AN OX

1st-Level Transmutation

Casting Time: 1 action
Range: Touch
Components: V, S, M (a 1-pound weight)
Duration: Concentration, up to 1 minute

You touch a creature and give it the capacity to carry, push, drag, or lift weight as if it were one size category larger for the duration of the spell. The target is also not subject to the penalties given in the variant rules for encumbrance. The subject can also carry a load that would normally be unwieldy, such as a large log, a rowboat, or an oxcart.

 At Higher Levels. When you cast this spell using a spell slot of 2nd level or higher, you can affect one additional creature for each slot level above 1st.

SUDDEN DAWN

3rd-Level Evocation (Ritual)

Casting Time: 1 action
Range: 100 feet
Components: V, S
Duration: Concentration, up to 10 minutes

You call upon morning to arrive ahead of schedule. With a sharp word, you create a 30-foot-radius cylinder of light centered on a point on the ground within range. The cylinder extends vertically for 100 feet or until it reaches an obstruction, such as a ceiling. The area inside the cylinder is brightly lit.

SUDDEN STAMPEDE

4th-Level Conjuration

Casting Time: 1 action
Range: 30 feet
Components: V, S, M (a horseshoe)
Duration: Instantaneous

You conjure up a multitude of fey spirits that manifest as galloping horses. These horses run in a 10-foot-wide, 60-foot-long line, in a given direction starting from a point within range, trampling all creatures in their path, before vanishing again. Each creature in the line takes 6d10 bludgeoning damage and is knocked prone. A successful Dexterity saving throw reduces the damage by half, and the creature is not knocked prone.

SUMMON AVATAR

9th-Level Conjuration (Ritual)

Casting Time: 1 minute

Range: 60 feet

Components: V, S, M (a vial of the caster's blood, a dried opium poppy, and a silver dagger)

Duration: Concentration, up to 1 hour

You summon a worldly incarnation of a Great Old One, which appears in an unoccupied space you can see within range. This avatar manifests as an emanation of elder darkness, augmented by boons from the Void. Choose one of the following options for the type of avatar that appears. (Other options might be available if the GM allows.) An asterisk indicates a spell described in this section:

- *Avatar of Cthulhu.* The incarnation is a **deep one** (see *Tome of Beasts*) that can innately cast *command* and *sleep of the deep** at will.
- *Avatar of Nyarlathotep.* The incarnation is a **dark voice** (see *Creature Codex*) that can innately cast *bane* and *semblance of dread** at will.
- *Avatar of Shub-Niggurath.* The incarnation is a **goat-man** (see *Tome of Beasts*) that can innately cast *Black Goat's blessing** and *unseen strangler** at will.
- *Avatar of Yog-Sothoth.* The incarnation is a human with 1d4 + 1 flesh warps that can innately cast *gift of resilience** (see page 71) and *thunderwave* at will.

When the avatar appears, you must make a Charisma saving throw. On a success, the avatar is friendly to you and your allies. On a failed save, the avatar is friendly to no one and attacks the nearest creature, pursuing and fighting for as long as possible.

Roll initiative for the avatar, which takes its own turns. If it is friendly to you, it obeys verbal commands you issue to it (no action required by you). If the avatar has no command, it attacks the nearest creature.

Each round when you maintain concentration on the spell, you must make a successful DC 15 Wisdom saving throw at the end of your turn or take 1d6 psychic damage. If the total of this damage exceeds your Wisdom score, you gain 1 point of Void taint and you are afflicted with a form of short-term madness. The same penalty recurs when the damage exceeds twice your Wisdom score, three times your Wisdom score, and so forth, if you maintain concentration for that long.

The avatar disappears when it drops to 0 hit points or when the spell ends. If you stop concentrating before 1 hour has elapsed, it becomes uncontrolled and hostile until it disappears 1d6 rounds later or until it is killed.

SUMMON ELDRITCH SERVITOR

5th-Level Conjuration (Ritual)

Casting Time: 1 minute

Range: 60 feet

Components: V, S, M (a vial of the caster's blood and a silver dagger)

Duration: Concentration, up to 1 hour

You summon eldritch aberrations that appear in unoccupied spaces you can see within range. Choose one of the following options for what appears:

- Two **ghasts of Leng** (see *Creature Codex*)
- One **shantak** (see *Creature Codex*)

When the summoned creatures appear, you must make a Charisma saving throw. On a success, the creatures are friendly to you and your allies. On a failure, the creatures are friendly to no one and attack the nearest creatures, pursuing and fighting for as long as possible.

Roll initiative for the summoned creatures, which take their own turns as a group. If friendly to you, they obey your verbal commands (no action required by you to issue a command), or they attack the nearest living creature if they are not commanded otherwise.

Each round when you maintain concentration on the spell, you must make a successful DC 15 Wisdom saving throw at the end of your turn or take 1d4 psychic damage. If the total of this damage exceeds your Wisdom score, you gain 1 point of Void taint and you are afflicted with a form of short-term madness. The same penalty applies when the damage exceeds twice your Wisdom score, three times your Wisdom score, and so forth, if you maintain concentration for that long.

A summoned creature disappears when it drops to 0 hit points or when the spell ends. If you stop concentrating on the spell before 1 hour has elapsed, the creatures become uncontrolled and hostile until they disappear 1d6 rounds later or until they are killed.

At Higher Levels. When you cast this spell using a 7th- or 8th-level spell slot, you can summon four **ghasts of Leng** or a **hound of Tindalos** (see *Creature Codex*). When you cast it with a 9th-level spell slot, you can summon five **ghasts of Leng** or a **nightgaunt** (see *Creature Codex*).

SUMMON STAR

8th-Level Conjuration

Casting Time: 1 action

Range: 90 feet

Components: V, S

Duration: Concentration, up to 1 minute

You summon a friendly star from the heavens to do your bidding. It appears in an unoccupied space you can see within range and takes the form of a glowing humanoid with long white hair. All creatures other than you who view the star must make a successful Wisdom saving throw or be charmed for the duration of the spell. A creature charmed in this way can repeat the Wisdom saving throw at the end of each of its turns. On a success, the creature is no longer charmed and is immune to the effect of this casting of the spell. In all other ways, the star is equivalent to a deva. It understands and obeys verbal commands you give it. If you do not give the star a command, it defends itself and attacks the last creature that attacked it. The star disappears when it drops to 0 hit points or when the spell ends.

SUN'S BOUNTY

5th-Level Transmutation

Casting Time: 1 action

Range: Touch

Components: V, S

Duration: Concentration, up to 1 hour

The sun's life-giving energy heals and sustains your body or that of a creature you touch. For the duration, you heal 1 hit point at the start of each of your turns whenever you are bathed in direct sunlight; 30 minutes or more of exposure also provides a day's normal nourishment.

In dim light, the spell's healing is reduced to 1 hit point per minute. Normal or magical darkness suppresses the spell's effect entirely. While in sunlight, the target can ignore one level of exhaustion. (The level is only temporarily removed.)

Undead are especially vulnerable to this spell. If a targeted undead fails its Wisdom save, it gains the poisoned condition and suffers radiant damage instead of healing while in sunlight.

SURGE DAMPENER

3rd-Level Abjuration (Ritual)

Casting Time: 1 action

Range: Touch

Components: V, S

Duration: 1 minute, until expended

Using your strength of will, you cause one creature other than yourself that you touch to become so firmly entrenched within reality that it is protected from the effects of a chaos magic surge. The protected creature can make a DC 13 Charisma saving throw to negate the effect of a chaos magic surge that does not normally allow a saving throw, or it gains advantage on a saving throw that is normally allowed. Once the protected creature makes a successful saving throw allowed by *surge dampener*, the spell ends.

SURPRISE BLESSING

5th-Level Abjuration

Casting Time: 1 action

Range: Touch

Components: V, S

Duration: 10 minutes

You touch a willing creature and choose one of the conditions listed below that the creature is currently subjected to. The condition's normal effect on the target is suspended, and the indicated effect applies instead. This spell's effect on the target lasts for the duration of the original condition or until the spell ends. If this spell ends before the original condition's duration expires, you become affected by the condition for as long as it lasts, even if you were not the original recipient of the condition.

Blinded. The target gains truesight out to a range of 10 feet and can see 10 feet into the Ethereal Plane.

Charmed. The target's Charisma score becomes 19, unless it is already higher than 19, and it gains immunity to charm effects.

Frightened. The target emits a 10-foot-radius aura of dread. Each creature the target designates that starts its turn in the aura must make a successful Wisdom saving throw or be frightened of the target. A creature frightened in this way that starts its turn outside the aura repeats the saving throw, ending the condition on itself on a success.

Paralyzed. The target can use one extra bonus action or reaction per round.

Petrified. The target gains a +2 bonus to AC.

Poisoned. The target heals 2d6 hit points at the start of its next turn, and it gains immunity to poison damage and the poisoned condition.

Stunned. The target has advantage on Intelligence, Wisdom, and Charisma saving throws.

SWIFT EXCHANGE

5th-Level Conjuration

Casting Time: 1 reaction, which you take when you or another creature within range is attacked

Range: 30 feet

Components: V

Duration: Instantaneous

When you or another creature you can see within range is the target of a weapon attack or a spell attack, you can magically switch your position with that of the other creature in an instant. If the creature is unwilling, it can make a Wisdom saving throw to avoid the effect. Otherwise, you and the creature change positions, each appearing in an eyeblink at the location the other previously occupied. Any attack that was about to occur against you or the other creature is resolved against whichever one of you now occupies the targeted space.

SYMBOL OF SORCERY

7th-Level Evocation

Casting Time: 10 minutes
Range: Touch
Components: V, S, M (a stick of incense worth 20 gp)
Duration: 8 hours

You draw an arcane symbol on an object, wall, or other surface at least 5 feet wide. When a creature other than you approaches within 5 feet of the symbol, that act triggers an arcane explosion. Each creature in a 60-foot cone must make a successful Wisdom saving throw or be stunned. A stunned creature repeats the saving throw at the end of each of its turns, ending the effect on itself on a successful save. After this symbol explodes or when the duration expires, its power is spent and the spell ends.

T

TALONS OF A HUNGRY LAND

7th-Level Evocation

Casting Time: 1 action
Range: 60 feet
Components: V, S
Duration: Concentration, up to 10 minutes

You cause three parallel lines of thick, flared obsidian spikes to erupt from the ground. They appear within range on a solid surface, last for the duration, and provide three-quarters cover to creatures behind them. You can make lines (up to 60 feet long, 10 feet high, and 5 feet thick) or form a circle (20 feet in diameter, up to 15 feet high and 5 feet thick).

When the lines appear, each creature in their area must make a Dexterity saving throw. Creatures takes 8d8 slashing damage, or half as much damage on a successful save.

A creature can move through the lines at the risk of cutting itself on the exposed edges. For every 1 foot a creature moves through the lines, it must spend 4 feet of movement. Furthermore, the first time a creature enters the lines on a turn or ends its turn there, the creature must make a Dexterity saving throw. It takes 8d8 slashing damage on a failure, or half as much damage on a success.

When you stop concentrating on the spell, you can cause the obsidian spikes to explode, dealing 5d8 slashing damage to any creature within 15 feet, or half as much damage on a successful Dexterity save.

At Higher Levels. When you cast this spell using a spell slot of 8th level or higher, the damage from all effects of the lines increases by 1d8 for each slot level above 7th.

TARGETING FOREKNOWLEDGE

3rd-Level Divination

Casting Time: 1 bonus action
Range: Self
Components: V
Duration: Instantaneous

Twisting the knife, slapping with the butt of the spear, slashing out again as you recover from a lunge, and countless other double-strike maneuvers are skillful ways to get more from your weapon. By casting this spell as a bonus action after making a successful melee weapon attack, you deal an extra 2d6 damage of the weapon's type to the target. In addition, if your weapon attack roll was a 19 or higher, it is a critical hit and increases the weapon's damage dice as normal. The extra damage from this spell is not increased on a critical hit.

TELEKINETIC PARRY

1st-Level Evocation

Casting Time: 1 reaction, which you take when an enemy makes an attack roll against you
Range: Self
Components: S
Duration: Instantaneous

As a reaction, you use a brief burst of kinetic energy to block an attack against you. The attacker has disadvantage on the attack roll. An attack that hits deals damage as normal. This spell works against melee and ranged attacks, as well as spell attacks that have a physical manifestation, including force effects, but not against spells that do not require an attack roll, such as *magic missile*.

TELEKINETIC TRIP

Transmutation Cantrip

Casting Time: 1 action
Range: 30 feet
Components: V, S
Duration: Instantaneous

You lash out with a burst of telekinesis, sweeping a creature within range off its feet. The target of this spell must succeed on a Dexterity saving throw or fall prone.

TERRIFYING LASH

3rd-Level Conjuration

Casting Time: 1 action
Range: Self
Components: V, S
Duration: Concentration, up to 1 minute

A faintly luminous whip of energy coalesces in your hand. The whip has reach, and you can take an action to make a melee attack roll against a target on your turn, using your spellcasting ability modifier as a bonus on the attack roll. On a hit, the target takes 2d10 psychic damage and must make a Wisdom saving throw. On a failed save, the target is frightened for 1d4 rounds. If you attack a target with this spell that is already frightened, you gain advantage on the attack roll, and the target has disadvantage on its Wisdom saving throw.

THIN THE ICE

1st-Level Transmutation

Casting Time: 1 action
Range: 60 feet
Components: V, S, M (a piece of sunstone)
Duration: Instantaneous

You target a point within range. That point becomes the top center of a cylinder 10 feet in radius and 40 feet deep. All ice inside that area melts immediately. The uppermost layer of ice seems to remain intact and sturdy, but it covers a 40-foot-deep pit filled with ice water. A successful Wisdom (Survival) check or passive Perception check against your spell save DC notices the thin ice. If a creature weighing more than 20 pounds (or a greater weight specified by you when casting the spell) treads over the cylinder or is already standing on it, the ice gives way. Unless the creature makes a successful Dexterity saving throw, it falls into the icy water, taking 2d6 cold damage plus whatever other problems are caused by water, by armor, or by being drenched in a freezing environment. The water gradually refreezes normally.

THORN CAGE

2nd-Level Conjuration

Casting Time: 1 action
Range: 60 feet
Components: V, S
Duration: Concentration, up to 1 minute

Thick vines studded with sharp thorns spring from the ground around a target of your choice. The target must succeed on a Strength saving throw or be restrained by the thorny vines until the spell ends. A creature restrained by the vines can use its action to make a Strength check against your spell save DC. Doing so causes the creature to take 2d6 piercing damage from the thorns. On a successful check, it frees itself.

THOUSAND DARTS

3rd-Level Evocation

Casting Time: 1 action
Range: Self (120-foot line)
Components: V, S, M (a set of mithral darts worth 25 gp)
Duration: Instantaneous

You launch thousands of needlelike darts in a 5-foot-wide line that is 120 feet long. Each creature in the line takes 6d6 piercing damage, or half as much damage if it makes a successful Dexterity saving throw. The first creature struck by the darts makes the saving throw with disadvantage.

At Higher Levels. When you cast this spell using a spell slot of 4th level or higher, the damage increases by 1d6 for each slot level above 3rd.

THROES OF ECSTASY

3rd-Level Transmutation

Casting Time: 1 action
Range: 60 feet
Components: V, S, M (a hazel or oak wand)
Duration: Concentration, up to 1 minute

Choose a humanoid that you can see within range. The target must succeed on a Constitution saving throw or become overcome with euphoria, rendering it

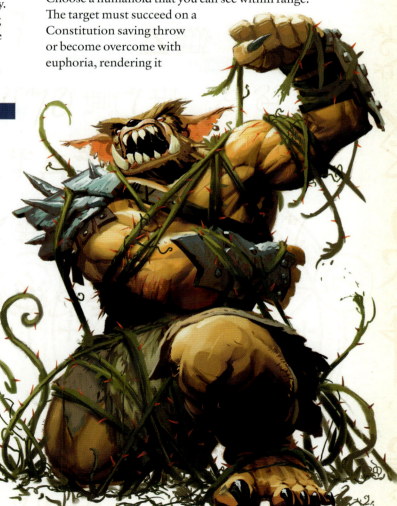

incapacitated for the duration. The target automatically fails Wisdom saving throws, and attack rolls against the target have advantage. At the end of each of its turns, the target can make another Constitution saving throw. On a successful save, the spell ends on the target, and it gains one level of exhaustion. If the spell continues for its maximum duration, the target gains three levels of exhaustion when the spell ends.

At Higher Levels. When you cast this spell using a spell slot of 4th level or higher, you can target one additional humanoid for each slot level above 3rd. The humanoids must be within 30 feet of each other when you target them.

THUNDER BOLT

Evocation Cantrip

Casting Time: 1 action
Range: 30 feet
Components: V, S
Duration: Instantaneous

You cast a knot of thunder at one enemy. Make a ranged spell attack against the target. If it hits, the target takes 1d8 thunder damage and can't use reactions until the start of your next turn. The spell's damage increases by 1d8 when you reach 5th level (2d8), 11th level (3d8), and 17th level (4d8).

THUNDERCLAP

3rd-Level Evocation

Casting Time: 1 action
Range: Self (20-foot radius)
Components: S
Duration: Instantaneous

You clap your hands, emitting a peal of thunder. Each creature within 20 feet of you takes 8d4 thunder damage and is deafened for 1d8 rounds, or it takes half as much damage and isn't deafened if it makes a successful Constitution saving throw. On a saving throw that fails by 5 or more, the creature is also stunned for 1 round.

This spell doesn't function in an area affected by a *silence* spell. Very brittle material such as crystal might be shattered if it's within range, at the GM's discretion; a character holding such an object can protect it from harm by making a successful Dexterity saving throw.

THUNDEROUS CHARGE

1st-Level Transmutation

Casting Time: 1 bonus action
Range: Self
Components: V
Duration: Instantaneous

With a thunderous battle cry, you move up to 10 feet in a straight line and make a melee weapon attack. If it hits, you can choose to either gain a +5 bonus on the attack's damage or shove the target 10 feet.

At Higher Levels. When you cast this spell using a spell slot of 2nd level or higher, the distance you can move increases by 10 feet, and the attack deals an additional 1d6 thunder damage, for each slot level above 1st.

THUNDEROUS STAMPEDE

2nd-Level Transmutation

Casting Time: 1 bonus action
Range: Self (30-foot radius)
Components: V
Duration: Instantaneous

This spell acts as *thunderous charge*, but affecting up to three targets within range, including yourself. A target other than you must use its reaction to move and attack under the effect of *thunderous stampede*.

At Higher Levels. When you cast this spell using a spell slot of 3rd level or higher, the distance your targets can move increases by 10 feet, and the attack deals an additional 1d6 thunder damage, for each slot level above 2nd.

THUNDEROUS WAVE

3rd-Level Evocation

Casting Time: 1 action
Range: 90 feet
Components: V, S
Duration: Instantaneous

You initiate a shock wave centered at a point you designate within range. The wave explodes outward into a 30-foot-radius sphere. This force deals no damage directly, but every creature the wave passes through must make a Strength saving throw. On a failed save, a creature is pushed 30 feet and knocked prone; if it strikes a solid obstruction, it also takes 5d6 bludgeoning damage. On a successful save, a creature is pushed 15 feet and not knocked prone, and it takes 2d6 bludgeoning damage if it strikes an obstruction. The spell also emits a thunderous boom that can be heard within 400 feet.

THUNDERSTORM

5th-Level Transmutation

Casting Time: 1 action

Range: Touch

Components: V, S, M (a piece of lightning-fused glass)

Duration: Concentration, up to 1 hour

You touch a willing creature, and it becomes surrounded by a roiling storm cloud 30 feet in diameter, erupting with (harmless) thunder and lightning. The creature gains a flying speed of 60 feet. The cloud heavily obscures the creature inside it from view, though it is transparent to the creature itself.

TIDAL BARRIER

1st-Level Abjuration

Casting Time: 1 action

Range: Self (10-foot radius)

Components: V, S, M (a piece of driftwood)

Duration: Concentration, up to 1 minute

A swirling wave of seawater surrounds you, crashing and rolling in a 10-foot radius around your space. The area is difficult terrain, and a creature that starts its turn there or that enters it for the first time on a turn must make a Strength saving throw. On a failed save, the creature is pushed 10 feet away from you and its speed is reduced to 0 until the start of its next turn.

TIME IN A BOTTLE

9th-Level Transmutation

Casting Time: 1 action

Range: Sight

Components: V

Duration: Concentration, up to 1 minute

You designate a spot within your sight. Time comes under your control in a 20-foot radius centered on that spot. You can freeze it, reverse it, or move it forward by as much as 1 minute as long as you maintain concentration. Nothing and no one, yourself included, can enter the field or affect what happens inside it. You can choose to end the effect at any moment as an action on your turn.

TIME JAUNT

7th-Level Transmutation

Casting Time: 1 action

Range: Self

Components: V

Duration: Special

When you cast this spell, you step outside the normal time stream, seeming to vanish as 1 round of time passes. You can make minor alterations to the scene being played out, becoming visible for an instant each time you make an adjustment that aids an ally or hinders foes. To everyone else, you disappear when the spell is cast, then flicker into and out of view during the next round, before reappearing for good in the space you vanished from 1 round later, whereupon the spell ends. You cannot be attacked by any means while under the effect of this spell.

As the round progresses, you can choose to bestow a single effect on each creature involved in the combat, choosing from the list below. You cannot take any other actions during the round:

- Give a creature advantage or disadvantage on a saving throw it is about to make.
- Give a creature advantage or disadvantage on an attack roll it is about to make.
- Alter the location of a mobile object to provide or remove cover for a creature.
- Shift objects into the path of a creature; the first 10 feet of terrain it must travel becomes difficult terrain.
- After an attack roll is determined to be successful, adjust the angle of the strike or the positioning of the target, either causing the strike to deal half as much damage or providing a bonus to damage equal to half your level.

Example of Combat. An adventuring party encounters four trolls in their lair. Initiative is rolled, and the order is fighter 20, cleric 15, rogue 14, trolls 12, wizard 10. Events unfold in this way:

Fighter draws sword and attacks troll #1.

Cleric casts *time jaunt* and disappears.

Rogue fires an arrow at troll #2. Cleric yanks the troll's arm, turning it broadside for a better target and giving the rogue advantage on the attack roll. The attack hits.

Troll #1 swings at the fighter. Cleric gives the fighter's shield a nudge to raise it just a little faster. Troll has disadvantage on the attack roll and misses.

Troll #2 throws a spear at the rogue. Cleric flips a table over between the rogue and the troll, giving the rogue cover against the attack. Attack roll is still high enough to hit.

Troll #3 charges the fighter. Cleric tips over an open barrel of pickled herring, strewing the contents across the floor and making the first 10 feet in the troll's path difficult terrain. As a result, troll #3 does not have enough movement to reach the fighter on its turn.

Troll #4 moves and attacks the fighter, scoring a hit. Cleric pulls on the troll's weapon arm so the strike is a glancing one rather than a direct hit, and the attack deals half as much damage.

Wizard casts *grease* on the area where trolls #1 and #4 are standing. Cleric gives each a swift kick to the back of the knee. Trolls have disadvantage on their Dexterity saving throws, fail their saves, and fall prone.

Fighter stabs at troll #1, scoring a hit. Cleric gives the troll's arm a yank, moving it just enough that the fighter hits the monster's chest rather than its shoulder, providing the fighter a bonus of +7 (half the cleric's level) on the attack's damage.

Cleric pops back into view, occupying the space where *time jaunt* was cast, then takes the next turn in round 2 as normal.

TIME JUMP

8th-Level Transmutation

Casting Time: 1 action
Range: Touch
Components: V, S
Duration: Instantaneous

You touch a construct and throw it forward in time if it fails a Constitution saving throw. The construct disappears for 1d4 + 1 rounds, during which time it cannot act or be acted upon in any way. When the construct returns, it is unaware that any time has passed.

TIME LOOP

6th-Level Transmutation

Casting Time: 1 action
Range: 30 feet
Components: V, S, M (a metal loop)
Duration: Concentration, up to 1 minute

You capture a creature within range in a loop of time. The target is teleported to the space where it began its most recent turn. The target then makes a Wisdom saving throw. On a successful save, the spell ends. On a failed save, the creature must repeat the activities it undertook on its previous turn, following the sequence of moves and actions to the best of its ability. It doesn't need to move along the same path or attack the same target, but if it moved and then attacked on its previous turn, its only option is to move and then attack on this turn. If the space where the target began its previous turn is occupied or if it's impossible for the target to take the same action (if it cast a spell but is now unable to do so, for example), the target becomes incapacitated.

An affected target can repeat the saving throw at the end of each of its turns, ending the effect on itself on a success. For as long as the spell lasts, the target teleports back to its starting point at the start of each of its turns, and it must repeat the same sequence of moves and actions.

TIME SLIPPAGE

8th-Level Enchantment

Casting Time: 1 action
Range: 60 feet
Components: V, S, M (the heart of a chaotic creature of challenge rating 5 or higher, worth 500 gp)
Duration: Concentration, up to 1 minute

You ensnare a creature within range in an insidious trap, causing different parts of its body to function at different speeds. The creature must make an Intelligence saving throw. On a failed save, it is stunned until the end of its next turn. On a success, the creature's speed is halved and it has disadvantage on attack rolls and saving throws until the end of its next turn. The creature repeats the saving throw at the end of each of its turns, with the same effects for success and failure. In addition, the creature has disadvantage on Strength or Dexterity saving throws but advantage on Constitution or Charisma saving throws for the spell's duration (a side effect of the chronal anomaly suffusing its body). The spell ends if the creature makes three successful saves in a row.

TIME STEP

2nd-Level Conjuration

Casting Time: 1 action
Range: Self
Components: V
Duration: Instantaneous

You briefly step forward in time. You disappear from your location and reappear at the start of your next turn in a location of your choice that you can see within 30 feet of the space you disappeared from. You can't be affected by anything that happens during the time you're missing, and you aren't aware of anything that happens during that time.

TIME VORTEX

4th-Level Evocation

Casting Time: 1 action
Range: 90 feet
Components: V, S
Duration: Concentration, up to 1 minute

This spell destabilizes the flow of time, enabling you to create a vortex of temporal fluctuations that are visible as a spherical distortion with a 10-foot radius, centered on a point within range. Each creature in the area when you cast the spell must succeed on a Wisdom saving throw or be affected by the time vortex. While the spell lasts, a creature that enters the sphere or starts its turn inside the sphere must also succeed on a Wisdom saving throw or be affected. On a successful save, it becomes immune to this casting of the spell.

An affected creature can't take reactions and rolls a d10 at the start of its turn to determine its behavior for that turn.

d10	Effect
1–2	The creature is affected as if by a *slow* spell until the start of its next turn.
3–5	The creature is stunned until the start of its next turn.
6–8	The creature's current initiative result is reduced by 5. The creature begins using this new initiative result in the next round. Multiple occurrences of this effect for the same creature are cumulative.
9–10	The creature's speed is halved (round up to the nearest 5-foot increment) until the start of its next turn.

You can move the temporal vortex 10 feet each round as a bonus action. An affected creature can repeat the saving throw at the end of each of its turns, ending the effect on itself on a success.

At Higher Levels. When you cast this spell using a spell slot of 5th level or higher, the radius of the sphere increases by 5 feet for each slot level above 4th.

TIMELY DISTRACTION

2nd-Level Evocation

Casting Time: 1 action

Range: 25 feet

Components: V, S, M (a handful of sand or dirt thrown in the air)

Duration: 3 rounds

You call forth a swirling, crackling wave of constantly shifting pops, flashes, and swept-up debris. This chaos can confound one creature. If the target gets a failure on a Wisdom saving throw, roll a d4 and consult the following table to determine the result. An affected creature can repeat the saving throw at the end of each of its turns, ending the effect on itself on a success. Otherwise, the spell ends when its duration expires.

d4	Mutation
1	Blinded
2	Stunned
3	Deafened
4	Prone

TIRELESS

1st-Level Transmutation

Casting Time: 1 action

Range: Touch

Components: S, M (an ever-wound spring worth 50 gp)

Duration: 24 hours

You grant machinelike stamina to a creature you touch for the duration of the spell. The target requires no food or drink or rest. It can move at three times its normal speed overland and perform three times the usual amount of labor. The target is not protected from fatigue or exhaustion caused by a magical effect.

TOLLING DOOM

6th-Level Necromancy

Casting Time: 1 action

Range: 150 feet

Components: V, S, M (a bronze bell)

Duration: Concentration, up to 1 minute

A deep, tolling bell seems to ring from somewhere above and beyond, judging your enemies and foretelling their impending doom. Up to eight creatures that you can see within range must make Charisma saving throws. Whenever a target that fails this saving throw makes an attack roll or saving throw before the spell ends, the target must roll a d4 and subtract the result from the attack roll or saving throw. You gain advantage on any attack against a target that has failed its saving throw against this spell. This spell has no effect on a target that has an Intelligence score lower than 3.

At Higher Levels. When you cast this spell using a spell slot of 7th level or higher, you can affect one additional target for each slot level above 6th.

TOME CURSE

4th-Level Necromancy

Casting Time: 10 minutes

Range: Touch

Components: V, S, M (an ounce of blood, and powdered onyx worth at least 50 gp, both of which the spell consumes)

Duration: Until dispelled or triggered

You protect a book by writing a curse in it with ink made from the material components of this spell. The writing is typically a couplet or a quatrain that warns of the consequences of disturbing your property. The curse is triggered by an action or actions that you specify (which typically involves someone reading the book without permission, trying to damage the book, or trying to steal it). When the curse is triggered, the creature that did so must succeed on a Wisdom saving throw or suffer its effect. You can choose one of the effects described in the *bestow curse* spell, or you can affect the target in one of the following ways:

- While the target is cursed, it is blinded.
- Beasts are unusually hostile to the target while it is cursed; they gain advantage on attack rolls against the target.
- While cursed, the target is an attractive mark to pickpockets and other thieves, and such individuals will try to steal the target's valuables when the opportunity presents itself. (Even if in the target's possession, the cursed book does not count as one of the target's valuables.)
- A cursed target that either receives magical healing or rolls Hit Dice to recover hit points after a long rest must roll twice and use the lower result.

A *remove curse* spell ends this effect. You can also stipulate other actions taken by the target that would nullify the curse (returning the book after it is stolen, for example).

TONGUE OF SAND

3rd-Level Illusion (Ritual)

Casting Time: 1 minute

Range: 30 feet

Components: V, S

Duration: Until dispelled

Tongue of sand is similar in many ways to *magic mouth*. When you cast it, you implant a message in a quantity of sand. The sand must fill a space no smaller than 4 square feet and at least 2 inches deep. The message can be up to 25 words. You also decide the conditions that trigger the speaking of the message. When the message is triggered, a mouth forms in the sand and delivers the message in a raspy, whispered voice that can be heard by creatures within 10 feet of the sand.

Additionally, *tongue of sand* has the ability to interact in a simple, brief manner with creatures who hear its message. For up to 10 minutes after the message is triggered, questions addressed to the sand will be answered as you would answer them. Each answer can be no more than ten words long, and the spell ends after a second question is answered.

TONGUE TIED

5th-Level Enchantment

Casting Time: 1 action

Range: 30 feet

Components: V, S

Duration: Concentration up to 1 minute

You make a choking motion while pointing at a target, which must make a successful Wisdom saving throw or become unable to communicate verbally. The target's speech becomes garbled, and it has disadvantage on Charisma checks that require speech. The creature can cast a spell that has a verbal component only by making a successful Constitution check against your spell save DC. On a failed check, the creature's action is used but the spell slot isn't expended.

TORRENT OF FIRE

4th-Level Conjuration

Casting Time: 1 action

Range: Self (60-foot cone)

Components: V, S, M (a piece of obsidian)

Duration: Instantaneous

You harness the power of fire contained in ley lines with this spell. You create a 60-foot cone of flame. Creatures in the cone take 6d6 fire damage, or half as much damage with a successful Dexterity saving throw. You can then flow along the flames, reappearing anywhere inside the cone's area. This repositioning doesn't count as movement and doesn't trigger opportunity attacks.

TOUCH OF THE UNLIVING

3rd-Level Necromancy

Casting Time: 1 action

Range: Touch

Components: V, S

Duration: Concentration, up to 1 minute

Make a melee spell attack against a creature you can reach. On a hit, the target takes 2d6 necrotic damage and, if it is not an undead creature, it is paralyzed until the end of its next turn. Until the spell ends, you can make the attack again on each of your turns as an action.

At Higher Levels. When you cast this spell using a spell slot of 4th level or higher, the damage increases by 1d6 for each slot level above 3rd.

TRACER

3rd-Level Divination

Casting Time: 1 bonus action
Range: Self
Components: V, S, M (a drop of bright paint)
Duration: 8 hours

When you cast this spell and as a bonus action on each of your turns until the spell ends, you can imbue a piece of ammunition you fire from a ranged weapon with a tiny, invisible beacon. If a ranged attack roll with an imbued piece of ammunition hits a target, the beacon is transferred to the target. The weapon that fired the ammunition is attuned to the beacon and becomes warm to the touch when it points in the direction of the target as long as the target is on the same plane of existence as you. You can have only one tracer target at a time. If you put a tracer on a different target, the effect on the previous target ends.

A creature must succeed on an Intelligence (Arcana) check against your spell save DC to notice the magical beacon.

TRACKING BEACON

3rd-Level Divination

Casting Time: 1 action
Range: 120 feet
Components: V, S
Duration: Concentration, up to 8 hours

You choose a creature within range to mark with a glowing orb of light, which floats 120 feet above the creature's head. The target must make a Wisdom saving throw. On a successful save, the spell ends. On a failed save, the light hovers above the target's location, moving as the target moves, which enables you to track the creature's direction and distance by staying within sight of the beacon. The beacon continues to function even when you cannot see it, as long as the target remains on the same plane as you. If either you or the target travels to another plane, the spell ends.

You can use a bonus action on your turn to adjust the height of the beacon, ranging from its starting point of 120 feet to as low as 5 feet above the head of the target.

TREASURE CHASM

2nd-Level Enchantment

Casting Time: 1 action
Range: 100 feet
Components: V, S, M (a gold coin)
Duration: Concentration, up to 1 minute

You cause the glint of a golden coin to haze over the vision of one creature in range. The target creature must make a Wisdom saving throw. If it fails, it sees a gorge, trench, or other hole in the ground, at a spot within range chosen by you, which is filled with gold and treasure. On its next turn, the creature must move toward that spot. When it reaches the spot, it becomes incapacitated, as it devotes all its attention to scooping imaginary treasure into its pockets or a pouch.

An affected creature can repeat the saving throw at the end of each of its turns, ending the effect on itself on a success. The effect also ends if the creature takes damage from you or one of your allies.

Creatures with the dragon type have disadvantage on the initial saving throw but have advantage on saving throws against this spell made after reaching the designated spot.

TREE HEAL

Evocation Cantrip

Casting Time: 1 action
Range: Touch
Components: V, S
Duration: Instantaneous

You touch a plant, and it regains 1d4 hit points. Alternatively, you can cure it of one disease or remove pests from it. Once you cast this spell on a plant or plant creature, you can't cast it on that target again for 24 hours. This spell can be used only on plants and plant creatures.

TREE RUNNING

2nd-Level Transmutation

Casting Time: 1 action
Range: Touch
Components: S, M (a maple catkin)
Duration: Concentration, up to 1 hour

One willing creature you touch gains a climbing speed equal to its walking speed. This climbing speed functions only while the creature is in contact with a living plant or fungus that's growing from the ground. The creature can cling to an appropriate surface with just one hand or with just its feet, leaving its hands free to wield weapons or cast spells. The plant doesn't give under the creature's weight, so the creature can walk on the tiniest of tree branches, stand on a leaf, or run across the waving top of a field of wheat without bending a stalk or touching the ground.

TREE SPEAK

1st-Level Divination

Casting Time: 1 action
Range: Touch
Components: V, S
Duration: 1 minute

You touch a tree and ask one question about anything that might have happened in its immediate vicinity (such as "Who passed by here?"). You get a mental sensation

of the response, which lasts for the duration of the spell. Trees do not have a humanoid's sense of time, so the tree might speak about something that happened last night or a hundred years ago. The sensation you receive might include sight, hearing, vibration, or smell, all from the tree's perspective. Trees are particularly attentive to anything that might harm the forest and always report such activities when questioned.

If you cast this spell on a tree that contains a creature that can merge with trees, such as a dryad, you can freely communicate with the merged creature for the duration of the spell.

TRENCH

2nd-Level Transmutation
Casting Time: 1 minute
Range: 60 feet
Components: V, S
Duration: Permanent

By making a scooping gesture, you cause the ground to slowly sink in an area 5 feet wide and 60 feet long, originating from a point within range. When the casting is finished, a 5-foot-deep trench is the result.

The spell works only on flat, open ground (not on stone or paved surfaces) that is not occupied by creatures or objects.

At Higher Levels. When you cast this spell using a spell slot of 3rd level or higher, you can increase the width of the trench by 5 feet or the length by 30 feet for each slot level above 2nd. You can make a different choice (width or length) for each slot level above 2nd.

TRICK QUESTION

1st-Level Enchantment
Casting Time: 1 action
Range: 30 feet
Components: V, S
Duration: Instantaneous

You pose a question that can be answered by one word, directed at a creature that can hear you. The target must make a successful Wisdom saving throw or be compelled to answer your question truthfully. When the answer is given, the target knows that you used magic to compel it.

TRIUMPH OF ICE

7th-Level Transmutation

Casting Time: 1 action
Range: 100 feet
Components: V, S, M (a stone extracted from glacial ice)
Duration: Concentration, up to 1 minute

You transform one of the four elements—air, earth, fire, or water—into ice or snow. The affected area is a sphere with a radius of 100 feet, centered on you. The specific effect depends on the element you choose.

Air. Vapor condenses into snowfall. If the effect of a *fog cloud* spell, a *stinking cloud*, or similar magic is in the area, this spell negates it. A creature of elemental air within range takes 8d6 cold damage—and, if airborne, it must make a successful Constitution saving throw at the start of its turn to avoid being knocked prone (no falling damage).

Earth. Soil freezes into permafrost to a depth of 10 feet. A creature burrowing through the area has its speed halved until the area thaws unless it can burrow through solid rock. A creature of elemental earth within range must make a successful Constitution saving throw or take 8d6 cold damage.

Fire. Flames or other sources of extreme heat (such as molten lava) on the ground within range transform into shards of ice, and the area they occupy becomes difficult terrain. Each creature in the previously burning area takes 2d6 slashing damage when the spell is cast and 1d6 slashing damage for every 5 feet it moves in the area (unless it is not hindered by icy terrain) until the spell ends; a successful Dexterity saving throw reduces the slashing damage by half. A creature of elemental fire within range must make a successful Constitution saving throw or take 8d6 cold damage and be stunned for 1d6 rounds.

Water. Open water (a pond, lake, or river) freezes to a depth of 4 feet. A creature on the surface of the water when it freezes must make a successful Dexterity saving throw to avoid being trapped in the ice. A trapped creature can free itself by using an action to make a successful Strength (Athletics) check. A creature of elemental water within range takes no damage from the spell but is paralyzed for 1d6 rounds unless it makes a successful Constitution saving throw, and it treats the affected area as difficult terrain.

TRUE LIGHT OF REVELATION

4th-Level Abjuration

Casting Time: 1 action
Range: 30 feet
Components: V, S, M (a small piece of phosphorus)
Duration: Concentration, up to 1 minute

A golden radiance spreads out from you, providing bright light up to 30 feet away, and dim light for an additional 30 feet. Any creatures or objects in the area of bright light that are invisible become visible while they are within 30 feet of you. Likewise, any magical disguises or illusions within 30 feet of you become feeble and transparent, their illusory nature obvious. These magical effects return to full potency if they move more than 30 feet away from you, or vice versa.

When a creature that has taken a different form—through spells such as *polymorph* or *shapechange*, or from inborn abilities, such as a druid's Wildshape feature—enters the bright light, it must succeed on a Constitution saving throw or be forced to return to its original form. Likewise, a creature attempting to change shape within the bright light must succeed on a Constitution saving throw in order to do so.

TWIST THE SKEIN

1st-Level Enchantment

Casting Time: 1 reaction, which you take when a creature makes an attack roll, saving throw, or skill check
Range: 30 feet
Components: S
Duration: Instantaneous

You tweak a strand of a creature's fate as it attempts an attack roll, saving throw, or skill check. Roll a d20 and subtract 10 to produce a number from 10 to –9. Add that number to the creature's roll. This adjustment can turn a failure into a success or vice versa, or it might not change the outcome at all.

UNCANNY AVOIDANCE

Divination Cantrip

Casting Time: 1 action
Range: 30 feet
Components: S
Duration: Concentration, up to 1 round

You extend a hand and point a finger at a creature within range. Your magic grants the target enhanced awareness of attacks directed at it. The next attack roll against the creature before the spell ends is made with disadvantage.

UNCONTROLLABLE TRANSFORMATION

7th-Level Transmutation (Ritual)

Casting Time: 1 action
Range: Self
Components: V, S, M (the bill of a platypus)
Duration: 1 hour

You infuse your body with raw chaos and will it to adopt a helpful mutation. Roll a d10 and consult the Uncontrollable Transformation table below to determine what mutation occurs. You can try to control the shifting

UNCONTROLLABLE TRANSFORMATION

d10	Mutation
1	A spindly third arm sprouts from your shoulder. As a bonus action, you can use it to attack with a light weapon. You have advantage on Dexterity (Sleight of Hand) checks and any checks that require the manipulation of tools.
2	Your skin is covered by rough scales that increase your AC by 1 and give you resistance to a random damage type (roll on the Damage Type table in the *frenzied bolt* spell description).
3	A puckered orifice grows on your back. You can forcefully expel air from it, granting you a flying speed of 30 feet. You must land at the end of your turn. In addition, as a bonus action, you can try to push a creature away with a blast of air. The target is pushed 5 feet away from you if it fails a Strength saving throw with a DC equal to 10 + your Constitution modifier.
4	A face appears on the back of your head. You gain darkvision out to a range of 120 feet and advantage on sight-based and scent-based Wisdom (Perception) checks. You become adept at carrying on conversations with yourself.
5	You grow gills that not only allow you to breathe underwater but also filter poison out of the air. You gain immunity to inhaled poisons.
6	Your hindquarters elongate, and you grow a second set of legs. Your base walking speed increases by 10 feet, and your carrying capacity becomes your Strength score multiplied by 20.
7	You become incorporeal and can move through other creatures and objects as if they were difficult terrain. You take 1d10 force damage if you end your turn inside an object. You can't pick up or interact with physical objects that you weren't carrying when you became incorporeal.
8	Your limbs elongate and flatten into prehensile paddles. You gain a swimming speed equal to your base walking speed and have advantage on Strength (Athletics) checks made to climb or swim. In addition, your unarmed strikes deal 1d6 bludgeoning damage.
9	Your head fills with a light gas and swells to four times its normal size, causing your hair to fall out. You have advantage on Intelligence and Wisdom ability checks and can levitate up to 5 feet above the ground.
10	You grow feathered wings that give you a flying speed equal to your walking speed and the ability to hover.

of your body to gain a mutation you prefer, but doing so is taxing; you can roll a d10 twice and choose the result you prefer, but you gain one level of exhaustion. At the end of the spell, your body returns to its normal form.

At Higher Levels. When you cast this spell using a spell slot of 8th level or higher, you gain an additional mutation for each slot level above 7th. You gain one level of exhaustion for each mutation you try to control.

UNDERMINE ARMOR

1st-Level Transmutation

Casting Time: 1 action

Range: 30 feet

Components: V, S

Duration: Concentration, up to 1 minute

You unravel the bonds of reality that hold a suit of armor together. A target wearing armor must succeed on a Constitution saving throw or its armor softens to the consistency of candle wax, decreasing the target's AC by 2.

Undermine armor has no effect on creatures that aren't wearing armor.

UNHOLY DEFIANCE

2nd-Level Necromancy

Casting Time: 1 action

Range: 30 feet

Components: V, S, M (a pinch of earth from a grave)

Duration: Concentration, up to 1 minute

Until the spell ends, undead creatures within range have advantage on saving throws against effects that turn undead. If an undead creature within this area has the Turning Defiance trait, that creature can roll a d4 when it makes a saving throw against an effect that turns undead and add the number rolled to the saving throw.

UNLEASH EFFIGY

9th-Level Transmutation

Casting Time: 1 action

Range: 60 feet

Components: V, S

Duration: Concentration, up to 10 minutes

You cause a stone statue that you can see within 60 feet of you to animate as your ally. The statue has the statistics of a stone golem. It takes a turn immediately after your turn. As a bonus action on your turn, you can order the golem to move and attack, provided you're within 60 feet of it. Without orders from you, the statue does nothing.

Whenever the statue has 75 hit points or fewer at the start of your turn or it is more than 60 feet from you at the start of your turn, you must make a successful DC 16 spellcasting check or the statue goes berserk. On each of its turns, the berserk statue attacks you or one of your allies. If no creature is near enough to be attacked, the statue dashes toward the nearest one instead. Once the statue goes berserk, it remains berserk until it's destroyed.

When the spell ends, the animated statue reverts to a normal, mundane statue.

UNLUCK ON THAT

1st-Level Enchantment

Casting Time: 1 reaction, which you take when a creature within range makes an attack roll, saving throw, or ability check

Range: 25 feet

Components: V

Duration: Instantaneous

By uttering a swift curse ("Unluck on that!"), you bring misfortune to the target's attempt; the affected creature has disadvantage on the roll.

At Higher Levels. When you cast this spell using a spell slot of 2nd level or higher, the range of the spell increases by 5 feet for each slot level above 1st.

UNRULY ITEM

1st-Level Transmutation

Casting Time: 1 action
Range: 30 feet
Components: V, S
Duration: Concentration, up to 1 minute

You animate an object in the possession of a creature within range, giving the object limited movement and a compulsion to thwart its possessor. The effect of the spell varies depending on the kind of object you affect.

    Weapon. A weapon being wielded by a creature fights and twists, trying to free itself from the creature's grasp. The creature must make a Dexterity saving throw. On a failed save, the creature has disadvantage on any attacks it makes in that round with the weapon. On a save that fails by 5 or more, the creature drops the weapon.

    Armor. The creature's armor shifts and moves, becoming noisy and uncomfortable. If the armor does not normally impart disadvantage on Dexterity (Stealth) checks, it does so while this spell is in effect. The creature wearing it must succeed on a Dexterity saving throw or take a 10-foot penalty to its speed and be unable to use the Dash action.

    Other Items. The effects on other carried items can vary at the GM's discretion. A potion might behave as a weapon, trying not to be drunk, falling to the ground and becoming ruined if the Dexterity save is failed by 5 or more. A backpack might try to empty itself, disgorging a random item each round on a failed save.

UNSEEN STRANGLER

3rd-Level Conjuration (Ritual)

Casting Time: 1 action
Range: 30 feet
Components: V, S, M (a pinch of sulfur and a live rodent)
Duration: 8 hours

You conjure an immaterial, tentacled aberration in an unoccupied space you can see within range, and you specify a password that the phantom recognizes. The entity remains where you conjured it until the spell ends, until you dismiss it as an action, or until you move more than 80 feet from it.

    The strangler is invisible to all creatures except you, and it can't be harmed. When a Small or larger creature approaches within 30 feet of it without speaking the password that you specified, the strangler starts whispering your name. This whispering is always audible to you, regardless of other sounds in the area, as long as you're conscious. The strangler sees invisible creatures and can see into the Ethereal Plane. It ignores illusions.

    If any creatures hostile to you are within 5 feet of the strangler at the start of your turn, the strangler attacks one of them with a tentacle. It makes a melee weapon attack with a bonus equal to your spellcasting ability modifier + your proficiency bonus. On a hit, it deals 3d6 bludgeoning damage, and a Large or smaller creature is grappled (escape DC = your spellcasting ability modifier + your proficiency bonus). Until this grapple ends, the target is restrained, and the strangler can't attack another target. If the strangler scores a critical hit, the target begins to suffocate and can't speak until the grapple ends.

UNSHACKLED MAGIC

9th-Level Enchantment

Casting Time: 1 action
Range: 120 feet
Components: V, S
Duration: Concentration, up to 1 minute

You designate a creature within range that has the Spellcasting or Innate Spellcasting special trait and imbue it with wild magic, causing it to lose control of its magical ability. If the target gets a failure on a Charisma saving throw, then on its next turn, it rolls randomly to select one of its available spells. The target then spontaneously casts that spell as an action. If the spell can be cast using a spell slot higher than its level, roll randomly to determine what slot is used to cast the spell. The target still determines factors such as the location of the spell's area or which creatures it affects, as normal, but it is compelled to cast that particular spell at that particular time.

    Each round while this spell remains in effect, the target makes another Charisma saving throw. On a successful save, it can act normally in that round, but the *unshackled magic* spell does not end.

VISAGE OF MADNESS

4th-Level Enchantment

Casting Time: 1 action
Range: Self
Components: V, S
Duration: Instantaneous

Your face momentarily becomes that of a demon lord, frightful enough to drive enemies mad. Every foe that's within 30 feet of you and that can see you must make a Wisdom saving throw. On a failed save, a creature claws savagely at its eyes, dealing piercing damage to itself equal to 1d6 + the creature's Strength modifier. The creature is also stunned until the end of its next turn and blinded for 1d4 rounds. A creature that rolls maximum damage against itself (a 6 on the d6) is blinded permanently.

VISAGE OF THE DEAD

4th-Level Necromancy (Ritual)

Casting Time: 1 action

Range: Touch

Components: V, S, M (a sliver of bone or piece of skin from an animated skeleton or zombie)

Duration: 8 hours

You infuse yourself, and up to four creatures you touch, with necromantic energy, taking on aspects of the undead. The targets gain immunity to poison damage and the poisoned condition for the duration of the spell, and they take on appearances similar to undead versions of themselves.

Undead that encounter a creature under the effect of this spell must make an Intelligence saving throw against your spell save DC. On a failed save, the undead mistakes the target for another undead creature. Typically this means the undead will ignore the target, especially if it is a less intelligent one such as a skeleton or a zombie, unless it is commanded otherwise. The response of more intelligent undead might depend on the conditions under which the encounter occurs, but if the target's presence would not be unusual, they too might likely ignore the target unless it acts suspiciously.

VITAL MARK

3rd-Level Transmutation (Ritual)

Casting Time: 10 minutes

Range: Touch

Components: V, S

Duration: 24 hours

You mark an unattended magic item (including weapons and armor) with a clearly visible stain of your blood. The item's magical abilities don't function for anyone else as long as the bloodstain remains on it. For example, a *+1 flaming longsword* with a vital mark functions as a nonmagical longsword in the hands of anyone but the caster, but it still functions as a *+1 flaming longsword* for the caster who placed the bloodstain on it. A *wand of magic missiles* would be no more than a stick in the hands of anyone but the caster.

At Higher Levels. When you cast this spell using a spell slot of 4th level or higher on the same item for 28 consecutive days, the effect becomes permanent until dispelled.

VOLLEY SHIELD

7th-Level Abjuration

Casting Time: 1 action

Range: Touch

Components: S

Duration: Concentration, up to 1 minute

You touch a willing creature and create a shimmering shield of energy to protect it. The shield grants the target a +5 bonus to AC and gives it resistance against nonmagical bludgeoning, piercing, and slashing damage for the duration of the spell.

In addition, the shield can reflect hostile spells back at their casters. When the target makes a successful saving throw against a hostile spell, the caster of the spell immediately becomes the spell's new target. The caster is entitled to the appropriate saving throw against the returned spell, if any, and is affected by the spell as if it came from a spellcaster of the caster's level.

VOMIT TENTACLES

2nd-Level Transmutation

Casting Time: 1 action

Range: Self

Components: V, S, M (a piece of a tentacle)

Duration: 5 rounds

Your jaws distend and dozens of thin, slimy tentacles emerge from your mouth to grasp and bind your opponents. Make a melee spell attack against a foe within 15 feet of you. On a hit, the target takes bludgeoning damage equal to 2d6 + your Strength modifier and is grappled (escape DC equal to your spell save DC). Until this grapple ends, the target is restrained and it takes the same damage at the start of each of your turns. You can grapple only one creature at a time.

The Armor Class of the tentacles is equal to yours. If they take slashing damage equal to 5 + your Constitution modifier from a single attack, enough tentacles are severed to enable a grappled creature to escape. Severed tentacles are replaced by new ones at the start of your turn. Damage dealt to the tentacles doesn't affect your hit points.

While the spell is in effect, you are incapable of speech and can't cast spells that have verbal components.

VOORISH SIGN

1st-Level Divination

Casting Time: 1 action

Range: Self (20-foot radius)

Components: S

Duration: Concentration, up to 10 minutes

For the duration, invisible creatures and objects within 20 feet of you become visible to you, and you have advantage on saving throws against effects that cause the frightened condition. The effect moves with you, remaining centered on you until the duration expires.

At Higher Levels. When you cast this spell using a spell slot of 3rd level or higher, the radius increases by 5 feet for every two slot levels above 1st.

WAFT

1st-Level Transmutation

Casting Time: 1 action
Range: Self
Components: V, S, M (a topaz worth at least 10 gp)
Duration: 1 round

This spell was first invented by dragon parents to assist their offspring when learning to fly. You gain a flying speed of 60 feet for 1 round. At the start of your next turn, you float rapidly down and land gently on a solid surface beneath you.

WALK THE TWISTED PATH

6th-Level Conjuration

Casting Time: 1 action
Range: Self (20-foot radius)
Components: V, S, M (a map)
Duration: Special

When you cast this spell, you and up to five creatures you can see within 20 feet of you enter a shifting landscape of endless walls and corridors that connect to many places throughout the world.

You can find your way to a destination within 100 miles, as long as you know for certain that your destination exists (though you don't need to have seen or visited it before), and you must make a successful DC 20 Intelligence check. If you have the ability to retrace a path you have previously taken without making a check (as a minotaur can), this check automatically succeeds. On a failed check, you don't find your path this round, and you and your companions each take 4d6 psychic damage as the madness of the shifting maze exacts its toll. You must repeat the check at the start of each of your turns until you find your way to your destination or until you die. In either event, the spell ends.

When the spell ends, you and those traveling with you appear in a safe location at your destination.

At Higher Levels. When you cast this spell using a spell slot of 7th level or higher, you can bring along two additional creatures or travel an additional 100 miles for each slot level above 6th.

WALKING WALL

7th-Level Transmutation

Casting Time: 1 action
Range: 30 feet
Components: V, S, M (100 miniature axes)
Duration: Concentration, up to 10 minutes

This spell creates a wall of swinging axes from the pile of miniature axes you provide when casting the spell. The wall fills a rectangle 10 feet wide, 10 feet high, and 20 feet long. The wall has a base speed of 50 feet, but it can't take the Dash action. It can make up to four attacks per round on your turn, using your spell attack modifier to hit and with a reach of 10 feet. You direct the wall's movement and attacks as a bonus action. If you choose not to direct it, the wall continues trying to execute the last command you gave it. The wall can't use reactions. Each successful attack deals 4d6 slashing damage, and the damage is considered magical.

The wall has AC 12 and 200 hit points, and is immune to necrotic, poison, psychic, and piercing damage. If it is reduced to 0 hit points or when the spell's duration ends, the wall disappears, and the miniature axes fall to the ground in a tidy heap.

WALL OF TIME

5th-Level Abjuration

Casting Time: 1 action
Range: 120 feet
Components: V, S, M (an hourglass)
Duration: Concentration, up to 1 minute

You create a wall of shimmering, transparent blocks on a solid surface within range. You can make a straight wall up to 60 feet long, 20 feet high, and 1 foot thick, or a cylindrical wall up to 20 feet high, 1 foot thick, and 20 feet in diameter. Nonmagical ranged attacks that cross the wall vanish into the time stream with no other effect. Ranged spell attacks and ranged weapon attacks made with magic weapons that pass through the wall are made with disadvantage. A creature that intentionally enters or passes through the wall is affected as if it had just failed its initial saving throw against a *slow* spell.

WARNING SHOUT

2nd-Level Divination

Casting Time: 1 reaction, which you take immediately before initiative is rolled
Range: 30 feet
Components: V
Duration: Instantaneous

You sense danger before it happens and call out a warning to an ally. One creature you can see and that can hear you gains advantage on its initiative roll.

WARP MIND AND MATTER

6th-Level Transmutation (Ritual)

Casting Time: 1 action

Range: 30 feet

Components: V, S, M (root of deadly nightshade and a drop of the caster's blood)

Duration: Until cured or dispelled

A creature you can see within range undergoes a baleful transmogrification. The target must make a successful Wisdom saving throw or suffer a flesh warp and be afflicted with a form of indefinite madness.

WAVE OF CORRUPTION

3rd-Level Necromancy

Casting Time: 1 action

Range: 30 feet

Components: V, S, M (a scrap of rotten meat)

Duration: Instantaneous

When you cast this spell, necromantic energy spreads out in a 30-foot radius around you, corrupting what it comes into contact with. Each unattended, nonmagical object within range takes 3d8 necrotic damage. All food and drink in the area, other than what is being carried, is fouled and made unpalatable. Magic consumables, such as potions, have a 50 percent chance of being ruined, but any such item in the possession of a creature gets a Constitution saving throw using the owner's save bonus to avoid this outcome.

At Higher Levels. When you cast this spell using a spell slot of 5th level or higher, the necrotic damage increases by 1d8 for every two slot levels above 3rd.

WAYWARD STRIKE

4th-Level Transmutation

Casting Time: 1 reaction, which you take when a melee or ranged attack is made against you

Range: 60 feet

Components: V, S

Duration: Instantaneous

You create a tear in the fabric of reality that protects you from an incoming attack by directing it through a second tear close to a creature you can see up within range. The attack plunges into one dimensional tear and out the other one, causing it to be resolved against that creature's AC. If the attack is successful, the creature takes the appropriate damage. You can even make the attacker hit itself, if you choose.

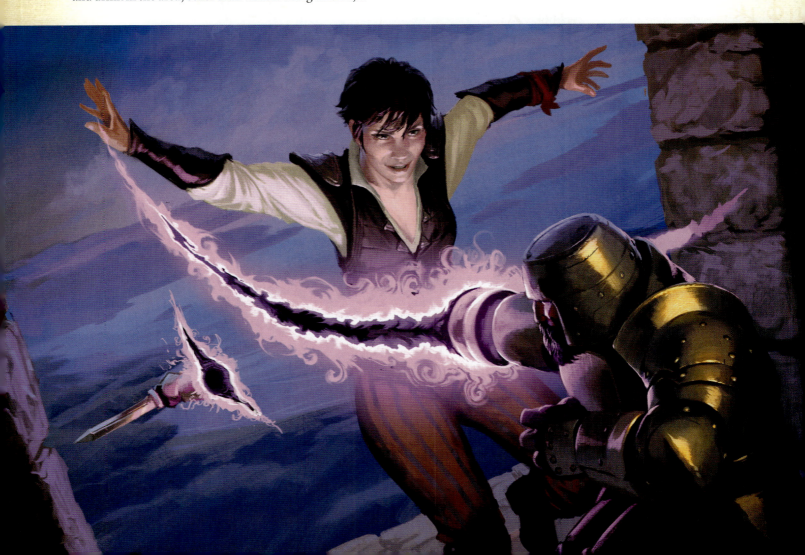

WEAPON OF BLOOD

1st-Level Transmutation

Casting Time: 1 action
Range: Self
Components: V, S, M (a pinch of iron shavings)
Duration: Concentration, up to 1 hour

When you cast this spell, you inflict 1d4 slashing damage on yourself that can't be healed until after the blade created by this spell is destroyed or the spell ends. The trickling blood transforms into a dagger of red metal that functions as a *+1 dagger*.

At Higher Levels. When you cast this spell using a spell slot of 3rd to 5th level, the self-inflicted wound deals 3d4 slashing damage and the spell produces a *+2 dagger*. When you cast this spell using a spell slot of 6th to 8th level, the self-inflicted wound deals 6d4 slashing damage and the spell produces a *+2 dagger of wounding*. When you cast this spell using a 9th-level spell slot, the self-inflicted wound deals 9d4 slashing damage and the spell produces a *+3 dagger of wounding*.

WEILER'S WARD

2nd-Level Conjuration

Casting Time: 1 bonus action
Range: Self
Components: V, S, M (a lock of hair from a fey creature)
Duration: Concentration, up to 1 hour

You create four small orbs of faerie magic that float around your head and give off dim light out to a radius of 15 feet. Whenever a Large or smaller enemy enters that area of dim light, or starts its turn in the area, you can use your reaction to attack it with one or more of the orbs. The enemy creature makes a Charisma saving throw. On a failed save, the creature is pushed 20 feet directly away from you, and each orb you used in the attack explodes violently, dealing 1d6 force damage to the creature.

At Higher Levels. When you cast this spell using a spell slot of 3rd level or higher, the number of orbs increases by one for each slot level above 2nd.

WILD SHIELD

4th-Level Abjuration

Casting Time: 1 action
Range: Self
Components: V, S
Duration: 1 minute

You surround yourself with the forces of chaos. Wild lights and strange sounds engulf you, making stealth impossible. While *wild shield* is active, you can use a reaction to repel a spell of 4th level or lower that targets you or whose area you are within. A repelled spell has no effect on you, but doing this causes the chance of a chaos magic surge as if you had cast a spell, with you considered the caster for any effect of the surge.

Wild shield ends when the duration expires or when it absorbs 4 levels of spells. If you try to repel a spell whose level exceeds the number of levels remaining, make an ability check using your spellcasting ability. The DC equals 10 + the spell's level – the number of levels *wild shield* can still repel. If the check succeeds, the spell is repelled; if the check fails, the spell has its full effect. The chance of a chaos magic surge exists regardless of whether the spell is repelled.

At Higher Levels. When you cast this spell using a spell slot of 5th level or higher, you can repel one additional spell level for each slot level above 4th.

WILD TRAJECTORY

7th-Level Transmutation

Casting Time: 1 action
Range: 100 feet
Components: V, S
Duration: Concentration, up to 1 minute

You create a 30-foot cube of magical instability that causes spell effects passing through it to diverge wildly from their original paths. When a spell with a visible or tangible manifestation (such as *fireball*, *lightning bolt*, or a ray or projectile such as *magic missile* or *ray of frost*) passes through the area, roll a d8. On a 1, the spell continues on its original path or toward its original target; on a 2, it diverts 45 degrees to the right; on a 3, it diverts 90 degrees to the right; on a 4, it diverts 135 degrees to the right; on a 5, it turns 180 degrees, back the way it came (striking the caster if it is a targeted spell); on a 6, the spell diverts 45 degrees to the left; on a 7, it diverts 90 degrees to the left; on an 8, it diverts 135 degrees to the left.

A spell that affects anything in its path, such as *lightning bolt*, continues to do so along its new trajectory, up to the limit of its range. A *fireball* spell will travel in the new direction up to the limit of its range before detonating. A targeted spell will strike the first viable target it encounters along its new trajectory.

WIND LASH

Evocation Cantrip

Casting Time: 1 action
Range: 20 feet
Components: V, S
Duration: Instantaneous

Your swift gesture creates a solid lash of howling wind. Make a melee spell attack against the target. On a hit, the target takes 1d8 slashing damage from the shearing wind and is pushed 5 feet away from you.

The spell's damage increases by 1d8 when you reach 5th level (2d8), 11th level (3d8), and 17th level (4d8).

WIND OF THE HEREAFTER

8th-Level Conjuration

Casting Time: 1 action
Range: 120 feet
Components: V, S, M (a vial of air from a tomb)
Duration: Concentration, up to 10 minutes

You create a 30-foot-radius sphere of roiling wind that carries the choking stench of death. The sphere is centered on a point you choose within range. The wind blows around corners. When a creature starts its turn in the sphere, it takes 8d8 necrotic damage, or half as much damage if it makes a successful Constitution saving throw. Creatures are affected even if they hold their breath or don't need to breathe.

The sphere moves 10 feet away from you at the start of each of your turns, drifting along the surface of the ground. It is not heavier than air but drifts in a straight line for the duration of the spell, even if that carries it over a cliff or gully. If the sphere meets a wall or other impassable obstacle, it turns to the left or right (select randomly).

WIND TUNNEL

1st-Level Evocation

Casting Time: 1 action
Range: Self (60-foot line)
Components: V, S, M (a paper straw)
Duration: Concentration, up to 1 minute

You create a swirling tunnel of strong wind extending from yourself in a direction you choose. The tunnel is a line 60 feet long and 10 feet wide. The wind blows from you toward the end of the line, which is stationary once created. A creature in the line moving with the wind (away from you) adds 10 feet to its speed, and ranged weapon attacks launched with the wind don't have disadvantage because of long range. Creatures in the line moving against the wind (toward you) spend 2 feet of movement for every 1 foot they move, and ranged weapon attacks launched along the line against the wind are made with disadvantage.

The wind tunnel immediately disperses gas or vapor, and it extinguishes candles, torches, and similar unprotected flames in the line. It causes protected flames, such as those of lanterns, to dance wildly and has a 50 percent chance of extinguishing them.

WINTER'S RADIANCE

6th-Level Evocation

Casting Time: 1 action
Range: 400 feet (30-foot cube)
Components: V, S, M (a piece of polished glass)
Duration: Concentration, up to 1 minute

When you cast this spell, the piercing rays of a day's worth of sunlight reflecting off fresh snow blankets the area, and the temperature drops precipitously. A creature in the area must make a Constitution saving throw, taking 4d8 cold damage and being blinded for the duration on a failed save or half as much damage with no additional effect on a successful one. Creatures possessing Sunlight Sensitivity have disadvantage on their save.

If any of this spell's area overlaps with an area of darkness created by a spell of 6th level or lower, the spell that created the darkness is dispelled.

WINTERDARK

6th-Level Transmutation

Casting Time: 1 action
Range: 120 feet
Components: V, S
Duration: Concentration, up to 1 hour

This spell invokes the deepest part of night on the winter solstice. You target a 40-foot-radius, 60-foot-high cylinder centered on a point within range, which is plunged into darkness and unbearable cold. Each creature in the area when you cast the spell and at the start of its turn must make a successful Constitution saving throw or take 1d6 cold damage and gain one level of exhaustion. Creatures immune to cold damage are also immune to the exhaustion effect, as are creatures wearing cold weather gear or otherwise adapted for a cold environment.

As a bonus action, you can move the center of the effect 20 feet.

WINTRY GLIDE

4th-Level Conjuration

Casting Time: 1 action
Range: Self
Components: V, S
Duration: Concentration, up to 1 minute

Upon casting *wintry glide*, you can travel via ice or snow without crossing the intervening space. If you are adjacent to a mass of ice or snow, you can enter it by expending 5 feet of movement. By expending another 5 feet of movement, you can immediately exit from that mass at any point—within 500 feet—that's part of the contiguous mass of ice or snow. When you enter the ice or snow, you instantly know the extent of the material within 500 feet.

You must have at least 10 feet of movement available when you cast the spell, or it fails.

If the mass of ice or snow is destroyed while you are transiting it, you must make a successful Constitution saving throw against your spell save DC to avoid taking 4d6 bludgeoning damage and falling prone at the midpoint of a line between your entrance point and your intended exit point.

WITHERED SIGHT

1st-Level Necromancy

Casting Time: 1 action
Range: 30 feet
Components: V, S, M (a dried lizard's eye)
Duration: Concentration, up to 1 minute

You cause the eyes of a creature you can see within range to lose acuity. The target must make a Constitution saving throw. On a failed save, the creature has disadvantage on Wisdom (Perception) checks and all attack rolls for the duration of the spell. An affected creature can repeat the saving throw at the end of each of its turns, ending the effect on itself on a success. This spell has no effect on a creature that is blind or that doesn't use its eyes to see.

At Higher Levels. When you cast this spell using a spell slot of 2nd level or higher, you can target one additional creature for each slot level above 1st.

WOLFSONG

1st-Level Transmutation

Casting Time: 1 action
Range: Self
Components: V, S
Duration: Instantaneous

You emit a howl that can be heard clearly from 300 feet away outdoors. The howl can convey a message of up to nine words, which can be understood by all dogs and wolves in that area, as well as (if you choose) one specific creature of any kind that you name when casting the spell.

If you cast the spell indoors and aboveground, the howl can be heard out to 200 feet from you. If you cast the spell underground, the howl can be heard from 100 feet away. A creature that understands the message is not compelled to act in a particular way, though the nature of the message might suggest or even dictate a course of action.

At Higher Levels. When you cast this spell using a spell slot of 2nd level or higher, you can name another specific recipient for each slot level above 2nd.

WRESTING WIND

2nd-Level Evocation

Casting Time: 1 action
Range: 90 feet
Components: V, S, M (a handful of paper confetti)
Duration: Instantaneous

By blowing a pinch of confetti from your cupped hand, you create a burst of air that can rip weapons and other items out of the hands of your enemies. Each enemy in a 20-foot radius centered on a point you target within range must make a successful Strength saving throw or drop anything held in its hands. The objects land 10 feet away from the creatures that dropped them, in random directions.

WRITHING ARMS

1st-Level Transmutation

Casting Time: 1 action
Range: 10 feet
Components: V, S
Duration: Concentration, up to 1 minute

Your arms become constantly writhing tentacles. You can use your action to make a melee spell attack against any target within range. The target takes 1d10 necrotic damage and is grappled (escape DC is your spell save DC). If the target does not escape your grapple, you can use your action on each subsequent turn to deal 1d10 necrotic damage to the target automatically.

Although you control the tentacles, they make it difficult to manipulate items. You cannot wield weapons or hold objects, including material components, while under the effects of this spell.

At Higher Levels. When you cast this spell using a spell slot of 2nd level or higher, the damage you deal with your tentacle attack increases by 1d10 for each slot level above 1st.

Y

YELLOW SIGN

4th-Level Enchantment

Casting Time: 1 action
Range: 30 feet
Components: V, S
Duration: 1d10 hours

You attempt to afflict a humanoid you can see within range with memories of distant, alien realms and their peculiar inhabitants. The target must make a successful Wisdom saving throw or be afflicted with a form of long-term madness and be charmed by you for the duration of the spell or until you or one of your allies harms it in any way. While charmed in this way, the creature regards you as a sacred monarch. If you or an ally of yours is fighting the creature, it has advantage on its saving throw.

A successful *remove curse* spell ends both effects.

APPENDIX

TALES OF THE VALIANT SPELL CONVERSION

This appendix contains guidance on how to convert any 5th Edition spell into one of the four circles of magic used in the *Tales of the Valiant* RPG and the *Core Fantasy Roleplaying* engine.

CIRCLES OF MAGIC

All magic requires energy. The four circles of magic represent the four primary sources of magical energy that fuel the abilities of spellcasters. When a spellcaster produces a spell, the caster taps into one of these energies using magical training, natural abilities, personal inclinations, or innate connections with magical entities. The section below details the four circles of magic and explains their roles in spellcasting.

ARCANE CIRCLE

The Arcane Circle of magic draws its power from the manipulation of forces that govern the material world, like heat, space, and gravity. In the hands of an arcane caster, the precise combination of words and gestures can ignite oxygen into roaring flame or link two pieces of land hundreds of miles apart. Arcane magic is governed by an extensive set of rules and calculations that make it highly complex. This complexity at times makes arcane magic more closely resemble science than mystical workings. Harnessing magic from this circle requires study, precision, and a talent for perfection.

The tools that define arcane magical working are varied and often highly personal to the arcane caster. The most common tools are runes, recitation, and hand gestures, but anything that engages the senses can be used. Casting arcane magic is only limited by imagination and an understanding of the formulaic laws of magic.

Conversion. When converting standard 5th Edition spells into the circles of magic, the following qualities typically indicate a spell belongs in the Arcane Circle:

- The spell detects, suppresses, ends, or otherwise interacts with the mechanical aspects of spellcasting.
- The spell harnesses elemental energy.
- The spell interacts with the five senses, whether to fool them or to extend their powers beyond typical capabilities.

DIVINE CIRCLE

The Divine Circle of magic draws its power from the connectivity that exists between beings. A divine caster can imbue a dying creature with the will to live again, channel the wrath of a divine being into a storm of fire, or miraculously restore the crops of a starving community. Whatever the specific effect, divine magic requires a connection between the will of the caster and at least one other being to function. Harnessing magic from this circle requires unwavering devotion, hyper-awareness of others, and belief in your ability to change the world.

The use of divine magic is often framed through the concept of faith, where an individual enacts the will of a mighty being known as a god. While this relationship between caster and god is the most common model, it isn't required to fuel divine magic. The Divine Circle draws energy just as potently for a caster who devotes themselves entirely to a community's needs, an evil coda set forth by a cult, or any other compelling source. Wherever need exists, there is the potential for divine magic. Casting divine magic is always done in the service of others, regardless of the morality of the caster.

Conversion. When converting standard 5th Edition spells into the circles of magic, the following qualities typically indicate a spell belongs in the Divine Circle:

- The spell specifically interacts with another creature's life force, whether to heal, harm, or imbue with undeath.
- The spell specifies interaction with a deity or includes the word faith in the description.

PRIMORDIAL CIRCLE

The Primordial Circle of magic draws its power from the primal energies of nature. A primordial caster can cause a forest to sprout from barren land, spur the rapid decay of flesh, or instantly restructure their biology to transform into a beast. Primordial magic redirect the forces of nature in accordance with the spellcaster's will. The Primordial Circle doesn't concern itself with creating new things but rather alters the energy already present in the environment to enact startling or subtle effects. Harnessing magic from this circle requires great awareness of the environment, extensive knowledge of the building blocks of life, and deep respect for the power inherent in nature.

The use of primordial magic always requires a source. Creating a primordial magical effect can be defined by how a caster interacts with energy that is present in the environment, whether amplifying, suppressing, altering, redirecting, or encouraging. A primordial caster understands that there is a finite amount of energy in the natural universe, and this magic concerns itself with tipping the scales of balance in just the right ways to enact the spellcaster's will. Primordial magic always draws from nature itself and can't be accessed without placing its interests first.

Conversion. When converting standard 5th Edition spells into the circles of magic, the following qualities typically indicate a spell belongs in the Primordial Circle:

- The spell alters or enhances a creature's biological characteristics.
- The spell specifically interacts with plants or beasts.
- The spell replicates an effect that could possibly occur as a natural phenomenon, such as fog or an earthquake.

WYRD CIRCLE

The Wyrd Circle of magic draws its power from the forces that sit beyond the material world. A wyrd caster can draw unnatural energy into existence to form a mass of writhing tendrils, summon another creature from a different plane to fight on their behalf, or banish their foes to the spinning void beyond reality. Harnessing wyrd magic requires spellcasters to free their minds from normal perceptions and open themselves to the possibilities of what lies beyond the measurable universe.

The use of wyrd magic requires a caster to become a conduit. The caster is the material anchor that calls unnatural energies into the world, then shapes those energies into the desired effect. Dealing with such bizarre forces antithetical to natural law is incredibly dangerous for a spellcaster, and tapping such powers usually requires the spellcaster to call on the assistance of beings familiar with the unfamiliar. Such spellcasters often forge pacts with extraplanar beings or invite spirits that dwell beyond the natural world into their bodies to interact with wyrd powers while shielding themselves from total ruin. Wyrd magic always breaks reality or the physical world to allow the forces from beyond to creep in.

Conversion. When converting standard 5th Edition spells into the circles of magic, the following qualities typically indicate a spell belongs in the Wyrd Circle:

- The spell summons a creature from a different plane or realm of existence.
- The spell harnesses energy that is not elemental in nature.
- The spell allows travel between different planes of existence.

MULTI-CIRCLE SPELLS

The guidance here gives suggestions for converting 5th Edition spells into circles of magic, but many spells possess the qualities of multiple circles. So, what do we do then? In those cases, the spell simply belongs to multiple circles. Spellcasters trained in different circles might access and use magical energy in different ways, but they often seek to cause the same or similar effects. Because of this, the way individual spellcasters use or cast a spell that belongs to multiple circles might be different, depending on the circle that gives that particular spellcaster access to the spell.

For example, the *detect poison and disease* spell belongs to both the Divine and Primordial circles. A divine spellcaster using the spell intuitively understands the target's lifeforce is in danger and know that the danger is posed by a poison or disease. A primordial spellcaster using the spell understands the target's natural rhythm is out of balance and can feel the unbalancing rhythm of the poison or disease as it courses through the target's body.

As another example, the *spider climb* spell belongs to both the Arcane and Primordial circles. An arcane spellcaster using the spell might change their personal static electricity to better cling to surfaces, while a primordial spellcaster might rearrange their physiology to gain spider-like qualities that allow for clinging to surfaces.

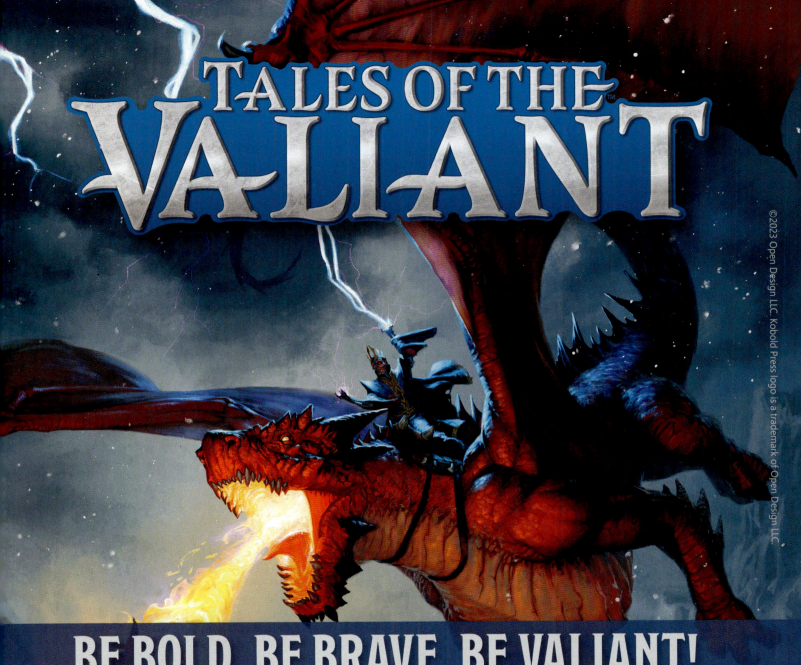

TALES OF THE VALIANT

BE BOLD. BE BRAVE. BE VALIANT!

Give your 5E game some very sharp teeth—with the Kobold Press take on Core Fantasy!

The Tales of the Valiant RPG adds new talents, heritages, spells, monsters, and much more to the familiar options from 5th Edition D&D.

As an independent 5E game, it is open to everyone and anyone who wants to create their own worlds and tell their own tale!

Join Kobold Press with a stunning new take on 5E, coming in 2024!

CAMPAIGN BUILDER
CITIES & TOWNS

A HOMEBREWER'S GUIDE TO FANTASY CITIES!

Campaign Builder: Cities & Towns provides a complete toolkit to create, expand, and enhance the cities and towns in your 5th Edition game, whether running an established or homebrew setting. From guilds to temples, and from craftspeople to criminals, this tome strengthens and expands your game's world immediately.

CAMPAIGN BUILDER: CITIES & TOWNS BRINGS YOU EVERYTHING YOU NEED:

- City character sheets to help build and track your settlements
- Guidance on all aspects of urban planning, from trade goods to architecture
- NPCs, rulers, guilds, and cults to populate your metropolis
- New character options to help urban heroes survive and thrive
- A bounty of tables, from name generators to urban encounters

START BUILDING BETTER CITIES TODAY!

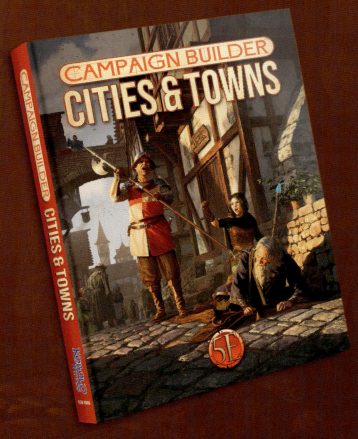

SMALL BUT FIERCE!

From hundreds of monsters, character options across all classes, dastardly adventures, and game design guides, Kobold Press has something for every table.

Kobold Press

SEE WHAT'S NEW ONLINE AT KOBOLDPRESS.COM

Open a Trove of Wonders!

Inside *Vault of Magic*, find a vast treasure trove of enchanted items of every imaginable use—more than 950 in all! There are plenty of armors, weapons, potions, rings, and wands, but that's just for starters. From mirrors to masks, edibles to earrings, and lanterns to lockets, it's all here, ready for your 5th Edition game.

This 240-page volume includes:

- More than 30 unique items developed by special guests, including Patrick Rothfuss, Gail Simone, Deborah Ann Woll, and Luke Gygax
- Fabled items that grow in power as characters rise in levels
- New item themes, such as monster-inspired, clockwork, and apprentice wizards
- Hundreds of full-color illustrations
- Complete treasure-generation tables sorted by rarity

Amaze your players and spice up your 5th Edition campaign with fresh, new enchanted items from Vault of Magic. It'll turn that next treasure hoard into something . . . wondrous!

©2022 Open Design LLC. Kobold Press logo is a trademark of Open Design LLC.

OPEN GAME LICENSE Version 1.0a

The following text is the property of Wizards of the Coast, Inc. and is Copyright 2000 Wizards of the Coast, Inc ("Wizards"). All Rights Reserved.

1. Definitions: (a)"Contributors" means the copyright and/or trademark owners who have contributed Open Game Content; (b)"Derivative Material" means copyrighted material including derivative works and translations (including into other computer languages), potation, modification, correction, addition, extension, upgrade, improvement, compilation, abridgment or other form in which an existing work may be recast, transformed or adapted; (c) "Distribute" means to reproduce, license, rent, lease, sell, broadcast, publicly display, transmit or otherwise distribute; (d)"Open Game Content" means the game mechanic and includes the methods, procedures, processes and routines to the extent such content does not embody the Product Identity and is an enhancement over the prior art and any additional content clearly identified as Open Game Content by the Contributor, and means any work covered by this License, including translations and derivative works under copyright law, but specifically excludes Product Identity. (e) "Product Identity" means product and product line names, logos and identifying marks including trade dress; artifacts; creatures characters; stories, storylines, plots, thematic elements, dialogue, incidents, language, artwork, symbols, designs, depictions, likenesses, formats, poses, concepts, themes and graphic, photographic and other visual or audio representations; names and descriptions of characters, spells, enchantments, personalities, teams, personas, likenesses and special abilities; places, locations, environments, creatures, equipment, magical or supernatural abilities or effects, logos, symbols, or graphic designs; and any other trademark or registered trademark clearly identified as Product identity by the owner of the Product Identity, and which specifically excludes the Open Game Content; (f) "Trademark" means the logos, names, mark, sign, motto, designs that are used by a Contributor to identify itself or its products or the associated products contributed to the Open Game License by the Contributor (g) "Use", "Used" or "Using" means to use, Distribute, copy, edit, format, modify, translate and otherwise create Derivative Material of Open Game Content. (h) "You" or "Your" means the licensee in terms of this agreement.

2. The License: This License applies to any Open Game Content that contains a notice indicating that the Open Game Content may only be Used under and in terms of this License. You must affix such a notice to any Open Game Content that you Use. No terms may be added to or subtracted from this License except as described by the License itself. No other terms or conditions may be applied to any Open Game Content distributed using this License.

3. Offer and Acceptance: By Using the Open Game Content You indicate Your acceptance of the terms of this License.

4. Grant and Consideration: In consideration for agreeing to use this License, the Contributors grant You a perpetual, worldwide, royalty-free, non-exclusive license with the exact terms of this License to Use, the Open Game Content.

5. Representation of Authority to Contribute: If You are contributing original material as Open Game Content, You represent that Your Contributions are Your original creation and/ or You have sufficient rights to grant the rights conveyed by this License.

6. Notice of License Copyright: You must update the COPYRIGHT NOTICE portion of this License to include the exact text of the COPYRIGHT NOTICE of any Open Game Content You are copying, modifying or distributing, and You must add the title, the copyright date, and the copyright holder's name to the COPYRIGHT NOTICE of any original Open Game Content you Distribute.

7. Use of Product Identity: You agree not to Use any Product Identity, including as an indication as to compatibility, except as expressly licensed in another, independent Agreement with the owner of each element of that Product Identity. You agree not to indicate compatibility or co-adaptability with any Trademark or Registered Trademark in conjunction with a work containing Open Game Content except as expressly licensed in another, independent Agreement with the owner of such Trademark or Registered Trademark. The use of any Product Identity in Open Game Content does not constitute a challenge to the ownership of that Product Identity. The owner of any Product Identity used in Open Game Content shall retain all rights, title and interest in and to that Product Identity.

8. Identification: If you distribute Open Game Content You must clearly indicate which portions of the work that you are distributing are Open Game Content.

9. Updating the License: Wizards or its designated Agents may publish updated versions of this License. You may use any authorized version of this License to copy, modify and distribute any Open Game Content originally distributed under any version of this License.

10. Copy of this License: You MUST include a copy of this License with every copy of the Open Game Content You Distribute.

11. Use of Contributor Credits: You may not market or advertise the Open Game Content using the name of any Contributor unless You have written permission from the Contributor to do so.

12. Inability to Comply: If it is impossible for You to comply with any of the terms of this License with respect to some or all of the Open Game Content due to statute, judicial order, or governmental regulation then You may not Use any Open Game Material so affected.

13. Termination: This License will terminate automatically if You fail to comply with all terms herein and fail to cure such breach within 30 days of becoming aware of the breach. All sublicenses shall survive the termination of this License.

14. Reformation: If any provision of this License is held to be unenforceable, such provision shall be reformed only to the extent necessary to make it enforceable.

15. COPYRIGHT NOTICE

Open Game License v 1.0a Copyright 2000, Wizards of the Coast, LLC.

System Reference Document 5.1 Copyright 2016, Wizards of the Coast, Inc.; Authors Mike Mearls, Jeremy Crawford, Chris Perkins, Rodney Thompson, Peter Lee, James Wyatt, Robert J. Schwalb, Bruce R. Cordell, Chris Sims, and Steve Townshend, based on original material by E. Gary Gygax and Dave Arneson.

Book of Ebon Tides © 2022 Open Design LLC; Authors: Wolfgang Baur and Celeste Conowitch.

Deep Magic: Alkemancy © 2019 Open Design LLC; Author: Phillip Larwood.

Deep Magic: Angelic Seals and Wards © 2016 Open Design LLC; Author: Dan Dillon.

Deep Magic: Battle Magic © 2016 Open Design LLC; Author: Greg Marks.

Deep Magic: Blood and Doom © 2017 Open Design LLC; Author: Chris Harris.

Deep Magic: Chaos Magic © 2016 Open Design LLC; Author: Greg Marks.

Deep Magic: Clockwork © 2016 Open Design LLC; Author: Scott Carter.

Deep Magic: Combat Divination © 2019 Open Design LLC; Author: Matt Corley.

Deep Magic: Dragon Magic © 2017 Open Design LLC; Author: Shawn Merwin.

Deep Magic: Elemental Magic © 2017 Open Design LLC; Author: Dan Dillon.

Deep Magic: Hieroglyph Magic © 2018 Open Design LLC; Author: Michael Ohl.

Deep Magic: Illumination Magic © 2016 Open Design LLC; Author: Greg Marks.

Deep Magic: Ley Line Magic © 2016 Open Design LLC; Author: Dan Dillon.

Deep Magic: Mythos Magic © 2018 Open Design LLC; Author: Christopher Lockey.

Deep Magic: Runes © 2016 Open Design LLC; Author: Chris Harris.

Deep Magic: Time Magic © 2018 Open Design LLC; Author: Carlos Ovalle.

Deep Magic: Void Magic © 2016 Open Design LLC; Author: Dan Dillon.

Deep Magic: Winter Magic © 2019 Open Design LLC; Author: Mike Welham.

Creature Codex © 2018 Open Design LLC; Authors: Wolfgang Baur, Dan Dillon, Richard Green, James Haeck, Chris Harris, Jeremy Hochhalter, James Introcaso, Chris Lockey, Shawn Merwin, and Jon Sawatsky.

Demon Cults & Secret Societies for 5th Edition © 2017 Open Design. Authors: Jeff Lee, Mike Welham, and Jon Sawatsky.

Margreve Player's Guide © 2019 Open Design LLC; Authors: Dan Dillon, Dennis Sustare, Jon Sawatsky, Lou Anders, Matthew Corley, and Mike Welham.

Midgard Heroes © 2015 Open Design LLC; Author: Dan Dillon.

Midgard Heroes Handbook © 2018 Open Design LLC; Authors: Chris Harris, Dan Dillon, Greg Marks, Jon Sawatsky, Michael Ohl, Richard Green, Rich Howard, Scott Carter, Shawn Merwin, and Wolfgang Baur.

Midgard Worldbook © 2018 Open Design LLC; Authors: Wolfgang Baur, Dan Dillon, Richard Green, Jeff Grubb, Chris Harris, Brian Suskind, and Jon Sawatsky.

Southlands Heroes © 2015 Open Design LLC; Author: Rich Howard.

Tome of Beasts © 2016 Open Design LLC; Authors: Chris Harris, Dan Dillon, Rodrigo Garcia Carmona, and Wolfgang Baur.

Tome Unbound © 2020 Open Design LLC; Authors: Mike Welham.

Underworld Player's Guide © 2020 Open Design LLC; Authors: Wolfgang Baur, Dan Dillon, Jeff Lee, Christopher Lockey, Shawn Merwin, and Kelly Pawlik.

Warlock 6: City of Brass © 2018 Open Design LLC; Authors: Richard Green, Jeff Grubb, Richard Pett, and Steve Winter.

Warlock 8: Undead. © 2018 Open Design LLC; Authors: Wolfgang Baur, Dan Dillon, Chris Harris, and Kelly Pawlik.

Warlock 10: The Magocracies © 2019 Open Design LLC; Authors: Dan Dillon, Ben McFarland, Kelly Pawlik, and Troy E. Taylor.

Warlock Bestiary © 2018 Open Design LLC; Authors: Jeff Lee with Chris Harris, James Introcaso, and Wolfgang Baur.

Deep Magic for 5th Edition © 2020 Open Design LLC; Authors: Dan Dillon, Chris Harris, and Jeff Lee.

Deep Magic Volume 1 © 2023 Open Design LLC; Authors: Wolfgang Baur, Scott Carter, Celeste Conowitch, Matthew Corley, Dan Dillon, Chris Harris, Jesse Jordan, Phillip Larwood, Jeff Lee, Chris Lockey, Greg Marks, Shawn Merwin, Michael Ohl, Carlos Ovalle, Marc Radle, Mike Welham, and Steve Winter.